The
Little Shadows

The
Little Shadows

MARINA
ENDICOTT

Doubleday Canada

Doubleday Canada and colophon are registered trademarks

LIBRARY AND ARCHIVES CANADA CATALOGUING IN PUBLICATION

Endicott, Marina, 1958-
The little shadows / Marina Endicott.

Issued also in electronic format.
ISBN 978-0-385-66891-0

I. Title.

PS8559.N475L58 2011   C813'.6   C2011-902496-9

Text and cover design: Kelly Hill
Cover art: Rosanne Olson | Riser | Getty Images
Printed and bound in the USA

Published in Canada by Doubleday Canada,
a division of Random House of Canada Limited

Visit Random House of Canada Limited's website: www.randomhouse.ca

10 9 8 7 6 5 4 3 2 1

For all my sisters

What is life? It is the flash of a firefly in the night.
It is the breath of a buffalo in the wintertime.
It is the little shadow which runs across the grass
and loses itself in the sunset.

CROWFOOT

Contents

OVERTURE

A summer evening. Moths dance in the lights outside the opera house.

A girl in a white dress slides into a seat on the aisle beside her father. The hall is crowded, many standing at the back. Ladies exclaim over the playbill while men, heads bent together, talk about the war. An older, greying soldier sits with his kind-faced wife. Her big black boot tucks out of sight behind his leg.

The curtain sways, curling along its bottom edge in a velvet wave, swept not by wind or the weight of the moon but by a company assembling backstage.

In the enfolding darkness of the wings, Aurora reaches out her hand on one side to find Clover's thin one; on the other Bella's, small and strong. Their warm clasp stills her trembling.

Silver-shelled footlights snap a scalloped arc of light onto the main curtain. Fresh red velvet: crimson lake, bright blood, the colour of love. Murmurs cease as the violins come creaking into tune, their mild excitable cacophony resolving into sense and meaning, into A, the one note they all seek. In the audience, silence falls. The cessation of visiting, the folding of programmes, the last adjustment to the seats.

Tips of shoes show beneath the bobble-fringe—a quiet rumpus, that must be the girls.

The bandmaster taps his stand.

It is about to start.

Breathe in—

ACT ONE

I.
Doing It in One

The Empress, Fort Macleod

We usually select a 'dumb act' for the first act on the bill—makes a good impression and will not be spoiled by late arrivals. A song-and-dance turn, a sister act, or any other little act that does not depend upon its words being heard.

WILL ROGERS

'*K*eep moving,' Mama told them. 'You will only be cold if you are slow, and we must get on. He won't wait.'

So they went quickly over the half-frozen field, in gritty snow that crunched underfoot but stung on their cheeks, and rubbed like sand between their hats and collars. Three girls in a row behind one round-bundled woman, who bent to the wind and made good headway on short, flicking legs. Aurora slid between snowbursts, smooth-sailing as a swan over a white lake. Bella was the smallest, hurrying to warm her hand by tucking it into Mama's pocket; Clover behind them, slowest and least desirous of their destination.

Everything in the little town was whirling and bright, late-afternoon whiteness unusual here where it did not snow deeply, being too far west into desert. But they could see through the squall the brick building of the Empress Theatre, and the black frame around its door, and the white placard tacked up on the door:

CLEVELAND'S STAR UNION VAUDEVILLE

And now they could hear a *plink-plink-plink* timpani of notes with depth removed by distance, and a soaring, scooping voice doing arpeggios. Aurora felt her own voicebox contracting in time, one octave up, tenor to soprano, reaching and then cascading down.

The door stuck—jammed—and their mama jerked her head so someone would help her pull. Bella did (no glove to soil, her right-hand one gone missing that morning and nothing for it but to keep her hand in her pocket, or in Mama's) and then Clover too. They yanked off-time—then again, together, and the door burst open. They fell back, then moved forward into a blur of darkness and warmth, with some-where in the distance red velvet and those arpeggios, very much louder now. Inside, a lobby gradually framed itself for their dazzled eyes, and a lighter square, two doors standing open into the theatre hall. An old scrubwoman, busy on the floor, grabbed her bucket away from their clumsy boots. Bella whispered an apology; after one glare the woman let her by and went back to her scrubbing.

Now that they stood still, the lobby was cold too. A little warmth curled out of the open doors, so the girls pressed their mother forward again, stepping quietly this time, Aurora's new boots almost skating over the glossy floorboards, to look through into the theatre.

It looked much larger inside. The space opened up and out—high, high ceiling with a silver sheen even in this low light. The walls were pressed tin too, but painted flat gold, so that it took a moment to make sense of the play of light and dark on the ornate lozenge patterns. The chairs had been pushed to the sides for floor-sweeping, topped by a tumbled mass of velvet cushions.

One skinny boy with a broom stood looking up at the stage: an eight-foot butte of bare boards, the frankly false proscenium decked out with advertisements in florid fancy scripts. Silver-shelled footlights dotted around the curve.

Up on the stage people were shifting furniture, moving carpets and hauling ropes. A man in a bright yellow waistcoat shouted down to the boy to make speed, and he dodged to the right of the stage and up, broom flying ahead of him like the flag *Excelsior.*

The scenery flats had been hiked high into the rafters and the cur-tains drawn as far open as they would go; the stage was bald. At the rim of the stage an elegant young man stood beside the piano, one arm laid along it while he sang. A small squirrelly fellow played for him, very flourishingly as to the notes but no folderol in his face.

The smell was port wine and dirt, velvet, greasesticks. And ashes, a frightening smell in a theatre. It was cold in here too—everywhere seemed like it would be warm, and then was not. Not till nighttime. Then the heat of bodies would help, when this whole space would be filled with breathing, laughing, sighing people crammed in side-by-each, all waiting and waiting for some beauty, some moment of transport.

Finished, the elegant gent bowed to the squirrel, received back his music, and took himself off smartly to the left, his top hat rolling down his arm and vanishing last. It was quieter in the hall then, so they could hear the slopping and brushing of the woman washing the lobby floor on her hands and knees behind them.

'Well—off we go,' Mama said. She made a complicated good-luck gesture, nipped at some fluff on Aurora's sleeve and gripped Bella's hand again, and they set off across the empty expanse of the hall. Their feet made no clatter at all on the shiny wooden floor, as Mama had taught them.

A stout man in a black coat stood mending a chair close to the stage. Mama stopped before him. 'The Three Graceful Avery Girls are here to audition,' she said, very haughty.

The man looked up at her, then at the girls. His black eyes shone in a long white tombstone face, and he looked them all over, staring the longest at Aurora, at the shine of her gold hair under the black hat, the huge velvet rose. Then he jerked his lipless mouth into a sideways, considering purse. 'Be a while. Stove in the dressing room,' he said. 'Stan'll fetch them when we're ready.'

Mama nodded and led the girls to the left side of the stage, where a hidden door now stood ajar into a bare brick passage open to the stage and the back workings. A little drift of snow lay in the bright patch of light along the back of the stage, where the flies above had been opened to the sky. Twenty feet along, stairs led up on the right, to the stage; down on the left, to the cellar under the stage. Aurora would not touch the makeshift splintery railing with her new mauve gloves, but the other girls held tight, stumbling down the steep steps after Mama.

Someone shouted as they were descending—'Maximilian! You're up!'—and a skinny dark man rushed up the stairs, pushing past, each one at a time having to endure him, a smelly man carrying a bird-cage and a box, and both those things banged into the girls but he murmured, *Oh dear, oh so, so sorry,* as he went, clearly in a panic, so they could not mind him.

Except that Mama said, 'Oh! *Never* cross on the stairs!' and stared up after him, frightened. This was a day for good luck.

On Our Uppers   At the bottom of the stairs was a close dark space. Mama found the door and Aurora went first, into a warm room glowing with light from the oil-stove and a lamp or two, a cozy room with benches set in front of tables lining the walls, mirrors showing a crowd of people—but half those people were themselves again, re-doubled in the glass. Still, the room was crammed, and very warm, with a strong smell of heating oil.

'Flora!' A little shriek, and then a pink hand clapped to a round pink mouth. A woman waved from one of the benches and leaned forward—so small was the room—to pat at Mama's arm urgently.

Mama peered through the glittering shadows, and then cried, in a whisper, 'Sybil! Of all delightful things! Now this makes me much easier in my mind—and you as pretty as—'

The woman got up (but was not much taller standing up) and hugged Mama. She was wearing bright-spangled pink artificial silk, very full in the skirt, which brushed too near the stove. Her eyes were shiny black sequins in a doll's face. 'You are a thousand years older now, Flora, and so am I. And who are these with you? Are they your daughters?'

'Aurora'—pulling her forward—'Sixteen! But we say eighteen, of course, and here is Amelia, not even a year younger, we call her Clover, her papa's pet name for her— Girls, this is Sybil Sutley, you'll remember me speaking of. Where are you, Bella? Arabella, she's the baby, now—thirteen, but sixteen, wink-wink, for the Gerry Society.' Mama patted them into order as she spoke, adjusting Aurora's hat around her face and pulling at the velvet flower's petals.

'And this is what came of your schoolmaster?'

'Yes, the very same, and very sad—' Mama broke off. She gritted her teeth and turned her face to one side, the palm of her small hand over her eyes and nose. An ugly gesture. Aurora turned to help, but Clover put an arm around Mama's waist as she continued, 'And my little Harry as well. But there, not now.' Then Mama was upright again, and Clover slid back into the shadow by the dressing-screen.

Bella was edging away, too, Aurora saw. Bella hated to hear Mama say Harry's name, or Papa's; she slipped out to sit alone on the stairs in the dark. Her skirt would get dusty, but they could brush it down for her. Aurora stood by a dressing mirror and carefully removed her hat, pin by pin, not looking (although she could see him perfectly clearly in the mirror) at the young man in evening clothes who had been singing upstairs, now lounging on one end of the table to draw on the wall an exact replica of a bottle on the table: *King of Whiskeys*. Many people had signed and drawn on the wall, so it must be all right that he was defacing it, but a whiskey bottle was not polite.

She stabbed each hatpin into a square of cloth that belonged in her velvet muff. Red scabs dotted her fingers, but she tried not to let herself pin them in the same holes each time, because that would smack of Mama, who had to count as she walked over the boardwalk back in Paddockwood—otherwise, what?—her long-dead mother's back would break, the mirrors would crack, seven years' bad luck would pour down on them. In sudden impatience, Aurora stripped off her mauve kid gloves. With her bare hand she swept dust from the dressing table before she set down her hat, then wiped off the dust on an inner fold of her black skirt. No towels set out, and they had forgot to borrow some from the boarding hotel.

Her mother and Sybil Sutley sat close together, talking *sotto voce*, reliving Boston and Chicago and their wonderful engagements with Keith's twenty years before (of which the girls knew every turn and every whistle stop), while the mad Maximilian pranced about the stage above their heads, sifting dust down on them all.

At least this was a proper theatre, if shabby. Not like the hotel in Prince Albert where they'd had their first professional audition, last summer. The conceited young man lounging on a sofa while they sang and danced for him, making them spin over and over so their skirts flew outward and their petticoats rose, then sidling too close to the makeshift stage in the hotel banqueting room to see what they had on underneath. Mama had left the piano, shutting the lid with a bang, and marched them out of there double-quick. 'Not for us,' she'd said. 'And besides, he has an unlucky face. I doubt if his touring company will come to pass.'

He had passed Aurora on the street as she walked to teach piano to the Sadler girls, and asked her to come for a second audition, on her own, and it was enough to make you laugh that he thought he was fooling anybody. Pulling her into a shadowed space between buildings, saying the number of his hotel room. If he'd had any skill she'd have thought it over, at least; as it was she just despised him. But he had a nice little tongue for kissing and he made her laugh with his bold unpractised wickedness, much as he made her angry with his superior air. She sang under her breath, staring at herself in the dim-lit mirror, *'He's a devil, he's a devil, He's a devil in his own home town!'* The elegant singer hummed along as he drew, but Aurora did not glance at him. A burst of jinkety music above: the piano playing *Streets of Cairo*—maybe the magician had a snake.

The pink-dressed Sybil woman leaned forward again to snatch at the knee of a dark old man, his massive head springing with wild gouts of grey hair, who sat hunched in a threadbare armchair shoved back into the alcove. Her hand like a bird's beak, pecking: 'And this is Julius Foster Konigsburg, my old man—we've been touring Europe, you know, after Australia, had a reversal there, but never mind that.' Peck-peck again. 'You remember me talking about Flora, Julius—we met in Boston on the continuous vaudeville—eleven o'clock in the morning till eleven at night and what a mercy *those* days are done.'

The heavy man's face was exaggeratedly made-up, lined with ochre and highlighted in strange patches; he must be a character actor in a melodrama or perhaps a single-man comic—but the pink lady was with him. Sybil's makeup was soubrette. She was still talking, though he paid her not the slightest heed.

'Touring with the Leddy Quartet, refined entertainment, Mr. and Mrs. Leddy and their son; Flora replaced their daughter when she ran off with a miner. Costumed mimicry—Flora, you was the best fancy dancer on any circuit from Ottawa to Corpus Christi. *And* you won a piano for dancing, in Minneapolis, just before you left us!'

'I did, but it's sold now, had to go. Left without a sou!'

That was not true. Aurora hated her for saying it, when Papa had tried so hard about money. It was just that the teacherage was not theirs and naturally they'd had to leave when the new man came, after Papa died—and everything cost so much—but they could always go to Qu'Appelle and stay with Papa's brother, only Mama would not. No reason they couldn't earn their way, she had said, and better. But she should not talk about Papa like that.

Aurora could feel her huge heart pounding, but half of her knew it was not for these small irritations, but for the terror of upstairs, and Mr. Cleveland, and getting the gig. And they wouldn't be paid less than a hundred a week; Mama would have to hold the line.

'Well, we're on our uppers, but the girls are greatly talented and we're going to make our way very-nicely-thank-you.' Mama ruffled her skirts and gave Aurora a chin-up look. 'You could be getting dressed, you girls: dodge behind the screen, nobody will mind.'

Clover was in a dream, so Aurora slipped into the space behind the cloth screen first, took off her long black skirt and hung it over a chair, fluffing out her shirtwaist into the baby-doll dress and pinafore of their costume. The stove-oil smell made her feel both comforted, because it was like the teacherage, and sick.

She *mmm*ed and hummed and worked her mouth in their exercises. There was not more than twenty dollars left in Mama's purse. One more night in the hotel here, then the fare back to Calgary. Or write to Uncle Chum in Qu'Appelle, begging for help.

Aurora breathed slowly. She stopped listening to everything else and became still.

Music of the Spheres   Out on the stairs, cold and cramped, Bella sat thinking of the dark staircase the Twelve Dancing Princesses travelled down when they went out to dance all night, dancing the soles right off their shoes. Her own feet felt pinched, but only Aurora had new boots. It was fair—Aurora was the eldest, after all, and maybe tight boots would keep one's feet from growing too gigantic.

'Have a bit of chocolate,' Sybil was saying to Mama in the dressing room, and the prospect almost made Bella go back in. But she would have to share, and she disliked that very much, and her mouth still remembered the hotel stew. She stayed on the step. The magician's patter that pittered down the stairwell sounded stilted. She could go watch from the wings. The other door at the bottom of the stairs, though, would be the tunnel under the seats to the lobby, like the one in the Prince Albert theatre. That would be better; she could pretend to be audience. She opened the wooden-slat door. Inside was a dirt-packed tunnel, a mine shaft. It was dark.

She stepped in, meaning to leave the door open, but it had a spring attached, like a front-porch door. Nothing to brace it with, so she would have to feel her way along the dirt wall. She stood inside the closed door to test if she could bear the dark. No, she could not—she opened the door. But the thought came to her that if she was brave enough, they would get the gig. So then she had to.

This cold-earth smell is what it will be like inside my grave, she thought. What it is like in Papa's grave, and Harry's. She saw Harry's small cold face, and how greatly still he had been. The floor was uneven, spills of dirt and pieces of lumber lying along it. Her fingers moved slowly over the dirt wall, scraping sometimes on a rock, jamming up against a beam every six feet or so. To calm herself she thought the hall was perhaps sixty feet long, so that would mean ten of those beams. Or maybe it was a hundred feet, and she could not imagine what the arithmetic for that would be. She stopped. Pretty soon she would be dead too, and packed in earth. There was no sound down here, none. Her own breathing, and a swimming sound. Papa had said it was the Music of the Spheres: you could only hear it when you were quite alone, when all other noise was absent, when your mind was clear. She loved that sound.

If She's Your Niece   A trill of music plinking—the magician upstairs, playing a ukulele, Clover thought. Quite good. She leaned against the wall, reading a posted sign with great concentration so no one would try to talk to her:

> Don't say 'slob' or 'son-of-a-gun' or 'hully gee' on
> Mr. Cleveland's stage unless you want to be cancelled
> peremptorily. Lack of talent will be less open to
> censure than would be an insult to a patron.
>   If you are in doubt as to the character of your act,
> consult the manager, for if you are guilty of uttering
> anything sacrilegious or suggestive, you will be
> immediately closed and will never again be allowed
> in a theatre where Mr. Cleveland is in authority.

'He stole that direct from Keith's, of course,' said a rich voice beside Clover. It belonged to the large man pushed deep into the armchair fitted into a hole in the wall; the bit of cloth draped around it was not enough to hide the dirt wall showing behind, hollowed out like a cave.

'Has ideas above his station, Mr. Kennebec Cleveland does. Aping bloody Keith. Bloody one-horse, miles-from-nowhere . . .'

The man's voice was swelling but the pink woman was suddenly across the room and up on his lap, her tiny paw stopping the large man's mouth. She whispered, 'No more of that, my dear, no more. Lucky to be here, and now my old pal Flora Dora, only Flora Avery she is now, and her baby-girl act—and no need for despair.' She turned her face up at a new noise from the stage. 'We'll get a thousand a week before we're done, you see if we don't!' As if listening to a lullaby, the large man subsided, until a raucous flapping above made them all start. Clover could see, between lines of dust filtering down through the cracks in the stage boards, a white feather.

The crooning, screeling noise of the birds was painful. 'And *there's my flock*!' shrieked Maximilian the Bird Magician. His big *finale*.

The door slammed open and Sybil jumped up, frightened. It was only a gawking boy to say, 'Julius Foster Konigsburg, King of Protean Raconteurs?'

The large man swept an arm forward, acknowledging the title. 'Yours to command, dear boy,' he said, and Clover could not help but laugh. Julius Foster Konigsburg liked that. He waggled his hand again.

'Mr. Cleveland says you have to wait a while. Knockabout Ninepins up next, and then he wants the Avery girls before you . . .'

Sybil told Mama, 'He does it in one, so he's much in demand, and of *course* would not be required to audition in the ordinary way. But Mr. Cleveland has asked to see his new material, thinking to put him number eight, next to closer on a nine-act bill—a headliner comedy smash for the big finish.'

'Nine, in such a little one-horse burg! Really!'

'I don't think you'll know anyone from the rest of the bill: a mind reader, but he's a sleazy type, and his assistant is beginning to show, poor little thing. Cleveland will be dumping them, his wife is a terrible prude. And of course there are the Wonder Dogs—' Sybil jerked a shoulder to the back wall, where a minor mutiny seemed to have broken out in the next room over. 'Now *he's* a character, quite a sweetheart but trouble with his temper, swears without meaning to. He keeps his cheeks stuffed with chaw and you can't make out what he's saying, so he gets by. I heard—but this is only gossip—that he cut off his own pecker in a rage one day. But the dogs are dear little things.'

Clover could not help wondering what that would look like, a stump like that. She tried not to think. She looked instead at a playbill pasted to the wall: *None are more Clever and Few Half so Good! Frederic LaDelle, the Man Who Mystifies! A very funny mystical effect that provokes laughter and surprise from the most blasé!* She filled in the first *e* in Clever to make a circle, so it read *None are more Clover.*

'Then there's the Sidewalk Conversationalists, East & Verrall, you might remember—*I can't go on! I'll go on!*—and Madame Minou and Her Living Statuary, never been top-of-the-bill and they've seen better days. He's lost the Hi-Jinx Jacksons, they got taken on by Keith's and are shuffling off to Buffalo! Good luck to them—that's why he's got the Knockabout Ninepins coming on—and for now The Italian Boys are the headliners. Lock up your daughters! But don't worry about them, good fun, but they're all nancy-boys.'

And what would that mean? Aurora caught Clover's eye, simpered. Oh!

'Then there's the pictures, of course, and *In An Artist's Studio* for the play. When it comes to little dogs, I miss the Lone Hand Four Aces,' Sybil said with some nostalgia. 'Not to mention Mr. Ace!'

'Girls, if we'll be next you'd better put your faces on.' Mama opened her valise and held out the pouch containing their greasepaint sticks and brushes. 'Still doing comic songs, Syb? Or is it a double act with Julius Foster?'

'Foster *Konigsburg* now, he's gone up in the world! A German routine. Things have been pretty dull in our line right now, most of the theatres closed up for the summer. Julius did not work last week, and does not work this week unless he can put it over Mr. Cleveland, but next week we'll work again and I think I can work the biggest part of the summer.'

Mama, giving a gurgling girly laugh: 'I remember you so well, doing *He's a Cousin of Mine*—that was the funniest thing, how many was it that one night, every available man in the company—'

'Fourteen kisses! The head carpenter, he was a lovely fellow, mmm . . . Don't listen, Jay! They didn't shut us down, but they're a bit more relaxed in Chicago. Then I did a follow-up, after you left us, *He's My Cousin (If She's Your Niece)*—did you ever see the sheets for that? It did quite well. I've got a mechanical-doll number now. Julius pulls my strings, it's a take on ventriloquy . . . with plenty of Clown White on my face I don't look an inch over fifty!'

'You are too modest, dear Sybil—you look wonderful, and that's the loveliest dress.'

'Only thing is, dear, I shouldn't say, but he's got *me* doing a doll, and he's got one baby-girl act already—the Simple Soubrettes. They do *Polly Lollipop* and what's that cheeky one, *Let Me Ride Your Pony, Daddy?*'

Mama blanched. She put her little hands to her cheeks. 'Oh God! This is the end!'

But Aurora laughed. 'It's all right, Mama, we'll just have to be better than them! Or do the sappy stuff instead—a bit of tone and a sentimental ending.'

Clover put pink cheeks on, number 5 greasepaint smeared into the palm of her hand, mixed with a tiny dollop of cold cream to enliven her usual all-over pale fawn. 'He does it in one'—that meant Julius Konigsburg didn't need the whole stage for his act, so the next turn could be set up behind the curtain while he played down in front by the footlights. They could do it in one too, if they did the sweet songs. For snappy numbers the dancing took more room, but in the hands-clasped soulful airs Mama had grouped them together. A little lip-bow with the brush and the skinny crimson-lake stick, and Clover handed the mascara pad to Aurora, who spat into the small dish and mixed the block into a paste, and damped the brush with it.

'Stand *still*!' she said.

'I was,' Clover said patiently. Aurora was always as nervous as a cat before an audition.

This was their ninth audition. Nine was lucky, wasn't it? It had to go well. The hotel in Prince Albert, three theatres in Regina, four in Calgary, now down into the sticks to the Empress—and there was no more money to go farther afield.

Clover stared into Aurora's face, trying not to let her eyelids tremble. The brush dabbed, dabbed; her lashes felt cold and heavy.

'You look lovely with your makeup on. Look how pretty,' Aurora said. Their two faces glowed in the golden mirror, pretty as paint, as pictures, as porcelain dolls. 'Where's Bella?'

Like a White Bird

In the darkness Bella had passed not ten but *twenty* of those supports. The hall could not be so long—or had she missed the count? Bella's teeth were chattering, she could not stop them. She laughed. It was truly like being blind. Perhaps her hearing would improve.

Swish, swish. Not, this time, the Music of the Spheres, but a scrub brush, overhead. The old woman cleaning in the lobby. Bella put her hand out and felt for the wall, but there was nothing—oh! it was a stair she'd hit. She crept up until there was a wooden door in front of her, a little light bleeding through the slats.

She had almost thought she would have to scream, which would make a commotion and the audition would be ruined and it would all be her fault. She found the handle and pressed the thumb, but it would not go down. She knocked, then knocked again, loudly. The door flew backwards, opening, and there was the broom-boy from the theatre. It was a very big broom.

'Stuck?' he asked. He had a sad, strange, flattened face, but it broke open in a moon-wide smile, and he took her arm and pulled her out of the dark stairway. 'Did you go under all the way without a light? You are brave!'

She nodded.

A clattering of pail and bucket: the old woman had finished the lobby cleaning, and she gave the boy a cuff. 'You're up, young Nando,' she said, eyes and mouth cold. She clumped through the double doors and down the long aisle created by the chairs, now back in their places. Bella and the boy followed.

He stopped halfway and held her sleeve. 'I'm not on yet, it's my dad and mam first.'

They stood still and watched what was happening onstage.

Two box-set pieces had been lowered, walls of a room with a window and a door, and a bedstead. There was a loud alarum, *clang-clang-clang*, so Bella was afraid it was fire, but a man in a nightshirt leaped out of the bed, higher than a human could, and landed with his feet *plump!* in his slippers. He found a giant wind-up clock hopping beside the bed, and threw it out the window—it came winging straight back at him and beaned him on the back of the head with a tremendous clatter.

'Got him good!' said the boy, close in her ear so as not to distract Mr. Cleveland.

The man stomped on the clock and hurt his foot. He leaped around the room one-footed, found and reached for his pants—but they whisked away on strings, to the right, to the left, as he lunged for them. The bed revolved as he was diving and caught him in mid-air, and he bounced once, straight up and then down, legs out, slippered feet pointed, and *whoosh*—straight into the pants now hovering over the bed—and *whoops* onto the floor all splay-legged and dazed.

'Set the strings right *that* time!' the boy said, laughing. 'Cleveland'll love that.'

The man pulled on his yellow waistcoat and reached blearily for his flask, but unstoppered his hot water bottle instead and took a big glug. He spat it out in a fan of spray, aggrieved, and went staggering round the room for his flask. No sooner had he found it than a vast pink elephant floated into the room, and as he backed away in horror from the elephant, a white-robed lady appeared from nowhere and grabbed the flask, holding it out of reach.

'Mrs. Cleveland ought to like that, Temperance herself!' the boy said, elbowing Bella. 'Whoops, I'm up, I'll miss my cue—' He flew down the length of the hall and vanished.

Onstage, the drunken man wrestled and danced with the pink elephant until he had vanquished it and tossed it out the window.

The beautiful lady held the flask aloft, shaking her finger at the man, but he hauled off and punched her—very hard, Bella thought— so that she seemed to float back, suspended in air, before dropping like a dead bird. Satisfied, he smacked the effort from his hands and walked right up over her flattened body to grab the flask from her limp fingers.

Just as he grabbed it, the door opened and in came the skinny boy with his broom at the ready, as if to sweep the floors. When he saw the lady lying supine and frail, he pointed accusingly at the big man, who was busy draining the flask to the lees and would only roll his eyes and shrug.

The boy shrugged too, and swept her up as if she weighed nothing, had no substance but imagination. She tumbled over and over, light as air, and when they got to the window somehow she was picked up with the broom, and the boy shook her out the window, nothing but a dust roll. She reached backwards once with a graceful hand, and then fell—it looked like she was falling thirty stories, like a wind-blown leaf, but Bella had seen backstage and knew she must only have fallen into a mattress.

The father seemed to take offence at losing the woman, then. He grabbed the end of the boy's broom in his huge hands and swung, and the boy rose in an aerial handstand as the broom rose, airborne at the end of it through the long arc, then came slamming down, the stage shaking with the impact. But he recovered and grabbed the broom back—then the *father* was diving up on the other end of the broom, as high, or higher, and letting go, vaulting and turning a somersault in air, grabbing, grabbing for a rope that was not there.

And then it was! The rope snaked gently down from the flies, the man relaxed and happy on its end, buffing his nails on his yellow waist-coat, cool as you please.

The boy had lost track of him. He bent to check out the window in case his quarry had flown out. The man crashed to the ground, grabbed the boy by the rump and upended him. He strode furiously around the room, sweeping the floor with the boy's hands and head and hair, his anger so huge and real that Bella had to put her fists over her eyes. When she looked again they were bowing, and the lady bouncing back in through the window like a white bird, bowing for Mr. Cleveland, who was clapping all by himself. So he must have liked them.

Bella heard the backstage man yell, 'Avery Sisters! Up next in one!'

She was still in her black skirt! She raced low and silent along the wall, through the invisible door, down the rickety stairs, unfastening her black serge skirt as she ran.

Avery's Ivories   It was too late to put proper makeup on Bella but her sisters helped her out of her black skirt and into baby-girl dress, and brushed the worst of the cobwebs from her hair and boot-toes. Mama's eyes had filled with tears of anxiety, so Aurora said Bella looked just aces and was the prettiest of them anyway, and Clover pounced at her with a carmined rabbit's foot and gave her a hectic tubercular flush, and they flitted out the dressing-room door, Sybil hissing good wishes and kissing the air behind them. The interior darkness had glimmered up into mere dusk, enough to manage the gimcrack stairs up onto the stage, and for Mama to find the piano and begin the vamp.

Aurora paused in the wings by the fire bucket and emptied her stomach into it, as neat as pouring tea. Clover found her hankie to wipe Aurora's mouth gently, not disturbing the set of her lips, and they went on.

Breathe. The footlights snapped on in their silver shells. The hall vanished in a pinkish glow, and the music tromped out its hokey bliss.

> *'Soft as the voice of an angel,*
> *Breathing a lesson unheard . . .'*

Aurora shifted her face to find the shaft of the Klieg light, to let it fall on her truly beautiful skin, her glorious eyes. She let her eyelids close, then lifted them as slowly as a shy girl might, at prayer.

> *'Hope with a gentle persuasion*
> *Whispers her comforting word.'*

Beside her Clover sang the alto clear and clean, no tricksy stuff about her. She held the notes as told to, she kept the others well in tune. Beautiful in service, her delicate hand flicked out to turn the page for Mama.

> *'Whispering Hope, oh how welcome thy voi-oice*
> *Making my heart in its sorrow rejoice . . .'*

Mama pumped away at the piano pedals, playing with great expression, pleased as punch with her dear girlies. Bella could see her thinking as she played, her face an open score: *This time! This time! They might think it was only her whim to insist on perfection, but now look.* Bella sang flat, but not by much; she shook her head slightly to set the curls swaying. She was the prettiest and the youngest but she was the worst singer, and she had the biggest feet already. It was sad.

> *'Then when the night is upon us,*
> *Why should the heart sink away?'*

Their voices blended, very pure, and the footlights glowed up at them, and the hall's sound rang clear. Bella thought this time they might succeed.

'And do these girls have a name?' The portly man who had been mending chairs pressed himself upright and came inching through the seats towards the stage. The scrubwoman had set her bucket down to listen. She pushed it out of his way but made no move to get up herself. So this must be Mr. and Mrs. Cleveland.

'Oh certainly, sir, they are the Three Graceful Avery Girls.'

'Avery's Ivories?'

Mama laughed obediently. 'Perhaps! Or we thought of using my name, you know. The Dora Belles? Their father's relations might not like to think of us having to earn our bread. But that's the way of the world, for dear Arthur had no kind of head for business and all we had was books and our lovely piano. *Which* the girls put to good use—'

Clover put quiet fingers on Mama's elbow; Mama ended on a false-trilling laugh.

'Repertoire?'

'Very sweet and tender lyrics and melodies—we've no aspiration to be confused with Tanguay, or that kind of display or licentious behaviour . . .'

Mr. Cleveland was not a conversationalist and Mama was irking him, Aurora could see that. 'We do *Daddy Wouldn't Buy Me A Bow-Wow,*' she put in, feeling the hypocrisy in the cold air on her white-tighted legs—and then regretted it. In Prince Albert, Mrs. Sadler had refused to let her daughters sing that song because Mr. Sadler had laughed his barking head off at some saucy meaning. But Cleveland waved his hand and Mama began the intro vamp.

Bella took the story part, lisping with all her might, while the others danced and pranced in on the horrible chorus.

> *'Daddy wouldn't buy me a bow-wow! bow wow!*
> *I've got a little cat,*
> *And I'm very fond of that!'*

(At this line, the girls grimaced in kittenish suggestion.)

> *'But I'd rather have a bow-wow, wow, wow, wow.'*

'See what you can do with this little ditty.' Mr. Cleveland handed a sheet of music across the shell-backed footlights. Clover, used to being helpful, bent down to take the music, but he snatched it back. 'The older gal, the blonde.'

Already bending, Clover was confused and nearly fell, but Bella was beside her with a small strong hand, and Aurora came forward to take the music. Clover and Bella retreated to the piano. A man had appeared there, the one called Mendel. He slid his sheet onto the piano's music rest and himself onto the bench beside Mama, who twitched her skirts and then herself away just in time. She and the younger girls stood in a clumsy group too close to the piano, till Clover backed them away.

> *'We heard little Willie cry in his sleep:*
> *I'll give it to Mary!*
> *Mary'll give it to John,*
> *And John will give it to the cook,*
> *She'll pass it right along.*

The cook will give it to Father,
Pa'll give it to Ma, you bet . . .'

Singing along as pert as was suitable to the jaunty tune, Aurora's brain caught up with the lyrics—how could Cleveland be known as a prude and offer her such a song to sing? Hardly even double entendre, it was pretty well single entendre: whatever the traffic would bear, she thought. Or, glancing down, whatever Mrs. Cleveland didn't squash.

She looked away from that tight-latched, crosspatch woman quickly, not wanting to spoil the buoyant mood of the piece—and there in the wings was the tail-coated young man from downstairs, smiling while he danced along to the tune, showing her how to do the step: a simple soft-shoe shuffle turned into a jumpy waltz. He waltzed alone over there, so she waltzed alone onstage, turning from one partner to another.

Once she'd got it, he saluted, hopped over the railing and left, walking straight out of the theatre so she could see him go, his nice straight back and springing step keeping time with her dancing. Infectious, like the song.

'And Ma'll give it to the ice-man,
That's the feller I want to get.'

A lighthearted finish and a flowery bow, and Mendel stretched out his arm with another sheet for Aurora to take, motioning the other girls to take sheets too.

He struck into the intro instantly, not waiting for Cleveland's say-so, and they were off. Grateful that it was familiar, Aurora could abandon the sheet and add a soaring embellishment, knowing the other two would hold the line. Mendel smiled at her; his face was altered by it, made bright and kind.

'My true love hath my heart, And I, and I have his,
By just exchange, the one to the other given

He loves my heart, for once it was his own,
I cherish his because in me, in me it bides.'

Clover loved singing this, one of Papa's favourites, and loved singing the bottom line while Bella and Aurora ran up above her. She loved being the true heart. Her heart was full of loving them both, and Mama; she had expected to be frightened but found herself lifted on the music to a serene pleasure in beauty and order.

But Mr. Cleveland hummed when they were done, and hawed his loveless tombstone face towards Mrs. Cleveland for confirmation, and Mendel, sober-eyed, took the sheets of music back and made a little bow to each of them.

Very Fond of That

'Nothing to offer us this week,' Mama said bravely to Sybil, whose upturned face was waiting for them at the bottom of the stairs. 'But *will keep us in mind* and perhaps when he's on the circuit—and every possibility in Medicine Hat next February. As if we can last until—'

Sandwiched between Mama and Aurora, Bella could not escape back upstairs, so she slid away from them and leaned against the tunnel door as Julius K. went up the stairs, taking them one at a time, putting a first and then a second foot on each step, waiting, then lifting to make the next six-inch ascent. He must be very sick, she thought, to go so slow up stairs. There was a scratching sound behind her, and then the door buffeted her gently. She turned and pulled it open, and there was the flat-faced boy, Nando, come through the tunnel.

'Are you hurt?' she asked, in a sudden fright for him, now that their own worry was over and they'd failed.

'Not at all! Or only when— Not more than a tad. The funny thing about our act is that Dad gets by far the worst of it, although it looks like he's wiping the floor with me.'

Bella laughed at that.

'It's all how you land limp, and break the fall with a foot or a hand. I've got the knack, because they started me so young—I been doing this twelve years, you know, and I'm not fifteen yet.'

She put out a hand and patted his arm because his face again looked so tired and flat.

'You got to land like a cat. Nobody can do that better than me.'

'I've got a little cat, and I'm very fond of that,' she sang.

He laughed and darted his head forward and kissed her mouth.

A Gallows Kind of Shout   Stuck at the top of the basement steps, Clover waited while Julius Foster Konigsburg climbed up painfully, stopping from time to time to crack a deep, throat-adjusting cough.

As he climbed she went to the props man's area to fetch him a paper cup of water from the jug kept there. When he reached the landing, Julius took the cup and drained it down before attempting the flight of steps up to the stage.

'Just a snatch of water, thank you—a paper cup—like drinking from a letter.' He coughed hugely again. 'Well, I'm off. All new material, naturally, stolen from the greatest modern masters. If I use anything of yours, dear miss, I will pay you five cents.'

He surged out onto the stage, into the pool of lights left over from when the girls had been turned down, and made a tremendous bow.

'Forgive me, dear sir, for my tardiness. I was performing my *toilette*— had squeezed out too much Toothpaste, and had the devil of a time getting it back into the Tube.'

He waited a beat for an imaginary laugh, striking a very professional pose, Clover considered. But she could see that he was not going over big with the manager. Mr. Cleveland slumped in his newly mended chair, one hand shading his eyes with a folded newspaper. Since the footlights did not shine outwards, there was nothing much to shade his eyes from, except Julius Foster Konigsburg.

'I have been Cognito in Vaudeville these many years, raconteuring to beat the band—to bedazzle the crowned fatheads of Europe—' Julius Foster Konigsburg's beautiful voice swam out, lush and confiding, from his ragged bearish torso, and Clover wanted to be kind to him, as Sybil was. 'It's close upon time that I retired from Treading the Boards myself and became a Writer of *The Melo-Drama* . . . I thought to pen a little thing about a Vampire, after the most blood-curdling tale of the last paralyzed century, but it's hard to be a Count, living on a long slim pedigree and what the neighbours bring in. That was a vein attempt at humour. In a Democracy, you know, your Vote counts—in Feudalism your Count votes.'

Clover could tell these were little throwaway jokes, as if Julius were making fun of the whole idea of jokes. But it was not funny and Clover began to worry that he was in trouble.

'A Count walks into a bar . . . No, no,' he corrected, and seemed to take himself in hand. 'Let's begin: I will play all the characters, on account of the current Hard Times.'*

This will be a thrill, she thought. Julius was a famous Protean, a quick-change artist—except he didn't use costumes, he just transformed himself with a hat or a length of cloth.

'Our scene is laid in Winnipeg—I forget the hen's name. A beautiful spot in Winnipeg, with not one mosquito—but this is all imaginary, of course.'

Julius seemed to be back on his feet. Clover could see only the back of his head, so she crept forward to stand beside the curtain-ropes. Others had come to watch, crowding backstage.

'The Villain enters, hiding behind his moustache. *Ha-ha!* He pulled his sleeve into a wicked cloak. 'Then retreats, mincing horribly, behind some scenery—then the Hero-een enters'—and he became a mysteriously lovely heroine—'wondering where Felix, her Lover, might be. She sings for him, a low flutter that gradually soars upward as fast as the price of coal. Felix is so handsome it hurts him. He enters yodelling, but has the presence of mind to put it back in his pocket.'

He was standing still and yet it seemed to Clover that he peopled the stage, flashing as he spoke from face to face, person to person, and though they were so ridiculous, they were real, for an instant—and she wanted to see that play. How difficult it must be to do this all alone, with no audience helping you. Their own turn was much easier. All they had to do was what they did at home: sing the right notes, dance on the right feet, watch each other, be sweet.

'You will see her return, pursued by the villain, who is pressing his wiles upon her, and much else—she holds him back: *Would you die for me?* But remember! Mine is *an undying love.* Ah, she was only a whiskey-maker, but he loved her still—'

Mr. Cleveland shouted, 'Move it along! Puns are scarcely accounted as humour in this house, sir.' He had a gallows kind of shout, rude and unkind. Clover hated him.

'But wait, there's more: the soubrette has a lantern jaw and can only sing light music.' Julius was going faster and faster—frightened, Clover thought. Too far out on some limb of memory barely attached to his original tale, he was busily sawing away at it regardless of sense or consequence, unable to clamber back to any kind of safety. 'She pulls out the last joint of her upper register—her mouth is a stab in the dark. She is accompanied in her flight by a running mate with straggling foliage round the front stoop . . .'

He blinked his boiled-onion eyes and stopped. There was a dense, active silence backstage, and no sound at all from the seats down front.

Julius K. said conversationally, looking up to the unpeopled balcony, 'If someone will bring me the river, I'll drown myself.'

'That's quite enough of that!' said Mrs. Cleveland, her tight voice a surprise from the darkness.

Julius K. remained still. Then his face gleamed as he changed direction: from a wide imaginary audience he brought his eyes to bear on Mrs. Cleveland, and shouted with great good humour, 'Let's have a good time, let's make it a party—all the men lean over and kiss the ladies in front . . . and the men in the front row can *kiss the ladies behind.*'

In the wings, behind Clover, Sybil's breath hissed. 'That's torn it,' she said. 'Now he won't get the gig. It's sheer pig-headedness, he's done it a-purpose.'

Mama put her arm around Sybil's plump shoulders and said, 'No, no!'

But they all knew it was true. Some managements might think the pun amusing but certainly not this one. Clover had read the sign. So had Julius Foster.

Sybil turned away from the stage. 'You let him know I'm down here packing, will you?'

'I will,' Mama said.

'With any luck we'll run into you farther down the line, Flor. Old times, old times.'

Clover could see she was crying a little, but Sybil ducked down the flight of stairs so they wouldn't have to watch.

Talked Me into It

They'd tidied themselves up and brushed their skirts and coats, and had no reason to linger, so Mama said, 'Well, girlies, back to the hotel, and perhaps the purse can stretch to a cup of tea to warm us up.'

Aurora drew her sisters into line and followed. As they filed up the aisle, Mr. Cleveland turned from where he was talking to a stagehand and said, 'Madam . . .'

Mama stopped, her back tense. Aurora watched her soften her face to polite inquiry before she turned.

Cleveland did not step towards them, nor raise his voice, but said, 'My orchestra leader likes your girls. He's talked me into it.'

Aurora found that her heart was pounding. She could feel a tremor in her hands and thighs, but she bit down on her cheek to stop it, and to stop herself from speaking.

'Well, I'm sure!' Mama did not specify exactly what she was sure of.

Mendel smiled at them from the stage, his mild squirrel's face seeming to know them well. Cleveland said, 'I've lost my opener. I'll

take your girls to do it in one, right off the top. Start tomorrow. Dispense
with the baby frills, let them sing in shirtwaists and skirts. More high-
tone, if you get me. And stick with the heartfelt ballads for now.'

He held out a booking sheet. 'We're here till Tuesday, then packed
up and a one-night stand in High River and then we're out to Crowsnest
for three—'

Mama found her voice again: 'And the girls can perform on Sunday,
Sunday acts not in costume being permissible. They have the dearest
little dove-grey challis walking suits, almost nun-like if you take my—
oh, you won't regret this! When they performed in Prince Albert,
Saskatchewan, at the Sunshine Sunday Concerts at the Prince Albert
Hotel, the boards were an inch deep in nickels and dimes and quarters.
Not a penny to be found among them!'

Aurora could not bear that Mama had mentioned the Sunshine
Sundays, as if it were a real gig instead of an amateur charity concert.

Mrs. Cleveland had been crouched, winkling at something stuck
on a chair-seat, but now she stood. 'Well, they'll need a better name.'

Mama pinched Aurora fiercely, for something to hold onto. 'Aurora,
Amelia, Arabella, my three lovely girls. The Adora Belles.'

'There's a set of them already at a box-house in Montana—you
don't want a mix-up with them, skirtless hussies,' Mrs. Cleveland said.
'Aurora Dawn, how about?' Asking her husband, rather than Mama.

Mendel swung round on the piano bench and said, 'The Belle
Auroras. Got the French tone and the dawn thing, got a ring.'

Mr. Cleveland shut his eyes and seemed to think. Then he nodded
his stiff head once and made to turn away, but Mama had not finished.

'And we would not be prepared to commit for less than $200 a week.'

He turned back, eyes darting into sharp focus.

'$150. Offer is final.'

'Well.'

Mrs. Cleveland piped up. 'And we play a split week, so half of that,
Cleveland.'

He looked irritated, but nodded his head at Mama. Stuck in a cleft
stick with that wife, Aurora thought.

'Done, then,' Mama said. '$75 for *this* week.' And out went her hand to shake on it. 'I'—she bowed—'come gratis, as their accompanist.'

She was good with exit lines and stepped smartly, spinning the girls before her, up the aisle and out.

'First show 2 p.m., band call at noon, keep strict to time,' Mendel called after them.

Gold Silk

Clover tucked one mouse-coloured glove into the other, a bit sad that she was left out of their new name. But as she was feeling sorry for herself she spied Julius Foster Konigsburg limping down the street in front of them, heading for the hotel—and then where?

Back in their crowded room at the hotel, bread and milk for supper, they were subdued. Julius K. and Sybil's room was close down the hall. There could be no congratulating themselves when all this had only come about by the miserable loss of the work for Julius. Mama pulled out the sealer jar of brown sugar and sprinkled a dusting on each bowl. 'We won't despair, my chicks, they'll get back on their feet,' she said. Clover watched the silver apostle spoon clink in the glass jar, flutter in the air above the bowls.

But although truly distressed for her old friend, Mama could not be sad for long. 'And of all the lucky breaks, when you think of it! We're on our way! *A hundred and fifty!*'

'Seventy-five,' Aurora said softly.

'You'll get a thousand a week, a thousand a week yet. Oh, I can see your names in lights, pricked out in silver on the bill of the Pantages, or Keith's—true talent will rise to the top, you'll see. If only we had a bit of cream this would be so nice.'

Each with her own bowl. When they were travelling, Clover would sometimes think of their supper bowls during the day, the little dishes nestled safely in Mama's humpbacked trunk. Bella's was pearly-white with a clump of bright flowers in the bottom, revealed as she ate her porridge or bread and milk. Clover had the Irish bowl with clovers on it, thin and delicate, Papa's mother's bowl—she'd been called Clover too, when she was a girl. Aurora's was lustreware, golden as her hair. The shine had tarnished on one side and Aurora always ate with the shine out, the tarnish turned towards her so no one would see, even though it was only them in the room. And Mama ate from the pot, crying again, as she often cried over her supper since Papa and Harry died.

They sat in a row to put their hair up in rags: Mama doing Aurora; Aurora doing Clover; Clover, Bella. Then the girls climbed into the big bed under the gold silk coverlet, last remnant of home, and Mama blew out the lamp. She lay along the end of the bed warming their feet and talking for a while, as she had always done, telling them stories of her life on the circuit and her miserable childhood in Madison, Wisconsin with Aunt Queen, who would hardly ever let her have a bath. Tonight she made plans for costumes and new songs and ways to keep the audience tacked to the edge of their seats, though the girls were only openers, until she had talked out her excitement and could rest. She ended: 'One week with the Star Union, a good start with a good company—we're on our way. Go to sleep, my clever girls, your dear papa is looking down from heaven on his daughters, with our little Harry in his arms, warm and peaceful and so happy to be together.'

She lay at their feet, murmuring of Harry's blond silk curls, how his darling sweetness bound them together—and how she should have ate better while expecting, or not run the last bit uphill with the water pail that one day when she cramped up, or what other thing she had done to leave him so weak that the pneumonia could take hold and carry him off.

She let herself sigh and cry then, and they all lay still in the cooling room, frost creeping over the window like a blind.

But Clover could not sleep. It was funny how that stage name left her out. Belle–Aurora with a blank space in the middle, because she was the blank among them, really. Clover turned again in the bed, making the others turn, and put her arm over Bella this time, who slid backwards into Clover's knees and thighs more tightly, warm under the gold silk. Mama had been right to bring the coverlet, though it had to be tied so tight to pack into the trunk every morning. They were getting faster at packing. Rags out of their hair, stays tied, stockings on, petticoats, skirts and waists, boots rubbed and retied—there was a complicated sequence to dressing, and the peacefulness of thinking about it let Clover drift away.

Moth-Girls

Later, when Mama tiptoed out to knock on Sybil's door, Aurora woke. She lay curled beside her sisters, thinking of what they would do tomorrow, how it would go. Down the hall she could hear the women comparing money outside Sybil's door before going down to the hotel bar by the back stairs, to get blissfully drunk on two of the last twenty dollars. The Italian Boys came down the hall and joined them as they went, so it sounded like to be a cheerful evening all around.

Wakened by the noise, Bella begged for a fairy story, as she used to when she was small.

'You are on the boards now, too old for fairy tales,' Aurora said. But she looked around the darkness for something to tell. Nothing, nothing— 'Well, there, under the windowsill, in the shadows, is a clutch of moth fairies' eggs. They will hatch out soon into a little troop of moth-girls in feathery dresses, dancing in and out of the candlelight and trying not to get singed . . .' Aurora felt Bella's knees cosy closer into Clover's, feet tucked under her bony heels; she spoke softer as Bella's breath slowed, sinking to sleep again, thinking of moth-girls, or maybe that boy— Nando?—who flew round the room on a flagpole broom.

Aurora slid her arm from where it had gone numb under Clover's neck and hugged her more tightly round her narrow waist.

They would do it in one and charm the house. They could do that, easy.

2.
First Night

JANUARY 1912

The Empress, Fort Macleod

. . . and there we were, not on the list.

FRED ASTAIRE

*S*nowlit wind, brilliant with ice-chips, swirled them along paths shovelled like tunnels through the drifts. Without the bunched baby-doll petticoats, the cold cut sharper. Aurora could feel it chafing to bright red the bare skin above her stocking tops. She breathed through her muff to keep her voice from freezing.

Clover held fingers over her eyes, leaving only a narrow slit to see through, as her father had said the Esquimaux did in the farthest North. A shorter journey to the theatre today because they knew the way—Clover had noticed that before. Or because she was dreading this a little, the band call and how that would be.

Bella walked through the snow thinking of Gerda's trail to the Snow Queen. Except Bella and her sisters were glad to be trapped in this palace. They would sing and dance for their supper because they were the luckiest, and too bad for poor Mr. Konigsburg. Her boots said *Konigsburg-Konigsburg* crunching over the snow. She wondered what Julius and Sybil were doing, where they had gone.

Mama's tight, black-gloved hand was on the handle, but the door flew open of its own accord, and there was the Ninepins' broom-boy, Nando Dent.

'Mendel sent me to look out for you,' he said, flat-planed face cracking into a creased grin. 'Welcome, ladies!'

'We are not behind time?' Mama asked, anxious.

'No, no, he wants to give you an extra bit, that's all.' Nando hurried them, still snow-dazzled, through the lobby, encouraging and clucking as if he were shooing chickens. He swung the inner door open, and the girls stopped in a clump—the velvet darkness again assailing them with its complicated smell and music. A little band assembled at the left in front of the stage was twiddling away: fiddle, clarinet, piano, one uncertain double bass. Another player, stretching his slide trombone to oil the long brass bones of it, inserted himself behind an array of odd percussion. Would they be heard over all that? Clover caught her cheek in her teeth and then let go. They were on their way. Her chest felt tight, and she could see the pulse jumping in Aurora's tender neck. Bella did not seem at all affected.

'It will be all right,' Mama said, softer-toned. 'You are very good girls and good performers, there is nothing to fret about.'

Her black hands pushed them in.

Bella skipped round the others and went first, Nando Dent bounding to run beside her down the slightly sloping floor to the small clear space in front of the stage. Half the chairs had been set up; part of the noise was the rest of them being crashed into place by a couple of skinny hands. Up on the stage Mr. Cleveland stood barking some order up into the fly gallery, then calling for '*Silence!*'

Which fell without delay, musicians and chair-movers milling around the house all stilled and expectant. Cleveland came forward to the lip of the stage and peered down, looking for Mendel. 'When you are ready, Mr. Mendel, we may begin?'

'*Uno momento,*' Mendel called up from the piano.

Aurora watched Cleveland make his way down the moveable stairs and midway up the house to his station at a two-legged table propped on seat-backs, strewn with papers and props; a squat, ugly man sat scribbling there already and looked up to murmur something.

The musicians huddled around Mendel once more. Nando danced back and pulled at Mama's sleeve. 'Your sides? The band arrangements?'

'Oh, mercy! I forgot. Here!' Mama held out the worn piano music, and then (with a grimace, for she knew it betrayed their lack of experience) brand-new sides, on very crisp paper, for violin, woodwind and double bass. 'But stay—is there a programme?'

He pulled one out of his pants pocket and bestowed it like a rose on the beloved, and Flora laughed and smacked at him affectionately, as if he were one of Arthur's big-boy students. A nice boy, with easy manners and some thought for the feelings of others.

They took their seats in the front row, crowded with other artistes waiting their turn. Aurora, in the middle, held the programme so they could all see. A long slim booklet of flimsy pinkish paper, with *Cleveland's Empress Theatre* on the front. She flipped over the pages, sifting through the rich black, decoratively lettered words, and finally—there—on the first page, all alone in a sea of advertisements, their new name:

THE BELLE AURORAS, ART SONGS OLD & NEW

So it must be real, Aurora thought.

'Openers, yes, but we'll work our way up from that, you'll see!' Mama whispered.

Pretty Little Gal   Aurora sat beside Clover and breathed through a light commotion in her stomach. This was only the band call— nothing, nothing to worry about.

Mendel's hand rose and the musicians dodged back to their stands, and they broke into a roistering little march, a lovely encouraging *come-in-and-enjoy-this* piece. Too soon for Aurora, Mendel's hand rose again and the band straggled to a stop, the violinist a bit behind the others, having had his eyes closed. The musicians were dressed in tight old suits, the patina of long use on knees and sleeves. One, the trombone player, had a slight dusting of flour all down his right side, which he brushed at whenever he was not playing. Perhaps he was a baker the rest of the time.

'Cut to . . . eight bars from the end,' Mendel said. 'Belle Auroras?'

'Present!' said Aurora, then blushed. *Present*, as if they were girls at school.

They ran up the backstage stairs and found another stagehand waiting there, who cried out to Mendel, 'In place!' The band struck up the cantering march and rode it to a happy crash of cymbals—a brief pause—then the opening bars of the *Whispering Hope* intro began. The stagehand motioned them to *go, go!*—and on they went. The stage was dusty and dirty, but Aurora could see the marks painted to show where to stand to do it in one. They arranged themselves sufficiently ahead of the marks to let the curtains swing closed behind them, and (brushing down their skirts into pretty order) stood still, breathed in all at the same moment, and sang—

Mendel's hand shot up on their third note, and the band stopped. Only Bella kept on singing, her wobbling voice echoing through the hall on *An-gel* . . . But she stopped when Clover's hand pinched her waist, and clamped her mouth shut with one hand, and the little audience of performers laughed, kindly enough.

Mendel consulted his sides: 'And then *Bow-Wow*—I thought we cut the *Bow-Wow?*'

Mama hastened onstage, explaining, 'Well, my dear sir, Mr. Cleveland required a twenty-minute length, and *without* that number we come in just a trifle under eighteen.'

'Better short than long,' Mr. Cleveland intoned from the worktable, waxy face gleaming in the lamplight as he leaned forward. 'Anyhow, *Bow-Wow* is Simple Soubrettes material. Clear the stage except performers.'

Mama's gloved hand waved frantically at Aurora and she vanished back into the wings, where Aurora could see her shifting from foot to foot in a small circle, like a lost bee.

Aurora turned to Mendel. 'Then we'll go straight to *Buffalo Gals*, with *Don't Dilly-Dally* after, and save *Last Rose of Summer* for the closer.'

Mendel considered, nodded, and made a pencil dash across his sheet. 'On to it then, boys, bridge from last four bars of *Whispering Hope*, vamp until I sign you in to *Buffalo Gals*.'

The band struck up at once, sliding from sorrowful minor thirds into the jaunty *Buffalo Gals*. Aurora and Clover darted into promenade steps behind Bella, who did the first verse in speak-song, her funny voice perking up the place. The waiting performers lifted their heads in sudden attention when she squeaked out, '*A pretty little gal I chanced to meet, Oh, she was fair to see!*'

Mendel called out, 'Last four bars—' and the girls skated into their final positions, to sing, '*. . . and dance by the light of the moon . . .*' They took it to their bow, and on into the intro for *Dilly-Dally*. Bella and Clover retreated, and Aurora moved up for her solo.

To demonstrate her professionalism, Aurora looked up to the lighting-booth window above the balcony and called out, 'Now the follow-spot should move to me alone.'

'I'm right here, you don't got to shout,' said the squat man sitting beside Cleveland.

Aurora went white. *Amateur!* She ought to have known that the lighting man would not be in the booth during band call.

'I got your notes right here, anyways,' he said. 'I'll follow you all right.'

'Of course,' she said politely, and bowed a little—even more stupid. 'Very sorry.'

Mendel, pressed for time, swung the band on into the lilt and sway of *Dilly-Dally*, crashed it to a halt and skipped to the end, when the girls came back to stand together in a nice tableau for *Last Rose*. 'When *true* hearts,' he prompted.

'*When true hearts lie withered, and loved ones are flown.*' Aurora took the rising trill solo at the end of that, and then their voices subsided together into the peaceful sighing ending— '*Oh, who would inhabit this bleak world alone?*'

'And the bow—and off you go, girls.' Dismissing them completely, Mendel turned to the band. 'Wonder Dogs, no vamps, long set-up so we riff the whole of *The Chicken Dance*.'

Not Simple

Four girls, preening and fluffing, had taken over the dressing room: too-short white skirts, dashing slippers with no stockings, lips kissing air in the mirror. A thin older one, strong-looking with a sharp, vivid face; two pudgy ones with blonde curls; and a thin little one, whose mouth was pulled into a tight knot on one side by an old scar. She had sparkling eyes.

Mama had spread their own things over a bench in front of one of
the mirrors, the only space left untenanted. She bustled importantly,
hanging up tartan shawls and pulling tissue out of dancing slippers.
Clover took the tissue and folded it along its original lines, watching
Aurora take a few quick steps into the room as the strong girl, the oldest
one, turned from the mirror to meet her. Aurora stared into her eyes.

'Mercy,' the girl said, holding out her hand.

'Oh! Aurora Avery,' Aurora said. She took the narrow hand, held
it for a moment.

They were enemies, they must be, Clover thought, but they had a
brightness in common. Mercy laughed and looked away.

'Simple Soubrettes?' Mama asked.

'That's us. Fifth up, right before the break. Bring 'em back alive,
Cleveland says.' Mercy laughed again, immoderately. Like a boy's, her
voice was deep and hoarse.

The larger blonde turned from the mirror and asked, 'Dumb act?'

'Not dumb!' Mama was quick to refute it. 'The Belle Auroras, a
selection of simple airs to recall tenderer years gone by.'

'Not *simple*,' the blonde said, puzzled. '*We're* Simple Soubrettes, so
you can't be.'

Mercy turned her back to the mirror, hands on the big girl's shoulders. 'Old songs, that's all they mean, Patience. And this,' she said, tap-
ping on the prettier blonde girl's arm, 'is my sister Temperance, and
the little one is Joyful.'

Clover folded another sheet of tissue, a chirp of laughter in her
head—such ridiculous names for flip-skirted foamy dancers.

Mama said, 'Plymouth Brethren?' and the older girl, Mercy, nodded.

'A great escape for the lot of you, then,' Mama said, nodding too.
'My aunt, *not* by blood, was Plymouth Brethren. She wanted me to be
renamed, but Thankful I was not. Clover, you carry on here while I
run back to the hotel to fetch the pincushion. I knew there was something I'd left behind, and ten to one we'll need it.' Wrapping a scarf
around her neck, she was gone almost before the words were out.

With the same brisk command, Mercy said, 'Joy, go show that

youngest girl where the necessary is and how to do the latch stage right so you can get back in. Mrs. C. will not have shown them.'

Of course she hadn't, thought Clover. Nobody'd said a thing about the arrangements.

Scampering Mice   Bella was very glad to go exploring. She wanted to see the Nando boy again, so she ran up the stairs with Joy like they were scampering mice. In the theatre the Living Statuary (willowy ladies and men in scandalous skin-coloured clothes) were setting up their props in three, on the last slice of stage. The backcloth showed an Italian courtyard in clumsy perspective. The girls sidled to the rear of the stage where a door stood inched ajar, latch hooked back in the jamb and a cloud of cold white air curling in.

Joy whispered, 'Someone's out there already, see, so that's useful too, then you don't wander out and have to wait there freezing. It's a two-hole biffy, but only if you go out together—nobody knocks if the door is shut. People are very cultured here.'

The biffy out the back of the schoolhouse and teacherage had four seats, and was only too often chock full of girls. Bella had no interest in seeing another. When they were famous she would only ever have an indoor toilet, *ever*. 'But I thought it was stage right?'

'This is stage right,' Joy said.

But it was on the left, on the side that their dressing room was on.

Joy laughed, the scar-knot lifting her cheek, even her eyelid. 'You have to think of it from *onstage*, not from as if you was watching. It's from our eyes that they named the two sides, because we're the simple ones!'

The Belle Auroras were not simple. Even if Joy and her sisters might be, in their saucy skirts and no stockings. 'Aren't your bare legs awfully cold?' Bella asked—then she and Joy both laughed, because it was such a silly, mean thing to say.

'Bone-chilled! But in the show when it gets so hot, when all the people come, I'll have to flap my skirts for air,' Joy said. She tugged Bella's sleeve to pull her behind a velvet curtain, so a stone plinth could be rolled on for the Living Statuary—stone in appearance only, Bella realized, because the stagehand was pushing two and pulling another on a string.

'This change is taking *too long*,' thundered Cleveland out of the darkness.

Everyone onstage jumped. Music crashed in, ending the underlying murmur that had been Mendel talking to the band. Joy and Bella clutched each other behind the curtain, trying not to shriek because everything was so funny, especially the men suddenly moving very quickly, like toys wound too tight.

Pincushion

Flora scuttled along the cleared path through the snow. Her left boot had a thin place and the cold seemed to come up in a fiery line straight through to her hip. '*Pincushion, pincushion*,' she sang to herself beneath her breath—not wanting to find herself in the hotel room, unable to recall why she had come. Her head ached, and after the theatre's darkness the morning sun was dazzling, sun-dog prisms glittering too bright to be borne. She put her gloved hand up to shade her eyes. One eye was not behaving properly; she ought not to have spent so long out with Sybil and Julius last night, and then she had been plagued with dreams.

What joy to see her girls onstage. Cleveland was one to watch out for, though; and he had eyed Aurora too openly, which would earn them all Mrs. C.'s dislike. Flora had seen enough of that. Aurora was too unseasoned to realize how careful she must be, but—

A patch of black ice nearly sent Flora tumbling—*phew!* A broken leg at this juncture would be disastrous!

More slowly, she stepped along the snowy edge of the path. Life on the stage was like a pincushion, she thought. Sharp points all around: useful, but you needed a silver thimble to manage. She must keep her thimble over her girls. The thought of Cleveland forcing himself on Aurora made her face break into a fearful heat, even in this prickling cold. Behind her black glove she could see it happening, an upsetting vision of Cleveland tugging at Aurora's hand, pressing it to his trousers—oh! Flora shook her head to clear it and redoubled her speed.

It was an advantage that she knew the way of the vaudeville world very well, its blessings as well as its dangers. She must simply be determined, and not let weakness or tiredness, or useless visions, distract her from keeping all her girls safe and sound.

An Instant Liking

'How'd you get the gig?' Mercy asked Aurora. Clover was there too, but Mercy did not bother with her, seeing at once who was in charge of the Belle Auroras, and speaking to her equivalent number.

'Auditioned yesterday,' Aurora said, as brief as possible.

Silence. Tongue out in concentration, Temperance drew on a crescent of eyebrow.

No reason not to be honest, Aurora judged. 'We didn't get it, but Cleveland was angry with Julius Foster Konigsburg, so then he had no opener and called us back.'

Mercy was kind, though. 'Oh, he could have used Maximilian the Bird Magician, if he'd been desperate. Maxie can do it in one if he's got to—less comfy for the birds, is all.'

Aurora gave way to an instant liking for Mercy. Her soldierly air, her lean arms, her eyes which were both sharp and melting. Her lips, too: full, but cut cleanly around the arching edge. Little chin. What was their life like, with no mother or manager to be seen?

'How did *you* get the gig?'

'Gave him a French job under the lighting table.'

Aurora looked blank.

'Where he sits with Lights. Sent Lights off to check for a burnt bulb.' Mercy laughed at the look on Aurora's face, at Clover staring too. 'It's not so bad—quick work, and no danger, you know. I'd far rather that than the other.'

Aurora did not want Mercy to see that she did not know what a French job might be. Whatever it was, how had it come about? How had Mr. Cleveland introduced the subject—or had Mercy? Would she herself be expected to do whatever it was? But she had Mama. She would have to watch out for Bella and Clover. She looked up and caught Clover's eye, and saw that she too was speculating as to what exactly it might be.

Clover rose and slid out of the room, the knuckles of her hand grazing the back of Aurora's neck gently on her way by.

Mercy said, drawing her own brows, 'Well, see you keep the gig now you've got it! Mrs. C. will ding you with her carving knife if she catches you at hanky-panky. She sent poor Melvin packing this morning, and his Tina, only because she was getting big in front.'

'Is that Neville Melvin Reads Your Subconscious Mind?' Aurora turned pages in the programme to find him, there, fourth on the bill.

'Yes. East & Verrall are coming. Cleveland got them on their way down to the Death Trail.'

'I love East,' Temperance said. The only thing she'd said so far. Her eyes were thick-rimmed with black, and she was painting a line of palest blue along the soft pink inner edge of her eyelid. She was spectacularly pretty, if you liked an armful. 'He gives you fudge.'

Mercy nodded. 'No girl with them. We wouldn't want to follow a girl.'

'Comics?'

'Double act, three hundred dates a year, but they run down to the Montana circuit to make that many. But what do they do with the money? They never seem to have any.'

Aurora watched Mercy paint her eyes. It was peaceful in that warm dark rabbit-hole of a room, while the work went on above them. In a droning, listless voice, Patience sang, *'What's my name? Poon'tain. Ask me again, I'll tell you the same.'*

Living Snake

Dogs were surging up the stairs stage left as Clover went to look for Bella. A moving river of white and black fur flowed onstage behind the curtain. Bella was there, watching the fray. Mama had returned, and she did not like dogs. Holding the pincushion out like a bone to tempt them, she backed away. One little dog, a ball of white fluff, snapped up at her with pointed white teeth.

'Oh, help! Save us!' Mama cried, and the Wonder Dogs man ran up behind the dogs and called them to order with a quiet whistle.

He avoided Mama's eyes, but grunted, 'Thorry,' and dealt with the dog by a short punch on the nose, his expressionless face rough but soft, like bread-dough torn into halves. Was he mad, a little? He must be, to have cut that living snake away. Clover shuddered. She was glad Bella had not heard what he'd done to himself, the poor man.

Mama gathered Bella's hand, clutched tight, and pulled her back down to the dressing room. Clover stopped to adjust her stocking (Mama's—too big, it sagged gradually down, however tight she tied her garter) and stayed to watch the dogs: twelve of them lined up on a row of stools behind a long table. Mendel pulled the curtain aside and said in a careful voice, as if talking to someone slow or deaf, 'Take that new opener all the way through, Juddy, Lights hasn't seen it yet . . . Make it an Italian if that suits the dogs, but go through the whole dinner party—after that we'll skip from cue to cue.'

Mama had made them do an Italian run of their songs at the hotel, speaking very quickly, to make sure that everyone remembered the lyrics. *Nothing* more inexcusable than forgetting lyrics, she said; some acts might be able to make them up, but the audience would know their old favourites, and any false word would jar. Clover was cold with dread that she might forget.

The Wonder Dogs man sat in the middle of the table, a row of dogs behind, led by a cock-eared black terrier. He whistled and they settled, with that same tight attention and excitement that Clover felt herself when standing ready to perform.

As the curtain opened, Juddy rang a brass bell for service and a maid-dog entered, prancing on hind legs, dressed in a darling little white cap and apron. As she set a plate in front of Juddy, a tiny poodle, nosed by the black terrier, jumped from the row of boxes behind and stood quivering upon the table. The maid-dog chased him off—but the same rascally black terrier nudged another onto the table, and another, until the maid found a whisk broom under the table and whisked the little dogs off, chasing them right offstage.

Juddy rang the bell again. No answer but a blat from the trombone, so he flung his dinner napkin down and went haring off after the maid-dog.

As soon as he'd gone, up jumped that rascally terrier—the instigator, Clover thought—and began to wolf down the abandoned dinner. Some commotion occurred offstage and the dog looked up, one ear cocked. He jumped down, grabbed a new dog, a hairy Pekinese-looking thing, by the scruff of her neck and plumped her down beside the plate.

Then the black dog nipped back to his box and sat, angelic—just in time, for his master came storming back in. When he saw the Pekinese at the half-eaten plate, Juddy lost his temper, scolding it in a torrent of hideous triple-speed curses, stamping his feet in a rage, then drawing a pistol and training it on the poor pup.

Clover was frightened. She thought Juddy truly was mad, and was going to kill his own dog like that, shoot him right there on the stage, for having ruined his number. The gun was very black and real. The substitute thief shrank, cowering, a masterpiece of abject apology, as Juddy cocked the pistol and prepared to execute the poor little creature.

But the black dog leaped up from his box and jumped onto the table between the gun and the Peke, begging piteously for his master to spare its life. Juddy dragged him off the table onto the floor, and instead—oh no! He shot the black dog!

The dog rocked back on his hind legs as if he were a man, and staggered about the stage, one paw over the wound, the other across his eyes. His whimpering was loud above the suddenly hushed music, and then—he died.

Appalled by what he had done, Juddy fell to his knees weeping. A huge dog—the biggest dog Clover had ever seen, in a police jacket and helmet—came in and grabbed Juddy from behind, nipping him on the seat of the pants, and dragged him offstage, straight to pokey where he belonged for killing his clever little dog. From the wings Clover could see how Juddy looked like he was being dragged when he was actually pushing himself along; he was very convincing even so. She was so sorry for the dead black dog—until, after a long funereal trombone blast, he jumped up onto the table and coolly finished his dinner.

'Right!' called Mendel. 'Out of time for you, Juddy—we'll wing it with part two.' He turned back to his band. 'Minou's up next, vamp sixty-four bars while they strike the dogs.'

The curtains swirled shut, and the stage was a welter of hands shifting stools and plinths in the blue working lamp, silent under a winding French café tune from the band.

Out of the darkness close beside Clover, a man said softly, 'Fresh blood?'

She jumped, then stood very still.

'New to this the-ayter, I mean to say? Humbug?' He proffered a paper bag to entice her. He had reddish hair and bright eyes that looked blue in the bluish light.

Another man emerged from the velvet curtain's shadow. 'Now, East, don't tease the lady.'

'This is no lady, she's a *soubrette*,' said East. They stood very near.

'Oh, I think not, I think she is not—I'd lay you odds she's as prim as you please.'

'Verrall, you back away slow and you won't get hurt. I've got dibs on this young miss.' East ran his arm behind Clover and pulled her quite close, but not close enough to be serious. There was a joke in everything he said, you could not be cross with him—besides, Clover was never subjected to this kind of attention, standing beside Aurora as she always did, and she found it interesting.

Verrall extended one long thin finger at East and twitched it side to side like Papa's metronome. 'Mrs. C. is watching. You'll find yourself in hot water with the management, my dear old East,' he said.

'D'you think? When he needs us ever so desperately?' East squeezed Clover's waist, measuringly, and then used both his hands to set her a little apart, like a doll he was putting back in the toy box. 'But perhaps he don't need *you* so desperately, my tidy tenderfoot, and it would never do to get you canned.'

Still Clover had not spoken a word. She could not say anything at all witty, so she tore herself away from watching Madame Minou's Statuary and trotted down the stairs to the dressing room as if she were quite confident and pert. Only her legs, trembling slightly, showed the lie.

The Doorstep

Aurora watched the Soubrettes running out as Clover ran in, and shortly back again, their call brief because they'd been with Cleveland's so long.

The Italian Boys had the last band call, coming next-to-close, before the pictures. Here at the Empress those were little more than a magic lantern show to harry the audience out of their seats, Cleveland saying that if the Keith–Albee circuit didn't bother with them he didn't see why he should pay through the nose for bad celluloid. The current picture was *A Natural History Study Showing Fifteen Phases of Bee Culture*; not even Bella wanted to see it. The girls were free to stay by the stove and keep warm for the hour before the first show.

But Aurora could not sit. Wrapping her shawl around herself she went up the stairs and outside as if to the privy, then turned round the side of the theatre and kept walking as far as she could in the cold. She took quick strides on the packed-snow path and watched her new boots peeping in and out beneath her swaying skirt, and thought of a blank blue sky over their old home in Paddockwood, of lying on the stone fence by the schoolhouse after all the others had gone in to supper; her father's shuttered face, bent over papers at his desk on the dais, when she went to call him in long after supper was cold.

'What a voice you've got,' he'd said one evening, after the Victoria Day concert. 'Wherever it came from.' Mama had never had much voice. Everybody said so, it was not disloyal. Aurora had more talent, and more beauty, but Mama had fiery energy and gumption, and those things counted high. Talent was only a tenth of it.

Aurora's feet were ice-lumps, so she turned and strode back. It was exciting, she told herself. It was—the doorstep of their professional lives. She took one last breath of cold air, feeling the well-known shock as the cold's bite reached down her chest.

The heat of the theatre warmed her skin on her way in. She passed grey-banged, whey-faced Mrs. Cleveland, but shy of being thought to have been at the outhouse, Aurora went on without speaking, aware of those flat eyes swinging to watch. She walked, in consequence, very straight and smooth.

 Openers

At ten to two the lobby doors opened and the house came in. The audience made a breathing noise, a subtle tidal movement beneath the excited chatter and the noise of Mendel's band playing warm-up music.

Openers, the girls stood dressed and ready in the wings: Aurora with her eyes closed, Clover looking a bit pinched but calm enough. Bella leaned up against the proscenium facade, peeping through an unstitched line in the velvet curtains to see what waited out there for them. People of every kind, wide and middling and narrow, anxious-looking or happy, in groups or by twos or alone, moving down the aisles to find a good spot, shuffling through the crowd to get to an empty seat in the middle.

All those velvet seats filling, all the feet trampling, all there to hear them—Bella was lifted up, buoyant deep in her belly with the pleasure of what was to come. Here we go, she thought, and it seemed like her whole life had been waiting for this particular minute. She turned to see how her sisters were—Aurora had not yet thrown up but Mama had brought up a slop pail and set it behind the second leg. Poor stuff! Bella was glad not to have a queasy stomach. Had she smudged her lip on the curtain?

They could hear Mendel winding his little orchestra down, and then there was a pause, and then it would be them. Aurora turned blindly in the dark. Clover pushed the slop pail to her, Aurora threw up quickly, and Mama wiped her mouth.

And then the stagehand was holding back a fold of curtain and the music rose, and it was time to go on. Clover went first, Bella second, and then Aurora, out into the liquid brilliance of the footlights, drinking it like wine or how they imagined champagne must be. Bits of people's heads and eyes and teeth showed in the darkness, that same breathing noise continuing, the swell and ebb of the audience's desire to be pleased.

Third bar of the intro, fourth bar of the intro. Now the climbing notes that made a ladder into the song:

> 'Soft as the voice of an angel,
> breathing a welcome unheard,
> Hope with her gentle persuasion
> whispers a comforting word . . .'

Were they loud enough? There was still some talk and some movement, but that was all right, that was to be expected, since they were the openers. Mama had coached them to carry on good-naturedly even if it seemed that no one was listening at all. 'We won't be in this spot for long, dear chickens,' she'd said. 'But make the best of it while visiting.'

Clover's dark, steady voice split for the chorus, her gentle low notes letting Aurora reach upward and keeping Bella grounded—'*Why should the heart sink away?*' Aurora was so gratefully fond of Clover that she could not help smiling at her, and then she could feel, almost like the press of a hand, the returned pleasure of the audience in their singing, and in their liking for one another.

> 'Making my heart, making my heart
> In its sorrow rejoice . . .'

They did not make too much of a meal out of the ending, but allowed the audience to remember being sad and then feeling a bit better. No going up on that last note, as some singers did; Mama felt anything show-offy ruined the song's genuine sentiment.

After that, how enjoyable to feel the tempo change to *Buffalo Gals*, and slip behind Bella while she glided forward, close to the glowing footlights that cast such a rosy shine onto their faces, Bella's now mischievous, happy to be in the blushing light, the limelight. She knew she was a very good gal, clowning: she found the crowd happy as she was herself, on her gangly feet.

> '*Her feet took up the whole sidewalk,*
> *And left no room for me.*
> *Oh-oh-oh! Buffalo Gals, won't you come out tonight . . .*'

Aurora and Clover danced shuffling swoops behind her, almost mocking her—but that was just what the song had in mind, for someone to poke a bit of cheerful fun at themselves. She was the gal with the hole in her stocking whose heel kept a-knocking, and weren't they all lucky to be having such a good time? *But wait*, Bella seemed to say, when she waved a flip goodbye at the end, *because here's the real treat!* The band swept into *Don't Dilly-Dally*. Many people in the audience perked up and started to hum along. 'Not too much of that,' Mama had warned. 'Cleveland won't like it if you turn his vaudeville into a common music hall, but you don't have to squelch them either.'

Aurora grabbed the birdcage from behind the downstage leg and went into the spotlight all forlorn, a lost girl in the city. '*My old man said, "Follow the van, And don't dilly-dally on the way . . ."*' Nice as it was to be centre stage, taking sympathy from the sea of faces down below, Aurora disliked this song. She wended through long verses about chamber pots (which they'd ditch tomorrow if Mrs. Cleveland happened to carp), into the chorus again. But by then the crowd was turning its attention to the programme, wondering what came next. She could see them shift in their seats, and only managed to keep panic from entering her voice by pushing it louder, which did not work.

Chorus again, this one the last: '*My old man said, Follow the van, don't dilly-dally on the way!*'—and then, a terrible blank.

The music went on alone. She had forgotten the lyrics.

She looked over at Mendel in a panic and saw his head swivel quickly to look at her, and then an eyebrow lifted—he reached the end of the bar and swung his hand around in a circle to the band as if he'd meant to do that all along. A cheerful broad-faced lady in the audience took that as encouragement and sang along gaily, '*My old man,*' and when they got to the second line it came back into Aurora's head and she sang on, '*Off went the cart with our home packed in it, I walked behind with my old cock linnet,*' while cold horror ran through her: she had forgotten the words. The stupidest of sins.

Bella nudged Clover to join in, and they sang along with the lady in the front row, rising up into a loud triumph on '*Can't find my way home!*' Aurora bobbed a curtsy to thank her for the lines, and knocked her head to show that it was empty.

Then the audience was all clapping, as much for their own woman as for the girls.

It was over. Except that they still had one song to go, and it was mostly hers to sing. So Aurora had to put despair aside. *The Last Rose of Summer* was Papa's favourite. She knew the words inside her bones, because the sentences made perfect sense; it was the saddest song in the world, except you could not let the audience feel so much sadness, so you tempered it a little.

> '*So soon may I follow when friendships decay*
> *And from love's shining circle the gems drop away.*
> *When true hearts lie withered and fond ones are flown*
> *O, who would inhabit this bleak world alone?*'

Papa had not waited to follow, he had gone before them. His true heart lay withered in the Paddockwood graveyard and Aurora knew it was only because she was good at pretending that she could sing the song at all, hating him as she did for leaving them. Effortlessly, as if it required only to be unleashed, she let her clearest voice soar up above Clover and Bella, flying into the clouds on *flown*, and then sinking back to inhabit this bleak world alone.

Not alone, though. Together they were bowing, the lights dazzling in their eyes as their heads and backs dipped forward, their skirts curdled into curtseys.

Drop the Other One

A respectable amount of applause, Clover thought, but Aurora was prostrate with humiliation. She sat with her cheek down on the dressing-table, a shawl over her head to shade her eyes. So Clover took Bella with her, creeping into the wings to watch East & Verrall, the Sidewalk Conversationalists. Seeing the act from behind meant mostly the backs of their bowler hats, but from time to time one would turn to fit in some false teeth or twiddle a prop out of a pocket, and he (carrot-topped, rascally East, or darker, gentlemanly Verrall) would wink at them, which made both girls feel deliciously at home in this new world.

East was the good-natured fool, Verrall the educated man. They wore tidy black boots, and their black suits were too tight: East's too short in the legs, Verrall's too long.

'Well, I don't know nothing, Mr. Verrall,' said East, rudely, when Verrall schooled him in some little fact or other.

'I don't know *anything*, Mr. East!' said Verrall back, trying to teach him better grammar.

Delighted, East crowed, 'You neither? I *thought* not!'

They walked along in front of a backdrop painted with a seafront scene, a promenade on a summery afternoon. Their walking was cleverly, expansively done: long legs moving in a loping stride, but each foot placed down only an inch in front of the other, so they made hardly any progress at all and could spend five minutes sauntering across the stage.

Talking about their lodgings, Verrall undertook to correct East again: 'I say, East, you must be less noisy tonight. The sick man in the room below us is so dreadfully nervous, he jumps out of his skin at a sudden noise. When you pull off your boots, don't drop them down the clattering way you always do! Set each one down soft.'

'Well, I tried that, Verrall, my old companion, because I remembered you saying that. I was careful as could be, creeping upstairs, inching open the door . . . I read for a minute and smoke my cigar, and then, phew, I'm sleepy, so I blows out the lamp, and—'

They had reached a handy park bench and East sat, suiting the action to the words.

'And I pulls off'—pulling off his boot with a tremendously agile flourish that took his leg nearly to vertical—'my boot—*bam!*'

The boot crashed to the floor with a great *bang*, helped by the percussion man. Verrall flinched and jumped, as if he were the nervous man himself. 'Ahh, but then I remembers!' East said, calming his friend with a soothing hand on his sleeve, then attending to his second boot. 'So I pulls the next one off easy—and slow—and sets it down so feather-soft it could not be heard at all . . . and off I goes to sleep.'

He arranged himself on the bench, forgetting to say his prayers, and then, poked by Verrall, murmuring and crossing himself piously. Taking off his bowler very carefully, he lay down in peaceful rest with the hat for a pillow. Then sprang bolt upright again: 'Four in the morning there's a terrible banging from the floor below and the sick man shouts out, Say! Pull off that other boot! I've been waiting for four mortal hours! I can't sleep till you *drop the other one*!' And Verrall, nodding and grimacing at the ripeness of the line, said it at the same time: '*Drop the other one.*'

Even Clover and Bella had heard that one, but they had not heard East tell it, so droll and innocent and misjudged. They laughed so loud a stagehand shushed them.

'Enough of your nocturnal adventures!' said Verrall. 'We've been asked to keep it very clean here in Fort Macleod, because this is Refined Vaudeville at its most elegant.'

East had his boots back on and nodded, jumping up with an absurd flurry of his skinny legs, to begin their walk again. 'Yes, and so I have a biblical query for you, Mr. Verrall: Why can a man never starve in the Great Desert?'

'I suppose the Great Desert is a place where many a man has starved to death, East.'

'Ah, you would think so, Mr. Verrall, but no! A man can never starve in the Great Desert, because he can eat the *sand which* is there.'

'But what brought the sandwiches there?'

'Why, Noah sent Ham, and his descendants mustered and bred.'

'Oh, Mr. East, oh, Mr. East, I fear you tread the boundaries of decency. Bred, indeed!'

'Man cannot live by breeding alone, you know, Mr. Verrall—much as we might like to,' said East, with such a roll of his eyes that Clover worried the lady in the front row might have an apoplexy and stop the show.

'Mr. East, I beg you, beg you—conform to the niceties of polite discourse.'

'Oh, Mr. Verrall, absolutely. I look up to you as the arbiter of all politesse, noblesse oblige, et ceteratera.' Then East shouted, with a comic-spasmodic helter-skelter jump of sweet alarm, '*Drop the other one!*'

The Fancy of the Management

The foaming rush of the Soubrettes flooded onstage, baby-doll frills and cross-tied black slippers, their skirts hiked up a good deal farther than Mama would have allowed, Bella thought.

Mama came up after the Soubrettes and stood watching beside Bella; Clover went down to see if Aurora would like to walk back to the hotel to rest before the second show. Bella thought it very sad that Aurora should be so overset by a tiny mistake.

'They're graceful enough,' Mama remarked, as the Soubrettes began *Pony*, their skittish bare-knee–baring second number.

'Marry me, carry me, right away with you.
Giddy up, giddy up, giddy up, whoa! My Pony Boy.'

'And pretty—you can see why they've taken the fancy of the Management.' (By which, Bella knew, Mama meant not Mrs. but Mr. Cleveland.) 'Those routines are nothing more than ballroom steps. They hardly sing, they certainly don't act. It's all costume and knees.'

Poor strange Patience stayed in the back row, watched by Joyful at her side. Mercy was the main singer, but Temperance did a bit to help, with a lisping babyish poetry recitation. She closed her mouth with carefully pursed lips at the end of every line—Bella made a note to herself not to do that. Anything tight or ungenerous became tiresome very quickly, she had noticed.

Exquisite

Aurora told Clover to go away, that she was going to die under this shawl but would be better presently if only she could be alone, so Clover went back up to watch. In a minute the door clicked open again and Aurora twitched the shawl off her head in a violent temper, whispering passionately, 'Can you not leave me in peace?' as she whirled around to strike at Clover.

But it was not Clover.

'I did not intend to disturb you—' the elegant young man said. He was very well turned out, in a Bohemian suit with a flowing neck-tie.

Aurora turned away, blushing, and found herself staring straight at his drawing of the *King of Whiskeys* bottle, looking quite friendly and familiar there on the wall. She couldn't turn to face him. 'No, I am sorry,' she said. 'I thought you were my sister.'

'I'm Jimmy Battle,' he said. 'Jimmy the Bat, they call me. And you're the Belle Auroras.'

'Did you see our number?'

'Nicely done, I thought,' he said carefully. 'The way you got out of that little mishap.'

She looked up and saw him smiling in the mirror.

'I was so stupid,' she said, without any airs.

'Happens.'

'Not to me, never before.'

'Well, you wasn't a professional before, then.'

The door opened again, and again it was not Clover. A tall woman flowed into the room on a wind of perfume and glamour. Dark hair clouded around her face, which was broad and open, with dark-hollowed eyes outlined in soot and a short nose above a very wide, mobile mouth. She must be Eleanor Masefield, the actress in the play. She wore something wonderful, a shimmering dark blue travelling costume in dull satin, elaborately cut and trimmed, but playing second fiddle to her magnificent head.

Jimmy the Bat jumped this time, standing almost at attention, some way off from Aurora.

'Oh, I'm early,' the apparition breathed, in a smoky whisper. She smelled of flowers.

Aurora tried to vanish back into her corner, but the woman's head turned gracefully and she fixed Aurora in a charming stare, with a glimmer of a laugh. Of mockery?

'You were the opener! You have an *ex*-quisite voice, my dear.'

Aurora found herself standing, and almost curtsying. Bah! She stood straight.

The woman turned from Aurora, dropping her out of the clutch of her attention to find the young man.

'Jimmy, good—I've left my fur wrap in the carriage, and it's gone back to Bell's Hotel. Sprint along and get it. It's cold in here. And give me your arm up those unspeakable stairs. I shouldn't be down here before the interval, those galloping girls will be back.'

He bowed very slightly, a gentleman even while being a flunky. As he helped with the sweeping skirt's exit he looked up at Aurora, a difficult expression on his face. *Help!* it said, and yet, *Don't worry, I've got her wound around my thumb!* Rueful, and partly apologetic. It made Aurora quite sad to see that lowly apprentice look, but she was still lightly vibrating from Eleanor Masefield's electric presence. '*Ex*-quisite!' She must find Clover to tell her.

At the bottom of the stairs, Aurora bowed again to the rickety steps, the bow she should have given at the end of their turn. Strong beginning, strong end, doesn't matter what happens in the middle, Mama said, and that was right. She looked up, and there was Jimmy the Bat, smiling down at her over the banister. He applauded, hands not quite touching, and threw her an invisible rose before leaping off to do Miss Masefield's bidding.

Then Aurora had to dash herself, because the tunnel door opened and there was Mrs. C. with her bucket, come to do the dressing-room floor. Aurora hoped she had not seen the bow.

A Broken Spell

They were allowed to find a seat at intermission, if they were out of makeup and costume. Bella was poring over the melodrama script she'd found tucked into the old velvet armchair in the dressing room. She and Clover leafed through it—lines underlined, cryptic notations—before returning to the first page:

IN AN ARTIST'S STUDIO

Scene: *An artist's studio in Bohemia, in the heart of New York City. A model's throne, Stage Left, heavy draperies behind a chaise longue. A great easel dominates the room, on which stands a full-length portrait of a beautiful raven-haired woman, carrying lilies. The woman of the portrait is caught, as the curtain rises, in the act of securing a diaphanous robe around her waist—had the curtain risen an instant before, her nakedness would have been exposed.*

Nakedness! But they had to stop reading, as the lights were lowered and the music began for the Knockabout Ninepins. The Ninepins were just as startling as their audition had been, the fury of Mr. Dent if anything more ferocious than before. Nando, hair standing out like Struwwelpeter's, was a shock-headed boy-broom whisking around the stage upside down. Mama gave a shriek, with the audience—impossible to believe that he was not being hurt in the act, but after yesterday's run he'd had no bruises, no scrapes. Bella winced, as he whirled up into the air at the end of that long broom, to see his hands tightening in what looked like terror. But the crowd adored it. They had merely clapped before; now they stamped their feet, and when the beautiful Mrs. Dent rose up unhurt as well, there were cries of relieved admiration from the people sitting nearby.

Soon after the melodrama began, Nando came crashing into the seat beside Bella and filled her and Clover in on the plot: 'She's a wealthy society queen—that's her portrait. He wants her to pose in the altogether, but she won't do it. A good thing too, though she does keep her figure pretty well hitched in.'

Bella thought Miss Masefield very beautiful. Massive eyes under arching, piteous brows, masses of dark hair heaped behind her head like a Gibson girl. Nando told them she was on loan from the legitimate theatre—like Ethel Barrymore, only older, or Sarah Bernhardt, only younger and not so famous. Another actress deigning to come around the vaudeville circuit with a play. The surprise for Bella and Clover was that the man in the play was Jimmy Battle. They'd thought him a singer, or a dancer, but here was where he had been hiding! He was lovely, Bella thought: wavy dark hair, dark eyes, and a look of sophisticated and desperate loneliness.

The first part was waffle about her broken heart and the young artist's empty bohemian life—his need for a woman who could teach him to love again, *purely*. He begged her to cast aside the shackles of society, and yield to him her soul. The words were racy, like those lyrics that Aurora'd sung yesterday, pretending to be chaste in order to be fast.

'Hey, they cut the bit about him wanting to paint her in a state of nature!' Nando whispered. 'But they kept the sheer curtains on her. Need to for the plot, you'll see.' Bella clamped her hand on his arm to make him hush. The woman was moving about the room in her trailing draperies, dark and passionate, practically writhing in the throes of some terrible dilemma. Finally she subsided onto a low couch, close to Jimmy.

> MRS. FARQUHAR: I must be true or I am nothing, can't
> you understand?

Her great eyes stared up at his slim figure, his hand resting negligently on the pillar. Bella wondered if he really did love her; he looked so hurt that she wouldn't be his own. He was a good dancer, and he liked Aurora, so maybe he didn't care about Mrs. Farquhar.

> MRS. FARQUHAR: I married him—that is sacred.
> AUBREY: I understand. You do not love me enough to
> brave the world's disdain.
> MRS. FARQUHAR: It is not disdain I shrink from, but I
> would not have you smirched.
> AUBREY: Oh, you—darling!

Jimmy raised Eleanor Masefield up, and then drew her near. 'They've cut the kiss,' Nando said in Bella's ear. 'Couldn't get it across Cleveland. The old girl was in a snit about that, said it's played the toniest gigs from Boston to Topeka.' But they nearly kissed, *nearly.* Jimmy the Bat's long nose touched the actress's long nose, and brushed along it until—she turned suddenly away. Her noble profile, the studied grace of her movements, made Bella's stomach swoop. Eleanor Masefield walked away from Jimmy, holding out a white arm behind her, begging him to stop. She crumpled to her knees, then knelt, back straight, a white flame in a lonely chapel. How does she make herself look so holy all at once, Bella wondered—while busy believing it with all her heart.

> MRS. FARQUHAR: I have a sacred duty to my husband, for
> he was the father of my little son—my son, passed

on to heaven at three years old. That hallowed
memory keeps me locked in my golden cage.

She smiled, a soft, sad smile, and lifted a serenely grieving face
heavenward.

At that Bella's fascination ended with a cool click in her mind. No.
That is not how Mama looks when she talks about Harry.

Bella pulled her arm out of Nando's and decided not to watch
any more. But then there was a tramping sound, and Aubrey and Mrs.
Farquhar turned as one towards the door in dramatic attitudes of
apprehension and alarm which, now the spell was broken, struck
Bella as funny. It was her husband! They sprang apart. He picked up
his palette and she clutched her negligee around her once more, and
shrank back onto the platform as if to hide behind it—but the artist
was a smarty, and moving her arms into place as if she were a statue,
he picked up the sheer drapery and flung it over Mrs. Farquhar.

The veil was barely in place when the husband came in. He was in
a storm, thundering round the studio, looking for his wife in the corners and behind the dressing screen. He stopped, transfixed, in front
of her beautiful portrait. Then his eye caught the veiled form, and he
went to tear the veiling off, but Aubrey stopped him.

> AUBREY: A statue, in its early stages. The clay cannot be
> exposed to air.

Oh, what a piffle! Bella did not expect the husband to be fooled
by that—but he let his hand drop, and went back to staring at the
portrait.

> MR. FARQUHAR: I raised her from obscurity, a poor girl,
> daughter of a country schoolmaster—she knew
> nothing of the ways of high society. I schooled her.
> Now she leads the social world. Or has, till now . . .

The draped figure moved, one arm yearning towards her husband.

AUBREY: And you seek to upbraid her for her sins?
MR. FARQUHAR: To beg her forgiveness, before— I have
failed her. The truth is, I am a failure. Cracked up,
business in ruins. I came to say—farewell.
AUBREY: You take the coward's way out, sir?
MR. FARQUHAR: If it is cowardly to rid the world of one
without worth, yes.

Bella was back in the story now with the stumpy businessman, whose round stomach and twiddly moustache might have made him ridiculous, except that he was so downtrodden by bad luck. He grovelled onto the model platform and collapsed at the feet of his wife's statue.

MR. FARQUHAR: She will be better without me. Free to
love, again!

He was still. Aubrey looked up at the statue and held out his hand, beckoning to his love with the imperiousness of youth. But lo! A rustle of silks, the veil cast aside, and the goddess knelt to the crumpled creature at her feet and touched his bald pate. The husband gasped; his head lifted. (Like one of Juddy's dogs sniffing a bone, Bella thought.)

MRS. FARQUHAR: I love you better in your failure
than ever in success. Come to me, my dear.

She cradled his head upon her bosom. Aubrey looked at the pair with a sardonic air. Swept a bow, picked up his hat, and left the two alone, in an artist's studio.

Watching Jimmy Battle come back for a curtain call and smile off into the wings (which she'd bet a nickel was where Aurora stood) Bella had a revelation. It came clear to her, about performing: there was the imaginary version, the vision of how the thing was going to be—how they would dance, how the people would be transported on wings of song. But then there was what really happened—how she almost came in a beat too soon and that threw them all off, then Aurora forgetting the words—which was the truth of it.

But not the whole truth of it, because they would be good, some-day they would be. And it seemed to her that the part of herself that would be good was the same part that tripped and fell, that came in too soon, that held the notes too long. As the part of Aurora that was best was the part that nearly killed her every time she did anything less than perfect—her privacy, her unwillingness to fail. And Clover? Clover was a puzzle. She thought nothing of herself, but that was so pure! That self-ignoring made Clover nothing but music when she sang, made her *self* disappear and the notes come forward. Maybe that was her goodness? And Mama was good at the vision of how things could be, at continuing on, no matter what.

Where We Want to Be Tea was served onstage during the break between shows, a nice surprise; the girls had thought they'd have to tramp back to the hotel or go without. A cup of stewed black tea and a biscuit one step up from hardtack, but they were not asked to contribute a penny each as Clover had feared they might be. Jimmy was there, and Clover nudged Bella to give him back his script and beg pardon for steal-ing it. He laughed and said he did not need it any longer, only kept it as a talisman. 'I figure I can't be fired if I've got my script in hand!'

Mama did not like that, she thought talk of trouble courted trouble. She knocked quickly on a wooden tabletop. 'Oh, it's all right,' he said, seeing her do it. 'I'm in pretty good with the management, at least until the wind changes.'

'You poor boy, all alone in the world, and in such a perilous busi-ness as this!'

Jimmy smiled at her lovingly. (Easy to see how well he went over with the older ladies, Clover thought.) 'Well, it is lonesome sometimes, but as for hating the work and wanting to give it up, no! Not as long as you can get booked and get a good salary, for there is no work in the world as nice and easy as this business when things are coming right.'

'That's exactly what I say to my girls. How long have you been with Miss Masefield?'

'Just this year. I was with Pantages for three years, and before that on the western tour with the Barnabas company in *East Lynne*— abridged version, twenty minutes, start to tagline. Headlining smaller theatres on the Sullivan–Considine circuit. Three days then to get from Helena to Spokane—that's halved now, only two changes, and a sleeper on one of the legs. But'—he lowered his voice—'I'd certainly rather play out east, wouldn't you?'

'Keith's family vaudeville is where we want to be,' Mama confided.

'As if that isn't where everybody wants to be!' Bella said. She went to talk to Nando, who was standing by the tea cart eating biscuits as if that were his vaudeville act: *How many will one mouth hold?*

Then tea service was over, since Mrs. Cleveland was waiting to wash the floor again, her grey hair pinned clumsily back and her hands dark red with soap-rash. Clover could not help thinking that she might be better to hire a floor-washing woman, to keep her own position a little more dignified, but perhaps the saving in money was too tempting.

Imaginary Monster

In the half-hour before the second show Bella slipped down the tunnel to the lobby and took a look from the audience side, to remind herself of the people sitting close-packed and hot, still bundled up after travelling through the cold maybe for miles and miles, waiting for the only wonderful thing they might see all year. It was so touching that they came, and she found that looking at the people made the audience less of an imaginary monster. The safety curtain shone like the aurora borealis, its white metallic surface covered with fancy-lettered ads from all the local businesses, a thousand messages obscured by rippling lights from buttons and mirrors and glass in the theatre—where was that light coming from? Then she saw: a banjo's silver plate, flashing as the musician strummed, made the footlights dance on the pressed-tin ceiling, light sparks reflecting everywhere. What a pretty halo everything had!

Bella was as happy as she could ever remember, watching all this.

Time to go on: she nipped back through the tunnel and up to the stage, and saw that from behind the curtain Mama was motioning her to hurry. Like walking to the theatre that morning, everything in the act went faster because they knew what was coming, and how things would go. They stood in the wings waiting for their cue, they sang, and before they knew where they were, they were done.

Dilly-Dally

Aurora did not forget the words to Dilly-Dally, though she could feel Bella and Clover alert beside her, ready to chime in with them if needed. She sang *Last Rose* even better than before, her throat funnelling the song upwards and hanging up there at *flown* . . . with Mendel following perfectly. The audience was livelier, or perhaps better fed. The applause at the end of their turn was gratifying; they heard two separate whistles. Even Clover was pink with pleasure as they came off, and Mama was clapping for them backstage. She shepherded them down the stairs to change out of their flowered shirtwaists. They'd been onstage for all of fourteen minutes, but it seemed an hour.

Aurora hung back—she had spotted Jimmy the Bat watching from the darkness beyond the second leg. She dodged in there, just for an instant, and he said, 'There! Told you so, you are a professional now.'

Aurora laughed and went to leave, but Jimmy caught her wrist and pulled her in close, one arm about her waist as if they were about to dance, and then kissed her.

Exactly what she wanted: the silkiness of his lips surprising and familiar, and the smell that hung about his mouth, fresh, a bit of cinnamon.

Aurora looked up into his dark eyes, one glance. She knew him.

'We would dance well,' she said. He would rather dance than act with Eleanor Masefield, she thought. She would rather that too.

Off she went. As the Wonder Dogs rose onto the stage like the tide, she turned back for a moment and saw a flash stage left that emanated from Mrs. C.'s searchlight eyes. She hoped Mrs. Cleveland had not seen that kiss; she would be a devil for anything of the kind. Jimmy was fording through the dogs, away from Mrs. Cleveland, who stared after him with blank, tight eyes and a mean mouth.

Not Allowed a Bath

The hotel room was warm from the Quebec stove bravely hissing. Mama sat sewing lace saved from her wedding peignoir to the collars of their ivory shirtwaists, and recalling her own mother, who'd had some success in the legitimate theatre, long before the current refinement of vaudeville. As she sewed, Mama retold stories of the pleasurable touring of her childhood, before her disapproving father snatched her up and left her with Aunt Queen and Uncle Elmore, the Plymouth Brethren and the dentistry. As she talked, her mouth filled and emptied of the pins necessary to keep the lace perfectly straight on the collars.

Almost dreaming already, Clover closed her eyes and listened to the rambling reminiscence. It was sad, that Mama could never forget a kindness or a slight or snub. She was as angry now over Aunt Queen not allowing her to have a bath in Madison before the dance concert as she must have been at that very moment—'Can you feature it!' she asked, as if she had not asked them all to feature it a thousand times. Clover sighed out and breathed in, and never minded Mama.

They would get better. It had not been a good show, except for the very last song, and a dull feeling accompanied that realization. But they'd practise tomorrow morning, and Clover felt the satisfying stability of being in a good company. Lying on her side in the quieting night, she could hear East and Verrall arguing along the hall in the hotel.

'. . . your boot?' That was Verrall.

Then East said more loudly, '*Hurts!* He wants to know if it hurts!'
More murmuring as Verrall shushed him, then a bump.

East said, 'Does it hurt?' and Verrall answered sadly, 'He wants to know if it hurts.'

They tramped on down the hall.

White Feathers

Bella woke slowly in pale morning light. A noise outside gradually turned into sense—shovels catching from time to time as men cleared the boardwalk. It must be late; there was sunlight on Aurora's hair, straying on the pillow beside her. A thousand colours, not just one gold: white and silver and caramel and pale, hardly ripe apricots, gleaming in the sun, the prettiest thing in the world. Her own hair was taffy-brown, dull and ugly.

Clover brought her porridge in the little flower-bottom bowl. 'We let you sleep, but come, eat. We'll have to climb through drifts today.'

When they left the hotel the sun was hung with sun-dogs, huge blinding brackets in the sky. The wind had died and glittering motes of snow stood suspended in air. Every branch, every twig of every tree and bush was furred and blurred with white feathers.

Too soon, almost, they were at the Empress. The same bustle and darkness, but Nando was not at the door to welcome them. They stood in the lobby to let their eyes adjust to the twilight, and saw a notice posted on the door, NEW ORDER, listing the order of acts for the day's shows.

'Now, look! Perhaps Cleveland has seen the light and placed you later in the bill!' Mama said with satisfaction. She peered at the list but could not make it out in the dimness. 'Clover?'

Obedient, Clover bent to the list, and found herself in a strange pause, not feeling as if she could breathe or had breathed for some time. *Opener, in one: Maximilian the Bird Magician,* she read. She ran her eye up and down the list, again, again. How could she say it out loud? Aurora and Bella leaned in to see.

They were not on the list.

Aurora felt it in her hands and feet, the coldness of the blood drained away. Bella in her stomach, a great swoop—it was her fault, it must be. Clover's breath would not come. Mama jerked her head and blinked, to insist her vision re-form: but still they were not on the list.

The list swam away from them through the darkness as Mendel opened the door to the theatre, a metal weight ready in his hand to prop it open for air.

'What does this mean?' Mama asked him, without histrionics.

'Sorry,' Mendel said, not even pretending not to know. 'Cleveland decided to make a change. You could find him in his office, but he'll only tell you that.'

The four of them, young and old, looked at Mendel, at his wise pitying face.

'I'm sorry. You've been cancelled.'

Aurora felt her hands as juggernauts, the weight of them threatening to sink her down through the floor. It was her, forgetting the lyrics—she had jinxed them at that very moment.

Bella cried, 'It's all my fault!' and Clover said, 'It's me, not you. It should have been the Belle–Aurora duo.'

Mendel looked over his shoulder quickly, and said, 'I understand it may have been the Mrs. who decided. Sometimes she does take a sudden whim.'

Mama somehow drew up her chin, her proud carriage returning. Small rapid tears were coursing down her cheeks, but there was no muffle in her voice. 'Girls, it's just the way it sometimes goes. We move on to the next gig, that's all.' She put an arm round Clover and one round Bella, leaving Aurora the dignity of the eldest.

'If—' Mendel hesitated, still holding the heavy weight. 'If it's not beneath you, I do have a pal in Calgary, in the burlesque house there. I could put in a word—'

'Thank you, but no, not at all,' Mama said.

'No,' Aurora agreed.

Schedules of trains, wagon rates, hotels, cartage fees, the fifty cents gone on supper last night riffled through Aurora's head like a magician's deck of cards. They'd be broke in a week. In this snow it was unlikely they could get to Qu'Appelle so soon.

Mendel came out into the lobby, shut the door, and put the weight down. 'I don't know how you're fixed, maybe you're fine—but look—it's nowhere near the money you'd get in burlesque, but I know Johnny Drawbank is hiring down in Helena, on the Ackerman circuit through Montana. I don't mind tipping him onto you, you're nice gals, a nice enough act, no reason you couldn't shine down there. No guarantee, but I'd say it's a good chance.'

Mama looked at him without gratitude. 'I did the Death Trail, twenty years ago. I have seen the elephant down there, Mr. Mendel.'

He almost laughed. 'It's not so bad these days. No more storefronts. Theatres, every one a plush-seat house. They're building brick, sprouting up all over. Keith's is looking to purchase in Great Falls, that's how far it's come. You'd be with the same artistes for a couple of months, they tour together through there. Down into Montana, Idaho, the Dakotas, but not rough like it used to be. Half-pay weeks, I know—but it'd be good training and a good start.'

The girls had heard Mama's account of the Death Trail, its privations and indignities. Mama had turned her face into Clover's shoulder, pretending to comfort her, to try to regain composure.

Watching the brown swirl of her mother's hair, trained into a respectable chignon, Aurora weighed the likelihood of Qu'Appelle, how it would be there when none of them knew Uncle Chum (and when Mama felt true hatred for Papa's family, possibly with some cause). As far as Aurora could see at this point, the only alternative was to return to Calgary and try to get taken on as domestic servants. That might easily be a fate worse than the Death Trail, and anyway it would take too long. They'd be starving at a soup kitchen before then.

Now Aurora touched Mendel on his sleeve, and smiled into his melted-chocolate eyes, because he was kind, and because it would help that he liked her.

She said, 'Yes, please, yes. If you could give us a note for Mr. Drawbank, that might ease our way.'

3.
The Death Trail

JANUARY–FEBRUARY 1912

The Parthenon, Helena, Montana

Apply to the manager of some obscure Vaudeville or
moving picture house, and obtain an engagement, even
if for a very small salary, and at the conclusion of the
engagement you will find out your weak points, if any
. . . Do not feel ashamed because you are compelled to
make such a humble beginning, as a great many
professional acts do this very same thing when they
have something new and untried. This is what's called
breaking in an act, or hiding away.

FREDERIC LADELLE, *HOW TO ENTER VAUDEVILLE*

$\mathcal{T}$he beauty of the snow faded as they went south—blown by the constant wind, leaving fields bare beneath a light dusting of white. The world was the colour of their old dog Tray, dun and white. Bella's eyes itched, remembering Tray. She and Papa had found him, lying by the tracks, as if asleep—and then so plainly not asleep, but gone. She hated the train they were on for Tray's death, for Papa's, even Harry's, without rational cause. Then, more sensibly, she hated herself for not being better in the act so that they could have stayed in Fort Macleod for the whole week and gone with the company to Crowsnest, with Nando, who was her sweetheart now. She hated being cancelled when she thought of Nando but it also made her laugh secretly, to think of him. *'I have a little cat, I'm very fond of that...'* she sang into her beret.

It would take all night to get to Montana. The girls sat propped in their seats, bolstered with packages and bandboxes, the trunk safe in the baggage-man's care. Aurora tried to calculate how much he would expect for its return. Would a nickel be enough, for a straight journey without a change? If only she knew more about the ordinary business of being in the world, in cities and trains.

She was learning, though. She had gone straight up to Cleveland's office after Mendel told them they were cancelled, to get their pay for the one night. Mrs. Cleveland was on her knees in the auditorium scrubbing again, but it would not take her long to scramble up and come after, so Aurora had made it quick: 'Only the one night, we'll take $30.'

Her upright bearing, or her cool stare, must have made it seem a good idea to comply. His flat-pouched eyes never leaving her face, Cleveland had forked out three ten-dollar bills. By rights it should have been $25. Being cancelled was a terrible blow, but she was extremely glad to be away from that shocking hypocrite. *And* a coward, and a bad judge of performance, she said to herself, not proud of getting the money out of him, but relieved to have it in Mama's grouch-bag, since train tickets to Helena had taken all the rest. She leaned her forehead on the cracked green leather to stare out the window above the frost. *Amateur-night, amateur-night,* the clacking wheels said, but riding over a siding the rhythm altered, and she made it turn into *we-will-be-better.*

Flora woke from a doze and looked around the jouncing carriage: Aurora, Bella—where was Clover? Oh, here, sleeping beside her, almost invisible under the ulster but keeping Flora's right side cozy and sheltered from the window's ice. She had been dreaming of the girls when Bella was tiny—in Medstead, it must have been, one school before Paddockwood. Dreaming of Arthur, not yet succumbed to melancholy, blowing bubbles into bright sun to propound some scientific principle to his class. They ought not to have moved from there, but bubbles do burst, no matter how carefully one touches them. Now back to the States—Flora's drowsy mind veered off from failure and drifted to her daughters again: dear Clover who would never leave her; Bella, the darling girl; her first-born Aurora whose beauty and talent must shine through and take the girls to the top regardless of stupidity in high places or vicissitudes so far, and never burlesque, not for her girls. Talent would out, cream would rise, a thousand a week quite soon.

Afterwards they slept, leaning on each other's shoulders as comfortably as they could; then Bella changed seats to lay her head on Aurora's lap. Even in the dusk, and later in clear, moon-relieved darkness, Aurora could see the hills marching south along with the train track, how they folded, alternating patches of shadow and pale moon-grey, until the folds gradually turned into mountains. When the train shifted on the track she saw her reflection in the window in the darkness—her face looked beautiful, but that was just the angle, and the darkness. She could see herself better in the crooked mirror of Clover's and Bella's eyes. They saw her true face, not this train-window beauty or the stage-makeup looks, and kept her from thinking too much of herself.

'My sweet friend Sybil went on the burlesque for a while,' Mama had said earlier, in the peace of the evening train. 'I went too, once, when we were broke. If it looked safe, she would toss her garters into the audience and they'd throw money back—once in a way she'd leave off her stockings, but that got her a night in jail in Dubuque. Of course she wasn't charged as Sybil Sutley: if she'd played under her right billing, her value on the medium-time would have been lowered, you see? Many people did it from time to time, went to burlesque when the wolf was at the door. We don't look down on them for it. You do what you have to do to get by. She went under the name of Saunders, Saucy Saunders.'

'We should have tried to stay in Paddockwood,' Clover said, before she thought.

'How can you say so!' Mama took her up quickly. Clover looked away. 'You'd rather have the life of a farm woman? Ought I to have looked about for a farmer? You know I would have done it if I'd thought it for the best.'

All three girls shook their heads quickly. Mama had not been good at the ordinary work of householding in any of Papa's teaching posts. Even in Paddockwood, where they'd lasted four years.

Mama made delicious macaroons, if they could get coconut. If they had eggs—if the chickens had not all died. Aurora gave a quick hoot of laughter, but bobbed her head at Mama to apologize, because she was no kind of good at all that herself and she completely *loathed* chickens, spiteful creatures who pecked at each other's corpses while you were trying to pluck them. Clover had a light hand with pastry, Bella made fudge. But if the choice was worry and turmoil and travel, or staying in one place forever with the chickens and the milking pail, Aurora was happy to be on the train.

Was He Weeping?   At Helena, the train station was plunked in a grim field. One good sign: the wind brought dodgers floating, flapping round their ankles, over the train platform. Bella picked at one and said 'Look!' The flimsy slips advertised Ackerman–Harris's Parthenon Semi-Continuous Vaudeville, '*fun and frolic, melodeon and concert saloon.*' Left to blow around the streets and sidewalks instead of handed out, dodgers were even cheaper than handbills, but it was good to see that the Parthenon existed.

'An omen!' Mama exclaimed. 'I believe our luck is turned, my chicks.'

They used the ladies' waiting room to pull themselves into proper order. Mama had packed the flowered waists carefully at the top of the trunk to keep them pressed overnight. 'Perhaps an extra wrinkle or two, but we won't repine,' she said, taking off her ulster in the freezing waiting room and beckoning Clover to help her hold it up across a corner so that Bella could change. Then Bella held it carefully for Clover, who was quick as lightning; Bella knew how she hated to be vulnerable in a public place, however deserted. Aurora went last, and they used the flat-steel mirror nailed to the station wall to tidy their hair. Even Mama was careful, arranging the curls of her fringe, and using the rouge-box first on the girls, delicately—'Roses blooming in the snow!'—and then on herself.

They asked the lonely stationmaster to show them the way to the theatre, leaving the trunk 'to be called for,' and set off through wind-blown emptiness to find the tallest-fronted buildings in town, Mama exclaiming at the beauty of well-established architecture and how this was more like it, a city with scope for great performances, and other observations calculated to console them for being firmly on the Death Trail now.

The Parthenon manager appeared be-hatted, a chewed cigar in his mouth. Bella thought he looked like a cartoon of a tough customer, except for his wide-apart pale blue eyes.

'Mendel!' he exclaimed sorrowfully, when Mama introduced herself and handed him the note, saying it was from Mendel at the Empress. He held it by one edge, doubtful. '*Mendel* sent you to me? Well, that's a great thing, a great thing. To hear from a guy like that. He's a trump card, Mendel.'

He took out his cigar and stared at the letter, in some distress of spirit. Taken aback, Mama waited for him to recover from the shock. It seemed to Bella that he might be in pain. Was he weeping?

He stretched his mouth wide, contorting his face like a baby, pulled one massive dirty hand over his whole bald scalp and down to hide his eyes, and shook his head, turning the envelope over in his other hand. 'So what's he think, I got a spot open?'

Aurora put her hand through Mama's arm and said gently, 'Perhaps we could audition?'

He seemed surprised all over again. 'Well, that's the ticket, but the thing is, I don't make those decisions. I'm the front man, I'm the business head, but I don't know beans about acts or booking 'em. I leave all that to Gentry Fox.'

At that name Mama's head rose, eyebrows arching up her forehead. 'Gentry Fox is your musical director, your manager?'

'*Is* he? I'll hope to tell ya. Manages the hell out of me.'

'Well,' said Mama. 'That puts a different complexion on it. I think Gentry will see me, for old times' sake.'

While Drawbank disappeared, Bella tugged Clover to look at the posters on the wall for the coming attractions (VICTOR SABORSKY, MANIFEST ECCENTRIC! THE GRAPHOPHONE GIRL, A BOWERY ROMANCE), and the present playbill: SUNDERLAND & PETTIBONE'S EXCURSION OF SONG, SWAIN'S RATS & CATS, and MAURICE MACKENNA KAVANAGH, ELOCUTIONIST. After the break, the OLD SOLDIER FIDDLERS, CORNELIUS THE BUBBLE JUGGLER, and the pictures. A lean bill. Kavanagh, a famous Irish actor who toured in vaudeville between theatre engagements, was the only name on the bill they'd heard before. Only the pictures to close, too. It was a paltry kind of place, but Bella did not say so.

They Do a Royal Tea

Gentry Fox was the shortest man Clover had ever seen, shorter than she was by far. As if someone had pressed down on the head of a normal man, but some time ago, so he'd had time to get used to it.

He had to look up, even at Bella, which he did with a sideways glint. 'What—have—we—here?' he asked, his voice both gravelled and silky.

The girls stood in a line, not sure whether to proceed. He waved a hand, beckoning them to the stage, and they went stiffly down the raked aisle, not entirely sure of their footing in the thicker darkness of the auditorium. Mama patted Clover, who moved aside to let her through. She took two steps and stopped, perhaps afraid, Clover thought.

But no. She had paused only to make a better entrance. Mr. Fox looked up, inquiring, when she did not speak—then, looking again, gave Mama a very warm, familiar smile. He laughed and bowed, and bowed again, coming forward as he bent and rose and bent.

'Oh, my dear sir, you may recall that I have had the distinct pleasure of making your acquaintance before,' Mama said to the little bowing man. Bowing now herself.

'But of course, of *course* I recall,' Mr. Fox said, murmuring and mincing. 'With the *greatest*, my dear Flora, the greatest of pleasure.'

Pleasure, pleasure. They were nodding dolls, bowing and re-bowing. Clover felt Aurora pull her close, then slide an arm behind to pull Bella into place.

'And these?'

'Oh, *these*! My dear Mr. Fox! You see before you—my daughters.'

Dark eyes gleamed in his dark rumpled face, turning from one girl to the next. His squashed neck was supple. Inspecting Aurora. Then Clover, Bella. And back to Mama.

'They are jewels,' he said with great simplicity. 'They sing? They dance?'

'They do!' Mama clapped her hands because he was so clever. 'May we?'

'Will you? Will they? Johnny Drawbank! Clear those hands away, if you will. Lights!'

This was a much bigger stage, a much bigger theatre. Not a jewel box like the Empress; the floorboards not as clean beneath the dirty chairs, and the stage not clean either. Deep, though, and high—four long curtain-legs before the backdrop. Clover thought doing it in one here would be a pleasure, because the stage bowed outwards and left an acre of room in front of the great red curtain (its ragged bottom draggling on the boards, gold bobble-trim gappy and dimmed).

Work-lights shone on the piano, and on the stage. As Mama and the girls climbed the moveable gangplank over the orchestra pit, on came the footlights, the gas flaring gently, and the stage became welcoming.

'We'll start with an old song,' Mama said, twinkling down at Mr. Fox. '*After the Ball*,' she murmured to the girls, and sat herself at the piano gracefully. Her little hands raised themselves over the keys, and paused, and then were off, playing with unusual care and a rippling dash—the conservatory glass, the palms, the tinkling waltz heard from a distance . . . They told the sentimental story plain, the way she had taught them, not as a tired tale but as if this were their Uncle Chum explaining his bachelor life to them. None of the girls could remember meeting him, but they all had affection for him, from this imaginary memory. It made Clover believe that Mama must have a soft spot for Chum too, after all.

> '. . . oh, Uncle, please.
> *Why are you single; why live alone?*
> *Have you no babies; have you no home?*
>
> *I had a sweetheart, years, years ago;*
> *Where she is now, pet, you will soon know.*
> *List to the story, I'll tell it all,*
> *I believed her faithless, after the ball . . .'*

Watching the girl he loved being kissed, standing empty-hearted with two glasses of punch in his hands . . . How plaintive the old man became, and what a small, stupid thing to ruin someone's life: '*he was her brother!*' Then they were into the chorus again, waltzing in place to prove they could do it in one:

'After the ball is over, after the break of dawn—
After the dancers' leaving; after the stars are gone;
Many a heart is aching, if you could read them all;
Many the hopes that have vanished
After the ball.'

Mama ended with a fading chord, well in keeping with the natural delivery of the song, and left a dainty hand poised in air for a moment as the girls bowed. Then she twirled on the piano stool, face out to the audience, to Gentry Fox. He rose from his seat in the front row with a hearty 'Bravo!' clapping his hands delightedly.

Coming forward to the stage, he stretched out a hand to Mama as if he could reach hers, which not even a tall man could have, and she reached down to him without moving from the stool.

'Lovely, lovely girls! *Lovely* to hear that old song again, so freshly rendered! And how well I recall you, my dear Flora—at the Hippodrome, was it not?—with that little number.'

'Oh, Gentry, a hundred years ago,' Mama said, blushing and bobbing. Bella laughed too, to see her so pleased. Clover looked at Mr. Fox with attention: a living clue to Mama's old life. But beside her she could feel Aurora waiting, tense, and her own confidence drained away.

'Now you must let me give you some lunch,' Gentry said, taking out a card case. 'Hand my card to the girl at the Grandon Hotel, they do a royal tea there . . . and thank you for warming an old man's heart. You are visiting in the neighbourhood? With family?'

Mama got up from the piano, her face fallen into a polite parody of her earlier happiness. 'You have no work for my girls, then, Gentry?' she asked—her voice sad, but her face remaining cheerful.

'My dear Flora, they are young and charming, and I am inundated with acts. Between you and me and your eighteen best friends, this is a poor place I find myself. We have only seven on the bill—all but continuous, you know—three shows a day, a hardscrabble life.'

'But what a training ground!' Mama said lightly—still working, still arguing, however her words might be disguised as chat.

'But such delicately reared girls, my dear Flora, could not be expected to— And my bill is full for this and *several* weeks to come.'

'But I see you lack a closer,' Mama said. Her last effort.

'Oh, as to that, I use the pictures as a closer. Nothing beats a very old pictograph for encouraging an audience's hearts for home.'

'I bet we could chase them better, if we're so bad!' Bella called over the footlights at him, laughing at her own audacity.

Clover pinched her quickly, but Gentry laughed too, darting a sharp look at Bella's cheeky, lively face. But he still held out the calling card. Lunch, not life.

Gentry

'Well, thank you, Gentry, for seeing us. It was a piece of old times to find you here,' Flora said, folding her music as if they hadn't a care in the world, as if they were, in fact, visiting family and perfectly easy. As if they hadn't spent twenty-three dollars on train fare.

She and Aurora looked at each other, and she lifted her chin and smiled.

'Off we go, then,' she said. 'But perhaps we had better return to our friends for luncheon, thank you all the same.'

Aurora lighted down on the first step, lifting her skirt delicately over her tight-laced new boot. The second step, the second boot (and above it, a stretch of smooth white stocking). The third step, the fourth. 'But, Mama,' she said, smiling into Gentry's upturned face. 'I think *I'd* like some tea.'

He held out his hand with the card again, and she took it, and then his arm, for help in navigating the last steps.

'Thank you, Mr. Fox,' Aurora said. She stopped to pull on her elegant mauve kid gloves. 'And will you come with us? My sisters and I would love to hear how you and Mama come to know each other so well; how you come to be in this theatre, and what wonders you are working in this out-of-the-way place—we see your dodgers all over town!'

Gentry blinked, but resisted, even though her eyes were so clear, their colour shifting from blue to green, a dark line around the iris. Beautiful, yes. The curve of her clear warm cheek and jaw ran enticingly into the hidden reaches of the neck, under that glossy pile of bright, ruly-unruly hair.

'Alas, no, I shall be engaged all afternoon with wretched business,' he told her sadly.

Aurora gave him a beautiful smile, exchanged his arm for her sister's, and walked up the raked aisle. The tiny waist of her jacket remained steady; below it the skirt swayed, its length tantalizing along the ground in an eddy of dust. The youngest one, the filly, hopped off the last step and sparkled at him, then dashed after the elder two.

'Look at her, the darling! All legs and heels and promise,' he said to Flora, before he could check himself. 'But I am sentimentalizing. Time to retire to the country!'

Flora took the steps without assistance, pulling on her own gloves, her music in its leather case beneath her arm, and at the bottom, bowed to Gentry. He looked at her soft face, brown curls at her brow. Still pretty as paint, even softened into middle age. A loving heart, if a silly one.

She stepped down onto the floor, not wanting to tower above him more than she could help—for his sake as well as her own. A stroke of luck to have found him here. It could not be wasted.

'Gentry,' she said, then drew in a breath. 'I wonder—I've done my best with my dear girls, but they need polish, of course. I wonder if you would consider taking them on for a few weeks, for nothing—well, or for just the usual travelling expenses, alone—to gain experience, to be introduced to the profession.'

She had caught his attention. Either his pockets were to let, or his native stinginess was stirring. How much this would cost her, coming and going, she thought she knew.

'I'm sure we could go farther afield and find paid work, but it's you, the association with someone of your calibre—oh! I know very well how much good you did me, all those years ago, and I wish that same good for my girls. Can you find it in your heart to blame me?'

'The thing is, Flora,' he said, not unkindly, 'your dainty girls are too refined for this place—it would be cruel. They are not—'

'They *are*. I promise you. They are better by far than I.' Her urgency led her to put a hand on his arm. A small hand in a black cloth glove, it vanished on his black sleeve.

'Gentry, for old times' sake—I beg you.'

After a moment, he bowed one last time. 'Madam, that plea is impossible to refuse. Not today. But bring them here at nine tomorrow, and I will see what can be done.'

She found it hard to look at him, after putting herself so low before him, but busied herself with her music case.

He gestured towards it: 'Have you a lobby photograph for the girls there?' He saw from her face that they had none. 'After your lunch go to Leroy's Studio on 8th Avenue. They will not overcharge you.'

As Flora went up the aisle, he called after her. 'What happened to your schoolmaster?'

'Oh—' She shrugged and almost smiled. 'Oh, he died.' She nodded, and went through the bright doorway.

A Very Quick Service

'He has offered a tentative booking' was how Mama put it to the girls. 'Two weeks' work with him in the mornings, and he'll use us as the closer, and see how we get on. No need to tell you what a chance this is, and how we must take prime advantage.'

She did not tell them how she had wangled it. Aurora wondered, but did not pry. The French job haunted her thoughts; but whatever it was, there could not have been time—unless it was a very quick service? Her mind went on down that path for an instant and then she shut it out. You do what you have to do, Mama had said about Sybil.

Mama let the younger girls walk on ahead of her to the train station, where they had left their trunk and boxes, while she and Aurora went to secure rooms. ROOMS UPSTAIRS, she saw again, the sign she'd half noted

in the Pioneer Restaurant window on their way to the Parthenon. And
beneath it the smaller handwritten sign: WAITRESS WANTED.

They climbed the steps and Mama rang the bell; Aurora tucked
her hair more carefully under her hat, tied her scarf tight round her
throat, and assumed a modest expression. It was soon enough worked
out: they would take the back room on the second floor, two weeks,
$10 per if they did for themselves, $12 if they had maid service. They
would do for themselves, and no thank you, no meals—working at
the Parthenon, they would be unable to do justice to the full board.

They did justice to the luncheon Aurora ordered at the Grandon,
the best they'd had in months. Rare-broiled porterhouse steak was the
special, and it arrived dressed with boiled potatoes and corn alongside,
which the waitress promised them was canned right at the hotel, none
of your tinned stuff. Bella and Mama had two helpings of cake.

They made a little stir going through the lobby, three bright-
faced well-fed girls on the way to Leroy's Studio—where a plump,
avid young man seemed only too happy to take their photograph,
divesting them of their coats with speedy competence and sitting
them in a succession of poses against his painted backdrop, Aurora
in the centre and the other two in various attitudes around her. He
disposed Aurora's coat tenderly over her shoulders when they were
done and looked meaningfully at her, but she contrived to be very concerned about the tying of Bella's shawl. Three poses, ten prints, to be
sent to the theatre in the morning—$2 more out of the grouch-bag,
but Aurora decided not to fret about that. They would soon enough
be paid—Gentry had all but promised.

Hey-Go-Mad

The Pioneer was a board-hotel, intended
for longer residencies, and the room
was bigger than in the last hotel. An
old chaise at the foot of the iron bedstead would make a couch for
Mama so the girls could have the bed. Their trunk had been delivered
and Clover and Aurora set about unpacking and making themselves at

home, while Mama put up Bella's hair in rags and chattered about Gentry Fox, the old times and his beautiful theatre, the Daystar in Philadelphia. Clover was very tired, not having slept well on the train, and once the gold coverlet was in place she climbed into bed to lie down, listening to Mama.

'He gave me a place in front in the Hey-Go-Mad Girls, and of course I had my usual dance turn. He made me the Queen of the May in our company finale number with a solo dance. Oh, my costume! Palest blue chiffon over silk to match, with inch-wide moiré ribbon edging the skirt; over that a three-quarter coat of cream lace. I was the favourite of the moment, and might have gone far, except we toured up to Toronto to play the Elgin. Your papa came to the theatre one night with his brother, one last hurrah before they headed off to the wilderness and left civilization behind, perhaps forever . . . And that was it for me. Poor Gentry begged me not to go, tears in his eyes, real tears—but I was head-over-ears, over-the-moon struck, and besides, I was already—oop!' She broke off and caught up the stack of bowls before Bella could sit on them, tired enough from travel and confusion to flop onto any flat surface and fall straight off to sleep.

'So I had to let Gentry down—how he terrified me. He worked with Nellie Melba, you know! What can have laid him so low as to be beached in this no-horse backpot of a tired old town? I suppose he is somehow tied to that unsavoury Drawbank. Perhaps he owes him money, or perhaps Drawbank owes him and Gentry doesn't want to let him out of his sight.'

Clover was accustomed to Mama's theories—a labyrinth to fall asleep in, wandering down alleys of possibility . . . Clover was over the stile and asleep, not worried, for a blessed change.

But the wind rattled round the hotel all night long, shaking the windowpanes. One buffet woke Clover, or perhaps it was a boarder slamming the door tight, coming back from the privy. Coming out of her dream she thought of Papa again, lying on the front walk, covered with snow. And then, shying away from that, of Harry, whose face was always there. Like an infected finger, which some part of your mind was always protecting. And now a new finger to hurt—that they had failed, and failed again, and yet they still had to go on.

An Idiot of the Voice

First thing next morning, standing in a straight line as he had arranged them on the empty stage, the Belle Auroras gave Gentry Fox their best repertoire, ending with *The Last Rose of Summer.*

As they sang, Gentry did not move from his chair or raise his head. Eyes closed, he leaned one elbow on the wooden armrest. His left leg was crossed tightly over his right; the ankle twined round and round very slowly. Up into the boughs their voices soared for the last of the lastness of the rose, to '. . . *inhabit this bleak world alone.*'

Then came the silence Aurora dreaded: someone who had power over their livelihood considering how best to let them down easy and get rid of them. Mama must have felt it too, even if a moment before she had been revelling in their performance. She rushed into explanation, dragging Gentry's attention to her. 'We have been most diligent working on their upper registers, they are all soprano of *course*, but perhaps Aurora has the most colour in the head voice, in the fourth and fifth registers . . .'

Aurora hated to hear that self-important tone in her mother's voice, although it sprang from nerves, she knew. Gentry closed his eyes briefly and swung his great head on its neck as if it pained him terribly. 'Flora, Flora! You were a skilful and enchanting dancer and I see that these children have been delightfully trained à la foot—but you are an idiot of the Voice. Registers! We do not encourage registers, we work for one voice without delineation. Because of the resonators employed, we will hear chest, middle, and head voice, I grant you. But when by bad habit or bad practice these demarcations are exaggerated, the uneven voice rises like a funicular railroad—*clunk-clunk-clunk*—rather than shading and melting, one register leading into another, imperceptibly— you see how it must be?'

It seemed to Aurora that this complaint was a mere difference in vocabulary; certainly Mama had never allowed them to clunk.

Gentry's black eyes were snapping, his ire barely contained. 'Beyond the shrieking quality in the top notes when you push for volume, dear girls, confounding *voice* with *register* creates a hopeless confusion, from which only the best of teachers may succeed in extricating the singer—and I am no Tosi, no Lehmann.'

'But, my dear Gentry, you are! You have the direct line, you studied with Lehmann.' Mama half rose from the piano bench, impassioned. 'You have a duty, a sacred trust, to pass the knowledge on.'

'I am an old man now,' he said pitifully, and indeed Aurora thought he was, very.

She shook her head to dislodge insult and impatience, both his and her own. 'Mr. Fox, we will work very hard, I promise. My sisters and I are aware that we are beginners, and we truly desire to mend our faults and to learn from you.'

He was not proof against this pandering to his vanity; and she carried her absurd young head with ridiculous dignity, and seemed intelligent. And if too much in the head, her voice was well enough, when she did not push. It was a puzzle, what to do with them all. The little one would do very well, no need for him to put himself about on her account. The middle one with serious dark brows—the watcher—had not grown into herself yet but had gravitas; her voice was low and well-pitched, once released from the soprano range foolish Flora had forced her into.

Aurora watched him calculate their potential.

'We can improve at a pace that will surprise you,' she said, somehow not plagued by self-consciousness. Almost as much as they needed the work, she wished to learn from him: because of his authority, his air of having been in all the best houses, of not belonging in this shabby place.

Gentry turned to Mama, his face wrinkling in disgust. 'Sopranos? No *of course* about it.' Clover laughed, then, and Aurora thought the rare sound seemed to please Gentry.

'I sing alto,' Clover said.

'Well, so you do, my dearest, from time to time, but someone must,' Mama said, but Aurora could see Gentry puffing himself up like a pigeon. Mama turned back to the piano and waited for instructions.

The Grand Scale So Gentry put them through a test. He spent an hour teaching them a plain scale without accompaniment, which he called The Grand, and for another hour made them sing it alone and together, over and over, till each note rang to the back of the hall and resounded in their inner ears. He ignored their music and their songs; he tapped them on the stomach where he wanted them to breathe, which each sister separately found objectionable and which they whispered about together while he struggled up the raked aisle on his half-sized legs to the very back of the auditorium.

'Do not push,' he said—and although he was almost out the lobby door, they heard him perfectly. 'Give me the first line of *Early One Morning.*'

They had not sung that for him—how could he know they knew it? He knew Mama. She turned on the piano bench and gave them an F and they sang, '*Early one morning, just as the sun was rising...*'

'Do not push,' he said again, his voice tender and young, coming from that wizened wizard's face. 'Just sing to me.'

'*I heard a maid singing in the va-alley below,*' they sang. The notes streamed out of their open mouths and through the empty twilit air and slipped into his ear, and he nodded (even at that distance they could see his head bob on his squat body) and said, 'Enough, for this morning. Your photos have arrived and look very pretty in the lobby, I am relieved to say; you may perform tonight, and this rehearsal will preclude the requirement of a band call. Take them away and sponge them, Flora, and after today's pictographs they may close with that song—and *Buffalo Gals*, with a bit of dancing. Not *After the Ball*, I beg you.'

'We've no sides for *Early One Morning*,' Flora said, hesitating to mention it.

'Caspar will manage—won't you?' At the bandleader's nod, Gentry waved them all away. 'Now sponge!'

Sponging they knew; Mama always made them do it when they were hoarse or had a cold in the throat: she poured boiling hot water into a bowl, let a sponge suck it all up, and (with a towel to protect her hand) squeezed it firmly out again. Then they sang scales in half-voice, breathing through the sponge for ten minutes, so the hot steam would act upon the bronchial tubes and the mucous membranes. The sponge had to be squeezed quite dry or it would make you choke. Having only one sponge, they took turns; while one was wheezing and singing, the others teased and distracted her until Mama made them stop. She would not let them go out into the cold air after the sponging, so they spent an endless hour lying flat on their backs on the bed going over the *Early One Morning* lyrics—until it was time to spring up and dress quickly (in their white wool challis, because the theatre was so cold that Gentry had forbidden them to wear the flowered waists) and trot cross-lots to the theatre.

Miss Belle-A-Clovers

No need to be on time for the opener since they were the closer, but they heard the tail end as they slid quietly in the stage door. Clover caught her breath, already winded from racing to the theatre, when she heard Julius Foster Konigsburg's rolling voice.

She dodged up to the wings and, craning around the last curtain-leg, saw his massive silhouette against the footlights, one arm flung dramatically out as he intoned, '*Do you love me so much you would die for me?* Ahhh—but remember! Mine is *an undying love.*'

Clover hid her mouth in her sleeve, so as not to make noise. She loved that bit. Julius was well in flight and the audience was laughing—how glad Clover was that he and Sybil had landed here where they were! And now they were balanced again, since the Belle Auroras had been cancelled too. He would be able to like them again. She kept her sleeve wrapped around her neck, hugging herself to get warm in this cold coffin of a place.

'The soubrette has a lantern jaw and so has to sing light music, *tra-la-la-la*,' Julius sang, mangling a bit of operetta with the most ridiculous exaggerated face, chin dropping to his middle waistcoat button, eyes rolling back in his head. 'She sings with impressive strength, strangling up to that last petrified high-C. Rising to the last screech of her upper register, her mouth looks like one long red Tunnel to Perdition.'

Couldn't have said *perdition* at the Empress, Clover thought.

'A flat flounder of a running mate with straggling pink moustachios accompanies this heavyweight Harpy in her flight . . .'

An in-drawn gasp beside her made Clover jump, and she saw that two people in costume had come to stand in the wings. They must be the next turn. One was a towering prow of a woman in a tight sateen gown, the other a fish-mouthed young man in ill-fitting tails, with a reddish moustache—the longest and limpest she had ever seen.

On the stage Julius continued: 'Her fervour is enough to shake the rafters—the poor young limpet thanks his stars it's not the ballet, so he doesn't have to hoist his *Inamorata* to the heavens, which would mean serious damage to his Inner Works and probably a perpetual Truss.'

The woman gasped again and grabbed at the stage manager—who Clover now saw was Johnny Drawbank, dressed for the work in a grey collarless shirt and no hat.

'Stop him!' the woman demanded.

Drawbank goggled, and the tenor goggled too. They were twin frogs and Clover had to clap her arm over her mouth again. This must be how Bella feels all the time, she thought, this crazy laugh wanting to come out. On the stage Julius had worked himself up into a frenzy, shielding his eyes as from a burning glare: 'But soft! What light is this from yonder balcony? It is a vast explosion—an *explosion of song*!'

'*Stop* him,' the woman hissed, and Clover saw the uniformed boy ready with the signboard:

AN EXCURSION OF SONG

SUNDERLAND & PETTIBONE

'Please, Miss Sunderland—' Johnny Drawbank began, but at her glare, his drooping eyes blinked and he bent to whisper through the speaking tube to the orchestra pit. 'Change music! Change!' and then as the piano cut in, covering Julius, Johnny murmured to the lights, 'Follow down, and let him off, and . . .'

Clover watched Julius draw out the applause and bow and bow, acknowledging quite imaginary *bravos* and kissing his hand to the non-existent balcony. He raised himself to his great height and strode off into the wings, where the tenor and the woman waited.

'I think that went rather well, would you not say so, dear Drawbank?' he inquired pleasantly.

The boy had run on to change the placards and a sudden wave of laughter broke, as the audience read the new one. The opera dame empurpled, and seemed to double in size. Clover wondered if she would burst. 'I will not go on. After *such* an insult? How dare you fit *me* into your paltry act,' she demanded of Julius.

'Happy accident, ma'am, I'm forced to say—you fitted hand-in-glove-like into a patter I had long been in habit of using. But I can see, looking at the dangling whiskers of your little friend here, how you might forgivably have wondered if I was referencing your *Execution of Song*—forgive me, *Excrement of*— but no. In-credible. No one who'd heard you sing, madam, could possibly believe that my poor comedy could in any way hope to approach its sheer horror—'

The soprano reached out one big paw and slapped Julius Foster Konigsburg's face. The sound must certainly have carried into the audience, but the music started up, operatic, and the lights rose again. Miss Sunderland sailed onstage, her arms held out to receive the slavish clapping of Pettibone the tenor. Her long green sateen train swam behind her like the tail of a giant fish. A scattering of applause from the audience, and quite a lot of laughter.

'My dear young miss—it is the middle Miss Belle-A-Clovers, is it not?' said Julius, in great good humour. He took her hand to draw her arm through his, and walked her towards the dressing-room stairs. 'Delighted to see you gracing this hectic Hebron of theatrical delights, however it comes about. My comrade-in-arms will be in *alt*, to find your Floral Mater restored to her.'

Clover matched her stride to his, not feeling the faintest desire to stay and hear *An Excursion of Song*.

A Really Well-trained Rat

They had a dressing room of their own. Or, if not quite all their own, they were only sharing it with one other number, the strawberry-haired woman from Swain's Rats & Cats. The cats, and most fortunately the rats, were housed with her husband in another dressing room, and the woman assured Mama that never, not once, had a rat been known to escape.

'These that we have in our act are not your run-of-the-mill rats,' she explained kindly. Her name was Letty Swain. Her nose and teeth were pointed and her chin slightly lacking, which made it easy to remember which act she was. As she talked she burnished small leather harnesses with mink oil, one after another, laying each one neatly down and picking up the next with small leather fingers. 'Ours are highly educated rats on whom no expense has been spared. The cats alone are worth in their tens of thousands, but the rats, well! There's no placing a value on a really well-trained rat.'

Bella agreed, the skin shivering up and down her arms at the very thought of one rat, let alone a plurality of them, but promised herself she would watch their turn if she could creep away. Tiny swords lay waiting to be polished, and a pumpkin, which had been hollowed out and made into a pretty travelling coach, and she longed to see these things in action. Let alone the rats.

'It's the cats who are the trouble,' Letty said. 'Always sickening for something, and my Greymalkin has a tumultuous growth behind her ear needs draining from week to week, but they're a lot less bother than a fistful of daughters would be, and if I feel like an evening out, all I've to do is fill the water bowls and lock the door behind me.'

(And hope that the cats don't eat the rats, Bella supposed.)

'Hubert can feed them, if I tell him every nig-nag detail, and he keeps the rats in order during the act, but it's I who doctors them and sits up with them nights when they are ailing.'

The boy stuck his head in the door. In this on-the-cheap establishment it was Mattie, the uniformed placard boy, who did the calls, too. 'On in ten,' he told Letty.

'Have you knocked on Room 3 yet?'

'Course.'

'Any answer?'

'He banged on the table and cursed.'

Letty jumped up and grabbed the tiny harnesses. 'Oh Lord, he's late,' she cried. 'Hopeless, hopeless!'

She ran out, and Mattie laughed and followed to see the fun. Smothered shrieks wound back along the hall as she harried the poor man, never mind the rats and cats, into harness.

Interested Red Eyes Impatient with the long wait, Aurora went up and stood in the wings to watch Maurice Kavanagh, Irish Elocutionist. She'd caught a glimpse of him earlier, striding into his dressing room, and wanted to see if he was as striking as his photographs.

Oh, he was. His voice was like port wine, she thought. Dressed in a dark velveteen jacket, a luxurious darkness, mauve velvet tie graceful at his throat; long hair flung wildly back over a broad, speaking brow. In the pool of light his feet were planted in a romantic stance, one leg thrust forward, as if the emotion of the moment had nigh unbalanced him. His arm rose as he declaimed:

> *'The star of the unconquered will,*
> *He rises in my breast,*
> *Serene, and resolute, and still,*
> *And calm, and self-possessed.'*

Aurora found her hands clasped at her collar, and dropped them. The velvet curtain-leg was close by her; as Kavanagh turned onstage she slipped quickly behind it to hide. To be caught watching!

He took a drink from the glass on the table—a tinted glass, which most likely meant the liquid was not water—and set it down, his face downcast and hidden. He came to stillness, to a profound thoughtfulness that was shared by the audience, judging from the silence, then filled his vast barrel of a chest and cried, in a sharp shout of loathing, '*Rats!*'

Aurora's skirts jumped into her hands, and she scanned the boards beneath her feet, frozen in terror— But he went on,

> '*They fought the dogs and killed the cats,*
> *And bit the babies in the cradles . . .*'

She had to lean on the rope-bed, weak with relief. It was only Browning, *in fifty different sharps and flats.* Kavanagh did the wild beginning of *Pied Piper* in a galloping, ranting screech that made her laugh as the audience did, then broke off and moved into *My Last Duchess*, changing himself in an instant into the cold, ferocious grandee with his *gift of a nine hundred years old name*, hating his young wife:

> '. . . *Just this*
> *Or that in you disgusts me; here you miss,*
> *Or there exceed the mark.*'

And then he had her killed, as easy as that: '*I gave commands, then all smiles stopped together.*' It was so cruel! As if Browning himself recited, Aurora thought.

Kavanagh moved stage left, cajoling the audience. 'Longfellow speaks to the inmost heart of us, in accents gentle enough to praise the hidden flowers of womanhood . . .'

> '*Standing, with reluctant feet,*
> *Where the brook and river meet . . .*'

It was such a man's piece of poesy to leave her meek, bewildered and damp. But Kavanagh was beautiful to look at, and besides his skill, the strength of his build pleased her very much.

Into the wings came a rather portly man, panting, carrying two cages with difficulty because a third perched between them. A score of interested red eyes peered out between the bars. Aurora yelped and dodged around the curtain before she could help herself, her skirt's tail whisking into view for an instant, and then out again. In the wings again she looked back and found Mr. Kavanagh staring offstage at her, an arrested look on his broad countenance.

She fled.

An Ocean of Joy

Mama and Sybil sat side by side in the dressing room, hemming the girls' ivory wool skirts to a sprightly six inches off the floor, and having a very satisfactory sentimental reunion, as touching as their last only three days ago.

Clover found it strange to see Mama so at ease with another woman, telling stories and laughing. In Paddockwood Mama had not had any friends. When out in company, uneasy with farm people and anxious to raise Papa's stature in the community, she had overplayed the gracious lady; at home, she was almost embarrassingly vulgar, an easy fountain of stories and songs, spending whole days in her wrapper. Clover watched her now with Sybil, giving back joke for joke, exchanging opinions about the success or failings of people they'd known, and thought that it was odd, how someone as inward and melancholy as Papa could have loved a person so transparently light. Light-hearted, light-minded. Or perhaps it was not odd at all.

She resolved not to think any more about Papa. She wetted the mascara brush and did her lashes again. She thought of them too often. After Papa the memory of Harry always came tagging along: sadder but cleaner, at least less complicated, the poor lamb. Clover was tired. We are far away, she thought, from what we've known. This small room, this momentary warmth and crowding, is what we have now instead of our old life. The table under her elbows was pitted and scarred, more than a school desk even, and the wooden plank walls between and above the mirrors were dotted with signatures and notes from artistes who had travelled through. She leaned on the heels of her hands and stared at *Eulélé Josephine, 1911*, the accents cut sharply into the wood, and tried not to think at all for a moment.

Sybil's catalogue of vaudeville stitched gently on, her tinny voice sharp and helpful as any needle. 'Julian Eltinge, he's *from* out here, you know. Years ago, when things were wilder, he made his living as a lap-girl in a box-house out in Butte—a very *respectable* girl, I'm sure—they were short on females in the area, so they'd dress a boy or two,' Sybil added quickly, with an eye towards the girls. 'His father found out and beat the tar out of him, so he went east—the suavest thing in shoes, a lovely dancer. This was in Boston, after you'd left us, Flora. Before he struck it big as a female impersonator, he was with Cadet Theatricals, but then E.E. Rice saw him, and he was made. In '03 he was already getting a thousand a week with Keith's, so he told me, and much more now, I'm sure. We did the galop, a private party at the Lyceum there in Cincinnati—I'd show you but there's not enough room to swing a cat, let alone a rat!' Sybil took a turn around the ballroom in her chair, little feet peeping out from her pink petticoat and fluttery hands dancing in the air. She sang, '*Waltz me around again, Willie, around, around, around*—' and ended in a skirt-gathering kick.

Clover could see what a hit she would have been as Miss Saucy Saunders, when broke and nothing for it but burlesque. '*I feel like a ship on an ocean of joy . . .*'

For herself, Clover thought she would rather do anything—go to Normal School to teach, be a telephone operator—than take that road, burlesque or box-house. They would just have to make some money. Mama was right. A thousand a week ought to do it.

A Dreadful Jig　　　The Old Soldiers sawed away at tunes left over from the Civil War. Several were blind or maimed, their faces old and blank. One fiddler sat playing with a bow strapped to his foot, having lost his arm. Another, blind, danced a dreadful jig as he played, thin legs darting lightly ahead and behind, and while he jigged he made his mouth into a grin that had no meaning. Bella said she could not bear to watch, and left Mattie to finish his apple alone; but it seemed to Clover, standing unnoticed in the wings, that the audience did not mind at all. They could not know how terrible it would be to have a skill, to lose it, then turn freak to get a portion of it back. Or was it still the same—did one still lose one's misery in the music? Clover curtsied as the soldiers filed past when their turn was over, silent in the backstage gloom.

Cornelius the Bubble Juggler was nothing but that, a stooped man with an outsize bubble-pipe and a carefully guarded Proprietary Mixture for making bubbles, which he patted up into the air from a silk cushion like a large glove on his hand. It was tedious, and he insisted on counting each pat, starting over when the bubble burst, as it always did. His was the first act Clover had seen that left her feeling flat and critical, and she did not like the feeling. Especially when they had to go on themselves in so little time.

But the pictures came between Cornelius and their turn. Clover ran down to help Aurora cope with Bella. She was only thirteen, even though they had to say she was sixteen. She'd been the baby for a long time—until she was eight, when Harry had come along, Clover and Aurora had called her Baby.

In the dressing room Clover found Aurora panting and sighing, standing against the wall. Clover panted too, filling out her narrow chest gorgeously as if she were Miss Sunderland, whisking an imaginary green-satin train from side to side and trilling to make her sisters laugh. She finished Bella's makeup and re-did her own frog-pond eyes, taking a pin to separate her own and Bella's thick-blacked eyelashes.

The challis shirtwaists had been fresh-pressed with sizing, skirt hems ironed to a knife-edge; the dressing room smelled deliciously of laundry. Mama had rigged an improvised board from their placard, two coffee cans and a towel.

'*Ge-ge-ge-ge-geh*,' Aurora sang. '*Ke-ke-ke-ke-keh.*'

'If you need an encore . . .'

But Clover said, 'We won't, Mama, we're just the closer. They'll be wanting to go home as much as we want to send them.' Which was true, of course.

The boy knocked at the door, and they were up and out in a flurry of skirts and boots, a herd of young horses rising suddenly from a field.

The Life

Gentry was not backstage, but the girls knew he must be watching. Clover breathed in through the bottom of her boots, as Gentry had said to do, determined not to look so serious.

Mattie held his hand out for their placard. Oh, the placard! The ironing board!

Bella raced down on galumphing feet, grabbed it, nearly throwing the rats' tack into a tangle, and jumped back upstairs three at a time, to the music already beginning over the end of the pictograph reel.

Mattie marched the card onstage and set it, and the music swelled, and they were up.

They ran prancing on to the music, holding hands. Into position. The lights were brighter in this theatre. Hot onstage—and they were ready, and the piano slid into the verse.

> 'Early one morning, just as the sun was rising
> I heard a maid singing in the valley below,
> O, don't deceive me, O, never leave me,
> How could you use a poor maiden so?'

In the song's story Clover was the low-voiced singer, and Aurora the maiden. Bella—another happier maiden, unable to contain her delight at being up on the boards again. She stood by Clover as Gentry had commanded; she did not swish her skirt or fidget.

They opened their mouths like caves and let the sound flow out, running smooth to the back of the house—Aurora opened up the top of her head and opened down the bottom of her jaw, the sweetest and most dreadfully deceived of girls, wandering there back of the castle all pregnant with her apron not fitting any more. Bella almost laughed as she thought about that humped-up apron. But they were using the

more refined lyrics with only the *garlands that you pressed on my brow* . . .
Even Mrs. Cleveland could not have objected to them.

There was a difference this evening, Aurora thought, a change
clearer in the house than in themselves: the audience was relaxed, as if
knowing the girls would sing well right from the start. Their act wasn't
just good in spots, it was good all through, and the back-and-forthness
between them and the people was made of pleasure rather than kindness.
If they kept working, they could be good like this all the time.

Then it was time for *Buffalo Gals*, where Bella could cut loose and
kick up her heels, and the audience became more lively. One of her tap-
ping heels encountered a smear of soap bubble left by the juggler, whisked
out from under her, and nearly took her whooshing off the stage—but
she recovered, with a windmill of arms that shook a huge laugh out of
the audience, and the applause at the end was such a cascade of happiness that Bella laughed as she bowed. This was the life for her.

A Kick

'Very—energetic,' Gentry said, waiting in the wings when they came off.
'My dear Bella, your poise and aplomb
was never more evident than when you did *not* land in the front row
after slipping. Head voice well released—it is a beginning. If you continue to give me that forward tone, I will let you do it in two, with the
park backdrop, well behind the Bubbler's soap scum.'

Aurora considered the honour. They had never yet been in two.
Mama pressed Gentry's hand and said, 'It is like you to be careful of my
girls, dear Gentry, thank you.' And then it was all to do over again for the
seven o'clock show—the waiting, the climbing up and down stairs, makeup removed and their faces cleaned, as Mama insisted, between shows.

The dressing room became a cozy snug, Sybil and Mama continuing their rambling catalogue of every gig and artiste they had played,
or played with, or ever seen; Letty Swain showing Bella how the harnesses worked and roping her in to polishing brass; Clover and Aurora
brushing each other's hair a thousand counted strokes.

After the second show, in the welter of prop-setting for Julius, Gentry stopped Aurora backstage with one twisted, arthritic hand on her arm. 'At the garlands verse, take a turn farther left to find the light. Your mama can find steps for that—*allemande, pas de bourrée,* not too lively. I'm pleased with you,' he said. 'Much as it pains me to say so.'

Aurora laughed, and caught the eye of the Elocutionist, passing behind Gentry just then, and no doubt hearing what Gentry had said. Kavanagh gave her a nod, a note of his eyes.

Gentry glanced over his shoulder to see who Aurora looked at. 'But I'm putting you back in one,' he told her, ignoring Kavanagh. 'I'll move the Soap Juggler back into two, so he won't sully the apron-stage with his suds. Distance is required for that illusion; and I still can't hear you dear girls when you are in two.'

Oh well, Aurora thought. A compliment, and then a kick to chase it. She gathered Clover and Bella, and they went down to wait the long stretch till the closer.

A Night Out

Maurice Kavanagh was served late supper at the Pioneer Restaurant, a favour granted by Mrs. Burday because she found him so romantical. When the girls and Mama trooped through the restaurant on their way to the back-hall stairs, he twisted in his seat, judging his timing to a pin, and called softly, 'Miss! Miss!'

Aurora, trailing the others, turned and gave him a delicious smile, in honour of his brilliance and the mauveness of his soft-folding tie.

He reared his head back and eyed her with a look pleasantly askance, considering. 'I'm a stranger here myself,' he said.

'Oh, so are we, Mr. Kavanagh.'

'But so familiar with the layout of the place?'

'We are lodging here, you see.'

'I do see,' he said, looking at her as a man might look at the menu at Delmonico's, then shaking his head. 'But I don't see—what is to be done.'

'What kind of a thing needs doing?'

'Well, here am I, with an evening on my hands, and no guide to this Underworld.'

Aurora laughed. He was quite old, probably thirty. Long thick eyelids under very dark brows. He liked her extremely. Everybody did! She was beautiful, at least this one evening.

'Will you?'

'Will I?'

'Be my Beatrice, lead me through at least the first circle of this Inferno of a town.'

She laughed again, but said, 'How can I? I know it no more than you do.'

'Accompany me and we will root out its terrors together. At least, eat supper with me,' he said. 'Mrs. Burday has promised a supportive meal, to restore the overextended nerves.'

In the stair-hall beyond, Mama paused by the newel post. Aurora could certainly use a good supper. If she should take the fancy of an artist as well-established as Kavanagh!—although it was not entirely clear whether he was on his way up or down. What harm could come from it when she was right here in the same building? She craned her neck back, holding the newel, and nodded to Aurora.

'Well, if you have no other company,' Aurora said.

She gave a hint of a bow and sat opposite him at the table, then reached her arms up and made a small show of taking off her hat. They had laid out too much on clothes when they were starting out, and after all, what was the point in a black velvet hat if you did not make use of it?

Mrs. Burday made no difficulty about bringing another plate. 'There's plenty, I'm sure. The potatoes is fresh fried up, the shin left over from suppertime. You'll want a glass of milk,' she told Aurora, making her very angry.

When supper had been disposed of, Mr. Kavanagh sat on, seeming in no hurry for his bed. It was after midnight, but he was into his stride, telling Aurora about his engagements in the legitimate theatre—his Alving in *Ghosts*, and how Belasco wanted him for Chicago, and (in a

generous nod to her sex) discoursing on the art of elocution as it per-
tained to females. 'The penetrative quality of every woman's voice may
be improved,' he told her. 'Elocution can hardly make women orators;
it cannot confer intelligence or discrimination; but it can tune that disordered instrument, the body.'

Abruptly he stopped, pulling out his watch. He stood, and commanded, 'Come!'

Aurora gathered her coat and mantle and stabbed her hat into
place, trying not to disorder her hair too badly. 'Where?'

'Do you care? I asked for Beatrice, and the Underworld awaits!'

Virgil led the poet through the Underworld, not Beatrice, Aurora
thought, but she did not complain. They went a long way over icy
paths, down empty, snow-packed streets to wherever he was going. He
did not talk much, trotting her along like a prize calf to market, but at
last they came to a square, brick-built house on a corner of State Street,
snow cleared from its edges and gaslight gleaming from the windows,
music sending fronds of spring out into the winter darkness.

'Just a private party,' he said at the tall black door, as he knocked.
'Jenny won't mind that I've brought you.' Bullying through the crush of
backs and arms, Maurice introduced her to a high-cheeked woman who
seemed the hostess. Older than Mama and taller, almost stern-looking,
in an elegant ruby silk dress, with dark coils of hair piled on her head.

'Make this little bird welcome, Jenny. She's dancing up at the
Parthenon, she and her sisters, new to the boards but she'll learn.'

'A dancer! You're in good company here, my dear, we were all
dancers once—but those days are past and it is much more respectable
here than formerly.'

Aurora gave her a hand, not certain this was correct, and said,
'Aurora Avery.'

The woman laughed, but not unkindly, and took her hand, then
tweaked her elbow, fingering the billowing flannel sleeve.

'You're a pearl, all right.' The ruby dress split as she swayed, revealing inner slashes of pale peach-fuzz velvet. 'Now, Maurice, you find her
a cup of the punch, and tell Ricardo to fetch you the usual; if you'd rather

something stronger, my dear Miss Avery, say what you want, I'm sure he's got every kind of liquor. We haven't gone Temperance here, not yet!'

Aurora bobbed her head to thank her, and at Maurice's pressure on her arm went into the shifting noisy crowd, musicians adding their own noise. Although Aurora kept drinking the punch (and found herself very thirsty) and nodding her head, she quite often had no idea what was being said to her. She felt very happy to be here, to be a woman in the world.

Maurice fell into animated argument with several different people who of course she did not know (though some of the orchestra members were familiar, moonlighting from the Parthenon); she was hard put to keep up with him as he moved from place to place. The room was smoky, hot after their cold walk to get here. Wherever *here* was. Suddenly weary, she thought of leaving, but found she could not reconstruct their route in her mind, and into the small hours, now, she would not be safe, wandering the streets to find the hotel.

She tried to be patient, but Maurice's conversations were full of names and people she did not know, consisting of highly coloured stories that left out all details. 'Jerry *did*, God-damned hound—nobody's fault but his own, we told him that—never saw her again nor wanted to . . .' in quick exchanges along the same lines with several different sets of men.

The women did not do much talking, but some were beautiful, and they wore dazzling dresses and jewellery. Aurora stood by a massive mahogany pocket door, tucked in, her punch-glass held carefully out of the way. It was delicate crystal with thistles etched upon it, and she feared to break it.

Almost Empty   Bella poured hot milk into the bread, feeling Clover's careful eye upon her lest she scald herself or spill. Mama had taken off her boots and sunk upon the sofa, feeling every inch of her years, she said, so Bella had gone down to the kitchen to get the milk while Clover combed Mama's hair out and rubbed her temples with a dab of perfume to help her aching head. The scent bottle was almost empty. Papa had given it to Mama for Christmas before . . . all the rest of it. Bella did not like the smell. She leaned over the bowls, warm sweet bread sending a curl of comfort to her nose. Aurora's lustreware bowl sat clean and empty on the dresser, but she'd be having something lovely downstairs, and probably cake. She was taking a very long time over supper.

Mama waved away her bowl, saying, 'You eat mine, Bella dear. You jump around so, you need the extra.' Clover shook her head, though, so the two girls helped Mama to sit up and Bella pressed the bowl into her hand.

'Look how nicely Bella has made it, Mama,' Clover said. 'All stirred smooth for you.'

So Mama opened her eyes and exclaimed over the perfection of the mixing and how her own mama had made it for her while touring long ago, and wasn't it lucky that they were cozy in this nice hotel. But after a spoonful or two she leaned her head on the arm of the sofa and let damp trails of tears fall down her cheeks.

Bella put the bowls on the dresser and brought the gold silk coverlet; Clover took Mama's stockings off and tucked her feet under the warm folds. The girls let her lie quiet while they undressed themselves in silence, and got into bed.

A lively evening is often followed by a sad ending, Bella thought, staring through the darkness at the paler rectangle of the window.

A Fool

'Hot in here,' Kavanagh said in Aurora's ear. She turned quickly and he gave her a loving, slow-growing smile that took in all the details of her face and hair and hat. 'Still got that hat on? Let's take you up—we'll find the cloakroom or something of the sort.'

The stairs were crowded too, and dark, though all the wood shone; dark doors lined the upper hall. In the first chamber, two people sat on the edge of an iron bed, the woman on the man's lap with her legs quite bare. Aurora looked quickly away. Maurice backed her out and closed the door with exaggerated care, and swung his arm out dramatically to open the next door, like a genie conjuring up a robbers' cave.

Nobody there—a small stuffy room with garments heaped up on the bed and couch; no lamp lit. He pushed the door farther open and manoeuvred her inside, not that she resisted.

Once inside the darkened room he cupped her chin and cheek in his hands in a well-practised fashion and tilted her head up. He missed her mouth when he bent to kiss her, smearing her eye, and then pretended to have been planning all along to plant kisses around her face, murmuring broken love-notes as he did so.

But her mind, which had been confused and unthinking, suddenly became a clean open space: *He is a fool*, she thought. Well, that was not a useful thing to be thinking. She returned his kiss, tipping her head so his mouth, smelling of rum and pastilles and tobacco, met hers. He seemed younger as she kissed him. She touched the cleft in his chin.

'You're a beauty,' he said. He wrapped an arm around her waist, and the hand on the arm circled around her breast while the other fumbled with the hooks on her bodice, but he soon gave up and merely mashed her chest in his hand, the other hand brought into play as well, lurching her into the wall, first, then to the couch covered with dresses. The fabric beneath them shifted and slid—they were going to flump onto the floor, but Aurora hoisted him up as well as she could. She did not know whether to stop him or go on, and found that she did not even care which, but she was uncomfortable.

'Beauty, beauty,' he kept saying, and she thought that really, an Elocutionist ought to have more eloquence at his disposal. But he was very handsome, and she recalled the mastery with which his voice had teased the meaning from Browning and Longfellow.

A quick rap at the door, and Jenny came into the room, skirts swirling, bright velvet visible and invisible. She took in Aurora's confusion and Maurice's heavy-lidded glare at the interruption, and spoke only to Aurora, her tone pitched as if they were quite alone.

'You shouldn't be here. You go on home, now.'

Aurora stood. She pulled at her skirt and smoothed the waistband. She straightened her hat, turning her face away to give herself time for breath.

To Maurice, Jenny said, as if she knew him very well, 'Out, you! Take this little girl safe home and then I might let you come back. You're a twister.'

He laughed and overbalanced, crashing into the nightstand but not quite to the floor. Then was up again, still laughing. 'You heard her, my dear, take me home safe, and then perhaps I will be let back into Paradise.'

Aurora looked at Jenny's strong-boned face, at her clean skin and long eyes. Old enough to be her mother, but seeming young and full of energy, and she gave back look for look, so that without the least bit wanting to, Aurora decided she was right. 'Yes,' she said. 'Thank you, ma'am, I had best be leaving.' She took Maurice's arm and steered him to the door, saying, 'They will be looking for me at home, sir.'

The Playbill

Clover could not quite sleep: the Parthenon playbill ran through her head continually, so that at one moment she was haunted by fascinated fear lest Julius cause another scene or be injured by the vast Miss Sunderland; at another, in an almost-dream, the rats and cats were the ones who fought. Aurora had been too long with the Elocutionist, some page of the programme said. Another page, and there was Mama, left alone in the world. Clover could not turn the next page because there would be her father lying on the front walk with the dark stain seeping under him, so she riffled back through the pages to Julius, to Gentry calling out from the back of the theatre.

She struggled to wake. The room shaped itself around her: the leaning square of mirror tilted over the dresser, the coal-fire's last ember in the stove, a small mountain of Mama on the sofa. Montana. From Paddockwood to Prince Albert, to Regina, to Calgary, to the Empress in Fort Macleod—now Helena. Clover pushed out of bed and stood. Her feet gripped the linoleum, one hand on the rough sheet still. No Aurora.

Across the room Mama lay uncovered, the coverlet fallen to the floor. Too slippery. Clover took the wool blanket off the bed, easing Bella's fingers from its edge, and tucked that around Mama instead. She laid the coverlet gently over Bella and stood a moment longer, silent in the dark room, before she made herself climb back into bed.

In Drink   Aurora hurried along beside Maurice as he straggled through silent frozen streets, seeming to know the route more as a horse knows the stable than as a thinking man. She put her hand through his arm, as his hands were shoved into his topcoat pockets, and took the longest strides she could. She feared that if their pace slowed he would forget what he was doing. She had many times seen men in drink, and it did not seem to her that he was too far gone, compared to how Papa had been once or twice, let alone Mr. Dyment from the land office, but she thought he might walk ahead and forget she was with him. From time to time she spoke; he did not seem to hear.

At last she spied the Pioneer on its corner, a block ahead, and felt some relief. Just then Maurice dodged away from her into a dark entryway, the cobbled tunnel to a yard behind a store. She stopped and moved towards him, but he flung out a beautiful white hand.

'Wait!' he cried. 'Nature must be answered!' and then she saw his arm braced against the bricks and understood that he was relieving himself. Hot piss made a curl of steam in the air. She felt more tired than she had for a very long time. And they had a lesson with Gentry in the morning.

'Sweetness? My beauty? Girl?' Maurice's voice came out of the passageway in a stage whisper, and she realized that he did not know her name.

'I'm here,' she said.

'Come, come,' he said.

No one in the street. The moon lay on snowy ruts and drifts impartially. She stepped into the shadow, keeping to the opposite wall from where he had been leaning. He opened his topcoat and folded her inside it, keeping her warm, and she found she was fond of him, of his looseness and greatness and strength, however fallen and come low. He kissed her again less clumsily, his mouth cooler after the long walk. With one hand he kirtled up her skirt and then, pinning the gathers between their two bodies, he nudged a knee at her legs to open them, and then his fingers touched her under there, opening her there, pushing through her legs to touch all through her, beneath her drawers along the silky tops of her legs above her stockings, and the feel of that hand on that skin was one of the things she was looking for, she thought, or perhaps she should push him away, she could not tell. After that first soft sweeping his fingers shoved into her too strongly, so he hurt her, and she did not know how to tell him she did not like it. His eyes were closed. Then he paused, pressed against her fiercely, paused again, and said in a reasonably sober voice, 'Your mama will be waiting. We must go.'

Once he had stopped pushing against her she could be kind in her thoughts towards him, and she supposed that they would continue like this, only not outside in the cold but in some rose-petal-strewn hotel room in Chicago or New York, where it would somehow be easier, or once she could get it right, all right.

He stood waiting for her to shake her skirts down and did not look at her, nor speak, the rest of the block to the Pioneer. Mrs. Burday had left the side door unlatched for them and he pushed her up the stoop and swayed on the doorstep.

'Lovely child,' he said. 'Lovely Silence.' She looked at him, puzzling out his face to see what his expression was: nothing but a smile there, and a quirk of the eyebrows.

'Wicked Jenny was right. But I'll make her sorry for that!' He shut the door and she could hear his feet clumsy on the steps, then making off down the street.

Upstairs, Mama woke from where she had been curled on the sofa, and asked in a clouded voice, 'Aurora? Did you have a good supper? You were an age down there. I hope he entertained you kindly and was not . . . I meant to come down and—but I dropped off . . .'

'Oh, it was fine, Mama. Mrs. Burday gave us shin of beef and fried potatoes, and when we'd eaten we went for a walk.' Enough to make Mama sigh and sleep again.

Clover sat up and watched her as she took her clothes off in the moonlight. Being Clover she did not ask anything, but Aurora lay down beside her and was very grateful for her thin arm around her for comfort. After a while she whispered, as if answering, 'I do not know. I think it was a bordello he took me to. The punch was delicious. The room is going round the bed, or the bed going round me, oh . . .'

She felt like a ship on an ocean of shame.

Before she slept she thought of Jimmy Battle, and felt the arch of bone inside her pelvis as she turned over in the bed to lie farther away from Clover. The spread of that bone, how her hips had opened and were waiting for women's work. Not children, she did not mean that, but the pressure of a man, however that would be. She would not expect love, because that was a weakening thing, but passion would be useful in her art.

Innermost Heart   Drops of water raced down the dark window as Bella opened her eyes. She put out a finger to touch one drop, splitting it into two pearls that ran onward to the sill. It was not a thaw, but the hip-bath steaming in front of the stove. The sky was still dark, it must be early. They had let her sleep till last again. She stretched under the gold coverlet, taking up the whole bed luxuriously, and rolled her head to see who was in the bath: Clover, her thin back bent, each nub of bone raised like a long set of knuckles, running down her spine.

Bella watched Clover stand, hugging herself as the water drained off, steaming in the cold air, hip bones a-jut and every side rib visible. Mama put a sheet around her. Aurora poured another kettle of hot water into the hip-bath. Clover bumped up into bed and under the coverlet, and laid her cold feet against Bella's legs so that Bella shrieked softly—and was shushed by Aurora, mindful as they always had to be of the sleepers in rooms beside theirs. The walls were thin as card-board. Even with the steam and the stove it was too cold for Bella to be happy about taking off her nightgown, but it had to be done, so she stripped and stepped into the water. Once she had scrubbed herself she braced against the lip of the bath and Mama and Aurora poured water over her head, soaped her, and took the suds out in a towel. They rinsed her hair with bathwater and then twice with new water, with vinegar in it for shine, but that was very cold, and then she stood and they helped her out to stand shivering on the linoleum in front of the stove until, wrapped and warming like a loaf in a napkin, she could get back under the coverlet while Aurora and Clover laced their corsets. Aurora said, 'Tighter, tighter,' and Clover pulled. Aurora had a beautiful corset: cut-away hips and a short back, made of French coutil with écru lace trimming and pale blue ribbons. God only knew what it had cost, Mama said. It was from the Queen of the May costume.

She ought to have a corset too, but Bella was still treated like a baby; hers was only a band, even though she had a bust beginning, and per-haps with a little cotton stuffed inside a corset she would look more like the sixteen she was supposed to be. Aurora was as cold as winter, and Clover only loved Aurora. They did not care about her, no matter how much she tried to be good and no trouble to anyone and to dance as well as the others. She dug her head under the coverlet and went back into the darkness for a while, into the misery of nobody, nobody knowing her innermost heart or loving her at all.

Sentimental Bilge-Distiller   'You have laced yourself too tight to breathe. You cannot *sing* if you can-not *breathe.*'

Gentry's stick whisked at Aurora, flicking like a carriage whip on her stiffened midriff. 'Take her to the dressing room and loosen her corset,' he told Flora, not troubling to make it a request. His impatience was always on fire in the mornings. A bad time for classes. But they had the choice: learn, or go. He cast his pearls before them! What was it to him if they chose to lace themselves into asphyxia for a pair of booze-soaked Irish eyes?

Clover and Bella ran through the Grand Scale twenty times before Aurora came back and joined them in the line, cheeks hot and bodice loose. They continued together, but Gentry flung up his arms and left the stage, struggling down the portable stairs with his cane, each step a contortion and spasm of limbs and hips and angles.

At the scale's downward arc, they fell silent. From the darkened auditorium they heard Gentry's voice in a smooth, powerful undertone that grew louder without tightness or exertion, imitating and correcting the tones he criticized. 'When you push, you create tension in the heart and in the brain—so the voice goes up in pitch and acquires a spindly, questioning, uncertain tone. If you try to make your voice big by pushing from the throat, you cut your voice in pieces, lose all the undertones and individuality. In the *throat*, you must feel no effort at all.' Gentry paced up and down the aisles, ending by shouting 'Throat!' at them, with as far as they could detect no effort at all in his own.

Aurora felt dizzy and sick, and had to remember to blink her eyes; Clover beside her was straight as a pillar, no colour in her face. Bella seemed to be struggling not to laugh, but glancing at her quickly, Aurora sent a dagger look. At the smallest infraction Gentry might dismiss them, and she needed him to tell her everything, everything. She could feel her understanding stretching to take in what he said.

At Gentry's command they sang *Buffalo Gals* again, and again, and again, *a capella*. At length he relented, came towards the stage, and softened his tone. 'Of course extra force is required to fill the theatre. You must find the fire to fill this space, and learn to release it without constriction. You prepare, prepare, prepare, and then you let it go, give your work out freely in your singing, and your audience will receive it as freely. Generosity is the lesson I would teach you.' He turned away, then back again. 'And focus.'

His own focus was ferocious. Aurora nodded but did not dare speak.

'Use it like the violin, your voice-box. Do not draw those strings tight so that they squawk and squeak—let them vibrate freely, with firm control, flowingly.' Then Gentry slammed the end of his stick down on the stage, making the girls jump. He shouted, 'Mr. Caspar? Are you there?' and the mousey bandleader ran down to the pit. *'Early One Morning,'* Gentry barked to him, and almost instantly the piano intro began.

Aurora stepped forward into her usual position and the girls began, following the song until Aurora took it alone: '*O don't deceive me, O never leave me,'* she sang, with the rise and plaintive fall of '*How could you use a poor maiden so?'*

'Stop, stop!' Gentry's stick hit the stage again. 'Why is this so hollow? Why so icy? Come! It is not enough to sing on key. You must give me something from your—'

He paused, seeming not to want to say *heart*, although he was pounding his chest. 'From your own pain. Don't you have some sorrowful love in your past? Has no one ever betrayed you?'

Aurora stood still.

Gentry came close to her. 'If no one has, rest assured that someone will. Imagine it.'

She looked into his face, below her own. He seemed to be trying to convey something vital to him and so she put aside her resistance and her pride, and let out a breath.

'Well, I am only young, still, sir,' she said. She gave a great smile, suddenly, and said, 'And still quite pretty.'

At that his ferocity broke, and he laughed and opened his arms wide, bowing to her. 'You are a brave girl, and an honest one, you rascal,' he said. 'As you sing that song, think of the poor girl who has been done wrong, rather than of your own safe prettiness.'

He turned away, saying, 'And give me a little of your father, and your young brother, in that dying fall.'

They none of them moved or spoke. But their silence felt charged, as if the sisters and their mother stood together against him.

Gentry paused. Then he turned back to Aurora, and bowed slightly, in what might have been some rare species of apology. 'All right. We need more of you. I want you to do a new song tonight, so some hard work this morning.'

She kept her astonishment carefully to herself. Clover and Bella said nothing either, although she could feel them tremble on either side of her.

'*My Rosary?*' Mama suggested, hurriedly searching through her music case for those pieces for which she had sides. 'We have a sweetly pretty arrangement for three voices, by Nevin himself.'

'*My Rosary!*' Gentry seethed to a dangerous boil all over again. 'A bastard get of the popular song—unbearably pretentious, pandering to the crowd, with the finicking touch of "Art" which makes all things false and vulgar. A sentimental bilge-distiller.'

Mama shut her case with a ridiculous little bob of apology and the girls stood frozen, waiting for the end of Gentry's rant.

'So, a new song!' Gentry said—suddenly, bewilderingly cheerful. '*I Can't Do the Sum* from *Babes in Toyland*. Victor Herbert, who has never written an original strain and is a plagiarist from first to last, whose music is execrable—but not, per se, immoral.'

He banged his cane again and Mattie rolled a large blackboard onto the stage, deposited a chunk of chalk on its ledge, and handed the girls their music. The jaunty little tune started up. They allowed the music to move them out of their stillness, and they sang.

> *Oh! Oh! Oh!*
> *Put down six and carry two, Gee, but this is hard to do,*
> *You can think and think and think, till your brain goes numb—*
> *I don't care what Teacher says, I can't do the sum!'*

Gentry decreed that Bella take the first verse, as a little girl trying to solve arithmetic stumpers; she could wear baby-girl and a giant bow. A quick change after the song, therefore a couple of minutes for Clover and Aurora to fill with a dance number—Mama recalled the *Musical Snuff-Box* routine from the last school concert before Papa died. They could easily work around Bella's absence.

Gradually, gradually, Aurora thought, their minutes were extending. From two songs to three, now a dance interlude. Unless Gentry turned it down for sentimental bilge.

He did not, again praising Mama's attention to their steps and telling the girls they were luckier than they knew to have such a fine instructor. By noon he seemed tired, and they were happy to run out of the theatre and back to the Pioneer. Bella would need her baby-doll shirtwaist and perhaps the prop lollipop. 'If we were paying for this,' Mama told Aurora, hurrying them along the cleared walks, 'we would not be able to. Whatever the cost to your self-pride.'

'Yes, it is worth it. At least he is not too hard on the others.'

Clover took Aurora's left hand as they ran, and Bella took the right.

A Living Hell At the dressing mirror Aurora took great pains with her hair and eyes, and was made up before Julius finished his opening turn at the first show. She perched on the edge of the makeup table in a state of light carbonation, one eye on the hallway through the open door.

Sybil fretted, afraid that Julius had gone too far the day before in quarrelling with Miss Sunderland and might go farther today. Duetto Paradiso—a new placard had been made the day before, Miss Sunderland refusing to perform under the name Excursion of Song ever again—was warming up in half-voice across the hall. Sybil confided to Mama, in a stage whisper, that Julius had touched a drop at breakfast, and that Italians always set him off.

Neither singer was truly Italian, Aurora considered saying, but she left it.

'Everybody *knows* it is necessary to get along with all the artistes in a company, and Jay has never done such a pointed thing before—why should he have taken against them so? Except that Miss Sunderland does a little resemble Jay's mother, who was a terrible tyrant and made his early years a living hell,' Sybil continued, in a running commentary that soon drove Aurora out into the hall.

She leaned against the doorjamb, staring at the piece of publicity letterhead Kavanagh had pinned to his dressing-room door: *Maurice MacKenna Kavanagh, Elocutionist*, in glossy black letters above his sketched profile. Remembering (with a delightful swoop of dizziness) his nose on her cheek, his black beard-shadow and the sharp cleft in his chin, she thought that the Belle Auroras needed some publicity letterhead of their own. Clover could draw their three profiles, that would be stylish. She wanted to see his face. His fingers had hurt her, but she had not said so; it was necessary to be brave. His glinting eyes were navy blue.

She could not linger in the doorway. He would think she was waiting for him when he came, as he must do very quickly, or be fined for missing his half-hour call. She started up the stairs on quick feet, planning to find a quiet corner where she could watch the show and not be seen at all.

But—her heart jumped—Kavanagh thundered through the back-stage door above. He came pelting down the stairs towards her, his hair dull and tousled.

Aurora flattened against the railing, twinkling up at him (with just the right laughing touch of *aren't you late, rascal!*) as he brushed past.

He glanced at her, then aside. She put out a hand to catch his sleeve, and he knocked it away roughly, saying, 'Get the fuck out of it. Leave me be!'

Her legs trembled so, she thought she might fall. He was in a hurry (she heard herself telling herself), late for his call. The railing felt very shaky.

Kavanagh slammed through the door of his dressing room and swore again.

There was no place to be in the theatre that was dark enough. After a minute Aurora walked up the halls past the dressing rooms (his door not quite closed, she could see him grinding greasepaint stick into the palm of his hand, dark head bent over the job) and, grasping at any door, went into the coal cellar—where she stood on the cleared space of floor waiting to catch her breath. She wanted more than anything to walk casually back and open his door to say something fine and witty, some little remark to let him see that she was perfectly un-affected; but she could not trust herself to get it right. It had been—displeasure. In his eyes, at seeing her.

Not displeasure, *disgust.*

She felt quite stupid, trying to think.

He had smelled strongly of liquor. And he had looked away, aggrieved that she would be in his way, demanding something of him. The coal dust left on the scraped floor would ruin her white skirt, she had to keep it heaped into her hands—as he had lifted her skirts, last night. A deep worm crawled and turned in her belly. But she would not be sick.

She gathered her skirts in one hand, opened the coal-cellar door with the other, and walked out, back straight and a dainty smile on her face. She went up to the wings to listen to his turn.

His elocution was as brilliant as before.

A Poor Maiden So   Coming into the dressing room Aurora took a fistful of cold cream and covered her face, rubbing it in for what seemed to Clover like a long time, and wiped it off, leaving a clean canvas. Then she began afresh, giving herself more colour by an extra screw of number 5 in the palm of her hand. Once she had her complexion perfect, she made her eyes magnificent.

Clover watched Aurora draw on her eyebrows (which she always thought too light) in delicate strokes, a long arch down to the bottom edge of her eye, and finally add two dots of crimson lake in the inner corners of her eyes to give them brilliance. She stared at herself blank-faced.

Then she re-did Clover's eyes, which needed it, and looked about for Bella. When Mama came to adjust her lace collar she gently pushed her hand away and did it herself. A powerful pall had descended on the cozy little room. They had all heard Kavanagh cursing.

Julius Foster Konigsburg surged out of his dressing-room door and caught Clover's wrist, delaying her, as the girls were going up for their turn. He leaned down from his height and murmured, in a richly articulated aside, 'Listening out my door just now—that Kavanagh bag of wind is a reprobate, a degenerate, and manifestly a popinjay, if you like that sort of thing … *Not* the answer to a maiden's prayer. Caution the rosy-fingered Dawn.' He coughed and bobbed his head, winking heavily, a conspirator.

Clover smiled at him, but did not answer.

Their new number went over big, Sybil said. She and Mama had gone round to the audience to watch them close the first show. The blackboard was wheeled on at the end of the pictures, making the audience expect a dull lecture to go with the pictograph, *South Sea Adventures with the Turtles*. But instead Bella appeared, puzzling out the numbers while her governesses Clover and Aurora added more arithmetical riddlers—till they all gave up and danced instead, a frisky jig of frustrated abandon. The older two were prim and Bella was joyful, and her joy gradually infected them so that they all danced like mad.

Mama had added a firecracker rolling-wheel kick that looked very hard to do until you got the hang of it, and at the end Bella went twirling-whirling offstage to do her quick change, the blackboard zoomed off, and the older girls paused as the music segued, then waltzed into their sashaying dance number.

After that, there was a quick shift of mood into *Early One Morning*. Aurora had been wondering how that would work. Up there in the light and warmth, with the audience warm too from Bella's charm and their tinkling *Snuff-Box* dance, she stood in the extended pose and thought, *Well, it's all right—I can use this. Here you are, all of you: I've been betrayed.* She let the damage to her pride rise almost to the surface for a moment, and looked in her mind's eye at Kavanagh's clever, romantic face.

Clover began alone, gravely, as one who had witnessed a sad thing. '*. . . just as the sun was rising, I heard a maid singing in the valley below.*'

Then Aurora stepped forward. She took a breath and thought of Gentry Fox's maxims, let it all go, and sang about the brick-walled passage last night, and the small room upstairs at Jenny's house, and even a tinge of how much of the punch she had drunk.

> '*O, don't deceive me, O, never leave me,*
> *How could you use a poor maiden so?*'

As she sang she dipped into the deep reservoir of how dreadful she felt, however little there was to complain of, really, in what Maurice Kavanagh had done. She had gone with him perfectly willingly. He had not forced her or even had to ask her. But she was bewildered and made miserable. And life was miserable enough already.

> *'Remember the vows that you made to your Mary,*
> *Remember the bower where you vow'd to be true . . .'*

Of course he had not vow'd to be true, not for a second. She kept telling herself how it was her own choice and her own doing, but she was pure, plain miserable—and yet it could go into the song instead and be used. That was good.

Gentry Fox was waiting backstage when they came off, and he laid a light hand on Aurora's shoulder. 'That's the ticket, my love' was all he said.

Here You Miss   Miss Sunderland had been watching in the wings as well; she gave Gentry a cold nod, and one to Aurora. The other girls went clattering down to the dressing room with Mama and Sybil congratulating them on the *Sum* song, no need to be quiet since the show was over and the audience clumping obediently out above them.

Aurora followed more slowly, a bit numb now that they'd come off all right.

At the bottom of the stairs Maurice stood waiting for her, lustrous eyes beseeching her forgiveness, asking a humorous question along the lines of *Isn't all this love business droll?*

'I was in an unspeakable temper, forgive me,' he said simply (but assuming, Aurora saw, that because he was an artist, there was nothing really to forgive). He held out his pale, long-boned hand, and she remembered the strength of his fingers. She gave a stiff smile, it being necessary to get along with all artistes in a company, and made to pass by. He caught at her arm, saying, 'Sweet Dignity—so injured—but you mustn't love me, you lovely creature. I am not at all trustworthy.'

Aurora was suddenly cleanly furious, as angry as she'd ever been in her life. All the dressing-room doors open, and the show ended, people milling about: everyone could hear. She could not look at him any longer for anger.

'Do not turn away, sweet Modesty. Your beauty, your grace—'

And he still did not seem to know her name. She wished to hit him but felt violence would only please him, as evidence of the depth of her affliction. She could not trust herself to speak coolly, or to say something clever. Instead she removed her arm from his grip as if he were a raspberry bush, saying nothing at all.

She went into the dressing room and cold-creamed her face again with shaking hands. What was it they had done?—nothing but a kiss and a fumble in the street. Disgusting. She was disgusted with herself.

Here you miss, or there exceed the mark . . . She would be that cold old Duke to her stupid self. She would give commands.

Another Rat

At the beginning of the eight-thirty show, Gentry sent Mattie down to the dressing room with a message asking Aurora to put on a wrap and join him at the back of the house for the turn of Duetto Paradiso.

Surprised, but glad of distraction from unhappy consciousness, Aurora obeyed, to find Gentry on the aisle in the very back row.

'You wait,' he said, promising a rare treat. 'The cavern that woman has for a mouth—talk of an upper register! Note how her head lengthens: how deeply the chest fills, how that massive jaw drops and sound comes pouring out. *She* is not afraid to let her face look foolish in service of sound.'

Imperious in her green satin dress, La Sunderland sailed onstage, into the small circle of respect carved by Pettibone's applause, and held out her hands for the audience (which was not clapping) to cease. Pettibone ceased.

She began with *Una Voce Poco Fa*, a general audience favourite. Aurora knew it from her father's Victrola record of Tetrazzini, who sang it with lilting lightness. Sunderland's voice was deeper, powerful and agile. She made the most of every legato and sostenuto, and trifled archly with the trills. 'Remarkable for a woman of her age,' Gentry murmured.

Aurora wondered what her age might be. 'Fifty-six,' he said, as if she'd asked, and she blushed. 'Since I'm seventy-six, she ought to seem youngish to me. I was fond of her once,' he added, without much emotional investment that Aurora could hear.

The soprano was laughing *ah ah ha ha ha ha ha ha*, up and down the scale, turning into a viper when crossed—and her mouth did open to an amazing stretch. At the end of the aria she flung both arms wide, beaning poor Pettibone who had come forward to guide her into their duet. She flicked him away, nodded to the pianist, and dropped those marble arms into a languid pose of regret.

The opening notes started, and the hair rose slightly on the back of Aurora's neck.

> *'Early one morning, just as the sun was rising,*
> *I heard a maid singing in the valley below . . .'*

She was not—she could not be—singing their song, could she? Aurora turned to look at Gentry and found him leaning forward, then standing, gnarled hands gripping the back of the empty seat in front of him.

But you could not help listening. *'How could you use a poor maiden so?'* The newly tender voice, the inflection—and the darkness underneath, or pain. Sunderland made the song heartbreaking. She did not seem to expend any technique in the singing of it. There was only the broken girl reaching through castle walls to the faithless lover. How could someone so old sing as a maid? Listening, Aurora did not think of Sunderland's face or figure, or skill, only the sadness of the song. It was so much better than her own rendering that she could feel no jealousy.

Gentry Fox, however, was not hampered by humility. He whipped Aurora out of her seat, into the lobby, and straight up the stairs, where he threw the startled Drawbank out of his little office and slammed the door shut, without regard to noise.

'She would, would she?' he demanded. 'And what was Caspar about, to play it for her?'

Aurora did not know what to reply.

He opened the door and barked at Drawbank (still gawping on the landing), 'Get those other girls!' Then slammed the door again. '*Last Rose of Summer*,' he commanded Aurora, and from then to the intermission he worked her through it at half-voice—Bella and Clover too, once they appeared, terrified, at the door. They sang under the noise of Swain's Rats & Cats and right through Kavanagh's turn. When Gentry was satisfied he dismissed them.

Bella and Clover ran round to the stage door and relative safety.

Aurora, moving more slowly to keep the words in her head, saw Gentry climb down the steep stairs to the lobby, open the glass case and remove the photographs of *Edith Sunderland, Coloratura Soprano & Thomas Pettibone, Tenor*. He locked the case.

Then he opened it again, and removed the photograph of *Maurice MacKenna Kavanagh, Elocutionist*.

Underhand & Cheekbone

The Last Rose of Summer went over very well—it was the best turn they'd done yet, Clover and Bella agreed. Aurora was still not talking much, but some colour had come back into her face. She had not had the relief of pretending to be the wounded maiden, since that song had been cut out from under them, but the *Last Rose* gave vent for their general loneliness, and something about the girls appealed to the late-night house that evening. The applause was prolonged and the girls came off pink-cheeked, to be greeted by a crowing Sybil and their delighted mama. ('Oh, if only you'd had an encore ready!')

'Gentry handed them their photographs, cool as you please,' Sybil told the girls and Flora, having witnessed the dismissals after the girls went onstage. '*Underhand & Cheekbone, No longer required at this establishment*—and her without a word to say, after what she did.'

In the dressing room Aurora found a note stuck to her mirror with a bit of moustache wax. *To the Fair,* it read, in dashing viridian ink. Inside, a couple of lines:

> It's been a great gig. In this roistering life there are a multitude of partings and meetings—
> I will look for you along the way—
>
> M.M.K.

She looked at the handwriting for a minute, the over-curled ends on Kavanagh's *g*'s; then crumpled the note and tossed it in the scrap basket. But she had liked being in the crowd at Jenny's, she decided. The cigars and the music.

Not for Long

The bill was short the next day. Gentry told the girls to begin with *Early* and end with *Last*. The departure of Sunderland and Pettibone took up most of the backstage talk; nobody asked why Maurice Kavanagh's run had also been cut short. Even Sybil knew nothing, beyond his photograph not being in the case.

Once the girls had gone onstage on Saturday afternoon, Flora caught Gentry. 'Mr. Kavanagh has left the bill, I see,' she said, gently probing.

'Mr. Kavanagh is a limited-term engagement wherever he appears, of late,' Gentry said. 'He suffers from depression, never sleeps, falls indiscriminately in love with unsuitable artistes, and is too often an ugly drunk with a hair-trigger temper, which makes difficulties in the town. It was time for him to be on his way.'

It was extremely kind of him to have made the change, she knew. Even if it was also in the best interests of his theatre to have no scandal that might reach Mrs. Ackerman's ears.

But still he made no move to pay them.

Something had to be done. After two weeks, Flora could no longer stretch the remaining coins out for porridge and milk. She had trotted around to the pawnshop with six of Arthur's mother's apostle spoons— that would give them an extra week. But she must get the spoons back before they had to move on, for Arthur had treasured them. That meant finding money somehow.

On Tuesday morning, instead of staying at the theatre to watch Gentry put the girls through their paces, she walked back through bright drifting sparks of snow to the Pioneer, enjoying the city's surprising grandeur and how far from the Death Trail's stigma the great buildings and prosperous houses seemed, to ask Mrs. Burday if she still needed a waitress. It was quickly enough arranged, as their room had been in the first place, and Flora was grateful for Mrs. Burday's practicality and experience. It was set that Flora would work lunch and dinner sittings, and help with the last cleaning of the kitchen in the evening. She dreaded telling Aurora, but hoped that it might be a day or two before she noticed. Meals would improve, because Flora could take a dinner-can with beans or stew, whatever the most plentiful dish of the night was, and run it over to the theatre between the matinee and the seven o'clock show, to share with the girls.

But after tallying again she saw that it was still not enough. Money never was, in her experience. The hotel bill could be paid (would definitely be paid, since Mrs. Burday would stop it out of her pay) and meals managed, but Bella's boot-soles were worn through, and in winter that was serious business. They'd padded them with cardboard and a piece of moleskin cut from a coat lining, but that would not last, and she could not dance without boots. Clover's would last another few months. They needed slippers for dancing—white kid with a stacked Louis heel, button or bow strap, that didn't matter—at least $1 a pair. Perhaps the ones in the window of the New York Store they passed every day, going to and from the theatre. Her locket would have to go, Flora decided. It ought to bring enough to buy new boots for Bella and three pairs of kid slippers, and perhaps fresh collars for the girls, and also to redeem the apostle spoons, which had lately not been letting her sleep.

Of course Aurora discovered the whole the first night. She was surprised when Flora arrived with a nice can of stewed chicken and dumplings. Mrs. Burday had been generous with the ladle, most likely knowing perfectly well that it fed the four of them. Flora hurried them through it and snatched back the forks. The younger girls had been hungry enough to eat without question but Aurora followed her up the stairs to the stage door, and pulled on her sleeve to say, 'What? Have you pawned more spoons?'

'No!' Flora played indignant, but did not manage to fool Aurora.

'Where did the money come from, then? Has Gentry decided to pay us?'

Mama's oh-ed mouth made Aurora laugh. 'Well, I knew he was not paying us, or we'd have had cash in hand. It was a very good plan to work for free. Did you suggest it?'

Flora nodded, relieved to have that out, and let her guard down enough that when Aurora asked, 'Have you taken a job?' she had no time to dissemble.

'Are you maiding at the hotel?' Aurora pressed her.

'No!' Indignant again, but weak this time.

'Then—cook? No, that can't be it, you would not have time to run back here.'

Flora was glad the afternoon had clouded, so if she had reddened Aurora would miss it. 'I am waitressing, lunch and suppers,' she said. 'But truly, truly, it is not bad, my dear, I'm not run off my feet and the boys are very cheerful. I quite enjoyed myself today.'

Biting one cheek, Aurora looked at her in the dimming light.

'Don't be angry,' Flora begged. 'I don't mind it, really. It's a bit like being onstage.'

They stood in the cold alley behind the theatre, both of them getting colder, and then Aurora leaned forward and kissed her mother's cheek. 'We'll do well,' she said. 'It won't be for long.'

Flora nodded, and turned and ran over the icy streets to the back door of the Pioneer Hotel.

Unusually Wide Awake When Sybil—who had missed Flora the night before and tracked her down at the Pioneer to pry the whole tale out of her—told Julius that the girls were not being paid, he at once went up in flames and announced to Clover, and anyone else who would listen, that he was on a dumb strike. For the seven o'clock show the next evening he did a mad scenario, enlisting Mattie the placard boy, and paying him ostentatiously for his work. As the music swelled and the curtain rose, Julius was revealed asleep in a dishevelled heap against a potted palm in front of the painted drop of a Georgian terrace.

In tattered costume and beard, he snored operatically, the newspaper over his face flying up and down like sheets snapping on a line, like sails filling on a brigantine. After a full minute of virtuoso log-sawing from Julius, Mattie appeared from stage right, sans placard-boy jacket and hat, an imp on roller skates. He whisked past the sleeping tramp, communicated to the audience by a wide dawning grin the gag he had in mind, and bent down to untie his skates and re-tie them on Julius's feet.

Then he pulled a brown paper bag out of his pocket, blew the bag up, scrumpled the neck tight, and smacked it with the other hand, to make a great explosion in Julius's ear. The tramp started awake, leaped to his feet in a flurry of newsprint, and sailed on the roller skates straight into the orchestra pit—

But no! He veered left at the very verge, one leg swinging out over the pit, then whirling him in a fancy spin while he batted newspaper here and everywhere, except the sheet which covered his eyes, to the delight of the audience and of Mattie—until Julius fell spectacularly on his commodious behind, arms and legs clutching to retain his prizes. Since there came an enormous crash of cymbals at exactly that moment, either the timpanist had been forewarned, or he was unusually wide awake, thought Gentry, watching from the observation window.

He sighed and began the long climb down the stairs on swollen and aching legs.

Julius struggled to his feet but fell again, again and again, wheels rolling out from under him no matter how he placed them.

Clover, watching all this in the wings, believed he'd have to stop, but then would come another attempt, another roll. Mattie was laughing so hard he could barely stand up, this being the first time he'd done the turn, his hilarity pitched the higher since he could not know how badly Drawbank was going to take all this.

'In what way is this to blackmail me?' Gentry asked Julius interestedly, as he came offstage.

'My voice shall not ring out in this Ephesus, this Delphi of the mind,' whispered Julius into Gentry's ear, crepe beard tickling considerably, 'until the Bella–Clovers are compensated commensurate with their endeavours! I say this to your ear alone,' he added prudently, gesturing with one fan-shaped hand to make Clover recede behind a curtain-leg.

'Well, Julius,' Gentry confided, 'the awkward thing is, *you* are compensated commensurate with your windage, due to your unexpected arrival like an orphan on my doorstep, and Syb's skilful playing on my heartstrings . . .'

'You! You have no heart to string,' Julius pronounced.

'. . . and therefore the exchequer is entirely empty, my dear old boy—and since the busting of Sunderland and the Irishman I am merely going into a fraction less debt, daily. There is no more compensation to be had, unless you would like me to direct Johnny Drawbank to divvy up your allotment and hand a portion over to the delightful girls. No? Ah, I thought not. Good day to you then.'

Not cowed, but pensive, Julius did his German professor at the nine o'clock show.

A Tenderfoot Act

After watching Julius cavort in their cause, Aurora gathered her courage and went to Gentry herself that evening. Her mother had not come to bed till after midnight the night before, and her hands were red and split in the morning. Aurora calculated the odds of Gentry firing them on the spot, and concluded that on balance, he would want to keep them. But it was clear that the theatre had no money to spare, and possible that Drawbank was pressing Gentry to reduce the numbers on the bill. The matter needed delicate handling.

She found him putting on his topcoat in his cubbyhole office.

'I believe my mother is shy to speak to you, sir,' she said, trying not to halt in her delivery. 'But I know there was a plan to revisit our arrangement, and I hope we have been—' She couldn't say *giving satisfaction* as if they were parlourmaids. 'I think we have been pleasing the crowds.'

Gentry looked hunted.

'Here's my proposal,' Aurora said. 'Your lessons are worth a great deal to us, at least half of what we might expect to get, I think $60 or $70 a week for a tenderfoot act. If you'll keep teaching us, we'll work for you for $30 a week, and keep that arrangement to ourselves—but you'd have to let us have the Act 1 closer spot, and more time for dancing.'

'That's the second-best spot.'

Did he think she didn't know that? She waited, trying not to reveal anything. Like a game of beggar-your-neighbour with Papa and Mr. Dyment.

His discomfort seemed to express itself in a stiff neck. He rolled his grizzled head wildly, staring up at her. Then he sidled crab-wise a step or two to his door, and closed it. '$20 a week is the outside I can stretch to,' he said. 'But you've worked hard, you are good girls. As a consideration for your efforts, I will give you the opener.'

'But—Julius—'

'No, no, no need to fret about Julius. I'm moving him and Syb to open the second act, with their ventriloquy number. She pinned me down for that one months ago.'

Aurora had not realized they had a double act. She had not paid the least attention to Sybil, but now remembered that she'd been wearing a pink tulle costume when they first met her, at Cleveland's—all that time ago, it now seemed.

'Done,' she said, and gave Gentry her hand.

'And the ghost will walk on Saturday, as usual,' he said, only faintly sighing.

After she'd gone, Gentry pulled out his watch, a beautiful gold turnip from his father on the occasion of his twenty-first birthday, lost now in the mists of time, and polished it once more on his sleeve. Only 9:18. Time, still, to knock on Hiram's door. He picked up his watch and the old French ebony carriage clock from the tiny mantel, then looked into his bowler hat, its rich silk lining agleam in the lamplight. He set it on his head and, pleased with the conceit, went round to the pawn-shop to see what could be got for the time he had left.

4.
A Change of Scene

FEBRUARY–MARCH 1912

The Parthenon, Helena
The People's Hippodrome, Butte
The Digby Parthenon, Missoula

If you open the show, you have a considerable advantage in not having the stronger acts appear before you, so that the audience might compare them and applaud accordingly. Whatever place you are assigned by the management, take it uncomplainingly.

FREDERICK LADELLE, *HOW TO ENTER VAUDEVILLE*

*A*t the end of February an announcement was posted at the theatre: the Fox–Drawbank Parthenon company would spend four weeks touring the circuit. Gentry assumed Flora would accompany the girls, but she laughed and said she'd have a holiday; Aurora was perfectly capable, and they would have Sybil and Julius to rely on in need.

In truth, she'd been totting up what they would spend in costs— every bit of their new-won pay—and had nervously determined that she must retain her waitress job. Even as she talked airily to Gentry, she was figuring in her head. Numb to worry for some time after Arthur's death, she now felt it descend heavily on her; it seemed there were cart-wheel grooves that her tired mind slid into over and over: hotel bills, supper, thread, shoes . . . She refused to allow the faintest tinge of fright to appear on her face, knowing nothing was more fatal to success than the appearance of failure.

The one thing that gave her pause was Bella—almost fourteen, and still not yet begun her womanly cycles, but ten to one she would do so any day, far from her mama's guidance.

Aurora, hearing this fear, told her not to be silly; she and Clover could do all that was necessary, and Bella already knew all about it anyway, having watched her sisters washing out their monthly rags these last four years.

But as if to iron their path, that last worry vanished the day before the cavalcade was to set off: between the five and seven-thirty shows Bella came bursting into the dressing room with her face glowing, back from the privy, and announced, 'It's come! I've *got* it!'—so tickled to have achieved womanhood that nobody could be in doubt as to what she referred.

Her sisters clucked over her and rigged a temporary pinning, and warned her about the pain that might attend her, but Bella laughed and pooh-poohed them. Kitted up with the unfamiliar wad between her legs, she danced around the room to test it out, pleased as Punch. She did not even protest when Mama could not refrain from telling, yet one more time, the well-known tale of Aunt Queen in Madison, when Mama had rushed in from playing one day, 'with no more idea than a bird of what had happened—I thought I'd cut myself! And she said, Well! Now you can have a baby. I asked, How on earth? And here's what she said, the only knowledge she gave me: *The man will stick his thing in you, and you'll have a baby*—can you feature it?'

All Mama's stories ended that way, Clover thought: in disbelief at the lack of understanding in this cold old world. Except those ending '. . . then Arthur and I had our lovely children and all was worth the struggle.' But she had made certain that her girls knew how babies came to be, even if her description of the mechanics was flowery and sun-dappled, and slightly vague as to biology.

Louis Heels

After an anxious morning of packing and repacking, Flora went with her girls to the station to participate in the general jollity of the company's departure. She stood beside Gentry Fox to wave them off, the girls swathed in their warmest wraps. If only they'd had furs, which make leave-taking so festive! They had tried on their new dancing slippers the night before—white kid, Louis heels, tied with satin ribbons criss-crossing up the ankle—and their delight had been enough to stave off any slight regret Flora might have had about her locket. Arthur could not know, and what use had she for sentiment if the girls were ill-shod? She'd bought Bella proper boots at the New York Store too, and had even got the apostle spoons back from Hiram in the deal. She beamed wholeheartedly at the girls as they left, her mind at ease for once. They had good shoes and were guaranteed on the bill of the Ackerman–Harris travelling company for a solid month—programme sheets printed, and nobody the wiser about the cut-rate pay they'd be getting, which was still much better than nothing! She knew they would do well.

Gentry gave her a cup of tea in the station waiting room after the train departed, and she headed back to the Pioneer (allowing Gentry to assume that she was off to enjoy her leisure) more happily than her daughters might have expected.

The Jump

They would play the People's Hippodrome in Butte the first week, meeting up there with several new acts. Swain's Rats & Cats were off to Chicago, with a cheery wave of too many tails. Instead they would share the bill with the Furniture Tusslers and Victor Saborsky, Eccentric, whom Sybil and Julius knew well.

'Oh yes, from a babe,' Sybil told Bella and Clover, sitting across from them on the first leg of their trip. 'His ma was an English variety dancer—well, she was Polish in fact, but married English, and him some kind of fiddler. Fabians, you know, *very* free, and then they took up with some heathen madman or other as well, odd as anything. Over they came, three or four years, with the little tyke in tow. This was after your ma had left us. He did his schooling in the dressing room, but his father was determined he get an education, very, so they upped back to England for a time, for him to attend a high-toned establishment, because the father, you know, was Someone in his own right before taking up with the Polish dancer. She was sweetly pretty, but a bit black in her moods from time to time; she struggled with her temper. Well, you'll notice his nose, that was her doing. Not that she was alone in that—look for example, if you need one, at those poor Ninepins, Missus and the boy, and how they must creep around that Joe Dent, who has a kind heart I'm sure but is a demon when in drink, and you can't tell me that boy is not being brutalized no matter how they blandish the authorities. And now he's a certified *Eccentric*, working without a net—I mean Victor Saborsky, not Nando. Odd to see a little boy all grown up now, makes you feel a bit old. His face so thin and sad, he looks as old as us, however sweet his expression may be—but his turn is spectacular, ever an honour to be on the bill with him. Always excepting of course my dear Jay, Victor's my favourite act on the circuits, this or any other year.'

From Butte, they would head east to Billings for a week; retrace their steps for a second week in Butte; and then shuffle west to Missoula for another week's engagement before making their way back to Helena—which now seemed like home.

The green leather seats felt sticky under Bella's tucked-up shins. In the warm train she had pushed her black stockings down from their elastic and rolled them tight-tight-tight around the tops of her new boots. *Butte boot.* Bella stared out the window at the hills rising oddly out of flat plains, the bones of the earth showing through, no decorations at all beyond a scrub of trees; here and there a blackened patch from fire.

Butte was always on fire in Mama's tales of the old Death Trail—one of her best stories was the fire in the butcher shop in Butte where her company was playing on her very first tour, how the pigs in the back squealed through the crackle of the flames, and the smell of roast pork beginning—extremely gruesome. Bella could not get it out of her mind; it ran horrified prickles up and down her scalp. Mama had been in no danger, she had said so over and over, but Bella could not help imagining that her feet were burning, Mama's feet, on the boards rigged over the butcher's counter for a stage—little feet in embroidered satin slippers. The horse-drawn fire wagon had scrambled up to the front door of the butcher shop as all the audience was streaming out. Mayhem! But it was better to think of that little fire than the big fire in Butte, the explosion in 1895, before Mama left vaudeville and married Papa and had Aurora and left this life. That explosion was far from the theatre, but onstage they'd heard the roar of it, and when they stopped the play and went out into the street there was a boy's body, blown several blocks by the blast—the whole thing like a scene from the war, dead bodies everywhere and blood seeping into the dirt of the road, and brains spattered here and there, parts of human beings. Bella had read the clipping in Mama's scrapbook: 'the cries and groans of the injured and dying and some of the bodies still quivering, remnants of human beings, legs and arms torn off . . . *shapeless trunks quivered and died in the arms of the living*.'

She shook her hands out quickly and lay down, her head on Clover's lap. A boy like Mattie, perhaps, or—not Nando! After a moment she whispered, 'In Butte there was a boy lying dead outside the theatre, and when they walked to see the explosion they passed parts of people quivering on the ground.'

Clover smoothed her hair. 'That was years ago—we will not be exploded this time, I promise.'

'I love you, Clover,' Bella said, digging her cheek into Clover's knee as if they were about to be separated by some great cataclysm. 'I love you.'

Clover's hand passed gently and constantly over her hair and her ears and presently she stopped thinking, and the swaying of the train over the tracks lulled her to sleep.

Stroking Bella's hair, Clover was lonely. Bella's childishness made her feel old and calm. Farther down the carriage Julius played pinochle with the leader of the Old Soldiers outfit, John Wendt Hayden. The son of a soldier, he had not seen action himself and bore no terrible wound; he had a lovely friendly voice. She could change seats and join them, but was disinclined to move. After the usual hubbub of the theatre it was nice to have quiet.

She could hear Julius holding forth to John Hayden: 'I *did* attempt blackface for a year or so, travelling in the Antipodes. No more. The young comic Jolson goes corked for Sullivan–Considine—a mouth with a man attached. I saw him perform in San Francisco, unfazed in the aftermath of the earthquake; I won't compete with him. I'd rather mock the German.'

Julius was easy to hear, but John had a low voice, so their conversation was an exchange of booms and murmurs, like Clover imagined the sound of the sea might be.

'Yon Jolson transcends the genre because he is in some sense sending up his Hebraism, of which the audience is perfectly well aware. But it's a pesky makeup to do. I have disliked it ever since, in my youth, I was persuaded to use coal dust one evening. Took seven months to rid my skin of the blue tinge. I looked like a damned Taffy, fresh from the mine.' Puffing on a cheroot, Julius expanded. 'When you work in concert with someone like Bert Williams, the race ceases to be abstraction, and becomes a collection of human beings, as noble, nasty, sharp or foolish as our own. Oddly, this transmogrification does not seem to attain with the German, whom I am never loath to loathe, and ever find more loathly on closer acquaintance—for example a railway journey, during which your German will always be provided with a frumious wurst of blemished origin, and an unsharp pocket knife to saw it with.'

As Julius's trumpeted over John's voice, his blatant body trumpeted too, lounging legs laid out into the aisle. 'In New York last year, Flo Ziegfeld signed Bert Williams to star in the Follies—blackface over his own black face—and when the cast (a collection of gabies) threatened to walk out rather than appear onstage with him, Ziegfeld's response was simple: Go if you want! I can replace every one of you—*except* the man you want me to fire!'

Clover thought of blackface as a costume. It startled her to think of the person under the makeup.

Across the aisle, Aurora stared at her own reflection in the train window, the abbreviated slant of her un-made-up brows and the jut of her too-strong chin. She tried to pull it in, experimenting with the angle to find how to make their next photos more flattering, and let the words to *Last Rose*, which Gentry had put permanently into their turn, run through her head: *Thus kindly I'll scatter thy leaves o'er the bed, Where thy mates of the garden lie scentless and dead.* A manual for deadheading in the garden; that practical coolness could be used in the song too. But when it came to *From love's shining circle, the gems drop away*, you could let the throb in there, open the coolness to the dark heart that lay under everyone's life. All the dead sisters and brothers, the lost fathers and children of everyone in the audience would come and sit beside them briefly, because she was singing. Perhaps Gentry meant that it was a better thing to do with grief than just being sad alone.

A Thin Man, Not Too Tall

The Hippodrome in Butte was a brand-new theatre, but only one of seventeen operating in the wealthy copper town. The Grand Opera on Myers Avenue was the largest; the Lyric Opera the most notorious (according to Sybil, the fancy name was a front for gambling and prostitution); and the Hippodrome the newest. The girls climbed dirty-snowed streets from the train station, following the straggling artistes, and were rewarded. Inside and out, it was a beauty. The opulent lobby was freshly painted, the smell of linseed oil still strong.

Inside the house, Clover stopped on her way down the aisle to turn around and around, staring up at the ceiling. A bright wreath of flowers painted around the ventilated dome in the centre of the roof held four figures (ribbon-sashes for *Music, Dancing, The Drama,* and *Tragedy* draped prudently over bare chests) and a fruit-basket-upset of musical instruments. Instead of advertisements, like in most theatres they had seen, the front-drop curtain featured a painted Greek scene: ruins on the shore of a lake and a dangerous mountain range behind.

Bella and Aurora went down to the dressing rooms, but Clover stayed to watch the flymen run through the ropes, testing the rigging. Myriad backdrops swept up and down, each with its own wing pieces: a fancy drawing room with folding doors, a poor kitchen, two different streets (one elegant, one shabby), a ship dock, dawn in a forest glade, a rocky pass fit for brigands, and many others. As she delightedly inspected the detail of a starving artist's garret (two mice fighting over a bit of cheese, a baby's fat little fist visible above the rim of a cracked cradle), a voice spoke behind her.

'Looks comfortable enough, and cheap, shall we move in?'

She turned quickly and saw a thin man, not too tall, with fluffy brown hair and a sharply bent nose. The sweetest face she'd ever seen: mild, interested, open to excitement. She liked his face on sight, more than any man's she could remember, except—perhaps it reminded her a bit of Papa's, abstraction combined with a suddenly present attention. He was attending to her at this moment.

'Victor Smith,' he said, indicating himself.

'Clover Avery,' she returned automatically, thinking he must be manager here. He did not look like a manager, but neither did Gentry Fox, and this man had something of Gentry's air of being not from the place he found himself in. She held out her hand and he laughed, and raised it almost to his lips—in a European way, but jokingly.

'I think you must be one of *Les Très Belles Aurores*?'

'Well, we're just the Belle Auroras,' Clover said. 'My sisters are Bella and Aurora, you see.'

'No Clover in that name—does that mean I can pluck you loose from them?'

'I sing alto,' she said, as if that explained the whole thing.

'Then you must definitely come over to my act. I need some sweet meadow flower to pull the bees. I am Victor Saborsky, when I am on the boards.'

'Oh! Our friend Sybil Sutley knows you, sir.'

'So she does. She was a good friend to my mother.'

'As she is to mine,' Clover said.

'Then we are cousins,' Victor said. He bowed to her, but shyness descended on her under his continued regard, so she turned again to watch the drops being raised and lowered—they were now in a stone square lit by shafts of moonlight, some European capital waiting for a princess to trip lightly down the stairs, or a king to abdicate—and when she raised her eyes he was gone. Vanished without a sound. She found herself looking up, as if for a bird. Nothing.

One Silver Dollar

The dressing rooms were shining clean, bright with mirrors. At one side a darling stove puffed heat into the room. Bella held her boots out one at a time to admire their gleam in the rows of electric bulbs. The first time they'd had electric lights in a dressing room, too. This was the fanciest place. Aurora had checked the bill and there were no other females on it—only Sybil, who had a dressing room of her own with Julius—so she let Bella pick the best spot and set out their things, with a place for Clover between them. Clover is the best friend of each of us, Bella thought, she is always between us. But she loved Aurora too. In some ways she and Aurora were the most alike: strong and bold. Clover was the sweetest of them, though.

A thousand thousand Bellas found the ranked mirrors entrancing. Their placement round the room showed her herself as a regiment of girls, all those shards, and ghosts dainty and slim, ready to dance. The Parthenon's old mirrors had not been so flattering.

A tap on the door—and two heads poked around it, like another doubling mirror.

'Mr. East and Mr. Verrall!' Bella exclaimed, happy to see old friends. 'Come in!'

'Oh, we will not intrude,' Verrall was saying, but East burst through his arm and into the room, to give each of the sisters a warm and slightly over-personal embrace.

Verrall flapped an envelope in his long fingers. Not entirely clean, Bella saw, after their railway journey, but her own hardly ever were either.

'We were charged with, given, we—'

East snatched the letter from him. 'Jimmy the Bat got us to bring this,' he said, rolling his eyes at Verrall's politesse. 'Not knowing what hotel you would be putting up at—and do you know yourselves?'

'I believe we are at Mrs. Seward's,' Aurora said. 'It is only a boarding house.'

'We will *call* it an hotel,' Verrall declared. 'We are there too.'

'Mrs. Seward's is the *only* place to stay in Butte,' East announced, sunk in gloom.

'Fine testimonial,' Verrall said. 'Not a paid endorsement.'

'We are thinking about hotels, because our present routine, that we are breaking in on this western swing, is hotelly.'

'It has a hotellishness about it,' Verrall agreed.

'A dark and hellish hotellishness.'

'So, Miss Bella, we were wondering if you could be purr-suaded—'

'We need, we have need, we are in need of, a good little girl . . .'

'. . . to hotel for us tonight?'

No matter how they talked over each other you could always hear each one, Bella noticed. East was the funniest. Or maybe Verrall, with his sad eyes and bluish teeth.

'We would add to your consequence the amount of *one silver dollar.*' Verrall flourished the coin as if it were a king's ransom.

'Per diem,' East put in hastily. 'Not per showem.'

'To help you in your act?' Bella was astonished.

'That very thing. You would have one or two lines, just old hokum, but would carry the day, and could wear whatever pretty little frock you've been singing in, without a change to trouble you.'

Aurora said, before Bella could agree, 'We'd have to see the lines. There cannot be any suggestive nonsense.' That chafed, but Bella knew that Aurora felt herself to be Mama while they were here, and was determined to look after their reputation as delicate girls.

'What, *none?*'

'No, no, East,' Verrall said. 'None of the kind, nothing, no. Only a sweet girl receptionist, a little stupid.'

'A very stupid, but such a pretty little hen!' said East, chucking Bella under the chin and almost kissing her, but managing to make Aurora smile about it.

Bella spun around till her skirt spread wide. 'Oh yes, yes, yes, please!' she cried.

Balance

While East and Verrall set about coaching Bella, Aurora read the letter they had brought her:

Dear Miss Aurora,

Miss Eleanor has decided to return East, which means I must go too for now. We've lost Mr. Hanrahan (who played her husband in the melodrama you might recall) and cannot do the show longer so she pulls it back to NY or Boston and we will do 'The Slap' again.

So it may be some time before I make it back Out West again and I am sorry for it. Keep up with your dancing and one of these turns it will be you and me.

Yours already, without any Right to style myself so,

JIMMY BATTLE

No, he did not have any right. It made her warm to think of it, but almost equally irritated. He was the puppy of that actress, even if he was working on a song-and-dance routine on the side. But it was comforting to think of him. She touched the signature, *Jimmy Battle*. Small writing, but not cramped. He would not ever shove her away and curse her. He was a good match for her; they were the same in many ways. But there ought to be some balance in things. Perhaps she too would find a patron for a while.

Glass Crash

The orchestra master knew his work and put the Belle Auroras through their cues like lightning, wasting no time at all on compliments but treating them like veterans, which was better. He nodded them off and turned to the more difficult cues for the Furniture Tusslers, a robust pair of young men with small eyes and ham-shaped arms who threw tables and chairs, and each other, across the stage at predetermined intervals, to the loud crashing of cymbals. The wood-crash operator was irritably busy stage right—when the girls crossed his line of vision he missed a cue. They fled.

Bella (who had looked back at the younger, quite-handsome Tussler) stomped on the foot of the waiting glass-crash man. He swore horribly, but gave her a black-toothed grin when she apologized. She loved his glittering basket of glass shards and the spare bottles he had lined up to break in it; but the wood-crash machine with its heavy handle frightened her. It sounded too much like a real man falling down stairs, or landing in a woodpile, or breaking a spindly Sheraton desk, depending on the velocity at which the handle was turned.

East and Verrall were quarrelling on the stairs as the girls went down, as they seemed almost always to be doing, when not performing or testing out their routines on personable girls. Bella knew that Aurora felt herself to be above them, although she could not have said why; and Clover liked them well enough but was still shy of their patter-schtick. Bella, however, was one of their company now, and they put out black-suited arms to stop her halfway down, and got her to run through her lines again at a whisper. *'Would you like to take a bath?'* *'No thanks, I'll leave it right where it is!'* and all the rest of the old gags. The second time through, Bella's tongue tripped up and she said, *'Would you like me to take a bath?'* Quick as lightning East said, *'Whoo-hoo, absolutely!'*—eyes goggling happily out of his head, hands somehow conjuring a claw-footed tub.

She didn't hesitate either, but asked, as if it were his luggage, *'Where would you like me to take it?'* which made East laugh out loud instead of carrying on—and that was winning the trick, so she was proud of herself.

But Verrall said the gag would get them tossed out of the theatre, even in the more relaxed environs of Butte, so they went back to the usual way. At the end of the whispering rehearsal Verrall shook her hand and told her she was *histrionic*, which she gathered was a good thing to be.

Butte was not Helena, no. The crowd was rougher—there was a woodsy smell in the theatre, a Paddockwood kind of smell, tobacco and tanned hides, drink, men's working clothes; although there were women in the audience, they were well outnumbered by men. Faces visible in the spilling light were white and owl-eyed. Some of the men stood up when Aurora and Clover danced the *Music-Box*, the better to see them twirl.

And opening was not closing. The stone-cold crowd talked generally through the first number, *Buffalo Gals*, and gave only a smattering of applause. Bella, who had grown used to being liked, found that she was almost angry not to have that appreciative cushion; she put more vim into *I Can't Do the Sum* and seemed to win the attention of the house. Aurora—and even, dutifully, Clover—twinkled and glimmered at the boxes and caught what eyes they could, but it was uphill work, and then went all downhill during *Early One Morning*, for which that crowd was definitely not in the mood.

As they cleaned their faces, Aurora said, 'If we'd had another number prepared, we could have caught them. Something with a little pep—or maybe a sentimental number?'

Bella shook it off. But she did think Gentry was wrong about the crowd down here.

Had 'Em, Lost 'Em

Bella trotted up to the stage-right side to be ready for East & Verrall's number, and caught the last of the Tusslers' act. That younger one had rangy legs curving in strong lines front and back. Arms bare beneath a brocade waistcoat, clean-boned and taut. He saw her watching and stared at her so boldly that she looked away and went through her lines in her head.

East and Verrall crowded into the wings beside her, kissed each side of her face, and went on. With an afternoon of hard work they had whipped their hotel number into slightly better shape.

It started in one, the seafront olio drop covering up the terrible mess left in two and three by the Furniture Tusslers. Behind the drop the hands raced to clear that mess.

Bella loved the dual view she had from the wings: East and Verrall's chatty number going on in front, bathed in the sweetness of the pinky golden light, all alive—while at the same time, behind the olio, deathly silent in faint blue light, stagehands going through their practised moves, soundlessly crouching, lifting slowly as if they were in a dream; the Furniture Tusslers walked like ghosts through their old life to retrieve their props.

In front, Verrall opened their number, minding his own business in a straw boater on the promenade, whistling idly till East came rolling onstage as if punched, brought up short and saved from the ocean by Verrall's foot.

'I was living the life of Riley,' East said, dusting off his coat.

'And then what happened?'

'Riley came home.'

Verrall was sympathetic. 'Women! You got to keep moving, Mr. East.'

East, looking nervously behind him: 'Now I'll *have* to move. Can you recommend a hotel?'

Their turn went on, light pattering music up and down under their voices in the same absurd style as their pattering conversation. On cue—exactly as the last of the stagehands whisked across behind a broom—the seafront olio rose to reveal a hotel lobby drop and a desk, in two, and Verrall strolled back to become the hotel manager.

Sidling up to the desk, East took out a cigar and chomped it between his teeth.

Verrall cried, 'Hey, put that out, there's no smoking in here.'

'What makes you think I'm smoking?' asked East, eyes wide open.

'You've got a cigar in your mouth!'

'I got boots on my feet, don't mean I'm walking.'

Verrall told him, in deep disdain: 'You're going to make some woman a wonderful husband.'

With a wild, agonizing roll of the eyes East said, 'I'm afraid so!'

'You don't even know what a husband is.' Verrall's superiority was massive.

'Oh, yes I do!' East snapped back, uncrushed. 'A husband is what's left of a sweetheart after the nerve has been killed.'

After they'd tangled a bit over the price of a room, Verrall tinged his little desk bell and yelled, 'Front! Show the man the elevator!'

But East said, 'No, no, I want a room with a bed in it.'

'Will you be needing a bath, sir?' Verrall asked, very cold.

'How rude!' Then, anxious, 'Would you say I do?'

Verrall rang his bell again with vigour, and Bella went skittering on in her dancing slippers, eyes wide as saucers for her first dramatic role. She was as helpfully unhelpful as they'd rehearsed and she said the lines as they'd told her to, and when she got a laugh she could not help checking the audience and laughing too—her naive pleasure making it all the funnier; she was quick enough to play with that, the way East and Verrall played.

When they came off after their turn they told Bella she'd saved their bacon.

'Cat-calls off, wolf-whistles on. That was all for you, cupcake,' East said as they bundled her down the stairs at the intermission. He gave her bottom a thoughtful pat.

'That last gag of yours was a three-person joke,' Verrall told East. 'I hope those three enjoyed themselves.'

'Over the heads of the rest. Had 'em, lost 'em, had 'em, lost 'em— one long recurring nightmare. I'd hang myself if my belt would hold.'

'It'll be better at the second show, when the audience is half-cut.' Verrall pulled the script out of his pocket and a pencil from the ribbon of his bowler hat, made a few swift strokes and scribbled a note. 'Lose the dining room bit, lose *They raise chickens in the cellar, the guests are fond of dark meat.* Too highbrow for this house.'

'We'll have to put the girl back in,' East said.

'*She was knocking on my door all night, but there were complaints and I had to let her out—*' Verrall scratched.

'Good, that'll lead into *There's a dead girl in the other bed . . .*'

'*Yes, but how did you find out she's dead?*' Verrall said, accusing the imaginary guest. 'Or do you think that's going too strong?'

Bella was laughing too hard to talk, so exhilarated she could have turned right around and gone back out again; and the best of it was, she'd be able to do it again at the second show, and at the third, and then all this week! She put her fist over her mouth and made herself calm down so she would have something left for the next two shows.

An Artiste

Later in the bill, Clover slipped backstage again to watch Victor Saborsky. His act used a very complicated technical rigging which he checked and rechecked during the Old Soldiers' performance, and right after the intermission Clover had seen him standing motionless at the very back of the stage behind the last olio drop, lost in thought, or in prayer.

'A true artiste,' Sibyl had whispered as they filed past him. 'Nothing comes before performance, with him. You don't often find that in this business, really, that kind of concentrated effort. People work hard— look at East and Verrall!—but he's a maniac.'

Clover had not mentioned him to her sisters, and she went up alone into the wings to watch him. Her white skirt and waist would be too evident in the wings, she thought, so she wrapped herself in a grey shawl and stood like a modest ghost just outside the hemp-bed's painted line. The blue light from the prompt box shone on her pale, pointed face and haloed her hair. Victor saw her and smiled, because she had come up for his turn, then looked quickly away.

He wore a great-collared black velvet dress-coat, threadbare and ornate—he might have stolen it from an opera wardrobe, or inherited it from Beethoven. High-waisted black trousers made his long legs twice as long; he wore elongated boots that flapped slightly but retained a worn elegance of line. Clover could see the pattern of soft cracks filled in with black polish. The lights dimmed, the music changed, and the curtain opened to reveal two.

A country road, a tree. Evening.

Tattered silk battens, blown gently by a stagehand on the wind machine, gave the appearance of mist drifting over the stage. The drop, keeping the stage in two, showed a blurred grey landscape with the suggestion of a moon hidden behind clouds. Victor wandered onstage as if he had walked for a long time in those long black boots, and began to talk to the people in front. Clover had never imagined anything so charming and easy (but it was not easy, she knew, to make them yours).

'Long ago I was a boy, and all alone,' Victor told them, confidingly. 'My father having died, and my mother being lost. She went to the Fabians, you know, and from them to even stranger company . . .' He was a portrait of sadness. 'But one must not repine.'

His feet flicked in a low flutter of ecstatic dance, then stilled. The wind began to blow, small particles of paper scudding towards Victor

in the wind machine's draught, and he was blown askew, farther off
gravity than ought to have been possible, before he turned to face the
wind and was tumbled backwards into a slow-flurrying roll. He picked
himself up and carefully brushed his coat.

'Life is not without its difficulties,' Victor said, and a sudden imaginary gust blew him back through three standing flips—his hands
never moved from holding his coat, his body merely seeming to revolve
on a still fulcrum. Lightning flashed in the blasted landscape. The
thunder-sheet was directly across from where Clover stood—she could
see the man yank mightily on the metal to make it crack, but jumped
anyway when the thunder boomed out.

Victor staggered back again and hid behind the small tree, clutching at it—and as the wind continued to blow, his feet lifted off in the
gale until his body flew straight out sideways, a black pennant waving
in the wind.

At his farthest extent the wind dropped, the lights changed, music
rippled through a discordant change into an old minuet, and Victor
leaped into a story, which he told while tuning a battered violin (where
had it appeared from?), rosining his bow, and finally playing it. In a very
few words he sketched an ancient Polish music-master teaching him to
play. The violin slid from dominating virtuoso to hopeless student, and
back again: shimmering from the violent, impatient commands of the
master to the trust and willingness to learn of the boy, Victor seemed to
waver from seven feet tall to three. The pupil's music grew from squawks
to mastery, and then the master died, and Victor assumed his greatcoat.

Clover found her eyes aching for her father, for how he as much as
Mama had set their feet on this path from her earliest memory.

Then the violin vanished into thin air, and lighter music began
from the orchestra.

'My next trick!' Victor announced. He swept the black frockcoat
into a wheeling circle and from it retrieved an egg, a feather fan, a
bowler hat and a bamboo walking stick. He juggled first the egg, then
the egg and the fan, then hat-egg-fan while twirling the bamboo cane
in a windmill. The cane landed on his nose, the hat flipped up onto

the cane, and he juggled the egg while fanning himself. While he was so occupied, with understandable concentration, his feet began a clattering dance, the boot-ends clacking a gay percussion.

His absurdity, thought Clover, is not of the idiot variety, but of someone wanting too much, reaching for the moon. Every motion was comic, every flex of foot and straight-edge of elevated leg.

'Yes, for some time I made my living rationally, as a juggler. But too much influenced by the moon, I became—if not an out-and-out lunatic—an eccentric. I shiver to see the moon each night, preposterous and separate. Why should we be so far from what we long for? But how to reach it?'

He pulled from his coat a large brass compass. 'My only inheritance,' he said, showing it off. 'From my father, a moral compass . . . My great treasure!' Flourishing it, he dropped it—oh no!—but caught it, dropped it, batted it forward, ran fast enough to be below it when it fell; he sighed with relief and shook it, and it all fell to pieces in his hand.

Clover was as horrified as Victor seemed. In a fumbling jumble he reassembled the pieces, making the compass into a birdcage, a lantern (lit!), and a drinking goblet before managing to shuffle it once more into a compass—although larger, and wilder. There was one piece left over: the glass cover, which he could not get to fix. Instead, abandoning the attempt, he stuck it into his eye as a monocle. It shone in the light and showed that eye magnificently magnified.

As Victor goggled at the audience, seeming to see everything new, the second drop rose and the stage was revealed in three: a dark forest of bare trees. Behind them a huge full moon and the night sky peppered with salty stars. Clover thought perhaps it would be a lady-moon, but saw no face—a faint suggestion of a rabbit was only shadows of pits and craters. Or *was* that a face, yellowy-green, hanging upside down?

Victor checked his compass to see how he should proceed, and showed the audience its needle wildly spinning. As the light increased, seeming to shine from the moon (but from the wings Clover could see the Klieg light), a path appeared in the darkness behind Victor, shining upwards, like a moonbeam. She took a breath, as the audience did—as Victor did, when he spun and saw the road shining before him.

'My destination!' he cried, looking back over his shoulder to bring the audience along with him. He tried to walk up it: fell through, of course, because it was only beams of light. He backed up and ran, and somersaulted through as if it were a cobweb, seeming to stick . . . and fell.

Victor picked himself up and hobbled back to teeter on the edge of the stage, between two silver footlights. He raised himself on his long toes and leaped, dove forward into a handspring and a cartwheel and a fan of arms and legs and somehow—how? even in the wings Clover could not tell!—up onto the ribbon of light descending from the moon. She saw the stagehand hauling on his harness from the other side, but Victor moved so naturally as he strode up the sky that it was hard to connect the two. He leaped over the tall trees and forward and at last he put out a hand and touched the moon's strange face, leaned in and kissed it, and exhorted the moon to explain to him: life, gravity, the persistent eternal pull of the tide, and of course, Love.

Receiving no answer but the hoot of a lonely owl, he brought out a silk kerchief and philosophically polished up that pallid face. 'Until we meet again,' he told the moon, with a lover's caressing promise. Then he turned away from the moon and leaped—so far forward that Clover was in terror—and landed again on the forestage, precisely in one, and stood triumphant.

The people went wild and Saborsky bowed a gigantic bow, wheeling his arms in a wild sunburst-rolling jump and bowing again, shouting '*Encore!*' for himself. He took fourteen bows, tossing and picking up (with enormously vulnerable gratitude and some elastic-string mechanism) the same two bouquets of red silk roses over and over, terribly reminiscent of Sunderland and Pettibone applauding each other, and almost the funniest bit of all.

Clover's whole heart and self was won.

Standing at the back of the hall beside Sybil, who had made them come up for a rare treat, her sisters watched too, and each in her own way saw how Saborsky's true skill outshone every little thing they might do themselves.

A Chance Not to Be Missed

Mrs. Seward's boarding hotel was a large, noisy place full of vaudeville people visiting with acquaintances from other theatres in town; a general movement through the house seemed to go on almost all night.

At 3 a.m. Mrs. Seward emerged in awful dudgeon and rang a little bell, and everyone went back to their own rooms, as East and Verrall had promised Aurora would happen. Finally something close to silence fell over the house and the girls could sleep, though Aurora was kept awake a little longer with the sick knowledge that they'd have to be up in four hours to make the band call for the next day's performances.

The next night, Friday night, a proposal floated through the dressing rooms, to go after the show to hear members of the Hippodrome orchestra moonlighting at a roadhouse in the nearby countryside. Most of the company were going. An important visiting impresario was to put in an appearance.

'A chance not to be missed,' Julius confided, leaning in to their dressing room. His eyes popped at Aurora earnestly: a surprising pale green, like peeled grapes floating in custard. 'We work, we strive, art is all—but at a certain juncture, management is a necessity. Mr. Fitzjohn Mayhew is a rising man and was last winter at the Follies. I think it worth the excursion.'

Aurora considered the proposal as she creamed off her makeup, listening to Sybil's rippling account of how such a party would be perfectly permissible and even educational. The hotel would be in a din till three again, anyway. She and Clover had been to country dances at home in Paddockwood, some quite rambunctious, and could certainly take care of themselves; besides, they'd be with all their friends from the Parthenon company. She did briefly wonder whether she ought to leave Bella behind at Mrs. Seward's, but Bella heard her saying as much to Clover and scotched that plan.

'Cat piss! I am just as fit as you to go out in the country without Mama,' Bella cried. 'You can't leave me here while you two go gallivanting!'

'I'm thinking of your good,' Aurora told her sharply. 'You're still a child.'

'Ha, no, I'm not any more, and *you know it*! Don't you treat me like a baby.'

'Only our own dear Baby,' Clover said, using Bella's old pet-name. 'We must look out for you.'

'If I'm old enough to be in the show, I'm old enough to go out with you.'

Aurora would have fought her down, but the boarding hotel with its wandering artistes was no safer a place for a girl alone. Instead she did a quick job on Bella's eyes, then Clover's and her own, as if looking older would better fortify them to cope with any questionable doings they might encounter. In any case, they had done nothing but work and strive for many months—it was delightful to think of a trip to the woods.

After the last show the whole party together rode the streetcar till the track ended, at a blank crossroads. After a chilly wait, a long cutter came jingling out of the darkness. A man with surprisingly few teeth jumped down to help them up into the hay that filled the wagon-bed, and then to plump carriage robes around them, paying some special attention to the girls' knees and feet until Julius growled at him; then they slid slowly off into the night woods.

The full moon had risen long before and rode above them, a silver orange dangling just out of reach. Clover was squashed in beside Mr. Verrall, but if she craned her neck slightly her cheek grazed the coat of Victor Saborsky, sitting on the wagon's sidebar. At one corner the wagon lurched and Victor put out a hand to save her from being tossed out. It was too dark to see his eyes but his hand felt warm right through her melton coat-sleeve.

The silence of the forest was broken by a chuffing, a huffing. The cutter drew to one side of the narrow track; the clattering sewing-machine sound rose, and a touring car burst out of the shadows behind them. It squeezed past, honking, headlamps flaring in the darkness, and off around a bend, the commotion gradually fading.

'Fitzjohn Mayhew,' Julius pronounced. 'His imprimatur.'

It was peaceful once the automobile had gone. The cutter slid on, runners scraping over gravel—winter was drying out to spring. Before long music twined out of the woods, and around another dark, piney dogleg they found a warm-lit huddle under the trees, a low log-built house with small windows under its eaves, each one a prick of light; buggies and wagons ranged alongside. Aurora took Bella's arm on one side and Clover caught her other hand, and they followed Sybil and Julius, and went before East & Verrall, Victor Saborsky, the Tussler boys and the musicians, crowding up into the ante-porch and through a cracked, moss-packed door into a cacophony of noise and smoke.

Aurora tried to make out the room through the haze. A low dive, she thought, and the smell was fierce, but there was music playing over the racket of talk, and none of the men seemed instantly violent. Miners, she thought, and officials at the mines. Girls moved through the crowd, a sprinkling among the men: well-dressed working women, a few drunken drabs. Wan, skinny chits who looked like God's last leftovers carried tin jugs of beer and unlabelled bottles. Although it irked her, Aurora saw she had made a mistake in coming. It was not a box-house—the kind of place she'd heard Sybil tell of, where girls went straight down from the stage to dally with the patrons in small enclosed boxes, for a little extra income—but it was not at all a respectable place. She kept a good grip on Bella's hand.

Across one end of the long room a slightly raised platform held the musicians. Silver plates on an accordion flashed in the lamplight as the musicians squashed together to make a larger empty space on the plat-form. Blurry forms of dancers waited to begin.

East took Clover's elbow to steer the girls to a half-empty table, then vanished with Verrall, reappearing with small stools to crowd in tight about the table. Aurora did a quick check of the room. No sign of the promised impresario. There was no one who could possibly have come in that touring car. There must be other rooms—or perhaps a different class of entertainment, in the outbuildings crouched around the wagon yard. She settled herself to watch, but kept one eye on the room.

A Little Less Sad This was a wild place, Bella thought. Just what her mood required! The thin girls serving and the thin men drinking interested her equally. The trampled floor was dark dirt; the long, low-ceilinged room felt dank with a distillery brew of yeasty sweat, but the woodsmoke and deer-hide smell reminded her of country dances in Paddockwood, and the theatre people seemed like old friends too: East and Verrall, of course, but Saborsky and the Tusslers too. The older Tussler gave her a wink and she gave him a twinkling one back, so he elbowed his brother and guffawed, winking again and again. Bella decided he was not entirely right in his head.

Fitful light fell from oil lamps set on tables and hung from beams, not bright enough to make it truly cheerful, but she felt like she knew the ropes here. In a back L of the room—closer to the still-room, she guessed, since the jugs of beer came from that end—men and a few women were playing cards.

The dancers came on: a man and woman, both wearing tattered street clothes and caps. The music changed to a *danse Apache* rag, and the man grabbed the woman's arm. He pulled her to him and slapped her, hard! But she didn't seem to mind. Still holding her arm, the man and his partner did a cocky strut till he grabbed her into a bear-hug and a rough little quickstep. They clung together, then the man threw the woman to the floor and yanked her back up to dance a squatting parody of a waltz. It was tight and harsh and none of it pretty; exciting to witness, like a fight on the street.

Next up was a singer, an older woman with a rasping voice and low-slung breasts that threatened to burst out of her stained satin dress. She did music-hall stuff at a rattling pace, with no stinting of lewd gestures and eye-rollings. Ugly, but with enough assurance to put her songs across, and the music was lively.

At first it had been lovely to sit in the warmth, cozied up between Clover and Aurora, but now Bella was hot and the place seemed only ordinary after all. She got up and wound round tables to the back of the long room as if she might be looking for a way out to the privy, but she had no need, only restlessness. Aurora had let her wear her dainty-flowered shirtwaist. She must look as old as her sisters, with her eyes darkened so.

There was a stronger odour back here, a hay smell or a burning-barrel. She supposed it was some unusual cure of tobacco. East had followed her and caught her sniffing at the air. He said, 'That's loco weed, that's all, hashish cigarillos.' Verrall came up beside him, and added, 'Makes these folk feel a little less sad, for a while.'

'But *you* wouldn't want that, no, no,' East said, steering her slightly wide of that table. 'Although *we* are as sad as can be. We need it to be comic in our Art.'

'No sadness for you,' Verrall agreed. 'Cards, though—we could all use some of the innocent joy that gambling brings to the hectic personality.'

At home in Paddockwood Bella had frequently played with the men. Her papa had taught her how to play poker, how to make it look like she couldn't play very well. Though that joke worked only once, she did enjoy trotting it out. East tucked her into the crowd watching a small table where a heavy-set woman was dealing and talking, talking and dealing. Bella could see that she was good.

The younger of the Tusslers was playing at the table, but he dashed his hand down in disgust as East and Bella joined the group, and the older brother replaced him. The younger stood beside them to watch a hand or two, commenting scornfully on the play under his breath to East, who stayed silent and watched; admiring his detached alertness, Bella copied him, a trill of pleasure running under her skin to be out in this wild place, at night. She was not the baby sister here. She was herself.

A Very Fine Suit

Near the end of a song from an angry woman with lank blonde hair, there was a commotion at the door and a large man came in, a bevy of theatre people around him chattering and showing off, oblivious to the performance going on. From his white silk scarf and pointed beard, from the cut of the astrakhan-collared overcoat, and from the very fine suit revealed as he doffed his coat (which was whisked to safety by one of his entourage), Aurora knew this must be Mr. Fitzjohn Mayhew.

The singer onstage knew it too—she snapped urgent fingers at the bandleader and the music changed to a hotter song, syncopated and loud, and she shouted a welcome over the heads of the crowd: 'Fitz! About time you came back to the sticks!' Mayhew raised his cane and saluted her, everything fine about him, even his manners. He waved to encourage the music, and the singer went on with a bawdy piece about her loving cup and the man to fill it up. Sybil, sitting alert in the shadow of Julius's bulk, pressed an importunate hand on Aurora's arm. 'You must sing next,' she hissed.

'Oh, no,' Aurora said, surprised. 'They've got plenty here to entertain.'

'Julius will work it. It's your best chance for Fitz Mayhew. He's got an eye for a pretty girl. You go ahead. You can't say no!'

Aurora could not, of course. Julius had already lumbered up and was talking to the band captain, gesturing back at the table.

But what to sing? Not their Parthenon act; Mayhew might have caught the show. Something different for this crowd. They've been riotous, she thought, violent and loud, so we'll be simple and sad. *After the Ball*? But it was long and didn't make sense without all the verses, and she wasn't sure she and Clover could get through to the last without losing the crowd. And the band didn't know them, and they had no sides. Julius came back and escorted Clover up to the stage. Bella was nowhere to be seen, but Aurora dared not hesitate or they would lose this chance. She needed something to catch the heart, to catch the attention of this Mayhew. Aurora leaned across to the fiddler and asked him, with her most engaging smile and a small, apologetic, enlisting shrug—*what is to be done?*—if they could borrow the loan of his violin for just one song. He blushed and handed it over.

'*Songs My Mother,*' she whispered to Clover, who gave her a strange eye back but dutifully tuned the fiddle, *plick-plick-plick*, swung it under her chin, and with her thin hip, edged behind Aurora into better position for her bow arm to begin the intro. Obedient to the music, the crowd quietened to listen. Aurora sang alone, not too high but rising into alt at the end of each line.

> *'Songs my mother taught me,*
> *In the days long vanished;*
> *Seldom from her eyelids*
> *Were the teardrops banished . . .'*

There was nothing to that song: just a little door opened to the mother that you missed so dreadfully, who had loved you as nobody else ever could; and now that she was dead, who would pray for you? As the verse ended Clover went soaring on the fiddle, a yellowy amateurish-looking thing that wept convincingly. Aurora sent the song streaming straight from her sadness, confusion stripped away and only one-bladed pain remaining. *Missing you, missing you,* the violin sang. Missing Papa's violin too, which had been sold in the first batch of selling, because they could hope to get another someday. The piano had not gone for another six months. Clover's bow pulled strongly down and rose sweetly up. Then Aurora, with the verses again, no embellishment:

> *'Now I teach my children,*
> *Each melodious measure.*
> *Oft the tears are flowing,*
> *Oft they flow from my memory's treasure.'*

It was a sentimental song and therefore could not be sung senti-mentally. Back in Helena, Mama would be washing dishes and cleaning tables, humming to herself to keep her cheer—but not this song, which always made her weep uncontrollably.

Aurora's clear voice freed the audience to be sad, in their own hearts, or glad of their mothers, or perhaps to mourn for never having had one. But she herself only thought of Mama's cracked red hands and empty purse, and that they'd better make some money very soon and double-quick.

At the back of the smoky room, she could see Mayhew's head turned, watching them. He had a dramatic, upright bearing; an air that hesitated between distinguished and raffish, like she imagined Florenz Ziegfeld must look. He'd left off his beaver hat, so his silver-dusted hair showed, but his stiff collar kept him looking formal in this rough place.

The lines of the song ran out, after the same two verses repeated, and then there was no ending, as there is no ending to remembering, only fading a little and folding and refolding, and the violin wept one last short chord, and they were done.

Aurora curtsied, accepting with grateful modesty the applause of this difficult crowd, won over. She took Clover's hand to pull her forward, and they curtsied together. Clover gave back the fiddle with a little bow. At the side of the platform the jagged dancers kissed them, the woman weeping quite openly. 'Dvorak!' she sobbed. The girls nodded, clasping their arms in return, and then the band started up again into a reeling Irish tune and two cloggers came out onto the stage, and Aurora and Clover could sit.

Clover had an empty stool beside her. Victor came out of the shadows to perch on it.

'I did not know you played the fiddle too.'

She bent her head. 'No, I'm out of practice, I believe I must give it up for good.'

'I like your playing, so clean and warm. I am myself in need of a fiddler.'

Clover looked up into his face. 'For my act,' he said. 'I work best without orchestra, only a ghostly fiddle in the wings. Will you consider playing for me?'

'I have no violin,' she said.

'Let us go out of this oppressive room and figure out a way for you to find one.' He stood and offered her his hand. 'The woods are good for walking, here, and it is not too cold.'

Clover looked at Aurora.

'May I take your sister for some air, dear miss?' Victor asked.

Aurora considered him. Friend of their friend, gentle-seeming, and well-known to the vaudeville folk. His had been the best number she'd ever seen. And Clover's face was shining, as she had not seen it shine since—for ages. She turned her own face away so Clover would not see that in her eyes.

'Of course,' she said coolly, engrossed again in the musicians.

Victor tucked Clover's hand in his arm and led her through the maze of tables. Aurora turned her head and watched them as they went, lifting her chin in a bob to acknowledge Mayhew's wave of appreciation as he caught her eye, and his kindly nod to Clover when she and Victor passed him at the door.

Penny-dreadful   Mayhew had watched the singer and her little sister, the two of them reminding him forcibly of the penny-dreadful play *The Two Orphans*: Henriette the orphan girl and her blind sister who sang in the streets of Paris and were, naturally, discovered to be aristocrats. Maybe the play could be adapted . . . His agile mind trotted the idea through its paces and discarded it. Unless he had a pretty pair of sisters, one a singer.

The singer's face—open planes, flat eyelids over lustrous dark orbs, the pearly skin illumined even in this dark place, drawing the lantern-light—was as much a part of her charm as the abundant floss of golden hair. Delicate line of cheek and chin. He calculated her value.

But it was difficult to stick to the task; the heart kept attempting to fly out of his breast as he listened. A young swan, looking up to catch back bright tears; the odd, thin bird behind her playing a borrowed fiddle. Not the usual run of artiste at Leary's roadhouse.

When the song was over the little sister left their table, going out with Victor Saborsky; that was interesting. Victor was famous for his reserve; held himself aloof, as Mayhew knew to his slight pain. For him to single out one of the sisters, that suggested a higher value than he'd tallied himself.

A space vacant beside the beauty. (The line of her neck taut as she looked towards the door; a little aloofness of her own in her bearing.) Mayhew made his way across the room, shedding his jolly party as he went, like drops of rain from an astrakhan collar.

Sham Pain

'Champagne for my true friends,' Mayhew told Julius, saluting him, 'and true pain for my sham friends.'

Aurora laughed as her ear leaped to his joke. As if champagne were available at this out-of-the-way place. But a tray was coming, one of Mayhew's minions balancing glasses and two bottles with foil-wrapped necks. Aurora had never yet had champagne.

'Brought it out from Butte,' Mayhew murmured in her ear, as the others exclaimed. He took the first bottle, ripped off the foil and untwisted a little metal trap, and very efficiently swirled the bottle while holding the cork—which promptly exploded out of the neck of the bottle, foam spilling in a rush over the table and onto Aurora's dark skirt.

'Damn it all!' he cried. 'You've shaken the bottle, Bert.' He let champagne flow into glasses as he dabbed at Aurora's skirt with the napkin from the bottle, until they were both generally damped, except for their spirits. The champagne was sharp, sweet; Aurora did not let herself gulp it.

It Is Spring

Victor and Clover walked in the winter woods, Clover thinking, *It is spring, it is spring.* Victor led her away from the buildings and noise, out along a deer path cut through a stand of pale birch, winding off into the darkness.

'Is it true that your mother is a Fabian?' Clover asked.

'Everything I ever say is true,' Victor answered. 'Someday I will tell you all about her adventures with the movement, and about her teacher, Galichen the moon-mad.'

The white-paper bark of birch trees caught the moon as they went farther into the woods. It was a paler version of Victor's empty forest backdrop.

She said, when he asked, that her father had taught her to play the violin.

'My own father is dead,' he told her. 'A year ago. Long enough that I am resigned.'

'My father, too,' she said. 'Two years ago. And my little brother, before that.'

'Yes, Sybil told me. I am sorry.'

'It set us off on our travels,' she said. Without those deaths, they would still be in Paddockwood together, cozy in the teacherage but dreaming still, not yet awakened into the world. Papa reading to them in the evenings, Mama trying to keep cheerful in her long exile. Impossible to say that was better.

But Clover's breath stuttered anyway at the thought of Harry walking beside her, as he always used to. 'He did not talk much, my brother. We all understood him, so he had no need. I cannot remember his voice. I think it was . . . a little croaking.' She remembered the feel of Harry's small fingers, delicate on her closed eyelids in the morning, seeing if she was awake. 'He was not yet four,' Clover said to Victor, as if to apologize for sadness at such an ordinary death.

Victor took her hand. A plain handclasp, restful and ordinary. 'There is no going back,' he said. 'So we keep our eyes open and go forward.'

'Yes.'

'You are a dear thing, Clover.'

She smiled, shielded by the dark.

'I ought to tell you what I already know,' he said. 'That you are she, for me.'

She could not help but laugh.

'You only saw me yesterday—how can you know?'

'My eyes are open.'

There was no snow left under their feet. The leaves had faded, winter-cured to a thick, soft carpet. Clover put out a hand to a young birch, to touch something, as if it were a lightning rod.

Perhaps a Dead Mouse From the back of the room, Bella had stared after Clover walking out into the night with the tired-faced genius. Her arms goose-prickled again, thinking of his number. Aurora must have let Clover go out.

Humph! They'd sung without her, and Bella had not decided yet whether to be cross or let it go. Very likely they'd only had a moment's notice, and had not been able to see her. But she still hadn't found a way to join the card game, and this was dull stuff, stuck watching all night long.

'Need some air,' the Tussler beside her said, suddenly. 'Want a walk?'

Bella was surprised.

'Or don't you dare to walk in the darkness?'

Bella laughed. She was never frightened of the dark. And why not go for a walk? Clover could. So could she.

Black-velvet country darkness made the roadhouse clearing seem like the entrance to a fairy tale. The woods that swallow Snow White when she runs away, Bella thought. Clover and Victor had disappeared up a trail into the birch woods, so Bella made the Tussler walk the other way, towards the dark hill. She had not been told his name and it felt a bit foolish to ask.

'Ought to be a still-room out here somewhere,' he said. 'Could find us a beer, you'd like that.'

She would not, she did not like beer. But a search for treasure was always to her taste. He took the lantern hanging above the chopping block, and she took one sitting by an empty wagon and lit it from his with a tuft of straw.

The straw flared up and almost singed his eyebrows, and he dodged backwards, making her laugh. He did not like that, she saw. She stopped.

They set off, the Tussler looking for some telltale smoke or a lit door, but there was none to be seen. The huge darkness of the night was shoved back by the light from the oil lanterns. They could not see the stars for the jangling, swinging light around them.

Bella caught a glimpse, a gleam of metal—there—it was a handle. A door cut into the hill. She pointed. 'A root cellar!'

'Might be good in there,' he agreed.

He must think of nothing but his stomach. But sometimes neither did she. He was a gangly boy, and not very bright, she thought. His bottom lip hung sulky and loose. She'd almost rather be back inside watching the card-play with East and Verrall. But it would be good fun to explore the root cellar.

It was nothing but a cave dug into the hillside, a tiny wooden door making it look like a fairy house, where the moth-girls might live. The door stuck a little, then gave way, leather hinges letting it fall askew after she dragged it open over the snow.

Bella loved dark places—nothing to be afraid of in the darkness. It was people you had to fear. Shadows shifted around thin pillars, like inside a mine—perhaps there were jewels down there, or a dragon's hoard of gold. The Tussler crowded behind her, so she stepped forward into the low space. Once her eyes had adjusted she saw straggling shelves lining the dirt walls, some with dull jars, some empty, furred with dust. Trays of carrots and apples in sand, jars of beets, pickles, jam, crocks of preserved eggs in isinglass. It was a treasure trove, but only of food.

'We ought not to be in here,' she said, sadly, and turned to go.

But he was in her way, blocking the passage to the door. He had set his lantern on a shelf and he fumbled with something she could not see beneath his coat. He took her hand and pulled it towards him, and she thought he was going to put something in it—an egg, or perhaps a dead mouse.

Instead he yanked her hand between his legs where he had something bulging. His manhood, she supposed. She had only seen down there in quite small boys, who went swimming in the slough behind the schoolhouse in Paddockwood and jumped into the air, little front-tails waggling; it was a surprise to feel how springy and hard his was.

She felt it jump under her hand and then he pulled her harder and hurt her wrist and at the same time he smeared her mouth with his flabby lip. She had not minded Nando kissing her, she had liked it very much, but this was a different thing. It— She wanted to stop.

'Stop,' she said, her voice too soft. She could not make it louder, the wind had gone out of her. She hated her own weakness.

After three thudding heartbeats she wrenched her face away, but he found it again and twisted it back to his mouth, thick fingers like a vise on her cheek. She still held the lantern, and if she dropped it, it would break and the wooden shelves would catch fire. The dirt wall behind her and the roof above them seemed to be moving, the earth closing in around them, and he was still pulling her, his rough jacket scratching her face and the button at the top digging into her neck painfully and all the time he was trying to tuck her hand into his pants, unbuttoning them with one hand and panting—that was maybe the worst of it, the snuffling *noise* he was making. She was pushed backwards into the shelves and the jars were going to shake together and the crocks on the bottom shelves would break, there would be beet juice and isinglass from the eggs all over her new boots, but she could not make her hands do anything but push vaguely at him. She had forgotten about breathing, even.

Then Verrall, outside in the clearing, called, 'Bella? East?'

The Tussler was still, his mouth open and the bottom lip hanging purplish. She could not think why she had ever found him handsome.

'Cunny-cunny fucking cunny,' he said in her ear. 'That's all you are.' The air of him speaking was hot inside her head.

'Bugger you,' she said, and with her free hand slapped his face with all her strength. It made a mighty noise. Her hand stung and her forearm ached.

He slammed her back against the wall. She gasped at the pain, at the shock of it, how strong he was, and his fist came at her—she jerked her head and he almost missed, catching only her cheek instead of her nose and eyes.

She had never been hit before. Her whole skull tingled and rang. He ground her hand into the hard-packed earth-wall for good measure, and shoved out of the cellar past Verrall, cursing him on the way.

Bella took her one hand in the other and rubbed it. She did not want to touch her face and feel that pain from the outside. Her face felt broken.

'He was bothering you?' Verrall asked.

'No, no,' she said. She ought not to have come in here with him. She had taken him for a weak sister. That was stupid.

'I could fetch Miss Aurora—let me—'

'No! No, no, no,' she said, shaking her head too many times, to stop him.

'What were you doing out here anyway?' East said roughly, coming behind Verrall. He held a fist-full of snow up to Bella's cheek and pressed. The cold scorched her face. 'You are like a bad kitten. You must learn to look after yourself better! And not to lead men on.'

'Oh no,' she said, more pitifully. 'I did not— I only meant—'

'Yes, yes, that's the usual,' East said, clearly disgusted. 'You only meant to have some fun and next you found him excited.'

'Let me get your sister,' said Verrall, in some agitation. His delicate hands flapped.

'Oh no, no!' she cried, quite desperate. 'You must not—she will be angry, she will say it is because I am too young. Please do not tell her.'

'Well, you are only a little thing—how were you to know how he might be?'

East snorted. 'She is a woman, ain't she? Born to be one, born knowing.'

'You are too hard on her, East. It's only a baby still.'

'I am not,' Bella said stoutly. She brushed down her front and tried to sweep the dirt off the back of her skirt. 'And I did not get beet juice on my boots, so you need not tell.'

'Well, come with us,' East said, long-suffering. 'We will look after you. And no more going off into corners or you will get what comes to you.'

Bella opened her eyes wider and the tears welling there did not fall. She shut her teeth together and refused.

Joy of the Moment   Side by side with Mayhew, who had commandeered the stool next to hers, Aurora sat watching a dancer—the one Mayhew told them he'd come to see. He was looking for a bit of flash for his next venture, he said, and a quick man could find treasures in these dark woods that the slower-moving producers in Boston and New York might give their ears to book.

'Elvira of the Regiment,' the band captain called, and Elvira came prancing on, in a tight military jacket with a soldier's cap, long plaited tails dangling down her back; her small worn boots had brass heels that clicked prettily to the music. Now she seemed only lazily beating time; now she rushed along as if seized by the joy of the moment. Those little brass heels! They gave a tantalizing syncopation to the dancing. Aurora looked round for her sisters. But Clover was still off with Victor Saborsky—and Bella? She could not crane her neck far enough to see Bella at the card tables.

Elvira smiled as she danced, with predatory, evenly spaced teeth. Off came her jacket and cap, revealing a scrap of bodice and a loose-laced cummerbund. Off flew her jaunty skirt, and she was dancing in what appeared to be her underthings, a red-dyed rag-bag with a wild gypsy air. Tapping-mad, she reeled and stamped and flew. At the conclusion of the dance she swirled the skirt up to make herself an officer's cape, then trotted along the edge of the platform in an orderly fashion and took leave of her public with a right military salute. As she wove through the crowd there was no doubt that she was making a series of appointments with various of the men.

Not that for us, Aurora thought. We don't have to; we're going to make money on our feet. And they had Mama, who knew the ropes and meant to keep them in the first flight, both in art and respectability.

Mayhew had risen to clap hands for the little military dancer, but he did not leave Aurora's table entirely, only reaching across to give the dancer a pasteboard card and hold her in a moment's conversation.

Mayhew's acquaintance could not be wasted—Aurora knew she ought to sit with him, work the conversation round to their act, and invite him to see them at the Hippodrome. But while he was occupied with

Elvira, she thought she'd run and check on Bella, whose absence was suddenly causing her a cramp of fright. She had forgotten how rough the men were, how green Bella was. She made her way among the tables.

But Bella was nowhere to be seen—no East or Verrall, either. Bella must have gone outside. The air was thick with smoke back here, and the stink stronger. Aurora stood still for a moment, thinking; then side-stepped back through the crowded tables to get her wraps. Too cold to do without, if she had to search for long.

She reached for Bella's things on back of her chair, and told Sybil that she had to go. 'Keep him entertained for me till we get back,' she said, relying on Sybil's good nature, Julius's love of exalted company, and their pressing need to keep Mayhew's interest aroused.

The Girl in the Other Bed

The door closed behind her and shut half the noise away with it. Aurora pulled on her wraps, and (after a pause to gather her courage) felt her way along the log wall, half blind in the darkness, heading like a moth for the glow of light from the wagon yard. She could hear strange noises, and felt someone pass a few feet from her as she rounded the corner of the roadhouse. There were the rails of the corral fence. She made her way along by touching the poles every few feet—but there were fearful shapes in the darkness. She was never easy without light.

A mound. What was that crumpled thing, lying there? Not Bella, it could not be . . .

Aurora stood still, uncertain whether she could bring herself to touch the bundle on the ground. A lantern—she was turning back to get one when she saw a bobbing light coming through the trees, and then another beside it.

'Miss Avery? Aurora?'

It was Verrall, with Bella on his arm. Aurora ran stumbling over the packed snow to reach her sister quickly. 'Are you—?' She did not know what to ask.

Bella had a hand filled with snow pressed to her cheek. Tears shone in her eyes but she only sounded angry: 'I ran into a tree branch in the dark, I am so stupid!'

'It will leave a miserable bruise,' Verrall said.

'But you should see the other fella,' East said, irrepressible. From within Aurora's warm clasp Bella punched East's coat-sleeve.

'It is too cold to stand here,' Aurora said. 'I must find Clover, too.'

But then she remembered the bundle on the ground. Verrall was handing her his lantern already, courteous as always; she took it and went back to the corral fence, to the place where she had seen the fallen heap.

It was a woman lying there. Aurora set the lantern down beside her and gently took the woman's shoulder. 'Are you in difficulty?' she asked, feeling the inadequacy of the words. 'Can we help you?'

A shock-white face lolled towards them as Aurora turned the woman's shoulder. Red hair like fox-fur springing from the girl's forehead, blood coming from her nose. Her dress was torn, her skirt ripped away, and Aurora saw blood on the pallid, splaying legs.

'*How did you find out she was dead?*' East asked, after a little silence. Verrall groaned and turned away into the darkness, to be loudly sick.

Bella knelt by Aurora and lifted the girl's bloody head to her lap. She still had a clump of snow in her hand, and with that she touched the broken cheek and eyelids. Aurora found the girl's hands and chafed them.

The girl shifted, not moaning but making a small cat sound. She opened her eyes and stared at them, then looked away and tried to cover her skinny legs.

'Mr. East?' Aurora said into the darkness, where East had gone to help Verrall.

'In a minute,' he said. 'Finish off, for the lord's sake, Verrall! How much do you have in there?'

Then Mayhew came, full of authority. He bent and lifted the girl by the shoulders to help her sit up, and Bella and Aurora gave him room; he felt her head with practised fingers, then said, 'Upsy-daisy,' and lifted her right up to her feet.

She stood there swaying. Bella found the ripped end of the girl's skirt and tucked it up so the girl was covered. Aurora pressed the girl's limp hand. 'Can you see?' she asked. 'Can you speak to me?'

The girl licked her broken lip. A purple mark showed faintly on her neck in the dim light. 'My shawl . . .' she said.

Bella searched for it and found it caught on a splinter of the fence-rail. Aurora asked her, 'Who hurt you?'

'I—he—I—' The girl touched her neck, and felt along her chest. 'He took my—'

Mayhew still had hold of her back. 'Best not to pry into it,' he told the others, quietly. 'It's her livelihood, after all. You'd only get her sacked.'

Aurora felt so sorry for her. No bigger than Bella, and not much older, from her voice. Her matted red braid had come down. It lay like a rope around her neck. Her poor lip.

'It's nothing,' the girl finally said. She shook her head, slowly, experimentally. 'I'm lucky, this time.' She had a strong accent—Irish, perhaps, mangled through her swollen mouth. She put up one hand and tucked a strand of hair back into order. 'Let me go.'

Aurora fell back. There was nothing to be done.

'You sang so nice,' the girl said to her. She almost smiled, then put a hand to her mouth. She took her shawl from Bella and walked off, feet very careful, into the dark recess behind the roadhouse where the privy was.

Lamentations   Flora woke in the clutch of a sudden vision: fetching carrots from the Pioneer's cellar, brushing the preserving sand off a bunch of dull orange fingers, feeling the cold depth of the sand with her own raw fingers. In the dream she knelt back on splintery planks over the packed-earth cellar floor and looked from the carrots upwards, to see Bella in trouble, pansy eyes shocked, necklace gone. Bella's face, head shaking, no, no, no, don't, don't.

She woke sweating and afraid, but all was still and safe in her room.

A cock must have crowed in the darkness, to wake her. She should not have sent the girls off alone.

Indian pudding and Boston brown bread, ladles of soup into bowls for the hungry boys—Flora got through lunch service and put in her hour helping to wash up. Then she folded her apron, put on her threadbare ulster, and walked to Gentry's lodgings. She hesitated to intrude on his private life, but the dream of Bella's eyes would not stop plaguing her.

Gentry Fox, Impresario, read the card in the brass slot of the building directory. He lived on the top floor in the flatiron-shaped Hannasyde building: monumental red stone, a good address. But as Flora climbed from floor to floor she saw how the grand staircases narrowed and the carpets grew less plush, down to bare drugget.

When he opened the door to her, Gentry grimaced, but waved her in.

His room was high-ceilinged for an attic, but narrow, cut from a larger chamber, and she was absurdly shocked to see how poor and cluttered and unclean it was. She somehow had not realized that he was straitened himself. Of course, of *course* he would have paid the girls properly, if he could have done so.

It was, then, impossible to make any demand of him. He had been her good friend here, to bring the girls onto the bill when he was in this case. Advancing a few feet into the room, she took hold of a chair-back to give herself some balance.

'Gentry, I'm afraid I find you in a pickle, and I did not mean to inconvenience you.'

He waved his hands, taking in the whole sorry mess. 'Not like old times, is it—best of everything, the finest suite at every hotel. Wouldn't have demeaned myself in those days with a mere sixth-floor room.'

She did not know what to say to that.

'What is the trouble, dear girl?'

'Oh! You must not call me girl! I am—'

'Forty-three.'

'Well!' She laughed. 'Forty-nine, if we're honest. I scrubbed a few years off the slate in the old days.'

'They seem to fly, do they not? In the rough-and-tumble.'

His words made her gasp and remember her dream. 'Oh, Gentry, I came because I need to follow after the girls. I ought not to have let them go alone, you were right. Aurora is wise—but the others are very young still. I've got to follow after, but I have no money. I came to ask you for a—for an advance, and I am very sorry to do it. Ten dollars would do me.'

He pulled out his wallet at once, and extracted two five-dollar bills. 'Flora, be easy. I'm certain you are wallowing in anti-nostalgic visions of the various hells in which you found yourself in your own youth, but consider: you had no mama to shepherd you in the wilderness. You were alone—and pretending to be older, rather than younger, in those days. How old were you, when you struck out on your own?'

'Fourteen, when I left my aunt's house.'

'But these girls of yours are well-protected at the theatre, I promise you; those old days are done, when any ruffian could accost a girl backstage—and there are three of them! What harm could come to one with the other two hawklike in her defence?'

Impossible to tell him of the dream—the pain, and Bella's eyes.

He waited, and then went on, 'They are good girls, keen to get on, and—wait, I received the manager's report from Butte yesterday: here, let me find it—' He scrabbled in his papers and found a yellow telegraph form and read, scanning down the sheet, 'Foster, Ventriloquist: *Comedy rather talky and long drawn-out but holds the audience, secured a number of laughs*; East & Verrall: *Not a bad act though decidedly overpaid*; Tusslers: *All the bad features of the act were eliminated when the chandelier* . . . Ah! Belle Auroras: *Dancing is good and seems to please. All their numbers were applauded. They hold their own here.* So! You see they are very well.'

She shook her head. 'There's something wrong, that's all. I had a dream.'

'Don't tell me!'

'I dreamt that—'

'Don't tell me.'

'Who am I to tell my nightmares to, Gentry?'

'I'm sure you've been lonely, but you must have been enjoying your unaccustomed leisure while the girls are away,' he said, to divert her.

She laughed, and then, remembering that he did not know of her waitress work, said, 'Oh yes, twiddling my thumbs!'

Gentry stood by the door, but had not opened it.

'To tell you the truth, Flora, I did wish to speak to you; to warn you of a—development. I am not in the very best of health. My medical man informs me that I ought to get my affairs in order.'

'Gentry.' She heard her own voice, low and tired.

'He exaggerates, you know how those fellows are, but I'm going to ground.'

She could not bear how old he looked, how broken-down.

'You're a dear girl, Flora, and these daughters of yours will go far.' He shrugged into his velvet evening jacket, one sleeve, then the other more slowly. 'I can't do anything for you now, and it pains me to say so.'

'No, Gentry, don't.'

'I've spent everything I ever made. Or lost it other ways.' He passed both hands over his large, mobile face. 'We've staved off ruin, so far, but I think Drawbank will be out within the month, and I'm away before that happens.'

Flora felt hopelessness steal over her again and pushed it away. 'I wish I had some money,' she said.

'Oh, I wish it too, fervently, but you couldn't help me even if you did.'

'At least I could help you to get home.'

'Home! I won't be going home, any more than you ever could. Madison has nothing for you. A few street names you'd know. A church, a school—you'd walk around the town and wear out your fragile memory in a day.'

She laughed, because it was true. She could not even conjure up a church. Perhaps Uncle Elmore's dentistry office would still be there; Uncle Elmore himself, of course, was long dead.

'And no more for me. *London, a poem*—' He broke off.

'It's a long way to go.'

'Without the means for travel, yes.' He nodded, master of himself again. 'No, no, I am for Montreal, where an elderly relative, washed up on that shore, will permit me to share his flat. We have our own Gerry Society for the Prevention of Cruelty to Elders.'

'Do you know him well?'

'Oh yes, well enough to hate him; he is my brother.'

'I did not know you had a brother! You will be glad to be with him.'

'You don't know my brother. He is observant; he will force me to synagogue, and will call me by my real name, or rather, refuse to call me by my real name, which has been Gentry Fox these forty years. He will serve me lamentations on my long life wasted, and I can tell you that I am not at all happy about this. But if I stay here I will die in a rented room, swollen and purple, and they will take me out feet-first to the paupers' field and bury me unmarked, and somehow that does . not seem comfortable.'

Flora would have liked to touch him, to put her arm around his shoulders, but he had never been one for physical contact, even in the old days when she was pretty.

'Gentry, I cannot—what you have done with the girls—there's no payment we can make.'

'Our ledger is balanced: I gave them a first season, they gave me a last season. You will not mention any shadow of illness to them, if you please. I'd as soon they thought of me as hale.'

He was moving through the room now, putting objects in piles as if his packing had begun, his limp very marked. Flora felt her own legs twist and swell, every joint racked to match his. He was very old.

This is what comes to us, she thought—lonely exile, a time with those who don't know us, death. She could feel her heart beating; she could see, in a drift of snow, Arthur lying still.

'My husband killed himself,' she said.

Gentry came to her side, and took her hands.

'Our life could not sustain him. Our girls. After Harry died, he was not himself any longer, and then he—'

'I am sorry,' he said.

'For him? Or me?' She shook her head. No reason to have told poor Gentry this. Except to say that we all live in pain. 'I'm sorry, Gentry. I only meant to say, everything is so sad.'

He held her hands, and there was some shred of comfort in that. He had known her when she was a girl.

But her errand was wasted. Gentry had no money to spare; she'd have to wait till her wages were paid, and the apostle spoons would have to go up the spout again. Fiddle, she thought. Arthur is dead after all and will not know. She set Gentry's five-dollar bills on the table behind her and gathered herself to go, her natural buoyancy helping her to look cheerful despite consuming worry. She touched the back of his greyish hand, and then went out into bright sunshine, to do her duty at the Pioneer.

Bruise

The bruise on Bella's face could be masked with an extra application of 5 and 9. Clover's spidery fingers were gentler than Aurora's on the swelling. Bella stared at herself as Clover dabbed: the puffing-out gave her the appearance of mumps on one side. Her cheek still hurt every time she opened her mouth to sing or chew.

She had managed to avoid the Tussler by remaining with her sisters in their dressing rooms; he and his brother did not board with Mrs. Seward, so she was not worried in the night, walking the halls to the bathroom. He hated her now, and in the theatre she could not entirely escape his baleful eye. At the end of their turn the Tusslers were always waiting in the wings to go on. Bella had twisted her steps in *I Can't Do the Sum* in order never to look stage right; she was first off, now, and usually the first heading down the stairs. Aurora and Clover had not complained. They were being kind.

Bella could not stop thinking about the poor beaten girl, left in the snow in the darkness. But what could they do anyway? They could not bring her to live with them at Mrs. Seward's. Bella indulged for a while in a continuing story where she rode a grey horse to the woods and found the red-haired girl, and brought her up behind the saddle and galloped off to a peaceful farm somewhere; but that was stupid and she did not even tell Clover, who had not seen the girl, because she'd been off in the darkness with Victor.

In the second show, Bella stayed for a moment offstage to watch the Tussler fall down the set of collapsing stairs (feeling almost avenged as he conked his head on the bottom). She did not think there had been time for the Tussler to do—whatever had been done to the poor girl. But *someone* had done it, and even if she was a dance-hall girl, nobody ought to do things like that.

The wealthy Mr. Mayhew, too: he'd been Johnny-on-the-spot. Perhaps it was he who'd done it. He'd been masterful that evening, liking his own authority and liking to throw money about, as if it was still a thrill for him to take charge of helpless females and solve everything. Under his silvering beard, Mayhew seemed young in an odd way. Not confident interiorly, as Gentry was, or Victor; only polished on the exterior with his fine clothes and motorcar. He had talked importantly about 'the wrong kind of scandal' and had impressed the need for discretion on East and Verrall (poor Verrall still very green from being so sick), and then, reassuming his silk hat and astrakhan-collared coat, had bundled them all into his car, a Pierce-Arrow saloon car more magnificent than anything Bella had ever seen, let alone been for a ride in. Every piece of it shone in the moonlight. The seats were like leather clouds, but she wished she could have stood on the running board instead, to feel the speed as they rushed through the night back to the city and pulled up in front of Mrs. Seward's—as if Cinderella and her Beautiful Sisters had all come home together in the coach.

Then Mr. Mayhew had melted away, as perhaps impresarios always must, and they had not seen him again.

Adjustments   Arriving at the Butte train station late in the evening, Gentry found a porter and gave him a well-shined ten-cent piece to convey his one bag to Butte's best hotel. No economy would save him now, might as well shoot the moon. He had stopped at the Pioneer to leave a note for Flora before leaving, explaining that he would make sure the girls were safe; through the French glass doors from the lobby he had been very much shocked to see her decked out in a full-length apron in the lunchroom, serving beans by the ladle to a rowdy table of bachelors who seemed only too familiar with her.

He'd taken care that Flora not catch sight of him, and had made his way to the train on slow pins, making some adjustments to his thinking.

I Cast My Pearls A note from Gentry arrived in the Hippodrome dressing room in the middle of the nine o'clock show, where the girls sat mending their stockings and keeping warm as the stove died, before joining the rest of the company to make their way through the windy streets to Mrs. Seward's.

'A lesson!' Aurora was surprised. 'First thing in the morning.'

Clover paled. 'Do you think he has had a bad report of us?'

It seemed unlikely—Robson, the Hippodrome's manager, had made a point of congratulating the girls on their performance at the early show. But Aurora passed a restless night, and sat by the window watching the milk wagon clopping up and down the street, impatient for the time to pass till they could go to the theatre.

Although they arrived early, there he was: short as life, impatiently awaiting them on the stage. One sleepy stagehand stayed close by to do his bidding; the rest of the theatre sat empty and lonely, as always in the pale mornings.

Gentry paced back and forth on the stage in front of the Belle Auroras, occupying one as they stood in two. He seemed possessed of an urgent demon, or Legion—ideas and advice teeming from his mind and heart. They had missed him.

First, a lecture on The Voice, which he delivered at a high declarative volume, glaring into each sister's eye in turn: 'The voice must be flexible, to reflect what you think and feel. Able to surprise, to make the audience remark what you make remarkable. Life in the voice springs from emotion—you must keep that emotion fresh, so that each time you sing the song is new. Technique supports you, but the work is never dulled, never the same.'

Earnest and intent that they should hold to these tenets he was giving them, he seemed terribly old and vulnerable.

'Lehmann used to tell us, *I cast my pearls, I cast my pearls before you—are you swine, or humans who can benefit from this teaching?*'

Then Gentry abandoned philosophy and turned to technique, directing a series of exercises on the breath, breathing into the back ribs, opening out. He made them lie in a row at the edge of the stage.

They breathed obediently for an hour before he would let them up, never coming close to falling asleep because he continued to pace above them, snapping formidable fingers when they sagged in concentration. Then he put them through their repertoire, shouting or nodding his head as they pleased or displeased him. He was not unkind, even when correcting (mostly herself, and Aurora recognized that as an honour).

'You must trust me when I tell you that the voice you hear inside that lovely head is not the one we hear outside it. Brilliance and carrying power you have, but without the true warm chest notes your soprano will always be light, disembodied, metallic—a little contrived. Your natural honesty demands better. You must reach down into yourself for that true voice, the one that is rooted at the core of your being.'

Aurora did not speak, but nodded, seeing the justice of his criticism.

'Lyrics are specific and rarely subtle, yet their extravagance encourages you to do extravagant things which are *not untrue.* You use inflections which if they had been calculated would seem false, but which if they spring from the stimulation of a song are quite true. Rhythms, lengths of words, playing with suspending, overriding rhythm while the sense goes on—those tricks keep a song driving through the verse without rushing.'

Gentry waved an arm to the wings and the black-toothed crash-box man wheeled out their old *I Can't Do the Sums* blackboard, covered

with new lyrics. Aurora braced herself as Gentry grabbed the chalk and
began to mark the board, muttering to himself, '*The pipes, the pipes, are
ca-all-ling...*' He turned, whirling in an excess of driving energy, cracking chalk in dagger lines above the words. 'Sense-stress and metre-stress
go against each other; you can stretch or shorten words as you sing—
syncopate them, or linger on a syllable, a phrase, to enliven meaning.'

White lines dashed on the board: Aurora thought of Papa, teaching them dactyl and spondee, feet and metre, flashing white text, with
accents slashed in above. The stage blackboard merged with the blackboard in the schoolroom in Paddockwood—

And without any idea that she was about to do it, Aurora fainted.

Chicken Sandwiches   Bella and Clover crouched on the
stage beside Aurora's slumped body.
'Well! Now what's to do?' asked
Gentry, blankly. 'Is it her corset again?'

'She is hungry,' Bella said, angry.

Aurora's hand twitched under hers, and gripped to make her stop.

'Did you not eat this morning?' Gentry demanded. 'You are always
to eat before practice, I have said so.'

'We had no money left,' Clover said, speaking too gently for Bella's
liking. 'But we will be paid tomorrow.'

Aurora sat up. 'No, no, not—I was thinking of—I am very well,
please.'

Gentry walked to where his snow-damped coat lay, and pulled
out a paper bag.

'Come, sit, you girls,' he said. 'I had forgotten the lunch.'

Four wrapped bundles in the bag. It made Bella's mouth water just
to see them. Chicken, on white rolls! 'Thank you *very* much,' she said,
and bit ferociously down.

Clover stayed by Aurora's side, so Gentry took the bag to them,
where their skirts lay pooled on the boards, their thin torsos upright
in their white shirtwaists.

'Eat,' he said. 'Eat. You do not have very good voices, but you sing much better than you did.'

Even Bella could not be anything but grateful for this, especially as she ate.

'You are not singers—' he said, with what Bella knew he must think of as enveloping kindness in his tone. 'But you are delightful performers. Worry less about the singing, now. Take care over your dancing steps, and enjoy yourselves, as the darlings you are—make some art, give the rubes some pleasure.' He rubbed his hands over his face, and smearing up into his eyebrows and hair and on up to the heavens—a theatrical gesture, but not untrue.

'Aurora, I have a gift for you. A new song—lyrics by a lawyer in England with song-writing aspirations. His sister-in-law showed me the song, and I have fitted it to the Londonderry Air. It will do well for you, here amongst the Irish miners.'

They read the words and Aurora nodded quickly, as if she already knew them.

'It is possible,' Gentry said, 'that I have misdirected you against sentiment. Much as it fails to please my own tastes, there is no denying that for a large part of our audience a tug on the heartstrings is part of the pleasure of vaudeville, and who am I to disparage them? But when embracing sentiment, guard against the sentimental.'

They were certainly words to tug the heart.

> *And if you come, when all the flowers are dying*
> *And I am dead, as dead I well may be*
> *You'll come and find the place where I am lying*
> *And kneel and say an Ave there for me.*

'A lazy, fat-headed singer lards a song with emotion, signals what she is supposed to be feeling. The tremolo is a villain. In a song with great depth of feeling, when the *voice* is allowed to become romantic, you tell the audience that you feel, but you do not convince them of the reason for that feeling: they do not, therefore, believe you. Or a suffering quality appears which is tedious. Whatever you are feeling, work against it—that pull of contradiction entices the listener. When you find yourself about to weep in life, you try not to! So you must in song. Also, tears clog the voice.'

Bella disliked tears very much. She would rather scream than cry. She watched Gentry walk around the stage, unburdening himself of ideas and principles as if his life depended on it, on their understanding him. 'It is the same as pushing. One pushes at the audience, blasts them with noise and energy, but when the listener feels these emotions being pushed at him he steps back, because exhibited reaction makes people recoil. In real life when someone is over-anxious to tell you something you are irritated and want to get away.'

And that was true, Bella thought.

'In comedy as well,' Gentry continued, 'a song which is witty and extravagant is not made funny by telling the audience with a wink and a nudge and an eye-roll that it is funny. Humour comes from necessity, from the belief of the singers in what they are singing. If we tinge this with smug understanding of *why* it is funny, the gag does not work. You must come down to the simplicity and logic of those words—as in *I Can't Do the Sum*, where the important thing is the attempt to solve those impossible puzzles.'

That was how it was when the song was working; Bella shivered because she could see that he was exactly right. When her bit in the hotel sketch worked best, it was because she was trying to help, not trying to be funny. You could see the force of it in Victor's act, how his absurdly concentrated discipline drew people in with him. Aurora simply listened, chicken roll in hand—how could she forget to eat? Bella wondered.

The practice pianist arrived, a tidy, nun-like man who seemed out of place in Butte, and in the theatre. He opened the sides that Gentry had left on the piano and played it through for them, the mountainside tune going up and down. When he added embellishments the next time through, Gentry spoke quietly to him, and he returned to the plainest rendering possible, barely an accompaniment at all. Bella watched Clover finger the notes on an imaginary violin.

Aurora tried the words under her breath, as if to see how they would wind through the highlands. '*And I shall hear, tho' soft you tread above me, And all my grave will warmer, sweeter be . . . For you will kneel and tell me that you love me . . .*' and then down again into peaceful sleep.

Then she stood and went to the piano and sang it for Gentry, once through.

Bella was both sad and satisfied to see that he wept without shame.

And Say an Ave There for Me

Gentry stood in the open door of the Hippodrome—how had he embroiled himself in this, after all? A loving glance from Flora's brown velvet eyes, long ago, perhaps that had been it. However extravagant in other ways, a manager could never afford affection.

Before driving back to the train station, Gentry visited the Hippodrome manager's office and corrected the Drawbank–Parthenon company pay schedule to read, *Belle Auroras, sister act: $100 per week.*

ACT TWO

5.
A Change of Management

MARCH–MAY 1912

The Babcock, Billings
The People's Hippodrome, Butte
The Parthenon, Helena

There is no keener psychologist than a vaudeville manager. Not only does he present the best of everything that can be shown upon a stage, but he so arranges the heterogeneous elements that they combine to form a unified whole.

BRETT PAGE, *WRITING FOR VAUDEVILLE*

*W*hen Aurora opened their pay envelope that Saturday night, she sent the placard boy straight to the telegraph office with a message to Mama in Helena: ONE HUNDRED PER STOP GENTRY PRINCE STOP QUIT JOB STOP WILL SEND MONEY. In the ten-word reply, which Aurora had sensibly paid for, Mama answered: WILL QUIT TOMORROW STOP NEW WAISTS STOCKINGS BUTTE STOP THOUSAND PER NEXT.

New clothes would be tomorrow's task. Tonight's was supper. The girls had been managing on bread and milk both morning and evening, their only meal at noon (usually beans), to make their few dollars last till payday. Now they ordered a magnificent supper at the Palace Hotel, roast chicken and ice cream, such a blowout that Bella feared her skirt might not do up next day.

Mama felt she must stay out her notice at the Pioneer, and so missed their week in Billings. They played the Babcock, which had replaced the burned-down Opera House: it was plain brick, elevated only by columns with floral carving, and already dingy on the inside. But with their new-found wealth they stayed in a lovely hotel, and their superior room had two beds. At first they argued over whose turn it was for the single, but after one night each alone, Clover and Bella let Aurora have the narrower bed in lonely state, and slept tangled up together as usual.

The Babcock playbill remained the same, but for Victor, who had a month booked with Sullivan–Considine, and was travelling from Spokane down to San Francisco. He was replaced by Zeno the Human Calculator, a silent man sunk in apathy save when he stood onstage and dazzled the crowd by naming the day of the week in response to their shouts of birthdates from various years over the last century. It was a very dull show compared to Victor's extravagant glory. Clover retired into herself again, but lived in expectation of the letters Victor had promised faithfully to send; he had left her with such reassurance of his affection that she was not troubled. It was the vaudeville life to be separated, and vaudeville people did not repine.

Bella lived in a state of dread because of the Tussler. The bruise on her cheek faded from purple, to brown, to yellow. Aurora and Clover quietly helped to conceal the damage. The Tussler grinned when he could catch Bella's eye, happy to see her worried.

The reunion with Mama in Butte, the week after, coincided with their third real payday. At the dressing table Aurora opened their packet almost fearfully, imagining that Gentry had changed his mind without telling them, but there it was again, a short stack: ten blessed ten-dollar bills.

They were together again, and in the money.

Past Life

When the company returned to Helena in late March, the snow was gone, and so was Gentry Fox. On the train, Flora described her visit to his dingy rooms: 'Only feature, a dreadful shame, to be cast on the charity of a relation—he has so much pride! And so much to be proud of, but all in the past now, poor man.'

Flora was keyed up almost to giddiness with the overwhelming relief of their raise in pay, which over the last month had made every difference to their lives. She had been able to purchase silk taffeta to make plaid sashes that swooped over their shoulders and down their white skirts, and had added a graceful swinging reel for the girls too, of which she knew Gentry would have approved. *Danny Boy* made her boo-hoo every time, tears seeping through her fingers, even if her girls only sighed at her.

The first rains of spring had muddied Helena's streets and sent occasional sprinkles like sneezes chasing them from street to street as they hurried from the train station to the Parthenon on Sunday afternoon—they'd been told to attend at the theatre for a company meeting on first return. Flora had spent the whole train journey from Butte in gossiping conjecture with Sybil as to what the news might be. It was whispered that Drawbank was out of the picture too, along with Gentry.

At the theatre a Pierce-Arrow car gleamed under the portico, which sported a glittering new white-lettered PARTHENON sign. Inside, Flora felt a pleasant hum of change—apparent immediately in the immaculate polished brass and spotless lobby floor.

The girls stepped lightly down the incline of the aisle, as Flora strained her eyes here and there, gathering clues to the mystery of what might happen next. The company sat assembled in the first rows, murmuring as if repeating *rhubarb, rhubarb* to each other the way theatre crowds are told to do. A new Diamond Dye olio drop was down in two, with a view of mountain ranges; the stage looked freshly painted.

As Flora seated herself beside her girls, there was a disturbance behind them. The assembled heads turned. Julius frankly gawped, rotating his huge upper body and poking a vast finger at Sybil: '*Mayhew!*' he hissed, far too loudly.

Mr. Fitzjohn Mayhew, that well-known impresario, fresh from the East, from haunts of Keith and Albee, made his way down the aisle with the backward-leaning gait the incline forced.

Flora exclaimed softly. She'd missed his visit to the roadhouse, of course, but had heard various versions of that evening from the girls and Sybil and Julius. This was lucky—Mayhew was known to her of old. He'd been a dashing fellow in the '80s, although not at that time in a position of any importance, merely an assistant to Mr. Beckwith, the manager of the Rialto in Chicago. She and Sybil had been friendly with him again at Proctor's Criterion in '87. Flora felt a tickle of pleasure at the sight of his face: older, of course, and with that distinguished streak of grey now, but still handsome. He had liked her *very* well in the old days.

She gave him a sparkling smile of pleased recognition. Knowing him would help her daughters now—which just showed how foolish Arthur's fears had been, that her past life might taint their prospects.

A Showman

Clover turned to see Mr. Mayhew, as Aurora had turned too, tilting her hat and chin carefully to the angle that made her neck's ivory column very long. Clover set herself back slightly, to serve as a dark foil to her bright sister.

Mayhew was nicely turned out again today, Clover saw; nothing but the best in men's suiting. As he ascended the moveable steps to the stage and turned to survey the company, she watched Aurora give him a welcoming, acknowledging, second-degree-of-warmth smile, which he returned with a nod, oddly shy for an instant. Aurora had made a good start with him at the roadhouse; maybe they were safe after all.

Regaining his showman's poise, Mayhew stood cocksure on the forestage, chest proud and knees locked backwards in a kind of strut. His vicuña coat was magnificent. The company clustered in the front rows sat rapt, as if at a performance, Clover thought: a *tableau vivante*— assumption of the throne by the new king.

'The Ackerman–Harris Company will not maintain a theatre that is not paying its way,' Mayhew announced, a trumpet voluntary kind of opener. His hat this morning was a tan fedora, brand new or immaculately brushed. 'Well, they can't! I've been asked to sweep in, a new broom, and I can tell you now, I've done the job in spades. As of today, Mr. Drawbank's services are surplus-to-requirement at this establishment.'

None of the assembled artistes had liked Drawbank, but there was general silence all the same. Houses had never been more than half full at the Parthenon—Clover had not understood till they went to Butte how sparse the audiences here in Helena had been—but things could not have been *that* bad?

Julius Foster Konigsburg stood and raised the question they all feared to ask: 'And what, my dear Maestro, has become of Gentry Fox, our long-time comrade and the artistic vision behind this fanfaronade?'

'Well, he's gone too,' Mayhew said. 'But not with any stain on his noble escutcheon, as *you* might say, Mr. Foster.'

Julius shuddered visibly.

'Recall that Mr. Fox was well along in years—in fact it was he who wrote to Mrs. Ackerman suggesting she have a second look at the books here—no tinge of criminal suspicion, but merely to ascertain whether full benefit of box office was being rendered.'

Satisfied, or at least muzzled, Julius settled himself again beside Sybil.

Mayhew gathered himself into a nobler pose and deepened his voice. 'In fact, at this time I'd like to pay a tribute to our pal Mr. Gentry Fox, late of this theatre, who has gone to what we all know is bound to be a rewarding retirement off the boards, down Montreal way. A legend in modern vaudeville, who sounded the depths and the rarefied air above the clouds of theatredom; the general of many battles, often in an army of one. As they say of the great ones, he cried for the griefs of others—for himself he chuckled. A great man of the theatre, and of the world!'

And that was all the fare-thee-well Gentry got: gone and only semi-besmirched. Clover felt a stab of pity, or perhaps anger.

Turning to practicalities, Mayhew expatiated on the seismic changes to come, growing particularly lively on the subject of *the Press*, and of *Advertising*, the Key to Success in Modern Polite Vaudeville. He dropped tantalizing hints about publicity stunts and gimmicks, and urged the company to greater efforts. 'Don't tell me that you killed at the Palace—do it here! I'll tell you this for free: the audience is never wrong. If a performer fails to get across, it's the material or the manner of presentation—don't let me hear you blaming the rubes for not getting something. This is a discriminating audience here in Helena and in all our theatres, and we play to them and respect them.'

Which Gentry never had, Clover thought. He was a dreadful snob and elitist, but it was deeply kind of him to leave their pay increase on the books—for Mayhew to assume, it turned out. They had better be worthy of their hire.

Mayhew stepped down from rhetoric and into details: 'First off, we'll be papering the house for the next two weeks. No more playing to empty seats. We'll take advantage of the community friendliness here, oil the water and find you some good audiences.'

New acts would be arriving to fill out the bill that Gentry had gradually reduced. Mayhew extolled their magnificence in such a naive, hucksterish way that after a little while Clover gave up listening. Maintaining an outward appearance of attention, she secretly pictured the back of Victor's head, the tender hollow between two tendons at his neck.

Her attention was called back when a large curtained easel rolled out, with red-tasseled drawings displayed on it, and—she gave a gasp of pleasure—a beautiful photo of Victor Saborsky. New playbills were distributed among the company as Mayhew sang the praises of Thierry & Thierrette (magic/terp team), The Royal Cingalese Dancers in picturesque national costumes, Victor Saborsky the Eccentric (guaranteed back by audience demand), and the rest of the company, including Julius (listed alone, and praised by Mayhew as Our Celebrated Protean Raconteur, which made Sybil mutter to Flora that she was 'nobody's excess baggage'), East & Verrall—and to Clover's surprise, themselves in a new guise: *'Les Très Belles Aurores, renowned Paris Casino favourites, a trio of charming prima donnas famous for their personal beauty and their delightful, angelic voices.'*

This was news. Her sisters had come to attention too. What did Mayhew intend? They'd done very well with sentimental ballads, wearing demure dresses and plaids. Casino girls would not wear tartans; they'd require more revealing garments—and what would they sing, *Au Claire de La Lune?*

Onstage, Mayhew was winding up to a rousing finish.

'We have to engage in a spirited campaign, boys, and dear ladies. From this day forward, the Parthenon Company is on the move!'

There was a burst of applause from the performers, and the meeting was over. Clover was impressed, a little against her will, to see how Mayhew had shifted the mood from glum to anticipatory.

A Dozen Dozen   Aurora stood with Clover in the lobby waiting for Mama—and saw with some pleasure that they seemed to stand among a dozen dozen pairs of pretty girls, refracted in the repeating gilted mirrors.

Emerging from the theatre, Mayhew found them there. 'Today being dark—' he began, putting his hand on Aurora's elbow to speak more privately with her, as the rest of the company streamed out into the noontime sun.

Dark is the wrong word for today, Aurora thought. Light flashed on the marble floor and the glass and rebounded along the mirrors, almost hurting the eyes.

'I mean to say—no shows today, I hope I may treat you girls and your dear mother to lunch—talk about this French Casino angle. The name gave me the idea, you know. When I saw you sing, before.'

In the bright lobby, Aurora let herself look into Mayhew's eyes for the first time. Pale blue, with yellowing whites, a bit lost in his large face.

At the roadhouse he had been smooth, even glossy. In this light she saw that Mayhew was not so dapper, but slightly frayed around the edges. His moustache raggedly trimmed; his nails, which bent over the tips of his fingers, yellow and not quite even. The skin sagged at his eyes and ears. Around the pointed beard, white stubble had formed on his jowls after his morning shave; she saw the cracked edge of a half-healed snick. His hair was like stiff straw. Seeing these things, oddly, made him more real to her.

He looked searchingly at her own face, his eager heart on display, and she was sorry for him. She smiled, to see him liking her, and understanding leaped between them. So much that he stood taller and breathed in loudly. 'Well!' he said, patting his chest, maybe not even conscious of that. She could have laughed at what she did to him, but that would hurt his dignity.

'Well!' he repeated. 'Mademoiselle Aurora.'

Bella clattered into the lobby, Mama behind her. At the sight of Mayhew, Bella stopped short, making Mama stumble.

Mayhew moved quickly, to help her regain her balance. Aurora liked that in him too, his awareness of other people. 'Dear Flora,' he said, clasping her hand and shaking it strongly. 'Or rather, Mrs. Avery I must call you now! To make your acquaintance again! What joy.'

'So pleasant to see—after too many years—and you not looking a moment older!'

'Nor you, my dear,' Mayhew said, as he could hardly help doing. 'I have been arranging with your girls, to carry you all away to luncheon. We're booked at the Placer, where I have my suite. It is the newest and the best: their atrium lobby is a thing to behold. Come now! The chariot awaits!'

Hot-house   Over lunch Mayhew outlined his vision for *Les Très Belles*: ditch the sentimental ballads, move along to a whole new act—'the French thing,' as Mendel had said long ago at the Empress. Starting with familiar folk-songs 'in demure old-country garb,' then, after a rural tour through *Florian's Song*, a quick change for some Parisienne flounce-skirt dancing—nothing risqué, this was family vaudeville—a pert, uptempo rendition of *Plaisir d'Amour*, one last change, into spectacular (here Aurora caught the overtone of 'seductive') costume for (and this he was proud of) the Flower Duet from *Lakmé*.

'French as you please,' he said. 'Saw it in Boston last fall, it brought down the house. Had to reprise twice! High reach, but voices just like yours,' nodding to Aurora and Clover.

Aurora glanced at Bella, who was apparently to be left out of that one, but Bella was finishing her oysters Rockefeller in a philosophical way.

Mayhew ate in great bites between spates of talk; his lunch was over and done with before theirs, even though he talked the whole time.

'Do you plan to return to New York, dear Fitz?' Mama asked, no doubt trying to discern the future.

'Vaudeville's all sewn up out East,' Mayhew said, shaking his head. 'But here and in the North there's opportunity, and I intend to seize it. I've got an option pending on a brand-new two-a-day house up in

Edmonton. I call it The Muse. There's a venture in Calgary I'm looking at—fill you in on that later. For now at the Parthenon, we'll mount
a melodrama. I wonder—' He turned to Aurora and tapped her thoughtfully on the forearm. 'I wonder if you've ever thought of acting? I saw
a short play in Chicago as I went through—it strikes me that it might
adapt well for you.'

Aurora still found his partiality for her slightly shocking. But not
unreasonable, she supposed; it was the response one worked for, after
all. 'I would love to act,' she said, smiling for him. Her hand went to
her wineglass. She loved champagne, loved being in vaudeville, loved
being the object of Mayhew's attentions. Mama and the girls were
happy too, and the lunch was magnificent! Oysters and lamb chops,
meringues with hot-house strawberries, every kind of careful service
from three hovering waiters. She was so happy. Glorious golden-yellow
roses massed in a bank on the table—in April!

Mayhew touched her arm again, his fingers warm through the
voile, then turned and made certain that Mama had had enough, offering to call up more meringue. She demurred, but Bella said *she* could
manage another. Mayhew laughed and gestured to one of the waiters,
who vanished and reappeared like an Arabian djinn, a new plate in
hand piled high with meringue and fruit and cream.

'These darling girls need fattening up!' Mayhew said. 'You're going
to need a new set of photos, new placards—we'll get cracking on it all
right away and aim to introduce the new act in a week or two.'

The abacus in Aurora's mind clicked: cloth, lace, new slippers and
other necessities.

'An increase in pay, of course,' he told her solemnly, as if this was a
sad consequence, and added to Flora, 'And in view of the expense of
these costumes I'm demanding, we'll work out an advance, dear madam,
that will amply cover your outlay.' Inwardly, Aurora sighed with relief,
and wondered exactly how great an increase. She decided that her role
here was to be an innocent girl, and leave it all to Mama.

And indeed, Mama was claiming Mayhew's attention, in an
effort to draw him out about himself, asking if he had created acts

himself in Ziegfeld's operation. He laughed. 'Oh ho! You don't create around Flo! He takes care of the direction—I mined the raw materials. I've always had an eye for remarkable talent. Well, didn't I say, my dear Flora, that you had a gift for enchantment, in those old days at Proctor's?'

Her nostalgia appealed to, she gave a great heart-shaped smile, blushing a little in happy confusion. 'You did, dear Fitz, and I've often remembered that over the years,' she admitted. 'But the girls don't need to waltz down memory lane with us!'

'Beauty and grace,' he said, almost turning serious. 'That's what the vaudeville stage can never have enough of. And with a voice and a face like your daughter's, my dear—well, these girls are going to go far.'

We Need the Eggs

Bella thought about Mayhew as she sat on the hotel counter in the wings, waiting for East and Verrall's sketch during their first show back in the saddle in Helena. She did not mind him, but he had no value for her or Clover except as Aurora's appendages. And he thought her a child, which she was *not*.

The stagehands rolled the counter on and she fluffed her skirt higher. The curtain parted and there she sat, knees jauntily revealed, and here was East, coming on to book a hotel room. Laughter rolled from the audience at the sight of her perched on the counter, and again at East's admiring double-take. It was much better to be playing to full houses—Mayhew had got that right.

'This is where my wife and I spent our wedding night!' East told Bella, while they waited for Verrall to answer the ping of the desk bell. 'Only this time *I'll* stay in the bathroom and cry.'

Her job here was to be dumb-Dora, and look fetching while the audience laughed.

'It is a little difficult to travel these days,' East said. 'My wife thinks she's a chicken.'

'Goodness! You should take her to the hospital!'

'Well, I would,' East confessed. 'But we need the eggs.'

'I think it's mean,' Bella said, very shocked. 'Your wife ought to be your soulmate!'

'Well, she was my *cell*-mate—that's where we first met, in pokey.'

'How romantic,' Verrall said, popping up from under the hotel desk as if he were climbing the stairs from the basement—he did that false climb so brilliantly that every time Bella had the urge to check behind her for the trap door.

'*You again!*' he said, when his head was high enough to see East. 'No room till we see the colour of your money!'

East looked ashamed. Since he could not pay—and still owed Verrall for his honeymoon visit—East was shanghaied into a job as waiter in the hotel restaurant. The desk spun round and disgorged a café table complete with red-checked cloth, and Julius already seated at the table in a black wig, the only customer, with a full roster of complaints and problems, from the first fly in his soup to the last corn on his toe, set to be stomped on by East's extra-long boot. More ridiculous nonsense, plates of soup and flying loaves of bread and egg-juggling (by everyone but Bella, who simply could not get the hang of it, try though she had). From time to time Julius's patently false black toupée would be dislodged by East or Verrall—and set back in place, so delicately that Julius continued in blissful self-satisfaction whether it was backwards, forwards, or drenched in soup.

She was Julius After the intermission, Clover joined Bella, Mama and Sybil at the back of the house to watch Long Chak Sam, a copy-cat Chinese magician Mayhew had booked in for the week before Thierry & Thierrette. Myriad three-named Chinese magicians worked the circuits—this one, at least, was truly Chinese. A silent, unsmiling man, he had a little daughter who spoke no English, but carried a document swearing she was sixteen. It was obvious to anyone with an eye that she was ten or twelve.

The daughter's name was Xiang, Bella whispered, and she had discovered the name's meaning also: *cloud*. Her own name meaning *beautiful*, she said in Clover's ear, under cover of the tinkling Eastern music,
was nothing but a joke these days: there were horrible spots popping
out on her face and the pudge around her middle had stayed even when
there was not enough to eat. She hated herself, she said, but Clover
squeezed her hand and told her to be patient, and she would be the
most beautiful swan of all of them.

Clover did not like the magician's act, in which he swallowed a
long length of thread followed by a bristling quiverful of sewing needles. She could feel the needles entering her own mouth and throat,
and had to close her eyes. At his command, his daughter-assistant
began drawing the long thread from his mouth, and there, suspended
at regular intervals, were the needles, *all threaded*, on it. It made Clover
shudder. She did like when he turned a child's dollhouse on a lazy
Susan to reveal a tiny Chinese doll standing in the inside rooms. He
twirled the house again, and the doll inside had grown much larger,
straining at the rooftop. At the next turn, the doll was Xiang, and she
rose through the roof to jump into his arms.

Julius Foster Konigsburg was up next, by himself, in full Protean
mode with his Voices of Kipling medley. He began in a great mysterious cloak with *If*, using the cloak (wire rigging built into it) to mask his
gyrations as he changed costume for each new poem. He ended in a
torn and stained Indian army uniform, for *Gunga Din*; the cloak,
dropped, formed a muddy battlefield.

'Ah, this brings back memories,' Sybil whispered, with a sentimental squeeze of Clover's hand. 'Julius used to do *Gunga Din* regular, you
know, he was famous for Kipling.' She gave a quick quiet laugh. 'As they
say, *I don't know, I've never Kippled!*—but he only does it now out here in
the sticks, because Clifton Crawford has been doing it in Boston and
New York and Albee asked Julius to stop. *Asked*, don't make me laugh!
As if he'd have a choice, when Albee *asked*!'

'But this isn't even an Albee theatre!'

'As you say! Except that now, whenever he does the bit, someone is sure to come up and accuse him of copying Crawford, and you know there's nothing sooner puts poor Jay in a rage than being accused of any kind of stinginess of spirit like imitation.'

'No wonder—it is entirely unfair!'

Sybil squeezed her arm and cozied a little closer. 'You're a dear girl, Clover. We never had a daughter, but if we *had* had, I'd have liked her to be just like you.'

Clover was abashed. She could not imagine being Sybil's daughter.

Julius had come to the end and shouted the last line, '*You're a better man than I am, Gunga Din!*'—then ripped his uniform away and stood in Gunga Din's filthy linen wrap and shawl, bandy legs brown and bruised—which worried Clover until she realized it was only his dreadful ochre makeup. Then there was a terrifying blast of artillery fire and a vile puff of smoke, which drifted off into silence to reveal the linen clout, empty on the floor.

The audience applauded with moderate enthusiasm, but one lady in the front row, in a great black hat with red feathers and a veil, kept clapping wildly, and jumped up crying, 'Do it again, Sonny, it's great!' Her escort tried to quiet her, and the people close by *shh*ed, but she would not be silent. She announced in a *forte* voice, 'I paid my money, and if I want to encore an act I'm going to do it.'

By this time the audience had become interested. Mattie stepped out from behind the proscenium arch and asked the woman not to talk so loud, as she was stopping the show.

'I don't care,' she shouted. 'My money is as good as anyone else's, and I mean to have that handsome quick-change man on again. He's the best thing in the show!'

'Behave yourself, madam,' Mattie warned. 'Or we will send for the police!'

With a banshee shriek the woman brangled down into the orchestra pit and took three wild leaps—piano bench, keyboard with a reverberating dischord, piano lid—and then hopped up onto the stage, where she began to wrestle Mattie, bringing whoops and shouts for the manager from the audience.

She got the poor boy into a headlock, but he wriggled around like
a greased pig and managed to tear the hat and veil off the lady—

And *she* was Julius.

'If you can't amuse 'em, amaze 'em,' Sybil whispered to Clover.
Under cover of the renewed applause they slipped out the back.

Not Pity Alone

Mayhew, standing to watch at the
back of the house, followed the women
down to the dressing rooms. He was
thinking about girls and women, as he often had in a long life spent in
theatres of one kind or another. Sybil, that old warhorse; Flora. Game
old girls, a sad life behind each one. But pity was not everything, not
anything much at all. Not pity alone.

He was not affected by Clover or Bella. It was all Aurora for him:
the soft rounding of her chin, the eyes. And the mouth—at odd
moments her mouth would look like she'd been hit, and must be
shielded. It was the frailty that caught at him. How they were not quite
professional, no matter how they twinkled and light-stepped. That was
the charm of *Les Très Belles Aurores*—it would translate especially well
if they were foreign waifs. He could make something of them . . .

He knocked at the door of their dressing room.

Aurora had taken down her mass of pale hair and was brushing
it out, silk tatters, silk ribbons, dark yellow, paler yellow and gold,
black brush sliding through the silk over and over. Smooth-spun
floss, curving feathers at the ends. Black velvet ribbon down the back
of her neck where the knobs of bone showed too clearly—and yet the
softness of the line!

At first she did not see him; then she did. She did not turn around,
but remained at her table, brushing her hair, watching him in the
mirror. A self-conscious ploy. Her idiotic youth tore him open. Anxious
fingernails bitten to the quick, beneath the pretty net gloves. Her
mouth's betraying softness that no hard expression could control. Her
eyelashes were black against the white lids, thickly mascara'd. Yet he

had seen her without stage makeup and knew them to be genuinely dark, set delicate as mink paintbrushes in the porcelain eyelids.

He had not thought like this for so long. He had not thought he ever would again.

Contagious

Flora and the girls were invited again, with East and Verrall, Julius and Sybil, to an early dinner on Sunday, a special feast prepared by the Placer chef. Mayhew held forth on the future of vaudeville as they waited for the first course to be served. 'The Parthenon circuit is going to get a tremendous boom from this new stagehand expense deal in the big-time. Big-time acts will come to us where they can play in decent houses at smaller salaries, but with consecutive bookings and a family atmosphere behind the curtain as well as out front.'

One arm draped along Mayhew's chair-back, the other occupied in draining a large brandy and soda, Julius had merely to raise an eyebrow to encourage the flow.

'But that does not mean,' Mayhew said, 'any diminument in our loyalty to the faithful medium-time acts which have stood by the company in times past.'

Verrall choked, then quickly asked whether there might be holes in the big-time, at this rate. Mayhew thought there might be, for a suitcase outfit that could travel without sets or stagehands. 'It will be contagious on you to take every advantage of the situation,' he said.

Flora did not mind the occasional miswording; she basked in Mayhew's golden spotlight. He'd been a jumped-up boy in the old days and was much the same now, with a patina of prosperity overlaying his familiar charm.

At the end of the evening, while the party was fetching wraps from the cloakroom, Mayhew managed to lead Flora apart from the others into the lee of the shining oak staircase.

'Thought you'd like to see this,' Mayhew said, showing Flora a yellow telegraph form he'd pulled out of his inner pocket. The manager's report from their last week in Billings:

BELLE A's: AS SQUARE AND HIGH-TONED A LITTLE
TEAM AS EVER CAME ROUND THE CIRCUIT. IT'LL BE A
PLEASURE TO READ THEIR NAMES ON THE BOOKING
LIST AGAIN. ON THE JOB TO THE MINUTE, STRAIGHT
HOME AFTER THEIR ACT, EACH ONE A LADY AND NOT
ONE A QUEEN.

'You can be proud of those girls, Flora,' he said.

Flora did not speak, but nodded. *Each one a lady.* That was what mattered, that's what she'd been able to give them. She and Arthur between them, give him his due.

Mayhew looked at her earnestly. 'What a job you've done! No time just now, but—'

She looked up, dashing wetness from below her eye.

'Could you grant me a few moments alone, my dear Flora? Perhaps tomorrow, right after the first show goes up? I'll take you to tea,' he said. 'It's a delicate matter.' He seemed to hover between smiling and embarrassment.

Flora stared at him for a moment. Then he reached out and squeezed her hand, and she saw that his eyes were—*beseeching* was the word that sprang to her mind. She returned his smile, and the pressure of his hand. 'I'd be very happy to have tea,' she said, gently taking over. 'I'll be in the lobby as soon as the overture begins.'

She would wear her new dove-coloured walking suit. And the pheasant-wing hat, and her locket, which she'd been able to redeem. It was time to re-enter the world, her period of mourning done.

But that night Flora woke in a panic from a dream: kneading bread in the summer kitchen at Paddockwood, watching Arthur walk over the field from the schoolhouse—her hair unpinned, arms floured to the elbows, the apron loose around her middle, which was big with Harry. Arthur walked in, lifting her easily up onto the dry-sink edge to kiss her without ceasing, bundled belly and flour and all. He did not speak, did not need to, only enveloped her, loving her for her true self, as she did him. The girls were singing in the parlour and she was beloved and the bread would rise and Harry would be born—

Not Harry. She struggled awake and put that aside. Travelled backwards in the dream and found Arthur again walking across the field and the shape he made against the pale sky and the full-carved shape of his mouth after love, and how she had loved him.

Mayhew was nothing to her. A dynamo of a manager, pleasant company.

But she ought to accept his proposal, whatever it might be, for the sake of the girls. She ran her hands down the bodice of her nightgown to her child-bagged belly. How could she bear to? When she was so old. But people did. You often heard of late marriages. Or late arrangements of convenience.

Flora pushed the covers aside and fit her feet into her house-shoes. She let herself out, leaving the door on the latch, and made her way to the privy through the darkness of the yard.

Wafting Like a Ghost

When Clover heard Mama come inside again, she pushed past the panel of the hall curtain and went towards her.

'Oh, Clover!' Mama whispered. 'You took ten years off me, wafting like a ghost!'

'I heard you get up,' Clover said. 'I heard you weeping.'

'No, no, no need. I just had a dream.'

Clover was shivering. Mama wrapped her arms around her and the shawl about them both. 'I'm to have tea with Mr. Mayhew tomorrow, during the first show, and I will try to let him down as easy as I can. Your father's memory is sacred to me.'

Clover looked down at the floor, at the parting line between the drugget carpet runner and the whitewashed floorboards. Snow on the front yard. Her father sprawled, snow on his black back and legs, red underneath him. Only a body, though, nothing left of himself. She trembled a little and her mother tightened the arm around her.

'I am sorry,' Mama said. 'Never mind it. Forget what I said. He loved us so.'

Clover wished she could erase the parts of her memory that did not tally with Mama's sweet remembrance. 'I thought it was Aurora that Mr. Mayhew wanted,' she said, pretending to be puzzled—the only way she could think to save her mother from humiliation.

'*Aurora!* She is thirty years younger than he!'

Clover went down the hall, feeling indeed like a ghost, one who could not make people listen.

Permission

Flora stayed in the dressing room after the girls had gone up, giving her skin a lustrous glow with just a very little ivory 5. The least suspicion of mascara under the shading black velvet brim. She looked very well, she thought. A dash of powder. There. He understands this world, that is the great thing, she thought. She would not have to justify the frippery nature of theatre, or patiently soothe fears of licentiousness, as she'd had to do even after fourteen years with Arthur. Outrageous, since he had been so wild himself: but it was no wonder, once Chum had put the bee into his bonnet . . . Fitz understood you had to set preference aside from time to time, to secure a place. It was a business.

She pinched her cheeks but did not add rouge. Arthur had not liked too high a colour.

The car was waiting, but Mayhew said, 'Will you walk? It's a lovely evening.'

The five o'clock sun was still striking the bright windows of the city. He took her arm as they walked up the length of State Street to the Grandon, which surprised Flora a little, knowing that the Placer was his favourite. The route took them past Gentry's building and she could not help a pang—how pleasant it would have been to form a partnership with him, odd as he was. She'd always had a soft place for Gentry.

At the Grandon, Mayhew settled her into an easy chair in the tea-lounge. A small bustle of waiters, then a lovely pot of tea steaming, and a tray of nice things to eat. It would be like this, to be married to Mayhew. All the superficial things would be delightful.

She excused herself, and went to the ladies' powder room, where she carefully washed off the 5 and dabbed her face back into plainness. Because Arthur—

All the superficial things—but beneath that, the immovable rock of memory. The silence in the night when Arthur was outside and she'd known he was out there and unable to bear his life. He'd been infinitely more to her than any other could be, and it was her fault that he died. It was her fault that Harry died.

She leaned on the marble counter, then pushed herself away and stood straight. In the mirror she saw a very tired older woman, with a stricken face and a long past behind her. A bundle of lies she'd told her beloved husband and a package of make-believe she'd sold her daughters, and with all that, she could not bring herself to take on Fitz Mayhew.

'I'm sorry, your tea must be growing cold,' she said, gliding back to the table.

'Neither the tea nor my heart!' His humour a little ponderous as always.

'Oh!' Then she was at a loss. She poured a cup of tea.

'I don't know how to begin,' he confessed, looking up with a frank expression of hopeless vulnerability. 'It's caught me late. I'm not used to this!'

She truly did feel sorry for him.

'You've probably seen how it is for me,' he said. 'I'm head over ears, but I wasn't sure how you—'

She began to stop him, but he broke in.

'Oh, Flora, just tell me, can I have your dear girl? I would keep her very well.'

She looked up then, suddenly, into his eyes. Pale blue and staring, straw-coloured lashes standing stiff out from them, faint blueness under the skin around the eyes. So old! For a brief instant she stared. Then she lowered her eyelids, and then her face, and bit the inside of her cheek till it bled.

He leaned forward. 'I see you are not prepared for this.'

She shook her head, rapid, almost furtive. Eyes still downcast to her hands, twined in her lap.

'Maybe you don't like to think of your daughter—'

Up came her eyes again, and he stopped.

They sat without speaking for a moment.

'Flora, I think you have got the wrong end of the stick.' He shifted a little in his cretonne chair, yanked it slightly off its line, put his stiff hands on the armrests. 'I'm not—I'm not suggesting anything you wouldn't like, you know. I want to marry the girl.'

She was unable to make herself speak.

Fitz leaned back again and gave a gusty sigh. A waiter zoomed to his side. 'A whiskey,' Fitz ordered. 'And the bottle.'

The locket around Flora's throat was choking her but she did not think she could make her fingers undo the catch. Such deep shame had bloomed in her belly and groin that she was afraid she might hemorrhage. A wave of heat poured upward from there, up her chest and throat. She must be a hideous colour but could not for the life of her manage to breathe, to get rid of the shame of it, of thinking it was she—

Fitz poured himself a whiskey and she reached for the bottle and poured a slug into her tea. He laughed. He knocked back his, and she took a good sip of hers.

'You've surprised me,' she said. 'You are right. I—a mother . . .'— try again!—'She was my little girl, you know, for a very long time.' Clover! Clover had known, last night. She took another drink of tea, wishing she'd poured a more generous dot from the bottle.

'Oh, Flora, I know.' She knew he was going to say it, and then he did. 'But you will not be losing your daughter,' he said. Some lightning must have alerted him in her eyes. '*Or* gaining a son! Hardly that! We are contemporaries and must always be!' His arm flew out and the waiter was there in a trice, and back again in another with a second glass.

Mayhew poured a couple of fingers and handed the glass to her. 'You can't drink that in tea.'

Then she could laugh and drink her shot. They laughed together and he poured another for each of them, and the worst of the shame receded, heat borne backwards on that wave of reliable warmth. There was some consolation in being pole-axed by someone who could afford a very good whiskey.

The Old Soldier

Mama had been drinking. She flitted around the dressing room, hanging clothes and tidying, an agitated moth brushing against things, her cloud of soft brown hair passing too close to the gas-jet every time she went by, so that Clover's attention had to dart after her.

Mama halted by the table where Aurora was doing her face. 'Has he—made up to you already?'

She stared into Aurora's face in the mirror, her own beside it. Clover saw how alike they were in certain ways, in expression rather than shape of face or colouring. Aurora had their father's fairness. Then Mama was off again, moving, picking up Bella's boots and brushing mud from their tips with a fold of her new dove-coloured walking skirt, so that Clover went to her and took them, and smoothed the skirt down. Mama flicked at it and turned away, jagged motions, saying, '*Stop*, Clover. Don't fuss at me.' She sat in the armchair.

'No, he hasn't,' Aurora said.

'Hasn't what?'

'Hasn't done a thing. Hasn't fondled me or made sheep's eyes at me or anything. He probably felt a little awkward, being your old pal.'

Bella came bursting in from the hotel sketch. 'Julius's toupée came off, but the bald wig underneath came with it!' she told Mama. 'They're fixing it on with spirit glue— What's going on?' She could see that Mama was not attending.

Clover took pity on her. 'Mr. Mayhew spoke to Mama this afternoon, to see whether he might—he wants to—'

'Oh!' Aurora cried. 'Out with it! He wants to marry me, that's all.'

Bella stood still, staring.

Aurora stared back, as if reading Bella's thoughts. 'He likes my looks, I suppose.'

Mama shook her head, and was going to speak, but she looked suddenly up at the ceiling and then bolted out of the room. Clover looked after her.

'I'd leave her, if I was you,' Aurora said. 'It'll take her a day or two to talk herself round.'

Clover nodded.

'Mayhew?' Bella asked. 'Will you be rich?'

Aurora laughed. 'It's not so strange. Look at Evelyn Nesbit. Sanford White was thirty years older than she. It happens all the time.' She set her brushes at the edge of her towel perfectly even, and then, telling Clover and Bella to hurry, went out and up the stairs.

Maybe not the happiest analogy, Clover thought, seeing that Sanford White ended up murdered.

'He asked permission before he even spoke to her!' Bella said, hurrying into her white skirt for their number. 'He is a strange customer.'

Clover shook her head and put a finger to her lips, in case anyone could hear.

Bella said quickly, 'I mean, it was extremely polite of him.' And then, more quietly, 'He is the oldest person we know, now Gentry is gone. But I'd rather marry Gentry, wouldn't you?'

Clover turned away from the dressing mirror. 'Maybe it is like the Old Soldier in *The Twelve Dancing Princesses*—how at the beginning he is so decrepit and exhausted by the wars, but he is brave and resourceful and kind, and then he marries the oldest daughter.'

And Bella seemed happy enough with that explanation.

A Practical Proposal　　Aurora was not surprised, of course, but did not know how to proceed. Especially since she was not sure how Mama felt about Mayhew, and the whole idea. A card came down at intermission to say that after the second show the Pierce-Arrow would be waiting for her, to take her out for a late supper.

Mayhew had caused a bower to be built in the ballroom at the Placer Hotel: white gauze cascading down from a ring in the ceiling to make a silken tent within the golden room. The white carpet laid as a path across the polished floor to the tent was lined with lilies, looking to Aurora's eyes rather funerary, but unquestionably opulent. A roving violinist played Kreisler, never wandering too near. Waiters appeared, vanished; plates materialized upon the table and her glass was refilled—bubbles rose in straight, slow-moving, perfect lines from the stem to the lip.

Aurora thought about bread and milk for supper, about holes in shoes and kerosene cans around bed-legs.

'You'll have been told,' he said, and she thought perhaps he blushed in the candlelight. 'What I proposed to your—to Flora.'

She nodded, smiling at him; unable not to smile.

'How would we deal together? Hey? Do you think?'

She set her glass down; it was again replenished. Mayhew's flick dismissed the waiter. Was this the entire proposal? She'd imagined something more flowery.

'You and the girls, and your mama, need protection. A weary business, booking and managing: I offer my poor efforts at your service. A practical arrangement.'

Aurora had already determined to accept him. He would not keep them on the bill otherwise; there was a vein, a lode, of untrustworthiness in him, and she did not think his support would outlast a refusal for long. She had that lode of selfishness herself and did not shy away from seeing it in him. This was their ticket. They'd seen over the past week what life in his train would be: good hotels, good service, no more worrying over pennies and pawnshops, no more hungry nights for Clover and Bella. Already Bella's eyes were bright again; even Clover looked less tired after a few days with lots to eat.

Mayhew sat watching her, one leg crossed over the other in a lazy, confident attitude; but the look on his face was not lazy. Not confident either. It was very gratifying to be so admired. He leaned forward and reached for her hand across the table, and when he had captured it, sat staring at her smooth-skinned fingers where they wound in and out of his.

'I'll tell you true, you have enflamed me. My soul is not my own.'

He did not seem entirely comfortable uttering these high-flown statements, but there was no doubt that he was sincerely struck by her.

She rose from the table, and stretched her hands up to touch the white silk roof with her fingertips, letting her back arch. Her hair felt heavy on the back of her head. Clover had coiffed it in the Gibson manner, with an extra rat to give it superabundance; Mama had finished stitching her ivory satin bodice during the second show, sewing up the back seam right on her: décolletage more daring than she'd had before, and she was wearing the gold locket they'd reclaimed from pawn. The plum velvet cummerbund matched a tiny bunch of velvet pansies on the bodice, pinned so that their weight pulled the satin down a little, a sweet revealing swoop.

He was waiting for her to speak.

'I think we will deal very well together, Fitz,' she said. 'I think we will be the best team in vaudeville!'

When he stood and took her in his arms to kiss her forehead, all that was appropriate with the waiters and violinist still present, she felt him, his—prodding between her legs, as if it knew its place. He did not grind at her, as Maurice Kavanagh had done, but pulled back a little, releasing her.

'Don't be afraid, I would not demand too much of you,' he said.

She kissed him, then, leaning forward—his mouth much fresher and sweeter than she had expected. He was older than Kavanagh, even. (Older than Papa, in fact, but she shut that piece away from her thinking because it contained Papa and was not to be dwelt on.) She had the power, but he had the purse strings and the authority. She liked his clothes and his money, she told herself. And the fearfulness in his eyes at her gaze. She would have to take care of him, in certain ways, and that was appealing too. Jimmy the Bat was in Winnipeg with Mrs. Masefield, probably taking a bouquet of white roses to her boudoir, probably walking across the floor in his polished dance-mules, offering her his arm, his evening coat brushed and his white tie snugged tight. And Mrs. Masefield would be putting one of her alabaster arms around his neck *anyway*.

So what was she to do but take Mayhew?

A Sparkling Eye   Sybil claimed the credit for it, having introduced them, as she repeated to Mama eighteen times a day: '—and I said how it would be, at that instant!' Julius bent from his remote height to wish Aurora the best, in ornate prose. East laughed; Verrall turned away abruptly before turning back to tell her with some ferocity that Mayhew was the luckiest man in the world.

The thing was done, more or less, though there were details to be decided.

'Not sure we want a long engagement, but we don't know each other too well just yet,' Mayhew had said, and Aurora was grateful for it. 'Don't want to attend with wedding plans immediately . . .'

Did he mean *contend*? That was the biggest stumbling block for her, Mayhew's occasional lapses in language. Sometimes she couldn't even trace back what word he had meant to say. She could see that Clover despised him slightly for it. But it was an innocence in him, too. It made her feel like Papa in the schoolroom, waiting patiently as poor Oscar Meller's meaning emerged through his broken English. As she had loved that patience in her father, she loved that Mayhew brought it out in her.

'We'll make a thing of it in the press,' he'd said. 'Use it as a draw— what are we, April now? Let's say late May, to make you Mrs. Mayhew.'

Next night the dressing room was filled with flowers—twenty dozen white roses, Bella counted for her. At the end of the show there was a boy at the door with a box of chocolate bonbons and a bottle of champagne. But no Mayhew. From some unexpected delicacy he stayed out of Aurora's way for several days, letting business take him down to Butte and Missoula on a quick tour of theatres there.

At first it was a relief, not to have to see him. But as more days went by it was odd, then irritating. She *wanted* to marry him, wanted to have him look after her, after them all. That was a slightly delicate matter: how responsible would he make himself for her sisters and Mama? There was a great deal that had not been said and she did not yet feel able to make him say it.

In his photograph, newly posted in the lobby—top hat and cane and white kid gloves—he was not unhandsome. She tried to see past the stiff rustiness of his hair, the wrinkles around his mouth, age every-where. His air of fashion could only survive at a distance. Close up, nothing about him wakened her or made her warm, nothing caused the delicious snake to curl over in her belly. But she would go through with it, she told herself. She would get pleasure out of making him cry out, out of her own supremacy. And the whole idea of crossing into the real world of marital love was exciting to her.

One morning, walking alone down State Street looking in shop windows, Aurora heard her name called. Behind her ran Mercy of the Simple Soubrettes, from their first gig at the Empress: bright face and black-jet eyes. A wholly unexpected pleasure—off guard, Aurora reached out in happy welcome, and they embraced and laughed in the empty street. Mercy pulled her into a nearby café, and had them at a table with tea in front of them in a twinkling of her clever eye. The Soubrettes (now the Good-time Girls, not wanting to soil the name Simple Soubrettes) were booked for a two-week gig, to start next day—at the nearby Variety theatre.

The Variety was a burlesque house. Aurora had to school her face, not to let shocked pity show.

'We only had the two weeks booked with Cleveland, and he let us go after that, the stinker! Then our Calgary jump fell through, and alto-gether we had a hole in the schedule—next Patty turned her ankle and we could not coach her to work round it, so we had to send her home to Spokane, which she does not like. And neither does my brother, of course. But it's only for a little while, and there's no denying that we get along faster without Patty. My brother says we'll be on Pan-time soon with this new look, since we've given the act a greater wow.' Mercy bent to drink her tea, but could not repress a doubtful shrug. 'Hope he's right! But tell me, what's this gossip about Fitzjohn Mayhew being at the Parthenon. I was never so surprised!'

Aurora was surprised herself, to hear Mayhew's name said with such relish. 'Why, what do you know of him? He's come from Ziegfeld's company, to take the reins after Drawbank was pushed out.'

'Fancy!'

Something hidden there. 'You know him?'

'Oh, no, not to say *know*. One hears things, that's all.'

Aurora waited.

'I used to know a girl who knew him, as you might say. He left Boston in a hurry. And he came back PDQ from San Francisco, too. Not that *that* means anything—I think it was around the time of the 'quake. I don't know—' Mercy pressed her lips together into a pink pucker. 'Have you gotten yourself mixed up with him?'

Aurora puckered in turn, twisting the little sapphire ring that Mayhew had given her. 'I suppose it is mixed up. I am to marry him in May,' she said.

'No!' Mercy laughed, loud enough to make heads turn among the café patrons. 'You are quick off the mark! You one-up my friend—he never thought of marrying *her*. I'll bet your mama had a hand in deciding it! Hearty best wishes for a prosperous union, et cetera—send me a card for the wedding.'

She and Aurora regarded each other across the table. 'Where are your sisters?' Aurora asked.

'Dozing! Where are yours? Nice to have a jaunt without them, ain't it?'

Aurora nodded, but was surprised to find it so. She had not been conscious of feeling crowded.

There was a silence.

'All prepared for it?' Mercy asked.

'What is a French job?' Aurora asked, at nearly the same time.

Mercy did not laugh, but took up the salt shaker. 'Good thing to have up your sleeve, they like it very much. Hold firm, but not too

tight. I always think of a fry-pan handle, that's about the right grip.'
After a quick look around, she bent over the table behind the menu
and demonstrated the action. It was only as she proceeded that Aurora
made sense of what she was doing.

'Into your—mouth?'

'It's what they like,' Mercy said.

'Where did you learn it?'

'Ship's steward on our way over from Bristol, when I was twelve.
Taught me all I know.'

Aurora had been half laughing, but she stopped then, truly shocked.

'Don't fret! It's been a boon to me all this time,' Mercy said. She set
down the salt shaker and scrubbed at its head with her napkin. 'It's often
good for a night off, when the other seems—well, a bit of a burden.'

'Oh, good God!' Aurora said.

'Have you done It yet, with him?'

Aurora shook her head.

'With anyone?'

'Not—not fully.'

'It hurts a bit, the first time. The thing is to be patient. And stay
calm. It's only natural, it's what we're built for. If you get lucky with
the man, it can be a very good time.'

But that was not her consideration, anyhow, Aurora thought. She
wanted to be expert, to bind him to her. The sentimental part of it was
not necessary—Mercy was proof of that. And she did not wish to be a
prude. 'I will be brave,' she said.

Mercy looked at her and grinned. 'Ho, yes, you will be!' she said.
'Ain't we all.'

My Man Famble   Back from Missoula, Mayhew began
work on his melodrama. After running
lines with Aurora in every spare
moment, Clover sat in the empty house to watch the first rehearsal.
Aurora was Miss Sylvia; East became the theatrical producer Fibster

Malverley, 'a handsome demon,' and Verrall oiled on and off in the minor part of Malverley's agent, Flink. Sybil was given a brief but poignant role as Miss Sylvia's white-haired mother, who spent much of the play visible through a window, tied up and gagged.

> MALVERLEY: Of course we can wait for your dear
>   mother—what can have detained her?
> *(aside)* Perhaps it was my man Famble and his blackjack!
> *(to Sylvia)* We are honoured by your presence. Can I
>   give you a glass of ratafia?
> SYLVIA: I do not know what ratafia is, sir.
> MALVERLEY: Oh, it is a mild soft drink. *(aside)* Along the
>   lines of Madeira or Blue Ruin . . .

East enjoyed his villainy hugely, chewing with relish upon his moustache as he inveigled the innocent miss into a state of drunken compliance and made his hideous assault, against her maidenly protests.

> MALVERLEY: It is entirely your own fault for enflaming
>   me, Sylvia. My heart has been yours since first
>   setting eyes on you. Let me call you—my Own.
> SYLVIA: *(blushing)* Please, sir! Unhand me, I beg of you!
> MALVERLEY: *(aside)* She maddens me! But her *beaux yeux*
>   will not make me marry her . . .

Knowing the play as well as Aurora did by that time, Clover was leaning forward in her seat, mouthing the lines, when she felt a touch on her arm and Victor Saborsky sat down beside her.

He was back! She jumped and would have shrieked, but he caught her arms and stopped her mouth with a kiss. 'Yes, yes,' he said, in a barely audible tone. 'I am back—we are reunited—but first, what is this appalling tripe they are playing on the stage?'

Clover explained, filling him in on the plot so far, and settled into the crook of Victor's arm to watch the rest, as if it were a private showing just for them. In the end it was revealed that clever Sylvia and her mother had planned the encounter themselves; Sylvia gave Malverley knock-out drops and robbed him of the papers which would have compromised her mother. Nonsense, yes, but Clover thought Aurora did a beautiful job of conveying the pure-minded maiden who was so put-upon by the Producer, willing to give up even her Virtue if that could save her Widowed Mother.

Going down to the dressing rooms to help Victor unpack, Clover murmured that she found it quite impenetrable that Mr. Mayhew would be interested in staging a melodrama that so closely resembled his own life—except he did not seem to have a Man Famble.

Victor suggested that perhaps Mayhew did not see the similarity. 'We have not always nose-past acuity,' he said, beginning a set of pull-ups on the dressing-room door.

She laughed, and he dropped down to the floor to kiss her. She blushed.

'I love that you blush when I kiss you,' he said. 'But you have no need.'

'I know! I do not know why I do it. Because I am so happy!'

'Reason enough,' he said, reaching to kiss her again.

But Aurora and East came running down the stairs, arguing about a bit of business with the ratafia glasses. Clover straightened her dress as Mayhew followed the others down.

'We'll put it on the bill at the beginning of May,' he told Aurora. 'Just time enough for a new gown for the beautiful Miss Sylvia.'

Aurora laughed and turned, arms in air, to show off the exquisite dress she wore: a float of embroidered lawn, pin-tucks and lace that Clover had helped her pick from the dressmaker's shop. 'Will this not do?'

'No, no,' Mayhew said, seriously. 'Your opulence in dress is your stock-in-trade, my dear. Never underestimate the importance of being well turned-out. For a woman especially, variety in dress is a necessity. Order one in ivory peau de soie. When that's done we'll put the melodrama on the bill, and not before.'

Gumballs

The older brother of the Tusslers was called Walter Middleton. Bella knew the name of the younger brother now too, but she refused to use it, even in her mind. Every show, at the end of their turn, the younger Tussler was there in the wings staring at her, and she remembered again the slam of his fist, those ham-knuckle bones. When he was hit onstage, or fell down the trick-collapsible stairs, she felt hot pleasure. Even so, she would have left it alone, hating herself for the mousey way fear made her behave; but then he began to bother Xiang.

The Chinese girl was unknowable—they had no common language, and her father required her constant presence both offstage and on— but Bella loved her straight-across bangs and mincing, dress-hobbled step. Before Long Chak Sam's act, Xiang carried a red lacquer tray of assorted magician's props upstairs. She wore big-soled black slippers with a divider between the toes and cotton socks that split her toes to match, and they were not easy on stairs. Perhaps wearied of worrying Bella, the Tussler started lying in wait for Xiang during the intermission. He had prop-work to do himself, clearing up the clattered furniture their act left splintered about the stage, and would engineer it so that he finished just in time to arrive at the top of the stairs as Xiang began to climb from the bottom. He'd have something large and awkward in his hands, wooden slats or a drawer, and would slip, stumbling down as she was going up. It was loud and terrifying, but he was very practised at falling; his wood slats were aimed with skill into Xiang's painstakingly arranged tray of props, scattering them. The first time Bella happened to see this, she was frightened enough to leap to help, although she usually avoided being within twenty feet of the Tussler. He scrambled up, pawing at Xiang's dress, and made as if to do the same to Bella, except that Bella fled back into their dressing room. Out of the corner of her eye she saw Xiang fly to the top of the stairs as if by magic.

It happened again at the next show. And again, and again. Afraid to tell her sisters what had happened to her, Bella could not tell them what was happening to Xiang; but she could not leave it as it was. She woke one night from bad dreams and lay in the dark, cold even under Clover's arm. He would have to be stopped.

She had no poison. Oil on the dressing-room stairs might kill him, but the Tussler was very good at falling. Oil on his collapsible stairs would kill only him, but the brothers checked their set-up before every show and would certainly notice oil-slick. For a moment she thought longingly of the bright spears of broken glass in the glass-crash box—but could not bear to imagine how it would cut her hand to use one to kill the Tussler.

Mattie could not help, he was just a boy. Verrall was so fearful of any trouble that he would only clasp his hands and beg her to take no notice. East was more of a firebrand but did not care for anybody but Verrall. No point in asking him. Maybe Aurora could get Mayhew to fire him? But she'd have to tell Aurora why, and no matter how she scolded herself she found she could not bear to speak of it, of the shame of being hit.

She needed Nando from the Knockabout Ninepins. She thought with pleasure of Nando dropping the gumballs that his wicked father danced and fell on later. Victor Saborsky had returned—maybe he could help somehow, he was good at elaborate machines. But she was shy of him, of his formal speaking and his intense, un-ironic energy. It was as if he could only speak to one woman in his life, and that was Clover. It was tiresome also because Clover was so mad in love with him that she was in a daze, a dazzle-ry, distracted and prone to fits of slight bad temper, unlike herself. And Bella could not bear her to know about this, anyway.

What would be the worst thing for the Tussler—humiliation during a show? To be injured, to lose confidence—to be afraid, to see how that felt. Except maybe that was why he liked to do it to her, because he already knew himself.

Les Trois

The theatre was warmer during the day, now that spring had come, and a good thing too, Bella thought: their costumes for the peasant number of *Les Très Belles* were cut scandalously low, and high. Mayhew came to watch the girls go through their paces. He wore the astrakhan-collared coat, though it was a little too warm outside, and in Bella's eyes he looked the perfect impresario.

They'd started rehearsing by singing *la-la-la* because they did not know how to pronounce the French words properly, but Victor spoke French, and had coached them till they were at least comfortable, if not entirely accurate. In fun, Clover and Bella had begun larding ordinary conversation with *eus* and *entrezs* and carrying on as if they were actually French, which pleased Mayhew so much that he insisted they ought to keep it up always. 'No need to inform the press of your nationality—ah, but I forgot! You are true *Canadiennes*—we merely stress the Frenchity of your native land.'

After listening, he reluctantly agreed that the uptempo *Plaisir d'Amour* did not work—they would try *Mon Homme* instead, Clover singing in French with Aurora and Bella in English after. It was Mistinguett's cabaret song and possibly the only genuine thing in the act, and Bella liked the song very well. Sad or funny, she could work it either way, depending.

> 'Two or three girls has he,
> That he likes as well as me,
> But I love him—I don't know why I should,
> He isn't true, he beats me too . . .'

Mayhew also approved *Sur le Pont d'Avignon* and their bridge dance, which Mama had blocked out to echo the children's game, London Bridge. 'That's the ticket,' he said. 'Familiar, yes—but Frenchified. No more of the Scottish numbers, that's clouding the issue. You'll have to stick to *La Françoise.*' Naturally, they would do as they were told.

Did they have to obey him even more, Bella wondered, now that he was going to be Aurora's husband? She had thought it might mean Aurora could jolly him out of things. Now they were working on the *Lakmé* and that meant she could sit out, a good thing since she'd been the one running through the bridge in the previous number, and was covered in a gleam of sweat. She retired behind the piano to watch, running a cloth over her face and neck and (screened by the piano's bulk) down her chest. The wads of cotton pouffing up her bosom were soaked through, but she looked much older with them and would not even rehearse without. Cleaned up, she could listen to Aurora establishing her own authority over their act, little by little.

'The key is too high for us,' Aurora was saying. Mama protested, but Aurora nodded firmly to Caspar, who rustled his paper making a little note, and took it down a few notches to the key of G. 'But we'll only do the first third,' she told him. It was Mayhew who objected this time, so that Aurora had to stop and smile and tell him that perhaps he was a little biased—and that maybe this week, for Clover's sake, they could begin with a short section and expand as they went along. Bella saw her apologize with her eyes to Clover, who obliged by looking downcast and incompetent. She shuffled her sides and held one upside down, until Aurora walked in front of her again and whispered, 'Enough, I think!'

The harmony was demanding, and the accompaniment did not match the melody—Aurora and Clover could not catch it till Caspar cleared his throat and sang each part separately for them, which Bella could only be grateful that Gentry Fox did not witness. As she sat waiting for *Lakmé* to be done, Bella wrote him a letter in her mind:

> Dear Gentry Fox,
>   You were right, we are not singers. But we do what you told us to do and somehow people are fooled. We miss you very much, and thank you, and wish our sister was marrying *you*, if you were not quite so antique.
>   Your young friend,
>
>   ARABELLA AVERY

What Beauty Awaits   Clover and Victor leaned on the lip of the false front of the theatre. Spring snow fell delicate and whole-flaked around them but none of it stayed on the black tarred roof. It was late in the season for a cloudburst to slink down the mountain driftway from Canada, but the snow was pretty, not threatening. The moon shone through torn clouds, bright as afternoon.

Inside a corner of Victor's greatcoat Clover was warm, and she loved heights. He had found her watching in the wings after his turn, and had spirited her away up the steel stairs beyond the catwalks, out onto the roof through the trap door which even Bella had not dared to open. He was an adventurer, an explorer. Music from the pictures clanged and banged, so far below that it was like faerie music.

'This is a night for Galichen, my teacher,' Victor said. 'I will take you to see his tall thin house, his all-white garden in the moonlight, and he will see that you are a sliver of moon yourself.'

Clover looked down at the street below, the black footprints of the audience being erased by whiteness. 'Well, I will have to get there on a moonbeam.'

'My mother will love you,' he said. She saw that he was quite serious. She did not speak, did not need to speak. After a pensive moment he added, 'As long as Gali does . . .' and she laughed, having heard about this master or monster of eccentricity who had ensnared Victor's parents. He lifted her to sit on the parapet. 'When you are old enough you, ma mie, will be the mother of my children.'

'Will we have children?'

'Before, I believed that it was irresponsible to usher infants into a world well-conditioned to cause them pain. But Galichen says: as pain is the human condition, love is its alleviation, and we must train. We endure the pain that visits us in order to be capable of enduring the flashes of sudden joy.' I *now* want to have children, because I have met the mother of them. The ridge of his nose stood dark against the light spilling upwards from the lighted Parthenon sign. His skin was too thin, and showed if he was tired or overwrought.

'You will be a good father.'

'I will be. Our children will be good children, because they will have found their true parents. *Little do you know, children!*' he shouted, his voice falling off the roof and down into the silent street where no one stood or walked any longer. '*What beauty awaits you! This is your mother!*'

Aurora would be waiting for her, she should go, she should go.

'Do not talk about being married any more,' Clover said, turning away from the roof's edge. 'It makes my chest hurt to think of it. I have to look after Mama.'

A Hundred Jawbreakers In the second show it happened: the Tussler fell. Bella had stayed in the wings after their turn to watch how the Tusslers' number went, to see if there was some weak spot she could use—she had been thinking again about gumballs. Nando had shown her how the hollow gumballs squashed when stepped on, so that his father could control exactly how his feet flew out from under him. But jawbreakers were not hollow, they were hard as iron and slippery as hell's slope, and if she let loose a hundred jawbreakers under the Tussler's feet he would go down, for sure.

Watching him in the act, though, she gave it up. He hardly set foot on the stage floor, but only ran up and down the twenty-foot set of stairs that was their central prop, carrying chairs and tables, hooking them out of the air as his brother tossed them. And now that she thought about it, a hundred jawbreakers would cost a dollar, and she had no money at all. Which was also infuriating, since she worked as hard as any of the others and never saw a red cent to call her own. She could feel her jaw tighten and the muscles under her eyebrows bunch up, but was making herself shrug and move away when the small thing happened. A small noise, a *tink* on the floor.

She turned—and saw a shape behind the scaffolding of the Tusslers' staircase-flat. In the backstage darkness, the shape was half as high as the staircase, and moved like a tall, stiff man. A man nine feet tall. Impossible. It must be a trick of shadow and the footlights.

The staircase shook and rumbled again as the younger Tussler crashed up to the summit, to receive the emptied desk which his brother tossed. In a minute he would toss the desk back and the brother would work the mechanism that turned the staircase into a slide, and the Tussler would slide all the way down for their big finale. He got to the top, and reached out his arms to catch the desk, which was careening through the air towards him—and the stairs went flat.

The Tussler seemed to hang in the air, still reaching up for the desk, before his feet came out awkwardly and his body tried to twist into a hook to grab somewhere, and—all unready, off balance—he crashed backwards onto the flattened stairs and down down down the twenty feet.

After he landed, seconds later, the desk crashed languidly down on top of him. And after that, the top half of the stairs themselves folded over and came cracking and breaking down until they lay in a dreadful heap.

The orchestra was still thumping away; the audience went wild for what they took to be the biggest finish of all. Bella stared at the wreck on the floor, then turned to look through the backstage dusk for the tall man. Nobody to be seen.

Xiang stood at the stairwell beside her father, shorter than him by a foot, and slighter. Their identical eyes gazed past Bella to the rumpus onstage: the older Tussler calling for help as the main curtain rippled shut, stagehands running to lift the wreckage off the under-Tussler. Him at first frighteningly silent, then yelling blue murder with the pain of something—everything—broken.

The Same

Aurora ran up the stairs and out into the auditorium. She should have seen— She *had* seen, that hideous bruise! She had known perfectly well that Bella was in trouble that evening at the roadhouse, and that the trouble had not gone away. Aurora hated herself. Mercy from the Soubrettes, with no kind of education, looked after poor Patience far better than she had looked after Bella. And now, what, what had Bella done?

She sped up the aisle to the lobby, hardly able to see her way in the after-hours gloom. The theatre had been emptied, the stage cleared, the Tussler hauled away to the hospital—all cacophony had ceased while they were down in the dressing room dealing with poor Bella's hysterics.

And it might have been worse—what if he had died from the fall?

The door to the upstairs offices was closed, but not locked. She ran up those stairs too, into Mayhew's office. He was still sitting over ledgers laid out under a green-shaded lamp, but looked up at her step. She could not speak.

'What is it?' He came round the desk to catch her hands, which she had held out without knowing it. 'Sit, sit—' He looked around the barren office as if a chair for her would materialize. Then he took her to his desk chair, saying easily, 'What a dingy place this is! Unfit for you.' He sat down in the chair himself and pulled her to his knee.

Aurora sat off balance at first, resisting—then caving in. What luxury, to let someone else be in charge. She lay against Mayhew and closed her eyes.

'Quietly, quietly. We'll fix it. What is the bother, my dear girl?'

Tense again, she straightened, but did not climb down off his knee.

'The Tussler—Verrall has just told me that he *hit* Bella, when we were in Butte—you did not see the bruise she got, the night we met.'

'The night we met, all I thought of was you,' Mayhew said.

Aurora shook her head. 'No, no—that girl, lying in the snow. Because she was so badly hurt I did not let myself think more about Bella. But what if he had—' Her brain was spinning. What if he had died tonight; what if he had killed Bella that night, or raped her? None of those could be spoken. 'And ever since she has been plagued by him.'

'So it's a timely thing that he has gone.'

'Bella has made herself ill, crying about it. Bella never cries.' She could not tell him what she feared: that it was Bella who had pulled the pin from the hinge on the stairs and caused them to crash down. If she had done it, nothing to be gained by saying so.

'Those two were unreliable, and their equipment ill-maintained,' Mayhew said. 'Walter's been in here giving me a song-and-dance about how he can continue on his own, he's got a single act, but I've told him it's no go.' In the circle of Mayhew's arm Aurora let herself subside. 'They'll be gone, and unable to make any more trouble for us, either of them.'

And unable to make a living, Aurora thought. Two gangly boys, no older than herself, as precariously perched in vaudeville. Now off their perch, Arnold hurt and Walter with no partner. But it was their own responsibility to check and recheck their equipment, and she could believe they'd neglected it. Everybody was in the same boat as far as injury went—if you could not work, you would not earn.

And perhaps, perhaps, as Bella had sobbed out to them below-stairs, it had been the Tussler who had hurt the Irish girl; and then good riddance to bad rubbish. Bella would be safe now, this way.

'All right,' she said into Mayhew's ear.

His arm gathered her in more strongly, almost rocking her. She turned her head until she could see up into his face, in the dim green dusk of the office. He was staring at her with a sad intensity.

'It will be all right,' she said to him.

After a minute he said, as if afraid to ask, 'What will?'

'Us,' she said. She touched his cheek, his forehead. 'Don't be worried. We are the same kind of person,' she said. He buried his head in her bosom, and she cupped her hand to hold him there.

Hurting Each Other   On Sunday, one of their dark-days, Clover persuaded Mama to invite Victor to tea at the Pioneer. Mayhew was there too, as he always was these days. The landlady, Mrs. Burday, offered the hotel's fancy parlour for the formal visit. Looking round the hideously refined room, with its lace-edged mantel and skirts on every chair, Clover thought it a fine example of the false ease that money brings. Mayhew had increased their dot to $150 per week, and they were finally able to put something away—now that they had no need to, because Mayhew looked after everything.

But of course they must not relax too much. Out of Aurora's hearing, Clover and Bella had decided they'd need a stake, in case Mayhew got tired of two sisters tagging along and decided to make Aurora into a single act. And they'd have to look after Mama as well. Bella wanted to work out a sketch bit with East and Verrall, but relying on those two made Clover no more confident. On a secret piece of paper she was figuring what they'd need to set off on their own: at least $200, she thought, to be comfortable for a month, and not very comfortable for another two or three. Even if they started with an engagement elsewhere.

She was too sick with apprehension to enjoy the tea. Mama turned prickly around Victor; and she thought Victor might find Mama's pretenses abominable. He would see through everything and perhaps, perhaps— Clover shook her head. He would still love her.

But they were arguing already. Mama had started in the moment he arrived, telling Victor how much he must have loved, and would now sadly miss, the Tusslers, since they were so very much like his own act. Victor had bowed, rather than speak, keeping the unspoken pact not to let Mama in on the true tale of the Tussler and Bella.

'And you must be looking forward to the Melodrama which Mr. Mayhew is proposing! So high-toned and instructive, just the thing to raise our vaudeville above the common run.'

Clover bit the inside of her cheek.

'But I like the common run,' Victor said. He pulled a red rubber ball out of his pocket.

'You are a certified genius and must scorn us mere mortal dancers and singers! But there is good in every type of act,' Mama said.

'I could not agree more,' Victor said, but his voice was flat.

'We agree, really!' Mama said, to jolly him. 'You like the same lovely things we do.'

'Sometimes I do. Sometimes we agree.'

'We enjoy a good laugh—like the Tusslers.'

Victor was oddly serious in this little argument. 'I laughed at them because I was afraid they were hurting each other.'

So Mama became serious as well—or rather, Clover saw, she began playing A Serious Artiste, nodding sagely, invisible spectacles settling upon her nose. 'Oh yes, I quite agree, Art must educate! That's what we both believe. It must be *understood*.'

Victor broke into a quick laugh. 'How can we presume to understand the mystery of art? It does not ask us to understand it, only to be present.'

'Well, I consider that Laughter, you know, makes the Message easier to hear!'

The pompous sentimentality of this was apparently too much for Bella. She jumped up from the settee with a small, impatient shriek. 'There is no message, Mama! Especially not in the *Très Belles* Bull-Roarers! If the turn is good, it's good, that's all—it doesn't need a moral, or to be interpreted.'

Mama continued her irritating nodding. 'Oh, dearest child, that's very true—they understand us, because we're just ordinary folk, like them.'

'We are nothing like them,' Victor said. He lounged against the table, idly winding the red ball through his finger. 'They are citizens, we are not.'

Like a spectator at tennis, Clover looked to see how Mama would return that serve—since to her *citizen*, like *worthy*, meant the despised Aunt Queen, she could not very well class herself as a citizen too. 'Now, my dear, dear Victor,' Mama said. 'You will admit that here in polite vaudeville we are all one happy family, now that certain standards are adhered to from town to town. And that we all get along beautifully, like you and my sweet Clover.'

'On the contrary, we quarrel often. The better to love.'

'Well, all I say is, we can move in the first circles of Society; and we work very hard to do the best we can to make the words clear and to show the purity and beauty of our girls. Crystal clear!'

She was almost defiant, and Clover was relieved to see Victor give her a tender glance. 'Not everything can be clear,' he said, suddenly kind, speaking to Mama's confusion. 'Sometimes I have no idea why I do something! I do it to provoke, to stagger—not to clarify.'

Mayhew raised his head from his paper, reminded. 'Speaking of stagger—I've invited the newspaper critics to lunch at the Placer next week, and I'll need you girls on hand all togged out.' He nodded to

Aurora, where she sat studying her lines in the window seat. 'Getting them well-buttered will help with publicizing your melodrama.'

Victor bowed in his direction. 'Machiavelli in spats.'

Mama commended Mayhew on his initiative, but Clover could see she wasn't giving up the argument with Victor, who seemed to make her as worried and confused as a small dog with a huge bone. Mama stretched out a hand to him, imploring him with great shadowy eyes to yield, to agree, to be at one with her in understanding. But Victor laughed and tossed the ball up into the air, where it became three balls, cascading down and flowing up again. Still, Mama reached out to him again. 'The girls give people Hope, and that is so important, you know. To Entertain is a great calling, a great service. We send the audience home happy and strengthened, better able to bear their burdens.'

Victor laughed, whistled a twiddly bit of tune, and turned the red balls into a rose, which he handed her with an apologetic bow. 'No. Not I, at least. I wish to send them home shocked, exhausted, discontented with their lives, and amazed.'

Amazed, yes, always, Clover thought. Even if you *can* amuse, amaze. Amazement is the best of all, in vaudeville.

6.
Headliners

MAY–JUNE, 1912

The Parthenon, Helena
The Starland, Calgary

The highest salary acts are usually placed last on the
bill and are referred to as headliners or features.

FREDERICK LADELLE, *HOW TO ENTER VAUDEVILLE*

*A*nd then the axe fell. They were still eating breakfast the next morning in the Pioneer dining room when Mayhew appeared, wearing his motoring-coat. Aurora could see he was in a taking. His face was a thunderstorm—mouth in a tight line, dark air seeming to swirl around him. He took Aurora's arm to pull her out on the porch with him, and—an afterthought—tweaked Flora's shoulder too.

Bella stayed at the table with Clover, unable to eat. It was frightening to be in the presence of someone so very angry. Papa had rarely given way. From the porch they heard Mayhew's raised voice, and after a bit, a slight shriek from Flora.

Then Aurora put her head in the dining-room door, and jerked her chin. The girls got up in haste, found her already racing up the stairs, and followed.

'We're to be packed in half an hour,' she told them as they ran. 'He's taken all his papers, the accounts, everything, out of the theatre—some intolerable slight that Mrs. Ackerman has dealt him. Mama is finding out more, but they sent me to begin.'

A very dreadful development. Bella felt ready to screech with feverish excitement.

Clover kissed her cheek and whispered, 'Don't! It will be all right!'

They'd cleared out their dressing room, as always on a Saturday night, to let the porters clean thoroughly over the dark-days—so all their things were in the room. And they had laundered their smalls last night and hung them by the stove.

Flora came flying up the stairs—then down again to give Mrs. Burday the news that they would be leaving without notice—and came back in a taking of her own, because *La Burday* had insisted on being paid out for the week, though this was only Monday. Conscious of the clock, Aurora grabbed the grouch-bag from her and went, slick black shoes skating on the drugget, to settle up with Mrs. Burday; as she went she shouted for Clover and Bella to come sit on the lid of the trunk once they had added the gold silk comforter.

Clover let Bella go, and snatched the chance to run three doors down to Mrs. Denham's boarding house, where others in the Parthenon company had rooms. East opened the door, his own case in hand, and Verrall behind him was clapping his bowler on his head—they were off that morning on a long jump to Portland for their next gig.

'Victor?' she asked, out of breath. Yes, he was in—his head appeared over the banister rail. She ran up two steps at a time. 'Mayhew has told us we are to leave—Aurora says we're going to Calgary, then Edmonton. He's had a wire from Mrs. Ackerman that sent him into blind rage.'

Victor stared at her, still not properly awake. His fluffy hair stood up in a rooster's comb.

'We're leaving!' She stamped her foot. 'I will never see you again!' Then she burst into soft weeping and pulled her arm up over her eyes.

'No, no, no,' Victor said.

'Yes, I am telling you!' Her voice was muted by her sleeve.

'No, I mean, no, you will *not* never see me again! We are conjoined! There is no other for us—and we are vaudeville people, used to separation. I am booked for San Francisco next week, but up the coast on Pan-time to Vancouver next month, and then in Edmonton myself. Come in, come in.'

Clover stood inside the door of his bedroom while Victor rummaged through his suitcase to find a booking sheet, then copied it out in his black European hand, 7s crossed with sharp lines, *d*s made with long rising tails. *San Francisco, Eugene, Seattle, Portland, Vancouver*—the cities formed under his pen, each with a theatre and a bracket of dates beside it, and then *Edmonton, The Empire (June 25–July 11)*. She had never been to Edmonton. She had never been inside Victor's bedroom before. His jacket, hanging limp on the cracked closet door, broke her heart. He was wearing a shirt with no collar, grey flannel trousers; his socks were clean as new snow. The room smelled of him, his arm smelled of him. She took the paper.

'I will see you soon, then,' she said. She nodded her head and pressed her hands to her cheeks. He put his arms around her again, and then she ran back, before Aurora might notice she was gone.

Within the allotted half-hour they were arrayed on the front porch. Mayhew's long Pierce-Arrow touring car wheeled up. No train trip for them this time! Bella was thrilled to be travelling by car. Only Clover was unhappy, because she always felt sick in a car, and dreaded Mayhew's fury. And because there was no happiness in the world. The paper on which Victor had written his dates crackled in her pocket.

The Open Road

'It's the lack of vision—that's what frosts me,' Mayhew said as they drove away, shouting to Aurora, in the seat of honour beside him. 'I can handle any kind of slur, but what makes me impatient is abrogant stupidity.'

Did he mean arrant, or arrogant? Ignorant? Aurora closed her eyes and concentrated on the slight tremble of the wind whipping at her hat-feather, even tied under the motoring veil. Mama and Clover sat with Bella between them in the back. Aurora felt she must be grateful they'd not been left behind. Their trunks had been directed to the train station and would meet them in Calgary, which had meant a quick reassembling of overnight things in two hat boxes, now strapped up behind the boot of the Pierce-Arrow.

'Wait!' Aurora cried, her hand flashing to the dashboard as if to stop the car. 'My gown! My new peau de soie, for the melodrama— please, Fitz, *please*, can we stop?'

The dressmaker lived behind her shop. Although fussed about the unturned hem, she was persuaded to give up the gown when Mayhew signed the bill to the theatre. As they pulled away, she ran after them down the street with a small package, shouting, 'The sash!' Bella leaned out the back and grabbed it.

They whirled past the theatre and the train station, and onto the main road rising north out of town, moving just faster than their dust. As the car swayed, the three in the back swayed together, nobody daring to say a word after that last interruption.

'Mrs. Bloody Ackerman—bloody fool, never been the same since she took the reins, you can't tell me he actually meant *her* to take over when he popped— It's the lack of—' The wind or the sound of the engine whipped away some of each sentence. Aurora sat looking straight ahead, sometimes nodding. Once she put her gloved hand on Mayhew's knee, and he took one hand off the wheel and set it over hers.

He had talked himself into an expansive temper again by the time they stopped for the night in Shelby, at a plain-looking place that Mayhew had heard was the best hotel in town. Certainly the sheets were clean and there was a good fire in the parlour, where they sat after supper. Before long, Mayhew excused himself and went out 'to see about the car.' They did not see him again until morning, when he was waiting outside the hotel, in the Pierce-Arrow.

Rather than ask him to come in and pay for their room, Aurora paid. She could not help feeling the weight of the grouch-bag lessening. A momentary panic overtook her, to think that they had left the Parthenon. Mama came down the stairs with Bella, the strings of their hat boxes tangled, and Aurora did not wish her to see that she was paying their bill. But it was too late—Mama looked up and caught Aurora's eyes, and they turned together away from the desk to look out the door at Mayhew.

'What's his is yours, soon,' Mama said. 'But what's ours has to do for Clover and Bella too.'

'Do you think I don't know that?' Aurora whispered, stooping to pick up a hat box.

Mayhew sprang out of the car as they went down the steps, to open the doors for them. 'All aboard for the open road,' he said, all geniality this morning. He had found a barber: his face was still bright pink from the hot towel and he smelled of bay rum and the spring wind. Aurora took some comfort from his sheer cleanliness, if not his godliness, and did not ask where he had spent the night.

A hundred miles from Shelby up to Lethbridge. In the late afternoon Aurora looked back at Mama, Bella and Clover, cramped in the
rear seat—bedraggled and silent, their hair choked with dust, mouths
parched—and knew herself to be in the same sad state. Only Mayhew
remained spruce.

During the long drive Aurora had kept her face turned to the window,
staring at the blank spring landscape, seeing only what she'd got herself
into—and her sisters, and Mama. It was all down to Mrs. Ackerman, it
seemed to her: if Gentry Fox had not been pushed out, they would have
continued to learn from him until they were ready to make the leap to
the big-time. Now Fitz was pushed out too, and they were left in mid-air,
halfway between their old act and their new. And (but this was childish)
she had been looking forward to the melodrama very much.

Firmament of Beauty   One night in Lethbridge, and they
reached Calgary the next afternoon:
a broad, wide-open place, with not a
tree to be seen, nor a paved street, the riverbanks crowded with tumble-
down shacks and garbage dumps. Indians were common in the streets,
walking in parties of six or seven with their horses and women. It was
a raw city, Clover thought, but had everything laid out as if it one day
might be as civilized as Helena, and trolley cars already zipping along
the thoroughfares.

She and Bella walked the straight streets while Mama and Aurora
fought through sessions with the dressmaker. The *Très Belles Aurores*
would be opening at the Starland in a week. The peasant blouses,
casino skirts and *Lakmé* costumes were a rush job, and much was still
to be discussed: ribbon, depth of flounce, and for the *Lakmé* costumes—
perfect!—short hoops like lampshades, worn over tight pantaloons,
enchantingly oriental.

Clover had heard talk of a wedding dress, as well, but Aurora had
put a stop to that, insisting that she would wear the peau de soie from
Helena: an ice-cream vision, needing only to be hemmed. The wedding

was set for the Saturday before they opened, to garner the most press possible. Mayhew was busy sweet-talking editors from the eight newspapers; he had himself paged in hotels and restaurants, interrupting with messages of bogus urgency the lavish luncheons he gave. He'd installed the *Très Belles Aurores* in Mrs. Hillier's, a small boarding hotel catering to respectable vaudeville, only six streets from the Starland.

The Starland itself was a plain box on 8th Avenue, not near as grand as many of the other theatres, one of a small string with theatres in Winnipeg, Brandon, Calgary and Lethbridge, and on the other side of the line, in St. Paul and Omaha. Although most were moving-picture houses, the Omaha theatre had been running vaude, and management had decided to try it in the Calgary branch. Mayhew arranged, in what seemed like a matter of hours, to helm the effort until the Muse should be ready to open in Edmonton. He seemed to have twenty irons neatly arranged at his fire, Clover thought. Twenty *she* knew of, probably another dozen he'd kept up his sleeve. He dashed in and out of the theatre, where rehearsals had begun; in the evenings, Mayhew squired the three girls to the other theatres in town to check the competition— never paying for a seat, so successfully had he established himself as an impresario to be given every entrée.

Mama begged off each time, saying that Mayhew's escort was enough; she was working in secret, Clover knew, on an embroidered wedding veil for Aurora. Between the fire and two gas-lamps, she sat stitching late into the evening, a garden of white-on-white flowers growing under her silver needle. Clover had heard her murmuring a series of wishes, like spells, into the veil as she sewed: that Mayhew would treat Aurora well, that he would be kind to her sisters, that Aurora would be happy, or at least safe and well. Nothing more ambitious. She was careful not to prick her finger, saying blood on the veil would mean a wound or a broken marriage.

The girls wore their best lawn to the fashionable Bijou Theatre. They had carefully dressed their hair, but were overshadowed by the extravagance of dress and coiffure in the audience around them, let alone onstage. Made shy by the noise and crush and sheer number of people, Clover felt they were country mice as they settled into red velvet seats, lights dimming and the chatter finally lessening.

The opener was a comic, Joe Whitehead. His catch-phrase was 'squeaky good!' and he used it every other line; Clover whispered to Bella, 'I miss East and Verrall, and Julius.'

What the Bijou Theatre bill *did* feature was beautiful girls. Even Aurora was not a candle to them; the Avery girls could barely register in the firmament of beauty there. The Eight Palace Girls, ravishing nymphs in complicated costumes, changed three times during their number—each time into rather less. Each of the eight was equally well shaped; all seemed good-natured. While music played they stood in graceful poses, altering slowly from stance to stance. Like matched ponies at a horse show, Clover thought, and just as tedious.

The Dahlia Sisters closed the first half: two very beautiful, modestly dressed girls who sang, and did not dance at all. They wore pretty gowns, but more, they seemed to glow with good nature and kindness, and Clover wanted to sit through their number again from the beginning.

December–May

Aurora asked Mayhew to take her backstage at intermission, if he was able. He laughed at the notion that anyone would try to keep him out, and they trooped down.

The Dahlia girls were even lovelier, close to. Aurora found she could not look them in the eyes for long, as if she were drinking in too much light. The fair-haired girl's cheek was flushed with apricot; her eyes were grey or green or blue, pale brows giving an odd impression of vulnerability to her open regard. She seemed unknowable. The dark-haired girl's sprinkling of tiny freckles could be counted, this close. Her eyes were bright and sad at the same time, perhaps some trick of birth, the lift in the upper lid coming at the exact point for tragedy. Her underlying sorrow gave a sombre quality to their songs.

Thoroughly humbled, Aurora saw that she and her sisters had been mistaken to think themselves anything out of the common run. And she had been lucky to hook Mayhew, it now seemed to her. He was dallying with the fair Dahlia Sister but he kept Aurora in the corner of his eye, and from time to time gave her a warm look.

The orchestra pit door opened, and through it came a creased squirrel-face that was pleasingly familiar: Mendel, the bandleader from the old Empress, with a bundle of music. Aurora remembered how he had tried to help them. It seemed like such a long time ago.

'Miss—Aurora,' he said, after the briefest of pauses. Then he added, 'Looking like a dozen roses—I see vaudeville has been good to you!'

She smiled, too broadly, tickled that he could see the shine on her. 'You gave us a good steer,' she said, nodding quickly. 'We worked with Gentry Fox down there, you know.' She stopped herself before she said 'for free.' No one should know that.

'I can see you've prospered—and your sisters, your mama, all well?'

'Oh yes! And you are here at the Bijou?'

'Yes, found I couldn't stomach Cleveland any longer. There's plenty of work at theatres in Calgary, and many old pals. Eleanor Masefield's company is at the Orpheum now, with Jimmy Battle, you'd remember him. Coming along a treat as a hoofer and a juvenile tenor. He'll branch out from the Masefield troupe one of these days.'

She nodded again. Cast a quick eye to where Mayhew was immersed with Cleveland.

'Are they touring the same play?'

'No, *The Undertow* now—December–May romance kind of thing, turned upside down, you know, because the man is the younger. A tragedy, I believe. He walks into the sea at the end, or maybe it's the woman who does.'

'Yes,' Aurora said, as if she knew all about the play, and the relationship, and the general tendency of the world to pair people who were completely unsuited to each other in the name of various conveniences. She found herself about to weep.

A Cage-Bird

The next night the Belle Auroras attended the Orpheum, though Bella felt tired almost to frailty from rehearsals, and was glad when Clover suggested that they stay at home for a night. But Mayhew had arranged for a box, and would not hear of missing it.

The Orpheum's melodrama was *The Undertow*. Bella, who seldom bothered with the printed word, was taken by surprise when the curtain rose on the drawing-room set of the play and Jimmy Battle was discovered sitting at a writing desk. She jumped, and clutched at Aurora's arm excitedly—then, as quickly, let go and sat abruptly back.

'What's to do?' Mayhew asked.

Eleanor Masefield was making her entrance just then, so Clover gestured towards her and said, 'We shared a bill with Miss Masefield long ago.' Which made Mayhew smile indulgently.

Bella did not dare turn her head to look at Aurora. Instead, she watched as Jimmy and Miss Masefield circled each other. It was a tedious, hackneyed play, only elevated by the tension that emanated from the thin young man and the wilder, darker woman, who did not look at all old until she chose to do so. Eleanor Masefield—Evaline Burton, in the play—confessed with fitting and beautiful shame that she had lost her heart to him, in a light, drawing-room comedy sort of way, until suddenly her deeper heart was revealed.

> EVALINE: And so I—must ask you to leave, Jerry.
>
> JERRY: But, Evaline! Miss Burton! I thought we were having such a ripping time.
>
> EVALINE: Like seabirds, cavorting in the wind! But—
>
> JERRY: But what?
>
> EVALINE: Society—does not like—
>
> JERRY: Is Society to dictate to our hearts?
>
> EVALINE: You are in your first youth, Jerry. I am—in my second.

An uneasy laugh from the audience. Bella heard Clover whisper in Aurora's ear, 'Her *third*, more like.'

But Jimmy's graceful kindness would not allow them to laugh at Mrs. Masefield. He knelt at her feet, the picture of rational adoration.

JERRY: Ten years means nothing to people in love!

'Ten!' Bella said. 'Try thirty!' Then she shot a scared glance at Mayhew.

Onstage, Jimmy the Bat knelt again at the actress's feet and begged her not to consider the world's judgement, '*When Love is at stake!*' ('Good title for a vampire play,' thought Bella) but marry him instead.

The instant they became engaged, a gentleman entered: her lawyer, come about her father's will. He shooed off Jimmy the Bat and wormed it out of Miss Masefield that she was planning to marry. They moved to the other end of the room to discuss the papers he had brought for her to sign, and Jimmy, who had been listening at the door, had a dramatic monologue where he spoke to her photograph:

JERRY: I cannot be the ruin of you. (ruefully) And I
cannot live without money. I am no seabird, happy to
wheel in the wind. I'm one who needs a gilded cage.

He stared out to the ocean, looking terribly romantic in his tennis flannels and faintly nautical blazer. A rotter, an adventurer, a cad. ('I do like him,' Bella whispered to Clover.) The lawyer came back to question the cad's motives, while the woman watched in silence, posed in a frozen tableau, one arm along the mantelpiece, head bent but her glorious chest still heaving, diamond pendant flashing—usually during the lawyer's speeches, Bella noticed—drawing focus.

Then Miss Masefield sent Jerry away and gave the lawyer what-for, magnificent in defence of her lover. But the lawyer had the parting shot, telling her that she would ruin the young man. '*That* is your real sin,' he said, and Bella concurred.

Evaline bowed her head and called Jerry in, to renounce him by pretending to care for money.

> JERRY: I see now that I was your plaything.
> EVALINE: Yes. And the time has come to put away
> childish things. To put away the toys . . .
> *He looks at her, in hurt rage, then whirls and leaves the room.*
> EVALINE: . . . And go to bed.
> *She walks out the French doors, towards the cliff.*

There was, some seconds later, a muted splash. Bella had to stifle a giggle—after all, the audience could have had no doubt as to what Evaline was planning, with that tragedy-face she'd pulled as she went out. She was a seabird, after all.

Nobody's Fault

Aurora knew they must go backstage. Mayhew's consequence demanded it, and business contracted during the backstage crush was their whole purpose for being at the theatre. Clover and Bella walked one each side of Aurora, closing her off from Mayhew until he reached back to take her arm.

She went forward, eyes and mouth well controlled, prepared to see Jimmy Battle. He would not be prepared to see her—that worried her a little. But in the event it was all right. Mayhew knew Eleanor Masefield—Norie, he called her—and she flew to his side and took all his attention, giving no sign of recognizing Aurora.

Detached from Mayhew by Miss Masefield, Aurora watched Bella run ahead to where Jimmy was receiving a velvet box from one of Eleanor's admirers. Bella waited till Jimmy turned, then kissed him and clapped her arms around him in childish pleasure, whispering something in his ear. Then Clover pulled Bella along and they melted away.

Aurora stood alone in a shadowy part of the hall, spectators and artistes milling around them, and Jimmy Battle came down the hall to find her. She was angry, without the least right to be. The privacy of the noisy crowd let her speak without restraint.

'We did not fall in love,' she said. 'Back then.'

'No.' Jimmy's chin, his cheeks, were thinner. 'Did we not?'

'You were under contract.'

'Yes, I was. I am.' He was angry himself. He must see that she was with Mayhew, now twenty feet away, deep in flirtatious conversation with Eleanor Masefield.

His anger melted her own. In an instant she was nothing but broken-hearted, that the infant thing between them must be squashed. She wanted to comfort him.

'Sometimes these things just do not work out,' she said. 'It is nobody's fault.'

He bit his lip, and fumbled with his cuff, his wrist. Then he handed her something, his fingers pressing it into her hand. She looked at the shape of them, strong and narrow, well groomed, nails trimmed very short. No hair on them, brown as if from sun.

'Keep that for me.'

She met his anxious eyes, and managed a smile.

'I know,' he said. 'We do what we must do. But keep that, anyway.'

She looked down at what he'd given her: a plain silver chain brace-let, not at all the sort of thing she would have thought he'd wear.

'It was my mother's. I'll come and get it back from you one day.'

'All right,' she said.

The crowd was breaking, and Mayhew and Eleanor were louder.

So Aurora and Jimmy separated, each taking the arm of a patron, and laughed at what was said. Whatever it was.

On the Starland Bill

Flora was pleased to see that dodgers for the Starland Theatre already littered the streets, advertising the starting bill, head-lined by *The Très Belles Aurores de Nouvelle France.* Mayhew sent a packet to Mrs. Hillier's boarding house so the girls could see themselves written up:

> ... widely-known through Europe for their excellent
> singing and the very best in stage dancing in the
> flamboyant French style, the three very *jolie Très Belles*
> *Aurores* are making their first American tour.

The other artistes on this first bill were impressive, Flora had to credit Mayhew, and his write-ups hit the heights of hyperbole. Paul Conchas, The Military Hercules, for example: Mayhew had penned a startling tale to go with his title, about Conchas serving in the German army, his magnificent physique drawing the personal attention of the Kaiser. '*When his term of service expired he came to America and since then has been a marvel and inspiration to thousands of young men.*'

'As long as he is not in the vein of the Tusslers,' said Clover. 'But listen: *The Ioleen Sisters, twin Amazons from Australia with a double set of accomplishments, slack-wire walking and sharp-shooting.* Why those two skills? For crossing a river as an alligator attacks?'

Flora frowned at her to stop, lest Mayhew take offence. Clover seemed so quiet, but she had a vein of humour that could deflate the fragile male.

Jolly Banjophiends were the dumb act opener ('*from the most raggy of the popular and up-to-date music to the highest classical selections*'), and Alberick Heatherton, Romantic Violin ('*experience the passionate intensity of his selections*') was to play between the melodrama and themselves in the second half.

Turning the dodger over, Clover exclaimed to the others, 'East & Verrall!'

Bella shrieked, and read it out: '*The Sidewalk Conversationalists, vivacious vagabonds of the road, contracted to this engagement at considerable expense.*'

Mayhew came tearing up the stairs to the hotel sitting room at that moment, vivid and energetic in a new plaid suit. Bella ran to thank him for booking East & Verrall.

'Now I can still do the hotel number! And we were working on a golf sketch.'

'Not golf, in this cowtown,' Mayhew declared. 'Nobody'd get the gag. I want to bring our own melodrama, *The Casting Couch*, along here,

and the boys will save us rehearsing. But that East is a champion dick-
erer. I'll be paying them twice over when the play goes up.'

Paying for things had been a repeated refrain in the last week,
Flora thought with some dismay. Clover glanced at Aurora, and went
back to the dodger.

Flora gathered her courage and said, 'The pretty dresses for *Lakmé*
are ready, dear Fitz, but the dressmaker won't deliver them here without payment. Shall I . . .?' She let the words die away, and sat rather
tense while Mayhew stared out the window to 8th Street.

'Hmm?' he said, seeming to wake to her inquiry. 'Dresses? Have
her send them to the theatre, tell her to make up an invoice for the
package. The fellow there will deal with it.'

Flora had been awake all night, obsessively counting over the dollars they had left, extremely reluctant to part with sixty to take pos-
session of the new outfits. She ought to have been more prudent, she
knew, scolding herself in the darkness, but what was to be done?

She watched as Aurora went to the window and touched Mayhew's
arm. 'I believe we will need summer frocks as well, Fitz. We could
make them ourselves, if Mama and I—'

He pulled out his money-roll, and peeled off several bills. 'New
dresses, new hats, new buckles to my lady's shoes. Outfit yourselves
with this, my dear. Next week we'll be raking in receipts at the Starland
hand over fist, and you'll have to look the part.' He closed her hand
over the money. 'Now let me listen to your rehearsals for a moment,
and then I'm off to meet the *Herald* editor, at his club—*club!* In this
pioneer place! Never mind, I'll invite him to the wedding. Two more
days!' He sat on the window-ledge in the weak May sunshine, and
waved a hand for them to begin.

The wedding was another worry, Flora thought, moving to the
piano (a boarding-house nag, tinny but in tune) to play for the girls.
Two days! Mayhew had booked the ballroom at the new Palliser Hotel,
very imposing, and was issuing invitation cards to every pressman he
encountered. The whole thing had the air of a stunt, but Flora could
not remonstrate with him; she could not even mention it to Aurora,

who had sequestered herself in silence. She sang at rehearsal, and shopped and stood for fittings; but she was . . . remote.

Nobody seemed at ease any more. Clover and Bella did not take to Mayhew's company, as they had East and Verrall's, say, or Julius Foster's. That was unfair of them—Mayhew always had a joke for Bella and a greeting for Clover, no matter how busy and distracted he became, thought Flora, as her tinkling accompaniment flowed without ceasing, as the girls sang on. She had a constant feeling, lately, of holding her breath.

Milk, Honey, Cream   Mayhew sat on the window-ledge with the light behind him, intending to listen critically; but he became fascinated by the three mouths moving at the same time, the shape of their mouths so much the same although their faces differed. When all three sang together, it was richer, deeper—a surprise that three young sylphs like these could produce that tone. Gentry Fox, that training showed. Their bird-waists and the small cages of their ribs, and then the pleasure of pretty girls' profiles: milk-pale skin on Clover, warm honey on Bella, full cream on Aurora.

Mayhew found himself pitifully aroused by her, and wished it were not so. He thought for a moment of the Irish girl they had found lying in the snow.

The complications of his business interests were extreme, but would be solvable without this baggage. The mirror over the piano showed him the backs of their heads, the coils and rolls they had pinned carefully into each others' coiffure. They were darlings, and he was as happy as he'd ever been, in fact. And they would help with the Starland, no question.

Oughtn't to have handed Aurora so much of the roll, though.

'I'm off,' he murmured, in the middle of verse two. He grabbed his hat and was out the door before the piano's notes had ebbed away.

A Sudden Fall of Snow On the night before the wedding it snowed. Silent, constant, nickel-sized snowflakes fell all night, in no wind, and in the morning when Clover awoke the light in the room was blue.

Mama gasped when Clover pulled open the curtain to show snow heaped halfway up the window. Snow covered the entire landscape like fondant on a wedding cake, smoothing definition of curbs and corners. The street was deserted, and snow was still falling, fifteen inches already on the ground—late May, and the worst blizzard of the year. A shell of ice waited on the water jug.

Clover's first feeling was relief. We'll never get there, she thought. Now they can't be married. Bella had jumped out of the blankets and come to join Clover at the window. She said out loud: 'Aurora! A blizzard has come—you'll miss your wedding!'

But Mrs. Hillier knocked on their door soon afterwards with an offer from her son to take them to the Palliser in the draycart. His big horse Clem had famously got through to the train station in the worst storm of 1910, and Hillier was itching to match the feat today.

The girls and Mama spent the morning washing and putting up their hair; in the afternoon they dressed in their wedding clothes—and all the time the snow fell.

The draycart's wheels shrieked and the snow squealed as they lurched along, but it was a pretty drive, through slow-falling flakes that dazzled in occasional spears of sun. Mama raised her white lawn parasol to shield Aurora's veil. When the wedding party disembarked at the Grain Exchange building, where the justice of the peace had his office, it was to silence. No streetcars were running, no carriages or cars rolled through the streets.

The Grain Exchange lobby was icy cold—no furnaceman had come to make the furnaces up. They left their galoshes by the door and climbed the stone stairs to the third floor, and there was Mayhew waiting in the hall, as if nothing were amiss with the world.

Bella and Clover were ahead, climbing the stairs, but they parted and let Aurora go through, and Clover was touched to see how Mayhew's face changed and steadied when he saw his bride.

The justice of the peace, a hardy man who laughed at the thought of a little snow keeping him from his work, dispensed the marriage proper within three minutes; it was little more than a quick 'Any reason they cannot be joined?' and a stamp, and signatures.

Mama shed a crystal tear, but at Clover's nudge and Aurora's impatient glance, she caught it in a lace hanky and put it tidily away. Then the party trooped down two flights of stairs (the elevator, like the furnace, being out of commission due to the storm), cut cater-corner across the deserted, snow-blown street and up more stairs into the Palliser lobby.

Nobody waited there but one greatcoated major domo, and one stick-thin bellhop in a hat too large for him. Mayhew gave a great snort, shook snow off his coat and divested himself, then assisted the women to take off their wraps. The bellhop disappeared behind a mountain of steaming wool.

'Well! On to the feast,' Mayhew exclaimed, as if expecting trumpets to strike up.

Silence prevailed. Clover stole a look at Aurora: her face seemed frozen. They walked across the marble hall and up the marble stairs. At the door of the Maple Leaf Room they were met by a fatly smiling waiter and not another single soul.

Inside, a dozen tables stood spread with white cloths, and a head table heavy with flowers. No guests were waiting here, either.

Space had been left clear on the glossy parquet floor for dancing; four members of the Starland orchestra sat at the ready. The bandleader, Tony Carrera, lifted his baton and applied himself, and a ragged-up rendition of Mendelssohn split the peaceful air.

'Mrs. Smarty gave a party,' Mama said. 'No one came.'

'Then her brother gave another, just the same,' said Bella.

Clover could not help laughing, then Bella and Mama joined in.

Aurora twiddled her ridiculous parasol and took Mayhew's arm where he stood, stiff as a poker, by the door. 'You know, Fitz,' she said, 'I don't think I was ever at a handsomer wedding feast. I'll tell you what we'll do, we'll have a good time.'

They were accustomed to making light of disaster. As chief attendant, Clover had two funny stories to tell about Aurora's childhood; Bella rose next, to compliment Mr. Mayhew on his accomplishments, not least of which was the winning of her dear sister's hand. Then they all did their best to drink a jeroboam of champagne. At least the waiters had turned up, and presumably, somewhere in the bowels of the hotel, the cooks.

Intermittent waiters served them turtle soup and roast capon with hot-house peas, a fine spring menu. Plates were set on all twelve tables, and carried away again untouched. Bella whispered to Clover that she was tempted to run down and eat a pea from each plate—such a scandalous waste!

A great cake was wheeled in on a trolley. Mayhew and Aurora stepped down to have their picture taken cutting it—and then Mayhew saw that the photographer had failed to appear. He turned to the cake, picked up the top layer and dashed it down to the floor. Icing roses slumped into the pale floor, petals smudged.

'Take the thrice-damned thing away!' he shouted, and the two waiters did so, as fast as their canter-wheeled trolley could go. Mayhew ran a few steps after it as if he would kick it, beside himself with rage.

Aurora stood still, keeping her peau de soie skirt out of the crumple of cake and cream. Clover held Bella's hand tightly under the high table's cloth.

Mama stood up (very nobly, Clover thought) and proposed, in a bravely raised voice, a toast. 'To Fitz and Aurora,' she cried. 'The best of good fellows, as I know you'll all agree, and the loveliest of girls. And so say all of us! Join me in *three rousing cheers for the happy couple!*'

No doubt when Mama had planned that phrasing, she had expected a genial, well-fed crowd of pressmen to shout *Hurrah* along with her. Clover was too frightened to speak, and Bella had bent her head in ferocious concentration so as not to giggle with nerves; Aurora and Mayhew could not very well cheer for themselves, and the four bandsmen, addressing their dinners, had forgotten to pay attention. So it was only Mama's single nervous *Hurrah!* that rang through the ballroom, at least as far as it could reach. She said again, *Hurrah!* and, not being able to stop, *Hurrah!* and then sat and drank down her champagne punch— and then, without noticing it, Clover's.

Folderol   Aurora stood on the vast parquet ice-field, a floating sensation invading her head and chest. For a moment she felt again the peace that had come over her, looking out that morning at the snow which would make the wedding impossible.

What ought to be done, just now, to help? She wondered in a detached way how much money Mayhew had laid out on this, or would have to, when the bill came round. A thousand dollars, perhaps. How many months she and her sisters could have lived on that in small-time vaudeville, doing their own work, thinking their own thoughts, trying to be better. What a folderol this was.

She bent to pick up a broken shard of china cake-pillar, and it nicked her finger. A minuscule drop of blood welled out, trembled for an instant on her fingertip, then dotted the wedding veil she had not yet removed. Very red on the white net. She looked up and saw Fitz staring at her, his face crimson as rare beef and his eyes deeply unhappy.

'Oh, Fitz,' she said. 'Don't— It doesn't matter. It was the storm, my dear.'

He nodded.

'And here are all the people I'd have wanted—except perhaps for East and Verrall, and Julius and—' She stopped. None of this was help-ing. 'Tony!' she called, looking back over her shoulder. 'Strike up the band, please! We need a waltz. *Casey* would be good!'

His brain was so loaded, it nearly exploded,
The poor girl would shake with alarm!

They twirled round the floor, the impresario and the girl he adored, but Aurora refused to shake with alarm.

Nor His Dinner   Mayhew danced with each of the girls, with Mama—who had continued to tidy up the champagne cup and asked Tony please to give her a slow song—and with Aurora again, and then the evening seemed to be over. Clover looked out the ballroom window into the still-falling snow and wondered what on earth they would do now. However well behaved they had been, the long day had clearly strained everyone's optimism.

The storm had worsened, and Mayhew, his temper restored, announced there was no question of making their way back to Mrs. Hillier's. 'The honeymoon is a double suite,' he said. 'I'm sure Aurora won't mind giving up one bedroom—will you, my dear?'

Far better, Clover thought, than to ask him to fork out for another suite, after all this waste.

Up in the suite, a blazing fire in the sitting room made things more cheerful. The same waiter who had served them in the ballroom appeared with a tea tray, and Mayhew poured brandy for himself and Mama. Aurora drank tea. Clover sat with Bella, wedged beside her on a small settee, and tried not to laugh or cry.

They had not been sitting for more than five minutes when, with a desperate lurch of delicacy, Mama rose and asked Bella and Clover to come with her to discover how palatial their bedroom might be. She could not settle, but walked about touching the lace curtains, the mantel cloth, the bedposts. Clover was very tired, but too tense to sleep; Bella, on the other hand, had drunk enough champagne while no one was watching that she could hardly keep her eyes open. Clover opened the bed for her, helped her to slip out of her blue dress and cami-band, and then Bella climbed up into the middle, exclaiming for a brief last waking moment over the softness of the sheets.

Clover slowly unfastened her own dress. An empty ewer stood on the washstand. She did not dare go into the bathroom, in case Mayhew might be there and might have forgotten to lock the door— but in an alcove round the corner of their wardrobe she discovered a sink. She filled the ewer with water from the hot tap, so piping hot that it burned her hand and she nearly dropped the jug. But did not. She wondered what Aurora would be doing, how the consummation would be. She touched her chest, unbuttoning her chemise to wash. Mayhew might ask Aurora to take off all her clothes, she supposed. It would be chilly.

Clover had only a hazy idea of what went on between a husband and wife. Or two who were not husband and wife—it would not matter to her, whether she and Victor were married. His family believed in Free Love and Vegetarianism, as part of their Fabian ideals. He would never make her into his property—nor his dinner, come to that.

'I ought to have warned her,' Mama suddenly said. 'It is— unexpected—unless you love him, and then—oh, Clover—'

'I think she expects it, Mama.'

'If you *love* the man, you cannot conceive of how different—' She stopped, and smoothed down her skirt. 'Well, she does love him, of course, or she would not have agreed to marry him.'

Clover turned down the bed and climbed in beside Bella, who was already deep asleep, sprawled flat on her back, mouth open like a little flowerpot.

Mama sat in the chair by the window, her hand over her eyes.

A Balance Sheet

In the sitting room, Aurora watched as Fitz left the bottle of brandy on the table, and called to Flora to feel free, if she needed a nightcap; then he stretched out a hand to Aurora and opened the other bedroom door.

All this felt unreal. Ever since coming to Calgary, none of the days had felt real. They'd had no work to do, perhaps that was it. Fitz was unbuttoning his jacket, loosening his tie, pulling it off. The lamp was still on—would he leave it on?

He turned the mantel lamp down low. The firelight caught his legs, but left the rest of him in darkness. 'That mother of yours will be snoring in a moment. She drank enough of the champagne.'

Aurora did not like him saying that. He had drunk enough of it himself.

'Come, come to bed,' he said, and then, 'I am sorry. She's a treasure. Only your family is a bit more present than I expected. And I will have to bunk in here with you tonight.'

'I thought that was what one did,' she said. 'On a wedding night. Bunk in.'

He stopped, in the act of pulling his suspenders off his shoulders. Looked at her in the lowered lamplight, as if trying to make out what she meant.

She felt some danger, some amusement, in being so powerful. He was angry, she knew, because of the imbalance between them. He was too old. She was beyond him, except for his position and his money. This was no way to go about the beginning of being married.

She had one hand on the bedpost. She leaned forward, letting herself swing around in a slow arc, and pulled his head towards her, to lay her cheek against his. She could give him pleasure, and let him believe himself loved. Since what was love anyway, but a balance sheet of what one respected the other for, what one could do for the other, what one needed from the other? Perhaps a jot of the mysterious thing that caused attraction, but that was not the whole. Even with Jimmy the Bat, attraction was only part of why she liked him. He was a good hoofer, that was a great part of it—and Mayhew, oh, Mayhew was an excellent manager.

'Will you kiss me first?' she asked him. She knew she could make herself a little drunk with kisses.

It was only her body, nothing she could not stand.

Agamemnon

Flora went out to the sitting room for another brandy, and sat on the settee reading the Bible by firelight, the only book to hand. Another small brandy. She did not know how Arthur could have done it, could have left them, how he could have been so cowardly or so deep in despair as not to think of what his daughters would do without him. That ugly Old Testament father sacrificing his son on the hill in the thicket, that's what she thought about, while she read the Psalms in the sitting room on the wedding night. But it was her own father she was thinking of, killing her before he went off to war. No, that was Agamemnon. In the other room she heard panting, shoving. No noise at all from Aurora. She never cried as a baby either.

The champagne and the brandy told on her. Before the sounds stopped, Flora had fallen asleep on the settee in the last of the firelight.

A White Knife

Clover found Mama on the settee an hour later. She covered her with an extra blanket from the chest, and sat watching her slackened face, shining a little in moonlight, now the snow had stopped falling. She has tried her best with us all, Clover thought, and she does not drink very often.

Then Aurora crept out, thin as a white knife in her shift, and padded to the bathroom. She stood in the middle of the tiled floor until Clover came and helped her into the bath. Her legs were shaking. Clover poured hot water over her head, down over her face, the silk hair sleek around her shoulders like otter's fur, and they both tried not to look at Aurora's poor underneath where pinkish blood kept seeping even after she was washed.

Clover dried her with a large, clean hotel towel. She braided her hair, wrapped her in the peignoir from her scant trousseau, kissed her cheek and went quietly back to bed. After a moment Aurora followed, sliding in on the other side of Bella, warm and soft. Bella sighed and turned on her side to make room, and the three of them curled together until dawn.

Then Clover watched Aurora glide back to the other room, to lie beside her husband as he woke.

But Can She Do This?

The snow was gone by Monday, not melted so much as evaporated in the dry prairie sun. By Tuesday it was spring again, almost summer, and the few trees loosed their tight-furled leaves like a girl might shake out her hair. The air was soft and smelled delicious. When they were not rehearsing, Bella and Clover walked out along the new-laid sidewalks as far as they stretched, not talking much. The subject closest to their hearts, Aurora and Mayhew, seemed disloyal to discuss—although Bella did tell Clover the reason that East and Verrall had not been at the wedding: because they had never received an invitation.

'Like they were bad fairies at the christening,' Bella said, indignant. 'And just what you might expect from—'

Clover hushed her, saying, 'It is a pity they were forgotten, but he had a great deal on his mind.' (Although privately she thought Mayhew had calculated the usefulness of the two comics, and given their seats to pressmen instead.)

On Thursday they opened. The Starland was lit up with brand-new electric lights around the sign, every surface festooned with garlands and flowers, and although its facade was plain, Mayhew had ordered a huge banner to be hung with the playbill painted on it, and there they were, in beautiful ornate letters, the headliners:

LES TRÉS BELLES AURORES DE NOUVELLE FRANCE

Bella was so excited to see it up there, Clover could hardly drag her inside.

Mayhew had papered the house to the rafters—every pressman who had not turned up for the wedding was artfully blackmailed into attending the opening in recompense.

The lineup stretched around the block when the girls arrived at six. By the time the curtain went up there wasn't an empty seat in the house, and a considerable crowd stood bunched at each arched entrance.

The openers, the Banjophiends, were playing their first gig in Calgary, although well known in the east. A self-contained little group who spoke only to each other, they stood glumly in the wings, one man tuning his instrument obsessively with soft plinks, until the stage manager gave the word, and off they trotted in a sudden froth of mirth.

Clover had crept up to watch, tucked into a corner by the hemp-bed. She laughed to see their sober frowns turn upside down as they hit the light and instantly cavorted. They played well, but it was the harum-scarum nature of the banjos that did the trick, and their wit. The leader and the littlest Banjophiend carried on a back-chat throughout their turn, about courage, which they called pluck, and how the little one could get up enough of it to finally propose to Miss Minnie Abernathy, the love of his life. At the end the little fellow did a soulful solo of *Silvery Moon*, and cried out in anguished ecstasy, 'Good night, Miss Minnie Abernathy, I looove you!'

The audience, which had been slow to settle, was good-natured. They cat-called and whooped for Miss Abernathy and gave the Banjophiends plenty of applause.

Paul Conchas, the Military Hercules, had been readying behind the curtain all that time. It rose to display him in an Olympian marble arena (his own special Diamond Dye drop), attired in nothing but a large paper fig leaf, tied round his hips with an inadequate-seeming piece of string. His pale skin shone like the marble pillars of the backdrop. Clover stared in awe at the classical indentations of his musculature, particularly the fascinating downward-tending ridge of muscle which separated the torso from the thighs. She felt her own being concentrated in that corresponding area, and shook her head to dispel the sensation. She had seen Victor half-clad, changing for his act as he talked to her—he too had that ridge, not so prominent under his silky biscuit-coloured skin.

Bella came crowding into Clover's corner, dressed in her saucy hotel uniform, an extra row of frills sprucing up her black serge skirt. Up next, East and Verrall squeezed in too, East blowing good-luck kisses to Clover and Bella and Verrall with great abandon. With no Julius, they had re-vamped the hotel sketch to lean more heavily on their own banter, and

Bella was to come on later, to apply for a job. She and Clover watched East and Verrall begin with their own kind of classical indentation: two clerks who had worked the same shift for too long.

> VERRALL: I'm afraid I'm going to leave you, East. I've
>   found the love of my life.
> EAST: But can she do this? *(turning a triple pirouette while
>   snapping fingers)*
> VERRALL: Well, yes, she can—she's a Spanish dancer.
> EAST: *Can she bake a cherry pie, Verrall boy, Verrall boy?*
>   *Can she bake a cherry pie, charming Verrall?*
> VERRALL: Well, East, but neither can you.
> EAST: But, Verrall, I could *learn.*

Then Bella pranced on, after a quick kiss from Clover, to apply for the job soon to be left vacant by Verrall. Her eyes danced like her feet—any hotel would have been glad to have her on the front desk. But of course East wanted no one but Verrall, and was determined to make things difficult for her.

> BELLA: I've come for the job you advertised in the
>   paper.
> EAST: Have you had any experience?
> BELLA: *(biting her lip and confessing)* Once a fellow got me
>   out in a car. He told me he ran out of gas . . .

Verrall kept dodging out of the restaurant to report on kitchen disasters, each worse than the last ('The chef backed into the meat grinder and got a little behind in his work . . .'), causing some in the audience to groan, and others to convulse with pleasure. 'One important thing I've learned in the kitchens,' Verrall told Bella, earnestly. 'Time flies like an arrow; fruit flies like a banana.'

During the sketch, Clover watched the slack-rope for the Ioleen Sisters being set up in three. The sisters walked back and forth along the rope, testing and retesting. They were like Amazons, Clover thought, their harsh Australian voices only adding to that impression. They wore lots of glitter but very little cloth, and in the blue backstage light they glowed.

But it was time to go down to the dressing room. Aurora would need help with her hair and her nerves. Clover did not wait for Bella to flounce offstage, but trotted down to find Aurora in a dreadful state, bone-white, very still, an occasional shudder passing through her body. Clover knew she had not eaten. She pulled out a folded napkin to give Aurora a torn bit of Mrs. Hillier's homemade bread. Aurora turned her head away, shutting her eyes, but Clover persisted. 'Once *The Casting Couch* is done, you will feel easier,' she said.

Aurora nodded. She was not dressed, but had her Miss Sylvia costume half-on, bodice and sleeves folded down and protected with a light towel. Her makeup was done, but she looked tired and listless. Clover set to work quieting Aurora's nerves.

The Play Unfolding   Flora sat out front with Mayhew to watch the second half. She did not entirely enjoy the melodrama, seeing herself as Sylvia's aged and foolish mother. In lieu of Sybil, the part was now played by the violinist Alberick Heatherton's maiden aunt, formerly on the legitimate; Flora *had* wondered whether Mayhew might ask her to do it herself, but Miss Heatherton got the nod.

Flora watched the little play unfolding, her hands nervously twisting in her lap. She had a band of pressure in her head and eyes, and often these days felt her heart pounding unexpectedly. As it pounded now, watching Aurora pleading with Malverley for her virtue. East was a devilish mimic, and had put something of Mayhew into his walk, even his voice. Flora hoped Mayhew would not notice—people often did not see themselves in caricature. It was cruel, and in any case inaccurate. Nobody had ever made Aurora do anything she did not want to do.

MALVERLEY: It is entirely your own fault for enflaming
me, Sylvia—my heart has been yours since first
setting eyes on you. Let me call you—my Own.
SYLVIA: *(blushing)* Oh, sir! Please, sir! Unhand me!
MALVERLEY: *(aside)* She maddens me! But her *beaux yeux*
will not make me *marry* her . . .

But he *had* married her. It was a kind of triumph, Flora supposed, to have her daughter so well settled. The bothersome pressure behind her eyes made them prone to seeping. She dabbed at the wetness and smiled, as Sylvia and her mother confounded Malverley's malevolence with a neat bit of foolery.

Now there was only the foppish violin to endure, and then it would be her dear girls, bursting upon the audience in all their loveliness.

Little Bird　　Backstage, Bella stood in the wings behind the violinist Alberick Heatherton, the handsomest boy she had ever seen. Mercurial wings of dark hair swept above the most romantic brow, the darkest and most haunted eyes. She could feel something straining in her chest, like a bird struggling to be free—she must be in love, she thought. She had watched him rehearse that morning, lost in a passionate dream of playing, swaying alone onstage, hairs flying wildly off his ferocious bow. He was so lonely, so sad—and his aunt, playing Sylvia's aged mother in the melodrama, was a dried-up prune with no understanding of the artistic temperament, prone to scold.

Her heart squeezing, Bella stepped closer to Alberick and put a hand on his sleeve, meaning to wish him good luck.

'Don't!' he exclaimed in a fierce whisper. 'I must not be touched!'

'Oh!' she breathed. 'I am sorry.'

He stared at her, all the fervour of his glare bent in hatred. 'Do you know who I am?'

'Of course! I only meant—'

She broke off. The stage manager had held up a hand to still their voices. Alberick hissed, his face jutting close to hers, 'Don't *mean* anything! Don't come near me!'

Goodness. Bella swallowed, even that sounding loud. She nodded, not wanting him to have an utter tantrum, and backed away and out to the stairs. He was not romantic at all, but had something wrong with him, she thought.

Aurora came dashing offstage and hurried Bella in front of her. 'Quick, quick! Oh quick!' she cried in a quiet panic. 'You are not dressed!'

Bella ran.

No Veil Between Them

In the applause that followed the violinist, Clover shifted from foot to foot, her lovely new slippers not quite broken-in to comfort yet. Aurora was pale but calmer; Bella (rushed into costume and pinked-up quickly in the cheeks) irrepressible but stoppered, like a shaken ginger-beer bottle. Clover let herself rest within their arms for an instant. They would be all right—headlining only differed from opening by how warm the audience was, how willing to be happy. She wished Gentry could be here to see them.

The music began, *Florian's Song*. Hands clutched, on they went, right foot first, in the chain-step of the village maidens, '*Ah, s'il est dans votre village . . .*' The backdrop was charming and they were charming, and the audience was led into the French countryside. When the dirndl skirts flew off as they went round a maypole, and they transformed into Moulin Rouge petticoat girls with that funny-sad song *Mon Homme*, the crowd went there too. Clover and Aurora slid off stage left, where Mama was waiting for them with their quick change into the *Lakmé* costumes. They could look over their shoulders, in between ducking and fastening, to see Bella still translating *Mon Homme*, making it both sadder and funnier than she ever had before, maintaining a hint of a French accent in the English version.

'Two or three girls has he that he likes as well as me
But I love him!
I don't know why I should—he isn't true—he beats me, too—
What can I do?'

She will be very good someday, Clover thought, letting Mama swing the pearl-beaded *Lakmé* dress over her tiny hoop. She already is!

Bella drooped off stage right, betrayed and downtrodden but with some inexhaustible sprig of optimism still springing in her gait, and the lights swirled through a transformation.

Scrim forest-panels descended to the cello-swoops of Delibes, and revealed a Brahmin princess and her maid-servant, gathering flowers and singing the interweaving, looping, many-petalled duet—Aurora finally at rest on the wings of this absurdly pretty song, Clover happy to serve her: the two of them able to sing to each other with no veil between them, as there had been ever since the wedding night.

'Sous le dôme épais où le blanc jasmin,
Ah! descendons ensemble!'

Their voices, sweeter in tandem than they could ever be apart, twined on as they descended, together, together . . . The flowering lights dimmed, and the audience took that priceless moment to pause and remember, and then broke into a wave of applause.

As the wave went on and on, the girls were rushed back onstage for another bow, all three of them—they had no encore ready, and in the fluster of the moment did not dare return to one of their non-French old favourites in case Mayhew might disapprove, so they merely bowed again, apologetically, and danced off, and the pictures began.

A conquest, Mayhew declared. He appeared in their dressing-room doorway within minutes of the final curtain, bearing in one hand a bottle of champagne, and in the other silver-wrapped boxes for each of the girls.

Mama came close behind him, weeping a little with the excitement—her girls, their first night as headliners! She admired the pretty coral beads that Bella pulled out of her box, and the pearls curled in Clover's, and gasped at Aurora's box: diamonds set in small flower clusters, pretty as falling water when Mayhew clasped the necklace round Aurora's neck.

The crowd descended, and Mayhew drew Aurora out into the hall to meet some of her admirers, pressure on her elbow indicating the more important of the pressmen.

Clover turned back to her mirror to steel herself to follow, and found a long parcel on the dressing table, marked with her name. Another present from Mayhew? Then she saw the sender's address: San Francisco. Inside, scribbled in Victor's jagged hand: *Only a fiddle, made by a Métis in Montana, they tell me, but it has a sweet true voice. Like you.* She folded back the velvet that cradled the violin, and gazed at its chestnut glow. Then wrapped it, quickly, before anyone else could see.

An Honest Charm

The papers in the morning were as fulsome as the night's admirers. *The Herald's* man reported that the entire bill made for a red-letter week at the Starland. Aurora read aloud that article, which hailed Mayhew as a bona fide New York producer, a boon to the city's artistic life. One reviewer called East & Verrall's hotel sketch 'horseplay and low comedy, which everybody wants at least once on a vaudeville bill; people laughed until they were ashamed of themselves.' East & Verrall were used to good notices. But it was new for the girls, basking in the parlour at Mrs. Hillier's (where Aurora and Mayhew had moved into a double front room), to read about themselves:

> The newest sensation on the vaudeville circuit, *Les Très Belles Aurores de Nouvelle France*, have an honest charm about them. Musical modesty, refined and accurate, without strain or artifice, gives their vocal acrobatics warmth without ever succumbing to egoism. The charming dual-language rendition of *Mon Homme*, a Mistinguett cabaret favourite, will

remain with this reviewer. Two of the sisters gave us
the finely executed *Flower Duet* from *Lakmé*, accompanied by a pleasing Oriental dance, with fragrant hints
of musical exoticism.

Miss Aurora Avery's performance was crucial to
the success of the playlet. The melodrama *The Casting
Couch* is an examination of innocence. The production
was not laden with excessive emotion or elaborate
gestures, offering simplicity, grace and directness.

And now, Aurora thought, they had to do it all again.

Men of Vision

As it turned out, the climax to their
Starland time came sooner than
expected. After little more than a
week, the consortium that ran the Starland out of Winnipeg sent their
Mr. Cocklington to inspect the operations. He congratulated Mayhew
on his management and foresight, and paid extravagant compliments
to Aurora. The praise continued through a lavish dinner and both
evening performances—lasting in fact until Mr. Cocklington came
back next morning, after having spent the night at the Palliser Hotel
poring over the ledgers.

At which point Mayhew and Mr. Cocklington closeted themselves
in the manager's office, and the shouts began.

Mayhew slammed back to Mrs. Hillier's before the women left for
the theatre and warned Aurora—as an introduction to his topic—not
to take over to the theatre any costumes or accoutrements she didn't
mind losing when the locks were changed.

Aurora stood stock-still in the parlour, one glove on and one off.
She saw how quietly Clover set her violin case behind the sofa, and the
way Mama sat down, holding her side and breathing very shallowly as
if at a sudden cramp. Bella crouched beside Mama, fingers crammed
firmly into her mouth.

It's a long time since we've been at the mercy of a man's temper, Aurora thought, surprised at the thought. She looked at Mayhew, searching for signs that he was worth it.

Mayhew prowled round the room, laying it out against the Cocklingtons' cowardly, penny-pinching ways, beginning with a controlled disquisition on Smallness of Outlook and Mishandling of Opportunity but soon descending to diatribe and invective, until Mama put her fingers tight into her ears.

'Men of vision is what modern vaudeville requires!' he shouted, so loudly that Mrs. Hillier came to the parlour door. Seeing him in a rage she backed away again, but she gave Aurora a grimace of sympathy and stayed behind the door in case she might be needed.

'Had the opacity to question my management decisions,' Mayhew cried, banging his hat down on the card table in the centre of the parlour. 'I can't be overseen by a chump! You don't get an enterprise off the ground without expense of the most rudipentary, and who is he to question what is paid out? The door receipts, *that's* his business! And my only argument!'

He crashed the lid of the piano down as he went past. Aurora remained silent, and so did the others, although Aurora could see Bella biting down hard on her hand not to let that laugh burst out.

The echoing bang of the piano lid seemed to give Mayhew some relief. He took up a pose by the fireplace, stared into the middle distance for a moment, and said in a grave, reasonable tone, 'I've cabled Winnipeg and Duluth. They will rescind this pup's admonishments, but it's too late for that. We'll take the high road and head out of here on Monday—work out the week so as not to leave bad feeling behind us, that is never good policy. Arriving a few weeks earlier in Edmonton will suit my plans very well.'

Mayhew pulled East & Verrall off the Starland bill as well, insisting that *The Casting Couch* required them and could not be remounted with new actors, and producing their contract, which held them to his production company, rather than to the Starland. Standard practice, he assured Aurora, and only the petty incompetence and lack of true vaudeville experience caused the ire of the Starland types.

That ire extended on Mr. Cocklington's part to talk of 'papers being served'—whatever that might mean—and led to a buzz of scandal among the vaudeville people in all the theatres. When Mayhew took the girls to luncheon at the Palliser on Sunday, a steady stream of newsmen and producers visited their table, bewailing their impending departure or prodding Mayhew for more information.

Aurora held her breath when the first plump producer came to the table with a jolly laugh and a sting in his conversation's tail. But Mayhew had had his flash of temper and was perfectly urbane, dismissing the curious and the comforting alike with a laugh. 'My interests in Edmonton proceed apace,' he told the pressmen, genially. 'It's the City of Tomorrow, and I aim to be top of the heap up there.'

Aurora could not help but applaud his resilience. She'd expected him to stay in a temper for days after this new setback.

'Happens all the time,' he told her. 'All we need is a free hand, free rein—and that's what we're going to have at the Muse. Besides, we're no worse off for a couple of weeks' receipts from the Starland. Calgary is a terrible one-horse town, I've always hated it,' he said, glaring out the window at the broad expanse of 9th Avenue, empty on a Sunday of anything but his car, left parked on the dusty street, and a single lonely wagon.

The Pierce-Arrow shone in the sunlight, hungry for the open road again, even if it was heading farther north.

INTERMISSION

7.
North Pole

SEPTEMBER–OCTOBER 1914

The Muse, Edmonton

Always leave the audience wanting a little bit more, but by all means take your share without overdoing it, as you will find at times some audiences that seem frozen to their seats with a North Pole expression to their faces.

FREDERICK LADELLE, *HOW TO ENTER VAUDEVILLE*

September in Edmonton—sixteen months they'd been stuck in this North Pole city. The streetcar ran through backyards on its way to the High Level Bridge, as they rode home from the Muse after the matinee. Bella and Clover liked to stand along this stretch, ready for the dizzying view off the top of the bridge.

Aurora sat with hands clasped in her lap. Overgrown rhubarb reached up rusty fluted leaves to the car window; small leaves shifting on the city's spindly trees were tinged with yellow. Everything was aging, turning back to winter. It made Aurora want to leap up and run south.

But you don't run from the lap of luxury. Fitz had moved them out of the King Edward Hotel (last June, when things began to run tight at the Muse), but the Arlington Apartments were luxury too, the newest and best in the city. The very desirable top floor, riverside corner, for their own suite; a separate apartment for Mama and the girls, two floors down, so they were not living in each other's pockets. Bella took great delight in the Murphy bed in their suite's parlour, swivel-flipping out of its shining mahogany pocket like Long Chak Sam's conjurer's boxes; her pleasure made Aurora happy. Pretty kitchenettes let them do for themselves, at least breakfast and cups of tea. Aurora had caught herself resenting it when Fitz told her to have eggs and bacon on hand, and then laughed to think how quickly she could progress from fearing for their lives and dining on bread-and-milk—if at all—to being too fancy to cook an egg.

Fitz was not often in for breakfast these days. He was busy doing the rounds of the other theatres, wooing backers and the press with all his might. The Muse was teetering, although her sisters and Mama were not to know that. Aurora could not bear Mayhew to fail again, at another theatre, with no one else to blame.

The streetcar jolted, coming round the tunnel for the run across the bridge—Aurora did not like it. And did not like that she did not like it. Stupid to feel so low in the belly as the car swung. A daring dash across a chasm was just what she used to love; now she was mouse-like, tremulous, squelched and afraid, hiding in Mayhew's big fur coat.

She thought of Lady Conan Doyle, who had been like this, yielding to her man. A natural-enough pliancy, but it chafed Aurora somehow. When the Conan Doyles had visited Edmonton a few months ago, also staying at the King Edward, Mayhew (who'd been unable to get a leg in when Sarah Bernhardt was in town) had arranged a dinner for Sir Arthur, whom he had met in London years before and wanted to cultivate. It had been a difficult evening for Aurora, and for Mama and Clover too; even for Bella, who had sulked for days after Mayhew refused to let her attend. War was imminent—was declared a few weeks after—but Sir Arthur had talked of nothing but suffragettes, how they put all thinking men out of patience and would never get the vote. An insufferable man. Especially beside Mayhew, always on top of the joke. If she was older, she would be an equal partner with him, not a—a concubine.

Aurora had not despised Lady Conan Doyle for being a chattel until she'd leaned across the table to confide in a stage whisper that her husband was 'quite silly when she was about.' Sir Arthur had stretched his hand across the table, declaring with a sentimental smirk that she had been a wonderful companion to him. 'Not one clouded or grey moment since we started from England!' (Unlike the suffragettes, who must be down-pouring regular monsoons on *their* husbands, Clover had said, when she and Aurora left the table to tidy their hair.)

Delightful, Aurora reminded herself, to be in company with the great men of the world. To wear a fur collar to one's coat. To take the streetcar as a treat, an outing, rather than as the only way to get about.

To eat. Although she had no great appetite these days.

Clover saw Aurora's white face, and let down the upper window for a breath of autumn air as the car came out into the light, out of the coal-dust smell in the tunnel. Up the trundling incline, then out onto the beautiful iron height of the bridge, lost in air between the two high banks the river had cut through the city. There were the old fort palings, the tiny clustered houses along the riverbank, and rising up from that the fine built-up city. Clover loved cities. The pale provincial buildings (the pattern of civilization, exactly like Helena's capitol building) hid the Arlington, but over the bald stretch of hill she could see the water tower, even the edge of the *Journal* building, where the man painted the day's headlines on the bricks each morning.

At the end of June, Clover and Bella had stood in the street watching the *Journal* man on his ladder, painting WAR DECLARED. And now there were soldiers in the streets, and you could hear shots and the shouts of them training, and already audiences had fallen off; every time a new shipment of soldiers left, the house emptied by another row of seats. Clover remembered the crowd watching the painter, more and more people stopping as they saw the word WAR. There had been sighing and cheering, except for one foolish old man who moaned and held his jaw with the toothache of patriotism.

She and Bella had been on their way from the King Edward to mail a letter to Victor, whose latest letter, from the Pantages Theatre in Cincinnati, she held tight-folded in her hand now. She knew it by heart already.

> I am a pacifist, as are all followers of Galichen. But
> it is hard to bear—hearing wild rumours, not knowing
> what is true. With his usual contrariness, Gali tells my
> mother he can help me into the London Territorials,
> having some pull. I will work out my remaining tour
> dates till Christmas but I feel an urgency to be there.
> I know those fields very well from childhood.
>   The Fabians say, for the right moment you must
> wait . . . but when the right moment comes you must strike
> hard. It is not that I sentimentalize the politics, or feel a
> patriot pull, but on the ground, in the towns I knew in

Belgium and France, people are in dire need—and I am strong and wily. If I cannot help, who can?

Clover, I must enlist.

I will make my way back to London after Christmas.

But before then I will find my way to you, my heart.

Clover wished she had not opened the letter. It was not real, anyway, the war—Mayhew said it would be over very soon: posturing in Europe, not to be indulged. Even thinking about it felt false and romantic. A little fanfare of tin bugles.

Bella returned from talking to the driver, strolling back along the car as it ran forward, feeling she was walking in air because she was so high-transported above the river. That would be Life, if she could ride the streetcar all day long like the driver did, and wear a nice little uniform! But girls could not be streetcar drivers or train drivers, could only prune-and-prism, pout and marry well, or be schoolteachers (which Mama had made them promise they would never be, considering how Papa was treated by the superintendents, who never appreciated his learning or his temperament); or else get out of all that and go on the boards—and marry anyway, like Aurora had.

But she herself would not marry very soon, Bella thought. The Ninepins were at the Muse this month, and she saw Nando every day, but even if she was old enough and he wanted to, his father would never let him marry. And Nando could not abandon the act, because then who would look after his mother? It was too bad that Joe Dent would not let her train for knockabout, because she thought she might do very well with it. She was as clumsy as anything, always falling down or tripping. It was good for comedy. Sadly, East and Verrall were out in Winnipeg; she missed them very much, especially since they were working on the golf sketch again, which was really about love and had many gags for her.

She snugged in beside Clover, slipping an arm around her waist, and was surprised to get a tight hug back from her. Clover tucked her letter away and pulled Bella back to sit on her knee beside Aurora, lacing fingers over Aurora's the way they both liked. The three of them together in one seat was comforting to Bella, who had not even known she was sad—but this was a dreadfully boring life, staying in one place for so long. The air was cold over the river; she would be glad of the brisk walk to the Arlington. Where Mama would be lying tangled in the blankets on the Murphy bed, dead to the world.

Mama had taken to missing matinees lately; she drank endless cups of tea, laced with a little sherry for her throat, that wavered into a smudged nap. Clover and Bella had the bedroom to themselves; Mama often stayed in bed till they came back to make her supper, the drapes left pulled across in the parlour for an all-day twilight that seemed to ease her head. Without meaning to, Bella thought, she and Clover were keeping that from Aurora. It was just that Aurora usually went straight up to her own suite when they got home, so Clover and Bella would rouse Mama and help her put her stockings on and make herself presentable before they all had to leave again for the evening show. There wasn't much time to rest. She had her bee-wings with her in the bag at Aurora's feet, because she had ripped a long tear in one. Mama would have to mend it before Mayhew sent the car for them at 6:15.

The Melee

The Muse's current bill, a short one, opened with the Novelli Brothers, tumbling twin violinists who were the antithesis of the Tusslers. Fey little men, they rolled and caracoled like two bits of chestnut-fluff on a zephyr. As the Novellis came running off-stage, Clover would duck behind the curtain-leg to evade the delicate sweat that sprayed off their foreheads, arms and heaving chests. She had never seen men so watery before. They played their violins with precise joy even while tumbling. When the first twin had heard her playing Victor's violin as he climbed the stairs past the girls' dressing room, he'd offered to play with her from time to time. 'To make a practice go more pleasing,' he said—by which Clover knew that she was not playing well enough. She was willing to be schooled. Novelli the Elder showed her

how to allow her fingers fall over the neck to let strings sing more silk-
ily, to make the notes fly crisp from one perch to another, no flailing in
between. He was involved only in music and never offered the least
effrontery; nor did Novelli the Younger. She'd have thought them nancy-
boys, if she had not had East's word on it that they spent all their money
at a fleabag whorehouse farther south into the boondocks.

Professor OK Griffith, Hypnotist, came next. Clover thought him
the strangest man! A round, buglike body supported on slender legs;
delicate feet, the toes of his shoes curling upward. Offstage, the
Professor sported a blue swallowtail coat, a vest of white duck stretched
across his wide body, and trousers of fawn-coloured plush—like a river-
boat gamester from the late century. For the stage, he donned a scholar's
gown of glistening silk, opening over a striped vest. His round black
eyes popped more than was strictly usual, but the expression on the
Professor's face was never unpleasant.

Suggestion was OK's first great trick. He suggested to the audience
that only the highly intelligent were susceptible to hypnotism, which
made them all wish to be susceptible. Reading people well was his
second: he could spot lonely women and gullible men a mile away, and
the ones looking for any excuse to cluck like a chicken.

Mayhew said the act stank of snake-oil, and was not intending to bring
him back to the Muse. Besides, he had lost a painful amount of money to
OK, playing poker one evening. Not a smart move on OK Griffith's part,
Clover thought. But perhaps he had read Mayhew, found him unsuggest-
ible, and already knew he would not be booked again at the Muse.

Bella came to coax Clover out of the wings before the end of OK,
to watch the Ninepins from the projection booth, which Clover knew
was her secret hideaway—the booth was empty till late in the second
half, when the projectionist would come with his oil can and prayer-
book. The projection machinery was ticklish.

Nando always blew a lavish kiss up to Bella, which the girls in the
balcony believed was coming to them. Twenty little arms would shoot up
into the air, but Bella turned her face to the light and caught it smack upon
her cheek. Clover would have worried about her except that Nando was

tremendously well behaved, and under his father's bloodshot eye near every minute of the day. Mrs. Dent was so sweet and weak, she could have used a girl about. If Bella had been eighteen, Clover thought, she'd have been off with the Knockabout Ninepins in a flash, taking her knocks as a fourth member of their troupe. Joe Dent would not take her until then.

But Joe might not last that long. Tonight he was struggling through their act. The Ninepins were working these days with a breakaway wall, spring-hinged windows and doors, and a couple of hidden spring-boards, all of which seemed to be nipping at Joe's heels. Nando said you had to be wide awake, or the scenery would spank some sense into you. When they were first setting up, he sat beside them and described everything: 'And that rotating thing there is the paraturn, of course . . .'

Clover bit. 'What's a paraturn?'

'About two bits an hour, if he's got good references.'

He made her laugh even more than East and Verrall.

In their *A Good Night Out* number, Nando and his father were two burglars in dark suits and half-masks, wild fake hair escaping from dark cloth caps. Each scaled the wall for separate nefarious purposes, scrambling over the bricks as if it were horizontal instead of vertical. Nando tumbled out through an upper window, Joe through a bottom—they collided—and the chase was on. Just as the schtick was getting a little familiar, Mrs. Dent appeared from a hidden alcove with a board, whacked Nando, and vanished again. Next time Joe went by, her arm snaked out and whacked *him* one. Clover always loved that, when Mrs. Dent got one in on Joe. Nando and Joe, each thinking the other had hit him, went for each other and fought in and out the windows. The business was repeated with a bucket of water—but just as Joe kicked Nando out the bottom window, both of them sopping wet, they spotted Mrs. Dent at the top with the bucket and realized she had done it.

Then the music picked up wildly and all three of them were in and out the doors and windows like mice or snakes. In the melee, Joe caught Mrs. Dent a good clip on the side of her head with his lump-filled burglar sack (*clang!* from the cymbals) that whooshed her in through the bottom window in a heap, and gave a terrible clout to Nando (*clang!*) that sent him flying ten feet straight up into the upper window. For an instant Joe stood victorious on the stage. Then Nando and Mrs. Dent flew back to the attack, and the fight was on again, in and out and up and down. Clover got dizzy watching—like a shell game, she had no idea who was where.

The music blared, and all three of them emerged from the same upper window, stuck fast, stuck—till their pounding caused the whole wall to collapse in a cloud of white chalk dust. The cloud hung for a minute, then the three of them emerged for a bow, in whiteface rather than blackface, coughing and wheezing. Even back in the booth, where they could not possibly hear her, Clover clapped like mad.

Down to Twelve

Bella slipped out of the booth and dashed back round the theatre in the cool night air, to help Nando towel off the white dust from his act. She didn't like that dust; it made Nando cough. Behind the curtain stagehands were busy with wet mops while the audience exploded into noise and swelled out into the lobby and the street for a breath of air. Bella examined Nando for bruises and cuts, as she always did, and he laughed and showed his unmarked face, saying, 'You should see the other fella.'

Joe was mopping himself down in a fairly good humour. It wasn't till after the show and back at the hotel that he became difficult. His excessive energy could be useful: the first place the Ninepins had stayed in south Edmonton had burned down—Joe had got them all out, and went back to get other tenants out too. When he came out of his berserker mood later, on the smoking grass, they saw the one treasure he'd managed to save from their luggage: a bar of soap. It was their third boarding-house fire, Nando said, and each time his father had saved a bar of soap. He was good in an emergency but a terrible fellow for ordinary life.

At the dressing table, Myra Dent pulled a washcloth over her face and stared blankly into the mirror. Myra still had a girlish figure, high breasts and slim waist, but her face was cut so deep in sad lines that it seemed she could not smile. Nando was not much of a smiler either. Only

Joe: big teeth grinning in his round face, little eyes stalking round the room for something to get mad at.

A knock on the door, and there was Fitz Mayhew, just the ticket.

'What were you doing a-standing there offstage like that?' Joe shouted, going from his self-satisfied hum to rage in a winking. 'Puts me off! It's dangerous!'

'Timing you,' Mayhew said. 'Seventeen minutes, Joe.'

'We've never gone over fifteen in our lives!'

Bella and Nando and Mrs. Dent all seeped back into the walls, white into whitewash, as Joe swelled and darkened with rage.

'Well, you're going down to twelve, tomorrow. Figure what to cut, and I'll see you at the band call at eleven.'

'You can't cut us! Who do you think you fecking are?'

'I'm the bloody boss around here, that's who. Cut to twelve, or you're cut for good.'

You had to hand it to Mayhew for laying down the law, Bella thought. He stayed steady even while Joe came at him, though Joe outweighed him by fifty pounds and was known as a scrapper. Mayhew's cigar came pointing out, that's all: 'Don't press me, Joe. I won't take guff from a drunk. You'll end up in the tank tonight if I have to call for help.'

'I'm not drunk!'

'If you were, you'd be fired.'

For a moment it seemed that Joe would jump Mayhew, and Bella felt Nando tense beside her. But he subsided, slumping his shoulders back down, turning his head from side to side. 'After a show, medicinal purposes only,' Joe said. 'Have one with me then, Fitzie.'

Mayhew smiled then, never one to say no to a shot himself. He took the glass from Joe and knocked it back. 'You watch it,' he said, still smiling. 'You've got a reputation for precision. Don't want to sully that.'

There was something about Mayhew that Bella found unsettling, lately. He was reckless in some ways, and acted unpredictably. Perhaps Aurora could predict him. Bella shivered and gave Nando a smearing kiss before she dashed off to her own dressing room, one flight down.

Far, Far Away   To revamp their number, and against their protests, Mayhew had insisted that they do *The Rosary*, which he called French on grounds of its sheer Catholicism. They obeyed, but with shame. Gentry had been entirely right to disdain it. '*Oh, how I hate this tawdry song,*' Aurora sang softly, as the intro ran on, turning her cheek into the light and making her throat into a silver funnel for false and holy prettiness. Clover hid a laugh. Mayhew would not let them sing it at anything approaching a bearable tempo, so they were forced to moo slightly.

> '*The hours I spent with Thee, Dear Heart!*
> *Are as a string of pearls to me,*
> *I count them over, every one apart,*
> *My rosary, my rosary!*'

'*My Gent-a-ry, My Gent-a-ry!*' Bella sang for Clover's ears only. '*O King of excellent taste, we loved you so.*' Funny that Bella would remember Gentry with such fondness; she was always asking for news of him, from any artistes who'd been out east. Not that they ever heard much; he had disappeared into retirement like a bear into a cave—but, Clover thought (stepping sedately through '*to still a heart in absence wrung . . .*'), they would have heard if he had died.

At last, *My Rosary* over, they processed mournfully offstage to a tiresome sprinkle of applause from the saps who actually liked the song.

The girls crowded back into the wings stage right to peel off their vestal-white gowns and scamper into their second costumes, low-cut waltz-length gowns with flower wreaths round the neck for the sappy *L'Air Printemps*. Mama adjusted the wreaths and they flew out, one-two-three: fifteen seconds in all.

They pas-de-trois'd Muse-like round and round, again feeling the energy leaking out of the act. The city was tired of them, and no wonder, after sixteen months. Clover and Aurora moved through a tricky series of arabesques while Bella danced off to get into her bumble-bee wings; they wafted into the ether of spring, the music metamorphosed, and Bella came clumping on in her bee costume: a comedy no matter how you tweaked the wings.

> *'Be my little baby bumble bee*
> *(Buzz around, buzz around, keep a-buzzin' 'round) . . .'*

Nothing fazes Bella, Clover thought, watching from the darkness. Bella's plump bosom filled up the stripey dress so nicely. Clover's own chest was two separate little teacups, but Bella had turned out almost upholstered, her rounded robin's front very appealing.

> *'Let me spend the happy hours*
> *Roving with you 'mongst the flow'rs*
> *And when we get where no one else can see*
> *(Cuddle up, cuddle up, cuddle up) . . .'*

There she went, flirting with the men in the first row of the balcony. Every few steps she'd hop-sidle, in sweet imitation of a bee landing on a flower clump. Mama had tried to infuse this dance with a bit more grace but had thrown up her hands in the end and told Bella to dance it her own way.

> *'I've got a dozen cousin bees*
> *But I want you, to be my baby bumble bee!'*

The stage manager, Teddy, grinned as he watched Bella, showing tiny upper teeth in a very even row, so that they looked as if they might have been filed off. He was decent and kind, as they had come to know, but Clover could never feel entirely easy with him. She waited till he'd turned his back before slipping her *Spring* dress off, and the *Per Valli* costume on, over her head.

Per Valli was her favourite song in the world, Clover had decided. It was Italian, not French, but Mayhew hadn't seemed to notice.

Perfect to sing with Aurora, whose lovely high register had got better and better while working with Gentry, and ever since, continued to put his lessons to use. Clover dashed across the dark stage behind the second drop, and slowed her breathing in time to enter as Bella bumbled off, taking advantage of the wave of applause the audience always gave her bee-costume and general odour of honey-sweetness.

The audience settled in the dark, seeing Aurora and Clover reappear. *Another damn song,* you could almost hear them thinking. But they would like this.

'*Per valli,*' Aurora called.

'*Per boschi,*' Clover answered, and they were off.

The song went over valleys and forests, searching for the beloved, Clover singing the darker second line and searching in her heart for where Victor might be, going through his calendar in her mind's eye. September 30, Cincinnati to St. Louis.

> '*Dimando di lei*
> *I call for him*
> *ogn' aura tacendo*
> *out of the silent air*
> *ogn' aura piangendo*
> *out of the weeping air*
> *sen passa da me?*
> *whither has he gone?*'

She sang for Victor. For whom did Aurora sing? Not Mayhew, watching in his box. For Gentry; or perhaps for Jimmy Battle, who was far, far away, under the aegis of Eleanor Masefield. Maybe she sang for Papa, and Harry. Or only for the idea of gone.

> '*Sweet echo replyeth, he is far, far away . . .*'

What Vicissitudes   Next morning, before it was light, Flora woke from a feverish vision and lay still, piecing together the dream: the empty house, bees clustering at the eyes of the dead woman, a policeman coming up the step: it seemed she was being lied to.

She moved her head, away from the dawn bleaching the window.

About Arthur, as always. But this was the Arlington. There was no one lying on the front walk, eyes staring at the ground. Arthur was a skeleton now, in his cold earth in Paddockwood, and Harry beside him ... The police had wanted in the front door but she wouldn't let them enter in the afternoon, so they came back in the evening and there was a little blood by the back door, and the bees.

No, that was from the dream, not from life. Bees meant a secret and death. The police: a secret, and possibly death. Blood, oddly, could be a journey.

She shook her head to dispel the fog, and wished Mayhew had not ordered the third bottle of wine at supper. A kind and generous host, no matter what vicissitudes. She fell asleep again.

Cheats and Whores   Later, the rasping apartment bell twisted and twisted. After a minute there was a rapping knock, then more twisting. It was ten, but only Clover was properly up—Bella was still in her nightgown, stirring scrambled eggs. At first Clover thought they should ignore what must be a peddler or the brush-man—unless it could be Aurora, needing milk for morning tea? Clover put her eye to the peephole and then stood back on her heels. After an instant she tiptoed backwards down the hall to the kitchen.

'Sybil and Julius!' she told Bella, who popped her eyes wide open and glanced round the kitchen at the truly dreadful mess they'd let build up since the maid had last been. Clover dodged into the parlour, where Mama lay tangled in blankets on the Murphy bed.

'Mama!' she whispered. 'It is Sybil at the door. And Julius!'

Mama opened one eye, then the other. Clover could see her trying to focus.

Then Mama jumped out of bed, flung the bedclothes towards the centre, shoved the Murphy bed back up into its niche and dashed for the bathroom, snatching her wrapper and a tangled assortment of sewing notions from the chair as she ran. 'Wait, just wait!' she whispered, and whisked the door shut, opening it again to release the sash of her wrapper. Her wild eye showed through the crack, and she nodded.

Clover opened the apartment door. 'Why, hello!' she said. 'Dear ma'am, dear sir—how pleasant to see you after this long while!'

'Yes, you'd think so! Sixteen months, as I count,' Sybil said, biting the words out. Her face was pinched and strange, not at all her eager, unsquashable self. She drew back her upper lip to display tight-clenched teeth. Julius looked at the ceiling.

Bella came from the kitchen, where she had been bundling dirty dishes quietly into the oven. She had tied a bib apron over her nightgown, and her feet were crammed into Clover's other shoes. 'Julius!' she cried, giving him a warm embrace; she turned to Sybil, but stopped in time.

'We are here to see Flora, *if* you please,' Sybil said, frost sharp in her voice and face.

The girls fell back and Clover showed their guests into the parlour. There they all stood awkwardly. The Murphy bed's rise had left the room disordered. Clover flicked the carpet into place and adjusted the armchair and the small table by the window. She opened the drapes to let in pale autumn sun.

Nobody spoke; there was only the wheeze of Julius breathing.

Then Mama was at the door, her hair tidied, girdle snug and everything dainty about her, as if she'd never had a bad night in her life. 'Dear Syb! And Julius,' she cried, her hands outstretched as she came forward. 'Here you are in cold old Edmonton, what a pleasure!'

Sybil tittered. 'Yes, here we are, back again like a bad penny. *Two* bad pennies!' Clover saw her eyes dart over Mama, taking in the new lace-point collar, the dove kid slippers peeping out under the silk morning-gown wrapper—noting, no doubt, the undeniable air of prosperity. 'We *thought* you would find it a pleasure,' Sybil said. The splotches of colour on her cheeks worried Clover.

Julius shambled to the single armchair and settled his bulk. One eyebrow waggled. Enjoying himself, Clover thought, the old scallywag. She sent Bella for more chairs.

'Got your address from Teddy Vickers at the Muse. We ourselves are staying at Mrs. Springer's, where the food is very decent—very. Performing later this week, Professor Konigsburg's Ventri-lectricity—at the Princess, south of the river . . .' He subsided, at a glance from Sybil.

'They'll know where the Princess is, Julius,' she said, with the sweetest of trills. 'Even though they theirselves are at the up-tone Muse, above our touch. Took us this long to get to Edmonton, to find a theatre that would book us here, but we made it.'

Bella came back, dressed, with two wooden chairs from the kitchen. She set them carefully for the ladies, but Sybil would not sit, so neither could Mama. Clover, queasy from the excess of ire in the room, saw that Sybil's eyes showed white all round the pupils.

There was a silence.

'When we left Helena so abruptly—' Mama began, but Sybil would not let her finish.

'Swanning it pretty well up here, are you? Cats that swallowed the cream?'

Mama turned her head in distaste.

'Oh, is that too coarse for you? Too materialistic for your fine sensibility?'

'You— I don't know what you mean,' Mama said. 'I'm sorry if you—'

'*Hist!*' Sybil said sharply. 'None of that! We need no apology from you!'

Julius turned from the window, pulling his chair beneath him without troubling to lift its feet. It set up a painful screech in the suddenly silent room. 'Sybil, my dear,' he said, mild as milk. 'Can it be you harbour some rancour towards our dear Flora?'

Sybil pounced on that: 'Oh, can it be? But how should I rancourize? You and I left high and dry without a gig and without a pay packet— Mayhew having come to Jay cap in hand *that very afternoon*, to ask for the loan of a hundred to tide him over to meet payroll! Fifty dollars he got off him! And if Jay had had more in pocket, we'd have been out all that as well, sure as shooting.'

Mama put out her hand towards Sybil, who leaped back as if the hand were a hot poker. 'Oh no! Don't you come the friendly with me now. Never a word we had from you, nor from Fitz Mayhew, not that I'd have expected it from him—and Jay ought to have known better—we've had enough words over that, thank you *very* much. But no word of warning that everything was done up! How much would that have cost you?'

Mama sat down quickly on the kitchen chair, as if her knees were not obeying her.

Bella had crept forward to Clover's elbow and now tugged very slightly on her sleeve, making bulgy eyes to pull her out of this. Clover was grateful—she knew Bella herself could stand the music and if there was to be a fight would not want to miss the fireworks, but Clover was likely to faint if she was too close to the action.

'I'd like to know how you could betray me so,' Sybil continued as the girls edged away. 'That had been your friend from olden days and forward, and would have gone to the ends of the earth for you—left with egg all over my face!'

The girls had reached the doorway; Clover halted there, feeling cowardly to leave Mama alone. But Mama was rising to the attack, cheeks flushed and eyes bright as if she'd been dancing.

'I thought it was you who had your finger on all the pulses, always up to snuff, queen of the prying noses—knew anything there was to know, long before *we* knew it, Sybil Sly.'

Julius leaned back in his chair, applauding this rejoinder. 'One to the solar plexus!'

Now Mama turned on Julius: 'You introduced my daughters to Fitz Mayhew in the first place, as I recall it, you old Pander.'

Sybil milled back in. 'So we did, as a favour, and look what good it's done her! And you!'

'If you call it *good*, for her to be tied to an old goat more than twice her age. Whom you now—when it suits your story—call unscrupulous.'

In the doorway Clover clung to Bella. Thank God, she thought, Mayhew is not here to add to this. Mama waved a hand at the girls, ordering them from the room. But Clover stayed rooted to the spot, as Sybil, towering to her full five feet, jabbed her jaw forward furiously. 'I don't say he's *unscrupulous*—I say he's a damned cheat, and I'll be damned if we'll ever work with him again!'

Julius hummed, his demon tickled by this excitement. 'Well, now, my dear Syb, where would we be in vaudeville if we refused to work with cheats and whores!'

Mama turned on him in a fury. 'And who are you calling a whore?'

There was a moment of silence in the room. But Julius never backed away from a fence. 'I suppose, dear lady, that I was referring to your eldest daughter.'

Mama stared at him, her eyes dark caves, her mouth fallen off its usual line.

Sybil cracked a sudden laugh. 'You'd rather he was talking of you?'

'That's enough!' Mama dashed her hand across her eyes to clear them and advanced on Sybil, step by step. Her wrapper had come untied, Clover saw, and the slip underneath drooped, revealing her slackened chest. 'After what you did to me! *Such a good friend* in those olden days—you made trouble between me and Arthur that nearly dished me, talking to Chum as if I was no better than a trollop.'

Sybil sobbed. 'I never meant to,' she said, 'I never meant it.'

'Well, you ought to have meant *not* to! You were jealous as a cat, and you are still, and you near as nothing ruined my life.'

Sybil gave a bleat of anguish and fell to her knees.

'Do you know how hard that was to fight against?' Mama demanded. 'He never truly believed me again—his whole *life*—' She looked at Clover and Bella, seeming to see them there for the first time. Her voice cracked and her fists flew through her hair, disarranging it.

'Girls, out!' She pointed to the apartment door. 'Go to Aurora.'

They ran.

Outside in the stair-hall, Bella and Clover stood shivering, almost laughing, unable to climb the flights to Aurora and Mayhew's suite.

Bella rang the button, but the elevator banged and clanged down in the basement region.

'Whore!' Bella said, behind her hand, her eyes bright and scared.

Clover put her arm around Bella. 'Oh, fish! Any girl in vaudeville might be called that. Even in the legitimate, to some people's mind.'

'I thought he liked us!'

'Think of Mr. Tweedie in Paddockwood,' Clover said. 'Everybody had him over to supper and felt so sorry for him because he was a bachelor and a sidesman. But nobody talked to Lily Bain or even let her come to church.'

'Well, but Lily Bain went with *all* the men.'

'Why should that make a difference? All the men went with her!'

'She looked like a scrag-end of mutton.'

'And Mr. Tweedie an old goat, they were well-suited that way.'

Bella laughed. 'All those scrawny goat-kid children!'

'I don't see why when a woman does that, she's a whore. When a man does it, there's no bad name to call him.'

The elevator came trundling up at last.

The apartment door behind them opened and Julius slid out, then shut the door again on a confused babble of women's voices. 'I've a mind to see Mayhew,' he said, with a bob of his massy head. 'And Miss Aurora—the virtue of whom has never been impugned, to my knowledge. Regrets! My devilish tongue cannot resist a quarrel.'

So Clover held the gate open, and let Julius ride up with them.

Charlatan   On the fifth floor Aurora was in perfect order, her rooms fresh as iced water after the overheated atmosphere downstairs. Bella and Clover vanished into the kitchenette, in fits of horrified laughter after attempting to convey the situation.

Aurora made a polite effort to entertain Julius—with whom she'd never had a cordial friendship, his heart having been given to Clover. She had noticed it often: people picked one or another sister to like,

not understanding how closely they were twined. There was no point
in his partisanship for Clover, because Clover herself was hopelessly
partisan for Aurora and Bella, and they for her.

She sought for some subject that might interest him. 'We had a
delightful dinner with Sir Arthur Conan Doyle last summer, perhaps
you have met him on your travels? I know he is fond of vaudeville.'

Julius gave a snort of mingled derision and amusement. '*Phoo!* A
charlatan, I believe. Authors always are. But I confess, I enjoy the hum-
buggery of his stories. A fascinating instance of Art surpassing the frail
human who creates it—who is the conduit for it, more like.'

Since that had been Aurora's own estimate of Conan Doyle, she
could not help laughing. 'It was only a month before war was declared,
yet all he could talk of was those uppity suffragettes and his moony
wife. He is a champion storyteller, though.'

The girls came in with a tea tray, and Aurora sighed as she saw that
Clover was thoughtfully carrying Fitz's good whiskey by its neck.

Some time later, when Julius had succumbed to the whiskey and
lay snoring in a corner of the upholstered sofa, Mama brought Sybil up
to see Aurora's flat and all her nice things. They had made up, by the
mysterious alchemy of long knowledge of each other. Aurora marvelled
at the cozy way the ladies walked arm-in-arm through the suite, con-
ferring over the latest rising salaries in the big-time.

Sybil spoke with earnest emphasis: 'Tanguay gets $3,500 a week.
Miss Barrymore asks $3,000—but vaude is on the up. The trick,' she
said, flicking a jaundiced eye over the slumbering form on the sofa,
'is making sure Julius doesn't give up. Which he will do, he's such a
one for losing heart. Only sixty-three, but you'd never know it; he's
got a decade to go before he really *can't* be hired, if I play his cards
right and keep him off the roller skates.'

Papa would have been forty-five this year, Aurora calculated.
Ten years younger than Fitz. Sybil bent over Julius, stroking his
shoulder to waken him, and for a moment Aurora saw herself standing there. Blonde curls, black smudged around starting eyes, elderly
husband.

Aurora promised herself that she would not let her eyes goggle like Sybil's. But the husband was undeniable.

The door opened. As if conjured by her thoughts, Fitz Mayhew strode in with a bundle of shirts, spiced meat from the Hungarian butcher, and an armful of gold chrysanthemums. 'Aurora! The car is waiting! You'll miss your call!' he shouted—then halted, seeing the array of women in front of him, and the bulk of Julius sleeping in the distance.

'My dear, you ought to have warned me, and I'd have brought more whiskey,' Mayhew said.

'Yes, and you'll need it,' Sybil said darkly. She prodded Julius. 'Jay! Jay! Here's Fitzjohn back. Tell him what you want.'

'I've no room at all on the bill,' Mayhew said, but he had a laugh in his eyes. He was entirely on the ball, as always, and Aurora found herself enjoying the scene, which had taken her some time to piece together. She wondered how much Mayhew owed Julius.

Not Brought Up to It

Excusing themselves on the grounds of their early call, Mama took Clover and Bella down to dress for the theatre.

'Can you feature it?' Mama said, as the elevator clanked down grinding its chain. 'What was Julius about to let her get into that state?' She polished her wedding ring on a lifted bit of skirt. 'He ought never to have lent Mayhew that money, but it's hardly our funeral—she was unreasonable, *distrait* even, during our little *tête-à-tête.*' (Clover could not help a gasp of laughter whenever Mama trotted out her French.) 'And Julius—*that word.*' She scrubbed at the ring, staring out into the bright brass cage that fell so slow. 'Can you *feature?*'

Must be close to the truth, or she would not be so distrait herself, Clover thought. She must have come pretty near it in Paddockwood, towards the end. Where is the line between being a weak, sweet, affectionate widow when the grocer comes for his bill, and being Lily Bain? A heavy *clunk*, and the cage opened, and they were set free.

Sham Friends   After the show Mayhew hosted a late dinner at the Shasta Grill, near the Pantages. Aurora hated going there; it always made Mayhew ill-tempered to see the Pantages Theatre's opulent appointments, compared to the little Muse.

As they drove through the rainy streets, Mayhew listed the evening's guests for Aurora: he had invited several vaudeville managers, including C.P. Walker, a Winnipegger who had taken over W.B. Sherman's enterprises in June (Sherman retreating to Calgary with his tail between his legs). Walker wanted to discuss continued rumours of Sullivan & Considine's demise, which would hurt them all; Mayhew discounted S&C, but had other fish to fry. He'd invited Mr. Penstenny too, the Muse's main investor. Mr. Penstenny's real estate wangling (he'd made a sudden fortune by being third in line when the Hudson's Bay Company sold off their lands) had financed the Muse. Penstenny was a stout ex-grocer with darting eyes and a pouted-out mouth, exuding stockyard breath. Aurora found him physically repellent, but always made an effort to hide that, out of courtesy as well as practicality. Penstenny now had a mortgage on his office block, and she did feel sorry for him.

The Pierce-Arrow whisked them along Jasper to the Shasta, where the party settled at a large table and began, as always, with champagne. Like that night at the roadhouse, Aurora thought, feeling unaccountably tired of popping corks.

Walker arrived with Charles Gill, manager of the Pantages. Both substantial men, but Walker the sharper-eyed of the two. Mayhew put Aurora between them, and she set about her work, to fascinate the new man, Walker, and jolly the dyspeptic Gill. Mayhew would manage Penstenny.

Aurora was surprised to find Sybil and Julius present. Mayhew must be feeling guilty, she supposed at first. But then she saw that he was using them as puppets, to talk to Walker and Gill. 'This city is on the verge of greatness,' Mayhew was telling Julius. 'Real estate speculation men have surveyed and laid out lots for a city the size of New York!'

Julius said, remembering his lines, 'Four and a half millions! That's what those chisellers at the Hudson's Bay netted when they sold their land.'

'A good bargain, for that land,' Mayhew said. 'Money is tight with the unsettling prospect of war—but it will loosen later, whether or not the war continues.' Under this, Aurora heard Sybil and Mama reciting a rude verse about the war, cackling at the end of the table.

Julius rode over them. 'Your house, the Muse—magnificent—full to bursting tonight!'

'Never better!' Mayhew lied and smiled with equal breadth. He leaned across to Gill. 'You may say the Pantages beats us, and for size you surely do, but not for high-class acts! East & Verrall, as an example: top-draw, top-class, travel all over the continent.'

So—the theatre was successful, land values were secure, nobody need worry about their money. Not looking at Mayhew, Aurora wondered how far in debt he was, and to whom.

The courses kept coming. By 2 a.m. the wine and the warmth had sent Sybil off to sleep beside Julius. A long day for them, Aurora thought, considering they'd been rampaging at Mama's door at ten that morning. Mama herself was having a grand blowout, and had found a kindred spirit in Mr. Walker of Winnipeg.

'Sherman had Marie Lloyd here in January,' she was saying. 'Now, she needs no publicity stunts!'

'A little of what you fancy,' Walker said, agreeing. He winked at Aurora.

Mama flung an arm out in Marie's dashing style—'*There he is, can't you see, a-waving his handkerchee!*'—and lashed a waiter who had just bent forward, Mayhew having directed him to fill her water glass. The waiter caught the pitcher, but Mama upset the glass as he poured, and icy water flooded the south end of the table. 'Oopsy-daisy!' she cried gaily, mopping with her napkin. 'Fitz! Fitz! Didn't Ziegfeld have them deliver four hundred bottles of milk for Anna Held? And when the pressmen didn't get hold of it in time, he sued the dairyman, saying it was sour. Anything to get her in the headlines.'

Walker laughed. Mayhew was turning a cigar under his nose; he snipped it and looked up. 'That's the ticket, Aurora, my girl, we'll have you bathe in milk.'

Aurora saw that Gill was a little scandalized that Mayhew would mention her naked body (or cause it to be imagined, at least) at the dinner table. Walker cast a speculative eye over her, which she caught, and returned with a minutely arched brow.

'Onstage, Fitz?' she asked, cool as milk herself.

She let her bare white arms float up in a flash of soap-sudsing, and the men shouted with laughter, that bursting basso shout that had flared up from her father's card-games in childhood. She loved how it mixed with the smell of cigars and liquor, loved her skill in provoking their big-toned laugh. Walker leaned towards her, his interest caught by the glimpse of wit beneath her polished surface.

But Mayhew raised an imaginary hat to her, not smiling, and she looked away, putting a hand across the table to ask Mama if she would like a soda water.

The night wore on, and the talk turned to the war, and to despairing, at least from Gill. Not Walker, who seemed a sensible man: 'Oh, war will be bad for vaudeville, take it from me—but we'll do better in polite vaudeville than the burlesque houses will, when their audiences disappear. My wife reminds me that when the men go off to war we'll still have the women and children, anxious to forget their troubles.'

Already, Aurora considered, they were seeing this very thing at the Muse.

'Unpleasant bully-ragging in Europe,' Julius pronounced, peering from his fug. 'Weeping sore, can be lanced. Strike hard and sharp.'

How Julius loves to look wise, Aurora thought. But she had begun to despise everyone. A darkness had slid over the world.

True Pain

The party broke up around four without anything secured, as far as Aurora could see. They were the last to leave

the dimming Shasta. Mayhew's flourishing signature on the bill, and a
fat tip in bills pressed into the maître d's hand, seemed to console the staff.

The elevator struggled up, first to Mama's floor to let her totter
out, then to theirs, doors clanging as they shut and opened, even though
Mayhew put out a gloved hand to damper the noise.

'You seemed to get along very well with Walker,' he said, throwing
his gloves on the table in the hall. 'He's hired Julius. Did he boast?
Given him dates in Winnipeg as well, the remainder of the year. Shows
his lack of discrimination, I suppose.'

Mayhew was jealous; Aurora had had to turn down her lamps at
dinner. Irrational, since he'd been using her to sweeten the table; and
now it likely meant a sleepless night while he railed at her misbehav-
iour and then took her with some force. Sometimes that was good, the
race of it making her blood thump, but tonight she was unaccountably
tired and only wanted sleep.

He came to take her cloak and held her, his fingers pressing underneath her arm so as to leave no bruise visible onstage. He was never
entirely blind to practicality.

'You're hurting me,' she said, gently pulling away. You had to be
careful not to escalate things, with Mayhew.

'Oh, it's a world of hurt,' he threw at her, and crashed the cloak
onto the table as he stalked into the parlour, ignoring the lateness of
the hour and the sleeping tenants below them.

Turn it aside to something else. She went to the piano, and lifted
the keyboard lid as if she would play to soothe him.

'How much did you give Julius?' she said lightly.

'I paid him back. He'd lent me a century—told his wife it was only
fifty.' The electric candles at the fireplace went on. Mayhew pushed with
his boot at the half-burned log in the grate, and bent to light it again.

Aurora's index finger touched a note, a note, a note. Very softly.
'With sixteen months' interest?'

Mayhew cracked a laugh. 'No! Only Julius's self-interest. The hope
I'll hire him again someday.'

She sat on the piano bench, where he could not comfortably follow her. Every inch of her body was weary and sore, and she had a strange taste in her mouth.

Mayhew turned from the fire. 'I'm taking *Les Très Belles* off the bill,' he said abruptly, with no softening introduction. 'You'll be the better for a transformation of some kind. Get involved in another vaude house, perhaps—you can work with Walker, or Gill.'

'Why?' She bit her lip. She knew why, all the reasons.

'Give the Muse's audience a goddamned rest, for one thing,' he said.

Aurora turned her head to see his face in the firelight.

He stayed by the mantel, staring back at her. 'You can take a break for four months. I'm working on the Spokane deal. We'll see how that pans out. In the meantime, you'll have to economize,' he said, closing the subject. He poured another whiskey and headed for the bathroom.

Four months—stuck in the apartment with nothing to do, and with less money! The collapse must be closer than she'd suspected. And she did not see how the Spokane deal could possibly come together.

Her trailing skirt caught on a carpet tack as she went to the bedroom—and when she pulled, it ripped. Another thing to fix. Mama would do it. The dressing table was tidy, Annie and Berthe had been in that afternoon. They would not be able to afford to have the maids every other day. Once a week, perhaps, at first, and then once every two, and then there would be a stiff little meeting where she handed them an envelope with a generous present for their service and a 'thank you very much, no thank you,' as Sybil would say.

Pulling out the velvet stool, she sat, bone-tired, took her hair down and ran the brush through it. It would be pleasant to braid one's hair for bed again, but Mayhew liked it loose. She took off her necklace. They were not diamonds, only brilliants. The glass laid over the fine wood of the dressing-table surface bothered her, she wanted to touch the wood. She ran a finger along the bevelled edge, careful not to cut herself.

Mayhew came from the bathroom with a damp face, scrubbing it with a towel. He shaved before bed, a custom he'd acquired from some fancy-woman so as not to scratch her delicate skin. Aurora was grateful enough, although she had not liked to hear him tell the story.

He often talked of former lovers. She had none, of course. But she'd known better than to mention Maurice Kavanagh or any of the boys from the old days. No reason on earth to mention Jimmy Battle. Mayhew's dignity was fragile.

She switched off the dressing-table lamp. Mayhew lay on the bed in his shirt-sleeves, waiting for her. He liked her to be naked in the bed and she had become accustomed, so that it was no longer anything odd, to let her peignoir drop away.

The moon fell in the river windows. Sounds floating up from the street below. Pieces of him were worth loving: his acumen, his energy, his definite, positive stance. But he was not honest, and never aimed for anything but the progress of Mayhew.

His hands moved over her like brick hods, one hand bigger than her breast pulling it, sliding downward, smearing the shape. She was cold, and wanted the comforter, but he lay sprawled across it, surveying her body in bands of moonlight that fell over the white bed. She arched her back when his hand moved lower. All she had to do was magnify the small responses that her body made. But she was tired, deep inside, of all this work: trying to please him by day and by night.

'Your mama had better watch the drink,' he said, as if he had only just now thought of it. 'I won't put up with that, I've told you so.'

Aurora lay still, not answering, Mama being a subject that could go either way.

His hand pulled heavier down her, moving into the cleft of her legs, pulling and pinching there the way he liked to do, feeling or fondling. He believed she would like it; maybe some woman in the past had told him so. She did not like anything, any of it. The spell that could come over her and make it all right was not working this night; her mind was too full of thinking.

She supposed they had been cancelled again, in fact. Taken off the list.

That thought made a vast lump in her chest, too hard, so she pushed it away. After a moment's stroking and pulling he unbuckled his cummerbund, awkwardly, then sat up to the edge of the bed to pull it away and unbutton his trousers.

'I won't take her to Spokane if she's in that state again,' he said, casually, in the brief pause between one trouser-leg and the other. Speaking as if she wouldn't care at all what was done to Mama. He flung the cummerbund into the corner, where his evening shirt lay crumpled. 'She's an embarrassment, in public.'

Aurora turned in the bed and found her peignoir with one hand; stood and pulled it on in one motion, not able to talk without at least that shield.

'What do you mean?'

'What I said!' He laughed at her ferocity. 'I'm not taking her. And the way things look, we'll be off sooner than later. The girls can come, but you'll have to ditch Flora.'

And for how long could the girls come? She must pull her wits together.

'If we're to shake this boondocks dust off our feet we can't be travelling with an old harpy—I'll tell you what, she and that Sybil hag get along so well, give her to Julius, he can have a *hareem*.'

Aurora's arm jerked as if she might hit him, but Mayhew was fast. He grabbed her hand as it came up, and he laughed. 'I won't put up with a drunk! Making a fool of herself, and of me.'

'Don't say that! You don't mind the drink in Julius, or your pals— or yourself.'

'I'm not supporting them to the tune of a hundred a week.'

Little enough, for headliners, she wished to say, but she could not fight with him. It was not safe to do so. She could not cajole him when he was close to anger. And he had drunk a great deal himself.

She let the lace peignoir drift apart, and put a hand on his arm. 'I'll speak to her, Fitz. She'd had a terrible fight with Sybil, and she's not feeling up to snuff these days, that's all.'

'Send her to grass, with that uncle of yours in Saskatchewan.'

'I can't do that, she wouldn't go. She needs us to look after her, you know that. She couldn't do without Clover and Bella—'

'Send them too!'

But he did not mean that. He saw her realize it, and he flung his trousers at the chair behind him, angry again, silver from his pockets spinning along the floor.

'Time for her to pack it in, the old cow!'

She shoved at his bare chest, at the grey wool and sunken paunch revealed in the cold moon—her temper suddenly lost, she felt a fierce need to make him lose his, and to hell with everything.

'She's no older than you! Time for *you* to pack it in? If you can't manage—'

He pushed her back into the bedclothes then with all his power, slamming her head down, hands on her neck and crushing her into the sheets, and she remembered that she had no strength at all, compared to him; there was nothing she could do. She did not panic, but waited, effort drained from her muscles. Thinking done with, pride useless. But she'd said what she thought, there was some virtue in that.

He stopped, and released her. 'No,' he said. 'I do not mean to hurt you.'

She lay still, pushed down into a nest of linens. Her eyes were slow to open.

'Poor darling girl, poor girl,' he said, as soft as the wind outside. 'Forgive me. Poor dear sweet girl, I love you so, and I torment you. You are a precious girl, my dearest one, don't fear me.'

Finally then she put her hand on his arm, and raised her head so her neck was open to him, submitting. Tears ran out her eyes and down the side of her face, but she did not cry out loud.

Later, she heard him speaking. She was almost asleep, not certain whether he spoke to her or thought her dreaming.

'I love beauty,' he said. 'I wanted to do beautiful things.'

Bella's bee wings had never got mended—I will do them tomorrow, she thought.

Legerdemain

Nobody at the Muse knew what caused Mayhew's patience to snap, but it was done. Bella stared at the new order-list that had been pasted on the lobby doors in the morning: the Knockabout Ninepins were moved to opener. A grievous insult for an act with the Ninepins' years of experience in the big-time. Not to be borne.

Everyone was scared and silent in the dressing rooms, wondering what Joe Dent was likely to do.

What he did was simple enough: he took an alarm-clock onstage with him, set for twelve minutes, and when it rang, he stopped the act without finishing the routine. Mrs. Dent and Nando stopped too, frozen in their window frames. Then they all walked offstage. The audience tried to clap, unsure what was going on; they had been only half attending, as usual with the opener, and the brief patter petered out.

There was a long blank silence, on an empty, lit stage, before the boy rushed out with OK Griffith's placard and his music started up.

That was the end of the Knockabout Ninepins at the Muse.

Up in the booth, Bella was beside herself with rage, so angry and frightened that for the first time in recorded history she was unable to speak. By the time she got back to the dressing rooms, Joe had the whole family packed up and out the back door, a feat of legerdemain that would have taken masterly planning—so he must have known they'd be done.

Late that night, Nando sent a note to the Arlington to tell Bella what was happening.

> Found a booking, so it's the Flyer south for us. We're off to the small-time in Spokane, a place Dad knows well. Ma not so pleased to leave the Muse and she remembers the last place we was at in Spokane, where we had to put the bedstead legs in cans of kerosene to stop the bugs invading nightly.
>
> No hard feelings, tell Mayhew. He's a hard man, but Dad's head is harder than anything.
>
> Spokane is just till November, then we're booked straight to Christmas, so don't be blue. Up to Winnipeg in January, two weeks at the Pantages, fine old Pan-time.
>
> See you in the funny papers, and don't forget that you are my, and I
> > your sweetheart,
> > > N. DENT

Bella declared secret war on Mayhew from that moment.

And he was making Aurora miserable too. In the morning, as soon as Bella was sure Mayhew would have left for the Muse, she went up to the top floor to get her bee wings, leaving Clover to wake and dress Mama. She found Aurora still in the bedroom, her head down on the burl maple dressing table. Still in her nightgown, cloudy hair in a bad tangle.

Bella picked up the comb and began to work through it. Having to be gentle made her calmer, and she told Aurora about Nando's letter, including the bit about Nando having no hard feelings. 'But *I* do!'

'Fitz is in trouble, Bell, it's not—it's not his real nature, to ditch them that way.'

'What trouble?' She pulled the comb through another long un-knotted section.

'Oh, too many things to say.'

Aurora bent her head to let Bella reach the last of the tangles, and to rest her forehead again on the cool glass protecting the wood. She spoke from within the dark shade her arm and head made. 'He left a hotel bill as long as your arm in Helena, for which both the Placer and the Ackermans are chasing him, and another in Calgary only half paid. All those dinners.'

Bella whistled. She let the ends of Aurora's hair curl around the comb, satin once again, and patted her neck.

'You comb so well, with your light hands,' Aurora said, turning her head to kiss Bella's wrist. 'He says it is perfectly justified, that every-thing was for the betterment of the theatres, even the wedding. All press is good press—you know what he says.'

'Yes, I do.'

'Yes.'

In the grey morning, rain drenching the windows, the bedroom was ugly, untidy. Tangled sheets on the floor. Bella began to set things in order again, ready for the maids to clean. She watched her sister lift her head and stare into the mirror, blank eyes making a cold assess-ment of her face; at least it was not the dumbstruck tragedy mask she'd been wearing when Bella came in.

Aurora opened a little pot and added a tinge of purplish ochre to one eyelid. 'The thing is, he is not a scrupulous person.'

'I know.'

'I think he will make us all do a bunk in the night. Don't tell Clover, it would make her unhappy.'

Bella nodded, coming to have her own eyes done. She spat into the little pot and stirred, then held out the mascara stick and leaned forward so Aurora could do her lashes.

'Hold still,' Aurora warned. She took the pin to separate the clotted lashes. 'He is not precisely bad,' she said, in a light, objective tone as she pricked and dabbed. 'He just does not operate under the same code— he was trained by Ziegfeld, and he goes on the way they do there. For these Ackerman circuit types to be slandering him is pretty rich.'

'They can't slang anyone more than they've been slanged themselves,' Bella agreed. She kept her head as still as marble.

Rain   Rain made the rooms at the Arlington cold, so that early October felt like November. Clover lit the gas fire and made tea before waking Mama. At first waking, as usual, Mama came back from the distance of her dreams, eyes moving frantically under tight-closed papery lids. 'Mama,' Clover said gently. 'Mama, here is your tea.'

She watched as Mama's eyes opened, rolled, trying for focus. She reached for a sip of tea and then pushed the cup away and turned back (bedsprings squeaking like a thousand baby mice) to catch at her dream, murmuring in a slurred, furred voice, 'One more minute . . .'

Fire within, rain without, suited Clover's mood. She sat at the window, rereading a letter from Victor about Galichen, the guru Victor's parents had espoused. How he demanded unthinking obedience from his followers, and often gave them ridiculous or conflicting orders '*to set their orderly brains at odds, so they might wake from what he calls their sleep.*' Once, Gali had made Victor's parents the floor-washers at his tall, thin house in Ladbroke Grove, a part of London. The stairs there were steep, five pairs of rackety narrow flights, ten landings to the attics—where they found Galichen waiting with freshly muddied boots, in which he stomped and slid downstairs so that they had all to do again. There was some lesson in there, but Clover decided she was too asleep, or too sensible, to see it.

There had been no news since the enlisting letter.

Mama stirred again in the bed and propped herself up on one pointed white elbow, smoothing a hand across her chest. She stared at the rain-smeared window, her hair crazy with curl-papers from the night before, half of them come undone.

'I've irritated poor Fitz,' she confided, picking at her lip with one unsteady hand. 'I must go in today and see if I can mend our fences . . . Bees in the caragana, and a stone leaning sideways in the churchyard. Collapsed because of the rain, it had flooded out the grave, you know. That would mean a change of scene.'

Mama always told her dreams in the morning now, as she searched for warnings. Clover put the kettle on again and brought a warm towel and Mama's wrapper, wondering if she ought to tell Aurora how unsteady Mama was these days. Her rough, misshapen feet peeped out of the bedclothes; Clover slipped carpet-shoes on them, and together they made their way down the hall to the bathroom.

'You ought not to spend so much time with Victor, dear Clover. It is not suitable,' Mama said, as Clover closed the bathroom door on her.

'I am nearly eighteen, Mama. I have not seen Victor for two months, I don't know why you're saying this.'

'Mooning over him. Just that one must be so careful—think of Julius, the other day, and how the least suspicion can destroy— You do not know how harsh the world can be.'

Clover thought that, actually, she did. Through the bathroom door, Mama had gone back to dream-recounting. 'One stone leaning, another crashed down . . . Moss grown into the letters, a missive gone astray.'

Papa's gravestone, she must be thinking of, or Harry's. Clover ran her hands over her face. The rain had got into her head.

Flood

It rained and rained and rained. A percussion pattered under all the numbers in the matinee. Water dripped from weak places in the roof, and steamed up from the pitifully sparse audience, who sat drying in the communal warmth. The wet-dog smell was terrific.

Between shows Teddy the stage manager took a couple of hands up onto the roof to sweep the water from the worst places that had pooled and begun to leak; wherever they pushed the water over, the white stone front of the theatre stained grey. Clover watched Mayhew stalk the aisles, directing one or other of the cleaning women to towel up wet patches or blot a seat down. Morose, distracted, he failed to respond at all to Mama's damp curtsy and trill of greeting, after she'd ventured out for buns from the Whyte Avenue tea room. Mama scuttled back up to the dressing room, Clover following; Mama found her needle again by jamming it into her thumb, but did not curse. The room was silent in the humming hive of the Muse, each sister locked in her own thoughts and Mama too anxious to sing.

But East and Verrall brightened the day when they knocked on the door, fresh in on the northbound Flyer from Montana. They'd come in early to replace the Ninepins, to start that night, although Friday was the usual bill-change day. Bella shrieked and jumped up to tell them the true story of the sacking of Joe and the others, which shocked Verrall.

East professed to have seen it coming, of course. 'Can't blame Mayhew,' he said. 'Joe isn't hardly fit for human consumption. He's a brute and treats that boy like a rented mule, and the sooner they start losing bookings, the faster Nando's going to jump ship.'

'He cannot leave his mother,' Flora said. 'He is too loyal and good a boy for that.'

East glowered at her, and said pointedly, 'She made her bed, and has lain on it these many years of her own choosing. What's the boy to do, submit to endless beatings? Kill his old dad?'

Clover intervened before they could brangle, asking how the golf sketch had shaped up. East clapped his hands. 'Capital, capital, we're ready to try it out tomorrow if you're game, Belle of All the World? Verrall has your sides—where are they, Verrall? Don't say you left them in the train or I will simply—'

But Verrall produced them, and they retreated to the Ninepins' empty dressing room across the hall to run the sketch through pronto. Clover could hear them through the flimsy walls: Verrall attempting to teach East, who had no idea how to hold a club.

> VERRALL: No, no, now take the stick again in your hand
>   and I'll show you . . . you swing back like this—
> EAST: Like this? *(smashing sound as the club connects)*
> *A pause.*
> VERRALL: *(very controlled)* What are you going to do
>   with that club now?
> EAST: Hit around corners?
> VERRALL: Stand over here—no, here, in front of me. I
>   want to examine your form.
> EAST: Examine my form?
> VERRALL: Yes, now I'll just stand behind you, and
>   put my arms around yours like this, and my hands
>   on your—
> EAST: Hey! *(smashing sound as the club connects)*
> VERRALL: *(yelping)* Hey! What did you do that for?
> EAST: You don't know me well enough for that yet. I
>   think you need someone more—female—to teach!
>   Hey, miss! miss!

Bella was a young golf widow searching for her husband with a bent club of her own. She told East and Verrall the whole sad story:

> BELLA: My Archie played golf yesterday—he came
>   home two hours late! He confessed the whole
>   sordid tale: he said that a beautiful lady had
>   jumped out of the bushes on the eleventh tee,

dressed just as she came delivered from her Maker.
She ravished him for hours, and he did not have
the strength to refuse her, and he was very sorry.
EAST: He made a clean breast of it, in fact.
BELLA: He did *indeeeeed*.
VERRALL: And did you forgive him?
BELLA: Ha! I know him far too well for that—I hit him
over the head with the rolling-pin. Lady, indeed!
The wretch had played another nine holes!

Her mama had told her that she must take up golf herself, if she wanted to preserve her marriage, and she was there for a lesson. Verrall taught her about golf, and East taught her about love, ending in a completely ridiculous song, the lyrics of which descended to a thousand rapid repetitions of the word *love*.

Clover continued her work, putting Aurora's hair up and tidying the dressing room, but it seemed to her that the song echoed and echoed in her own idiotic heart, *love love love love love*—and no one to answer it. No letter from Victor.

And now the rain had got into her eyes.

Lot's Wife   At the eight-thirty show, the girls pranced on for *Spring Song* to the basso accompaniment of a colossal clap of thunder. At least, Bella thought it was thunder—

But as everyone in the house looked up, the middle rows of the audience were stung with a sliding shower of water. Then a shining sheet— then the roof parted, through the centre, and a waterfall fell through.

Aurora and Clover had raised their wreaths for Bella to duck through, and they all stopped still, stone statues of the Muses.

The audience began screaming, starting with the people directly under the waterspout. Luckily it was a paltry house again, and there was plenty of room to run up the aisles.

The bandleader in the pit turned when he saw the stricken look on the girls' faces. He whipped his stick up in the air and shouted, 'Out, boys!' and the orchestra grabbed their instruments and hightailed it, the sudden ceasing of the music lost in the stampeding noise of the water still pouring down, and the ominous and quite dreadful shrieking of the ceiling.

The sidelights in the house went out, but the stage lights, wired separately in a new-built section, stayed on, so they could see it happen: the roof caving in. First the pressed-tin panels sagged, and a few drooped to the seats; then the great metal span bent down and down, and then it snapped, with another hideous wrenching noise, and more of the ceiling came down, in a terrific rush of smoking dust and water. The older girls huddled over Bella, but it did not occur to them to run. Teddy and his hands had come out to see the devastation. The stage was filling with silent gawping faces, turned audience themselves. The balcony emptied fast, but people were still streaming up the side aisles, some looking back like Lot's wife, then yanked along by their friends.

'Playing to the haircuts,' Aurora said, and the other two could not help but laugh. That's what was said when your act was so bad people left in the middle.

The fire curtain never did come down, as it was supposed to in any catastrophe.

Another span bent, another section of roof collapsed. And another. At the centre lobby doors, a brave or reckless group of men from the audience stood watching. Those onstage stared back, across the awful chasm that had been the Muse's seats. Just before they finally ran for it, Bella watched in fascination as Mayhew appeared in the window of the booth, shouting something nobody could hear.

Condemned

Mayhew did not come home that night. Aurora found him at the Muse, Friday morning, standing in the rubble of the house. His perfect boots dusty, a tear in one sleeve. The city building inspector (who'd had many a lunch on Mayhew during the building process) had placarded the bevelled-glass front doors of the Muse with BUILDING CONDEMNED cards. From the front, the theatre looked unharmed, as if it might all have been a bad dream. Rounding the building, though, the sad truth became evident. There was a plain of devastation, an expanse of jumbled white and grey, with here and there the red velvet of a seat jutting through, caked with plaster grime. *They won't come in their best clothes if they think their skirts will be dirtied,* Aurora remembered Mayhew telling the cleaning women, the first week the Muse was open.

She had never known that so much wire went into a building. Dangling ends and spikes stuck out everywhere. One of the balcony's grand pillars remained standing—sheared off in a long diagonal, the plaster-of-Paris foliage still curling rambunctiously. Like the broken pillar she had cut her finger on, when Mayhew hurled their wedding cake to the floor. Perhaps Sybil, with her forebodings, would have seen this coming, if she'd been invited to the wedding.

Aurora picked her way across the expanse of wreckage. All the way there on the streetcar, she had rehearsed what not to say to Mayhew. The rain had subsided to dribs and drabs, but her boots would be quite ruined by the combination of plaster dust and jagged wood and tar-muck.

'It's been a great gig,' he said, when she'd come close enough to hear.

The quiet interested her. After all the noise last night it seemed peaceful, even calm this morning.

'Edmonton, of all cursed places, to take me down.'

She looked at him. The astrakhan collar of his overcoat, slung over his arm, was as plush as ever.

'It's just the house, you see,' he said, gesturing right and left to where the newer additions were still standing—the stage looking naked, open to the elements. 'Penstenny will be able to rebuild, if he chooses. He can turn the front piece into a decent office block. He won't be ruined.'

She nodded. Workmen were moving here and there, one pushing a wheelbarrow piled high with detritus.

'Came at the right time,' Mayhew said. 'I couldn't have made payroll tomorrow . . . Might have had to fire the place anyhow.'

He offered her an arm, and she took it. They progressed together through the broken bits of wood, back to the street.

The Pierce-Arrow was parked in front, his monogrammed suitcases already strapped on the rumble seat. She had not noticed anything missing from the apartment, but hadn't looked inside his closet. He must have been ready to do a bolt for some time.

'I'd take you with me,' he ventured.

Weak autumn sun made an effort to turn the puddles gold; the boardwalk glistened grey and black. 'That's. kind of you, but no— there's Mama, and the girls.'

He nodded. He opened the car door, and hesitated with one foot on the running board.

'I love you,' he said.

Because that was so absurd a thing to say, and so stupid, her resolution from the streetcar ride gave out. 'Did you hurt that girl, the Irish girl?' she asked him quickly, wanting desperately to know.

Mayhew stared down at her, at the bright cloud of hair, the young rise of bodice and neck and cheek. At her face, so well known to him now, and her self—impervious to his love, not part of him, not his in any sense.

'No!' he said. 'How could you ask me such a thing?'

'I was not certain,' she said.

'Have I hurt you so badly?'

'No,' she said. 'Only a little. I don't care.'

From an inner pocket he pulled out a roll of money, pressing it into her glove. 'Won't last you long, but don't give the vultures any of it,' he said as he got into the car. 'Promise me.'

Aurora laughed, unable to resist his cock-eyed gall. The car door slammed, and off Mayhew went, white wheels skimming over the golden pools of rain.

There went her livelihood. What a fix to be in.

She felt ridiculously happy.

ACT THREE

8.
Butterfly Girls

OCTOBER 1914–JANUARY 1915

The David, Camrose
The Lyric, Swift Current
The Pantages, Winnipeg

Never carry more baggage than absolutely necessary.
Excess baggage rates are exorbitant on the majority of
railroads since the 2 cent a mile passenger rate has gone
into effect.

FREDERICK LADELLE, *HOW TO ENTER VAUDEVILLE*

*T*hey counted their money.

The roll Mayhew had given Aurora held fives and tens, adding up to a hundred. A month's rent on both Arlington apartments, with a little over for food. A month's grace, then.

With a sad feeling of virtue, Clover opened her letter-box and brought out seventy-eight dollars she had been hoarding for some eventuality (not so well-formed an idea as running away to find Victor). Bella was handed fifty in notes by Verrall, which he said was only fair, for many times when they had not bothered to settle up her contracted dollar-per-show. $228: once that would have seemed like riches.

Flora had been diligent in banking half the Belle Auroras' hundred a week (down again from the original $150 once Mayhew had settled them into the apartment and was paying for so much). Although they'd not worked every week, and had incurred large expenses for costumes and fallals—*exorbitant*, for the butterfly wings—she was confident, or at least hopeful, that there was more than a thousand in the bank.

When she went up to the teller the horrible truth came out.

Mayhew had set up their banking, as the man necessarily in charge, and his rubber Muse cheques had been assigned forward to empty all his accounts, including the one he'd set up for the Belle Auroras. The ledger showed, in fact, a deficit of eighteen dollars.

Flora came home in palpitations, the loss of the money far worse than the rather exciting loss of the Muse, and lay on the sofa in Aurora's suite at the Arlington, weeping in great sodden gulps, railing against Mayhew in an incoherent spate which even Aurora could not stem. She let Mama run on as she struggled to close the lid of Mayhew's rolltop desk over the nest of unpaid bills that feathered there.

Next morning, when Aurora was finally allowed to make her way up to the untouched office floor at the Muse, she found a matching bill-pillow squashed into his desk drawer there. She looked at the mass of papers for six thudding heartbeats; then gently shut the drawer and left, without another glance at the ruin of the Muse.

As she rode the streetcar home it began to snow. She put one grey-gloved hand out the window and caught a constellation of snowflakes. The river down below was slow-churning ice cream.

That afternoon Aurora spoke to the manager of the Arlington, to give notice. He explained, kindly, that Mayhew had signed a year's unbreakable, iron-clad lease. Aurora then explained, equally kindly, that Mayhew had absconded, and that Mr. Crumley could sue her vanished husband for the rent if he pleased, but might wish to consult a lawyer before making ugly threats to an abandoned woman. *Abandoned* was right, the manager said, and battle would have been joined, except that Aurora laughed.

'Dear Mr. Crumley,' Aurora said, giving him a bewilderingly happy smile. 'My abandoned sisters and I will stay on in the third-floor apartment till the end of November, but I'll be out of the top-floor suite by Monday—and the rent's been paid, so just think! You could have it twice over, if you move fast. Such a desirable residence will be snatched up, even if you were to *raise* the rent.'

Before he left he had agreed to take much of the furniture off her hands, to rent the place as a fully furnished gentleman's apartment.

Any proper woman would be shattered to lose her work and her husband in one go, she thought, watching Crumley's satisfied rump rumbling away down the hall. But as she shut the door she was still fizzing gently, like very cold champagne, with the consciousness of life starting up again.

Baggage

So they were off, although they did not yet know where. They had nice new trunks now, three of them—purchased by Mayhew, in a fit of prosperity, with his own monogrammed suitcases. Mama, when she emerged from her sobs, said the trunks should be sold 'along with everything else!' but Bella refused to part with hers, which was sapphire blue leather and very beautiful.

'No,' Aurora agreed. 'We have the props to look like headliners, and we must keep as much of our outfit as may be managed.'

Clover gave an internal sigh of relief because she loved hers too: mole brown, but with a pleated orange silk lining that pierced her heart with its beauty every time she opened it. And Aurora's was a sight to behold, a silver-grey upright-opening dresser trunk with mother-of-pearl knobbed drawers, too lovely to be dispensed with—unless she might dislike to have anything that reminded her of Mayhew; but Clover had not noticed that she was sensitive that way.

'Well, keep them, then,' Mama said. 'But when we are begging in the streets for a crust of bread I hope someone comes along who wants a trunk!' She sank her aching head back into one weak hand, and put the other out for Bella to refill her teacup.

Aurora's trunk stood open in one corner of the kitchen, acting as her wardrobe. In a fluttering of satin and silks she turned out her closet upstairs; Clover and Bella took the excess clothing to be sold—a long, weary tramp to the rag merchants, who paid far less than the girls had hoped. Then to the dairy and the butcher, paying off accounts. Bella was shocked that they were even bothering to pay what she saw as Mayhew's bills, but Clover held that after all they'd eaten the eggs and sausages, and could not cheat the tradesmen.

They brought home half a dozen brown eggs and a fresh loaf, and were eating a poached egg supper when the doorbell rasped, six twists, followed by a light-rapping knock. Julius and Sybil blew into the hall, stamping snowy boots, and followed Clover along to the kitchen, Sybil exclaiming and Julius declaiming. They had seen the ruin of the Muse.

'A Cataclysm,' Julius declared, raising his voice over Sybil's excited continuous yip-yapping of: 'Who'd have thought? Who could have imagined?'

Mama had stayed collapsed in the armchair they'd dragged into the kitchen for her. Julius pressed her hand, begging her not to rise. Bella brought two more chairs from the parlour, Clover set to making more toast, and they had a cozy party in the little kitchen.

'We saw it in the paper!' Sybil pulled out a cutting: '*The dull reful-gence of the chandeliers, now lying smashed and buried in the rubble of the auditorium* . . . So of course we rushed round to see, and there it is, displastered all to pieces.'

'Don't, don't read it,' Mama begged. 'I will have another spasm.'

'I took the liberty of bringing liquid refreshment,' Julius said, with ponderous courtesy. 'A bottle of sherry, now, brings comfort to the widow and the orphan alike.'

He pulled three bottles from his coat and set them in the middle of the table with a flourish. People like to be helpful in affliction, Clover thought—our kind of people do. All week small packages and bottles had been brought to their door, from the Novelli Brothers, from Teddy—also thrown out of work by the demise of the Muse, with reason to hate anyone associated with Mayhew. Even from Mr. Penstenny, for whom she felt terribly sorry.

'Not that you are a widow, precisely, dear Aurora,' Sybil said, receiving a teacup with a bob of thanks to Bella. 'Although I did *hear*—but no—oh! Toast! How kind you are, dear Clover.'

'And a free hand with the butter, a rare thing in a woman,' Julius said. He pulled a chair up to the little table and Bella made room for his plate by moving the cocoa jug.

'So what are you going to do?' Sybil asked.

The three girls looked at her in some dismay, and Mama burst again into damp sobs.

'Well, I'm sorry to bring it up, I'm sure,' Sybil said.

'No, no,' Aurora said. 'It must be—we do have to— What was it you heard, Sybil?'

Sybil covered her mouth with her small fat paws.

Clover said, 'We do not know just yet what we will do, dear Sybil. But what did you hear?'

'Oh!' Sybil's wide mouth came down into a small pursing whistle. But she had the eyes of all and her histrionic heart could not resist. 'It is *only* gossip, and I did not like to say, but I understand that he already *has* a wife, married some years ago, in San Francisco.'

Aurora could not have been exactly surprised, but Clover felt a hideous downward bend within her chest.

It was Julius who protested. 'Syb!' he shouted. 'No! Too much. There is not a man alive who does *not* have a wife down in San Francisco. I do myself! To suggest bigamy as the reason that the rascal has decamped—merely frivolous! He's a crook, that's all.'

He poured himself a glass of whiskey and knocked half of it back.

'Besides, he'd be a fool,' he added. 'Greatest beauty in vaudeville, why would he desert *la belle Aurore* for a previous marital error? Excess baggage, my dear, excess baggage.'

A Gig from a Pool Hall

As they sat in limbo, it snowed and snowed and snowed.

Used to this, the city dug in under a goose-feather blanket. Enough to drive you mad, Bella thought, when you had no work and had to stare at snow the live-long day. The furnace clanked through the building, loud as the elevator; pipes hissed and spat, and Bella discovered that if you whirled the radiator tap unwarily, a powerful stream of water hissed out and soaked your dress and burned your hand.

She was *so glad* they were leaving this stupid town. She had had no answer to her letters to Nando, so perhaps the Ninepins had not got to Seattle yet; or perhaps Joe had been thrown out of another gig. Nando ought to have written.

Glaring out the window, she decided that the real trouble was they did not yet know enough people in vaudeville. The only other person they knew was Jimmy the Bat, and he was in Winnipeg at the Pantages—the theatre where C.P. Walker, who had liked Aurora so well at Mayhew's last dinner party, was the boss. Bella stared into the bald white field towards the ice-bound river, thinking about Jimmy's face as he had stood talking to Aurora in the hall of the Calgary the-atre. Then she put on her coat and boots.

Going down the stairs she met East and Verrall coming up, shaking snow from their bowler hats, dank hair sticking up in spikes where they had dashed the snow away.

'You need better hats than that for this horrid winter,' she said, laughing at them.

'We need to be elsewhere!' East shouted, and she hushed him, looking back to see if the apartment door would fly open and one of her sisters burst out to stop her going anywhere.

East and Verrall had leaped straight over to the Pantages, missing only one night's work after the flood—they were employable any-where. East could wangle a gig from a pool hall if need be. A funeral hall. She ought to have asked his advice earlier.

'Come along,' she said to East and Verrall. 'I'm going to send a cable, and you'd like a walk.'

'We just had a walk,' East protested, but Verrall patted his (entirely flat) stomach and said he could use the exercise. They went back out into the snow-silenced street.

Dreadful Frozen City

Aurora had moved a cot down to the third floor and shoved Bella and Clover's bed right against the wall to make room. She could not share the Murphy bed with Mama, who was spending longer and longer hours in bed, in a state of sherry-induced stupefaction. Better to be back in the room with her sisters. Everything was tranquil now. And something would come up. If she held to that, she could manage.

But her bone-china composure broke one night. She woke from her first fitful sleep and lay in the little bed, choked by her nightgown, remembering Mayhew's hand moving down her side from shoulder to arm, slipping over her flank and down her legs, the bulk of him always behind her. The thousand countless humiliations of lying with him and never being loved, or known, only being of use to him, all mocked and redoubled now by the hopeless absurdity of missing him.

She broke into painful tears, seeing with eye-pricking clarity that Mayhew was gone for good, was a rascal. Worse: that she had dragged her sisters and Mama into the muck and was wholly responsible for them being stranded in this dreadful frozen city, probably forever, until they were obliged to find work as domestics.

When Clover, waking, slid into the cot and put her arms around her, she whispered all of that, unable to find the breath to speak out loud.

'No, no,' Clover said, pulling her fingers gently through Aurora's hair to comfort her. 'We are all much better off, even stuck here penniless, than we were in Montana. We ought not to be moving southwards, we need to go East, to where things really matter in vaude. To Chicago, and New York. Come, let me braid your hair for you, and you will sleep better.'

Aurora clasped her sister's narrow body close, remembering her wedding night, and how Clover had come to braid her hair. She was the best and kindest of all of them.

Painted Wings   The Belle Auroras had been headliners only by Mayhew's favour. To begin afresh, it was necessary to realize where they stood in the natural order of vaudeville. Not openers, they were too good for that. But they were a quiet act, a simple one, and it seemed to Aurora that simplicity was their strength: charming songs, charmingly sung, no tricksy gimmicks. Their dancing was good, but not of stellar quality; they were nothing at all out of the ordinary as far as looks went.

As they were debating how to begin again, a letter arrived from Gentry. When Aurora found the envelope in the mail slot she knew his thick-stroked writing. Even as she opened it, she felt a warm glow of returning life. He had learned of their predicament from Julius, and while regretting that he had no money to send them, he had taken the liberty of enclosing a new song he'd laid hands on—perhaps they could make something of it?

> ... Ray Hubbell, an associate of mine in olden days, sent it to me for comment—no harm testing it out before Hubbell finds a show to slide it into. Jack Golden stole the poignant story of an abandoned Japanese maiden direct from Puccini: perhaps its delicate fragrance might make up for the slight tinge of irony in its similarity to your own story.
>
> And if I may take a further liberty, may I remind you, my dear Aurora, that you did very well with the song *Danny Boy*. Sometimes it is the song that makes the singer.
>
> Yours aff'ly,
>
> et cetera,
>
> GENTRY FOX, ESQ. (RETIRED)

The song-sheet had been folded into eighths to cram into the envelope. While Aurora scanned the letter, Bella opened the sheet music, and laughed as she read the title: '*Poor Butterfly!*'

She flapped the music like wings, tap-tapping the sheets against the vilely expensive silk butterfly wings, which had been delivered days before and lay furled against the parlour wall, hooked on the ceiling moulding. Stiff painted silk stretched over bent balsa-wood frames. Mama and Clover exclaimed in pleasure: Mama for joy at not having wasted such a great deal of money, and Clover because the wings themselves were so fragile and lovely, and ought to be used.

'Perhaps we could make of it something that would please,' Aurora said. It was the first good thing in what seemed like a long while.

They cleared the floor and began to work (missing the expanse of the Muse's rehearsal hall), testing out ideas that Mama called to them. Sashays, grands battements, arabesques, cramped into the parlour-space: none of it made the scalp tingle or the breath catch, as the good idea will.

The painted design delighted them when the wings were open. But the *Poor Butterfly* tune did not work for dancing unless the tempo was jinked up, which bent the song out of true. After a while, Aurora stopped them. 'If we had a good dance with the wings—maybe *Spring Song?*—I could do *Butterfly* afterwards, almost as a playlet. With Bella's *Bumble Bee*, we could do a whole insect number. A kimono would be quick to run up in art silk, and I'm sure Clover could paint it to match the wings.'.

Bella was discontent. 'But why do I still have to be a bee?'

'Because,' Clover told her, 'you get the biggest laughs and the biggest hand of all.'

Clover and Aurora bent and fluttered and bowed, and Bella sang the tweedly *Spring Song* for all she was worth, but the thing lacked zing. The afternoon darkened into evening, and they still had nothing usable.

'Wear less,' Mama said. 'That's the ticket.' She snatched off their practice skirts and wrapped a tea towel round Clover's middle, leaving most of her legs revealed.

'Mama!' Bella said, but she was laughing—Clover's legs were spindly and insect-like, quite sweet. Aurora stood in her stockings, considering.

'Longer stockings will be needed,' Mama said. 'But it is all God's creation, no earthly reason not to display such limbs, in the service of transformative dance. You will need more accentuation at the eyes.' Then, overcome, she went to lie down on Bella and Clover's bed.

Thoughtfully, Aurora pulled Bella's skirt up, up—till most of her darling legs stood revealed. 'I think she's right,' she said. 'And Bella's right too. Bella should be the other butterfly, and I'll turn up alone with the song, afterwards. Ditch the bee, for now. But let's think of other music for the dance—*On Wings of Song* might be much better.'

Bella clapped her hands. 'Oh yes! Perfect, it is about sisters!'

The other two stared at her.

'Their lovely sister-flowers—*the lotus flowers await thee, their lovely sister-flower!*'

Finally Aurora's scalp sparkled, and they were off.

American Dollars   Four days later a telegram came, addressed to Bella. Clover answered the bell and gave the boy a nickel, and stood looking at the yellow envelope, thinking it must be from Nando. And an envelope in the mail slot too: from Victor. 'Bella!' she called, going down the dusky hall to the parlour, where Bella was curled in the armchair, discontentedly reading a three-day-old newspaper holding nothing but war news.

Aurora and Mama were playing Up-the-River on the Murphy bed. Bella had to edge around it to get to the yellow envelope, but she made good time and flicked it from Clover's grasp, opened and read it in the blink of an eye—and threw her arms into the air in joy. *The Journal* went flying, aflutter, pages like grouse lifting. 'Reprieved!' she cried. 'Look, look!'

Clover took the telegram and read it out to the others:

'WALKER SAYS SPOT PANTAGES WINNIPEG JAN I BELL
AURORS OPENERS SORRY J BATTLE.'

Aurora, sank to the bed, saying, 'Openers again. But thank God!' She began mumbling numbers: rent for December, food, train fare to Winnipeg.

Bella read the telegram again to Mama, who began to praise Jimmy Battle as the best boy in vaudeville, how she had known he would never let them down, unlike some, and how you could tell who was solid sterling worth, and so on.

There was an extra sheet in the envelope, Clover saw as she picked it up. 'He wired cash as well,' she said. 'Forty-seven dollars. Not a round number—perhaps it is all he has.'

But still not enough for train fare for the four of them. Mama and Bella debated hammer-and-tongs who should be left behind to find her own way to Winnipeg, on foot if necessary.

While they were quarrelling, Clover opened her letter from Victor, and three American twenty-dollar bills fell out.

The Casting Couch Redux East and Verrall heard the news and proposed that instead of stewing in their own juices, the girls come along with them for two jumps on their way to Regina, at small-time houses in Camrose and Swift Current.

'You'd waste the rent-paid place for the rest of November, yes, but you'd be earning all the way, and refining your new number at the same time,' Verrall said persuasively.

'And here's the bonus,' East said, holding her other arm. 'We thought we ought—'

'Well, we thight we might,' Verrall said.

'We think we ink, we thought, ought we not?' East joggled her arm. 'Agree! Agree!'

'To what?' Aurora begged.

Verrall swatted East to make him stop. 'Stan Bailey at the David Theatre in Camrose wants a melodrama more than life itself, he's been shopping everywhere: and we've got one in our pocket!'

'*The Casting Couch*? But we are missing Miss Heatherton for the mother, and—'

'Your sainted mama! She would be magnificent in the role! I itch to see it!'

Aurora pushed East away and turned to Verrall. 'You want to re-stage it?'

'Indeed, and we'd work on Stan to engage you for *Les Très* as well as the melodrama, so it might mean double pay—although at a sadly, even pitifully, low rate . . .'

East chimed back in, mournful: 'Worst pay in the West. He's legendary.'

In a flurry of telegrams, Stan Bailey refused to pay full shot but agreed to mount *The Casting Couch* at $120 for a two-week stint in Camrose, a town southeast of Edmonton—at least in the direction of Winnipeg. Aurora would have taken less to get them to Winnipeg on time and be able to repay Jimmy Battle's money. And Verrall thought he could also get them onto the bill at the Lyric, in Swift Current (farther south into Saskatchewan, still towards Winnipeg), where he had pull with the management.

For three days the girls rehearsed the melodrama and worked on the butterfly numbers, in a much better frame of mind and heart. The night before they left, Aurora counted the kitty beside Mama, listing additions and subtractions from the sale of their effects and the cash they'd shelled out for the new number: the purchase of sides for *On Wings of Song*, kimono silk, and new photographs.

After two counts, the tally came to $169, not including Jimmy Battle's $47, which Aurora had sewn into the bottom pocket of her grouch-bag, hoping not to have to spend it. Four train fares to Camrose cost $40.

One last brangle erupted when Aurora decided she should sell her fur wrap before they left, thinking to get a better price for it in Edmonton than she might in a smaller place. But Mama, recovered from her earlier vapours, put her Louis-heeled foot down. 'You must not sell your furs. Nothing succeeds like good clothes, and a fur carries unmistakable glamour.'

'None of *you* have furs,' Aurora said.

'You give us all cachet, by wearing yours. It's a great mistake, economy at the expense of the illusion of success.'

A dis-illusion, Aurora thought, but she did not say so, and she kept her furs.

Malingerer   On the way to the station Flora asked if they might stop to visit Sybil, laid up in the Alberta Hotel with bronchitis, lest it turn to pneumonia, to which she was prone. Verrall had told them that the Orpheum was famous for cold: 'An ungodly icy stand, where the audience knows to keep their overcoats on. Comes up through the boards as you stand onstage, shivering through your number—good for castanet acts.'

Sybil's button eyes shone out of the sheet Julius had wrapped her in, a dwindled mummy within a sarcophagus of flannel. Flora bent to kiss her hot cheek and asked whether they should perhaps crack the window—was she not sweltering in all that cloth?

'Oh no! I like to be toasty warm, you know,' Sybil said, coughing wretchedly with the effort of being vivacious. 'A sip—?'

Flora held the water glass to her lips. Sybil drank, then lay back against her cushions with a fine show of exhausted bravery. 'So you're off—and who knows when we shall meet once more?'

From the doorway, where his bulk would not impede the visit, Julius gave a grunting laugh. 'In three or four weeks' time, you malingerer! We are engaged to Regina next, then to Winnipeg ourselves. I doubt these maids of mirth will have had their photographs handed back by then.'

'It's a sad thing to be going down in the world,' Flora said. 'Camrose, of all unheard-of places—then the Lyric in Swift Current. A large house, we hear, but still small-time.'

'But *Winnipeg*,' Sybil whispered, after another coughing fit. 'Big-time! Very big!'

After a period of consultation and debate over which boarding houses to favour along the road, and which to avoid at all costs due to poor food or a history of bugs, it was time to go to the station, a block away. The girls bent to kiss her goodbye.

Sybil's eyes were feverish and fearful. She doled out dire warnings, one apiece. 'Dear Aurora! Destined for great things, my dear,' she said, with some of her usual fervour. 'Make sure you're eating enough for, you can't be too— And Clover, oh, there's a lover in your name, isn't there? You've a loving heart, that's why, but you think you'll be taken care of, and you end up taking care. Like me and poor old Jay.' She coughed, waited for breath, coughed. 'Baby Bella, last never least, the very best of all! What a merry dance you lead them! Such a tussle getting to the top, be extra careful of Mr. Pericles Pentangles, Alexander I *don't* think, unless Alexander was Lothario.'

Flora pushed Sybil's feet over and sat on the bed. 'Don't be pronouncing, Syb, you give the girls fits with your feyness,' she said.

'Oh, Flora, what yoicks we had!' Sybil wiped away a sudden tear. 'It's you I always talk to in my head. Jay wouldn't listen anyway! Nobody knows you like I do, nor me like you. Pretty thing I was in the olden days—never a candle to you for brains, but did we have larks!'

'You are smart as a whip and always was,' Flora said. 'It's you got Julius to where he is and kept him up to the mark—you'd have had a starring career of your own if you so chose.'

'Never!' Sybil was smiling, though, to think of it. The two women held hands for a little, and then Sybil said briskly, as if she'd got her health back all of a sudden, 'Where's that Jay? Jay! Come, escort the ladies to the station, they'll be missing their train. It's always nicer to go about with a man, I find.'

She blew them kisses with her fat little hands, each finger covered with spiked and sparkly rings. Tears welling out of her staring eyes, unregarded.

Snow on the Line

The train had a great pointed plow in front, a gleaming axe for snow. It seemed to Clover, settling into her seat, that they were a winter family—everything, good and bad, happened to them in snow: Papa dying—before that, Harry dying. Aurora's wedding, Bella's tangle with the Tussler. But also their first gig, and Gentry.

Clover leaned on the window, not sleepy. Victor's letter, sent with the money, had said that he would try to come to Edmonton: *If a way can be devised I will devise it.* But now—well, they would meet in Winnipeg, perhaps, where he had two gigs in February. Unless he went to England to enlist.

Their predicament had knocked the war out of her thinking, but not out of Victor's. There was a car of soldiers on this train, heading to some camp, not yet overseas. In uniform, though, very boisterous with each other, some already sprawled snoring across the seats. How would Victor the Eccentric fare with men like that? He would win them over, but perhaps not straightaway. Strange never to have seen him in any other circumstances but backstage in vaude. Or the night in the woods, at the roadhouse.

Emptying her mind of worry, she looked out at the winter landscape. Snow and sky in places indistinguishable because they were almost of one colour: the sky white-ash and the snow blue-ash. Monochrome, except that the blue-grey of the trees held inside it a suspicion of orangey life, ash over embers. A long, curling ostrich-plume of smoke trailed behind the train.

Three crows hopped from a snow-furred telegraph wire, knocking the snow free from the line and leaving a blank space—she now saw many such breaks in the wire-snow, where birds had been and gone like notes in music sitting on the staff.

Snow had drifted onto the tracks. The sun shone in a long low line; they would miss band call if the train was held up for long. Ahead, a small army of men in dark clothing, all wearing dark caps, shovelled and gestured while the engine steamed and stamped. The thick glass of the window did not let her hear their shouts. Their clothes were dotted with snow; more snow fell as they worked.

King of Whiskeys Bella thought Camrose was no kind of a town. A little spot on the blank earth, two streets, dirt blown bare of snow. Still, a certain lightness of heart came with being nomads again, rather than stuffy apartment-dwelling citizens. Apartments were for the audience.

The David Theatre, at the top of the main business street, had a new coat of paint: green, gold and white, garishly delineating medallions of pressed tin that covered walls and ceiling. As they waited for Mr. Bailey to appear, Aurora said it was refreshing to see a theatre with its roof on tight. In this wintry snap the David was as cold as Sybil's Orpheum, but that would remedy itself when warm bodies filled it to bursting, as East had assured Bella they would. In a moment, a short, carrot-headed man came up the auditorium aisle, eyeing them.

'The Belle Auroras,' Mama said, in her old grand manner. 'Here for *The Casting Couch*.' She held her hand out, as if she expected him to kiss it; he stared at her blankly. Clover touched Mama's elbow to restrain her, and Mama shook her off, with some irritation.

'Hello, Mr. Bailey!' Aurora gave him an ordinary smile, to make up for Mama's condescension. 'Very sorry we've missed band call—the train was held up by snow. We are here to join Mr. East and Mr. Verrall in the melodrama. I promise you, we are ready.'

Understanding seeped gradually into Mr. Bailey's stolid face. 'Ho!' he said. 'Down in the dressing room. Ladies stage left,' he added, pointing stage right, revealing himself not to be a true man of vaudeville yet; Bella felt pleasantly superior.

They went through a door into the bare brick-walled backstage—no wonder it was cold—and down the side stairs, Bella in a clattering rush, taking the luxury of being loud, since no one was working above.

The dressing room was empty, cramped, and hot: a Quebec stove in one corner churning out heat. The comforting sameness of lights and tables and small rooms to make ready in. Mama pulled a chair nearer the stove, sank into it, and shut her eyes.

'Oh my dears, I can't seem to get warm, since seeing Sybil shivering,' she said.

While Aurora unpacked their makeup boxes, Clover ran up again with the purse, to see if the boy had brought their basket-trunk yet. The other baggage had been sent straight to Mrs. Ardmore's boarding house, where East and Verrall were also putting up.

Bella called through the wall, 'East! Verrall! Are you there?' and received a muted shout in reply; she bustled out to ask when the run-through of the melodrama would be held.

In the men's room East was lounging on the dressing table, flat on his back, cutting his fingernails with a jackknife. He looked up. 'You're here, are you? Thought you'd mosey along?'

'The train was held up, snow—'

'Oh, there's always some excuse from women,' East said. Unfairly, of course, but Bella did not need Verrall to scold East for it. She laughed and demanded to know why they were not going to do the golf sketch at the David.

'Nobody golfs,' Verrall said. 'They don't speak the language.'

Groaning, East rolled over and sat up. 'Wouldn't get a single laugh. Out, wenchling! I disrobe. And take that to your mama.' His hand whipped out to toss a white paper bag of opera fudge. East always had something sweet about him, it was one way he acquired his lady friends. He did not usually waste it on *them*, though.

'Sybil's made her sad, the candy might cheer her up,' he said, and Bella understood: he was sacrificing his bait for the good of the melodrama. Fair enough.

Her Beaux Yeux Aurora inspected the dressing table, wiping it down so she could lay out, and polished the mirror. Reaching the edge of it she found a picture drawn in pencil on the wall: *King of Whiskeys.* She laughed, for the first time in a long while. So Jimmy had played here too. He had been so kind, campaigning for them, sending the money. Did it mean he was no longer associated with Eleanor Masefield? She had no one to ask, and had not liked to put such a bald question in her letter of thanks. She opened her dressing-box and took out the silver bracelet he had given her long ago.

The cast had rehearsed in Edmonton, but when the audition began that evening with the audience in place (breathing, sighing, emanating their anxiety for the innocent Miss Sylvia), Aurora found it different. Perhaps it was the deep golden warmth of the lit stage in darkness, or the costume slowing her movement. She had not worn the peau de soie for rehearsals—its heavy, luxurious skirt, trailing after her as she moved, gave greater gravity to the scene. She was brought to sudden attention by East's line, which she had heard a thousand times:

MALVERLEY: *(aside)* She maddens me! But her *beaux yeux* will not make me *marry* her . . .

That hissing whisper seemed to ring in her ears, hanging in the empty atmosphere above the stage. If Sybil's information about the San Francisco wife was true, then the line was true—Mayhew had *not* married her. The world ran still and cold. She turned, and the turning seemed to take an age.

SYLVIA: What's that you say, Mr. Malverley?

The audience tensed and gasped at her hauteur—

MALVERLEY: *(hastily)* I say I long for your sake to *marry*
      you! To smooth life's path, to heal the wounds that
      fate has dealt you, and your sainted mother.
SYLVIA: Sir! You deal with me, here, not my mother. Let
      us leave her out of our—negotiations. I believe I
      will have a glass of wine, if you will join me?

—and they were hers from that moment, as she worked to bring about Malverley's ruin. As she sang the aria for him and drew him in, as she doctored his wine, as the plot worked its tortuous and silly way, she felt herself unfreezing and coming to a fine and useful heat. Use this, she thought, *use this*.

The Only Possible

Verrall watched the nonsensical *Casting Couch* from the wings, enthralled. Half believing it. Having drugged the wine, Aurora bent to frisk old East—who was as ticklish as the devil and always had to bite his cheek not to giggle as he was searched. Right then, in that ludicrous moment of melodrama, Verrall realized that he must love Aurora. The only woman, ever, the only possible. He saw it very clearly.

Sad, he told himself, drawing a slow breath. An odd stick of a thing like himself, and too old, besides; and then there was East. You couldn't abandon a fellow.

But Aurora, the lovely girl. Everything about her fine and sweet; the vile stinking Mayhew ought to be bullwhipped or worse. Look at her, suffering there—ah, but she had the letter and was reading it, released from bondage, on fire with relief and joy. He found himself overcome, and had to turn aside to blow his nose, quietly but thoroughly, before gathering Flora up to chase her on for her big scene.

Close-Packed Teeth At the end of the first week at Mrs. Ardmore's, Bella and Clover joined the boarders for midday Sunday dinner in the dining hall. Two long tables filled the room, with not enough leeway between for either set of chairs to be comfortable; patrons on the inside were prisoners till the end of the meal. Twenty boarders at a sit, Mrs. Ardmore boasted. Many of the boarders had returned from church; they all seemed to have been awake for hours, working up an appetite; the noise was terrific as Clover and Bella sidled through to less-desirable inner chairs. East and Verrall were already ensconced, East in a prime window corner, Verrall wedged beside him.

Aurora had turned over in the bed that morning, not feeling well, and begged to be allowed to sleep, a very rare thing with her. Mama was still dressing. Bella and Clover had waited, tiptoeing around the darkened room, till Clover signed that they ought to go down ahead.

Now Bella almost wished they had not. A fat man covered in bristles speared his food with his fork, all anyhow, and sawed at it with his knife held awkwardly. Bella looked away. It was snobbish, wanting to eat like civilized people. Mama had been diligent in correcting them, quoting Aunt Queen. Table manners *were* a social delineator. The woman across the table was picking at something caught in her tooth, which she examined and then ate. Bella resolved never to do that again, although her close-packed teeth were prone to catching celery strings and meat. Clover's little pearls were spaced apart so she never had any trouble; Aurora's teeth were perfect. Oh, it was hard to be the homely; the youngest ought always to be the prettiest. Gawky and too buxom—and spots on her skin, now. Although her blue boots were very nice, she herself was hideous and she knew it, and so did the others, however they might try to puff her up.

Food was handed down the table: massive bowls of mashed potatoes, cabbage salad with cooked dressing, a crock of beans, a platter of bumpy sausages. Food piling into all those mouths. Clover, a surgeon with her knife and fork, reminded Bella of Papa. All around them men and women sat, chewing with their mouths open, knocking ladles onto the floor and putting them straight back into dishes; but Clover polished her teaspoon on her napkin and ate blancmange, calmly accepting everyone—not superior either, just being herself. Bella made a second resolution: to overlook the faults of others.

Mama came late enough to table that she could not forge a way to the seat Bella had saved. Instead she perched on the piano stool at the head of the table, under Mrs. Ardmore's elbow, flinching every time the landlady's wooden spoon banged.

A clanging came from the front doorbell. Mrs. Ardmore shouted to the back regions, 'Bridie! Come answer the door! *Bridie!*' until a small girl in a gunny-sack apron scuttled out from the kitchen, and opened the door wide, so that a whirl of cold air and snow blew in.

With it blew a man in a flowing dark greatcoat. He came to the archway and peered round the crowded room, searching for someone, it seemed. He undid his muffler and lifted his hat, revealing the fluffy coxcomb of hair, the thin tender cheek and interested eye of Victor Saborsky, the Eccentric.

Clover stood straight up, and cried out, 'Here I am!'

Victor laughed, and somehow made a straight path through the tables to catch her hands and then her shoulders, to pull her to him. They embraced in the centre of all those people, right out in public. Bella was a bit shocked. When Clover woke to where they were, she stepped back, or would have if there'd been room.

Mama gave a startling shriek and leaped up herself, wild-eyed in horror, hands clapped to her cheeks. Clover clasped Victor's hand, saying, 'Oh, no, Mama—it is quite all right— We—'

'No, no, oh no—just, I have broken a tooth,' Mama said. She burst into small childish sobs, and Bella went squirming through the crowd to help her.

The assembled boarders exclaimed, one or two of the rougher boys laughed, and Mrs. Ardmore banged her spoon on the table for order, bellowing that dinner service was over. 'Supper to be had at six sharp, for those who behave like civilized gentlemen!'

Victor, whose own teeth were awful, slipped out during the commotion and came back within ten minutes, having searched out and arranged for a dentist to see Mama right away.

'So kind,' Mama said earnestly to Clover. 'I see, now, what you love in him.' But she continued to mourn all afternoon. Even as the dentist (with the very latest in nitrous oxide equipment for pain-free dental excavation) prepared to pull what remained of her tooth, she wept all the harder, until the nitrous took her.

When she first caught sight of herself in the mirror afterwards, though, Mama's eyes were quite, quite dry. 'There goes the last of my beauty,' she said.

Bella and Clover clasped her hands. 'You are always beautiful,' Bella told her. 'The *most* beautiful.'

'We will have a replacement tooth made very soon,' Aurora promised, but Bella saw how carefully she folded the flap down on the grouch-bag, lighter by another five dollars.

A Quiet Walk

Victor had been set on their trail by Julius, whom he had found performing alone at the Orpheum. 'I am afraid for Sybil,' Victor told Clover, and the whole company, settled that evening in Mrs. Ardmore's tiny parlour for a hand or two of cards—East and Verrall having shelled out extra for the privilege of lounging there with guests on Sunday afternoons. 'Julius scolds her for a lay-about, but she is not shamming, and he knows it—high fever, eyes distressed. She pants.'

Mama turned aside, shuffling the old playing cards over and over.

'She seemed in a terrible state when we visited her,' Clover said. 'Julius had her tight-wrapped in flannel, but the hotel room was not warm enough.'

'No, but it will be the Orpheum's chill that kills her, you mark,' East predicted.

At Mama's face, Bella begged him to stop—and Verrall suddenly shouted, 'Don't be a bloody dolt, East!'

Everyone was silent.

Verrall shrugged and sank back to the piano bench, blushing a faint rose. 'Sybil is—we are all used to arctic air. Takes an iron constitution to tour, and she's been touring twenty years.'

They left the subject, no one wishing to think further on Sybil's illness, since they had no remedy and could not even take over a bottle of spirits to lift hers.

The wind had dropped, and it was not so cold. Slipping outdoors once Mama became engrossed in Racing Demon, Clover and Victor walked deserted streets under the full moon, by the light of which he regaled her with tales of Galichen the guru, whose philosophy ascribed eerie importance to the moon, and the follies of his own mother, now a full-fledged disciple. 'Working her way up through the ranks of acolytes as fast as her slim purse will take her,' Victor said, but with tolerance.

Clover kept step with Victor's beautiful flowing gait, and they soon passed out of the town along the empty road, which had blown clear of snow and was sheltered by drifted banks.

'I respect her fervour. Since my father died she has had no outlet for her energies; no way now to return to Paris, with the war.'

That word hung in the frozen air like the moon, Clover thought. Distant, constant, overlooking, undeniable. Victor did not pause at it, but continued his account of Galichen selling a carpet to the widow whose son he had cured, by hypnosis, of a terrible opium addiction. 'He is one of the great storytellers. That is half—three-quarters of his mystery. He travelled the east as we vaudevillians tour, performing, gathering tales, working with yogis. He swears there is no truth to the rumour that he was once a secret agent of the Russian Tsar—and the Scales are definitely not secret semaphore code.'

'The scales?'

He stopped in his tracks and laughed. 'Wait, I will show you. Sometimes his followers are not allowed to speak, but must communicate only by physical movements he has taught them—his sense of humour is so strange that I do not know what this means. It might be nonsensical gyration—or a powerful gathering and expending of energy. The movements, which he calls *directions of intent*, are arranged in scales, sequences as permutable as the layouts of Tarot cards.' He took off his overcoat, threw it to a bank of snow, and struck a twisted attitude, staring and reaching backwards with his arm across his face. 'The numbers go up on a notice board in the garden hall of the London house: *Eleven to three!*' he cried, and drew his right arm from behind him as if it wanted to go through his body, then slipping it round and out in front, stretching heavenward and to the right. '*Three to one, one to eight!*' The arm described a wide circle over his head, flung down and back, then reached out yearningly to the middle left as if begging a coin from a passing king. She had seen him doing movements like these before, alone on the empty stage after the band call. 'All the community comes pouring out into the garden in the yellow-green light of spring to convey unearthly concepts. Is he at an upstairs window, laughing at his foolish followers? But the movements feel wonderful. *Eight to four, four to twelve, twelve to seven!*' he continued, reaching to different points, like da Vinci's drawing in her father's book, a trebled man inside a globe.

'But *is* it a code?' Clover demanded. 'What are you saying now?'

'I am attracted to you, as to a vast electromagnet!' Victor answered as he swept through the compass. 'You are the light and warmth upon which life depends, the glow of the ray of creation—in the magnetic economy of the universe nothing is lost, *ten to six*, and the energy that entwines us, *six to eleven*, having finished its work on this plane, will go to another—*and eleven to three!*'

The scale complete, Victor pulled her down onto the overcoat which he had flung on the bank, sinking them into the drift as into a feather bed.

He pointed up. '*Man cannot tear free from the moon*, Galichen says. All our movements and actions are controlled by her. If one kills a man, the moon does it. If one sacrifices himself for others, the moon does that also. All evil deeds, all crimes, all heroic exploits, all the actions of an ordinary life, are due to the influence of the moon on our minds and hearts.'

She stared at the monstrous moon and then at Victor's face.

He caught her eyes and stopped playing the lunatic. 'So says Galichen, and I love him for his madness, but it is not true. You are the moon for me, Clover.'

They turned together in the warmth of his coat, as if true magnets were pulling them—no need to be apart. No outdated falseness, no propriety could keep them from each other. No buttons, no belts, no cold, no hollow, wall-eyed moon could slow their snowy marriage.

A Pair of Scissors

Across the fields, upstairs in Mrs. Ardmore's boarding house, Aurora lay in a trapezoid of moonlight, half awake. Mama and Bella had stayed to play cards with East and the others, but she had found herself unaccountably sleepy, and had slipped away. She ached underneath, as if from riding, and she did not know why. She held herself cupped in her hand, unable not to, needing comfort or company, somehow, in this new loneliness.

Clover was out walking with Victor, in the snow, but that was all right. Although Aurora could not imagine loving the Eccentric herself, he and Clover were as well matched as fireplace dogs, or the two halves of a pair of scissors. Neither useful without the other, it seemed, now that they had found each other.

No need to weep, Aurora told herself. But she had time before the others came up to bed, so she did.

A Drop Too Much A few days later, with East and Verrall but without Victor, they disembarked at the train station in Swift Current. A hilly place, pretty in the noonday sun. Motes of snow fell through still air. Clover was relieved to be out of the train and felt somehow freed by the height of the cloud-straddled blue sky, clouds like cotton batten pulled thin.

The Lyric had a woman in charge. Calm, barrel-bodied, Lyddie ran the place with an iron thumb strong upon the neck of all; she had even rented out the basement of the theatre for the drilling and training of soldiers, so there was a martial stir about the place. Lyddie slapped East's shoulder and gave Verrall an arm, and put them all straight to work. Her stagehands were well trained, and everybody involved in *The Casting Couch* relaxed, knowing it would go well that night.

It was a good house, too, the people of Swift Current being starved for entertainment with only two theatres open. At the end of the play, when the cast stood together to bow, the audience looked to Clover, peeking from the wings, like people who have been to an unexpected feast. Pleased and full, grateful to the cooks. That is what we are, she thought.

But Mrs. O'Hara's boarding house, booked on Julius's recommendation, was appalling.

The woman herself was fully drunk. They had been late arriving, it was true, past ten-thirty, and nobody would blame a poor woman for taking a drop in the evening, but Mrs. O'Hara opened the door in her nightgown, pulling a dirty plaid shawl around her, far gone in drink, reeking of sweat and homebrew. Her burnt-red hair was slipping down at the back and sides. She bunched it up and solemnly, stupidly, fixed a pin in it again. After thus repairing her hair, Mrs. O'Hara pulled herself up the stairs ahead of Mama by hauling on the handrail. She threw open the door of a double room with pride, wincing at the slam as the door met the wall behind.

Mama put out an arm to stop the girls, bidding them stay in the hall, and moved into the room, a squalid chamber with bare dirty windows and a sagging bed, ill-covered by a torn quilt. She pointed, and twitched one end of the covering, to reveal the bed-legs standing in rusted tin cans. She sniffed for kerosene.

'Empty, but you know what they are there for,' Mama said quietly.

The landlady leaned against the wall, seemingly dizzy. Mama went to the head of the bed and turned back the bedclothes—and something, many things, moved on the unsheeted mattress. Nothing matches the scuttle of a bug, Clover thought. Prickles moved up and down her arms.

'Bedding?' Mama asked, speaking sharply, to wake the woman from her stupor.

'I'll get sh-sheets,' the woman said. She coughed phlegm into a filthy hankie. 'Water jug, my son's supposed—but—he's away—'

'It's a wonder to me that you have not been closed down,' Mama said.

The woman laughed, 'Nobody minds my housekeeping when they've et my cooking! I'm the best cook in the province of Saskatchewan, and damn anyone who doubts it.'

'Enough!' Mama said, with a chilling absence of emotion. 'Never receive a guest when drunk again. You've lost the custom of many more than us by this disgraceful room—we represent the vast part of your clientele, and you'll find vaudevillians stick together.'

Pushing the girls before her, Mama marched down the stairs and out.

'My son has gone for a soldier,' Mrs. O'Hara said from the top of the stairs. 'And if I've took a drop too much that's the cause of it.'

Clover looked back up the flight to where the woman lolled against the banister rail.

'I didn't raise my boy to be a soldier!' Mrs. O'Hara fumbled with her shawl, heavy with the drink, almost fell and then stood upright again. 'I'll fight anyone who says I did!'

They went down the front steps and out into the street, a small phalanx with no bed for the night.

'You can't have your deposit back,' Mrs. O'Hara shouted after them.

Since they had paid none, they were not worried about that.

Above the Lyric   Arriving so late, they perplexed the prim hotel clerk at the Alexandra, a block from the Lyric, who was reluctant to admit he had a room available and made all kinds of difficulties. Aurora was reminded strongly of Verrall in the hotel sketch—then realized with a laugh (as East and Verrall sauntered in the door from the beer parlour) that of course the performance must be based on this very man.

East and Verrall gave them bona fides, and winked and worried the clerk into finding them a room with two beds—on the shady side, so the morning would not strike too harshly in their eyes, as Verrall put it, with a flowery bow that clearly impressed the clerk. When Aurora explained that they had come away from Mrs. O'Hara's, East shouted, '*No*, not there! What were you thinking?'

The desk clerk, succumbing to East's personality, or to Verrall's kindness, swivelled the register around to Mama, took a pen out of a glass of buckshot, dipped it in the inkwell and handed it to her.

Verrall took Aurora aside for a conference: he and East were not staying in the hotel, but were putting up in the small apartments above the Lyric—'Shall I ask Lyddie to fit you in there too?' Aurora snatched at this intervention. The next day, after a quick tour of the suite Lyddie had to let—four small rooms opening off each other, an ingenious arrangement whereby one large skylight served to light all the rooms—Aurora closed with the offer.

The Love Magician   East & Verrall had a new bit, twenty minutes all on love. Bella was featured in the middle sketch, but their act opened with East alone onstage, as a Love Magician in a vast flashy turban. He called out to the audience for a volunteer, in a ludicrous accent intended to portray the mysterious Hindu: 'I must have a man with the physique of Hercules, the courage of Napoleon—above all, with what we might delicately call *It*.'

At that, Verrall slid out of his seat and came down the aisle, slumped into a scrawny slope.

'Sir, did you not hear the particular criteria?' East demanded, turban bobbing. 'I am looking for someone with *It*.'

'Oh!' said Verrall. 'I thought you said *If*.'

Backstage, Bella laughed at that every time, a corner of curtain-leg over her mouth to muffle it.

East read Verrall's mind, retrieving from concealment in the turban a miner's reflector and a magnifying glass, and peering in Verrall's ear. 'Ahhh! Down here . . . down this very dark tunnel, I begin to see . . .'

'What, what?' Verrall asked, agog.

'No. I was wrong. Nothing there at all.' He tapped with a small hammer on Verrall's head. The orchestra timpanist made a lovely knock on the wooden block.

East promised to conjure up a wife for Verrall, but all his magic failed, as lovely visions (Bella, popping up from behind a screen in a succession of hats) appeared, took one look at Verrall, and vanished again in small puffs of smoke (which East continually begged the stage-hand to make *very* small, since smoke-powder was expensive).

Finally the magician tore off his turban and stomped on it. 'By jinks, I'll have to marry you myself!'

After a musical interlude they were back, in their usual bowlers, criss-crossing the stage with their loping lallygagging stride—Verrall saying sadly, 'If it weren't for pickpockets, I'd have no love life at all.'

East suggested that Verrall send for a mail-order bride.

'I tried that once,' Verrall confessed. 'Put an ad in the classifieds: *Wife Wanted*. Next day I had a hundred replies! Each one said, *You can have mine*.'

Pa-dum-cha! from the timpanist.

'I'm a married man myself,' East said, passing again. 'People ask the secret of our long marriage, and it is simply this: we take time to go to a restaurant every week. A little candlelight dinner, soft music, dancing . . . Mmm.' He stared dreamily into the middle distance.

'And does it work, Mr. East?'

'Works like a charm. She goes Thursdays, I go Fridays.'

Another cymbal.

Bella turned up in the second half of their act, in a very short skirt (now that they were wearing the brief butterfly skirts, nothing seemed too short, even to Mama) with a very large bow tying up her ruffly hair. She and East became instant pals, and he recruited her as a possible mate for his pal Verrall.

'Not for me,' he promised her. 'No no no no. I've *got* a wife, who is worth her weight in gold.'

He took out a photo to show Bella, who exclaimed, 'Oh my, I didn't think there was that much money in the world!' He nodded, proudly, then did a lovely double-take. Some nights he made it a triple-take— Verrall kept challenging him to try a quadruple.

Bella changed clothes almost without ceasing, but she enjoyed that, with always the laughable risk of going on in the wrong costume. Lucky the wings came first, she thought, and Clover now helped her to lay out her quick changes, since the night she'd missed one change and had been scolded by East and docked fifty cents of her pay—still one silver dollar per performance. They ought to address that ridiculous deal, Aurora had said, but it was only through East and Verrall that they'd got this gig at all.

Pie   In the street in front of the Lyric that evening, as they set off to the late-opening café for supper after the second show, a small crowd had gathered. The usual bold young men wanting to speak to East, shy ones sending furtive glances to the girls. A woman detached herself from the group and rushed forward to Aurora, who felt Clover move closer to protect her.

It was Mrs. O'Hara, from the filthy boarding house.

'Oh miss,' she cried, drunk again, but not as far gone as before. 'I wanted to tell you how good you was. I'm ashamed of how you saw me the other night and I—you made me cry so, that song.'

Verrall, leaving East to the young men, tried to motion Mrs. O'Hara away. He waved to the seven-foot-tall policeman strolling the sidewalk across the street.

'No, Mr. Verrall, it's all right,' Aurora said.

'My own boy, gone to the war already,' Mrs. O'Hara said. 'Not old enough to let him go. I live in fear, miss, and I can't bear, but needs must, you know, needs must, needs must, and there was no work here for him to—' She cracked into ugly weeping.

'You must be proud of your son for serving his King and country,' Aurora suggested. Clover took Mrs. O'Hara's arm and gave her a hanky.

The tall policeman had arrived; he bent to listen.

'He was a gentle boy,' Mrs. O'Hara said. 'He could not smack a fly, you know.'

Bella patted her other arm. 'Well, but he is going to defend poor little Belgium,' Aurora said.

'I've seen the last of him, I tell myself. I know it to be true. He always liked my pie.'

'Yes,' said Aurora. 'You told us you were a good cook, I remember.'

'So I am,' the woman said, and she turned away, hiccuping, and reeled up the street into the darkness, unquestioned by the giant policeman, who crossed the street again slowly on long stilt legs.

'You *belong* in vaudeville, you know,' East called after him.

They turned away to the lit windows of the Modern Restaurant.

All the rest of their time at the Lyric, a pie arrived for Aurora every afternoon.

Dummy

Their next stop, Regina, was a wasteland of snow. The day they arrived a blizzard came in behind them, and no sooner had they established themselves in Mrs. Mead's, the boarding house where East and Verrall always stayed, than the world went white.

When the storm finally let up they rushed to band call through fresh-sugared streets, in air so still and cold their nostrils froze together.

Wish as Flora might to run, her legs would not obey. Bella's gloveless fingers were beet-red with cold when they arrived, and Flora took her hands between her own to warm them—only just stopping herself from thrusting Bella's hands into her bodice, as she used to do when the girls were very small.

The Regina bill was sharps and flats, East had said. The Belle Auroras were preceded by a terrible act, Scintillating Songsters: two small bald men with wheedling smiles, a bull-shaped woman swaying between them, in rousing roundelays of slightly-off songs like *Mrs. Binns's Twins* in English accents. After them, it was a haul to retrieve whatever audience was already there. Stragglers, coming in as the girls began, were easier to catch.

East and Verrall were headlining at the Regina Theatre, but did not put on airs about it. They always behaved the same, whatever their position. The bill was filled out by a semi-amateur blackface troupe, Hubert's Loop-de-Loop. Eight slender young men, who ought to have had better things to do than sing college songs with shoe polish on their faces, Flora said, aside, to East.

'Once conscription starts up,' East said, 'they'll be gone. Make the most of 'em, ladies.'

The *Butterfly* number went over big, with those long fluttering wings, which Bella and Clover made fan and flicker in the footlights. In the cold backstage Flora confided to Aurora her worry that the costumes might edge over the line into tawdry: 'And the more high-toned an act, the better the pay, it has to be faced.' The butterfly idea was pure art—but seeing Clover's goose-pimpled arms and bluish bare legs, Flora imagined light-floating skirts (and perhaps pale green leather slippers?) when they finally reached Winnipeg and had some money to work with. The loss of that money in Mayhew's bank had bruised her deep in her soul, leaving a dank sense of foreboding, and along with everything else it made her feel very low.

Dread burst into flower one morning shortly before Christmas, as she sat in the audience waiting for the girls at band call. Hearing some noise, she looked back to the lobby doors and saw Julius Foster Konigsburg roiling down the aisle, carrying a huge valise. Alone.

She stood up and went to meet him, her hands outstretched.

'Sybil?' she asked, and he stared, trying to bring her face into focus. Her hand went nervously to her mouth, to hide the gap in her teeth.

'Flora Dora,' he said, after a moment. 'Yes, indeed, the *Dame aux Fleurs*.' He was not reeling drunk, but studiously, concentratedly so.

She took his hands, which were pawing at his pockets as if in search of a bottle, and he stilled, and stood there for a moment unspeaking.

'You've guessed it,' he said then.

'Oh, my dear,' she said.

'Two weeks gone.' He counted. 'Yes. Hah. Seems longer.'

Flora guided him into the seats, out of the way as the company moved up and down the aisle.

'Quite quick, at the end,' he said. 'She asked for you, if that's a comfort. Don't see why it would be.' His hand trembled on the velvet armrest. She did not quite dare to touch him.

'I put pennies on her eyes,' he said. 'One is required to do so. But they fell off, and her eyes flew open, and for a moment I persuaded myself—'

Kneeling, she took his hand and kissed it, but he snatched it away and flicked the air. 'Frees me up,' he said. 'I'll travel now.'

Flora looked at him, the bulk of him wedged into the velvet seat. He had not shaved, but his shirt was clean and buttoned, a string tie pulled tight at the neck.

East and Verrall, coming down the aisle, saw them and approached. Behind Julius, East gestured, questioning, and Flora nodded. 'Come on, then, old chum,' Verrall said. He took one arm and East took the other, and they helped Julius to rise.

'Foster & Foster, ventriloquy,' he told them, as if they were the management. 'I've bought a dummy. I'll do Syb's lines for her.'

'Come on, you bunk in with us,' East said. 'We'll take you back and set you up. Don't dawdle, now, we're going to be late.'

Flora sat back down and laid her head along the red velvet, and cried like a little girl.

Gone for a Soldier

Soon after Julius arrived, as if he had brought trouble with him, something went wrong with the furnace at the boarding house. Mrs. Mead's husband ran up and down stairs with buckets and wrenches; workmen trooped through the house, to no avail. Cold pervaded everything. Tea steamed in the cups, the air was so frigid.

Clover listened as Mama complained, heavy-eyed and listless, that she could not keep warm. In some form of mourning for Sybil's death, she took to her bed and stayed there for days, missing several shows. Julius reported for duty but maintained a rigid state of semi-drunkenness; the others tried to pull him into conversation or a hand of cards, but he would not be drawn.

Clover was silent too. A couple of days earlier she had found a letter from Victor waiting at the Regina Theatre. His mother had booked him passage on a ship to England, sailing in April from New York.

> She is weak from the after-effects of rheumatic
> fever, and begs to see me before she passes beyond—
> Galichen assures me in a postscript that she is not in
> peril of death, but reminds me that I had sought some
> way over, and here two birds can be dispatched one-
> stone-wise. I will write again before I go. V

Reading it, she'd felt her heart crack inside her chest. He would die in battle, she knew it. That was what happened to the ones you loved. She'd seen the last of him. Unhurriedly, she had folded the letter and put it in the pocket of her skirt.

That night was a rough one. The invisible manager, Mr. Cartwright, whom they had never yet met, had put up a new order, in which Julius took second spot and the Belle Auroras closed the first half. A good promotion, but in his present state Julius was a tough act to follow, no one knowing on what line, or if, he would end his act. Mama had remained in bed, which complicated Aurora's quick change after *Poor Butterfly*. They felt themselves on suffrage still with Mr. Cartwright, and

were anxious for everything to go well. So anxious, in fact, that Aurora
was sick twice in the fire bucket while Bella danced the *Bumble Bee*.

Aurora went on for *Poor Butterfly*, saying that she would be all right
now. But during the bridge of the song, drifting from one painted
cherry tree to another, Clover could see her breathing very carefully
again. And then the second verse, '*The moments pass into hours, The hours
pass into years, And as she smiles through her tears, She murmurs low . . .*' she
bent to murmur low to a bough of the cherry tree, the painted whorls
of its brown cloth bark, and spat daintily into the palm of her hand.
Her face was flake-white under the black wig, Clover saw, as she came
off and held out her arms for help with the kimono.

Bella was there to do Aurora's costume change; Clover grabbed her
violin and flitted behind the backdrop. She strolled out onto the stage
as the lights came up again, and began the intro to *Danny Boy*. At the
assigned phrase she turned to watch Aurora enter, for they liked to nod
to each other as they began.

But Aurora did not come.

Clover played the intro again, then—helpless, not skilled enough
to improvise—carried on through the song. The only other piece she
knew by heart was *The Minstrel Boy*. She played that.

As her eyes adjusted to the brightness of the lights in front she
could see Aurora in the wings being wretchedly sick, shoulders heaving in silence, Bella attending to her. Bella cast a frightened glance
back at the stage, but she was half-in, half-out of her Love Magician
costume, and could hardly run on in that state.

The song was finishing. Although a serviceable violinist for
accompaniment, Clover was not a strong enough musician to hold
the crowd for long—and this was their first chance at closing the
first half.

Three more phrases, two more, the final long pull on the last
chord of *The Minstrel Boy* . . .

Clover laid her violin carefully on the small flower table, and without too much thought, stepped forward into the light where Aurora
ought to be.

'*The Minstrel Boy to the war has gone*,' she said, not singing but letting the words ring. '*In the ranks of death ye'll find him.*'

The crowd stilled. Nothing like a bit of death to stop the chatter, she thought, but she did not slow. '*His father's sword he hath girded on, and his wild harp slung behind him.*'

She paused, unwound her tartan scarf from her shoulder, and lifted it into a shawl round her head. 'My son has gone for a soldier,' she called out, in the words of Mrs. O'Hara, the boarding-house landlady at the Lyric. 'If I've took a drop too much that's the cause of it.'

Nobody moved or spoke. The men at the back stood quiet.

'I didn't raise my boy to be a soldier!'

She fumbled with her shawl, she tottered with the drink, she stood upright again.

'And I'll fight anyone who says I did!'

Not much thinking was going on in Clover's usually thought-crowded head. Faced with the imminent death of the empty stage, she had slipped a cog and gone into a different way of being—just doing, rather than thinking. Since there was no sign of Aurora entering, and the audience seemed to be listening, she kept on going, still without any planning.

In Mrs. O'Hara's hunched posture she bustled back, turned around twice, as if going up stairs, and flung open an imaginary door. 'My best room, saved for you,' she boasted to an imaginary prospective boarder, one without as much gumption as Mama. 'Oh yes! I've had the windows painted shut a-*purpose*—that way there's no nasty draft. No, no need to shift the bedclothes, sir! Perfectly clean in there—well, now look at that—' (Seeing the bugs scuttling everywhere she twitched her dress away, stomping on one, then pretended not to have stomped, then casually brushed off the boot behind her skirts.) 'Don't that beat the Dutch? Mr. Ainsley in here last seemed such a cleanly gentleman!'

She bent to sweep the bugs off the imaginary bed, and the imaginary potential boarder pointed to the cans. 'Why are the bed-legs in tin cans, you say? Oh, well, you know, precautionary—no, no, there's no kerosene in there, but should we ever need it, well, you know, it's a particulous convenimence to have the cans already there!'

The audience laughed. Bella would have laughed with them, but that was her way. Clover paid not the least attention, but kept on convincing the boarder that hers was the best house in town. She gathered herself to assert the strictness of her propriety, reciting a cascade of rules: 'No eating, no cooking, no murder done, no smoking, no smoking *hams*, no playing cards, no playing piano, no playing of the piano *accordion*,' and ending with, 'Lights out at 3 a.m. and everybody goes back to their own room! Iron-clad, no deviagation from that one.'

Again the audience laughed, a good big rollicking laugh. But it was no good, the prospective boarder was leaving. She ran ahead of him to block the stairs, promising hot water, lowering the rent, begging him to stay. And when he would not, she burst into floods of noisy alcoholic tears, explaining and exclaiming that her son was gone to serve his King and country.

'I live in fear, sir, but needs must, you know, needs must, needs must, and there was no work here for him to— He always liked my pie . . .'

The boarder seemed to relent. She took his money and watched him go upstairs to the room, then turned away, dancing a rackety little jig as she counted the money, and tucked it away in her bosom.

Still for a moment, she put both hands flat on her chest, and shut her eyes. She spoke quietly, drawing them in to hear her secret thought: 'My gentle boy. I've seen the last of him, I tell myself. I know it to be true.'

Then she straightened her back and regained her ferocious air. 'Supper at six sharp for those who are civilized behaviers,' she shouted up the stairs to her new boarder.

Clover turned back to the audience, glanced around at the upturned faces watching her, took off her shawl and curtsied, a dainty girl again. The bandleader was on the ball; he struck up a bright recruiting march, and off she went in the noise of their applause.

'What on earth possessed you?' Bella asked, interestedly, when they were alone in the dressing room, Aurora asleep on the little sofa with a cold cloth over her eyes.

'I had to do something,' Clover said. 'Nobody came on.'

'I'd have run screaming, myself.'

'Oh, you would not! You'd have done a nice dance and given them a song that you made up.'

'Well, you did more than that, you did a whole monologue! You should write that down.'

Clover wished Bella would stop talking. The whole idea was too new, or too—holy. 'I've heard enough of Julius's,' she said, pulling her dress over her head.

'Yes, but not done by a woman—that was the best part of all. Although I did like your jig. You have spidery legs, but you are a beautiful dancer.'

The Wings

On the off-days in late December the girls had Christmas party engagements. They wore their tartan scarves and sang sentimental songs to please the crowds. Every ten dollars helped get them to Winnipeg; and it was instructive to see the telephone operator girls at their Christmas tea: pinched faces, higgledy-piggledy teeth, twisted stockings and thick eyebrows. Aurora thought how easily she herself might have been one of them, watching the performers with longing.

They'd worked out a dance number for a small area, pretty and flashy, and Mama (who always accompanied them to private parties, clad in forbidding black with an air of terrifying respectability) gave them notes afterwards: 'Sloppy on the pirouettes, Bella, *snap* round. And make sure there's something going on with your eyes, all of you. Dead-face, or thinking about your supper?'

Their last night at the Regina Theatre was December twenty-seventh, the evening before they were to leave for Winnipeg at last. Christmas revelries were over, and another blinding snowstorm made it a small house, half the seats empty. But it was payday, and on receipt of their buff envelopes, the artistes were cheerful. Verrall and East ran through jokes as they dressed, Verrall dabbing on the white makeup that let him appear more of a blister than he was.

The girls stood close together in the dark, waiting for the Scintillating Songsters to be through: Bella and Clover be-winged, Aurora wrapped in her silk kimono. The various silks clung to each other and to the girls' limbs, giving off sparks in the darkness when they shifted. 'Like the moth-girls in their cocoons,' Bella whispered to Aurora, 'all wrapped and furled inside themselves.'

The Songsters creaked through *I Don't Want To Play in Your Yard* with unbearable archness, and finally ground to a halt and went off in applause so sparse it was almost silence. The lights went to black, the boy changed the placard to THE BUTTERFLY GIRLS, and the stage-hand closest to them waved Bella and Clover on.

As he did so, his cigar stub, not quite out, caught on the edge of Bella's wing.

They swept and swooped as *Spring Song* started, and the fanning motion of the wings fanned the little spark too, which almost wafted off on a burned scrap of silk, but then clung, the electricity of the air keeping it hooked.

The lower-trailing wing caught with a tiny whoosh. Bella spun, as the dance required, and the wings spun with her, and then both wings were burning.

She turned her head in a sudden animal panic, fumbling for the straps that held them on, tied tight round behind so that they would not fall off. She shrieked a tiny cry to Clover, not needed—Clover had seen and was chasing her, trying to close her arms around Bella's wings to damp them down.

Then Clover's wings caught, and the two girls stood for a moment on the spot-lit stage, stock-still, burning.

The stagehand had been watching his ropes but turned to see the flames, and the audience rose as one person, their shrieks louder than Bella's.

Aurora grabbed the fire bucket, but it was only sand, and she did not know what to do with it. When she tried to bat at the fiery wings her kimono sleeves shrivelled up in a smoking ruin that she tore off and stamped into smoke before running back to help—but it was

Verrall, running down to the stage, who did the only thing possible. In the clanking rush of the fire-curtain's descent he grabbed the girls' arms and dashed them backstage to the alley door—dislocating his shoulder as he shoved it open—and threw them out and down the steps into the snow, landing all in a squalling heap, Verrall shouting with pain, flaring bits of silk drifting like ash.

Snow fell blindingly around them, and the girls lay looking up almost peacefully into a whirl of whiteness, separate dots spinning down, small hisses as the separate flames went out.

9.

In One, in Two, in Three

JANUARY–MAY 1915

The Walker, Winnipeg
The Orpheum, Winnipeg
The Pantages, Winnipeg

Personal advice: let your conduct at all times be that of ladies and gentlemen. This same suggestion holds good while you are around the theatre, as the manager knows everything that goes on in the back of the curtain, even if he never comes back there.

FREDERICK LADELLE, *HOW TO ENTER VAUDEVILLE*

*B*ella leaned on the train window to cool her forehead. Burn-blisters from where she'd slashed at the flames pained her right hand and arm, and she was edgy and sore with her monthly visitor as well. She hated that—something she'd wanted so badly to come; wasn't that just a little sermon for you. Nothing was wrong, only that she was tired of being nervous. Pressed against the window-ledge, she ground her fist into her eye socket. Nothing was wrong; the theatre had not burned.

Clover sat upright, as still as the train allowed, a cold statue of herself to take away the heat of the fire from her hands, puffed and seeping. Perhaps—she did not know, after all—perhaps Victor was the kind of person who hated a scar.

Aurora had closed her eyes, determined to sleep. She ached every-where, and the bandages on her wrists chafed. Once they got to Winnipeg she would have to pull herself up into liveliness, to charm Mr. Walker into taking them without their props. Those beautiful wings, gone. They still had their white dresses and tartan sashes. They had *Whispering Hope, Buffalo Gals, Danny Boy*—what they'd started with, and what Gentry had given them. Yes, but they were much better now than they had once been. Almost singers. She breathed slowly and refused to worry. She thought of Jimmy, but stopped that as well. Her stomach was tight enough.

Beside her, Flora made lists of what must be done. Kimono silk found, purchased, painted, made up; or ought they to cross *Poor Butterfly* off? Her pencil hesitated. A smoky smell clung to their hands and clothes, unless that was an illusion. She had forgotten to ask Aurora what pay-ment they would be getting at the Walker. Leaving her lists, she stared out at the snowfields going by, going by. Winter again, always winter on tour. Seeing the fields as she left Madison; seeing Paddockwood in winter, seeing Arthur lying face down, a black suit flung on the snow.

Real Snap, Real Vim

'The Butterfly number was piquant, but we felt it had staled a little,' Aurora told C.P. Walker with languid confidence, sitting in his spacious, high-ceilinged office—the first elegant manager's office they'd seen. He pressed a box of bonbons on her, and when she refused, on Bella, who took two.

Mama leaned in and took a chocolate in dainty black-gloved fingers. 'My dear girls are not a *variety* act, after all.'

Aurora gave Walker a modestly glowing look, inviting him into her confidence. 'Gentry Fox, who has been so kind to us, has given me first trial of a number of new songs, which we have paired with old favourites to present a simple, evocative medley with an elegantly distinguished air.'

She wondered if she'd gone too far there.

But Mr. Walker smoothed his foxtail moustache and bowed, according them carefully gauged status: recognized artistes, strong pedigree, some standing on the circuit and the admiration of their peers. No fame, but perfectly respectable openers for the Walker Theatre.

'*Elegantly simple*,' he said. 'I like the sound of that. I tell my artistes, the single most important job is to know your material. Pick songs to show yourself to best advantage, and you're halfway there. The rest is smoke and mirrors—not *actual* smoke! No, no, our theatre, the finest playhouse in the Dominion, is absolutely fireproof.' Perhaps he could smell the smoke on them.

They were to start as openers, in one, the next day.

'I think you'll agree, ladies, that the bill goes with a real snap and real vim,' Walker said. 'You're a harmonious and delightful sort of an act, then we've got Pantalon & Pantalette, the Singing Comedics; Bee Ho Gray, the Lasso Man—his horse is a wonder and his wife's a daisy too. The DeWolf Girls, they're a classy Grecian statue act—tasteful, you know. Then intermission, then the play (except that's done now); Nutt & Nuttier get off a lot of stuff that is mighty good—nothing to touch East & Verrall, though, who we have booked for a two-week stand but not till Feb-u-ary.' He waved his hand at a large and gorgeously coloured poster, and they saw that the bill was filled out by a knife-throwing Spanish dancer, a French poodle act, and the headliner Rouclere, with Mildredism ('*thought-reading with no words passed!*').

'Very nice, to be treated like artistes,' Mama whispered to Aurora, as Walker escorted them to his office door. He patted Bella absentmindedly on her swishing rump as she went by—but impressed by his office and his chocolates, she only gave him a reproachful look.

'Doors open at seven,' he said genially. 'Trouble begins at eight!'

They laughed as required and went through to the outer office. Two typists clacked in corners and a grey-crowned matron sat moored at Walker's door like a battleship ready to repel all comers, her desk fenced round.

The matron spoke through her nose about their particulars sheet, press clippings, photographs 'to be supplied in a timely fashion'— forestalled by Aurora producing these from her music case—and the vital provision of a telephone number as soon as that could be obtained from their lodgings. Aurora steeled herself to deal with this new hurdle.

But Jimmy Battle ran into the office, jumping the fence. Their friend. In a glow of high spirits he clasped each hand in turn, and told 'dear Dot' to cut the cackle. 'They're at Sadie Jewett's, same as me, you've got the number in your wonderful files!'

He opened the gate and waved them out and down the stairs. They obeyed, tying scarves and pulling on gloves, laughing at the bustle he was producing and very happy to see him—lean and black-clad as usual, legs like long matchsticks, and always debonair.

At the street door Aurora began a proper thank-you, but he would not let her speak. 'I'm on in two hours, replacing a man with the DeWolf Girls—we've got to get you settled in and figure a few things out.' As they emerged from the stage door he bundled them straight into a cab, flipped a coin to the driver and called out the address. 'Five in a hansom's a tight fit, but I promise it's only a few blocks,' Jimmy said. 'Which one's the smallest: you could sit on my lap, Bella, if you'd like?'

Bella laughed and said no, thank you very much, she was quite well placed.

'Break my heart,' he said, making a very sad face for an instant. 'Now, dear Mrs. Avery, are you well? I heard sad news of our poor old Sybil . . .'

After a few minutes comforting Mama, they pulled up in front of a dark brick house with a slim veranda. Mrs. Jewett was in the hall, a talkative lady with a false bang of yellow curls. Her boy took charge of the baggage, and Mrs. Jewett ushered Mama and the younger girls upstairs to see the two rooms she had set aside.

Aurora was left behind with Jimmy in the parlour-hall. She turned to the pier-glass, but did not lift her hands to take off her hat. Hidden by its brim she looked at him: unscathed. A little smoother, but the same. She was different now.

'I've had some time on my hands,' he said. He leaned on the tall newel post, arms gently crossed, one foot angled over the other in a graceful, athletic stance. Her blood rose in her throat. He'd been kind even long ago, when he danced to help her audition at the Empress— it was because of him that they had been hired, then and now.

He caught her eye in the long glass, and said, as if it didn't matter a whit, 'Working on a song-and-dance number—I need a partner. Might you be persuaded to join me?'

Aurora looked at him, charged with energy, bright in this stifling wood-panelled hall. An oblique bevel of the mirror seared his cheek with a scar of sun. She felt she knew him very well, and yet they'd only spent a few moments alone in these three years.

'A week to rehearse, two weeks' run. Walker will pay well for the number,' he said, as if she needed convincing. He joined her in the pier-glass. The two of them side by side, a pleasing combination of light and dark, well-matched as to size and build. 'Two hundred a week,' he promised, if it looks good when we get it sorted out,' he said. 'Strong placement, too: second-to-last in the first half.'

'What of Miss Masefield?' The play was off, Walker had said.

'She had an opportunity,' Jimmy said, smiling at Aurora with warm understanding. 'New York, a revival of *The Degenerates*, in which she had such great success some years ago. The cast was already filled, she had no need of another young man. And so!'

Aurora wished the story were otherwise, that he'd had the resolution to quit Miss Masefield's company. But after all, she had not quit Mayhew. She raised her arms to unpin her hat, her face bent away. The velvet cuff of her walking-suit fell back, revealing a bandage on one wrist. The silver bracelet she had worn for some time now caught on the gauze.

Jimmy put out a hand to touch the bracelet, then the bandage. 'What's this?'

'Oh!' She tucked her hands back into the cuffs. 'Nothing! A small fire, it was nothing. Only it burnt our props, so we are having to change our act.'

'Poor hand,' he said. He pulled her wrist gently out into the open, and kissed above the burn. 'Will you find time to dance with me, though?'

'I think so—but what about us?' *Us* always meaning the three of them, she and her sisters.

Jimmy laughed. 'Double acts come and go, sister acts are more rare. Never fear, Walker wants the Belle Auroras too. He's a man of vision, pays top dollar for good openers.'

Remembering, she pulled the grouch-bag out of her bodice and ripped the loose stitching from its inner pocket. 'Thank you for the loan,' she said. Forty-seven dollars; she counted them into his hand. Then she said, 'Now that we are quits, we can be partners.'

Brittle   East and Verrall, arriving on a later train, paid a call on the girls that evening. Verrall's arm was in a sling, but he swore he only wore it as a ploy for pity, to save joining up. East brought a white paper bag of peanut brittle, as well as the rundown on who all was in town, or had enlisted: the cream of vaudeville was rising in Winnipeg, three of its theatres counting as minor big-time—first-stringers abounded, with plenty of their old friends to round out the bills. Among East's other news: the Elocutionist, Maurice Kavanagh, was starring in a play at the Pantages.

'Kavanagh's a furniture actor,' East told them disgustedly. 'Acquits himself well enough sitting down, but the moment he stands up, he's a joke. Grabs the back of chairs, leans against the tables—rested against a wall last week and the flat collapsed. And he's got his lines written all over. Nice bit of business, picks up the picture of his dear wife—except when you look close, you see he's pasted his sides on it. Soused buffoon.'

'No, East,' Verrall objected. 'Nobody would know. He speaks as smooth as velvet and he's got grace, you've got to give him that.'

Bella glanced across to see how Aurora took this news of Kavanagh's decline. Not well—a pity to still be overset by an old drunk not treating her with respect years ago, Bella thought. Looking suddenly quite sick, Aurora dashed out of the parlour.

'Bit queasy these days, ain't she?' East asked Bella, in an interested way.

'She's always like that,' Bella said, around a mouthful of brittle. East took the bag from her.

'It's Julius that has me worried,' Verrall said. 'Since—you know—since *then*, he doesn't look after himself as he ought.'

'He told me he'd found the cure for a hangover: continuous drunkenness. I thought that was rather good,' East said. 'Continuous vaudeville used to do the same for me.'

Mama had drawn as close to the fire as the chair would fit. 'Sybil was my youth brought back,' she said, into a little silence. 'She always thought I was judging her, but I promise you, I was not.'

'No, no, Mama,' Clover said. 'We know that.'

'A good wife to Julius, a better wife than many.' She fell silent again, and in a little while East and Verrall took their leave, recalling that orchestra rehearsal would come early next morning.

Bella and Clover walked Mama up to their chamber, finding Aurora already asleep there in the alcove bed. They helped Mama undress, and put her to bed. Bella crawled in beside her to keep her warm. She smoothed Mama's hair with a gentle hand, watching the brown curls spring back, silver threads amongst the brown. Perhaps the man who wrote that song had been patting his mother's hair, soothing her after some sad trial.

In the darkened room she listened to Clover moving about, tidying their things and putting on her own nightdress, linens rustling as she climbed in with Aurora in the alcove bed; then silence fell complete. This was a cozy room. Winnipeg was the best city they'd been so far. If only their act went well tomorrow, Bella thought. She squeezed her eyes tight shut and begged the world, the universe, and the Almighty to let them make a great thing of it here, to find success.

Still Mrs. Mayhew

In the morning darkness, Aurora and Mama debated which numbers, in what order, and what the girls should wear. On the 'something glad/something sad' principle that even the dreadful Cherry Sisters obeyed, they would begin with *Buffalo Gals*, a rampageous starter that would do nicely to cover latecomers and grab the attention of the house; then the fragrant *Last Rose of Summer*; and end with *Danny Boy*. Clover took Bella through the harmony again, correcting her impatiently, while Mama ran the iron through Aurora's hair—and then the cab was at the door.

Their dressing room was shared with the two DeWolf showgirls, massive placid beauties who stood still and revolved on platforms; their ponies (smaller girls, who danced) made friendly greetings. The room was well mirrored, only two flights up; the hanging-space allotted for their costumes was if anything too much. Mama set out their things while they ran down for orchestra call. No hitches, in this smooth-running theatre. The fly-ropes ran like clockwork, the stage was clean as a whistle. The vast house, seating nearly two thousand, was a palace of white and cream and gilt. It was the most opulent theatre they'd yet played, so Aurora was interested to notice how soon it became like every other theatre: ordinary, home. Under their leader, Bert Pike, the orchestra boys were a cheerful bunch, famous for a long-continuing double-pinochle game. Even the backstage was warm, important in frigid January, and biscuits and tea were served behind the curtain before the matinee, a ceremony they hadn't seen since the Empress.

Walker strolled about the stage himself, and bowed kindly to Mama. 'Any word of Mayhew, by the by?' he asked Aurora.

She looked up at him. 'Would it matter, sir?'

'Ha! Not to me, my dear,' he said. 'But it might to you.'

'My understanding is that he has gone south, and will not be entering the Dominion again,' she said, remaining very cool.

'He mentioned an interest in Spokane,' Walker continued, not pressing exactly.

'I believe he did. But his affairs were considerably disordered after the ruin of the Muse, and I am not certain—' She broke off, and then laughed. 'To be candid, Mr. Walker, he found himself embarrassed before his creditors, and I doubt we'll ever hear from him again.'

He took her elbow and said, 'Well, well—you do right by the Walker, and I'll do right by you, Miss Avery.'

'Still Mrs. Mayhew, still,' Mama corrected him. 'Divorce being repugnant, and also, without Mr. Mayhew's assistance, impossible.'

'I intended only to use your daughter's professional name, which I trust she has retained,' Walker said smoothly.

Mrs. Walker had come down to greet the artistes as well, handsomely turned out in a brown walking dress with red velvet reverses; Walker introduced her to the girls and Mama.

'No need, I've known Flora these twenty years, my dear,' she said, extending her hand. 'I'm Hattie Anderson that was,' she said. 'I remember you from the Hey-Go-Mad Girls—you were the loveliest thing I'd ever seen, all pale blue and cream lace.'

Mama pinked with the pleasure of being remembered, and although unable to repay the compliment, thanked Mrs. Walker with a nostalgic and flourishing curtsy.

Black-and-White Puzzle The street in front of the theatre was crowded with carriages and cars by evening. Dressed for the first number, Clover wrapped herself in her shawl and ran outside for a breath of cold air. She heard the jingle of sleigh bells even through the jostling, jockeying street noise, and watched a red cariole sleigh drive up, the coachman bulbous in buffalo on the high front seat. He handed his passengers out onto the marble walk in front of the theatre and helped them slip out of their own buffalo robes; jewellery glittered on the ladies as they emerged from the dull brown cocoons.

For a faint instant Clover missed her butterfly wings. She had felt very graceful in those wings. Now she was a dull brown ball of misery. But must shake that off, for the performance. She made her way down under the house and up to the dressing rooms, with a brief detour to the convenience—where she discovered a streak of pink on her under-clothing and let out a soft gasp of relief, staring past her knees to the solved black-and-white puzzle of the tiled floor.

'Clover?' Aurora's voice came through the cubicle door.

'I'm here,' she answered, almost cheerfully.

'Are you all right?'

'Yes! Yes I am quite all right, I just—my visitor came. I will hurry.' She ought not to have given way to the relief, but Aurora did not seem to notice.

Warmer, Sweeter The house held the electric hum of a good night beginning. In the wings every rope was taut, all the hands alert. None of them with a cigar. As she checked herself, Aurora saw Bella checking—dear Bella, who could have been burned so badly, and was so brave about her poor arm and shoulder. But the music was changing. Aurora watched Bella gird herself to forget about fire and danger and just be joyful. Easy enough, on a night like this, the closest to big-time they'd yet worked in vaudeville—easy to be an opener. And there was the tune, and away they went.

'A pretty little gal I chanced to meet,
Oh, she was fair to see . . .'

Dancing behind her, Aurora thought that Bella *was* fair too—conscious of the brightness that she could command, letting it beam out to all the lovely people who had come, who were as happy to see her as she was to see them. Her heart visibly overflowing from pleasure into glee, Bella danced for her sisters and joked with them and enlisted them until they all stamped the *Buffalo Gals* stomp, and danced by the light of the moon.

The audience turned from their coat-arranging and coiffure-touching; they ceased to chatter and kiss and whisper, turned their sunflower faces up to the girls, and let themselves be carried away by nothing complicated, nothing effortful, just the enjoyable treat of a nice girl, clowning to make them laugh.

Quick change into their white dresses, and Mama had their garlands to hand—they were ready to fly back out even before the applause had stopped from *Buffalo Gals*. Aurora put out her hand and gave Clover's a clasp, wondering about her words in the convenience—she had not thought that Clover and Victor—but, no time. They danced on with the intro to *The Last Rose of Summer.*

Offstage right, and there was Mama waiting with Clover's tartan sash, her fiddle, Bella's sash—those two turned smartly and went back on—and Aurora's sash. 'Well done,' Mama whispered as she slipped the sash past Aurora's glimmering hair. 'In very good looks tonight, my dear girl!' She gave her a kiss and Aurora walked into the light, as the low-voiced violin began its strain.

'Oh Danny boy, the pipes, the pipes are calling
From glen to glen, and down the mountainside . . .'

She had not seen him before, but as she reached the end of the second verse she looked straight into Jimmy Battle's eyes, where he leaned against the arched entrance to a box. Since he was there, she sang to him, giving him a gift of fitting love, however separated by time and luck and cowardice and greed—none of that mattering.

> *'And I shall hear, tho' soft you tread above me*
> *And all my dreams will warmer, sweeter be . . .'*

Behind the violin she could hear Clover holding the line for her, deepening down so that she could rise, and she turned the lamp of her attention on every person in the audience, letting each of them know how she loved them, and always, always would.

The room was still for that ineffable instant before the applause began. Then the orchestra struck up the Pantalon music, and the Belle Auroras were done.

C.P. Walker visited their dressing room before the intermission, to say he'd heard open sobs from the audience during that last number, and to suggest that they might better work in two, with more room for their pretty dancing; he'd push Bee Ho Gray's set back into three.

'And future dates along our circuit into February or March, if your schedule will suit? I'll have my girl draw up an extension for you to sign tomorrow,' Walker told Aurora.

With a genial wave, he left them. Aurora smiled at his little girl, who had tagged along at his coattail and waved her hand too. Her coat and leggings were of curly Persian lamb, and she wore red boots.

If I Had You

Sufficiently energized by success, Mama roused herself from her lethargy to help with the choreography for Jimmy and Aurora's double act.

Walker had given them a new Irving Berlin, *If I Had You*—a silly, inconsequential ditty, but Berlin was the best of the Tin Pan Alley men, and Walker had an ear for the populist choice. 'Berlin's good for the average theatre-goer, you see—not the highbrow nor the lowbrow, but that vast intermediate bunch that is the soul of our market. Not the high end, those overeducated twits, nor the low, subnormal, jazz end. His public is the real people, the people I want in my seats.'

Mama sent Aurora and Jimmy around the room a few times to see how they went together. His arm on Aurora's back trembled, but they waltzed with discipline. Clover, watching, admired their upright carriage as well as their grace, and thought it fitting (but a little worrying, too) that neither smiled once. She wished Aurora could take it more lightly.

'Yes,' Mama said, stopping them. 'I think—yes. Make it very clean, very plain. That chassez at the end, let's develop that, but we'll work it into a one-step. Smooth gliding, never lift your feet from the floor, Mr. Battle. And, Aurora my dear, hitch up your skirt six inches—we'll make you go backwards the whole way round.'

The first time through Aurora nearly stumbled once or twice, but Jimmy caught her and Clover saw how quickly she adapted. He was a good leader: within a very few minutes Aurora relaxed to trust in his propelling. Mama insisted on military precision in the steps, declaring that the audience's pleasure would be ruined if they allowed laxity to creep in. 'Up on your toes the whole time, Aurora, to make the backwards runs work. Now we can add a little skip at the turn,' she called. 'A flirting flip with the outside leg, I think, but keep it fairy-dance, not folk—first you, Aurora.'

She did dance like a fairy, Clover thought. Her delicate ankles, her pointed shoe flung out like a narrow white petal, the tiniest sideways tilt of her head as they went round, as if she had heard, but was ignoring, a distant bell. Her relentless backwards motion was fascinating, too—Jimmy a sleek black ghost to guide her.

'The arm a little higher than usual, Mr. Battle,' Mama said. 'Yes, that gives the whole a nice *I don't care* flair that will serve very well.' She turned back to the piano. 'Maintaining detachment, clasp closer, I think, Mr. Battle. After the first round you should seem glued.'

They danced around the room again, and Clover was shocked to see the difference that instruction made. Jimmy's black leg knifed right into Aurora's white skirt; her skirt swirled and entwined him. The closeness of their lower limbs combined with the stillness of their sober faces gave the dance a curious airy thrill, compounded when they began to twirl and Aurora's pointed foot flicked up once, around once, and on the third swoop gave a charming waggle to the side.

'Light, light, chest up, chin up, all easy even when it's tricky—it's the style of it that will carry you through,' Mama said. 'I must say, dear Jimmy, you were born to dance with my girl. She's a bit of thistledown, with you to lead.'

Clover could see, when Aurora bent to refasten her shoe, that she was not feeling much like thistledown—it must be exhausting, running backwards all through the dance. But she stood up again with a smile, and as they circled the room, clasped tightly together, the twirling tightened and tensed to the point where they were simply spinning, their two feet planted as one foot, as if Aurora rode on Jimmy's feet the way they used to dance with Papa. Swing, swing, again, a full turn in only two steps, rotating around and around full-out at the climax of the dance. Mama stopped playing but continued singing the hokey little tune, and turned to give judgement.

'Yes,' she said at last, breaking off and clapping her hands. 'That will be quite the thing. I expect you will kill at the Palace.'

The Walk

Mama decided Aurora must have a new frock for the number, and sent Bella and Clover haring all over Winnipeg to dressmakers for the right weight of white lawn: 'Something with a sheen, nothing too transparent—it must float, you know, girls.'

Late at night she swept the bedroom floor carefully and cut out dress pieces. Bella hated the sound of the scissors creaking and clacking on the floorboards. Mama stitched away by day and night: peering at the sketch she had made, from time to time sighing or giving a small shriek when a sleeve turned out to be sewn in backwards. Aurora tried on the basted version, early one morning: it was a marvel. A suggestion of panniers, wide three-quarter sleeves so that it had a country air: a china shepherdess. The skirt, almost hobbled, rose quite ten inches off the ground, showing Aurora's graceful ankles and shins and her delicate white-heeled dancing slippers. She looked like an illustration from a fairy tale, Bella thought.

At breakfast, East told Bella that the Ninepins had arrived, booked for three weeks at the Orpheum, and her pleasure at this treat made her feel kindly towards her sisters, who had recently been difficult to live with—for perfectly good reasons, she understood. Aurora was an angel of grace and beauty, well deserving of Jimmy, and Clover was her darling and would always be so, however cross she became because Victor wanted to enlist.

The war was on everyone's lips. Another Canadian contingent of soldiers was being raised, but really Bella did not see that it concerned them. They were not citizens, they were of the vagabond company. No one would expect an artiste to enlist. East and Verrall (of complicated citizenry, but brought up in New York) were debating going to Australia for a prolonged tour they'd been offered: at least, East was debating it. Verrall waffled. Whereupon East clapped his hands and said, 'That's it, then—we'll get Julius to come join us for the Pantages dates, and run down into the States. Meanwhile, let's take Bella for a walk down to Mrs. Howell's to see her kid.'

Bella ran for her coat; there was time before orchestra rehearsal.

The wind had died down, and she pranced along with the two men, liking herself as a bright robin between two crows. In Mrs. Howell's parlour (an icebox, stiff with old horsehair furniture), they found Nando at the window, himself as always. Bella flew to him and jumped into his arms, as happy as she could ever remember, and they kissed—it was delightful, his nice mouth, and their two chests glued together. Mrs. Dent coughed and Nando took Bella's hands to push her gently away, grinning as if he was the broom-boy, the day they first met. He winked at his mother, and leaned forward to kiss Bella again.

Bella gave her hand to Mrs. Dent, and asked after Joe.

'We're here alone,' Myra Dent said, lips hardly parting over dark-edged teeth. Her hair had paled from ash-yellow to ash-grey. She took Bella's offered hand, and her eyes closed.

'Dad's off in the sanatorium,' Nando told them all. 'Last month down in Philly it got to be too much, and he saw it himself, so we signed him into Clifton Springs. It's only a couple of months.'

East sat on the sliding horsehair beside Myra Dent and patted her knee. He pulled a box of lemon drops out of his vest pocket, then stuffed them back in, perhaps feeling it was not the right moment. 'All the better for it,' he promised. 'Every time I go myself I'm glad I did.'

Bella was not sure she believed that East had been to a sanatorium, but Myra let up a little on looking like Death had come for them all. Bella considered it was a very good thing for Joe Dent to dry out; perhaps then he would stop lambasting his wife so badly—Bella could not credit how women did stick with brutal husbands. Like Mrs. Black in Paddockwood, covered with bruises, but would not hear a word said about Mr. Black, even when Papa had offered to help her. 'He is not hard on the boys' was all she said, in a saintly way that made Bella feel uncomfortable.

Verrall had perched himself on the piano stool, more crowlike than ever. 'But, pardon me, but—how are you to continue the Ninepins?'

'Yes, we was fussing about that,' Nando said. 'I've had an offer to make movies, but that's low class and the pay's to match, no point in slumming. A solo number's in the works, a trick wagon that breaks apart, only Dad never liked the idea. It is a bit fussy with the props.'

Nando's mother lifted her face, as if reminded of something. She had the prettiest blue eyes. 'Nando, I meant to say, they've brought the auto back.'

'Well, that's one good thing!' Nando jumped up and grabbed Bella's arm to pull her out the door, leaving his mother to East and Verrall. 'Let me take you out for a spin—you're warm enough dressed—we have our own flivver now, just like Misery Mayhew. I'll deliver you to the theatre in style, I promise you.'

Bella did not know how much of Mayhew's downfall Nando knew about. Perhaps nothing. She wondered what to tell him. He had not grown taller but had a different stride, a sort of maturity that surprised her, maybe from his father being gone. He helped her climb into the cushioned leather seat of the bright green runabout (an open car, its black cloth hood pulled up against the winter), then cranked the engine six or seven times till it caught. He jumped in beside her, worked the pedals, and they set off through the snowy streets.

'This is very nice!' Bella exclaimed, bouncing a bit to test the seats.

'An '08 Model T, a treasure, good as gold, needs a little adjustment from time to time. Just got her back from the blacksmith; he's been fixing the bumper and a few other things . . .'

There was a terrible grinding noise, and the motion stopped—and something sprang hissing from the hood of the car and flew up into the windscreen. Bella screamed.

'No, no! Nothing to fear!' His face still blank as a doormat, Nando jumped out again and went round to fasten the hood-cap back down. The windscreen had a crack in it; Bella did not think it had been there before but did not like to point it out.

He jumped back in, released the handbrake and started the car forward again.

'She's a beauty, we—' Another bang. Stuttering from the engine.

'What a pleasant thing it is to take a drive,' Bella said, gamely.

'Shut up!'

'How can you speak so unkind? I was only being pleasant!'

'Nothing pleasant about it. Someone's got something that matters to them and you make jokes. You're no different from your brother-in-law.'

'He's not my—' Well, she supposed he was, technically speaking. 'At least—Sybil said he was married already anyway, and never married Aurora at all! Besides, he's run off to the States and took everything we had, and left Aurora high and dry, so he's no more *your* enemy than he is *mine*.'

She ought not to have said all that. Not even Nando ought to know about the other wife. And poor Sybil was dead—Nando probably had not heard that, either. A cold finger of guilt crept up her neck. She turned her head away from Nando, who appeared to have paid not the least attention to all this news, but was swearing and attempting something complicated with the levers. The car limped along another few yards and then coughed and stopped, unpleasant-smelling steam curling in a weak spiral from the engine. Or perhaps it was smoke.

They sat in the cold, the silence.

East and Verrall, walking to the Orpheum for their own rehearsal call, passed by. East called, 'Get a horse!' Verrall gave a frivolous waggle of his glove, still careful with his hurt shoulder.

'Go piss yourselves,' Nando called back.

'Thank you *very* much for your considerate offer,' Bella said. 'I will walk with my friends. I see that they are going to be on time for their call and I fear if I stay with you, I shall not be.'

'Stay where you are.' Although he was as angry as she'd ever seen him, Nando's face stayed flat and calm, as if he didn't care at all what she did—even after kissing her, and being happy.

Bella cried, 'Ugh!' in exasperation and gathered her skirt, but Nando put out a quick strong hand and held her down.

Violent in her indignation, Bella stood up and smacked into the cloth hood. With a dreadful tearing noise her head went right through the roof. She pulled at her hat brim and sat down again, a ripple of hysterical giggles beginning in her chest.

She tried to keep it in. It was nothing to laugh at, the ruin of poor Nando's car.

But then he smacked a hand on the steering wheel and started to laugh himself. 'Your hat!' he said. 'I think it is worse off than the roof.'

There! She knew he was lovely. It was just his father being off in the sanatorium that made him grouch at life. Perhaps he would kiss her again.

Beneficence

After only a few days, sewing had to be interrupted on Aurora's frock, when Mama came down with a crushing headache. For several hours she blinked and scrubbed at her blurring eyes and made herself continue, trying to finish the long seam, but at last could sew no longer. Only Clover's gentle fingers stroking the papery eyelid skin seemed to help, and poppy syrup. Mama was loath to use laudanum because of dependence, but nothing else would do. She begged Clover to sit watch. She had a horror of being heard in a snore, which laudanum could produce, but her eyes were drooping, and her mouth too. 'Please, please do not leave me! If I should be noisy— Aunt Queen, you know, was a trumpet-major for snoring, and I cannot bear to— But I must be still for a little.'

Clover did not, naturally, tell Mama that she snored most nights, but doled out the drops with care and sat quietly, reading papers left by other boarders in the dining room, till Mama drowsed off and ceased her murmured complaints.

War news dominated the papers. Clover studied the map of the fighting line in Flanders and made herself read every word, trying to imagine the reality behind the accounts. The Germans had declared British waters a war zone, and anyone sailing to England would be at peril. She refused to think further about that.

Mama stirred and said in a fretful voice, 'Clover? You won't leave me, will you?'

'I am here, Mama. Go to sleep.'

'Thank you, dearest—you won't leave, though?'

Nothing could truly reassure her, not since Papa's death. Perhaps the fear was even getting worse, lately. 'I am here, sweetheart,' Clover said. She opened the dividing door, so Mama could see her from the bed, and be calm.

The German dead: 971,042 *'not counting Bavarian, Saxon, Wurtemberg and the naval lists.'* A million dead! How could that be true? But it was printed there, in the war diary. Every day as they walked to and from the theatre they saw groups of soldiers, natty in olive drab. More and more racing off to the Front.

Clover had a bump of patriotism, inherited from her father, that made her weep during the anthem. She had always mistrusted it. But it was impossible not to cheer the bravery of those honourable officers, and the Tommies slopping through muck, cocking a snook at the vile Prussians. Clover ran her eye down the columns, hurrying through accounts of sinkings and torpedoings. The first Canadian soldiers had been killed. Her cold foreboding was warmed by pride in Victor's need to be part of this enterprise, however great the cost. He was the best of men, best in the world.

The Double Act   For a week, Aurora and Jimmy rehearsed the double act in the back parlour at Mrs. Jewett's. Twice with Mama playing piano for them, once with Clover—but the fourth time, Mama's head was too bad and she wanted Clover to sit with her; Bella was out for a spin with Nando and Verrall, Nando having sworn that he'd fixed whatever was wrong with the Model T. Aurora said not to fret, she could sing the tune while she and Jimmy ran through the steps.

When Jimmy arrived Aurora took him to Mrs. Jewett's back parlour where the old piano was, then pulled the pocket doors back along their runner till the two sides met tight, and locked them top and bottom, brass sliding into brass in a silky glide and drop.

He opened the piano and set out the sheet music. Turning, he watched as she went first to one window, then the other, pulling down the blinds. It was just past ten in the morning and the house was quiet for a spell, boarders gone off to work or in their rooms, Mrs. Jewett and the help busy in the kitchen, baking pies for the boarders' dinner.

She took the big cushions from the window seat and threw them down onto the floor with soft flumps, and she undid her blouse with fingers that trembled and fumbled and worked fast.

'What are you doing?' he asked, walking over the polished floor towards her.

'There is not much time, don't waste it.' Her blouse fell, the ribbon cummerbund fell, and she stepped out of her skirt, but there was still so much fabric to get through. She kicked at the pool of froth and linen on the floor, and said, 'Please help me, please.'

He untied the waistband of her petticoat and knelt to draw it down, and buried his face in the smell and warmth of her, and she put her hands on his head. She hummed the tune as loudly as she could, and knelt beside him, and they sank together onto the pile of clothes and pillows—and really, Aurora thought, it was about time.

Turning her head away so as not to deafen him, she sang, '*I never envied the rich millionaires, I never wanted to have what was theirs, I never bother about their affairs . . . All that I want is a chance to be glad, I've grown so tired of being so sad, There's only one thing I wish that I had, That's you, just you.*'

As he pushed inside her, she had to stop singing or it would become an ululation.

Silent, then. Silence, silence, breathing carefully in and out, his arms under her hands and the fiery rage that he created spreading through her whole body, more than the blaze of the butterfly wings had been, spearing her or maybe going clear through her, their spirits dissolving into each other or knifing through and between, and there was no stopping it, their bodies in some trance of perfect time and beat, and beat, everything running between them like electricity, to shock them and to run the engines of them forward, until they died.

Very quietly, and very quickly.

She held him closer, closer, and then rolled him sideways and sprang up and dashed to the piano, playing the chorus through in a fine gallop, and then said loudly, 'All right, one more time—*I never envied the rich millionaires, I never wanted to have what was theirs, I never bother about their affairs*—' but when he reached for her she felt a warm liquidity run down the inside of her thigh, and she shuddered and laughed and shook her head, and step-stepped around the room (still in her shoes, they had not got so far as taking off her stockings), dancing as loud-clacking as might be while she grabbed one garment at a time and shrugged into it or under it, and he lay back on the cushions, laughing without the faintest sound.

'Perhaps we need a gramophone,' he said, when she was tight and tidy once more.

Four Months,
Maybe Five

On Mondays, when the rest of the town was open for business, the vaudeville people took each other out for supper to Mariaggi's or visited burlesque theatres, or danced at one of the big hotels. Jimmy and Aurora went dancing the Monday night before their premier at the Walker as the Double-Glide Duo. Aurora took Clover along for propriety; Bella had begged to come too, but Aurora had been hard as coal and would not let her. Mama told Bella she needed her to help with the finishing on the white dress, and that was the final word. Bella had thrashed off to the bedroom in a serious huff.

The Palm Lounge at the Fort Garry Hotel had a lovely little band, but it was not mere pleasure for Jimmy and Aurora to dance there: they were advertisements for themselves. Walker had taken a party there and all evening he directed their attention to Aurora and Jimmy.

Aurora was purely happy, spinning through the crystalled air, amid palm fronds and wineglasses and waiters and the polished parquet floor. The dance floor was sprung, with a horsehair cushion beneath it, so you could dance all night and never be tired. At the end of every dance, a scattering of applause broke out.

She was not tired these days, but full of vigour, with a little wellspring of pleasure—all the day brightened by the chance to dance with Jimmy. The sinews in his arm, masked by black broadcloth; everything about him so clean and fresh, the size of him just right and the steps that they knew well enough to ignore, to dream through the dances; even more, the perfect understanding that existed between them, and their alikeness.

It was too bad that Bella was angry, she would have to fix that. It was irritating; nothing was fun if Bella and Clover were unhappy. Mama's grief, on the other hand, compounded of sadness and illness, she could not fix. Around, around, around—counting without knowing that she was counting, her body knowing that they were nearing the end, the end, whirling twice more, once more, and then the sweet little dual kicks and the bow. There. The song was *Helen Gone,* a racy ragtime two-step, much more fun than the Irving Berlin they'd got to use for Mr. Walker. *Helen gone, she could dance all night until the dawn . . .*

They had supper after dancing, and as they ate Jimmy made every effort to draw Clover out. Kind, but mistaken, Aurora thought: Clover was not shy, only leaden. It was a niggling burden to see her so miserable over that odd fish Victor, who would probably sail through the war untouched, playing his strange tricks on the Hun. Catching herself thinking so uncharitably, Aurora stopped, and asked, 'Have you had a letter from Victor?'

Clover blushed, her delicate skin pinking from the cheeks outward till even her ears were rosy.

Jimmy said, with a comic leer, 'Someone has a beau?'

But that was too much. Clover, choking, stood up and left the table.

Aurora dashed down her napkin and went after her, but it was no good. Clover locked herself in a marble cubicle, only replying, 'It is nothing . . .' no matter how Aurora begged her to say what the trouble might be. Under the eye of the powder room attendant she could not bully Clover into telling. She went back out.

Jimmy was waiting in the hall. 'Walker paid our tab—decent of him,' he said. 'So we've got some coin left, and the night's a pup. Did you know that Mercy's Soubrettes are here, playing the little Lyric down by Annabella Street? We could catch their last turn.' Burlesque worked Mondays (though even those houses stayed dark on Sundays, lest the town make an example of them and shut them down permanently).

Emerging, Clover quietly agreed to go, and they set off.

Although delighted at the prospect of seeing friends again after many months, Aurora hesitated at the down-at-heels lobby of the theatre and the rowdy patrons. Jimmy grinned and elbowed them through to a box, where they sat in relative peace and watched the last of the show: a bad comic whose gimmick was that he hit himself with a rubber chicken; then a very doleful, illogical comedy-melodrama; and finally, Mercy and the Soubrettes. Billed as the Saucy Soubrettes now, instead of Simple.

Mercy wore a skimpy gypsy dress (but no more scandalous than the butterfly costumes had been, Aurora reflected); little Joyful danced behind her in a revolving series of hootchie-kootchie wiggles. Joyful, skinny as ever, stayed fully draped in a Nautch girl curtain; Mercy's seven veils, none very opaque, came off in due rotation. At the seventh, Aurora turned her head away, but found Clover staring in such surprise that she had to look back: Mercy naked, save for a peach-coloured full-body stocking.

Jimmy laughed at their shock, and after the show ground to a halt he took them round to the tiny dressing room where a dozen girls, the Soubrettes and others from earlier acts, were wiping themselves down in various stages of undress. With the tripling mirrors and the closeness and the lateness of the hour, it seemed to be a roomful of trembling rumps and breasts.

After the first exclamations, a bottle of plum brandy came out of hiding and they all sat down for a general reunion and exchange of news. The Soubrette sisters had split: Temp and simple Patience had been ill, and were in Spokane being bullied by the brother; Mercy and Joy would work the circuit till May, then go back and summer there too, so Patience could be happy. As Mercy and Joy were, to hear that the Belle Auroras were together, doing finely at the Walker, whatever vicissitudes might have come before. The room gradually filled with comics and trick jugglers who seemed to know Jimmy. Jimmy had pulled a new bottle from somewhere, and was filling glasses for the bandmen, some of whom were smoking reefer, which Aurora did not like the smell of. East arrived, without Verrall but with two hoydenish half-naked girls and a couple of pale boys; many toasts were drunk, and Clover settled in to a comfortable game of cards with Joyful, always the sweetest of the girls.

Rising from the drunken rabble to change into street clothes, Mercy pulled Aurora gently behind the screen, setting an arm round her shoulders and one warm hand on her belly.

'When is the baby coming?' she whispered, her eyes bright.

The floor seemed to buckle slightly. Aurora put her own hand over Mercy's, and then, moving Mercy's aside, over her midsection—feeling it gathered there beneath her hand, taut and firm. Oh, heavens.

'Did you not know?'

Aurora glanced above the screen to where Jimmy rocked back on his heels, laughing at some joke—then shook her head.

Mercy had seen the glance. 'Oh, you must be further along than that, to be showing. I'd say four months, maybe five.'

She skinned off her stocking-suit, whipped the legs straight, and rolled them efficiently to keep the wrinkles out; she slung her gypsy bandeau over the screen and wiped the makeup off her chest with a rough towel. In the shadows behind the screen, Mercy's naked midriff was as flat and smooth as a dish of cream—but so was her own, Aurora had thought.

'Have you not felt the baby moving? Though you're the type as won't show much, ever—I'd be over to the yard if it was me, which it won't be. I know how to stop all that.'

Moving? Aurora felt the blood humming in her ears, in her veins. 'What does it feel like?'

'Like a fish, like a secret. Like you et something that's alive.'

Then Aurora thought she might be sick again—but was too busy thinking, as a succession of images flashed through her mind: how long it had been since her last blood, Mayhew's face above her, Jimmy's. 'I have always had an uneasy stomach,' she said quietly.

Mercy laughed. 'Well, it will be uneasy now!' She put her arms round Aurora and kissed her. 'It will be all right, don't look so! The human race keeps on and on, and all of *us* were born.'

Come Up Trumps

At home, Aurora found Mama alone, nodding over her thimble, and stroked her cheek to waken her. 'Come, Mama,' she whispered, not to disturb her dream. 'We must put you to bed.'

The bedroom was still pristine—and Bella was nowhere to be seen. Just as she was about to panic, Aurora heard boots climbing the stairs, and Clover and Bella arguing, their voices boarding-house low. Mama sank onto the bed and put her feet up under the covers, turning her back so Aurora could loosen her corset, saying irritably, 'No, no, don't, just untie me, I'll sleep in my wrapper. I'm cold.'

Bella flung the door open, but caught it back before it could slam on the wall. 'You have no right to scold me!' she whispered, in a fury. 'Or to tell me what I cannot do. I'm almost sixteen—I can look after myself!'

'Not if you are so dead to propriety as to be out in the streets alone at this hour!'

'*Propriety*—' Bella fairly spat.

Clover's face was tight and cold. 'You might have run into terrible trouble, and none of us to know what had become of you.'

'I would not, so there! I was with Nando, and he would protect me, but there was no need, for we were not up to tricks but only gone for a drive for an hour to see the moon, that was all.'

Aurora tucked the gold coverlet around Mama's neck and kissed her cheek, murmuring that she and Clover would see to Bella; she drew her sisters through into the other room. 'Enough,' she said. 'Mrs. Jewett will throw us out on our ears, and if you went for an hour how does it come about that it is almost four in the morning?'

Bella gave a jumbled explanation about the state of the Portage road and the darkness and Nando being a very good driver really, except the automobile had given up the ghost five miles out of town: 'And a very good thing that I dressed warmly, because you know it is an open car, I freeze in it, so we could walk back without harm, and since there was no traffic it was a very good thing, *another* good thing, that there was a moon to light us, the lantern having broken when the car blew up.'

She got the desired effect from that, and laughed. 'Well, smoke came out of it and something melted, and Nando says it is not going to go again. But we have thought of the best thing: we're going to have it carted back to the city and turn it into a vaudeville act! Nando says he's going to call it "Bella's First Car," a very nice honour, I think.'

Aurora sat on the daybed and tried to unclench her stomach. 'Bella—you cannot run around with Nando in the middle of the night! You know what people will think of you. Perhaps Mrs. Jewett will already be composing her speech to turf us out. How could you be so naughty?'

'Naughty? I am *sixteen*! I cannot abide that superior coolness you pretend—you have a dreadful temper, if anyone crosses you!' Bella said, fierce as a fire. 'When you were sixteen you had all the money already and were looking after all of us. I don't even get to keep my own pay!'

'That's so, and it isn't right,' Clover said. She put her arm around Bella, who stayed stiff, but did not shout or pull away. 'We've been relying on you for too long to look after everything for us. We ought to divvy up the pay packet, and each put back into the kitty for lodging and food.'

Aurora could not sort her thoughts to argue against this: it was absurd, of course, and would lead to arguments and trouble, but she could not— She only wanted to be alone to think, and when was she ever, ever, alone? Through the door to the bedroom she could see Mama's mouth fallen open, head back in the doped sleep of exhaustion. Her finished white dress, hanging like a lily in the firelight.

And inside her, as she sat still and quiet, she felt a leaf tremble, a tendril grow, a finger drawn across her cheek. She said, '*Ohh*. The baby moved . . .'

Her sisters dropped beside her.

'Do not tell Mama,' she said.

Beautiful Doll

The Belle Auroras' original week at the Walker was extended 'by popular demand' and after two weeks with the *If I Had You* number, another big hit, they went on the road, down through the Walker chain into Minneapolis and points west. The houses there were not on the scale of the Winnipeg theatre, but were well run and well appointed. Bee Ho Gray travelled too, and Rouclere, so they had familiar company, as well as a few new faces to meet. They were in the money, and Flora was happy not to count the change obsessively at every tea shop. Out of town, the Walker people stayed in hotels, and that was very comfortable too, she and Clover taking one room, Bella and Aurora another.

Jimmy suggested he and Aurora work up a second song-and-dance number, another arrow for their quiver. Challenged, Flora studied sheets and chose *Oh, You Beautiful Doll*—a song that had never had much made of it. It made her think of Sybil, jaunty and nonsensical. Aurora would look very nice got up as an Eaton Beauty Doll. And she thought to herself, secretly, that the dance would work just as well if Bella were a little girl being given the doll—she worked the steps with that in mind. Jimmy was a dear boy, attentive, an elegant, expert dancer; but there was something not quite right about him. He had lost his clear look, from when they'd first met him back at the Empress. Little pouches under his eyes, a hesitancy, shame of some sort. He was—smirched, she thought.

In any case, not being a widow, Aurora could not marry anyone. When Flora thought about Mayhew her scalp tightened as if her head were swelling. She had learned not to think about him. She bent her mind to creating a lovely, adaptable set of steps, so Bella could do the trick if need be.

An Appetite

Aurora liked the new number very well. She had not told Jimmy about the baby; had not spoken of it again to her sisters, nor they to her. But it was never entirely out of her mind. When she crossed the street she was careful of trams and horses; when she was hungry she ate; when she was tired, she curled up on coats on the dressing-room floor and slept. It seemed that she had to, now that she knew. But the knowledge did not stop her wanting Jimmy— she had such an appetite for him, for the energetic exchange of their lovemaking, that it shocked her. She expected a kind of holiness to descend, instead of greater greed for their snatched opportunities. In the St. Paul Walker Theatre, a closet full of velvet drapes made a dark red bower; in Bismarck, a loose button on a dark, unused dressing-room's horsehair divan scraped the skin on her back till she bled. She felt terribly guilty about using Jimmy this way, as if he were no person but stood in for all men, as if somehow this action helped her to make the baby grow. Nonsense, of course, but then the need would seize her and she would rise silently from the bed she shared with Bella, and knock very gently on Jimmy's hotel room door.

It was exhilarating to be able to talk to him as an equal, to argue about the áct, to confer, to dance and make the new steps work. But consciousness of the child turned her inward, and even when most enwrapped and invaded by Jimmy, she was alone again. In some sense she belonged only to what was inside her. When she felt guilty, she told herself that, after all, letters from Eleanor Masefield followed him from theatre to theatre, and he did not mention them to her.

Maske of Cupid   Julius was in Winnipeg at the Orpheum when they returned in the middle of March, working with East and Verrall on a new number, a dark little playlet they'd created. *On Drunkenness*, East called it, saying Julius was just the expert required; they renamed it *Tipsychorean Tales* for the stage. Before the Belle Auroras went back on at the Walker, Clover went to see the show, sitting by herself in the gallery and having the first good laugh she'd had in the longest time. After the matinee, she walked with Julius along the stone bridge that crossed the river not far from the theatre, glad of his bulk in the fierce wind and the warmth of his dark coat-sleeve, smelling of tobacco and rum, where her hand was tucked. He rambled and rumbled about the other artistes at the Orpheum: '*The jolly company, in manner of a maske, enrangèd orderly.*'

She did not recognize the lines but did not ask their source, and he fell silent. Silence suited her. They watched the water curling under and springing forth from the edges of ice, spring awakening with a faint smell of green, the sun warm though the air was brisk.

'Your sister and this hatchling matinee idol, what of that?'

Surprised, Clover answered frankly. 'I think it is a passing fancy, only. She is happy to be with someone young, after Mayhew, but—she is—'

'With child, I know.'

She looked quickly at Julius's face, but saw no judgement there. 'They were legitimately married, as far as any of us knew, whatever the case may really be.'

'Oh yes, nothing to say Mayhew had *married* that Spanish floozy in Frisco. Poor Syb was wrong to bring it up at all, but gossip was her meat and drink.'

His face was calm, and his hands, on the stone parapet, were still.

'I heard your spontaneous monologue, at the Regina,' he said, surprising Clover again. 'Unplanned, I take it?'

She had almost forgotten that night when Aurora was so sick and did not come on; that must have been sickness from the baby, of course.

'You have—a facility,' Julius said. His mammoth head turned to pin her with an irritated glare. 'Use that intelligence,' he told her. 'One must not waste one's art.' ·

A carillon chimed from a church they could not see. Six o'clock.

'A most delicious harmony, in full strange notes,' he said. '*The fraile soule in deepe delight nigh dround.*' He tucked her hand in his arm and led her back towards the theatre. 'We will warm ourselves by the stove and watch the maskers march forth in trim array. And if the first be *Fancy, like a lovely boy of rare aspect*, well, we will be kind to him. If he is *Desyre*, I congratulate your fair sister . . . I myself am *Doubt*, the broken reed. Now if it was Victor, your own infatuate, I should have no hesitation. I trust his penmanship suffices you for now.'

Clover fell silent again. No letter, no letter. She had not heard from Victor since the night they walked out into the country, when he did scales beneath the moon.

But on her return to Mrs. Jewett's that evening, a small packet was waiting, sent over from the Walker. She slid a penknife along the manila and spread the packet open on the dresser, under the lamp's light. A red silk scarf, like a cardinal's wing—and something wrapped inside it.

She unrolled the scarf and out fell a picture postcard from Quebec, one from Montreal, and a steamship ticket for the SS *Alaunia*, sailing from Montreal to London, England, May 15, 1915.

On the back of the postcard depicting the port of Montreal: *I love you always. You know. My mother has a house, 24 St. Quintin Avenue, I wish you could*— then something scratched out, in black impatient strokes. On the back of the postcard of Quebec: *Come. Please come.* Attached to the ticket by a brass clip: a bank draft for fifty pounds.

Precious Prize

Settled at Mrs. Jewett's boarding house again, Aurora would get up as if making a trip to the convenience when Bella drowsed off, then tap on Jimmy's door and slip like a ghost down the wooden stairs to meet him in the dark back parlour. The doors slid soundlessly along the track which she had waxed with a candle stub; the heaviness of the doors matched the heaviness in her body, the ground-running depth of how badly she wanted him to drive inside her and make her climb that strange mountain again. One night she stayed in his bed almost all night, his velvety skin under hers. After Mayhew's body she was surprised by Jimmy's springing youth, and found a gratifying pleasure in giving him pleasure. The night sessions were driven, racing—for him too, murmuring in her ear, *precious, precious.* Since they did not ever make a public display, those night whispers were sweet.

She did not know what all this was doing to the baby. Now, in early March, a visible mound protruded when she took off her corset, so she stopped taking it off in anyone's presence, including Jimmy's. He laughed at her modesty, but was compliant. She could not lace tight any longer, the baby would not let her. Though cut in the new flowing line, the white dress was fitted enough that she could not bear to fasten the middle buttons. She made herself a bridging-piece to hold the edges together underneath the cummerbund. Clover helped her dress for the number and said not a word about it—but she had grown so silent, lately, that Aurora hardly noticed the kindness of that reserve.

As soon as the new number was ready, Walker had promised to slot the *Beautiful Doll* number in as his first-act closer. The Belle Auroras were resting; Walker's notion was to let Jimmy and Aurora have the limelight to themselves for a week first, and then put the girls back on to open the second act. Manager reports had been glowing as they played the western theatres, and Aurora believed he would be true to his word.

They refined the choreography with Mama on Monday morning till Aurora was out of breath and dizzy, begging for a rest. In the afternoon, she and Jimmy went over to the Walker to show their steps to Bert Pike, the orchestra leader, before orchestra rehearsal the next morning.

'Halloo!' Jimmy called, pulling open the doors to the dark auditorium. Aurora shivered—an empty theatre always spooked her. Far in the distance they heard Bert answer, then a snap and the work-lights glowed onstage. More hard metallic snaps: a row of house-lights came up, enough that they could make their way down the aisle and up the moveable stairs onto the stage.

She set their sides on the rehearsal piano and showed Bert the modifications they'd made to the lyrics; he worked through it once while they footed the steps, as one might mouth the words of a song, marking out areas on the stage they'd be able to use.

Aurora put herself into the Eaton Beauty Doll position, eyes staring and arms stiff, to let Jimmy carry her as they moved into the singing break:

> *'Precious prize, close your eyes*
> *Now we're going to visit lovers' paradise*
> *Press your lips again to mine,*
> *For love is king of everything.'*

In the empty space, with only the tinny rehearsal piano, the song sounded weak, even forlorn. *'If you ever leave me how my heart will ache . . .'*

'All right now,' said Bert, and they ran for their marks as he chugged into the jaunty introduction, four chords, then one, two, three, four: step-step slide, step-step glide, sweeping farther than they'd yet been able to with this number. *'Let me put my arms around you,'* Jimmy sang in her ear. *'I could never live without you—'*

They locked together to begin their cakewalk twirls, and because she was tired, Aurora felt the hard mass of the baby gathered into a tightening ball. She knew she ought to stop, but Bert had come in especially, and they had to start tomorrow. She eased back from Jimmy, to give herself room to breathe. When the run was done, she stiffened and posed as he went into the chorus again.

> *'I want to hug you but I fear you'd break—*
> *Oh, oh, oh, oh, oh, you beautiful doll!'*

Then the man stood still, admiring, and the doll danced. Aurora put her mind to it and held herself up through the sixteen stiff-armed twirls of her solo, and then there was only one more chorus for them to sing together, until the music ran out and she could stop. They held the final pose for a moment, and broke off to bow to Bert—and then, hearing applause from the seats, out to the house.

Thinking Walker must have come to see, Aurora went forward to the footlights and shaded her eyes to ask, 'Were we all right? Did you like it?'

'Very much indeed,' came the answer, in a voice like sherry-coloured velvet.

Aurora backed away. Not Mrs. Walker. Who was it?

The woman walked down the raked aisle into the spill of light from the stage, the prow of her dress leading, furs swaying behind her. A perfectly composed face looked up from under her shadowing hat-brim, great eyes glowing and hands held out to applaud again. Eleanor Masefield.

The two onstage stood still for a moment. Her hand still in Jimmy's, Aurora felt the contraction in his fingers, and then a second, purposeful pressure, before he let her hand drop and walked to the lip of the stage. Between two footlights he vanished; as her eyes adjusted, his silhouette reappeared.

'You, here!' he said, cool and detached, with an underlay of warmth that might be anger or affection. 'What brings you to the sticks?' His light voice almost laughed.

Beads of jet dazzled on Miss Masefield's bodice. Jet sparked in her hat as well, and as she lifted her skirt to climb the stairs, fabulously lovely black boots appeared. She was black-rimmed and beautiful; her complicated gown was a deep ocean-going blue. She beamed suddenly, showing the impish gap between her teeth as if she were a boy, and moved forward past Jimmy to hold out a hand to Aurora. 'Why, it's Miss—don't tell me—Evans. Ainsley. One of the little sisters.'

Aurora touched the outstretched hand, seeing no way not to, then reclaimed hers to pull her skirt out and drop a brief ironic curtsy. The white dress was no longer pristine and crisp, after an hour of vigorous dancing, but she stood very straight and braced herself, not knowing exactly for what.

Miss Masefield turned, hat hiding her face as a cloud obscures the moon, and held out her other hand to Jimmy. 'I've missed you so much, Jimmy,' she said, the laugh-note in her voice now.

He waited.

'You are the only one who understands me—I've had to fire that cub in New York.'

Jimmy came into the circle of light, taking Eleanor's hand, with such a concentrated gaze that Aurora felt invisible. She had faded, in her white dress, into the pale backdrop.

'Come, lunch with me, I'm famished from the train,' the actress said, turning abruptly, and catching sight, as she did so, of Bert Pike. 'Oh, Bert! How lovely to see you,' she cried. Bert gave a brief, almost rude salute, and Eleanor moved gracefully towards him, her skirt somehow flowing, although, in the latest fashion from New York, it did not touch the boards.

The luncheon invitation had quite clearly not included Aurora; she smoothed her hands down her white lawn frock, trying to remember how nice it once had been. Her mother's stitches amateur, but very tiny, very loving.

Miss Masefield had placed herself theoretically out of earshot, engaging Bert in an earnest (and to Aurora's eyes, entirely sham) exchange.

Jimmy clasped Aurora quickly to him, his cheek on hers. He pressed her hand again and said, in a low voice, 'I'd better find out what she wants.'

Asking for approval, which Aurora found cowardly.

'I think we are quite finished,' she said, cool in her turn. 'If Bert needs no more.' Bert's face peered out from behind that cartwheel hat-brim; he gave a quick, dismissing nod.

Aurora went backstage. But she could not climb up the dressing-room stairs as yet. Her middle was clenched and unhappy, almost hot. She should not have danced so long this morning. When she heard the others leave (Eleanor Masefield's mellifluous laugh easily floating up the aisle over the two men's voices), Aurora went back out to the empty stage to retrieve their sides, walking through the circles of light the electrician had left on.

The footlights still glowed, and the overhead lights ghosted. *Do not be afraid or lonely*, she told the child inside her. *The dead space will be alive again tomorrow.* The house sat empty, waiting, and what a lucky girl she was to have this stage, this life. She stood staring into the black void beyond the lights, then sank down to the boards, skirt pooling around her, and pressed her hands over her eyes to black out everything.

King of Everything

Jimmy returned to the boarding house that evening after supper. He found Aurora on the window seat in the back parlour. Clover, polishing her fiddle at the piano, wrapped it in a red scarf and left the room.

Jimmy stood at the door, looking at her, and then came across the floor.

'She wants me to go back to New York tonight. There's a sleeper—' He stopped, and Aurora was glad. Too much between them, and between him and Miss Masefield. 'I can't—I can't miss this,' he said. 'It's the *Palace*.'

Oh, well then.

'New York is assured. She's given me a contract for eighteen months. At a thousand a week.' His mouth closed at the end of each sentence, Aurora saw. Closed, like his face. She took up a cushion on the window seat. To give him room, he would think, but really to cover her middle where she had loosed her sash.

'I've come back to pack,' he said, not sitting down.

That too, she admired: that he could be so honest.

'I owe her a great deal. Everything.'

'Not everything,' Aurora said. 'You've given good service, over the years.' That was cruel, she should not have said it.

He did not flinch, he laughed. That was a bad sign. 'You know how to wound me.'

She laughed too, almost. '*You* know better.'

He stepped to one side, and then back to face her. Unable, it seemed, to stand still. Impatient. She felt very patient, very old.

'You know you would never—'

She wondered what he had intended to say. She looked up, but could not make her eyes focus properly on his face, to see what he meant.

'You are always alone, even when we are most together.'

That was true. It was a fault in her, she knew it. 'We might get to New York together,' she said. It was all she would do, to beg.

'In ten years! Or twelve, or never.'

'There is something other than success.'

'Not for me.'

'Or a better kind of success, than riding the skirt of an old woman.'

Then he looked entirely miserable. Unfair of her. What else had she done herself? They were both cheap at the price.

'The cab's to come at nine,' he said.

'I will help you pack your things.' She gathered her book and shawl, and went ahead of him up the stairs to his room, the third-floor front.

Everything is undone, she thought, watching him pile shirts into the leather suitcase he was so proud of. Eleanor Masefield had had it custom-made, with his initials in gilt. When he turned to the bureau, Aurora undid his mother's silver bracelet and let it slip from her wrist down into the suitcase.

The case was packed. He set it on the floor beside his trunk, moved her back onto the bed and kissed her, and kissed her, and pushed her skirt up. In the lamp's light his eyes were shining with tears.

'This is what I am good at,' Jimmy said. 'Isn't it?' He rose up into her.

Then it was over and she wished she had not, not one more time. She pulled herself out from under his leg, tidied her dress as well as she could, kissed him and left the room.

The Eleventh   Clover looked up the train schedule to Montreal. To be on the ship sailing May fifteenth, she must leave Winnipeg on the twelfth. Three weeks. The eleventh would be safer. Even in May, a train could be held up by snow, going over the lakehead by Port Arthur. Or there could be trouble with the track.

Ever since Bella had demanded her own pay, Clover had got hers too. She had enough for a sleeper and meals, and Victor's fifty pounds to spare at journey's end. If she did not go in May, shipping might cease for the duration of the war.

Perhaps he meant her to stay with his mother, to look after her. Or if that did not work out, she was sturdy and could do many things to earn a living.

What she could not seem to do was tell her sisters, or Mama, her plans. None of them knew Victor like she did; they would think him mad, and her mad to leave. But Aurora was partnered with Jimmy and the new number would lift them into the big-time for certain, Clover thought. Bella could tag along, and there would be a baby to look after too, so that would keep Mama happy, and none of them would miss her.

The moment would come—must come—when even her sisters, who ignored the war as far as they were able, would see she had to go.

You Need That Pride Mr. Walker agreed to see Aurora first thing in the morning, asking Dot to bring a cup of tea with an extra nod, which seemed to mean *call my wife!* For along with the tea, in very short order, came Mrs. Walker.

Aurora had had time to explain that she was without a partner and to offer the Belle Auroras as substitute for the first-act closing slot, which would now be empty; Walker waited for his wife to sit, and said, 'Seems we've lost young Jimmy to Miss Masefield's New York company, Hattie.'

Mrs. Walker, imposing in brown corded silk, pursed her full mouth and considered. 'Well, that's no bad thing in my opinion—you couldn't marry the fellow, in your situation, and I had my doubts whether it was suitable to book the two of you, smelling of April and May and dancing so romantic, with you not even a widow. And beginning to show, my dear,' she added, with a kindly glance that made bile rise in Aurora's throat till she thought it must burst out into screeching.

What could she answer? It was no slander but perfectly true, and Mrs. Walker had every right to say so. She ran a polite vaudeville house and must guard its reputation.

Aurora would not look down, however, but met her eyes and refused the shame she was being so benevolently offered. 'There*fore*,' she said, speaking low and careful, 'you may be happier with the same pretty number performed with my youngest sister, as a child with an Eaton Beauty Doll. The dance is whimsical and charming and so is my sister, as you know, and I'm persuaded we can pull it off this very day, at the evening show at least, for Bella has watched rehearsals.'

'You need that pride, to be a vaude artiste,' Mrs. Walker said, approvingly. 'To suffer through the constant trial of self and skill. You're a nice little dancer, and so was he. I could see you making a big hit. But without him, no. Your sister in his place—no, not for us, not so soon after you've played.'

'But we'll still take the girls for that spot I'd mentioned, eh, Hat?' Walker asked her. 'Second-act openers, not next week but the week after?'

Prisoners in the dock must feel like this, Aurora thought.

Mrs. Walker looked sober. 'I think we'll have to wait on that, Mr. Walker,' she said. 'I'm not sure that without the balance of the romance we can fit in the sister act.'

'We can do *Lakmé*,' Aurora said, and could have bitten her tongue out.

Mrs. Walker gave her a firm nod. 'A little resting time may be just what you girls need,' she said. 'I'll see her out, Mr. Walker, I'm going myself.'

Sweetness in Song

Verrall passed their door on his way to rehearsal call at the Orpheum, and heard Flora's first shrieking. He shrank against the wall and would have snuck down the stairs in a cowardly fashion, but then he heard Aurora give one cry, and then there was a smash—'Oh lord,' he said to himself. 'There goes the bureau mirror. Seven years' bad luck.'

Taking his courage in both fists, he gave a timid knock upon the door, and when nobody noticed, opened it. As he'd suspected, glass lay sprinkled across the Turkey carpet, a glittering mound on the hearth tiles where Bella was sweeping it with the little broom and coal shovel. He ought to fetch East, really.

'Trouble?' he asked, in as nonchalant a voice as he could manage.

'Only the usual ruin of everything,' Flora cried. 'A man too weak to break with temptation!'

'It was a thousand a week she offered,' Aurora said mildly. She was lying flat on the bed in a tangle of sheets, wearing her outside coat and the frippery blue hat that Verrall loved. Her boots, stuck out into the room, were still wet with snow.

'He's gone, is he? Well, good riddance,' said Verrall. 'I never liked him much.'

Hiccuping over the broken glass, Bella raised her head and said, 'No, no, it is all that nasty actress. He could not refuse a thousand a week. She is like a mother to him, you know.'

Aurora cracked a laugh and sat up. 'Verrall, could you take me to the Orpheum this morning? I met Martin once, with Mayhew. At least I can sound him out. I might be able to put it to him—'

'If you are looking for a gig,' Verrall said, 'I am your man. Martin asked about your bookings while you was gone to points south! If you care to come along that would be sound management, but we must make a mile because East is already shouting from the door.'

Indeed they could all hear him, now that Mama had subsided into mere moaning.

'I think you must sign up with our booking agent, Miss Aurora,' Verrall said as they went down the stairs. 'He does very well for us, and the portion that we pay him is repaid tenfold in extra dates.'

He wished he could say what was in his heart: that the doltish Jimmy was a fair way to a drunkard anyway, and of unsavoury habits, and everybody knew it to be so. But the cad had sloped off and what need, now, to hurt her more?

Earle Martin seemed to think he was stealing a march on Walker, snatching the Belle Auroras out from under his nose, and with a brand-new novelty dance as well. Their number would be filled out with a soldier song and (Aurora having a moment of inspiration) the sentimental favourite *Songs My Mother Taught Me*. Verrall remembered with approval that Martin had been very fond of his mother; he was damp in the eye by the time Aurora had run through it for him.

'We'll bill it as Belle Auroras: Sweetness in Song,' Martin said, blowing his nose horribly on a dirty handkerchief. 'In two.'

The Orpheum was no kind of class, and the floors were grimy, but on the snowy sidewalk outside, Verrall was rewarded with Aurora's quick, fervent hug, and a kiss on his hollow cheek.

Bella's New Car

With the Ninepins also booked in at the Orpheum the chance was too good to miss: Nando had decided it was time to test out the exploding car sketch. With his mother's doleful blessing (she took a few weeks off to lie weeping in bed, eating choco-lates), he and Bella worked non-stop on effects and banter.

Clover loved the new sketch. She watched it every show, seeing new bits of invention and precision each time. Bella had grown into her comic self so brilliantly. She and Nando were a perfect match, Clover thought; she also thought, with greater comfort, that it was *they* who would hit the big-time after all, now that Jimmy had decamped, and carry Aurora and Mama along with them.

The Orpheum stage was massive, made for stunts, but even so, when the rippling curtains opened in three, the crowd gasped to see Nando and Bella driving their flivver on from the wings (pulled by stagehands with a hidden rope, while the glass-crash man made a tol-erable engine racket on his machines). An automobile, onstage!

Hinky-dinky cacophony music travelled along with them, a jaunty outing on a summer day, Bella enjoying the sun and the breeze. 'Hold my head scarf for me, Tommy!' she begged in pretty flirtation. She had just rearranged her tumbling curls when the car's motor coughed and spat.

They lurched forward again, then the car coughed again, and stopped.

They sat, Nando staring blankly, until Bella said, 'Do something! Talk to it!'

Nando got out and lifted the hood, and disappeared into it, feet waggling. A moment later an ominous sputter like a fizzing ginger-beer bottle (exactly like, in fact, since inside the hood Nando had been shak-ing one like crazy) finished with a terrific explosion and a flash (as he lit the flashpan), and Nando (having hooked himself onto the flying-harness) was blown backwards away from the car, blackfaced and flail-ing, and fell *clump* onto the ground.

Bella shrieked and hid her eyes.

Nando wiped his face with his kerchief, then realized it was Bella's pink scarf, now blackened. He made a great show of hiding the ruined scarf.

Regaining some courage and human decency, Bella exclaimed and jumped out of the car and rushed to him, applying first aid in the form of blown kisses (no actual kisses being yet permitted onstage, even at the relaxed Orpheum).

She sat him up, and he fell down.

She stood him up. He fell forward, flat on his nose, except that she caught him in the nick of time, and they both fell sprawling in a very improper attitude (so that Clover caught her breath, hearing Sybil say, 'Begs for a blue envelope!')—and were up, next instant, Bella giving the cheekiest dimpling wave to the manager in the booth.

Nando dusted himself off and thanked Bella, but no, thank you *very* much, she was just a woman and he could fix the ding-danged car himself. He rustled in the trunk for a tool box, pulled out a gigantic wrench, and made his way round to the front of the car, legs rubbery from the explosion. He made his legs such instruments of comedy: stiff and limp at once, unpredictably non–weight-bearing, expressive both of excruciating pain and irrepressible gaiety. Just watching him walk round to the front of the car Clover could see why Bella was so fond of him.

The headlight fell off in his hand.

Oh! It was *hot*! He hot-potatoed it, tossed it up in the air, bright and fragile and dangerous. Bella, leaning forward to give helpful unwanted advice, caught it—*ouch!* She juggled it delicately, carefully (Clover knew how hard she had worked at that juggling) and tossed it back to him; he whipped it back, like a badminton birdie. They volleyed it twice, and then, being burned again, Nando gave it an angry smack and it smashed into the stage. The sugar-glass took forever to make each morning, Mrs. Dent standing fretting over the stove.

The front bumper fell off with a *clang.* Nando caught it up, handed it to Bella, and the back bumper fell slantwise with an ominous creak— he rushed to it and something exploded at the front, giving Bella instant blackface. She opened her bright eyes at the audience and leaned back over the car, in time for the radiator to spray out a jet of water and wash her face, till she jumped back, dripping.

The two of them danced around the car reattaching the bumpers backwards, and the audience-side door fell off. The wheels went flat, each one hissing in turn, till the last wheel hopped right off its axle and went rolling all over the stage, almost out into the audience. Nando raced, tripping over his own feet, hopping the wheel back and forth, and caught it each night, just before it beaned someone.

Then he was angry. He took Bella to task: 'You could have killed someone!' Finger wagging.

She wagged right back at him since the whole thing was his fault, and— *His* fault! why, it was she who was distracting him with her endless chatter— Then Bella leaned over and kissed him (the kiss not visible, of course, just the back of her head and her arm round his neck), and demurely returned upright, with a secret smile.

Nando's face went still, enraptured. His fist relaxed and his arm dropped, as he entered a trance of beauty. After a moment, his hand crept over and clasped hers.

Together they approached the car with dread. The horn toot-tooted: *watch out!*

After a breath, the car exploded, collapsed into twenty-five pieces.

A sway-backed horse wandered onstage, and they mounted and rode away.

Show after show, Clover sat in the midst of the cheering audience and ached to think of leaving Bella.

A Snow White Dove　Earle Martin, the Orpheum manager, brought the war in by insisting the Belle Auroras add a soldier song to their medley. He summoned Aurora to push for the sentimental number *Cradle Song*, a soldier's widow singing to her poor che-ild:

> *Father lies upon the plain.*
> *He is sleeping too.*
> *Mother's heart must bear the pain*
> *Heav'n hath sent her you.*

Over your bed a snow white dove
That watches the long night through . . .

The horror of crooning vile treacle to an imaginary fatherless babe, while conscious of the real fatherless babe within, made Aurora adamant against it. She argued that it was hardly an encouraging song, a poor fellow left dead on some Belgian field. '*Soldiers brave must fight and fall for their native land,*' she pointed out to Mr. Martin. 'I would think twice, myself, if that were the recruiting poster.'

The orchestra leader (a long-faced Dutchman called Vanderdonk, known as Donkey) agreed with Aurora and suggested instead a new song from Britain, *There's a Long, Long Trail A-Winding*, on the grounds that it could be almost a cowboy song, as well as a girl longing for her soldier-lad. He shuffled through his sheets to find the music, muttering about another new song, *Roses of Picardy*.

Aurora could sense Martin studying her—too closely—in the pause. She pulled herself up, and refused to smile at him. He was following, she knew, the little path down between her breasts, gleaming in the work-lights. She caught his eye and he looked upward to the fly gallery, checking the position of the second drop.

In the end Martin let the Belle Auroras off with *Long Trail*, but with two stipulations: they must add a brief, brisk gallop through a rousing song being puffed off as the latest thing.

We're the Boys from Canada
Glad to serve Britannia!
Don't you hear them? Well then, cheer them!
Send a loyal, loud Hurrah!

Not at all to Aurora's taste, but better than the snow white dove. And his final demand: he wished them to use Flora, whom he had known in years past, as accompanist for the *Long, Long Trail*. An old mother, he insisted, would lend the song authenticity.

Washed Up   When Aurora relayed Martin's request, Flora was taken aback, not having yet begun to consider herself an 'old mother.' But she was game for anything that kept her girls at the Orpheum. That evening when they'd gone onstage, she climbed the iron stairs to the dressing room and powdered her hair, to dim the brown and see how she looked. Very tired, very old, was the answer. She stared at herself in the mirror: washed up, finished. Her memory failing, her eyes impossible; there had never been time to get a false tooth, and the little gesture to hide the gap with her hand was second nature now—her hand had drifted up even as she thought.

When the girls came up ten minutes later, they found her in a state of strangled weeping. Flora could see that they hated her grief. 'It is *nothing*,' she said, to forestall them. 'A momentary spasm. I looked very ancient with white hair, that is all.'

Then they went to work to fix it, her good girls: to brush the powder from her hair, to kiss her and tell her how pretty she was, to scold her for dimming her beauty with tears, to chatter about which gown she ought to wear, perhaps the Alice-blue linen that had been Aurora's in Montana, a flattering yet maternal colour. Flora laughed and pushed them away and said she was all right, never mind it.

But she felt the strain—the move from the Walker, the danger of cancellation—in her chest. She was aware of Aurora's misery, and hated Jimmy and that Actress, whom she would not name even in her thoughts. He was a weak puppet, she a monster.

And there was something still wrong, some other axe to fall that nobody was telling her. She could not discern whether it was Clover's trouble or Aurora's, or even Bella's, because her girls did not confide in her any longer, because she was too old and they too strong and young, and the girls who had loved her best of anyone in the world, better than even Arthur had loved her, now found her foolish and had to *manage* her.

Which could not be allowed, so she must take courage and stiffen her backbone and do this small performing, without any more silly vanity.

Man in the Moon The Ninepins' flying apparatus was being wasted, since only the one rig was needed for *Bella's New Car.* But Nando could not stop his mind from thinking up new stunts, and he came to Aurora with an idea for a new number, a dreamy thing about the man in the moon that she loved the sound of; when he showed her the sketch, Bella pointing and explaining, Aurora had clapped her hands and laughed for the first time in ages.

Donkey had sides for *My Sweetheart's the Man in the Moon,* and he was happy to do the switch for the coming week. He would put it in three.

Nando had drawn a crescent moon, with a seat and a harness and a couple of girls dancing around on the ground, vaguely worked in, because he was only interested in the flying. Aurora scotched that, though. No dancing in this one. She needed a sit-down number, for a rest from the exertions of *Beautiful Doll.* And once she'd read the lyrics, she wanted three moons. 'One each, please,' she said to the stage carpenters. 'And each one different: silver and cream and faint, faint green—with a whiff of cheese.'

She sang it straight down to the baby, who had begun to swim and cavort inside her, who loved underdone beef (she realized when she ate steak at Mariaggi's one night, and received such a tremendous kick that she thought Mama must have noticed), and kept her awake at night with its constant exertions. During those wakeful hours she thought of how she would break this news to Mama, but always fell asleep before a sensible answer occurred.

The number began with an empty, cloud-strewn stage, just Aurora strolling on, already singing and dreaming, a pirouette to match the simple, winding, dreamy tune.

> 'Everybody has a sweetheart, underneath the rose.
> 'Everybody loves a body, so the old song goes . . .'

She found her mark in the gauze-and-batten clouds, and turned to tell the audience,

'I've a sweetheart—you all know him just as well as me.
Every evening I can see him shortly after tea.'

Behind her tiny stars sprinkled in the rigging, and the great creamy moon floated down from the night sky, a perfect crescent moon, closer and closer, until it was the right height for her to hop up into the seat nestled in its cupped point.

'My sweetheart's the Man in the Moon
I'm going to marry him soon
It would fill me with bliss, just to give him one kiss
But I know that a dozen I never would miss . . .'

And the moon climbed gradually with her into the night sky—but not very far, for she had no kind of a head for heights.

'Then behind a dark cloud, where no one is allowed
I'll make love to the Man in the Moon . . .'

Words just intoxicating enough to cause a slight, delighted gasp from the audience. Before they had time to settle in to another verse, another moon rose into view—this one cunningly contrived to sweep in from stage left, as if rising over an unseen horizon, Clover already in place in its silver curve. Dark hair gleaming, she sang the chorus, with Aurora singing wistful harmony.

And at last Bella came chiming in, her green moon sinking gradually down from the heavens (six flights of iron stairs on tiptoe, to get into position on the catwalk).

'Last night while the stars brightly shone,
He told me through love's telephone,
That when we were wed, he'd go early to bed,
And never stay out with the boys (so he said).'

All three moon-girls became aware of each other, in the venerable musical tradition of suddenly seeing what's been under one's nose for some time, and continued together.

> *'We're going to marry next June,*
> *The wedding takes place on the moon.'*

And each of them reached behind the moon's curve to produce a small bundle of joy.

> *'A sweet little Venus,*
> *We'll fondle between us,*
> *When I wed my old man in the moon.'*

If Mama doesn't get this hint, Aurora told herself, settling into better comfort on her moon's shelf, she can't really blame me.

True Moon

The Man in the Moon was a colossal hit. For the next two weeks, the theatre sold out night after night. No slouch, Earle Martin quickly switched them to the headliner spot, raised their pay to six-fifty, and wanted them to sign a long-term contract. But the idea for the number had not been his and on the advice of Verrall's booking agent (wired to in New York) they felt no qualm saying no.

The act was good because it was true, Clover thought. All their loves were on the moon, in one way or another: Victor, that night in Camrose under the moon's power. Anyone could see how much Bella loved Nando, the high-flyer, her hand in his, her face lifted to tell him something funny as they walked by moonlight ahead of the others, on the way home after the evening show. And Aurora was a moon herself, a small new moon burgeoning out of her. Then Clover shook her head to shake out fancy, and ran a little to catch Nando's other arm and be warm and close in company, rather than alone and cold like the moon in the darkness.

The second week with the new number, Martin upped the ticket price and still sold out. On Friday morning Alexander Pantages, of the Pantages chain, sent his Winnipeg manager Tom Brownlee round to Mrs. Jewett's to enter into negotiations with the Belle Auroras for a move to Pantages following their stint at the Orpheum. They would begin in Chicago, with jumps to the end of July, including Boston and New York. Further continuance in the fall if suitable to both parties.

He offered a thousand a week.

When Brownlee had gone, the girls sat quite still in the back parlour. Mama's eyes were shining, and the hand at her mouth trembled. She could not speak for happiness. 'It's Bella's little telephone that took the trick,' Aurora said, and Bella laughed. 'No! It's the three dollies that make it so good!'

Clover looked at the calendar. May fourth. One more week.

The Flower

Before going to the theatre for band call on Saturday morning, the eighth of May, Aurora made Mama stop at a dental surgery to have an impression taken for a new tooth. It was time and more—they were settled and prospering and little things could be looked after, she told Mama, blowing aside all objections happily.

But when they reached the theatre, Aurora decided to stay in the dressing room and let the others run through without her. She was not comfortable. Her back had ached all night and she wished she had stayed in bed. But you could not stop when the going was good.

In the last weeks she had been very careful not to stand in profile when Mama was watching; but Mama, tired and seeming queasy herself, had hardly been watching. She was making new skirts for the moon number, their old skirts now soiled beyond what was nice, and always had one with her to stitch the endless gored seams. She would have stayed in the dressing room for the band call, save that Aurora snapped at her to go.

A wave of cramping hit Aurora and she had to sit down, but that was not comfortable either, she had to squat, and then lie down, and no position made her better until it lifted in a moment and she could breathe again. She could not bear the couch; she spread a spare velvet curtain-leg, all there was, on the floor and tried to be calm, knowing she must have done something wrong—she had been tight all morning, and low in spirits, and had not wanted to eat her breakfast. She feared for the baby, suddenly. Another wave coming, another mountain of—*oh heavens*, Aurora thought, or did not think.

A Russian psychic, Madame Tatiana, had the next dressing room. It was she, hearing Aurora's stifled cries, who came in time to assist with the baby's birth. Aurora had hardly spoken to her before, but took her offered hands without the least restraint and obeyed every command she was given, and bit hard on a fold of velvet rather than shriek when her entire body was riven and split up the middle and her back exploded and cracked right open, and then with a surprising and quite different ease a tiny squaller slid out of her onto sheets of Clover's newspaper, which Tatiana had quickly spread.

'Oh, you are a rare one for speed,' Tatiana said, crowing with surprise. 'We will have to get you training all the women!'

Aurora could not believe it was done with. She wanted the baby, she wanted to stop it crying. With shaking fingers she pulled at the buttons on her bodice, and then the laces on her corset cover, and let all fall open, leaning up—all the time keeping her unfocused, focusing eyes on the round dark head and tiny red face of her baby, whose arms and legs were waving like water-fronds in this unexpected element of air. A firm hand pushed her back down, and laid the baby warm and damp on her chest, and a voice said, 'You wait, wait.' Her belly being swept with strong hands, and then there was another awful wave of clenching and turbulence and another push of something rushing out and such a deal of blood and mess, it would have been humiliating except that Tatiana was taking care of it and it did not matter. The baby's mouth was seeking on her chest, complaining and writhing with its arms, and she sat up a little to guide it to her breast and then it was all right: its mouth sucking for a moment, its fingers relaxing from fists to open and spread on her chest, red on white.

She closed her eyes, and let the flower feed.

'A lovely boy—maybe early, but in good heart. Did you not know this dear one was coming?' Tatiana asked, in a soft crooning quite unlike her *mysterioso* stage tone.

'I knew, I knew,' Aurora said. The baby, now that it had found its place, let go with his mouth and looked around the room with great attention, his black glossy eyes, like chips of shining coal, roving here and there.

Something warm was wrapped around her, and the baby wrapped too, in a spare petticoat.

'You are not much torn, there, lucky girl. I need some string—you stay till I come back, and we let nobody bother you.'

'The matinee,' Aurora said.

Tatiana laughed. 'You are true vaudeville, my dear.'

Bella was the first to see, running up after the rehearsal. She gasped in mingled horror, for the bloody cloths still heaped against the wall, and adoration, for the tiny squeeze-faced lump that Aurora held so lightly. 'It is real! It has come, then!'

Aurora laughed, a whisper of a laugh, at least. 'Real, oh yes—look at his hand.'

Bella leaned close to study the furled fist and the furled eyelashes, the perfection of the blistered lip. 'What kind is it?' she asked.

'It is a boy, it is my boy.' Tears welled out of Aurora's eyes and Bella seemed more shocked at that than at the blood.

Then Clover was at the door, with Mama. Who took in the scene and looked around for help, or air, and crumpled without sound into an untidy faint.

New Everybody in the company came round to see the baby, the news having zipped through the backstage like a quick fuse. Madame Tatiana and Clover had tidied the room remarkably well, Aurora found when she looked up from staring at the darling creature. She had not expected to like it so much—it was new, to see the thing that had been growing for so long inside her, but not frightening, because he was so instantly a person. He was not a stranger, but she did not know his name yet, and when East prodded her for one she only laughed and shrugged.

'Not George East, at any rate,' Verrall told him severely.

Julius bent to peer at the red thing and announced a solid likeness to Fitzjohn Mayhew, which was undeniable, but no one else was rude enough to bring it up again.

Clover and Bella did the matinee without her, but Aurora insisted on doing the moon number in the evening show. 'All I have to do is sit,' she said. 'I am not wounded, only a little shocked.'

Turned inside out was more like it, but able to sing. Eager to sing.

Mama had recovered from her faint and turned to frenzied cleaning, the one anchor she could hold to. She saw a likeness to Harry (so frequently that Aurora found herself superstitiously unable to use Harry even as the boy's second name), and drove herself into a frenzy watching over the baby—all with an eldritch air of stability, entirely invented.

The worst of it was that Mama had conceived a ferocious jealousy of Madame Tatiana and seemed to feel that Aurora had preferred to have another woman help her with the birth. Aurora felt guilty enough already for not having told her of the secret, but on the other hand, here was an excellent illustration of why she had chosen to keep silent.

For two days she watched as Mama cleaned, murmured to herself of lists and tasks, and smiled perpetually—showing off her new tooth, though she said she found its unaccustomed presence odd in her mouth. The only respite was when she held the still-unnamed baby. Then she fell quiet, seeming to be in a relapse of mourning Harry. She suffered frequent palpitations, needing to sit, just for a moment, begging their understanding. Aurora was no longer merely impatient with her: it was difficult to manage the baby with Mama bleating and getting in the way. She suffered bouts of unstoppable hiccups—her embarrassment heaping more fire on Aurora's head.

Nobody slept much, with the new one in the bed between Aurora and Clover (a less thrashy sleeper than Bella), and the necessity for keeping him quiet to placate Mrs. Jewett, who although reminded vehemently by Mama of Aurora's married state, had not bargained for an infant and said as much, twice.

Pole-axed

A week later, worn out from long days and nights of fretting, Flora sank for a moment onto the dressing-room couch before the evening show, wishing she could wake the baby to have an excuse to lie and hold him. But then Madame Tatiana came snooping about, and how could she lie down when that woman was there, thinking her neglectful no doubt for not realizing that her own daughter, her own—

The anxiousness became so extreme that Flora had to rise, and bustle to the drying rack to fluff out the girls'—what?—sleeves. The other fly-bite was that she had been forgetting words, quite simple words like *sleeves*. She smoothed her blue linen, and pinned up her hair in the mirror. Mouth sagging, no prettiness left in her. She could kill Hattie Walker for remembering her, and even yet dismissing her girls.

With a dreadful glut of hate in her heart, Flora went down with the girls, leaving Madame Tatiana (too tenderly thanked by Aurora, who was after all *paying* the woman) to rock the baby during their turn.

A person gets themselves into a state, she thought, as she made her way to the piano in the dark behind the curtain, and the body well nigh goes berserk. She felt she could not contain any more worry, nor endure it. She would have to leave the stage and lie down. There was no pain, only the weight of dread, something terrible to happen to the baby, or to the girls, and all of it her fault, and if she had been a better mother to begin with, Harry would not have died, and then nor would Arthur, because she could have jollied him along a while—

The girls were in place. Flora opened the piano, ready for *A Long, Long Trail A-Winding*.

As the curtain lifted and the glittering fragments of the house appeared, she lifted her hands to the keyboard to play the introduction.

The left hand line went as usual, but she found that she could not make her right hand play. She turned to look at Clover, sent a beseeching, apologetic look to Aurora, and then fell forward onto the keys in a jarring chord. She tried to muffle it with the soft pedal, but her foot would not catch, would not obey. Not fainting, not, but. Words suspended, she slumped from the bench to the boards.

Nice Little Number   Mama was brought round, one eye opening and closing, but she could not stand or respond sensibly to questions; she was in vague distress, but unable to speak or even to weep. Bella watched in shock as Clover, who had run almost in time to catch Mama before the fall, held her while Aurora spoke urgently to East, who stepped in front of the curtain to request any doctor present to visit the rear of the stage.

A burly, bullish man presented himself, and after examining Mama's inert form pronounced her to have suffered a paralytic stroke. 'Have her conveyed to the General,' he said, giving Verrall his card. 'I will attend on her.' He stood, and brushed stage grit from his knees. 'Nice little number you girls do,' Bella heard him say to Aurora—as if they cared for his review just then! 'My wife has seen it twice already, she won't mind leaving early.'

East took the card from Verrall's limp hand, bustled a stagehand into bringing round the theatre's wagon, and organized the transfer to the hospital; Clover went with her in the wagon while Bella and Aurora went back upstairs to dress and take the baby from Madame Tatiana— who must be onstage soon. Indeed, after a slightly extended intermission, the show continued, Martin never being one to hand out refunds if any alternative existed.

Bella's hands trembled as she buttoned up her coat and boots; then she took the baby, who mewled and cast his little head from side to side, alarmed by the upset. Aurora dressed in a trice and gathered Clover's hat and coat, and they followed Mama.

Dr. King was before them, already standing by the bed where
Mama lay, suddenly minute, beneath a hard white sheet. Knife-starched
nurses clip-clopped out as the girls came in; it seemed to Bella that the
oldest of them cast a sharp eye at the baby bundled in Aurora's arms,
but the nurse said nothing.

Clover stood, like a line of shadow in her straight grey dress, by the
long window at the end of the room, a small ward with six white iron
beds. Each bed had a white curtain pulled to the wall at a mathematical
angle, and the antiseptic bite in the air was ferocious. It was the cleanest,
most military place Bella had ever seen; nothing in that comforted her.
She rushed forward and knelt beside the bed, her face on a level with the
flat, deserted thing lying there. 'Mama, Mama,' she whispered, until
Clover put a hand on her shoulder. Then she clamped her mouth shut
and said no more, but stayed, stroking her mother's hand.

Possibly, Possibly

'It is an ischemic stroke, what you
would know as apoplexy, not the worst
of possibilities,' Dr. King said, taking
Aurora's arm to lead her out into the hall. The Matron, at her station
near the door, offered to hold the baby while they talked. Aurora gave
him into her arms and beckoned to Clover.

'She has lost the use of the left side, and is presently incapable of
speech, but that may alter. It is very likely that she will regain some
function, possibly more than with the usual run of patients. She is
relatively young, and looks to have been in general health before this—
was she under a great deal of strain?'

Aurora did not feel that the doctor needed a full account of their
recent years.

'She had returned to the stage,' was all she said.

'Possibly, possibly. There is often some instigating incident. But
the underlying condition of worry contributes.' He was a chubby man,
with a habit of leaning his weight over his heels, so that he seemed
about to fall backwards. 'We will bully her out of bed tomorrow, and

sit her upright as much as possible—difficult to say for a day or two what degree of impairment we may expect. Then there is the question of long-term care. Of course you lead a transitory life, but perhaps there is family? I do not recommend a sanatorium, or anything of that kind. With the best will in the world, the institutional tendency is for a patient to be left to rest, and that will not do for your mother. She must be cared for, but more importantly she must move and walk, the more the better. A sanatorium is a death-sentence. She must use those faculties which are impaired—you must demand that she speak, for instance.'

Aurora was grateful to have Clover standing beside her, hearing all this too. She would remember what must be done.

Then the Matron came out into the hall carrying the baby, newly washed and wrapped tight. The doctor went to consult at another bed, leaving Aurora with her little family.

Not the Belle Auroras   Time passed strangely in the hospital ward, compressed but empty. The afternoon shaded down—they would have to go back to the theatre for their call at 8 p.m. When the nurses came to change the sheets under Mama, Clover and Bella moved to the last bed by the window, where Aurora had retired behind the white curtain to nurse her child.

Bella sat on the end of the bed, and Clover stayed by the window, looking out.

'We do not need Mama for the act,' Aurora said. The baby had lapsed into sleep at her breast, petal mouth fallen open. 'But she cannot be moved about from hotel to hotel.'

Bella said, 'She would want to come—' And then, feeling that made Mama sound dead, said, 'She *wants* to come! A thousand a week!'

Clover looked back to the suddenly slight figure in the bed, hardly making a hump in the white sheet. *Stricken*, that is why they call it a stroke, she thought.

'Or—a sanatorium! Joe Dent is at one in Philadelphia—I will ask Nando—'

'Not a sanatorium,' Clover said. She had an obstructive lump in her chest and was finding breathing difficult, let alone speaking.

Aurora traced the round line of her baby's cheek with a delicate finger. Under downcast lids, her eyes flicked this way and that, considering. A decision had to be made, she must find the best solution—oh, but she was hardly used to the child yet and still fuzzy-headed. She looked up at her sisters. 'It is the tenth today, we are due in Chicago on the eighteenth—there is nothing for it,' she said. 'We will have to send her to Uncle Chum in Qu'Appelle.'

Bella exclaimed, '*No!* She would *hate* that!'

The nurse at the far end of the ward straightened from a patient and gave an admonitory *shhh!*

'The doctor does not think she is going to be fully aware for some time yet.' Aurora put it as careful as she could, not wanting to give Bella all his bad news. 'We can work it this last week at the Orpheum: two moons will be enough. Not as funny, but we can let the situation become known, and I do not think the audience will complain. We will ask to delay our opening in Chicago by a week, and if we cannot, then we'll start there, with two moons, until Clover gets back.'

'Back from where?' Clover asked, her voice more quiet than usual.

Aurora looked up, impatient. 'From Qu'Appelle, of course. You will have to accompany Mama there, see that she is safe, and then hurry back to us.'

'I cannot go,' Clover said. Behind her the window shone, and the dark blue, clouded sky outside. Bella stared at her, wondering why she looked stone-stiff, desperate. Clover never refused Aurora. Bella found herself holding her breath.

'I cannot take her,' Clover said. 'I am going to England tomorrow.'

Then Aurora stared too. Her grip must have changed, for the baby startled awake and began to wail, and the ward sister came hurrying down the polished black floor, shoes squeaking on the linoleum.

'I'm afraid you'll have to leave!' An officious whisperer. 'My patients really must be kept perfectly quiet!'

Aurora stood, furious, her bodice open and a damp-shining nipple eluding the baby's grasping mouth. As she guided him back, she said to the nurse, 'Have the goodness to leave us in peace. Most of your ward is catatonic, and if my mother wakes, so much the better for her to hear her grandson close by!'

'Well, really!' said the nurse.

'Oh, do go away!' said Bella, pounding her fists together in a passion.

Clover took Bella round the waist, pushing her to the window enclosure; to the nurse in a soothing tone she said, 'The baby is brand new, you know, and still learning how. Look, he is content now, and so tender, is he not?'

Which made the nurse leave off her huffing. After casting a softened eye over the now-suckling infant, she turned and went back to her work.

They sat in silence, then, the only noise the baby's gulping and grizzling.

'Victor has sent me a steamship ticket, to sail from Montreal on the fifteenth,' Clover said at last.

Bella felt so lonely then, so painfully lonely, that her icy fright dissolved and she felt tears come to her eyes. She said nothing, but let them well over and fall, trying to be interested in the cool trails they left down her cheek, and wondering which would fall first to her chest.

After several moments Aurora asked, 'Were you never going to tell us? What about the Pantages contract?'

'I was too cowardly,' Clover said. She twined her fingers together in a nervous knot. 'And I did not know yet whether I would go.'

That was a lie, Aurora thought; you'd go anywhere he asked. She looked down at the round head at her breast, and for the sake of the milk she tried not to let herself be angry.

'Well. We will have to refuse the contract,' she said, at last. 'We could do without you for a week, but not for longer. We are not the Belle Auroras if there are only two of us left.'

Clover looked at her sister, her cool grace not lessened by the recent birth, or by Mama's collapse, or by anything. Then you shouldn't have left me out of the name, she thought. But it was a childish thought, unworthy. Childish, not to have told them. 'I could not disappoint you both—I could not bring myself— A thousand a week! But I must go.'

Impossible to explain how she could abandon them, after all they had done to get to this place. And Mama in the bed like a dead bird on the road, flattened and helpless. To abandon her too was a dreadful thing. But if she stayed now, if she was dutiful, she would be the one to take Mama to Qu'Appelle, and nurse her there, and never leave that place—so they would be disbanded anyhow. And she would never see Victor again, because he would be killed in the war.

She turned from them and walked away down the long black road of the ward, straight and modest in her grey dress, carrying nothing.

Bella was crying openly now, leaning against the white iron rail. 'I'm going to die too,' she said in a clogged whisper. 'Like Mama.'

The baby unlatched, his arm flying open in ecstatic relaxation, with a popping noise and a vast, surprising sigh that made Bella laugh, she could not help it.

'She is not dying,' Aurora said, smiling down at the baby. An inexplicable calm possessed her—she supposed it was his doing. His little body, still curled like a fiddle-head, occupied her in some way that did not allow, at present, for worry or ambition. After adoring him for a moment she returned to the business of soothing Bella. 'The doctor does not believe so—but her recovery may be long. What will we do, Bella? We are in the soup now. We must both go with Mama, I suppose. I do not know how we will manage, without money to—well, never mind it,' she said quickly.

Bella straightened like a puppet yanked into life. '*I?* I am not going to that rinky-dink place, I promise you! Besides, we cannot both stop working. I have *Bella's New Car*—Nando and I will book more dates for it. Or I can work with East and Verrall—in their new number somehow.'

She was intent, her face bright in the evening sun streaming through the window, and Aurora saw her all at once as a person, not the baby sister. That was as it should be: there was someone younger in the room now. 'I wish you could take our Pantages dates,' Aurora said, thinking. 'It is all Nando's flying equipment anyway . . .'

'He could be the man in the moon!'

Yes, that might do very well, the second verse, and perhaps the telephone could stretch between them—or a tin-can phone. 'We would have to talk to Mr. Brownlee. You must be ready by the eighteenth, or he'd have no incentive to book you.'

'We can! Easy!'

'Nando—can he even sing?'

'No, but he don't need to,' Bella said, her eyes in happy circumflex as she thought of how it might go. 'He can have one moon, and I'll take another, and I'll do most of the singing. He plays the ukulele, we might let him strum.'

'You could put his mama on the third moon?'

Bella looked doubtful. 'She is not much for performing now, the life has been squashed out of her. But she is very pretty.'

It would mean income. Bella was sixteen—older than she had been herself when they set out from Paddockwood—and established. She would be safe travelling with Nando and his mother; East and Verrall would look out for her too. And Bella could send money to Qu'Appelle for their keep, so they would not be entirely beholden to Uncle Chum.

'One good thing,' Bella said, staring down the ward to Mama's bed with some of her buoyancy restored. 'That you insisted on her new tooth. She could not bear to go to Uncle Chum without it.'

But Aurora's eye had caught the big clock at the end of the ward, and she jumped up. 'We must dash back—we'll be late for the call.'

'Do you think Clover will even come?' Swept into sadness again, Bella kissed the uncomplaining baby's downy scalp.

Aurora fastened her bodice and settled the baby in an already-practised arm. She stooped to place a cool hand on Mama's cheek, and they went away down the echoing polished halls.

ACT FOUR

10.

Per Valli, Per Boschi

JUNE 1915–AUGUST 1917

Qu'Appelle, Saskatchewan
London, England
The Pantages Circuit, United States

Practice alone before a mirror, then before one or two
of your friends, and ask them to tell you of any faults
they see in your work. The vim and enthusiasm you
put into your act is often contagious, and many a
mediocre stunt will bring applause if presented in a
buoyant manner.

FREDERICK LADELLE, *HOW TO ENTER VAUDEVILLE*

*A*n Indian man crouched by the side of the road, smoking a long white pipe. His coat was a white blanket, roughly cut and sewn, edged with ragged fringe. He wore a bandana at his neck and a big silver ring on one long finger. His face was the leather of shoes, brown and hard, seams cut from nose to mouth and around his eyes, which sparked in swollen pockets. Hunkered on his heels in long grass, he looked up at Aurora. Earrings glinted under his fall of grey matted hair.

The sight of him pulled Aurora back to the old days, before their vaudeville life. Her father had bought his liquor from an old Cree woman who ran a still in the woods near the school in Paddockwood. Her sons had come to the teacherage with deliveries or to ask for payment. They made jokes. Sometimes the girls came, bright eyes and soft cheeks, big with babies, one on a hip and one in the belly. Now Aurora had her own baby, halfway between belly and hip, too small to balance there yet.

Dust kicked up by the horses had been sifting gently over them since they'd left the train station, sanding the blanket Aurora had set over the baby, sleeping in his basket. The wagon moved slowly, every wheel-turn rolling them closer to Uncle Chum.

Qu'Appelle was as far away as Paddockwood from flying rigs and marble foyers. Pretty in the afternoon stillness: brilliant green leaves frilled under mauve cones of lilac, and yellow-flowering caragana hedges bordering streets of oiled dust over hard-packed dirt. A girl walked along the ditch, white stockings tanned with dirt, dust-coloured ringlets and a fine white dress blowing vaguely about her.

It was hot. Grasshoppers creaked their gates.

Aurora clenched her knees together to stop from jumping out of the wagon and running back to the station. It would jounce the baby, and Mama could not be abandoned.

Mama sat in a daze, dully conscious but not talking. She'd been given a slate at the hospital; she had not used it yet, but Aurora was to remind and require her to write. Aurora found herself looking everywhere but at Mama's face, still dragged down on the right side, fallen from sense, from gravity.

Looking down instead, Aurora checked the baby in his basket at her feet and gazed at his sleeping face, beautifully abandoned, mouth slightly open, petal lip blistered from nursing. A delicious quiver filled her chest.

Half a mile past the edge of town, a big house rose behind a bank of caraganas. It was square-built stone, an imposing place with eight-foot windows and a white-roofed portico. Far grander than Aurora had expected. She was not sure whether that was good or bad. Uncle Chum had retired from the North West Mounted Police as an inspector, but he might still have family money, after all these years. Papa's remittance had been cut off when Aurora was ten—what a wailing in the house there'd been at that letter! Mama could not tell her now, if she knew, whether it had been punishment for some action of Papa's or a failure in England. Aurora put her warm hand on Mama's cold one.

Not a word between the brothers even then; they'd had no contact at all since Papa had married Mama. But when Aurora had written to inform her uncle of Papa's death, a kind letter had arrived by return, offering them help or a home—only Mama had been very angry, and had refused even to answer. In her right senses, Aurora knew, she would never have agreed to come here.

The wagon trundled inexorably down the long drive, and at length pulled up.

Aurora stepped out onto the gravel and grass of the drive, a little blinded by the sun. People stood on the porch, and one of them moved forward: a man in a dark suit coat, upright in his bearing. A pleasant shape of a man. His face, as well as she could see, was calm, with mild, well-intentioned eyes—not the martial personage she had expected from Mama's stories.

Familiar around the eyes, the nose, but not much like Papa, she thought. His thick hair was iron grey, for one thing. Her father's had been fair.

Her uncle came down the steps and reached to help her down, saying, 'Well now, you are no little girl, but all grown up!' He put an arm around Aurora's shoulders, to her surprise. 'With a great look of your father about you—that pleases me.'

'How do you do, sir?' Aurora set the baby's basket at her feet, and turned to help Mama down.

'And there's little Flora,' Chum said. He set Aurora aside and lifted Mama down from the wagon's step. 'I hear you've been through the mill, my poor dear. Come inside, let's have a proper talk.'

Mama was docile enough, but did not lift her face to look at Chum. She looked round at the garden as if dazzled.

'Sad to see her so burnt to the socket.' Chum spoke to Aurora, but kept Mama's arm tucked through his own as they went up the walk. 'And what's in the basket you carry so carefully?'

Until that moment Aurora had not realized that she ought to have mentioned the baby. All her telegrams had been of Mama, and the stroke that had befallen her, never the baby—he was her secret still, she suddenly understood.

'This is Mabel,' her uncle was saying. 'My wife's goddaughter, who is good enough to live with us and keep us company.'

His wife's? But—Aurora had thought him a bachelor.

'How d'you do,' said Mabel, her eyes careful, unrevealing. She was neat and narrow.

'And Elsie's somewhere close by. *Else!*' he shouted, suddenly parade-ground.

Another woman shadowed the screen door and came through: a warm face, brown braids pinned in a coronet; a round figure, well-corseted in a pretty flowered dress, with plump fluttering hands. A little older than Mama.

'I hear you, Chum, no need to holler.' She made a gentle buffer to his larger energy.

'Here's Aurora, and poor Flora, they're here.'

'I see them, Chum. What a long journey! But the best time of year for it.'

Mabel slipped back up the steps to help Aunt Elsie down, for she was lame in one foot, with a great-heeled black boot.

None of this was what Aurora had expected; her head was buzzing. And she had not mentioned the baby! People were apt to be doubtful about babies, when there was no father to be seen.

She set the basket down, shifted the blanket and lifted out her sleeping son, light as air, still curled into his fern-frond posture and gently complaining as the lifting roused him.

There was a small silence on the porch, on the steps, on the walk.

Mama moved, stepping closer to Aurora and raising her left arm to shield the baby, as if defending him. Aurora pressed her hand, whispering, 'Good! You are stronger already!'

Then Aunt Elsie moved forward too, and Mabel, to see the baby more closely.

'Oh! So *new*!' Elsie said. Her finger traced the baby's chin.

Chum was tall enough to see over his wife and niece, no need to move. He asked, 'What is the child's name?'

Aurora could not bear to admit that she had not named him yet. 'Avery,' she said—unable, though thinking she ought, to say *Chum*. 'Avery Mayhew.' She listened to the sound of that, wondering if it was any good. Poor babe, if it was not.

'And your husband?' Chum asked it gravely, as if expecting the worst.

'No longer with us.' Then, realizing that might cause them to think her a widow, she quickly added, 'My husband left us, I'm sorry to say. His theatre was destroyed and he—decamped to the States.' A military way to put it, perhaps that would be best.

Elsie gave a short sighing gasp, either sympathy or censure. Chum and Mabel looked at them without speaking for a few moments. Mama, who had been dully silent all day, looked up and tried to speak. Nothing emerged.

Mabel showed them up to a wide bedroom. A high spool bed, a dresser, a washstand with china bowl and pitcher, and a lidded pot beneath. The room shone, evening sun pouring through two open windows. Mama stood at the west window and hummed a droning tune.

'Mosquitoes aren't much this year,' Mabel promised, drawing the net curtains aside to show the view out over the prairie—nothing to see but grass and sky, and more of each beyond. 'But we keep the screens in place anyhow. I could hold Avery for you, while you help your mother,' she offered, with some awkwardness, and it was only fair for Aurora to hand him over.

Avery. In Mabel's arms she could see him better. It might suit.

When they had washed, Mabel took them down to supper in the quiet dining room: chicken stew and early greens from the garden, and rice pudding made plain without eggs.

This was a peaceful house. In lieu of children, Aunt Elsie kept fourteen cats in the kitchen, lolling close by the stove on a conglomeration of pillows, reminding Aurora of Swain's Rats & Cats. They were never allowed in the rest of the house, but Mama was agitated by them. It was the first thing she wrote on her slate: *overlay?*

Aurora laughed to see it, from relief that Mama had taken chalk in hand; kissing her mother, she promised faithfully not to allow the cats to overlay Avery.

The Dark Ship   In the darkness, the mass of people on the pier overwhelmed Clover, along with the smell, and the boat's bulk in the nighttime. Thick black shadows claimed its upper half, past the reach of the dock lights. She laid one hand on her mouse-brown trunk, to keep up with the porter, and watched the massive planks beneath her feet. Her kid boots (bought new for the moon number) had narrow teetery heels that might fit in the gaps.

A column of uniformed soldiers swung through, slicing the crowd into halves that rejoined as they passed. Perhaps Victor had enlisted already—she did not even know if he would still be in England when she arrived.

The porter lurched forward and she lurched after him. They joined the queue moving towards the gangplank and stopped again; the porter slumped into conversation with one of his counterparts, in French that Clover could not follow.

The press of people was frightening—a nervous crowd, shadowed eyes shifting like fish. The *Lusitania*, torpedoed by a German U-boat, had sunk in eighteen minutes. Twelve hundred lives lost. At the wicket the Cunard purser offered her a more desirable outside cabin for half the fare, because so many people had cancelled their bookings. But she had no money to spare. He winked at her. 'Ah, well, you'll have the cabin to yourself, at any rate, miss, and that's the best of all.'

The porter shoved against the shoving; Clover clung to the trunk. Pressed up against the rope at the water's edge, she could smell the river and the planking stained with oil. The dark ship rose vertical above them. Between the boat and the pier was a narrow strip of greenish air; far below, green-black water with an oil slick on it, and a dank slopping noise she could hear even through the shouting of the crowd. Clover stared into the black and green, down to where the water caught the lamps and swayed like oil in a jar. If she fell between the dock and the ship, she would be crushed or drowned or merely trapped until the ship had gone, and her chance gone with it.

But the rope held and she felt her well-known trunk beneath her glove. She was not afraid. In another quarter of the globe Victor would meet her in London, where there was a high brick house and a wall, and pavement stones along the street. The air would be sweet. A pear tree in the garden and Victor doing scales, birds singing in the darkness.

The porter cried *hup!* It was their turn to climb the gangway. He set his shoulder and pushed the trunk. Clover went beside it up into the hulk of the ship, ready to cross the Atlantic, a blue map spiked with German submarines and danger.

But there was kindness in the world, too. Her assigned door opened to reveal an outside cabin, rather than an inside one. The purser had switched her after all. She stepped over the high metal threshold, shut herself into the tiny cell, and lay on the bunk, vibrating gently in time with the unthinkable engine, all alone.

A Prodigy At the end of their first week in Qu'Appelle, Aurora walked down to the clinic with Mabel to have the baby weighed and checked for various deficiencies, of which he had none. A healthy boy, perhaps a little early, was the verdict. The stern district nurse, Miss Peavey, broke into a gap-toothed smile: 'Impatient to get here!'

Same teeth as Eleanor Masefield, same square forehead, but how nice this woman was, how well at ease in the world. Seeing the likeness took away some of the smart that had lasted all this time. Aurora wondered for an instant how Jimmy fared in New York, but Avery swam stomach-down on the white flannel sheet, trying to lift his head by furiously raising his eyebrows—far too early! a prodigy!—and that other life receded again.

A young Indian woman came in the door bringing a breeze with her, three leggy girls following and a bright snapping-eyed boy in her arms. One of the little girls darted over to look at Avery and touched his cheek. Miss Peavey looked quickly at Aurora, but Aurora put out a hand and touched the girl's cheek, saying, 'Pretty!'

Uncle Chum took Aurora out to the veranda after supper that evening and told her kindly that he and Elsie would be very happy to keep Avery with them, should she feel it urgent to return to her sister. 'He's a dear little chappie, and it's good for Mabel to have the occupation,' Chum said.

Aurora looked back through the French doors to Mama, frail in one corner of a sofa, lips moving in a mumbling song as she sat with Avery tucked into her stiff right arm.

On the Moon

Bella lay in the upper berth, behind cloistering Pullman curtains, and looked at the Belle Auroras publicity photo she'd stuck into her dressing-case lid, now that she and Nando had a new set.

Clover: straight nose, narrow face soft-rounding at the chin. Patient eyes. Too frail to travel alone. Only of course she would stay with Victor's mother or that mad guru. Victor! Who could stand to live with his oddness all the time? He was like oysters: interesting, but not for every dinner. Unlike Nando, her daily bread. Fitz Mayhew had been rib steak, underdone; and Jimmy, champagne.

The cable from Aurora was tucked under the photo. Bella fished it out and read again:

CANNOT LEAVE MAMA YET. CARRY ON WITHOUT ME.
WRITE SOON.

Was that a promise that Aurora would write soon, or an order: *write to me soon?* Bella had answered by return, wiring money as well. But no letter had found her yet. The train wobbled on through the night, without her other souls, her sisters. How can one live all alone? Nando was no help, in a state of perpetual nerves about his dad.

Too hot in this berth. Nando's mother in the berth below did not like the window cracked, and would fret if Bella turned over too many times. Myra had turned out to be considerable trouble: wistful and stubborn, only wanting Nando. Her ethereal face masked a hungry spirit, and no friendliness on Bella's part could satisfy her. Nando was kept on the hop all the time, and Bella too—if she would not do to *talk* to, she served very well to fetch tea and run baths in the hotels.

Bella stared up at the dented ceiling cloth, feeling straitjacketed in the berth. Maybe Joe was kept in one of those canvas jails, in his sanatorium. If Papa had gone to the san when he was so ill, he would have been, because he was *non compos mentis*, the doctor had said. But Mama had kept him home, however sad and wild he became. For the first time in ages Bella thought of Harry in his coffin, and Papa, and then the old thought followed that she too would be dead soon enough, lying under a low roof, under the creaking weight of earth.

Think of the prop moons instead. She sang on the golden moon now, a step up in the world. Nando had the silver. Myra on the green-cheese moon had not worked; her dreary delivery sent the whole number flat. The green moon was baggage, but no more trouble than the car. They had a big hit with *Bella's New Car.* Pantages had taken them on—at a reduced rate, of course, as everything always went, but Nando's booking agent said they'd still got a whacking good deal, seven-fifty a week to split between them, which amounted to three hundred each, once the expenses of touring the larger rig came off the top. Her grouch-bag was full to bursting—enough to send pots of money on to Aurora and Mama, and to Clover, if she needed it. Bella turned her face into the mingy Pullman pillow. Day after tomorrow was her sixteenth birthday. Nando would not remember. It would be shoddy to remind him. Aurora might think of her, if she was not too taken up with the baby. Clover would remember, on the ocean, as long as her ship was not sunk by Germans like the *Lusitania*. But it would not be, it would not.

Bella turned, her nightgown twisting into a shroud.

After a while she turned again, carefully, and pushed the curtain back to inspect the corridor. Nobody. She slipped her shoes on and manoeuvred down from the berth. The lower berth curtain did not stir.

Moving quickly down the corridor, she let herself through the connecting door (a burst of juddering noise and shaking, a rush of night air) and into the next carriage, where Nando's berth was—he had a lower, thank heavens, with an open curtain and empty berth above him. She undid the snap and slid her hand in to pat his face.

'Wha—!' he said, huffing and snorting.

She had woken him. Serve him right, being so dozy. She swung herself in, and the curtain shut, in a jiff. He jumped and bumped his head on the upper bunk, but that did not matter. 'Shh!' she said.

'What are you doing? Go back to your berth!'

Where was the boy who had kissed her in the tunnel of the Empress when they were children?

'I wanted to be with you.' She put her hand on his cheek in the twilight of the berth.

The moon was somewhere above the train, not visible but shining sometimes on the little ponds flashing by the window. Nando searched for his watch and held it to the window, tilting it impatiently to find the light. 'It's the middle of the night,' he said, giving up.

'Don't you want me here? Don't you want to cuddle?'

'No!' He sounded very angry.

'Don't you love me?'

'No!' He caught her arms and shook her, but not like his father shook him. 'You can't do this, it's not decent. Kisses are one thing but this—you must wait till we're married.'

'Will we be married?' Bella was smiling in the dark; he did too love her.

'No.' He was hard-hearted. 'I was dreaming! Why did you wake me up?'

'Don't make me go back, Nandy, it's cold and I'm lonely.'

'I've my dad to think of, and you're too young to know what you're doing anyhow.'

She started to cry, soft as a cat; he believed her, and opened the blanket. He thought he was the only one who could pretend! Much more comfortable under the blanket, even if he would not pet her or be sweet. He was so prickly. His father, and worry, had made him very ill-tempered.

'May I touch you here?' She did, without permission. He made no sound, but his whole body stiffened, not just the bit she had hold of. 'Just let me lie with you for a while, you would like me to,' she whispered. 'I want you to, please do, Nandy, please?'

They were like snakes twining then, his hands touching her all over and on her bosom where she thought they must leave traces like red paint, it felt so delicious. His mouth glued to hers kept them quite quiet, and they said no words even when he pushed his stiffness at her, trying to fit in, and pushed, and then—he gasped, and pushed himself up so fast he hit his head on the ceiling again. He swung her legs through the curtain and pushed her out, only her head left looking at him.

'No!' she cried. Her bare bottom was cold in the passageway.

'Shh!' he said in great irritation. 'Go back to your bunk!'

'But I love you, Nando!'

'You are a baby, and I won't do it.' He flung himself down on his side, turning away from her. She stared at his stupid back, his pig head. Then she hauled down her nightie and slammed the curtain along the rod, and slipped through the carriage and back to her own berth, furious to find herself so hurt.

Grave

In vaudeville, Sunday was the day for doing laundry. Church made a change, Aurora thought. She and Mama went with the household to the pretty brick Pro-Cathedral. So called because Qu'Appelle was meant to have been the capital of Saskatchewan—Uncle Chum described the ins and outs of the capital heist as they walked, calling Regina by its old name, Pile o' Bones, until a series of nine cataclysmic sneezes from Avery distracted him and he forgot ire.

Aurora wore her new afternoon dress, a bell-shaped skirt of Saxe blue over corded silk, ordered after the thousand-a-week contract and delivered just as she and Mama were leaving town. It was lovely, but the brilliant June sunshine made Aurora want to walk the fields in her old muslin dress, left behind long ago at some hotel. To stretch out on grass, to be pressed into the grass by— But the thought of Jimmy brought the face of Miss Masefield, and Aurora stopped thinking. Her body was her own, or at least belonged only to Avery.

The darkness inside was cool and smelled of hymn books. Mabel's father had been Rural Dean at St. Peter's before the present incumbent; Aurora saw her shyness dropping away as they entered her territory. She quietly introduced Aurora and Avery to the ladies of the parish, while Mama sat beside Elsie, prim in a pew. One prow-fronted, important dame, Mrs. Gower, looked exactly as Aurora imagined Mama's Aunt Queen.

This was a very proper place: exquisitely embroidered vestments, stained glass, the lessons read by men with strong English accents. Canon Barr-Smith gabbled through Morning Prayer at speed, but his sermon was thoughtful and Aurora had no need to feign attention. She felt she must be more proper than anyone, since she carried the thrilling taint of vaudeville, and a baby without a visible husband.

After the service the family joined the congregation in assorted wagons and carriages for the annual Sunday School picnic, jostled up beside more people to whom Elsie and Mabel introduced Mama and Aurora. Mama stared out at the scenery, or into her lap, but did not seem physically uncomfortable.

The picnic was laid out at the cemetery north of town, down an avenue of pines. An established place, unlike most windblown prairie graveyards. Fine stones had pressed down into the earth, and wild roses rioted between the rows.

After the ice cream and cake had been wolfed, a gang of tall boys set up races: egg-and-spoon, three-legged, sack. Mabel, who had taken the blue in last year's sack race, spread a rug in a bit of shade near the finish line for Mama and Elsie, with Avery between them, and went off to compete.

Aurora walked through the graves alone, not caring if she stained her white slippers in the bright grass. This was an ice-cream world, she thought, insulated by good behaviour and agreeable surroundings— even Aunt Elsie's chickens were clean and white as hens in a picture book. Paddockwood had been realer. Vaudeville too, with all its pretense, was mixed up in the grubby world, alive.

Among the headstones, Aurora paused to read inscriptions. Her arms felt pleasantly empty, not carrying Avery. Sunlight lay hot and fluid among the graves. A pretty place to sleep under the ground: she wished Papa could have been buried here, and dear Harry.

'You have such a look of my brother. I miss him,' Uncle Chum said behind her, startling her by his presence and the coincidence of their thoughts. Not unnatural to be thinking of the dead, she supposed.

'I miss my brother, too,' she said. 'He died when he was four.' She had not spoken of Harry for years. In the glancing sunlight, she saw it was not her father that Chum reminded her of, but Harry: his square, pleasant face and calm assurance.

Her uncle took her arm to walk on through the grass. At a pressure from his hand, they stopped by a small grave marker. 'Our little son,' Chum said. 'Only lived a day.'

ELMORE ARTHUR AVERY, the plaque read. SUFFER THE LITTLE CHILDREN—1905.

Tears sprang to Aurora's eyes, so quickly it seemed they would spring out to water the grass.

'No, no, you must not grieve, nor fear for your own babe. Elsie was well on in years; I dithered too long before marrying her. His lungs were weak, you know. It was God's will.'

Aurora turned her head so her uncle would not see anger spring into her face as the tears had. That was what the minister had said at Papa's funeral, with a solemn face, as if he did not know Papa had taken his own life. Not God's will, his *own* will.

'Arthur and I were close,' Chum was saying. 'Not as boys, you know, for he was twelve years younger. But when we first came out to Canada, then we were. Worked like slaveys on a farm in Ontario, had a spree or two together once we'd done with that. I was with him the night he met your mother. I hoped he would join the redcoats with me, but schoolmastering was more to his taste.'

Aurora found she could hardly remember her father any more, or be sure her memories were true. He had been melancholy so long, and not himself.

'We have a good schoolmaster here,' Chum said, pointing back towards the picnic. 'Talking to the Dean by the lintel-gate. The principal of the high school, Lewis Ridgeway. A learned man, I'll introduce him to you and your mother.'

Chum waved to Mr. Ridgeway, a spare man with dark hair, straight shoulders in a dark suit. Shadows round his eyes gave him a patient look. He looked up and smiled, lighting the gravity of his face, then came across the grass, a hand held out to Aurora so that his coat-sleeve displayed a creamy linen shirt cuff. No celluloid cuffs for this school-master, at least on Sundays.

'Mrs. Mayhew, I believe?'

She inclined her head in a demi-bow (internally amused that no matter how minor the audience, she could not help trying to present well), as Chum put an arm round her, saying, 'Aurora has come to stay with us while my poor sister recovers from an apoplectic episode.'

Mr. Ridgeway seemed to know all about that. 'Your mother is making a good recovery, it seems. I saw her reach for her slate, although she did not write. She watches the passing show with interest . . . A good sign.'

Aurora flushed with gratitude, and asked if he was familiar with the effects of stroke.

Her uncle clapped his hands. 'Ridgeway is up on all the latest! An educated intellect. Is Dr. Graham back, d'you know?'

Mr. Ridgeway tilted his head as if consulting an aerial calendar. His strong forehead and cheekbone stood out, caught by the noonday sun. 'Mid-July. He will be pleased to consult, he has a strong interest in apoplexy and ischemia—he'll be out to see Mabel when he returns, I'm certain.'

Aurora did not question, but her uncle explained: 'Mabel is engaged to Dr. Graham's son, Aleck, who is at the Front. Has she not told you? He farms near Indian Head. Yes, Lewis, we'll have Graham see if he can make Flora's lot easier. Your sisters worry me too,' Chum said, turning to Aurora. 'Their lives will be unsettled, alone and far away— now you and Flora are comfortable here, won't you write and ask them to come home too?'

Kind of him to call it *home*, Aurora thought. Kind to think of her sisters. Maybe this placid ice-cream life would be better for them. 'We are grateful for your help,' she said. 'But I believe the girls are happy as they are. My youngest sister Bella remains on the vaudeville circuit, Mr. Ridgeway, touring with friends of ours, in great demand. I do not think I could drag her away! My other sister has gone to England to stay with her fiancé's mother.'

'Were you frightened for her after the *Lusitania*'s sinking?' Mr. Ridgeway asked.

She glanced quickly up—it was almost too intimate a question. 'Very much. Clover was on the *Ausania*, which sailed a few days afterwards. I was glad my mother could have no grasp of the disaster. But the *Ausania* has come to no harm.'

'She may be unable to leave England for some protracted time, if shipping is halted.'

Aurora nodded; she could feel the light going out of her face and eyes.

'Lewis takes an interest in the war,' Chum said. 'He was at Cambridge, you know.'

'More immediately, Aleck Graham is a friend of mine. But I'd follow the progress of hostilities without any added stake. It is the proper study for all men, as long as the conflict continues.'

'You think—but it will not continue long, though?' Aurora asked, surprised.

'Now that both sides have dug in, I fear it will. This is not last century's war.'

Chum took Mr. Ridgeway's arm, saying, 'Aurora won't want to hear about all that.'

'Won't she?' Mr. Ridgeway said, looking at her closely. Seeing her glance at the grave marker for Chum's little son, he nodded.

'It seems wrong to speak of the war in this quiet place,' she said, grateful for his understanding.

Mr. Ridgeway walked away, with a word or a brief smile to one person or another as he went. He had Mayhew's breadth, but not Mayhew's expansiveness. A schoolmaster, all right.

Against her will Aurora felt suffocated in this peaceful, orderly place. The air was still, yet the noise of grasshoppers and birds trembled beneath every conversation, every thought. But amiable sociability was the least she owed Uncle Chum for taking them in. Money had not yet been mentioned. Before she rejoined Bella, they would have to work out a stipend for Mama's board.

Aurora went out of the shadow of the pines, back to the races and the blanket where Avery lay on his back in the grass watching Mama. She was singing to him as his bare legs kicked the air. In this week he had uncurled, showing his true length. He would be tall, like Mayhew. But not a man *like* Mayhew. She would see to that.

'*I heard a maiden singing in the va-alley below . . .*'

Mama was singing words. Aurora stood still, listening.

Free Love

A letter came from Clover in the first week of July, sooner than Aurora had expected or hoped. The British mails, Chum boasted, were terrifically efficient, even in wartime. 'Delay would have been in Montreal,' he said, shaking his paper to turn the page at breakfast.

Aurora skimmed the letter at the table, then ran up to read it to Mama, who was still drowsing in bed, Avery lying beside her making an interesting variety of conversational noise. Mabel had suggested that Mama might like tea and toast on a tray for breakfast, like Aunt Elsie had, rather than rushing in the morning. That allowed Uncle Chum to have his breakfast in peace, with only Mabel and Aurora for company.

Aurora did not read the whole letter to Mama, only the first two pages about the English air and the narrow brick house where Victor's mother lived, next door to Galichen's atelier, '*with a fine view of Wormwood Scrubs prison behind.*' There was a great deal about Victor, very little about Clover herself. Aurora did not read the next page aloud.

> . . . he is filled with joyful purpose to be doing what he knows he must. As I am. I hope you have forgiven me, but I don't know if Bella ever will.
>
> Victor met my ship at Plymouth—we had three days in a cottage on the edge of Dartmoor, did not stir beyond the garden except out to the moor each day. It is not like the prairie but made me homesick anyway,

except that now my home is him. I was already his
wife, his true wife. I cannot talk about that in a letter,
only to say that I had not known before that love poems
are real. I thought they made it all up, but now I see
that it is true.

(Do not read that to Mama.)

He is to embark on Friday. I cannot say more about
that either, but the Front is so close—he is promised
leave at home. His mother has been kind . . .

Aurora wondered if Victor's mother was treating Clover badly. The
stressing of *has been kind* gave a faint suggestion of unkindness, but his
mother was a Fabian after all, a believer in Free Love. Aurora could
hardly be shocked by Clover's decision to live irregularly. Her own
marriage was purely opportune, nothing like the love Clover had for
Victor; their parents' marriage, full of passionate storms, had been no
model. Seeing Uncle Chum, she also saw how unlike him Papa had
been, how rash and wild.

No storms left in Mama now, so tiny in the bed. But she would
improve, Aurora told herself. Avery reached for her, his face breaking
open in a dripping smile when he caught her eye. She unpinned her
bodice again, took him up, and began composing a letter to Clover as
they rocked.

A No-Hoper

The Minneapolis bill was chock-a-
block even in summer, from Chinese
jugglers to a horse act, and the best
magician Bella had ever seen, Harlan the Great. Harlan had adored
Nando's mother when Myra was a girl down in Florida; in his company
she was less despondent, basking in nostalgic admiration. As a bonus,
East and Verrall were at the Regent, the other Pantages theatre, with
Julius. They were all staying at the same hotel, patronized by Pantages
folk; it made for cozy visits. But it was hard for Bella to see Julius so

thin, legs like two sticks covered with cloth, his chest fallen. He did not meet her eyes but talked in a rambling way about Clover.

Julius only made one show in three, Verrall told Bella in a quiet corner. 'But he is right on the money when he manages to stay vertical.'

'Making almost enough to keep himself in gin,' East said, as he passed with a bottle. East had brought Bella a new song, *Pretty Baby*, which she and Nando were working up as a dolly comedy. *Everybody loves a baby, that's why I'm in love with you . . . I'd like to be your sister, brother, dad and mother too, Pretty Baby of mine!*

At the end of their first week in Detroit, a telegram came to the dressing room Bella shared with Myra, addressed to *N. Dent*. Myra pretended to think that was an *M*, opened it, and went straight into hysterics. Bella knew better by then than to fool with her, but ran for Nando. He dropped his greasestick and stepped across the hall to dash a cup of water in his mother's face, reducing her to fishlike gasps.

His face went tight when he read the telegram—he passed the yellow sheet to Bella:

> PATIENT J DENT NO LONGER COMPLIANT. REMOVE
> AT EARLIEST CONVENIENCE.
> GEO STURGIS, DIRECTOR, CLIFTON SPRINGS
> SANATORIUM, PHILADELPHIA, PA.

Myra sobbed helplessly (consoled by Harlan and other members of the company, who knew Joe's reputation all too well) long into the night at their hotel. In the morning she was out on the street, hailing a cab, when Bella and Nando found her.

Nando grabbed her suitcase and pulled her back to the curb. 'We've got to do three shows today, Ma, and talk to Burt. We'll take the train to Philly Sunday morning.'

Myra made no answer, but dissolved into a further wash of tears.

Harlan the Great came down the steps, his own valise in hand, and took Myra's case from Nando. 'She's coming with me,' Harlan said. 'Don't make it hard on her, laddie.'

Bella, standing in the doorway, thought her stomach would come right out her mouth. She hated Harlan and Myra equally. No, she despised Myra more, seeing her swoon on the big magician's arm. The quickness of his hand deceived the eye: he bundled her and the baggage into the cab and barred the door to Nando.

'I'm taking her to Florida,' Harlan announced. 'Where she'll be happy for a change. You're a good lad, don't waste your own life with that worthless drunk.'

Bella thought Nando might die right there on the pavement. She went down to stand beside him while the cab wheeled off, and pulled him gently out of the street.

'Well, I've got to go get Dad, anyhow,' he said.

'Of course.'

He would not meet her eyes.

She squeezed his elbow, all she could get hold of. 'He'll be glad to see us! We can do *A Good Night Out*, you know—I could do it easy!'

'Not you,' he said. 'Not without Ma, you can't travel with us.'

She gave a shocked laugh. 'What are you talking about?'

'Anyway, I don't want you.' He went up the steps, and would not say another word.

Best to let him alone till they went to the theatre, she thought, remembering Papa on his darker days.

Between the first and second shows, Nando had a word with George Burt, the Detroit manager, who looked fussed and said he'd deal with it after the second. As Bella was wiping the dust off her face and bosom from the *New Car* explosion-finale, Burt turned up, ushering in the big boss, Mr. Pantages. Burt went across to fetch Nando.

Bella shrieked and dodged behind her screen, and Pantages laughed. His heavy eyes creased, smooth as unbaked buns. 'Nice little number,' he said, peering over the screen. She turned her back but could not resist giving him just a very brief view of her pretty bodice. It could not hurt to keep the boss intrigued.

Nando came into the room and asked Pantages shortly what he could do for him.

'It's you wants to see *me*, boy,' Pantages said, good-naturedly enough. His shining hair was parted in the middle over a very white scalp. 'I hear you wants out your contract.'

'Can't help it, sir,' Nando said, stiff as a plank. He gave Bella not one glance. 'My old dad's in trouble and there's only me to help him.'

'And me,' Bella said behind the screen.

'I've got to head for Philly in the morning,' Nando said, doggedly ignoring her.

Pantages examined a hand full of rings. 'And that leaves me where?'

'I know it's putting you out, but I got no choice,' Nando said. 'If it means I'm sunk in this business, I still got to go.'

'Oh you'll *be* sunk, if you cross me,' Pantages promised, still genial, and glossy as shellac.

'Well, I got an offer for the movies and I'll take that. My dad and me together. It's the coming thing, it'll beat out vaudeville, you'll see!'

Bella ducked her head below the screen to hide her shock—Nando had baldly refused to have anything to do with the pictures before this.

'If that's all right with you, boy,' Pantages said. 'And what about your missus here?'

'She's not my missus, she's just a baby. She's not in on this. She's a good girl and a trouper—I know East & Verrall have been trying to get her for their new number over at the Regent, she'll be all right with them. I'm sorry you're out an act.'

He's arranging my next jump as if I was props, Bella thought, but she kept silence. As long as he didn't send her straight to Qu'Appelle to wither into dust.

Pantages stared at Nando for a beat, eyes like jet beads. 'I know your dad, he's a no-hoper.'

'Not for me.'

'Your funeral, boy,' the boss said, and he went.

After a minute Nando said to the screen, 'I'll talk to East. You'll be safe with them.'

There's only so much you can do, Bella thought, to throw yourself at someone who doesn't want you. She stayed behind the screen, pulling on her clothes, every piece of her body hurting like she'd been beaten up, and when she came out Nando had gone.

They did the third show. They yelled at each other as the car fell to pieces, and near the end of the number Bella hauled off and slugged him straight in the eye as hard as she could.

She sat back, aghast, looking at the eye already starting to swell. The audience broke into delighted hoots.

Nando pulled the string that set off the final explosion, and under it he said, quite quietly, 'Guess that's that, then. See you in the funny papers.'

'I hate you *so much*,' Bella said, and the car fell apart.

The Work

Left with Madame Saborsky now that Victor was at training camp, late night was Clover's only solitude. Lamp oil was dear, so she wrote to Aurora by moonlight at the barred window in Victor's third-floor sitting room, once a nursery. The bed was warm, piled with feather beds and comforters, the linens heavy and smooth. Madame Saborsky had fine taste in fabrics, and wore gorgeous embroidered velvet drapery on her person too. The plank floor was bare and the damp could not be beaten back by the stingy supply of coals for the tiny fireplace, but it was quiet. Down in the cellar Madame would be sorting her hoard of marmalade and tinned beef, her treasure-store against the starvation she expected inevitably to follow war. Small stone crocks of goose-grease— which Madame used as face cream—lined up like soldiers.

It seemed disloyal to send her sisters a full portrait of Madame. Instead Clover wrote of Galichen. Even in vaude she had never met such a person.

A head bald as an egg, a pair of gimlet eyes—one hugely magnified by a thick monocle. He stares into one's soul with that one moon eye. I creep about in terror, hiding in the skirts of Victor's mother. Gali's people put me to work washing stairs; but everyone about the

place scrubs floors all the time. The one to pity is
M. le Comte Filouski, who is detailed to Galichen's
own bathroom. I have never seen it, thank God, but
the legends are horrific. 'At times I have to use a
ladder to clean the walls,' he is supposed to have said.
But I see how people are swept under Gali's sway. He
puts them through The Work in order to clean their
spiritual houses, their soul's rooms; and they say they
are better for it.

Victor said I ought to call his mother *Belle-Mère*,
but it sounds fake-French, like *Les Très Belles*: I call her
Madame. She is unsteady in her spirits and keeps two
or three of everything—the house is crammed with
things she has collected. Her face puckers under a head
of flat black hair, which she dyes herself with some
walnut-juice concoction. I miss Mama. Is she writing
on her slate yet? Please give her a tender kiss from me,
and forward the enclosed note (which of course you
may read!) to Bella.

To Bella, she wrote:

There is a variety theatre not far from here, the
Gate. I watched the show with Victor before he left—it
is vulgar but very funny. They don't need any singers
thank you very much no thank you, especially not
ones with colonial accents, but I will keep trying to find
some work. I hope your new car is exploding explosively
and that you and Nando are headed straight for the
Palace. A-oooga!
Love love
Your Clover

Black Thread

The strings on the back of Aurora's neck tensed painfully when she sewed. But in this domestic life, she knew, it must be done. One summer evening, she went up to Mabel's room to ask for black darning thread, and found Mabel sorting through a box of letters. On the uncluttered dressing table stood a photo of her Captain Graham, two ivory-backed brushes, and a limp dun hairnet: an inexpressibly sad collection. The young captain's direct eyes stared from a wide, easy-natured face.

Mabel got up at once to find thread. Seeing Aurora's eye on the photograph, she held out a page of the letter she had let fall on the bed. Aurora read:

> . . . Tom is still in England, he was left in care of
> the horses, but—just on the q.t. between you and me
> May—he got 'cold feet,' savvy?
>
> I am sorry I have not written you more. When we
> go into the firing line for eight days and get about
> three hours sleep out of every twenty-four, one gets
> dead all over nearly, and during all the hours whether
> asleep or awake, one has always to keep his eye skinted
> down his rifle barrel. It does get one's nerves, some,
> but it's all right—

'This page is sad, the rest is more—well. I wish you knew him. You will someday.' Mabel's fingers refolded the flimsy page gently, her face lighted, shining.

Aurora experienced a dreadful pang of envy, seeing quiet Mabel transformed by love. She took up the spool of black thread to go. But Mabel, composed again, said, 'Won't you play for us instead? I can mend your things, if you will play. We get so little good music here, although the high school gives a charity concert from time to time.'

Happy to give over the needlework, Aurora fetched sheet music Bella had sent her, Paderewski's *Minuet* and a book of Field and

Chopin Nocturnes: suitable for drawing-room music, but a challenge to perfect. Mama sat by the piano, her head leaning on her left hand, the weak right arm abandoned in her lap, humming softly.

After that, Aurora played for them every evening once Avery was put in his cot. She played for him, too, as he lay sleeping right above the drawing room.

Words and Music

On his return to Qu'Appelle in late July, Dr. Graham came out to see Mama. He was a loose-jointed, surprisingly unkempt man with spiky hair that looked as if he'd just run his fingers through it; he had clever crow's eyes and an air of tolerance.

After listening closely to what Aurora could tell him of Dr. King's diagnosis, Dr. Graham spent most of the afternoon observing Mama, talking to her as if she would respond. He sat on her left side, chatting easily of Avery, who lay playing with a silver spoon from the old apostle set. When Dr. Graham moved to Mama's right side she ignored him; but when Avery fussed and Aurora picked him up and sat close to Dr. Graham, Mama's eyes followed the baby.

'There, you see! The child will be a help,' the doctor said. 'You must use whatever interests her strongly to reawaken her desire to use this damaged side.'

Aurora told him she had been placing Avery in Mama's right arm from time to time, to force her to hold tight; the doctor commended her and asked if she saw any improvement in Mama's speech.

'No, but—I don't know if this matters—she can sing.'

'I heard her humming to the babe, yes.'

'But she sings in words.'

That did surprise him. Aurora sang, '*O, don't deceive me . . .*' and Mama, without seeming to think at all, joined in: '*O, never leave me, How could you use a poor maiden so?*'—the words quite clear.

Dr. Graham's attention was truly caught, then. 'Has she any other songs? Does she appear to know the meaning of the words?'

'Sometimes,' Aurora said. 'The phrases she uses when she sings seem to fit what is happening. I have heard snatches of other songs, but this is the only one she sings all the way through.'

'You must keep note! This may smooth the path of her recovery.'

Dr. Graham made other recommendations: to maintain natural speech with Mama, including her in their conversations as if she could answer, and not to expect too speedy a progress. 'Try not to correct her, or grow impatient; the connection from brain to tongue has been broken and must be relearned. It may never be fully restored, I'm sorry to say,' he told Aurora. 'But we will expect the best. This singing business—I must write to King and some others . . .' He looked again at Mama. 'Have you tried her with drawing?'

'She does not like to hold the slate,' Aurora said. 'But she can form letters still, very slowly. One or two words, no more.'

'Yes, that is usual—well, we shall see! I will keep her under my eye,' he said.

Mama looked away from him and plucked with her left hand at her skirt until Aurora sat beside her, taking the fretful hand.

Dr. Graham came back across the fields for dinner that evening, bringing the schoolmaster, Lewis Ridgeway, with him. 'He's all alone,' the doctor murmured to Elsie. 'I knew you would not mind.'

While the men were smoking in the garden after dinner, Elsie whispered to Aurora and Mama that Ridgeway had had a disappointment in love. 'His fiancée left at Christmas—she has taken a school in Weyburn. And nobody knows, my dears, whether she will come back at all—no one is certain why she left. I have heard it said that she was *made* unhappy.'

Mr. Ridgeway must be to blame if his fiancée skittered off, it seemed. Aurora listened to Mama singing under her breath: '*Thus sang the poor maiden, her sorrows bewailing . . .*'

'Lewis can be a little daunting,' Mabel said quietly. 'But he is a good friend.'

Out of sympathy with ladies who talked secrets, Aurora played piano behind the gathering—Dr. Graham monopolizing Uncle Chum, with an occasional aside to Mabel; Elsie and Mama drowsing in their chairs.

Mr. Ridgeway seemed to attend to Dr. Graham's conversation, but when Mabel brought in the tea tray he came to the piano as Aurora played the final quiet chords of a Field nocturne. He leaned down to say, 'I can't recall when I've enjoyed an evening more, Mrs. Mayhew. I like to listen to you.'

She looked up, one arm stretched in the lamplight to close the book. 'I wish you could have heard my mother, before— She plays far better than I do.'

'My musical understanding cannot reach to anything better than your playing.'

Made self-conscious, Aurora straightened the edges of the music.

'Perhaps next term I could persuade you to play for my students?'

'Certainly,' she said. 'If you would like me to. But perhaps my mother's health will improve under Dr. Graham's care, and you may yet hear her play.'

He nodded, allowing this as a serious possibility, then said, 'I'm sorry to have missed the little boy this evening. He is very bonny.'

She smiled up at Mr. Ridgeway. She liked him, she decided, for his kindness to Mabel and his half-concealed unhappiness.

The Candy Habit

'Pantages has taken a fancy to her,' East told Verrall as they ran up the iron flights of stairs to their dressing room, Bella following like a puppy on a leash. 'And Julius—'

'A good name, but some nights you can't get him onstage,' Verrall said.

'If we've got her, we're flexible,' East said. 'If he's good, we do the old hotel routine. If not, we do the golf.' East opened the door to their dressing room and bowed her in.

Julius was in the armchair, a glass in hand. He looked up. 'Ahh, my boys. And.' He stared at Bella. 'Oh no, no. No, no . . . I've had one or two over the eight, my dear,' he said. 'Can't fulfill my—can't manage— take her away, boys, don't tempt me.'

Verrall blushed brilliantly and begged Bella to take no notice, but she found it horrible that Julius mistook her for a floozy. He'd never mistake Clover or Aurora that way, she'd bet.

East bustled about making cocoa while Verrall explained the deal.

'Pantages is a famous highway robber. Thirty-two weeks is only to tempt us; you'll see, the written contract will be for fourteen weeks. Six weeks to work our way out to the West Coast—then Pantages will hand us the choice of being cancelled and stranded, or taking a 25-percent cut in salary for the remaining eight weeks.'

'But he can't do that!'

'He won't do it to *us*,' East boasted. 'I'll see to that! We'll see our sixty weeks of work, because he likes us. And you, Pretty Baby—you're the icing on the cake this year.'

Verrall said, 'Pantages wants us—well, except Jay—to meet him for dinner after the show. He is generous, in his way, always ready with a bag of peanuts or—say, East, is that where you got the candy habit?'

'Penuche?' East asked, producing a crumpled bag.

Bella laughed and sang her chorus: '*Oh I want a loving baby and it might as well be you, Pretty Baby of mine . . .*'

Yawning

Uncle Chum and Aunt Elsie spent every August at their cottage at Katepwa, twenty-five miles up into the country on a long lake cut through prairie tableland. Aurora did not need more rest-cure, but thought the change might do Mama good. They drove out to the lake in Uncle Chum's new toy, a shining bottle-green Ford motorcar. Aurora wondered again how well-off Chum was; so far she had not been able to engage him in serious discussion about paying for their board, and had abandoned the struggle.

Aunt Elsie sat with Mama, Avery between them, in the back seat; Aurora, the only one not afraid of the car, sat up front watching Uncle Chum slash the gear lever violently in all directions until something caught. She kept the laugh caught in her throat, feeling like Bella, and did not let it come streaming out.

Katepwa was a huddle of pleasant cottages set in stone-walled lots along the lakeshore. Mabel had gone up a few days before (when Dr. Graham was going to his own place) to air the cottage and lay in supplies. When the Ford pulled up, tea was waiting on the porch: a pretty table set with a white cloth, and Mabel smiling from the steps.

Mama gasped with pleasure, like her old self—Aurora felt a hard double-beat in her heart, frustrated longing to leave combined with certainty that she was doing the right thing. She wished her sisters could see Mama here. Another thing: whatever rift there had been between Mama and Uncle Chum, clearly he had no memory of it, and she was blessedly blank now too. Aurora found it a great relief that Mama had put down that heavy baggage of past grievance.

At Katepwa there was nothing to do but listen to Victrola records and play with Avery. The dollhouse kitchen was too small for more than Elsie and Mabel, and even those two spent as little time as possible on housewifely duty. The lake community visited all day, or canoed at a leisurely stroke up and down the lake. Mabel and Aurora strolled the lanes while Avery napped in the afternoon. Mabel got freckles on her nose and was distressed; Aurora told her they became her very well, and Mabel glowed, briefly.

After dinner the lake stilled, only the placid, plangent popping of fish breaking the surface. Chum did his fishing in the morning, but kept an ear open in the evening. On Saturday night, when a band came to play for the weekly dance, Chum grunted and paced down to the shore to watch the fish rise, as music slid over the water. Aurora and Mabel canoed out onto the lake, under the brightest full moon Aurora had ever seen. They talked about dropping in at the dance—and paddled home down the moonbeam instead.

It was all excruciatingly boring. But restful. Aurora felt her breathing deepen, the muscles around her ribs loosening after years of tautness—as if she were unlacing her corset, as Gentry had ordered her to do so long ago. She thought of sending him a postcard, but did not want to sadden him with news of Mama's infirmity.

Dr. Graham came to the cottage one morning to work with Mama again. After spending an hour watching her play with Avery on the lawn, he said that he was well satisfied, though they might not see the tiny gradation of improvement. But once in a while, Aurora did catch Mama lifting the cream jug with the reluctant right hand; if frustrated enough she might scrawl a few words on her slate. Avery called forth greater effort; when Mama was frustrated or tired and weepy, plumping him onto her knee would stem her tears. She sang to him all day long, branching out from *Early One Morning* to snatches of *Last Rose of Summer*, and Aurora could hear the lyrics becoming clearer.

Mail and the papers followed them up to Katepwa, a day or two late. A letter from Clover on the peculiarities of Galichen's atelier was a galvanizing jolt of pleasure in the soporific haze. Aurora read excerpts to Mabel and Elsie as they sat playing honeymoon whist on the porch one rainy afternoon. Mama dandled Avery on her lap—her reluctant right arm put to work around his waist, keeping him safe.

> Gali issues dicta. Yawning is the latest: on Monday at the
> noon meal (we take it at the atelier every day; one piece
> of bread per person and a ladle of thin soup) he came out
> of his sanctum and spoke: we must yawn! Breath frees
> the soul and body to work more freely, yawning signals
> the moving of the mind to a new plane of discovery. So
> no one must be polite (always a cuss word around here)
> and repressed, but yawn mightily all day long.
>
> By Thursday I guess he'd had enough of our
> tonsils: the dicta was on the noticeboard in the morn-
> ing. Yawning would not be tolerated—a yawn is the
> sign of a disengaged mind, tending towards sleep, and
> we were all in need of waking up! If we find ourselves
> about to yawn we are to bend from the hips and
> breathe deeply six times.

A letter came from Bella, too, and required puzzling through as if it were the Rosetta stone:

Verrall has bouhgt a typewriter, the better to
seem proffesional!! I am traelling with him and eEast
now because Nando has gone to work in the movies.
Hiw father ~~maeoe~~ him. made him. Nando s mother
went off with a magician she used to know. that broke
his heart then he had to go get horrible Joe from the
san so he went. Also some man in New Yrok wanted
him to go int the movies but Nando does not want to
but he could take his dad there too so he went. But do
not worry about the $$$ becaues I will get a third of
E&V take now they've come over to Pantages because
Mr. Pantages likes me. He is faft. He wants me to do
the bumbble bee but I do not have the wings. I mgiht
do Pretty Baby in Seattle. Every body loves a baby
that's why I'm in love with you, Pretty Baby. tell mama
I miss her is she alll rihgt?

  xxxxXXXXXXxxxxx for you and mama and the
little dovey-boy

YOUR LOVING B.

  i like Avery for his name thats good

Did that mean Pantages was *fast*, or *fat*? The typewriter was no
better than Bella's handwriting. Disturbing to hear that Nando's mother
had run off—and impossible to tell exactly what was going on with
Nando, but perhaps it was for the best. Aurora had not been entirely
easy about letting Bella travel with Nando when she was so enamoured
of him, and still so young. It was a comfort that East and Verrall were
with Pantages now and would look after Bella. How lucky that Pantages
himself had taken a liking to her!

  Aurora took the baby upstairs, and thought as he nursed of the lively
lives her sisters were pursuing—and how this long hiatus was dulling
her own mind, making her unfit for work. Avery's hair was growing in,
bright gold. His fingers worked on her breast, muddling her thoughts,
and they fell asleep together, as they did most afternoons at Katepwa.

A King of Vaude   Bella lay watching, in an unlucky tilt of the dressing-table mirror, Mr. Pantages's heels pushing backwards against the polished bed-foot, his bandy legs in boots. He hadn't even taken off his boots. Black pants flurried around his ankles, caught his legs, tangled them, all lard fatness and the wool serge wrinkling. And in between his gasping—a sow searching out something rotten. She did not believe that Mayhew would have been so piggy, but comforted herself that Mayhew was only a faker, not a true King of Vaude.

Pantages went *ahh!* in one high-pitched squeal and then he slacked, he slumped, he pushed again, groaning and kicking the bed, and then he huffed, like the train engine coming into Paddockwood and stopping— you know that lurch is coming, and it comes.

Although it hurt more than she had expected, she did not make any complaint. All that lather and steam out of him and not a note from her.

That was that, then. Bella closed her eyes.

In the morning, waking with the sun spiking through a tear in the blind, her first thought was that she'd lived through it. How perfect a coincidence it was, that the sun would rise in that exact trajectory to blind her. Her eyes were sore and sandy from the night before. His leg was heavy over hers: girly-soft white skin, massive in the thigh, dwindling to a hard skinny shin. She supposed that she must love him or something, to notice that. But no, she hated him in fact and never wished to see his pasty face again. And she would have to smile or get cancelled, and she had East and Verrall to think of.

This was a no-good comedown for her. She was not the Belle Auroras any more.

She slid out from under Pantages—no reaction, he seemed unconscious rather than asleep—and padded into the marble temple of the bathroom, turning the brass lock. Mirrors filled the wall about the bath. This place had tone. Her body looked the same. If she pulled in her belly she could look quite pretty, rounded at the hip and bust but with a little bird waist, almost like Aurora. Perhaps she was going to have a baby now too; it could happen so suddenly. She felt stupid and also uncomfortable and did not want to identify exactly why. *You do what you have to do*, Mama had said. But where Mama had been was a vacant space Bella could not bear to think about. She sat for a while on the tiles in the clean morning light. It would be nice to cry.

Pantages took her to luncheon; then he flicked her on the chin and left, heading for St. Louis and San Francisco. What was the point, Bella wondered, if he was just going to drop her? Maybe she was not very good at that sort of thing, or she was not pretty enough.

Well, cat piss to that. She gave herself a good scolding, and decided to ignore how pretty or not-pretty she was from now on. She was different from Aurora, she never would be beautiful that way, but she could fool people into wanting her. The trick was not to let them follow through.

She had to write to Aurora, but she used a postcard, to make it short.

> We are staying put here in Chi for a while
> loonger becasue Mistrr Pantages says so.
>
> LOVE YOUR BELLA

The Tiny Knot

Clover managed to get hired as a dancer in a revue at the Tivoli: the show was not merely shabby but off-colour, a tired old Saucy Soubrette kind of gig. But she made a friend of the sole remaining comic on the bill, a wizened fellow named Felix Quirk. Perhaps because he reminded her of Julius, she told Quirk that she wanted to try her hand as a monologuist, and he offered to call a few pals and get her an audition. He was a haggard but functioning drunk who had been rejected for service. The theatre, indeed the whole of England, was full of drunks, to Clover's eyes. The streets as she walked home after the theatre were lousy with semi-conscious men, often in khakis, tottering from lamppost to lamppost, or being herded up drunk and disorderly by the police van. They were never troublesome to her, and the money was vital, because Victor's pay was small and he could not send them much.

And because Clover found that she was going to have a baby—in January, as well as she could count.

The chorus girls were cheerful in the dressing room, toasted by the reeking gas fire where they dried their washed-out stockings. After the heat and the noise, the silent walk home through dripping streets was a pleasure, but Clover often found herself tired and lonely. She could not tell Victor her news in a letter, and would not tell Madame or Aurora until he knew. The tiny knot of the baby inside her clutched and stretched, and she sometimes sang to it as she walked along. The London streets were dark with the Zeppelin blackout, yet she felt perfectly safe. She watched for a vast, ghostly shape moving through the skies, but never saw one. Only the great searchlights quartering the sky, and craters the bombs had left.

The baby was so much in the forefront of her mind that she almost told the gnome-like Felix Quirk as they were strolling away from the theatre one evening. But just then, in the grip of some necessity, he dodged into a public house for a quick snifter of brandy, leaving her to make her way home alone.

No. Not alone, for the child went with her.

Hole in the Heart

Late in September, Lewis Ridgeway invited Aurora to give a piano concert to the senior high-school girls. Remembering how she had longed for lovely clothes at that age, she wore the blue grosgrain afternoon gown with a linen jabot, and her best shoes; the half-mile walk would not ruin them. Mr. Ridgeway had asked for a mixed repertoire; she would sandwich two nocturnes around MacDowell's *To A Wild Rose*, which the girls could play themselves. The brass zip on her leather music case ran smooth and cool. She missed working.

As she left the house she passed Mama standing on the porch with a watering can for the stone jars of marigolds. '*O, who would inhabit, This bleak world alone?*' Mama sang, eyes fastened on hers, desperate to convey a message.

Aurora pressed a kiss on her cheek, and told her Avery was in his cot with Mabel writing letters beside him. Her present strategy was to expect Mama to understand, to be perfectly capable, as if that might *make* her capable.

Mr. Ridgeway was waiting for her at the entrance to the brick high school. The school suited him—it was an oddly significant building for such a little town. Walking down the glossy-floored hall they passed several empty classrooms. She glanced into yet another large bare room, and he gave a sudden smile. 'Yes, we have the facilities for a music room. Mrs. Gower has donated an instrument I think you'll enjoy.'

He ushered her through the last double doors into a pleasant open hall with folding wooden chairs and, on a raised dais, a vast black concert grand.

Aurora went to examine the piano. The high-school girls trooped in, taking their seats with decorum, and Mr. Ridgeway introduced Aurora as a seasoned concert performer.

Feeling a ridiculous blush rise to her cheeks, she turned to the girls to say, 'My sisters and I toured in vaudeville for several years...' Then she fell silent, alone onstage, missing Clover and Bella—as if her arms were gone, whole portions of her body. What could these girls know about vaude, the real life and ordinary beauty of it?

Taking herself in hand, Aurora bowed and began. Halfway through the Field nocturne she wished she'd thought to turn the piano, so she could see the audience. The audience. Even a handful of schoolgirls was worth working for—it was not vanity or shallowness of mind, it was the desire to do one's best by the music, and to—to elevate the listeners, or simply delight them.

She turned from the piano after *Wild Rose*, to find several of the girls in tears. 'It's *exquisite*!' said a cherry-ribboned girl—Nell Barr-Smith, the Dean's daughter. 'But does it have words, could you sing it?' And the others cried *yes, yes, please.*

Grateful and surprised, Aurora altered her plan and instead of the second Field piece gave them *Last Rose of Summer, a capella.* After singing it under-voice all these months to encourage Mama, it was a pleasure to let her full voice out—but a pity to do without Clover's mourning violin.

She sang, enjoying the song's frank sentiment and the long afternoon light streaming in the tall windows. At the end, smiling down at the flowery faces, she sank into a formal curtsy, one hand over her heart, to please them. The girls came in twos and threes to thank her and make shy compliments.

As the room emptied, Aurora was left alone on the dais, packing her music away.

Mr. Ridgeway regarded her from his position by the windows, twenty feet away. Happy to have been able to play for the girls, she began to thank him for inviting her, but he waved a hand. They stood silent for a moment.

'I don't know what to do,' he said, his look too direct for light conversation.

'About what?'

He turned his head away, then fixed his eyes on her again, across the room. 'You must know already, your voice is—you are—beautiful.'

Aurora was not shocked, exactly, but entirely surprised. She stared back at him, not smiling, unsure herself what to say or do.

Hurrying footsteps sounded in the hall: two tall girls rushed in with a bucket of blackboard erasers. 'All clean, sir,' the taller girl said.

The spell was broken, and Aurora picked up her hat and music case.

'Don't go, Mrs. Mayhew,' Mr. Ridgeway said, his voice very dry and scholarly. 'Miss Frye will want to see you about the Christmas concert.'

The girls said goodbye to her again, and to Mr. Ridgeway; he made a show of ushering them out and then turned back to Aurora. 'I should correct myself—' He shook his head, raised his hands. 'I cannot apologize. It was an observation of fact.'

She walked home deep in thought, conscious of a terrible appetite. Not for Lewis Ridgeway, who was so odd and angular—but for some flare of excitement. Maybe she was perfectly frozen, and never would love anyone. There were women like that, pathologically cold—one heard about them. She had not been cold with Jimmy, but was never his, not really. Not the way Clover was Victor's, unquestioningly, her whole heart open to him. Or Mabel, with her Aleck. For a moment Aurora wished very badly to have that. Perhaps one could be whole-hearted with Lewis Ridgeway. Except that she was still married to Mayhew, so there was no point in thinking of— And she did not want to think of it, any of it. Better to be alone.

Not alone; with Avery. She could be whole in heart there. A hole in the heart, perhaps that is what she had.

Better and Better   Do you remember that time when you were sick backstage—that must have been the baby coming!—and I did Mrs. O'Hara? Well, I have been earning a bit of money doing monologues like that for the Gate variety theatre near here. Most of their comics have gone to the Front and they are starved for artistes. Good to have a jingle of coins in my pocket although Gali is kind and so is Madame. (But I think she is a little mad.)

Clover had taken to writing to Aurora in snatches—never able to sit long enough for a whole letter. Her mind was nervous and her body could not settle. Still no news from Victor. That was to be expected in wartime, but she wanted so badly to let him know her own news. Tying her apron above the small firm bulge of the baby, she longed to tell Aurora, to ask her about the tight feeling and whether it was all right to be so terribly sleepy all day long.

Clover went to beat carpets in the garden, a useful and therapeutic occupation, but found she had to sit down on the dead grass—crouch, really—and pant for a while. It was uncomfortably animal.

Through the window she could hear Victor's mother in her bath, quietly chanting Coué's auto-suggestion trick, 'Every day, in every way,

I am better and better.' It was not really allowed. Gali did not approve of other gurus. When she visited the astrologer, Madame wore a mysterious grey veil as a disguise. Clover gave a hiccuping laugh and felt the baby inside her jump, and laughed again. To keep herself from worrying about Victor, she was working on a monologue character called Madame Scrappati. Victor would not mind her using his mother's eccentricity, even in the unlikely event that he was able to see the show.

The baby turned a somersault and kicked her hard in the ribs, and Clover determined to be more cheerful, more courageous, for its sake. Fear would hurt the baby. How brave Aurora had been, dancing right to the minute of Avery's birth. She could do that. Getting up, she danced gently in the garden, stretching her arms out to the view of Wormwood Scrubs prison. *Better and better,* she sang to the baby inside her as they twirled.

Every Unspoken Wish   In Seattle, Bella got a new song by Irving Berlin, which brightened the November gloom. Pantages sent the song from San Diego in an envelope marked, *BELLA AVERY ONLY,* which she supposed was nice of him. Very silly, no sentimental bilge-distilling—Gentry Fox would approve. She thought of writing to tell Gentry so, but she did not have his address and he'd always liked Aurora best anyway. It was a lovely song, a girl explaining the hidden charms of her new boyfriend, and Bella knew just what to do with it: all her own surprise, a little measure of shock, a dab of relish and a bit of a laugh, more at herself than him.

> *'He's not so good in a crowd, but when you get him alone*
> *You'd be surprised,*
> *He doesn't look very strong, but when you sit on his knee,*
> *You'd be surprised!'*

She was enjoying herself until she realized she was singing about Nando: *'But in a Pullman berth, you'd be surprised!'* The song was a big hit. Rather than giving her a blue envelope for the innuendos, Kleinhardt, the manager in Oakland, put her second-to-close in her own slot and changed the handbills that very week, with a paycheque all her own as well as her third of the E&V take.

Her grouch-bag was groaning, though she sent half of everything off to Qu'Appelle. Aurora wrote to say she had opened a bank account in Indian Head for a rainy day, and had wired money to Clover, and that Bella should be sure to buy herself nice things for ordinary as well as new costumes as required. Bella did need a new dress for the number, and she had the perfect thing made up. Mama would love this dress, she thought, and she had a photo taken to send to her: demure white lace, only six inches off the ground, with pink satin shoes and sash: a wallflower's dress, in which she could suddenly transform to a girl who has had every unspoken wish fulfilled, along with some she didn't know how to pronounce.

Mme Scrappati

Not trusting the British audience as she did the houses back home, Clover used herself, in the role of a naive traveller new to England, to introduce her monologues. She did Mrs. O'Hara regularly, and developed others: a gawky ballerina and an aging opera singer (a very free portrait of Miss Sunderland from Gentry's theatre). Madame Scrappati went over best—though Clover thought it would not work at home, being a portrait of a type only seen in England.

> Last week I met Madame Scrappati, an eccentric
> lady who teaches the violin to any number of unpleasant
> children, walking down Portobello Market. She carried
> an enormous basket, and from it fished a mutton bone
> for a dog that came whining, a penny for every poor waif
> she met, and a large bar of doubtful chocolate, which she
> offered to me. I proposed a cup of tea instead.

Having sketched Madame Scrappati's basket and movements, Clover transformed into Madame herself, sweeping a vast magenta velvet, marabou-edged stole about her shoulders as she turned to nestle herself, her draperies and her basket into an imaginary inglenook. *Dearest!* she began, in a breathy, overexcited voice: a hint of gin, polyglot phrasing, and every odd usage she was learning from the atelier.

> I have had the most *profound* session with La Sombreuse—opening the stars to me in all their power and influence. But perhaps do *not* mention her to the dear Vicar, for he is not in sympathy with the esoteric wisdom. Of course *you and I* do not credit astrology, but one cannot help finding the accuracy quite astounding! La Sombreuse warns of a conjunction, Neptune the trickster and warlike Mars. She sees real possibility of *international conflict*.

And then a rapid tour through various vultures of clairvoyants and charlatans, until:

> Oh, darling, I will be late for my Tarot reading: Signora Esmeralda, a genius of the mystical cards—her pack was passed down to her from Ahasuerus and Sheba, and she has the most *fascinating* insights . . . But do not tell the dear Vicar, *cher amie* . . . *(Donning a grey veil, she totters off.)*

It went over well, but audiences had little else to amuse them, with most male artistes gone to the Front. In Victor's regiment there were four former variety artistes—Victor had once sent her a cartoon featuring himself, drawn by Bairnsfather: a private juggling grenades to the mixed entertainment and horror of his troopmates. 'It was only tins of bully beef,' Victor wrote at the bottom of the cartoon. 'I would not care to waste a good grenade.'

Felix Quirk was the last remaining comic at the Tivoli. His withered arm was skilfully hidden, and his upper-class accent might even have been his own. He went Clover's way after the last show, heading for

Notting Hill, and walked a different route with her each evening, introducing her to London's geography. When he changed to the Vaudeville Theatre down on the Strand, he got Clover a few weeks' engagement there so they could continue their walks. He made a pet of her, calling her the Little Canadian. But Quirk was a more dedicated drunkard even than Julius, and Clover reserved herself a little too.

One night they came upon a line of ambulance carriages along the street. Clover asked what they were waiting for, and Felix pointed up the street to St. Pancras station, far distant. 'Wounded soldiers returning from France,' he said. 'Brought in at night, so the public does not panic at their numbers.'

It took twenty minutes to walk down the line. The wounded were brought out on stretchers, and a few walking, accompanied by nursing sisters and orderlies. Their faces were the colour of the stones; the darkness kept Clover from seeing their eyes. She saw them in dreams, though, after that night.

What's One to Do?   As he had promised, one November afternoon Dr. Graham came to see how Mama progressed, driving his open car. Beside him sat Lewis Ridgeway, so muffled up against the dust and chill that Aurora could not make out his expression.

The doctor asked after Mama; Chum collared Ridgeway and took him into his study for a chat. Aurora was glad not to have to enter into polite conversation. She and the doctor went to the sitting room, where Mama was engaged in building block towers with Avery.

Mabel came out of the kitchen, gave Dr. Graham a quick embrace, and offered tea; the doctor sat at once to help with the blocks, telling Aurora that she might go about her business. So Aurora slipped her coat on and went out, telling Aunt Elsie that a walk to the post office would do her good. Not—she told herself—avoiding Mr. Ridgeway.

The air outside had a clean, cold bite. Smoke rose in spirals from burning leaves as the townspeople cleared their gardens for the winter.

Everything smelled of winter, making Aurora long for snow. It was just past four o'clock, time to walk out and back before dark.

But she had not gone past the end of the drive before she was hailed, and turned to see Ridgeway striding after her, his long overcoat slashing through the air.

'May I walk with you?' he asked, wanting permission, it seemed, after their strange conversation at the schoolhouse. She looked at him. His narrow face did not show emotion easily, she thought; or perhaps he had no easy emotions.

'If you wish,' she said, laughing a little at her own cowardice.

He made no attempt to take her arm but suited his step to hers, and they progressed along the empty road.

'No snow as yet,' she said, after a silence of a few minutes.

'No.' He turned his head at her gambit. 'You are not usually a conventional conversationalist, Mrs. Mayhew, and I like that.'

'If you wish, I will keep Silence, like in the library.'

'I hope not. But—here, have you tried the path through the copse? It is smooth and clear.'

They veered to the left and entered a little wood that stretched out from the edge of town, poplars and scrub willows. Most of the leaves had fallen, soft-cracking underfoot; an early moon showed through bare branches. She waited for him to speak, glancing at his profile as they walked. He had a defined head: strong forehead and nose, sharp jaw and chin. She found it impossible to tell where his intellect left off and his human-ness began.

'Your husband left you?' he asked. Abrupt, in that quiet grey place. 'Yes.'

'My fiancée left me,' he said.

There was a pause. 'Yes, I'd heard that,' she finally said.

'What's one to do?'

Not an idle phrase, she thought, but a real question. He sounded still desolate.

'I'm sure your case is quite different,' she said, seeking to comfort him. 'Mine had gone bust, you know, and considered my mother and sisters excess baggage. I did not know about Avery yet, so he did not desert his child—but I have no way of finding him, nor any intention of doing so.'

A relief to be able to tell all this without emotion. She had not told Uncle Chum the full story. 'My husband was dishonest in every way,' she said. 'Not an honourable or admirable person. But I will find something good to remember about him, to tell my son.'

'My—Miss Parker was honest enough,' Ridgeway said. 'Quite brutally so.'

'I am sorry,' Aurora said.

He laughed, lessening the intensity of the exchange. 'Eloquent, in fact! But perhaps it was for the best,' he said.

And that was all. Through the little wood, they emerged into the open and saw Uncle Chum's Ford coming towards them, weaving its way tenderly along the ruts, to save her the walk.

'Kind of him, but you know he very much likes a reason for an outing,' she said. 'Good night, Mr. Ridgeway.' She stopped herself from saying *thank you*.

He said it instead. 'Thank you. I will see you—oh, soon, I expect.'

The Ford stitched up the road to the post office. While Chum filled her in on the smallest details of Lewis Ridgeway's antecedents and credentials, she thought about his face, so distinct in the moonlight.

Gas

The long silence was explained in letters brought for Clover and Madame by a London Territorial home on leave: Victor had been gassed at Loos. They were in his own handwriting, which Madame took as a sign. She was phlegmatic. Her astrologer had warned of catastrophe averted.

> I am sorry to have kept it from you, but it was our own
> gas, blown back over the lines. It's a shame you should
> be worried—I was convinced that it would be easier for
> you both if I could reassure you that I am perfectly

well again, rather than sending one of the tick-cards.
The headache was the worst of it, I was never as badly
off as many. Their coughing was the continuo at the
hospital, their yellowy-green faces floated upside
down, beseeching, heads hanging off stretchers to
get some relief.

The doctors bled me! I was under the misappre-
hension that bleeding was a medieval sort of treatment.
They kept us warm with good blankets and hot-water
bottles, a nice change from the trenches, and after a
course of saltwater vomiting, I'm pronounced fit for
light duty again. I'll work at the hospital this month,
and be back at the Front as soon as winking. If I'd been
sent to hospital in England, I'd have had some sick
leave. Only I can't wish for leave when things are so
desperate here. Perhaps you have heard some of it.

The Prince of Wales came to visit the Guards,
tell my mother, I forgot to put it in her letter. They
would not allow him near the Front, too dangerous,
but he ordered his car to stop near Loos and while he
was trying to get closer to the trenches to see the men,
his car and driver were blown to bits.

Unable to bear leaving him in ignorance any longer, Clover wrote
to Victor by return, telling him that he was to be a father. Within the
week she received the warmest of letters in return, promising faithfully
that he would return safe, and wishing her to take every care, as he
would too, so that they could be the most fortunate and loving parents
since the world was made. It was a letter in Victor's old manner, his old
poetic voice. She remembered him leaning over the edge of the Parthenon
roof in Helena, shouting into the snow, 'Children! This is your mother!'

Clover wrote immediately to Aurora and Mama (asking Aurora to
gauge whether Mama would find the news distressing) and to Bella.
She requested their best advice—but felt she needed none. She had

passed the uncomfortable sickish part, and was feeling stronger than ever in her life.

9, 10, 11　　　Joyful from the Soubrettes was at the Pantages in Spokane, posing in scanty clothes as a magician's assistant. In a happy reunion, she and Bella told all their sisters' tales, including Mama's stroke and Clover's defection to England. East had tried to find Mayhew when they hit Spokane, but apparently he had not stayed in the city more than a month before he'd lit out for parts south with a dancer called Estella, or Elvira, and even in the small pond of vaudeville, nobody had heard of him since. Good riddance, Bella told Joyful.

The Soubrettes were scattered, Mercy in Australia with a theatre company, and Tempy out at the farm, where she had married a fellow who didn't mind keeping Patience. Joyful whooped when she heard of Aurora's baby—and now Clover's, to come! After three or four glasses of sloe gin, Bella confided that she was quite afraid of being caught that way herself, especially now Clover was expecting too, and Joyful taught her about counting days.

'Have you had your womanly time since?'

Bella nodded, not shy with Joyful. 'Last week.'

Joyful nodded too. 'You're likely good, then. You take from then, from the first day, and count nine. Then you stay away from men— well, or give them only a French—for *ten* days, then you're mostly good for *eleven* days. Doesn't always work, but you can find a woman to help you. Mercy has special tea if you get a scare, if your visitor don't come.'

Nine, ten, eleven. She could do that. Bella started to mark off the days, using a carmine stick to smudge the day she started and counting nine, ten and eleven from there each month. She crossed her fingers that Pantages would not come at a bad time. He did not like it when she was on her monthlies; she could pretend to be, as long as she was reasonable about it, and get away with a French job or only canoodling.

So really she was hardly bothered by him. It was all right. When he gave her an extra present she sent the money to Aurora and asked her to send half to Clover, for the baby.

A Blanket from the Fire

In late December Clover ran out of work, the pantomimes taking over every variety stage. It was time, anyway; she was already much bigger than Aurora had been with Avery, and could only do Mrs. O'Hara and Madame Scrappati, whose costumes were loose round the middle.

Felix Quirk sent tickets to his panto. Madame sang along with the words on the screen let down from the flies, '*Keep the home fires burning...*' Clover sat hard as stone while the cheery patriots sang. Patriotism had burned out of her when Victor was gassed.

The last month went very slowly. Madame never seemed to worry about things but held that providence or the stars or Gali would provide—indeed, just before Christmas a large bank draft came from Qu'Appelle, so they had both heat and light, with plenty over for food. Although Clover had debated going to a lying-in hospital, wounded men were flooding all the wards, and she felt so well that she delayed making any arrangement. In the end, well into January, the baby was born at Galichen's atelier—choosing to come in the middle of the night. Clover woke in a pool of water, hit by a wave of pain so shocking that she cried out for Madame, who came with spritely haste and gentle shrieks. Not daring to take time to fetch help, she wrapped Clover up and took the mountain to Mahomet the instant the wave had passed, hurrying her out to the street and down the area steps to the atelier's kitchen.

The little girl was born on the well-scrubbed kitchen table, Madame exclaiming and Heather Jakes doing the work. Heather was a closed-faced woman. They had often met in the atelier kitchen, or crossed on the stairs, but during the long violence of the birth pains Clover came to love her. Not a talker, but her hands were sure and strong and she held Clover's knees, from time to time giving some useful direction: 'Hold off now, no pushing—a bit longer, but it won't be more than you can stand.' And because Heather Jakes had said so, it was not. But bad enough.

When the baby was born finally and Clover was lying still, holding the miraculous creature and not in pain any more, Galichen came to the kitchen to look her over, and the child. After close scrutiny he pronounced his satisfaction, gave permission for it to live, and dedicated it to the moon. Clover would have laughed, if she'd had the wind. His one magnified eye glared at her, and winked, and then he left.

Heather Jakes brought her a blanket warm from the fire, the kindliest thing Clover had ever felt. She was so tired. In case she died, she said to the women, 'Her name is Harriet, Harriet Avery—tell Victor.'

Luna   Snow heaped up around the stone house to the windowsills, a succession of blizzards keeping Qu'Appelle people more or less housebound in the first months of 1916. But mild spring air sent everyone searching for companionship. By April, dinners and teas filled the calendar, and Aurora watched the social life of the little town creaking to a start again.

Mrs. Gower was the queen of Qu'Appelle society, and a determined organizer. Her son was serving as aide-de-camp in Belgium; Mrs. Gower took war-work seriously. She and Miss Frye from the high school instituted bandage-rolling (in competition with the ladies of Indian Head) at the Opera House on Saturdays, and the Avery women were summoned to the first session. *Do bring Mrs. Arthur Avery as well, and your niece,* the invitation read, in flourishing peacock ink. *And any little items you can spare for packs for our brave soldiers.* A remarkably long list of those little items was attached, from tooth powder to warm socks to candy and *cigars, if any.* As well as the worsted socks they had knitted all winter, Aunt Elsie began obediently to gather whatever Chum could be persuaded to give up.

Since they were all going, Aurora brought Avery as well, a great consolation. In the shut-in months he'd grown from baby to child—walking on strong legs, talking when it suited him. He had acquired a thoughtful, considering air. His flaxen hair fell into curls that begged for stroking, but he shrugged away too much petting, and liked to be his own man. Aurora saw some of Mayhew's good qualities in him, in fact: independence, enterprise, the habit of command. He was a loving boy, and very good company unless enraged.

A photograph had arrived in February: Clover holding her tiny daughter Harriet. Aurora had shown it to Mama and Avery, the explanation as incomprehensible to one as the other, it seemed; but Mama still carried the photo with her from room to room. As they walked to town Aurora tried to imagine what Harriet would be like—what elf-child Clover and Victor had combined to make.

April sun warmed the steps of the imposing brick Opera House, companion building to the high school. The Dean and Nell Barr-Smith were arriving too; Avery knew them well and greeted them with warm embraces, which set all the parish pussies vying for kisses of their own. It was a happy afternoon, doing useful work in company with the ladies of the town. Aurora enjoyed watching Mabel in her element, moving among the women to gently encourage their efforts and smooth their frictions. Tea was served: crustless sandwiches and fancy cakes on tiered plates, courtesy of Mrs. Gower. Aunt Elsie was asked to pour and accepted the privilege; under the table her built-up black boot showed, turned sideways in a dainty flop over the smaller shoe.

Aurora found herself swept by an eddy of women into a safe backwater beside a screen, where she stood holding Avery, glad to have his weight for anchor.

On the other side of the screen, Mrs. Gower sat discussing the success of the day with Miss Frye. 'I believe we have every lady in the town,' Mrs. Gower congratulated herself, her booming voice perfectly audible even in this noisy room.

'And Mrs. Mayhew's dear little boy!' Miss Frye trilled. She had succumbed to Avery.

'*Mrs.*, hmm . . . A vaudeville dancer, I hear—*flamboyant.* Elsie Avery is a saint to take those two in. I'm told the mother is quite addled in her wits.'

Until then, Mrs. Gower's dominance had amused Aurora. But the word *addled* sent a hot poker through her chest.

She broke from behind the screen and cut through the tea line, still absurdly long, to find Aunt Elsie sitting at the head. Elsie sent up a pheasant-flurry of dismay when Aurora said she was walking home— Aurora held Elsie's plump hands to stop the flow. 'I want to, dear Aunt. Avery will enjoy the walk and it won't take us twenty minutes.'

Outside the Opera House, Avery squirmed to be let down, and Aurora bent to set him on the sidewalk. They all thought her no better than she should be, practically divorced—*if she was ever married at all*, she could hear them saying. And not without cause! She was a woman of low morals, as they defined these things; Mayhew's desertion had left her in an impossible position, at least to civilized society.

Avery's eye was caught by a swelling of green, a crocus leaf in the bare earth by the churchyard wall. They bent together to look at how it grew, Avery's finger tracing along the hairy stem. A careful boy, he was not one to grasp at things, but tested first. Aurora breathed in the delicious decay of last year's grass and the green scent of this year's growing, and ceased to fret.

As they crouched there, Lewis Ridgeway came running down the schoolhouse steps across the street. He paused when he saw her there with Avery, and after an instant's hesitation, came to join them.

'Have you escaped from the hive?' he asked.

Aurora laughed. 'I am a bad bee.'

He looked at her with curious fondness. 'You are no bee, you are a luna moth. You are in the wrong purlieu, that's all.'

She thought perhaps he was flirting with her. Not wanting that, she stood and said in a comradely way, 'I don't know what a luna moth does, but I did work hard for the first half.'

'It is pale green, long-winged, a nocturnal creature that always seems to be dancing. Unsuited to this climate, in fact.'

Aurora looked at Lewis. His whole being seemed to live in his skull: bright eyes and sharp angles, demanding and dissecting. He had a gift for appreciation. She remembered saying long ago to Mayhew, *we are the same.* To Jimmy, too. Maybe if she stayed here she could be the same as Lewis—intelligent, perceptive, sure.

A general locust noise rose from the Opera House door, tea-full ladies going back to packages and bandages and ordering each other about. Aurora picked Avery up, needing to walk. Leaning his head on her shoulder, he studied the crocus he had finally picked.

Lewis kept step with her, but did not speak until the sound receded behind them. Then he asked, 'What will you do with your life?'

She laughed at such a ridiculous question, out of the blue; shifting Avery to one hip, she shook her head and looked down at her feet passing over the boardwalk.

'This is not for you, this buzzing parish world.'

'Is it for you?' she asked.

His face grew serious. 'I believe it is. I am a schoolmaster bone-deep.'

'Did you know my father was a schoolmaster too?'

'I knew. Did you admire him?'

'For his learning, I suppose—but more for his wilder nature. He was a great gambler and a minor drunkard, and kept my sisters and me very well amused. But he did not have a happy life.'

'So Chum has told me. Melancholy is a scholastic deformation.'

She could not afford melancholy, herself. Children were too important to allow one to entertain maunderings about the purpose of life. You do what you have to do, Mama had said. What she had to do was keep Avery safe. And keep Mama from sinking.

Ladybug   February had come in like a polar bear; in France, soldiers froze to death frequently. Even into March, Victor was not able to get home to see Harriet. But in April he wrote:

> I put in for leave this week end, but with the best
> intention in the world they can't grant passes freely—we
> are the first line of defence now. I am longing to see her.

If I get a pass shall arrive 3.30 or 4—not issued till
Saturday p.m. and until then may be rescinded ... but I
am always with you, and now with her also, my beloveds.

Knowing he would not come, overcome with knowing it, Clover
wept so much on reading this letter that the baby's soft brown ringlets
were soaked. She could not work out whether she was crying for herself
or Victor. Then, recalling her vow to be more courageous for Harriet's
sake, she stopped and settled her back to the breast. Madame made a
great show of not having noticed the sobs, only brought a cup of cham-
omile tea and kissed her cheek.

Clover walked to Victoria with Harriet in an ancient perambula-
tor Madame had unearthed from the basement. It had been storing
onions, but worked very nicely once the wheels were oiled. The noise
at the station was fierce—trains toiling in and out, soldiers walking
about or lounging with blank stares, faces sharp and worried even
here in safety.

She wheeled the pram around the platforms and back into the
arcade, and saw—Victor!—detach himself from a bit of wall and come
towards her. A gas mask dangled from his rucksack. She could not bear
to think about gas.

'But it's not even *three*, you're early,' she said.

He folded his thin, real arms around her.

They were vaudeville people, they were used to separation.

She kissed him, his caved-in cheek, his tunic collar, his hand, again
and again.

He pressed her away, at last, saying, 'This, I take it, is the off-
spring?' Clover nodded, suddenly worried that he might not like
Harriet. He turned and bowed before the pram to introduce himself.
'Miss, I am your father,' he said.

Clover undid the snug shawl wrapping, so Victor could see Harriet's
flower face peeping through the wool. 'Has the baby been eating
onions?' he asked, leaning closer.

Her eyes opened, bright as blue glass, with a crazy expression as she tried to focus on his face. She reached out a hand and caught at his long nose.

'None of that!' he said. 'You are to be a dancer, not a vulgar comic. May I take her out?' It seemed both odd and correct that he should ask permission. Clover nodded.

As if picking up a glass bauble or a ladybug, Victor lifted the baby up into his arms, where she lay quite contented, only kicking a little with her strong legs. 'You see? Dancing on air already.'

Victor seemed all right, but as they began to walk Clover swiftly realized that he was not. New grooves showed in his face; at every step he seemed to ward off something invisible. She slowed the pram and looked about for a taxicab, and waved. 'You must rush home to see Madame,' she said, pressing a ten-shilling note into his hand. 'She has been so kind, do her this favour—she would love to have you to herself for a little while.'

Victor stood wavering on the street, then made a face and climbed into the cab.

She bent to kiss him. 'Harriet will have her airing, and I'll make a good tea. Don't let Madame take you to the atelier, it will be thin soup and marge, and I have tinned ham!'

Yellow Custard

We are proper tour poeple now, one week in each. Verrll says we weill get sixtie 60 weeks of worrrk. And there are ıı theatrees in Caliofrnia alone. So no holiday for mine.

Remember the Tuslers? The older brother is back on the circit, he's a gag weihgt-lifter now. Dosnt say what happened to the other one.

That was all Bella could stand to write about him. The smell of cold crumbling earth in the root cellar tumbled in her mind with the hotel sheets and the violet aftershave on Mr. Pantages, and her own shabbiness of spirit. The Irish girl's face outside in the snow, her dress so badly torn. Her blood-smudged thighs. It must have been the Tussler who hurt her. Now he was hurt and gone from vaude or maybe dead, his brother never said. Or else it was this older brother who'd done it, and then the wrong one got hurt. But the younger had hurt her, had hurt Bella herself.

One night as she was racing down the iron stairs for her turn, the older brother grabbed her arm and planted a sucking kiss on her neck. Not even enough time to hit him—her intro was starting! She yanked away and he let her go, laughing to see her stumble down to stage level. At the curtain's edge she found herself doubled over, arms around her stomach, which was on fire. She tried to think about Nando instead— but thinking of him made her so angry and miserable her stomach got worse. Biting her arm hard enough that the teeth-marks stayed for days, she went on.

Verrall placed himself between her and the tough any time he could manage. And of course East knew. Bella told them that she meant to put him out of business, and after Verrall had gently shrieked, East suggested pulling the old pie gag on him: 'No physical damage, but it does a fellow's reputation a world of hurt, and gives some satisfaction to the pie-dealer.'

Bella thought there was quite a list, actually, of people to whom she'd like to deal a pie. But the Tussler would do to begin with.

When East brought up the subject of free dates, the Tussler rose like a fish to the fly. 'I know a beautiful gal,' said East. 'Buxom! Lives with her father, but he's a trainman, works nights. Bring her a custard pie and she is yours for the night.'

The Tussler was more than willing, and next day a custard pie sat waiting on his dressing table. After the second show, East led him down dark alleys and round a few corners, circling to give the others time to get in place; slavering for the girl as he was, the Tussler did not notice. East carried the custard pie, just being naturally helpful.

He stopped at a side door and up they went into a stairwell lit by small gas lights—dim, rather than dark. East handed off the custard pie to Bella, who stood hiding in the shadows by the door.

East and the Tussler climbed the narrow stairs, and as they neared the top East called out, 'Annie, Annie! We've brought pie!'

At that cue Verrall, waiting up above in a riotous grey beard, leaned over the banister and shouted in a heavy Ukrainian accent, 'Zo! You would ruin my Anna? I kill you!'

At that, Bella hurled an old mason jar at the brick wall beside the Tussler. Exploding violently, it echoed in the dark stairwell like a shotgun blast. The Tussler skedaddled down the stairs three at a time. East and Verrall reached the bottom just in time to see Bella, lurking at the door, sploosh that custard pie into the Tussler's terrified mug.

East had twigged the cops to the gag, and they were posted at the corner in time to see the Tussler streak through the streets shouting for help, face yellow with custard, two eye-holes dragged through the mess with his thumbs. They said it was as good as a show.

Bella was so grateful to East for helping her to snapdragon the Tussler that she kissed him. He tightened his arm around her waist and with the other hand offered her a small white sack of sherbet candy.

She was everybody's baby—but not the Tussler's.

Gilt Wings

The ten days of Victor's leave stretched very long, chiefly because he could not sleep in the bed Clover had so carefully prepared. He lay down gratefully on the laundered sheets after tea, burying his nose in the down pillow, and was unconscious within seconds. But every noise of the baby woke him; every time Clover moved to her, he started upright. He took to walking the streets at night, sleeping in fits and starts during the day. He said he needed to get back into good condition and the walking would do him good. But he was white and silent in the mornings, never seeming fully asleep or awake. London was dark all day long, it seemed, the atmosphere plagued by fog, or rain too listless to fall. Air, water, darkness—no distinction.

Clover was dancing again at the Vaudeville, in a middling revue. If only Victor could have seen her monologue act! But there was one lovely number, a flitting fairy dance to *Up the airy mountain, Down the rushy glen*, and she had gilt wings.

On his third night home Victor saw the show and came to the dressing room in a seething rage, declaring it beneath her and demanding that she quit. She guided him down to the stage door laughing, thinking he was playing. Out into the alley—it was only there under the lit sign that she saw he was serious. She laughed again, for how absurd it was.

'It's not the Palace,' she said, 'but it puts coal in the fireplace!'

He fired up, blazingly angry. 'What am I to do about the coal? Should I desert?'

Now Clover was angry too. 'How can you ask that? I said nothing to deserve it.' That sounded like the quarrels of her parents' marriage. A black pall smothered her own spirits.

They walked home in silence. Clover took Harriet from Madame and left Victor to sit by the fire with her—the fire itself now in some unwanted way a reproach to both of them.

He did come to her in bed. He was always silent there, now; Clover did not feel able, either, to speak the soft besotted things they had once said.

Before returning to the Front, Victor was summoned to an audience with Galichen; he and Clover presented themselves as required, Harriet at their feet in a basket. Gali pronounced himself satisfied with Clover on eugenic grounds, congratulated Victor on his devotion to the cause of freedom, and reminded him to make certain to do his scales every day. He presented Victor with a handwritten chart of strengths and weaknesses, not unlike a school report card, and kissed him gravely on both cheeks, much moved.

Outside Gali's door they caught each other's eye and choked with laughter, but kept that silent too. And then Victor was gone.

Breakdown

In mid-June the congregation thronged to Mrs. Gower's garden for the Strawberry Festival: melting ice cream and strawberries. Aurora was observing a truce with Mrs. Gower, who had spoken very kindly to her and to Mama at the end of the Deanery working-bee; and since Bella's latest cheque had paid for a new moon-green silk dress which was at least the match of any other lady's there, Aurora prepared herself to enjoy the fete. She looked around (she could not help it) for Lewis Ridgeway, but did not find him. Perhaps he had end-of-term school work to do, or—well, it did not matter.

Avery was cranky and suffering from a surfeit of ice cream. Mabel took him into her arms, needing something to occupy herself. They'd learned that morning that an Indian Head boy had been killed in action: Frank Richmond, a schoolfriend of Aleck Graham's. Dr. Graham had brought the news to church with him. The doctor and Mabel were carefully not talking together, as if conversation could only tend in one direction, and that a useless one.

The night before, Mabel had shown Aurora part of a letter that a friend of Aleck's, John Levitt (wounded in action and invalided home) had brought from the Front. She'd handed the page over without a word, and retired to her room once it was back in her hand.

> . . . give me the rifle fire all day, every day instead of
> one of those hellish coal-boxes packed with nails,
> screws, anything sharp—no wonder to see men go
> plumb loony, nutty—
> 　　You read of such cases in the papers, how men
> suffer from breakdown.
> 　　Don't think they are nervous or weak or anything
> like that. Pity them rather—for the whine and sizzle of
> the shell in the air, and the awful suspense of waiting
> for the explosion to come is what does the trick.
> Enough of this—

Enough, yes. The sun was pale for May.

Aurora stood on Mrs. Gower's graceful veranda, listening to Mama's slight, sweet voice singing to Avery as Mabel held him, '*Whispering Hope, oh how welcome thy voice, making my heart in its sorrow rejoice . . .*'

Hearing an odd groan or gasp, Aurora stepped in through the French doors to see Mrs. Gower standing in the middle of her wood-panelled hall. Dr. Graham and Lewis and the Dean had come in through the front door together, looking grave or unhappy depending on their natures, and the Dean held a telegram.

Mrs. Gower's mouth opened very sadly, as if she were going to speak, but she did not. One foot pawed at the first of the grand stairs, could not lift to it. Lewis went to help her. She shied away from him too, now saying, 'No, no,' in almost her ordinary voice, and tripped, falling heavily onto the stair.

Dr. Graham knelt beside her. Seeing that she had the help she needed, Lewis led Aurora back through the drawing room, out onto the veranda again. 'Her son has been killed in Belgium,' he said. But she had already known that.

Mama's voice had dwindled to a whisper. Behind Avery's drowsing golden head, Mabel's eyes were like caves. Aurora took her hand.

Moon Flit   Victor's leave only worried Clover more. She did not see how he could carry on in that state of distress, in the dreadful conditions which were becoming known. And now so weak in body. He had not talked about the trenches in daylight, only in the half-dream state at four a.m. But she had seen his feet, and the hideous bruises coursing down his back and flanks. Greyer than before, Madame crept through the house and spent more time on scales and meditation at Galichen's atelier, seeking comfort. Clover wrote lightly to her sisters. To Aurora:

> Galichen requires his followers to be tested for
> purity, purpose and spiritual fitness before they
> reproduce, so we jumped the gun. But Harriet is such a
> darling, not even he could carp. While I work she stays
> with Madame or with Heather Jakes in the atelier

kitchen. Work has dried up, and these are my last few
weeks for now. I would like to go with that American
singer, Elsie Janis, to the Front—but Harriet makes that
impossible. I am not complaining. Victor did not want
to talk about the war at all when he was home.

That was all Clover could say about that. After Victor's visit she
found it harder to write to him, mired as he was in unimaginable terrors. He had talked of shelling that turned pretty woods into blank
prairies, land scarred worse than the mine pit at Butte; he had said (this
in fits and starts, in the dark, and she was not sure he was awake) that
one night they had camped in a bad smell, and only when a poor boy
went off his head, hacking at the ground, did they realize that they
were lying on a mud stew of shallow-buried bodies.

She did not want to hurt him more. At last she managed a few
sentences that were neither frozen nor frivolous: the first time she'd
ever thought twice before speaking or writing to him. When she had
addressed her letters, she wrapped Harriet up and took her along to
the postbox. The walk along wide pavements soothed her spirit a
little, and Harriet's slight weight gave her ballast. The moon flitted
between clouds. She tried not to think what its light shone on, over
in France.

Shadow Buff   At Katepwa that second August the
mornings were fresh and the weather
very fine and hot. Towards evening
thunderstorms swelled down the valley like a tide. In late August, when
idleness began to pall, Mabel organized a games evening for all their
acquaintances to join in: the Dean with his daughter Nell, Miss Frye
and her great friend Miss North who was visiting in the area, even
Mrs. Gower, Dr. Graham and Lewis Ridgeway.

Aurora went to settle Mama and Avery for the night. The thun-
dery air had made both of them fractious and demanding, and Avery

insisted Aurora hold him for a little while before he climbed into bed with his grandmother. Mama was trying to convey something in a cautious whisper. All that came out, though, was a thread of song: '. . . *sweetheart's the man in the moon* . . .' At last she gave up the attempt and opened the coverlet, singing instead, '*Come out tonight, come out tonight*' to Avery, who joined in her lento, lullaby version of *Buffalo Gals*. Aurora kissed them and dimmed the lamp.

Outside the door she stopped to listen to the two reedy voices in the room behind. She checked her reflection in the hall mirror: pale green dress, cloud of hair pinned up, her little necklace of brilliants. Fine.

She was not the Belle Auroras any more. A mother, a dutiful daughter, a matron in comfortable circumstances—thanks to Chum's kindness and to Bella's money, which kept coming and coming in slightly alarming amounts. Missing Bella very much, Aurora went down to the party.

Across the wide arch between dining room and parlour a white sheet hung. The piano stool sat lonely in the middle of the carpet, the furniture moved back. Well behind the stool, the strongest lamp in the house shone—its mica shade tilted to throw a bright beam.

Mabel explained to the little company, 'This is Shadow Buff. Someone must be *It*, and sit on the stool, staring at the screen. Then everyone else will parade behind, between *It* and the lamplight, so their shadows fall upon the screen like moving pictures—then *It* must guess whose each shadow is. You may disguise yourselves by changing your gait, rumpling your hair, or—look! Adding one of these ridiculous noses.' She and Aurora had cut and glued paper noses all the afternoon, laughing at each other's new profiles.

The Dean was unexpectedly good at the game. He identified more than half the strange shadow-creatures, saying it was due to long observation of his parishioners' idiosyncracies. Mrs. Gower, drawn in to take a turn, sat on the stool, calling out names almost at random. She had shrunk since her son's death. The opulent clothes hung on her frame; deep new lines fell from mouth to jowl. After five or six of the company had passed behind her she rose from the stool and retired, saying, 'Well, I am no use at this game, I'll give over to all of you.'

Miss Frye bounced up to take her place, pulling off the paper beak with which she had successfully duped the Dean, but did not manage to identify anyone but Miss North (whose bulk was undisguisable) and Nell Barr-Smith, a girl she had taught for six years. 'It would have been surprising if I'd missed you, Nell,' she cried, very jocular. 'Stand up straight next time and I won't know you!'

The darkened room, the parade of shambling creatures, had become nightmarish to Aurora. The thunderstorm was building, that must be it.

Lewis Ridgeway stood next and took the stool, and the line of disguisers moved behind him. He took the game oddly seriously, asking one or other to pass by again, or turn around. 'Dean, you are betrayed by the pitch of your head,' Lewis said. 'Mabel, no one could miss the kindness in your profile, nose or not. Dr. Graham—but what is the matter with your back, sir? Heal thyself!'

Dr. Graham straightened, indignant at being caught, for no one else had known him.

'And this—' Lewis paused.

Aurora walked slowly, putting a hitch in her gait, like Mama since her stroke—or perhaps like Aunt Elsie, with one lame booted foot. She waited for Lewis to name her, but he remained silent as she took the last few steps across the sheet.

At the edge her shadow paused and turned to hook-nosed profile with a giddy flourish. Lewis turned his head quickly to see who it was, to a roar of 'Cheat! Cheat!' from the crowd. Accepting disgrace, he yielded the chair and found a nose of his own.

The heat grew in advance of the storm. When the sheet was pulled down from the arch to reveal a late supper, iced lemonade was the first aim of the revellers.

No rain this evening. A storm would help, Aurora thought. She slipped out to the long porch and walked along into the shadows at the far end, wishing she could go down to the lake and bathe without worrying her aunt, who believed that anyone with a toe in the water would naturally be electrified during a storm. Bella would bathe with her, if she was here. Aurora longed for the company of her sisters, for the long-ago time when they'd slid into the water together as children at Christopher Lake. She and Clover had held Bella's hands the first time, but after that she was a little fish.

Bella would not come to Qu'Appelle, not while she was earning big money; she had not even come to visit when she'd played Regina last spring, had not let Aurora know until afterwards. She must be in trouble, but did not say what the matter was; her letters were short and funny and told you nothing. Clover's were just as opaque: she was caught up with Victor. A sudden wave of longing hit Aurora, to be loved like Victor loved Clover, simply for herself, not for beauty or skill.

A long rumble of thunder curled at the edge of the valley and receded. Uncle Chum had put the music on, Aunt Elsie was urging the others to dance. Aurora thought she'd rather stay outside than go in and dance with Lewis in that cramped space.

She heard the French door click and Lewis came out at the other end of the porch. He stood looking down to the lake, perhaps not wanting to dance with her, either.

He had not seen her yet. Aurora studied him in the light that spilled from the house. Arrogant, she told herself. Severe, over-fastidious—yet she also knew him to be perceptive and thoughtful. She must have sighed a little; a tilt of his head betrayed that Lewis had sensed her there.

Even then it took him some time to turn. Spontaneity was not his way.

'That dress is the colour of a luna moth,' he said.

'I know. I looked them up in the library.'

'I did not know it was you,' he said. 'Your shadow.'

Aurora smiled in the darkness.

'A remarkable example of pathetic fallacy,' he said, as the thunder rumbled out again. 'Of all this crowd, I thought it would be you I'd know.'

'I have a spell to cloud men's minds,' she said. One of Madame Tatiana's *mysterioso* lines. Lewis laughed then, at her accent and the mysterious swoop her shadow made.

'Walk down to the shore with me,' he said. 'If you are not afraid of the storm. I think it is some way off yet.'

They met at the steps and he took her hand to help her down. When she tried to retrieve it his grip tightened. They walked that way, hidden by darkness, to the edge of the lake and out onto the pebbly sand. East of the thunderclouds a horned moon had risen over the hills, ready to sit on like the green prop moon.

In the warm air Lewis brought her hand to his mouth and kissed her palm, and kissed it again. His mouth was cool and smooth as lake water. She felt the snaking curl in her belly and chest, radiating everywhere, the inner appetite wanting, wanting. But remembering the luna moth, which has no mouth and cannot eat, she took her hand away.

'What is to be done?' he asked her, as he had in the woods last winter.

'It is impossible, I know,' she said, answering all the considerations he had not said: her vanished husband, her child, Lewis's position.

Water lapped at the sand.

After a moment, she said, 'I don't know what you want.'

Lewis walked a little away along the edge of the lake. 'I know I am clumsy,' he said.

'No,' she said. Perhaps his fiancé had told him so. 'No, it is just difficult.'

'I want to be honourable,' he said. 'To honour what is between us.'

He was looking at her in the darkness, at her silk dress, her silk hair, her costume wings: not seeing her, herself. Naming shadows and fancy moths, this pampered life—it was all false, Aurora thought.

Also false: herself and Lewis.

'I want to be honest,' she said. 'I don't care much about honour.'

She took off her shoes and stockings, and walked into the water, certain he would not follow. He did not.

Imaginary Ladies

In Portland, East and Verrall stayed in Mrs. Kay's boarding hotel as they always had, Julius in the next room. Bella was at the Nortonia Hotel, but the delightful tea garden with its Japanese lanterns was closed for the winter. Mr. Pantages had gone south to see a very pretty quick-change artiste whose final change was Godiva. It was more peaceful without his attentions, but her contract was up in January. She continued to headline every bill—and had her picture on the cover of a song-sheet for *You'd Be Surprised!*—but could not help feeling unsettled.

She felt a fretful, pestering hunger for company, a loneliness as grey as the November evening. Restless and not at all tired, instead of turning in to the Nortonia, she walked down towards Mrs. Kay's hoping to catch East still at cards in the parlour; it was only just past midnight. She did love East, and he liked her too, however brisk he might be.

Everyone knew Verrall loved Aurora, but maybe East could like *her* best—he liked so many girls, why not her most of all? She was no longer a child, after all. Perhaps he would come back to the Nortonia with her, just this once.

A fast clip down cold, echoey pavement warmed her. Through hedge-grown back streets she arrived at Mrs. Kay's from the side and could see, across the grass, the lighted square of East's and Verrall's window—not asleep, then.

No, there was East in his shirt-sleeves moving about. Verrall stood behind him, brushing a coat with careful strokes. It was like the picture screen. Bella stood watching.

Taking off his shirt, his chest vulnerable and thin in the lamplight, East laughed at something Verrall had said. Just quietly, a joke between the two of them. Verrall wore a grin of calm pleasure, having pleased his friend. He came to the window—he would see her watching.

No, he turned back, hand on the curtain, to say something, and East came forward and laid his hand on Verrall's neck. An easy gesture. But it came to Bella, watching them, that East was Verrall's, and Verrall East's.

That it had always been so, whatever nonsense East might spout about imaginary ladies, whatever bonbons he might dole out.

Verrall pulled the curtain across.

Bella turned and made her way back through empty streets to the hotel.

Suffit

Victor had been wounded at the Somme. In November the official letter came, before any word from Victor. Both Clover and Madame stood for a long while in the gloomy front hall, trying to read the telegram. Three heads close together in the hall mirror when Clover raised her eyes. Madame's dark little head—how fond she had become of it—and Harriet's, remarkably similar.

'Wait,' Clover said, and stepped across to push the brass light switch. Before she could return to the paper, Madame had read it and fainted flat on the worn carpet.

Clover read it for herself and then sat down beside Madame, back against the wall and legs out in front of her, still holding Harriet. It was a relief, in a way, that it said *wounded in action*. That it had come, the thing she knew would be coming.

Harriet climbed off her lap and patted Madame's face, saying, 'Dama! Dama!'

In January 1917, Victor was sent to a London hospital, his leg badly infected. The pins the field surgeons had inserted to hold his leg together were causing a great deal of pain; the swelling was terrible to see, and the scar livid. Clover went to Wandsworth Hospital every day, a complicated trip involving two changes on the underground and several buses. Two hours, to be allowed ten minutes with Victor—'until his condition improves to my liking,' the ward sister said.

He was not always himself. He did not want to speak, but might return the pressure of her hand. Sometimes there would be a delay, and Clover counted the seconds until the faint squeeze came. The ward was full of men in worse case, very few in better. It was not a peaceful place, but they kept up the cheer—Victor's next-cot neighbour (who'd lost one leg at the thigh and one at the knee, but was game as a pebble) told her they had 'a few infectious spirits who rouse all the others: a very gay ward here, *very* gay.' She was grateful to him for trying to rouse her own spirits.

Once they left Harriet with Heather Jakes, so Madame could come. But the visit led to three days' hysterical weeping from Madame, and was clearly painful for Victor as well; they did not repeat the experiment.

Slowly, in snatches, he began to talk. One day as Clover bent over to kiss his marble face he said, 'I can't—' She stayed bent over his bed, close enough to hear. 'Tell them—you'll have to telegraph them. I can't go back.'

'All right,' she said. As if it ever could be all right again.

For days he kept his eyes shut. The nurse, and later the doctor, assured Clover that there was nothing wrong with his eyes. So she thought perhaps he did not want to see her. She visited anyway. Weeks progressed; his leg went from one infection to another as they pondered taking it off, alternately threatening or promising to do so.

At home, Madame was frantic. She often woke Clover, and Harriet, screaming in the night; she denied having nightmares but called them visions. She had been 'vouchsafed to know the possibilities' and Victor was not, *not*, to return to the Front when his leg had been patched together. Walking the floor with Harriet (who cried constantly these days, a colicky stomach or teething or the accumulating strain of everyone around her), Clover tried to reassure Madame—but the only reassurance she had in her quiver was Victor's leg, which seemed so bad to her that he would never walk on it again.

'*Suffit!*' Madame shrieked, finally. 'I will speak to Gali.'

After the Ball   Lewis often drove out with Dr. Graham, who found distraction in puzzling out new ways to tempt Mama into using her reluctant right side. Lewis always brought something for Mabel, a new book of poems or a bottle of Pelikan ink, hard to obtain these days, for her letters; cigars for Chum; something sweet for Aunt Elsie; a toy for Avery.

'Christmas every day,' Aurora said, watching him hand out presents.

She wanted Lewis to come, she found his visits energizing; she wished he would never come again. Each time he reawakened in her some vague dream of a peaceful life, an honourable husband. She had even mooned over Lewis's nice brick house—and that made her truly angry with herself—when Uncle Chum pointed it out one day in town.

In January, Lewis came for dinner and found Dr. Graham already in the parlour. Mama had Avery on display there, entertaining Uncle Chum and the doctor with his precocious tricks; she had been demonstrating Avery's command of the naval jig. Hands on hips, Avery followed Mama's beat, surprisingly controlled for a child not yet two. Mama motioned Aurora to dance with him and they did an exhibition waltz: step-two-three, twirl together, twirl apart, around the room as Mama sang, *'After the ball is over, after the break of dawn . . .'*

Mabel looked in from the kitchen, hair curled into tendrils by the heat of the stove. Aurora left off dancing and went to help her, but Mabel saw Lewis there and shooed Aurora back to the parlour.

Newly returned from a Christmas trip to Winnipeg, Lewis had brought a stack of sheet music for Aurora. He handed the pile to her with some diffidence, saying he'd asked for the newest songs in the shop. She was delighted with the gift, and looked through the sheets at once.

The third sheet down was *You'd Be Surprised!*—the cover a ravishing photo of Bella in a pink-sashed dress, powdering her nose with an arch sideways glance to the reader.

'It is Bella!' Aurora cried. 'My sister!'

Lewis came to look more closely. 'She doesn't resemble you,' he said—as if disputing that they could be sisters.

Looking up quickly, Aurora saw that he was disturbed. 'Does the photograph offend you?' she asked. It was a very demure dress, compared to most.

'It is vulgar, that's all,' he said. 'They have tinted the photograph with too vivid a colour. Nothing like you.'

Aurora laughed. 'No, no, that's Bella! She was probably brighter in real life.'

Mama came to see, and took the sheet. She seemed to be about to speak, then lifted the paper to touch Bella's photograph to her cheek. Aurora put her arm around Mama and kissed her soft hair. 'Never mind,' she said. 'She will come to see us soon. I'll write again.' She turned to take Mama up to their room.

Lewis was watching her, unsmiling.

At the stairs, seeing that Mama had the banister railing, Aurora looked back, her voice pitched to him alone, not even angry.

'You would not be judging my sister, would you?'

Mama had stopped on the stairs; she kept her face resolutely turned away, but Aurora thought she was listening.

'My father the schoolmaster had some difficulty with my mother's life in vaudeville,' Aurora said to Lewis. 'I wouldn't stomach that for an instant, in anyone I respected or whose respect I valued.'

For some while after that, Lewis did not visit.

Like the Rose

As Bella headed north on the long leg into Canada, Pantages headed to Seattle, to take his wife across-country, scouting for theatres to swallow up. He gave Bella a diamond brooch and signed her six-month contract as a solo artiste, till July 1917: a thousand a week for two comic numbers and one straight.

So she was rich. Surprising how flat she felt.

Then East & Verrall—disturbed by recent talk of the United States entering the war after all—announced they were stepping into an Australian tour that Julius and Sybil had had booked years ahead, but of course could not fulfill. Verrall felt they should not leave Julius behind; but East was heart-hardened.

'We've carried him more than a year, to what avail? He doesn't want to buck up, he wants to lie down in the road and die. Time to wash our hands and let him—he's on Pan-time all the way to Edmonton till his contract runs out in May. And don't think, Bella my girl, we're leaving you in charge of him, because that is not the case.'

Well, they were. Somebody would have to look out for him. Julius was eating again, pretending to be on the mend, but offstage he was still alarmingly disconnected. And he'd never taken to her. Nobody loved her, in fact, but that did not matter.

Nothing mattered. People kept company with other people just because the thought occurred to them, and only innocents or bumpkins followed the old society laws or worried, as Mama always had, about their virtue. Nobody cared, in the vaude world, if a person was pure. Perhaps it was different in the old days. But thinking about some things Mama had let slip, she did not think so. Drinking was nothing—she had a very hard head and could drink all evening and never feel it. Or if she felt it a bit, it did not matter. Only her stomach troubled her, and sometimes she had to lie in a warm bath for an hour before she could make herself dress for the theatre. She was no fatter, and she still had her monthlies, but everything hurt down there.

Anyway, off they went.

From the hotel in Butte, Bella wrote to Aurora and to Clover, whose shades she seemed to see on every street corner; she lay in bed till noon most days, staring at nothing. Julius gave her some reason to get up—he had to be hustled into dressing and got down for late breakfast or he would not eat, and if he missed another show from 'illness' she thought he might get canned. Without East and Verrall, he'd switched to an older number, the Sad Philosophizer. He ran with it for the rest of their tour, a lamentation on life and death that Bella could hardly bear to watch. The bit ended with a song, *Life's a Funny Proposition After All*, which was enough to send you searching for the razor blades.

> *'With all we've thought and all we're taught,*
> *All we seem to know*
> *Is we're born, and live a while, and then we die.'*

Spare me, she thought, the first time she watched. Julius pulled out all the stops: adding blue shadows to his own sunken eyes and cheeks, accenting his well-worn lines with carmine into a ghastly tragedy mask. But he was painfully funny, as the hobo preparing for bed in a fleabag hotel. His disrobing for bed was the peeling of his defences, the revealing of his starveling soul: horribly sad, and horribly entertaining. The melody unwound on drums and a squeeze-box, as played by the monkey in the park. Julius prepared to lay him down to sleep as if for the last time, making the bed tenderly,

praying, finally setting a bud vase with a gorgeous full-blown rose
on the upturned night-soil bucket. He pulled the sheet down gently,
like a shroud, then heeled back, his shock making clear that the bed
was alive with bugs. He brushed them one way and the other, counted,
gave up counting, shook hands with a few of them and asked permission to join their party, and gingerly climbed in.

> *'We're born to die, but don't know why, or what it's all about,*
> *Young for a day, then old and gray;*
> *Like the rose that buds and blooms . . . and fades and falls away,*
> *Life's a very funny proposition, anyway.'*

Last of all, he pulled a concealed string, and the petals fell from
the rose. And then the lights went out.

Though Bella resisted, and hated him for it, the number caught her
every time. Why do we die? Papa; Harry, who had faded from her
memory until he was just a flash of blue jacket running up the road;
Sybil. She hated death and knew her own would come too soon. So did
everyone's. It gave her a deep trembling in her legs, wanting to see
Aurora and Clover, Mama and Avery—and Clover's Harriet—but she
must keep working, to keep them all afloat. Maybe next summer,
maybe when her Pantages contract ended in June.

Loneliness swamped her, in the darkness of the wings, but there
was no one to joke or give her a candy or have a good time with. She
waited for Julius to come offstage, and she said *left 'em gasping in the aisles
with that one, you killed, you're a marvel*—all the things he needed to have
said, that Sybil had once said for him. Then she walked him up the
stairs to his dressing table, and ran down again in time for her own
number. It was all a very funny proposition, after all.

Bright Dark Red

Julius died in Edmonton.

Bella had got used to money. For
their two weeks in April she'd booked

a suite at the MacDonald, the limestone chateau on the bluff above the river where the Galician immigrants had lived like bears in their caves (it was of them that Bella always thought when Clover mentioned Galichen). Very handy for the Pantages. The suite was huge. Bella and Julius rattled in it like two dry beans in a can; the bathroom was a palace of marble.

Julius was not bad to travel with, aside from the massively disgusting nose-blowing in the morning as he dislodged the night's accumulated phlegm; he made far less mess than she did herself, and as long as he had his medicinal dose of gin (increased by half again, even while she'd been his minder) he kept himself in order well enough.

One night she stayed out for an after-theatre dinner at the Shasta Grill—trying to enjoy the old glamour—and walked home through streets she and Clover had so often walked in those old days, with a dog-leg to the Arlington to wave at their old windows.

When she let herself into the suite she stumbled over Julius's body, slumped like a suit of old clothes across the parquet floor of the vestibule. He was snoring painfully and she could not wake him. She rang the front desk for help and two liveried boys came up and carried him to his bed; after they'd left she discovered that Julius had soiled himself. There being nobody else to clean him, she did it herself, rolling him back and forth to undress him and wash his backside. The bedding would never recover.

When it was done she stood staring at him, pinned in the bed by a clean sheet from her own bed. He had shrunk. His still-massive head and wild grizzled hair made his diminishment less noticeable when he was awake, but the rest of him was just a bundle of kindling now. His hands lay flaccid on the sheets, long bones in gloves of skin. Julius had never had the time of day for her, really. It ought to be Clover looking after him, he'd like that better. They were the ones who'd been such friends. It ought to be Sybil.

It ought to be Papa she was helping, or horrible old Joe Dent.

Julius only made it to the theatre next day after she'd sent down for another bottle of gin. He was unsteady on his pins and his number did not make much sense, but the audience took it as a drunk act, and he got by. He could not eat the supper she brought to his dressing room. After a look at his grey face she did not press him. But he would not go to hospital, nor allow her to send for a doctor.

He opened a fresh bottle and took a tumblerful as if it were ghastly medicine, and the shaking that ran through his body lessened. At the end of the second show she bundled him into a cab and took him back to the hotel, where she propped him up in bed with water to hand, and of course the gin. She raced back to the Pantages and made her nine o'clock call by a whisker. In the glory of taking the chilly Edmonton audience by storm she was able to forget his cadaverous eyes, not beseeching her to stay but only staring at her face as if it were the last thing he would see.

Which it was, because when she got home that evening she found him in the elegant bathroom, blind drunk, clinging to the tub with clawed hands. His eyes almost sewn shut, so deep was his refusal to open them. 'Cannot, no,' he whispered, when she begged him to look at her. His belly was distended and stiff, and he quaked from time to time—she ran to the house-phone and asked the desk to send for a doctor or a nurse, and ran back to hold him till help came.

But Julius opened his mouth like a fountain's mouth, and like a fountain, a waterfall of blood poured out. The violent noise of the blood slamming into the bathtub made Bella dizzy. Towels—she reached for a towel and shoved it into Julius's mouth, but more blood came out, first leaking and soaking and then in a shuddering stream, and the bathtub was filling with it, and another towel, and another. She could not stop it. The blood was a terrible bright dark red.

No, no—the necessity of it remaining inside his body made her eyes swim and blacken, until she took hold of herself. She tried to speak to Julius, saying nothing useful, but just, 'No, no, don't, I will hold you—' To which he made no answer, nor did his eyes ever open.

The doctor took Julius out of her arms and laid him flat on the blood-swimming tiles, and a sigh came out of Julius's mouth but the doctor said that was just air, that he had already been dead for some time. Because the body cannot live without the blood that fills its caverns and tributaries.

A nurse helped Bella up from the floor and washed her hands and face till water took all that blood away and they put her in a different room, and that was the last of Julius.

Cartwheel   Clover reread Aurora's letters as she had once read Victor's. (She read Bella's, too, but they were so few she had to hoard them, like Madame with her last box of French nougat.) She knew the cast of people in Qu'Appelle and read between the lines when necessary; she was dismayed both by Lewis Ridgeway's entire absence from the letter, and the news of Aleck Graham.

> Dr. Graham has received a telegram reporting his son Aleck 'wounded, no particulars.' Dear Mabel spent a day in her room, and another day sitting in the darkened church; then she wrote to Aleck (the first of no doubt a thousand cheerful letters) and went back to her ordinary work.
>
> The Dean has an illuminated War Roll in St Peter's. All the boys gone from Qu'Appelle and Ft Qu'Appelle and Indian Head. Many of them already dead. This is the news: lists, telegrams, pride in one son's sacrifice.

Pride holds them up after their sons are gone, Clover thought. So we agree not to take that away. But pride was not helping Madame these days. She crept back and forth to the atelier like a mouse, shrinking within her draperies. Only calm, briefly, when feeding Harriet or playing at puppets with her.

The hospital discharged Victor in April, saying they'd done everything they could; the army invalided him out. His leg was useless; his vision and lungs were compromised from the chlorine attack in 1915, the army doctor told her.

'He can walk, in a dot-and-carry way—and will regain some strength for walking, but he'll always need the crutch. He won't be fit for any regular kind of life,' he said.

The doctor's moustache was cut straight across, perhaps with a special set of moustache scissors, Clover thought—so she did not have to think about Victor's leg, the suppurating sores, the mass on one side, the swelling that came and went, the constant tearing pain. Or about the impossible cartwheel into the sky that he had performed the first night she saw him, at the Hippodrome in Montana.

She brought him home in a hackney. The atelier acolytes came to visit, while Madame made potage. Victor lay in his old room, moving from bed to couch in a kind of stasis, not speaking unless driven to it. He could not bear Harriet to chatter, as she did now from morning to night; he had a very uncertain temper for the tuck of his sheets and the noise of the ticking clock two floors below.

One afternoon, after an unusually bad day, Clover knelt and begged him to tell her what he was thinking about that plagued him so badly.

'It is nothing to do with you,' Victor said.

He swung off the couch, grabbing his crutch, and manoeuvred himself downstairs and out the door. It was the first time he'd spoken to her in a week. Through the window, Clover watched him walking down the road. *Nothing to do with her.* She had never been accused of selfishness before.

They blundered on into spring. The difficulties of managing Victor and Harriet while finding, keeping and doing work piled up in Clover's mind in a great mountain range; she longed for the prairies. Victor tried to help—but would peel until the potato was all peeled away, or prune till the branches were all hacked off the bush. He could not look her, or anyone, in the eye. He did not speak easily, but sometimes she heard him telling stories to Harriet in her cot.

When Galichen returned in late April from one of his mysterious absences, he came to see Victor and carried him away, literally in his arms, to the atelier for two days. Clover went over to find him, the first evening, and Heather Jakes told her not to fuss. 'He's giving him the business,' Heather said. 'You'll be glad of it, when he's through.' Next morning Clover looked out and saw Victor in the next-door garden among the white-robed acolytes, doing scales. Gali had given him a knee-cup, a carved peg with a cushioned knee he could strap on to relieve the pressure on his shinbones. He looked absurd, a pirate strayed into a Greek chorus, but he was moving through the sequences and his eyes were open.

Forty-eight hours of penetrating attention from Galichen was enough to turn an invalid around, or knock one through death's door. Victor came back with his crutch, but not hobbling so badly, and Heather Jakes brought poultices for her to use, on Gali's orders, which seemed at least as effective as the carbolic and boracic acid the hospital had advised.

Clover talked to Madame, to Heather Jakes; then went next door, heart in her hands, and talked to Gali himself. At the end of the week she wrote to Aurora:

> Victor does not sleep. He lies beside me staring into the darkness. He falls into a drowse—then the jerking begins, twitching in his legs and arms, as if when he loses consciousness his body begins to fight again or fight it off, whatever it is. The things that I can't know about.
>
> Gali has arranged passage on a merchant ship to which he has some connection. They say shipping will be cut off in the next little while, and I don't dare wait—for his sake and for Harriet's, and even mine. Please ask Uncle Chum if we can stay there, till we get on our feet. Victor cannot work, but truly, I'll be able to get bookings. My monologues have done well here, even in the wartime theatre. They will get better, too. It's not like the violin.

Trusting to Aurora, Uncle Chum, Gali's string-pulling and her own instinct, she kissed Madame goodbye, and they boarded the ship.

Very Fond of That   Bella worked her way down the Pantages circuit as the spring wore on, to Los Angeles, where she would have a month playing the top four of the city's eight Pan-time theatres. As a single headlining act, she did an expanded version of the *Bumble Bee* song (with very beautiful new wings and clod-hoppy black boots) and had introduced a send-up of *Ah, Sweet Mystery of Life* from Victor Herbert's operetta where she played both lovers; she switched her straight song night to night, as fancy took her, between *Danny Boy* and a new song, *I'm Always Chasing Rainbows*, a glum little number about bad luck. She thought she might make a hit of *Life's a Very Funny Proposition After All*, taking it sad and poignant. If she could bear to do it—although hardly being able to stand performing something seemed to be part of the art of it.

Touring alone these last weeks, she'd worked out a plan for doing *Bella's New Car* alone—an elegant lady motorist driving herself in hat and veil, kind of a Gibson girl dame, until the disasters began and she could strip off one piece of veiling at a time, almost a burlesque number except of course that she would still be demurely covered until the contraption blew up and a pull-away frock left her in tattered underclothes.

She was enjoying herself, except when she was not. She had stopped drinking anything more than an occasional polite sherry (Julius's ulcerative stomach and hideous death being the best of dissuasion), and was sleeping better, except for the nightmares.

Coming backstage her third night at the Arcade on Broadway, she found a note pinned to her dressing-room door. She opened it without much thought, expecting something from the orchestra leader—and saw his name first of all, his initial.

There were no other *N*s for her.

Found you. I hear you're staying at the Alexandria,
good hotel. I know you might not want to see me, but
I'll be in the mezzanine at eleven tomorrow morning,
in case you do.

See you there, I hope,

N. (NANDO DENT)

He stood against the railing, hat in his hand. Nice grey suit, but it looked like it might be his only one. She had changed her dress eight times.

The mezzanine lobby was empty, the lunch rush not yet begun.

She had thought about what to say, but it flew out of her head. 'Why didn't you come up and see me after the show?'

'Not sure you would talk to me,' he said. 'Now you are headlining.'

That was not worthy of comment.

'Besides,' he said, turning his hat round and round in his hands, as if it were a stage prop. 'I tried to make you mad when I left.'

'That worked.' She put her hand on a pillar, casual, but needing a bit of support.

Nando looked up, his careful eyes checking her face, and he turned her to a nearby plush-covered bench. They sat, and she waited.

'You didn't know my dad, not really. Not when he was so far gone in drinking, nobody knew about that. I couldn't let you come along and see that. Look what he did to my mam. She wasn't bad really—she'd had the biscuit. I still can't blame her.'

'Do you ever see her?'

'Haven't heard a word from her all this time. We know she's alive, because Harlan the Great sends out Christmas cards to the industry and she's in them. Looks pretty. Happier.'

'It was a mean thing to leave you,' Bella said.

He moved on the bench, got up and walked to the railing. 'It was a mean thing to leave *you*,' he said.

Bella's eyes suffered an unaccustomed rush of water. Not for herself, but because he did not know what she had been doing. Maybe he thought they could still be partners, or something.

Nando looked at her. She looked over the rail to the staircase instead.

'I know you was with Pantages,' he said in a quiet voice. 'Some people told me, and I saw your photo with him once or twice. You still with him?'

'No.'

'He leave you in the lurch too?'

She looked at him again.

'I figure that's what *I* did, is why I'm asking. East and Verrall weren't fit to look after a girl, and Julius was a sad old drunk. But I couldn't see anything but Dad then. Without my mam around I've got to know him a bit better. He's still an ugly customer but he's mellowed a fraction. Got Christian Science now and swears he's off the bottle.'

'Is he here?' She could not help glancing round, half fearing to see that big surly mug.

Nando laughed. 'No, he's in the san again, down in Pasadena. I told them not to let him out till I get back, and he's behaving himself so far.'

'Well, thank you,' she said. 'I mean, for thinking about it. About leaving me.'

'Too late, though. Your mama'd have my nuts for nickels, and so would your sisters. Whatever you've got up to, you were not—'

'Don't say it!' Bella stood and found her hands in fists. 'Don't say I was not old enough! I did what I wanted and what I thought I had to do, and I'm not ashamed—you can take that Sunday face off.'

Nando sat silent on the railing, lazy leg dangling, his face flat.

'You don't get to scold me,' she said, still very angry. 'What have you been up to yourself? Saints all round, I suppose.'

He nodded. 'Except when I was with someone or other.'

She gasped.

'I'm not boasting of it, but you ought to know we're about even.'

Her own face went flat, she felt it. She could not bear to think about Nando with someone else.

'Only I never found any girl I wanted like you, or that fit my hand so well, and fit my mind, never anyone. How about you?'

Now would be the time to flounce off, all aggrieved.

'Liked me best of all, didn't you?'

She bit the inside of her cheek.

'I made a good bit in the movies so far—nothing like the money in vaude, but the work's okay. I can take my dad along, they find him something to do. But I'm not stuck on it, I'd come back to the boards if you wanted me. Dad can manage on his own now, he don't need much from me but a bank draft, time to time.'

'Why are you—?' She intended to walk out. She had an independent—She was a headliner, all by herself. All on her own bat.

He spread his hands open. Callused and squared, short crooked fingers, each one of them broken one time or another.

'*I have a little cat, and I'm very fond of that,*' he sang, rusty-voiced. Then he leaned forward, one foot hooked in the mezzanine railing, farther forward than a man could possibly lean, and kissed her mouth.

II.

Together Again

JUNE 1917

Qu'Appelle, Saskatchewan
Vancouver, British Columbia
Regina, Saskatchewan

After the band has rehearsed your music to your
satisfaction, thank them kindly and retire. This is not
necessary but customary and costs nothing, and is
generally appreciated. It does no harm.

FREDERICK LADELLE, *HOW TO ENTER VAUDEVILLE*

*T*he train announced itself at a distance, halved the distance, halved it again, and galloped into the station on a thousand horses, steaming and stamping. Aurora ran down the platform, looking for every opening door and hoping, and then there was Clover— wasn't it?—backing down off the stairs, a child in her arms, turning to help—and Victor, with a cane, hopping awkwardly down to the platform.

Aurora stopped for a moment to look at them whole: Clover much older, her hair hidden under a dark felt hat, glancing towards Victor. She was carrying the baby girl, a fairy, thin legs in red Viyella leggings buttoned under nice brown shoes, her face hidden under a red tam and crammed down into Clover's collar. Victor shook off Clover's hand and pointed to Aurora. His face was so changed, Aurora could not take it in. His pant-leg was bunched around some contraption, and he leaned on a sturdy cane. She remembered him flying through the air, landing so lightly that the stage made no sound.

Then they were all together, she and Clover pressed to each other like flowers in a book, and the little Harriet making sleepy mews at being squashed.

Luggage mushroomed on the baggage cart, a porter loaded it into the Ford—which Uncle Chum, relenting, had taught Aurora to drive— and they went tooling back up the street. Clover pulled off Harriet's tam, releasing springing dark curls, and then her own hat. Her hair, cut straight to the jaw, swung free.

'London style,' she said, at Aurora's admiring gasp. 'Fabian style, at least!'

Aurora pointed out landmarks (the church, Mrs. Gower's, the school, the Opera House) and kept up a flow of welcoming babble until they had passed out of town into the countryside. Then she fell silent to let the air and sky and the thin strip of endless land at the bottom of the window do their work on Clover.

Everyone was out on the veranda to watch them arrive. When Aurora pulled up in the drive and waved, Mabel let go of Avery's hand so he could hop down the steps to greet his long-lost aunt. Holding a limp bunch of white clover in his hand, he waited patiently for some-one to get out of the car who might be her.

Harriet clung to her mother until she saw Avery, whereupon her eyes followed him, fascinated. Aurora saw him afresh, looking very grown up, suddenly, compared to Harriet. Chum called Elsie to come and see Arthur in the children; Elsie countered that she certainly saw Flora in the little girl—'Look at those sweet brown eyes.'

By then, Mama had come haltingly down the stairs. She went round Chum in a slight hunch to find Clover. Once she had accepted Avery's tribute, Clover turned—and Mama insinuated herself through the press to catch at her sleeve, kissing her; but joyfully, not in the mysteriously sad way she sometimes had. 'Clover, Clover' she was able to say, and then, overcome, she sang, *'Wait till the darkness is over, wait till the tempest is done!'* Aurora saw that she used her right hand, as well as her left, to hold her dear lost daughter.

Mabel stayed in the background, as she did always. She had lunch-eon waiting on the veranda for the travellers. When they'd been fed, she and Aurora led Clover up to the bedroom waiting for her, and Mabel kindly helped her to settle Harriet for a nap.

'Perhaps you'd like to rest yourselves, after the long journey,' she said.

'Victor will, I think,' Clover said. 'But I am not—'

Aurora got up from studying Harriet's pale sleeping face. 'No, no, not yet. Mama will want to sit with you a little longer.'

'All right, then, Mrs.—' Mabel stopped, agonized at her own clumsi-ness. 'I mean—'

Clover kissed her reddening cheek and said cheerfully, 'It's all right, I don't mind. You must call me Clover anyhow. I'm still Miss Avery, as you may know, but I think I should be Mrs. Saborsky here in Qu'Appelle. I don't expect there are many Fabians around here to explain the concept of Free Love.'

What Every Wife Does In the pearly evening Aurora and Clover walked down to the garden and stood looking over the neat rows of lettuce and spinach, the first green lace of carrot tops and young bean vines trellising up behind the cucumber hills.

Clover asked, 'Did you miss the Paddockwood garden so much?'

Aurora laughed. 'I do very little to help—all Aunt Elsie asks is that I play the piano sometimes. Mabel even darns Avery's socks. She is much better at it than I.'

'Not Mama?'

'She cannot hold the needle well, it frustrates her. But she sorts beans and buttons, all the little things Dr. Graham suggested. She is still improving. You heard her singing *Whispering Hope*—it seems words come most easily from our old songs. She loves Avery; she will be very happy dandling Harriet too.'

Aurora turned Clover to walk back up the lawn towards the house. From a wicker chair that Mabel had brought out, Mama was watching the children play under a large spruce tree whose boughs hung down in places right to the ground.

'Avery's lair—he has play dishes and blocks there, to make a house or a fort. I hope Harriet won't get too dirty,' Aurora said.

'Avery's beautiful. I didn't expect him to be so fair.'

'His temper is mostly Mayhew, I think.'

Clover said, 'It is a little like seeing Harry again, but not sad.'

As they climbed up to the veranda, a rhythmic shout caught Aurora's ear: '*Eleven to three, three to eight, eight to four*—' On a flat patch of grass, Victor was doing scales, reaching and swaying and turning himself in knots, the strange cup-brace hampering but not stopping him. The women stood watching him shift and twirl in the lowering sun. His shadow was huge along the lawn.

'But what does it mean?' Aurora asked.

'Oh, it means *I love you, Clover,* over and over, of course. *I love you, Harriet, I am your soul.*' Clover closed her eyes.

Aurora looked at her thin face. The skin colourless, tiny lines drawn round her eyes by the finest brush, not aging her, but setting a shadow over her face.

'He is angry with me all the time,' Clover said, looking up again.

Lilacs growing close to the house partly screened the veranda, and the low words would not carry to Victor. Aurora put her arm round her sister's waist.

'Going to sleep is the worst. He is afraid to sleep—not just the dreams, but the letting-go moment before sleep, when all the thoughts he's kept at bay bleed in. So he stays up half the night until he falls into a heavy sleep, sitting in a chair or lying on the hearth-rug. It was just the same in London; I had to lie with Harriet to keep her warm. When he did come to bed, I was back and forth between them all night long.'

The veranda railing held Clover as she leaned slightly forward, her eyes always on Victor.

He had taken up a pair of ebony sticks and was working through a routine with them, sharp and graceful except when he had to shift from the sound leg to the crutch. Almost juggling, except the sticks slid and fell oddly. Sometimes a ball appeared between them and disappeared again.

'Did you—do you know a lot about the war?' Aurora asked. 'I mean, what is really happening there?'

'It is so close, the Front—like taking the train from Edmonton to Calgary, and there, right there, is the mud and the wire. But I did not know enough to help him at all. I ought to have gone for an ambulance driver, I would have liked that—no, not *liked*. I could have done it. I would have liked to see some of—' Clover gritted her teeth, spoke more carefully. '*Not liked*. I wish I could have seen what he was seeing. But there was Harriet and I could not go.'

Aurora found Victor's movements mesmerizing. 'When he came back, was he—?'

'Off his head? Not long. I think he might wish it had been longer. He was stuck with thinking. The nights are bad. You won't hear us, we have become good at silence.'

On the grass, Victor stood still, in as straight a pose as his leg allowed, hands clasped. He ceased to move. His stillness was very restful.

'I think of Mama living with the same thing, without the trigger of the war. But Papa was the same, you know he was, gripped by that hideous understanding of—the underlying horror of every single thing. Livid if Mama talked to Mr. Dyment in the street, you remember; suspecting that she gossiped of his weakness, or worse. How he squashed her frivolous mind, stopped her singing. I think of her.'

Aurora kissed the pale cheek, and smoothed Clover's hair while she talked.

'I am not always certain I can go on with him, living this way. It is bad for Harriet . . . and I must be so careful not to irritate or trouble him, or make everything worse by causing him anxiety. He can't decide anything. He can't choose what to eat in a restaurant. I just order for him as if that's what every wife does. I think he has forgotten that it's not.' Clover shook her head to erase all that. 'His leg, his wounds, are bad. But they will mend. He'll work again. It's merely a matter of my good sense to get us bookings again.'

She laughed suddenly, and all the heads turned to look up to the veranda, even Harriet peeking out from the spruce-boughs to see what had amused her mother. 'I sound like Sybil, keeping Julius off the roller skates.'

Victor removed the strange cup-brace and came slowly back to the house, cane sliding on gravel. 'I had some skill, once,' he said, looking up at Aurora. 'I seek to get it back.'

Spring Song

Next morning Mama taught the children to dance, just as she had taught the girls when they were small. A jaunty song that Clover had brought from England squawked on the Victrola: *'Hello, Hello, Who's your lady friend? Who's the little girlie by your side?'*

With her fresh eyes, Clover could see how well Mama had recovered—and after the horrors at the Wandsworth Hospital, Mama's impairment seemed quite minor. She had a clever way of hiding the stiffness on her right side by holding a hand to her mouth as if musing: the left arm and leg did the dancing. Harriet was working hard to learn the waltz-step. Tall and sturdy at two-and-a-quarter, Avery danced very well already. Clover's feet itched pleasantly.

She and Aurora left the children to Mama and Aunt Elsie and walked in to town with Mabel, three abreast down the empty road.

Breaking through her shyness, Mabel asked whether she had liked London, and a wave of bitterness flooded through Clover.

'I hated everything about it,' she said. Then checked herself: 'Not London. It was the war I hated—the talk of glory and noble sacrifice, the self-righteous politicians safe at home. Even the men, how they love each other so as soldiers, and how girls love them too. I did myself, the boys in the hospital, the men coming home in pieces. It's easier in England because all the men are in, anyone able-bodied, so everyone knows what you're—well, they don't look sideways at Victor when they see the crutch. People don't understand here.'

'We do,' Aurora said, no doubt to protect Mabel. 'Eight men from Qu'Appelle have been killed now, and many more wounded.'

Clover stopped herself from answering, streaming lines of ghosts in her mind. At that one hospital in Wandsworth, floors and floors of them, twenty boys in every room who ought to have been killed, who'd come out wrecked and maimed. The lucky ones. 'How I hate the idea of sacrifice!' she said, and then, her face burning, said to Mabel, 'I mean—that it is *asked* of them, of us. I'm sorry, I have heard from Aurora about your fiancé being wounded.'

Mabel had retreated into herself, and Clover tried to repair it. She put a hand on Mabel's muslin sleeve, warm with sun. 'I know what that is like, the waiting. Aside from the war, London is—oh, beautiful. A riot of flowers, and the air! Like here, you know. The water is sweet too.' She turned to Aurora. 'I loved it there, and I love Victor's mother, but I cannot work there. They will never let me be English, I'll always be a colonial. Variety is vulgar, too, nothing like true vaudeville. In variety you must be a coquette, good at engaging rowdy crowds, and enjoy being ogled. It is much better here.'

In town, Mabel suggested they show Clover the Opera House, one of Qu'Appelle's sights. Miss Peavey was closing the clinic door as they entered; she knew where the Opera House key was kept, and came along to keep them company.

The little theatre was charming and clean, with a border of advertisements round the proscenium stage—Clover laughed, her spirits rising, and pulled Aurora's hand to go closer. 'It's like the David Theatre, in Camrose, do you remember?'

Their steps made no sound as they ran down the slight rake of the hall and up the side steps to the little stage. '*Spring Song*,' Aurora said, and they wafted on, imaginary wreaths held high, and circled round and round, arms at each other's waists, *la-la*-ing the tweedling melody.

'We need Bella,' Clover said, when they paused to make the bridge for Bella to pass under—it was this number they'd been doing, and just here that they'd stopped, when the Muse was flooded and destroyed. 'Or waterfalls of rain . . .'

Aurora laughed, her face glowing. 'We've had quite a good time, haven't we?'

Here is what I have been missing all this time, Clover thought. She embraced Aurora, whispering, 'You are my sister!' as she kissed her velvet cheek.

Mabel and Miss Peavey broke into applause, and a man's voice added, 'Encore!'

Aurora's arm tightened a little around Clover. She murmured in her ear, 'Lewis Ridgeway, the schoolmaster. And Miss Frye, from the school. Come, I will introduce you.'

Miss Frye said excitedly, 'Oh, Mrs. Mayhew! Is this your sister? How wonderful! We must have you *both*—do say you will!'

Mr. Ridgeway put a calming hand on Miss Frye's elbow. 'This is a lucky meeting. Miss Frye has an idea of getting up a concert for Dominion Day.'

'You know Mrs. Gower thought of it last year, but then with her son's tragic end—*I* thought, let's *us* do it for her! Funds to send to our boys overseas, you know, war bonds, that sort of thing. But it would be meaningless without you, Mrs. Mayhew, so if we can persuade or entice you, or beg of you . . .'

Clover thought Miss Frye was shy, beneath the chatter. Aurora took pity on her, and said that since by lucky chance her sister (bows and introductions all round) was visiting, perhaps they could revive one of their old numbers? Miss Frye bubbled over in ecstasy and began to enumerate the other acts they had in mind: the dear girls' chorus from the high school, a highly talented child flautist, and an exhibition of embroidery. Perhaps not a bill calculated to sell a superfluity of bonds.

Lewis Ridgeway gave Clover a penetrating look and took her hand. 'Your sister has told me a little of your trouble—I've looked forward to meeting you and Mr. Saborsky.'

Clover nodded, examining his face as he did hers. Sombre, not much humour. Difficult to read. She hoped he had not been making Aurora unhappy.

Overflowing

On a sudden inspiration, Aurora cabled to Bella. Nothing but a brief line on a postcard had come from her since Easter, never more than *Very well, happy, don't be worried, more soon.* The last note had been scribbled on the back of a list of tour dates, so she had some idea where Bella must be, and sent the cable to the Pantages theatres in both Edmonton and Calgary.

CONCERT TROOPS JULY 1 WITH CLOVER AND VICTOR,
CAN YOU JOIN?

Many theatres went dark in July, there was a chance. She sent a prepaid answer, hoping that might ensure a reply, but did not mention it to Clover or Mama, for fear Bella would refuse. She did not allow herself to think how badly she wished for Bella's wildness, her bountiful overflowing energy—and for her to see Avery, and Harriet.

And Bella would help Clover, who seemed sunk into an understandable despair that Aurora could see no way to lift.

Like a Soldier   Clover watched as Uncle Chum and Victor walked down to the garden, turning at the bean-row hedge; back up to turn again at the lilac bushes that sheltered the south porch, over and over. Clover sat on the porch with Harriet sleeping on her knee, screened from view but able to see her beloved as he walked to and fro.

Nearing the lilac bushes she heard Chum say, 'What amazes me is that you were able to survive. I suppose the thought of your wife and child . . .'

She did not expect Victor to answer that. But as they reached the turn, she heard his voice: 'I survived by acting like a soldier.'

That was like opening a letter, one Clover could not quite read. Perhaps he meant that he'd shut off his questioning, curious, independent self. That he had yielded to his training.

Chum said, 'Yes.' Nothing more. They turned and walked away.

All men who had been in battle knew things she would never know. She was eavesdropping. But she, waiting without word for weeks, being with Victor when the visions plagued him, knew things that men did not seem to remember.

Harriet stirred and sat up, bewildered and afraid. 'It is all right, dear heart,' Clover told her. 'We are here in Saskatchewan.'

'Dama?' Harriet asked; she missed Madame still.

'Come, let's find Avery.'

The men were down at the hedge, Chum on the wooden bench and Victor standing, a cigarette in one thin hand. Harriet pulled on Clover's hand, and they went inside.

Aunt Elsie had invited several people for dinner, wishing to present their guests to the town—and there was the Dominion Day concert to discuss. Mrs. Gower was coming with Lewis Ridgeway and Miss Frye from the high school, and since it was a dinner, the doctor and the Dean might as well be included.

Clover went to talk to Uncle Chum in his study that afternoon, remembering how he had seemed to understand Victor's silence in the garden.

He put an arm over her shoulders, as if they knew each other well. 'Don't fuss, my dear. Victor will get along very well.' As Clover hesitated, not even knowing how to ask for help, he added, 'It's nobody but the doctor, the Dean and Lewis Ridgeway—the Dean was in the Boer War, you know, distinguished himself. I've seen a deal of trouble myself, in various ways. If he is having difficulties, I'll bring him in here for a bit of quiet. We won't make the poor fellow uncomfortable, I can promise you. Men understand these things better than you'd think.'

But they didn't know this war, Clover thought. She went away.

To Correct Myself

The doctor and Lewis Ridgeway were the first to arrive for the dinner party, while Aurora was still arranging tiger lilies in the big silver vase for the dining table; Clover and Victor had not yet come downstairs. Chum took Dr. Graham off to his sanctum; Aunt Elsie, smelling the cheese straws burning in the kitchen, pushed Lewis into the dining room, making a pleading face behind his back and saying, 'Dear Aurora, here is our first guest!'

'Hello, Mr. Ridgeway—will you mind if I carry on with these flowers?' Aurora said, tension making her slide into ridiculous formality. Aunt Elsie vanished again.

Lewis stood against the wood panelling, not fully entering the room. 'I would like to correct myself,' he said. 'I misspoke, about your sister.'

Oh dear, thought Aurora. 'Lewis, that was so long ago! I promise I have forgotten it.'

'Well, you have not forgotten,' he said, looking at her carefully. 'Or you would not have known which sister I meant.'

Aurora looked at his sharp, unhappy face; at his tired eyes. 'It is I who ought to apologize,' she said. 'I am tigerish in defence of my sisters. I'm sorry I spoke that way.'

'Your sister's—Mrs. Saborsky's—sterling quality is plain to see,' Lewis said. 'I made a wrong assumption about Miss Bella.'

He had better stop talking, Aurora thought. And always perceptive, he did.

She took up the last tiger lily, careful of its dusty black pollen. 'Bella *is* flirtatious and rascally—that is her beauty, her goodness. More than anyone in the world, she is entirely honest!' Unlike me, unlike Lewis, she thought.

He remained stiff. 'I hope we can be friends again.'

Aurora put out a hand, smiling at him. 'Yes, thank you, let's. It will be much more comfortable for Aunt Elsie.'

Dinner was surprisingly peaceful, for all the tension beforehand. Mrs. Gower was in a lighter mood these days, interested in the concert and wanting to hear all the plans. She took a fancy to Harriet's shining walnut curls, and offered to put up Victor and Clover if there wasn't enough room here. 'Don't want your guests to feel cramped,' she said, impervious to Elsie's bristling.

The concert was the central topic of conversation, led by Mrs. Gower, with interpolations from Lewis and Aurora in turn. Mrs. Gower had decided that Mrs. Mayhew and her sister should sing several numbers, not just one, 'Being as you are, in a way, semi-professional,' she said. Aurora understood that to be a form of compliment, as one might say *semi-professional prostitutes*, and—not looking at Clover—she promised that they would work up a few songs.

'Do a monologue.' Victor raised his rusted voice to carry around the table.

Clover touched his sleeve and gave him a twinkling smile. 'I will, if you'll let me,' she said to Lewis. 'To keep my hand in. Perhaps Miss Sunderland, the thieving opera singer.'

Aurora burst out laughing and clapped her hands, saying it had to be in; Lewis promised to add her to the bill.

In a kind way that made Aurora like him afresh, Lewis talked to Victor, not troubling him for much of a reply but holding the burden of conversation himself; genuinely interested in what Victor did say. Uncle Chum nodded at Aurora once, when he caught her checking the progress of their talk, to let her know he was keeping tabs as well.

During the length of dinner, as Victor remained calm, Clover seemed to allow her vigilance to relax; a glass of wine brought a little tint of colour to her cheeks. Aurora looked at her—then at Lewis. She found herself smiling with him and erased it from her face. She liked him very much, but she had had three glasses of wine.

Another Gig   The Pantages in Regina was an old hell-hole. With a new Pantages set to open in the fall, no repairs were being carried out. Ropes regularly failed, letting massive Diamond Dye drops fall slithering to the ground. Nando spent hours before every show checking his and Bella's equipment, with the professional fury he reserved for incompetence. He paced the dressing room nightly threatening to quit this tired outfit and haul Bella back to the movies, where if things were gimcrack and slipshod they'd know how to deal with it, and you'd only use a set once anyhow before you shot it to bits or burned it down or had a locomotive crash into it.

Then they'd go on and do their number to wild applause and find a bouquet in their dressing room from the manager, and he'd calm down again for the night.

'Are you turning into your dad?' Bella asked him one evening in mid-rant. 'Just that I'd like to know.'

He glowered at her. 'No!'

'A week more, and we're off. Do you think we'll live that long?'

'I don't guarantee a thing.'

She threw herself into his arms and locked her mouth passionately on his, saying, 'Then let us *live tonight*, my darling!'

He laughed then and stopped fussing, and sat in the armchair to hold her more freely; but they were interrupted by a knock on the dressing-room door.

A black bowler hat came into the room, trembling, and was joined round the edge of the jamb by another, lower down, and then the door burst open—to reveal East and Verrall.

Bella jumped up. 'Back! I thought you had two more months!'

'Australia, not a place you'd want to stay for long,' East said. 'But I got good boots there—see?' He stuck out a pudgy leg and waggled a shining black pull-on boot.

'Welcome home, welcome home,' Bella said.

Verrall climbed in around East—the dressing rooms none too large in this antiquated house—and handed Bella a pair of fine leather gloves. 'Doe kangaroo,' he said. 'Or I was terribly cheated.'

Nando was watching with a glint in his eye, and enjoyed the double-take when East discovered him. 'You! Here!' Verrall said, bemused, and East yelled, 'Unhand that girl, sir!'

'Can't,' said Nando. 'We're wed.'

That called for champagne. East sent one of the placard boys round to find beer at least, if champagne was not available, and they settled in for a good visit. Verrall told them that the tour had been cancelled half-way through, and they'd been lucky to get back. 'This war puts a crimp in everything,' he said. 'And now, what with the conscription here and the U.S. jumping in, it's enough to curl your liver. So I'm going to join up,' he said. They had landed in Vancouver on the only steamer they could get, and were making their way to Minneapolis, which was where Verrall planned to enlist. 'They won't take East—his feet, you know,' Verrall said. 'But they'll take me, and I think I shall enjoy it, in a quiet way.'

'He's all for adventure, you know Verrall,' East said, looking so miserable that the joke fell flat.

Then they had to be told about Julius, which cast a pall over the party. Bella did not want to dwell on it, so she told how she and Nando had come to be touring together, and the new numbers they were working on now; they went through all the vaude news, and who was where: Nando said that Jimmy Battle was in town, for one, with a solo song-and-dance act, comedy songs and fancy footwork.

'Finally pried himself loose from that harpy?' East said. 'She was a word, if you like.'

The placard boy came back with four bottles of beer, and a cable that had been forwarded for Bella. She opened it and laughed. 'Boys,' she announced, 'you'll have to pause one more time on your way to Minneapolis—we've got another gig.'

The Sweet Gay Life   Aurora watched the concert plan race like a riptide, once word came from Bella that not only she, but the famous comedy duo East & Verrall would donate their time to the cause. East sent a long telegram to Aurora, detailing what they'd need and what they'd bring with them, including a roster of musicians he promised to vouch for, *travel only* to come off the top of receipts (East was always practical). Band call was arranged for the morning of July 1; he and Verrall would arrive the night before, with Bella et al. A package came on the train with songs and music, new things East and Verrall had picked up on their travels—a George M. Cohan, written for the U.S. entry to the war in April, which East thought should be a company number at the end. 'Big finale, use all the kiddies, and the soldier-happy old ladies will shell out' was how he put it. Aurora planned to phrase it more circumspectly to Miss Frye and Mrs. Gower.

Clover and Aurora put their heads together over the bill, and showed it to Victor when he came through the empty dining room. 'Not *Danny Boy*,' he said. 'Too hammer-nail now.' So they cut that and replaced it with their true favourite, the limpid *Per Valli, Per Boschi*. As they worked they sang, in a trickle of sound that was very pleasing to them both.

Miss Frye was staggered when they took the proposed concert bill in to her at the lunch-hour next day. 'This is! *Far* too—! East & Verrall!'

She wiped her mouth with a hanky. 'I saw them in Regina in '09. Are they *particular* friends of yours?' Clover assured her that the stories of East and his thousand young ladies were merely apocryphal, publicity stunts in fact.

'It's rude to take over like this,' Aurora told Lewis, keeping the paper close for a moment. 'I think it's the pleasure of performing together again that has taken wing.'

She placed the bill before him.

DOMINION DAY CONCERT

Hello, Hello, Who's Your Lady Friend?..........Qu'Appelle High School Girls' Chorus

On the Banks of the Saskatchewan..............Mr. Geo. East, High School Girls' Chorus

Per Valli, Per Boschi........................ Miss Aurora Avery & Miss Clover Avery

A Recitation............................... Mr. Lewis Ridgeway

Bella's Flying Machine....................... Miss Bella Avery

A Monologue............................ Miss Clover Avery

The Golf Lovers........................... East & Verrall

They Didn't Believe Me.................... Miss Bella Avery

Over There (a new song by George M. Cohan)....................... East & Verrall, the Company

Lewis cast a cool eye down the sheet, and laughed. 'A nine-item bill! You've turned our concert into polite vaudeville, Mrs. Mayhew.' His own name caught his eye. 'A recitation?'

'I know you are a skilled elocutionist,' Aurora said, seeing that he was pleased. 'A valuable addition to the bill, if you could favour us.'

He bowed his head and said he would be honoured. 'I may choose my material?'

'Of course, you will choose best.'

'And you'll want to work with the girls beforehand?'

'Yes! They'll be wet rags by the time we're finished with them. We'll start this afternoon, learning the words and music—in a one-off revue like this their number should be more than just an opener.'

She saw that he looked blank, but it was not worth explaining.

Mabel met Aurora and Clover outside the school and walked with them to the Opera House, saying, 'I hope it's not too Machiavellian, but I've asked Mrs. Gower to take complete charge of the tea—she'll be in here redirecting the numbers if you don't keep her busy.'

'Perfection.' Clover gave Mabel a quick, surprising kiss. 'But you are going to help *us*, not her?'

Taking Mabel's other arm, Aurora agreed. 'Mrs. Gower can't have you. We need you for backstage mistress, if you are willing.'

Mabel was perfectly willing, and they went inside to measure and make more lists and wait for the high-school girls. By the time Aurora and Clover had driven them through an hour of singing practice and a strenuous hour of dance, all the little faces were red and puffing. Nell Barr-Smith gave a wild hoot at the end of one successfully executed set of steps, but the other girls were too winded.

'We'll have to bring Mama in tomorrow,' Clover said. Aurora was interested to see that Clover often realized better than she what Mama could do, not being used to thinking of her as negligible. Clover had left Harriet in Mama's care quite happily, for example, though she never left Harriet with Victor. It seemed to be doing Mama good.

Next day Mrs. Gower came by the theatre midway through rehearsal to announce that tickets had sold out, and they were going to add two more rows of seats.

'Nobody will be comfortable,' she said. 'But it's all in a good cause.'

The girls came trooping in for their first run-through, so Mrs. Gower sat and watched. 'Sprightly does it,' Aurora called. Twenty spines lifted, twenty chins came up.

> *'Hello! Hello! Who's your lady friend?*
> *Who's the little girlie by your side?*
> *I've seen you with a girl or two.*
> *Oh! Oh! Oh! I am surprised at you.'*

Mama pulled at Clover's sleeve, whispering, 'Knife, steel!' Clover executed the brushing movement of the entrechat more crisply—and the girls obediently sharpened up their motion.

'*Banks of the Saskatchewan*, please,' Aurora called, and the girls fluttered and regathered stage left. 'This will be a very quick turnaround, you'll have to be on your toes—' She played the intro and they were off, dancing during the tenor's verse, which Clover sang for now. East would do a lovely job of it.

> *'By the banks of the Seine live girls so beautiful*
> *It gives one pain to remain quite dutiful*
> *And yet I've sworn by the stars above*
> *Throughout my life to reserve my love,*
> *for the girl by the Saskatchewan, the girl by the*
>   *Saskatchewan.'*

At one end of the upright piano Lewis stood watching, with Miss Frye nodding her head gaily in time to the swooping music.

'Lovely,' Aurora called, as Clover gave the girls a round of applause for getting all the way through the steps. 'We'd better take one more run at *Hello, Hello*, please.'

Miss Frye, recalled to the world, said, 'Oh! The bandage-rolling is due to begin at five, and we're in their space—I'll just start setting up the tables.'

'Hello, hello, stop your little games,
Don't you think your ways you ought to mend?'

The girls stomped and wagged their fingers and had a hilarious time scolding Clover, then scurried in a swirling fan around her to carry her off.

Aurora began to fold the music away. Lewis put an arm over the piano to hold the sheets open. They looked at each other.

'Do you know that I—'

She waited to hear what he would say.

'I would give the world—if your circumstances were different,' he said. 'Or mine.'

'Yes,' she said. He had such a pretty brick house. She touched his hand lightly. 'I know you would.'

'How do we know love?' he asked her.

Another of his difficult questions. She did not know the least thing about love. When she looked back, it seemed that she was always happiest alone. Not pretending, not folding herself small to fit in someone else's grasp.

The girls were laughing, clanging the folding legs for the bandage tables into place. Clover gestured from the door to say she would walk home ahead rather than wait for the car. Her eagerness to return to Victor plainly showing.

Aurora brought her attention back to Lewis. 'I think we know, already, the ones we love. It seems that people—recognize each other. Perhaps one just has to be patient.'

San Fairy Ann

Having no community duty, Clover walked back alone from the Opera House in evening sun, thinking of the chattering girls and the women winding bandages like tiny shrouds. Thinking too of Victor's dream, which had woken him many times in terrible fear—that he was mistaken, that these corpses he was burying were not dead. Somehow their not being dead was more fearful. Burning of the bodies . . . He spoke only in fragments about it, and had only spoken twice, but she thought he had the dream often.

Tiny green bugs danced in the golden air as Clover walked. Her shadow fell very long, stalking into the fields beside the road. Perhaps she would still feel patriotic about the war if he had not come back a ghost. How could the eloquence she loved so much be gone? His romantic gall, his openness in declaring love—which had let her be open too, for the first time in her life.

At the door Elsie met her with a shushing finger: the children were already in bed, she whispered. Clover went up, making no noise.

Victor sat at the edge of the bed, talking quietly to the children to let them go to sleep. These days he could not seem to stop his hands from fiddling. He was stroking Harriet's hair with one hand and play-ing, playing with the old prop compass in his other hand. Harriet's eyes had half closed; in the cot Avery lay staring at the eastern wall, striped with long strands of late sun.

'*San fairy ann,* they say out there. When my mother speaks in French, Harriet, you hear her say that: *Ça ne fait rien.* It matters nothing. But San Fairy Ann, she's another thing altogether. She hovers over the world, sometimes sighing and sometimes laughing a little in her sleeve. Once long ago, San Fairy Ann went walking in a wood in France, where every leaf had fallen, but it was not winter. Bare trunks of trees stood up in serried rows and San Fairy Ann wound her way between them, looking for a lost child. That child's name was Harry—don't worry, Harriet and Avery were safe at home, being looked after by their mamas, but Harry had gone adventuring into the world, to find their three fathers, who had disappeared some time before.'

Close to sleep, Harriet's breath was given up, as Gali said to do in his breathing work. Gentry had said that too, years ago, Clover remem-bered. *Let the breath fall in, give it up.* Avery's eyes left the bars of light to watch his uncle's face, grave in the twilight.

'San Fairy Ann has a compass too—but hers can point to more than North. She set her compass for Harry, and the needle wobbled and wobbled, winding round until she bent her wrist and the arrow could point down. So then she knew that Harry had found some sign of his father, had gone into the maze of tunnels underground, where his father wandered lost and alone.'

Clover backed away from the room, going slow and light, so the wide plank floor did not creak. She felt light-headed, and a little sick. But she thought Victor had been working to make the story not frightening.

When Aurora and Mabel came back, Clover tugged Aurora's sleeve, pulling her sister out with her for a last breath of air. They walked around the loop of the drive, grasshoppers leaping at mad angles from their feet, and talked over the concert, less than a week away. Their skirts, shorter these days, still flowed around their knees in the wind that rose off the grass. At the end of the drive they turned.

The warm house lay in front of them, windows rosy in the darkness.

Aurora said, 'Don't you think you could stay here for a while? A year, for Victor to get better—Uncle Chum asked me to tell you that you'd be welcome as long as you like.'

'On charity? We haven't got much left, after the trip. I've got to find a gig soon.'

'There's plenty of money in the Indian Head account. I haven't needed anything but a little for Christmas presents. We could take a little house.'

'I don't want to live on Bella either! But it's not the money. It's— needing to go. Some people are citizens, and some are nomads, I think. We'll be glad to be on the move again.'

Aurora did not try further persuasion.

'Come too,' Clover said. 'When we leave, why don't you come?'

Quiet

The coyotes were loud that night. After the excitement of the day it took some time for the house to settle. When it was quiet at last, and they were all in their beds, the *ki-yi*-ing started outside. Clover listened to Harriet breathing, tucked between them in the bed.

Victor lay rigid, not asleep. She did not dare to touch him.

Tired from long rehearsal, Clover drifted into a waking dream, then deeper into sleep. When she woke, the first faint light was coming in the window. Four o'clock, perhaps. The coyotes were so close, at first she thought they must have wakened her.

Victor was not in the bed. She lay still, not yet thinking.

She heard a rifle shot, and the coyotes' yipping ceased.

Then everything was quiet.

Another minute she lay there. Then she thought, well, it would be quiet. If he was dead, there would be no more noise. I would lie here thinking how quiet everything was.

No conscious movement—but she was down the stairs and out onto the veranda, and there in the pale light saw Victor lying on the grass. Like a war memorial, the rifle on his chest with one hand holding it. Her mind looked for Papa's black suit, and the blot of red opening out on the snow.

But it was grass. She knelt beside him.

He opened his eyes. 'I didn't do it,' he said.

'No.'

She went inside and put the rifle under a pile of sheets on the top shelf of the linen closet, where the children could not reach it, and took out a blanket to wrap him in. He came with her willingly, using her instead of his forgotten crutch, and curled himself around Harriet in the bed. And finally he slept.

The Company Assembled Early Sunday morning, Bella was due on the Regina train. Aurora could almost not imagine it, after so long. East and Verrall and a handful of musicians would come on the same train, for rehearsal—East had booked rooms at the hotel, but Mrs. Gower demanded that these be left to the musicians; Bella and the famous East and Verrall must stay at her house. And she insisted on hosting a light fork-luncheon after the rehearsal, which Mabel warned Aurora might be anything up to roast suckling pig.

Aurora and Clover took the Ford to the station and drew up just as the train blew in. They flew up the platform to the first-class carriage as Bella fell out the door, and then Nando. Clover hugged Bella while Aurora kissed Nando, crying, 'Bella, you might have told us!'

'Wanted to surprise you with everything,' Bella said, moving Clover's arm to free her mouth. 'We even got married! Not high-minded like *you*, Clover!' She kissed Aurora and wrapped her springy arms around both of them. Nando smiled and smiled, his face pulling into an unaccustomed shape. He managed, Aurora saw, to keep one hand connected to Bella the whole time.

Then Verrall came sliding down the step. Standing on the platform his head was at the level of East's, poking out the door. There were more embraces and exchanges of best wishes, and complaints that the children were not present to be patted and compared.

'Later,' Aurora promised. 'They are to attend the concert, of course.'

'The concert!' East cried. 'I had forgot what we were here for. I must catch the baggage man—' He fled down the train, and Verrall shrugged and loped after him.

'We'll take a wagon,' Verrall called back.

The Opera House was an ants' nest of girls and women already, but Mabel had the musicians in place, tuning their assorted instruments. The man at the piano, to Aurora's great pleasure, was Mr. Mendel, from the Empress Theatre long ago.

'Made the switch to Pantages, years back,' he said. 'Never regretted it. The man's an ape but the theatre is run like clocks and I like my boys. I think you will too.' His wrinkled face peered over the piano and he gave out an A for the others to tune to.

The programmes had arrived from the printer, in a large flat packet which Mabel took to her prompt corner to open; the giddy girls were in Miss Peavey's clinic, which had been turned into the chorus dressing room for the duration. A banner hung across the proscenium:

FOR OUR BOYS OVERSEAS. It was bright red on white silk, like that of a Red Cross hospital—but never mind that, Aurora thought.

Riding a Bicycle

Bella and Nando did the visiting royalty business with the helpers, but with Bella royalty could never be completely serious—she felt a simmering, shimmering laugh under everything she did these days.

'Oh, there's one more thing that I forgot,' she said to Aurora. 'And here he is.'

The auditorium door was ajar, and in the arch stood Jimmy the Bat, posing like an advertisement for cigarettes, in a white linen motoring coat over a sylph-like suit.

It seemed to Bella, watching closely, that Aurora was holding her breath.

Jimmy walked down the rake of the main aisle. Nobody ever more graceful. At Bella's nod the musicians started up *The Double-Glide Walk*, and Aurora laughed and moved forward to greet him.

'Let's dance it one more time,' he said, reaching out a hand.

In the cleared space where the seats would be put up, they met and clung and held the pose—and then were off, circling circling, Aurora's lily foot flicking up from time to time in the most carefree way, as if she'd done nothing in her life but dance.

Clover turned away, white-faced, probably sick with nostalgia; Bella was not so sappy. She kept a sharp eye on what those two were doing: it seemed to her that they were chiefly having a very good time. But of course that was the whole purpose of that dance, and it might not be real. What the hell, she thought, it was worth a shot—I shouldn't be the only happy one in the family.

As the dance finished Jimmy and Aurora bowed to the musicians with a flourish. Aurora broke away, but kept hold on Jimmy's elbow. 'I'm winded!' she said, loud enough for the rest to hear. 'You are in top form, but it's two years since I danced.'

'Like riding a bicycle,' Jimmy said. His every gesture, thought Bella, was easy and cool as shaved ice.

Mabel came forward to show off the programmes from the printer, with Nando's name by Bella's, and the dance number in place: *Miss A. Avery & Mr. Jimmy Battle: The Double-Glide Walk & Oh, You Beautiful Doll*, between Clover's monologue and East & Verrall.

Aurora took the parchment programme. '*Et tu*, Mabel? Bella, you're a genius!'

There was one more task. Bella did not want to shirk the last thing she could do for Julius. Seeing Clover in a quiet corner, Bella took Aurora over to tell them together that Julius had died, keeping it very bare: 'He'd been out of sorts for ages, and then he died—it was the drink, of course. He said to give you his dear love, Clover, and a little to spare for the beautiful Aurora.'

She buried her face in her sisters' shoulders, both to hide his true death and for her own comfort. They could not have made it better if they had been there, after all.

You're What?

To Clover's surprise and relief, Victor appeared to watch her brief mono-logue set-up. His thin length lean-ing on the door frame gave her a surge of joy—she hoped it did not show in her face. He must have walked in from the farm, and he looked as if the sun had done him good. She was through in a moment, only her entrance and exit requiring cues, and ran down to stand beside him.

'Harriet's sleeping, and your mama is coming in with them after lunch,' Victor said. 'Let me watch in peace.' He clasped her hand, kissed it, and waved her back to work.

Bella's Flying Machine was the big number. Nando had adapted the prop aeroplane to fit it onto this small stage. Without flies there would be some effects missing. 'But it'll still be a whizz-bang,' he promised. At the run-through the propellers dropped off one by one in perfect time, as Bella chanted mournfully, 'He loves me, he loves me not, he loves me, he loves me *not*— Oh dear . . .'

Another necessary modification was discovered in mid-rehearsal. While Nando cranked and adjusted, Bella filled in Clover and Aurora about their plans. 'No point withering away outside the big-time any more—but Keith's won't book any act straight from the small-time now, even from Pan-time. You've got to have a whole new look to get in there.'

A wrench dropped out of the sky, retrieved by Nell Barr-Smith, who had designated herself Nando's assistant.

'The *Flying Machine* will be a step up,' Bella said. 'Nando has all kinds of ideas for really big-time, flying out over the audience, dropping candy bombs, you name it.'

Nando's face appeared upside down, hanging from a wing. 'Get me a roll of that cotton duck tape from the clinic, would you, Nell?'

'But the thing is—' Bella said, and then stopped.

'The thing is, she's not telling you the main thing,' Nando said. 'It puts a bit of a crimp in the Keith's plan, for a while—I'm going to enlist.'

Clover looked at him, at Bella.

'I've got to,' Nando said, apologizing. 'I want to go for a flyer. I figure they'll take me. I learned how for the pictures—wing-walked and flew a bit. Best thing in the world.'

'Hey!'

'Excepting Bella,' he allowed. 'I'm going to enlist up here, Royal Flying Corps.'

Bella stared upwards. 'It's all butterfly, him and me,' she told her sisters. 'All bumble bee.'

Clover turned abruptly, and got into the wings in time. That was the place for crying, and she felt dreadfully sick as well— There, the fire bucket was waiting for her, like it had waited for Aurora in the old times.

Leaning over, retching as quietly as she could, her mind caught suddenly. Hooked like a little fish. Oh yes—oh yes, she thought. Counted back, could not remember—must have been in March, not since they left England—oh. Oh.

She straightened, and wiped her mouth with a prop-table towel.

There was no silence to keep, like last time, though. Victor was right out there in front. No need to wait to tell him; she was instantly, absolutely certain. She slipped out around the proscenium arch and climbed up to the seats where Victor sat, his head back, eyes closed.

'You're *what?*' he said slowly, in the gentlest voice, when she told him. His still-dreaming eyes were peaceful and he reached up to touch her face.

The Point

They ought to be heading to Mrs. Gower's luncheon. It's only a country concert, Aurora told herself, and laughed to see Clover up on stage muttering through her monologue one last time.

'An encore for the concert,' Verrall said, gliding up with music in his hand.

Aurora protested that they would not need such a thing, but he insisted. 'Oh, believe me, you're going to need one. Here's just the thing: you can be Colinette with the Sea-Blue Eyes, with Bella and Clover to back you. The ladies will put an extra dollar in the soldiers' box once they've had a good cry—the gents will put in five. Do it in one, then we'll open the curtains to reveal the assembled company, all bowing again like trained seals. Lovely!'

Mendel ran through it on the piano, a trilling beginning and a peaceful, lilting tempo. It would pull up tears, Aurora thought—not a bad thing, when raising funds for a good cause.

'But there's one rose that dies not in Picardy
'Tis the rose that I keep in my heart . . .'

She called Clover and Bella up to try it through with Mendel, keeping it very simple.

'It ought to be a tenor,' Clover said. 'But to sing all together again— let's keep it!'

They walked to Mrs. Gower's, finding the spreading house packed full of every citizen of note from Qu'Appelle and Indian Head, with a few from Fort Qu'Appelle. Aurora stopped in front of a small shrine in the hall to show Clover the photo of Mrs. Gower's son—a sweet face, serious and young, with the least tinge of Mrs. Gower's popping eyes, and a faint irrepressible smile.

Their uncle found them there and told Clover about the boy.

'Mont Sorrel,' Chum said, putting an arm out to draw Lewis Ridgeway in as he came near. 'He was aide-de-camp to Arthur Williams: taken prisoner, badly wounded. I knew Williams well, you know. He was an inspector in the Mounted Police before he went off to run the cavalry school. I'm told that Williams may still be alive, but rumours of war . . .'

'Facts of war, this morning,' Lewis said. 'Two more boys from Fort Qu'Appelle killed. And word of a major offensive in July.'

Walking on, Chum and Lewis settled themselves on a sofa near Dr. Graham. The doctor sat with his head in his hands, Mabel beside him. He had delivered both the boys from Fort Qu'Appelle.

Aurora had taken Clover's arm, and now bent her head to rest on her sister's shoulder. 'There's nothing—no point, in any of it,' she said. 'We dance and sing, and all these boys go off and die.'

A plush bee mumbled out of the flowers on the mahogany table and floated, lost for landmarks in the indoor world.

'Well, I don't know why we ever thought there was a point,' Clover said. 'Dancing, singing, dying, that is all of it, I think.'

Victor lifted his head from the sofa. 'You know better.'

The women turned to look at him. He had not spoken to anyone but Clover yet that day. After a moment he turned his head away slightly, and spoke again. 'Perfecting it. Making it—realer, or less real.'

Aurora watched him struggle to find words.

'I mean, the *point* is the point. To make the joke so perfect—' Victor paused, eyes up on a line of reflected light dancing on the ceiling. 'We are only pointing at the moon, but it is the moon.'

He saw Clover watching him, and lifted one hand into a sketched salute.

Aurora opened the glass door to let the bee drowse out into the garden. 'I will go with you when you go,' she said, leaning out into the summer day.

FINALE

JULY 1, 1917

Qu'Appelle, Saskatchewan

And now we have come to the act that closes the show.
... Many have only waited to see the chief attraction of
the evening, before hurrying off to their after-theatre
supper and dance. So we spring a big 'flash.'

BRETT PAGE, *WRITING FOR VAUDEVILLE*

The lights outside the Opera House blazed, and inside, the lobby glowed with electricity of all varieties. The heat of the day had begun to cool, and the open windows let in a small occasional breeze, gratefully received by the audience moving slowly through the ticket line. Nell Barr-Smith peeked out from the clinic across the hall to count the people going in, but gave up when she saw them jumbled by the door, excitedly pushing. She went back to have Miss Peavey tie her sash, happy to have been allowed to keep her cherry ribbons, to have helped with the aeroplane and listened to the vaudeville people talk. To be one of them.

Then they were lining up, and the music which had been *trumpety-trum* changed to something more important, a march, so the girls' feet began to move—but did not clump, since Mrs. Avery (Mrs. *Arthur* Avery, the dancing mistress, not Mabel's Aunt Elsie) had whispered fiercely not to. White slippers, white dresses, like a graduating class, except better. Miss Frye raised an arm for complete silence—and opened the door. Through the back hall, down to the secret entrance by the Town Clerk's office, up the little set of stairs into the wings. It smelled so good back here, half church, half (Nell blushed interiorly, to think the word) bordello. The music rose up suddenly loud and the curtains were swinging open, it was time. On they pranced, right behind Mr. East and Mr. Verrall, who were doing a nice little soft-shoe shuffle up in front, where they called it 'one.' '*Jeremiah Jones, a ladies' man was he, Every pretty girl he loved to spoon.*'

The ridiculous Mr. East ogled each of the girls in turn while Mr. Verrall sang the tweedling story, and then it was their turn to burst into finger-wagging song. This was the best thing in the world! '*That isn't the girl I saw you with at Brighton—Who—who—who's your lady friend?*'

Mrs. Gower sat enthroned in her usual seat, two rows up, smack in the middle. In front of her, Miss Frye leaned over to whisper to her friend Miss North, down for the concert, that the Avery sisters knew Mr. East *very well*, 'And they assure me that the stories are only publicity stunts.'

Mrs. Gower rapped Miss Frye's shoulder for silence, and turned her attention back to the stage. The romping, rampaging girls went galloping along, scolding and laughing, and trit-trotted off the other side, subsiding as the curtains swung to and the music crashed on in a festive climax.

Finding the break between the front curtains, Mr. East stepped out into a beam of light as the curtains closed gracefully behind him. 'Happy to welcome you all to this patriotic event, in honour and support of our troops overseas. All donations kindly accepted, gifts of knitted goods are always welcome. The recruiting officer could not be here, he's dealing with a rush of business in Regina, but feel free to find him At Home in his *salon* there, any day from ten to four. I'm speaking to you, young fella!' (Here East pointed with some ferocity at Chum.) 'I'll let you in on a secret. I'm going to be waving goodbye myself pretty soon—no, no, sadly they've turned me down. My feet, you know, so I'm stuck doing what I can to entertain, but my dear partner in crime, Mr. Didcot Verrall, is enlisting in the United States Army next week.'

Hearty cheers from the crowd as Verrall dodged out through the curtain break to doff his bowler with a shy grin. Mrs. Gower clapped, raising her hands to show her appreciation.

'Huzzah! Yes, but I don't know who will plaster my corns for me now ... It may be some time before he sees these shores again, so let's show him what he's got in store for him in gay Paree!'

Music wound out again, a clarinet taking the lead, pinging chimes. East trilled, '*By the banks of the Seine live girls so beautiful ...*' And here came the lovely Saskatchewan girls, with a poignant refrain, '*Flow, river, flow, down to the sea,*' and then more of the thrills of French life, absurd but entertaining. Mrs. Gower found herself keeping time with one heavily ringed finger.

'When you live by the Seine you suffer awfully
If you refrain from enjoying, lawfully,
the sweet gay life in a gay sweet way . . .'

Backstage, Mabel watched Clover and Aurora put their heads together for a moment, humming quietly before their number. Mabel allowed herself to love, for a brief span of time, everything about them. Their grace, their children, their closeness. Their mother, broken as she was. Mabel wondered how Chum and Elsie would manage without them all; it was perfectly plain to her that Aurora would go with her sisters when they left. She did not know how she could bear it herself. They stood straight again, arms around each other's waists, and then the music began. Clover walked out first—but Aurora turned to see Mabel watching, and sent her a wink and a blown kiss. Mabel waved, and Aurora flew onstage to join Clover in the fast-flowing duet.

At rehearsals they had sung in half-voice. And Mabel had heard Aurora sing many times over the last two years, in the confines of church or parlour, but she had never heard this soaring and reaching. The blending of the alto and soprano line was both exact and smudged, as if their two voices blurred into each other slightly, like the flow blue on Aunt Elsie's good china. Mabel clasped her list and listened.

'I know,' Bella said beside her. 'Aren't they good?'

Mabel turned to her, tears threatening to overflow her eyelids. Bella handed her a hanky. 'Take mine,' she said. 'I never need it.'

Lewis Ridgeway was behind Bella, next up, and it seemed to Bella that he was also moved. She had no second hanky—she hoped he'd keep it bottled up.

Mabel motioned Lewis to the podium that had been set up stage left, in one.

In the audience Miss Frye and Miss North gathered themselves to listen dutifully to the part of the programme that was good for you. Mr. Ridgeway opened his book, as they had seen him do so often in the classroom, and ran a finger down the page to flatten it. He began very quietly, his tone no different from the last song's lonely finish, *non ve, non ve . . .*

> 'The night is come, but not too soon;
> And sinking silently,
> All silently, the little moon
> Drops down behind the sky.'

What a fine figure of a man he is, thought Miss Frye; it makes one proud. If one had to work for a man, which was inevitable within the scholastic profession, what pleasure to work for one so upright, so intelligent, and in whom stern justice was ever diluted by the milk of human kindness. She would have liked to repeat this to her friend Miss North, but thought it better to wait till the intermission.

> 'There is no light in earth or heaven
> But the cold light of stars;
> And the first watch of night is given
> To the red planet Mars.'

In the wings stage right, Aurora crept up to the first curtain-leg to watch Lewis reading. This had been one of Maurice Kavanagh's selections, Longfellow's mysterious *Light of Stars*. Lewis had none of the false, high-flown passion of Kavanagh. Instead he read with awareness of the war and the soldiers in the room, as a cool, measured directive.

> 'The star of the unconquered will,
> He rises in my breast,
> Serene, and resolute, and still,
> And calm, and self-possessed.'

If she had heard *this* five years ago, she wondered, instead of Kavanagh's excesses, before she'd married Mayhew, what then?

Lewis's profile as he looked up to the audience was straight and definite. His ordinary purity made her wish, for a moment, that she had met him then. But Avery—no regret or reforming of the past was possible if it denied her Avery.

Ignoring the stodgy poetry, Nell Barr-Smith ran to the back of the auditorium to be ready for the *Flying Machine*. Having worked on it, being backstage, she knew just what they were doing behind the curtain as the music played and the audience visited. So many people! Mrs. Gower's extra two rows had not been enough, and thirty or forty people were standing at the back. But Nell wriggled through as the music came twirling into a cyclone and the curtains were opening.

Clouds and blue sky were revealed, then trundling through the clouds, making a remarkable sewing-machine noise—there came the plane! Nando had told her (he was *so kind*!) that it was a Red Albatross, a biplane, single propeller. It only had two blades, really; they'd added more propeller blades just for the daisy joke.

It was a pleasure ride at first. Nando had brought along a picnic basket because he was going to propose. He handed things to Bella: a sunshade (inside-out, whoops! whipped backwards, and gone), a dozen boiled eggs, a waggling string of sausages, long sticks of French bread—they all went flying backwards and *yipes* off the end of the plane. Bella grabbed the tablecloth to wrap around her, since her hat had flown off long before. Nando would turn and steer a little in between each thing. Finally he brought out a large bottle of gold-foiled champagne. He shook it to boast a bit, took hold of the cork, and the bottle blew off and out onto the wing of the plane.

Sausages were one thing, but he couldn't lose the champagne. He made Bella sit up front and fly, wearing the goggles he'd been using. They wrestled hilariously on the top of the plane to change seats, Bella nearly coming out of her dress, oh my goodness! Mrs. Gower wouldn't like that, but Daddy was laughing so hard he'd choked. Bella got the goggles on every way but right; at one point she landed head-down in the cockpit, flying with her feet.

Nando, meanwhile, inched out onto the wing of the plane—all this time they'd been swaying and fidgeting their clothes as if they were in a high wind—forward, forward, and then the plane dipped, dipped, until he went slithering down to the end of the wing—and grabbed the bottle just as it rolled slowly off. He lay back on the wing and took a big glug from the bottle.

The hectic music and the way Nando and Bella played with each other made it all go by so fast—Nell wanted to see how they did the bit where they lassoed the tail with Bella's sash to pull her backwards to get the blue velvet engagement-ring box. When they were chasing each other over and under the double wings because she was so mad at him for losing the ring and Nando lost sight of Bella—that was priceless—her feet dangling in air so you were really dizzy, but he saved her, and she kissed him and they were going to fall—oh, it was the best thing Nell had ever seen and it was—it was over.

The curtains swirled shut and in a minute Bella and Nando peeked out through the split, her head way on top of his, and out they came for a bow, another and another. Then the intermission music swelled and the lights came on . . . Oh, run—she was on to help with tea!

The noise and swelter and the startlingly good tea provided by Mrs. Gower's army restored the fractured spirits of any who had been frightened by the aeroplane, and the audience sank back into their seats, ready for a little peace and quiet.

But the curtain opened only to an empty stage—perhaps too quiet. Offstage, a fiddle started playing *Minstrel Boy*, and Clover came on in a plain dark dress with a tartan scarf.

'*The Minstrel Boy to the war has gone*,' she sang in a gentle, thoughtful tone. '*In the ranks of death ye'll find him. His father's sword he hath girded on, and his wild harp slung behind him.*'

She paused, unwound her tartan scarf from her shoulder, and pulled it into a shawl around her neck, tucking it into her belt to become a suddenly belligerent fishwife.

'My son has gone for a soldier,' she called out, an ugly drunk. The horror of that sacred word *soldier* combined with drunkenness kept the hall entirely silent. She staggered, caught at the chair-back, and missed.

She grabbed it on the second try and hauled herself up again, joints creaking, dizzy.

In the audience, Victor made himself breathe out. He was afraid for her.

'If I've took a drop too much that's the cause of it. My own boy, gone to the war already,' the old woman said, with a sobering effort. 'Not old enough to let him go. He sang so sweet— I live in fear, sir, I can't bear, but needs must, you know, needs must, needs must, and no work here for him to—'

She broke into ugly weeping.

'I didn't raise my boy to be a soldier!' She fumbled with her shawl, and stood upright again. 'I'll fight anyone who says I did!'

Hunched, she bustled twice around invisible flights of stairs and flung open an imaginary door. 'My best room, saved for you,' she boasted to her imaginary boarder. 'Isn't it spacious!' A great bumping noise: 'Oh, watch your head, there, that's a nasty crack.'

In the wings, Mabel stood very still, holding herself tightly in check. As she was always in check, she thought, except with Aleck. The old hag showed the client round the room, boasting, disguising flaws. The cans at the bed-legs: 'Well, you know, it's a particulous convenimence to have the cans already there, and I won't have the boarders using the po-po for the keeping away of bugs!'

That got a laugh, surprising in this straight-laced town, Mabel thought. Perhaps they'd already been shocked into submission.

'Lights out at 3 a.m. and everybody goes back to their own room! Iron-clad, no deviagation from that one.' But it was no good, the prospective boarder was leaving. 'Well, go then! Who needs you! But needs must, you know, needs must, and there was no work here for him to— He always liked my pie . . .'

The boarder relented—his weak will and small stature almost visible, as the landlady took his money and watched him go upstairs to the room. She turned away, with a rackety jig as she fingered the cash and tucked it away, and turned to them again, to speak as if to a fair judge. 'There's no word can ease a mother's grief. Only the knowledge that my boy was not alone, that he was one of all those tens of thousands, hundreds of thousands, who are doing what they believe to be . . . That he had good company out there! He wrote to me, you see, although he was never one for writing, and he says, *we strive together*, that's what he says. *I'll see you again, dear Mother*, that's what he wrote.'

'Somebody must go,' the old woman said. 'But oh, my boy.'

Mabel stood against the proscenium arch, just touching it. Clover had spoken to her beforehand, had asked her please not to listen, but she could not bear to miss it. In the audience, a woman began to sob. Mabel hoped it was not Mrs. Gower.

Ferocious again, the old Irishwoman straightened and stepped up one stair, shouting, 'Supper six sharp, for them as can mind their manners!'

On second thought, Mrs. Gower can stand it, Mabel told herself. She has good company here.

Miss Peavey and Miss Frye were sitting directly behind Victor Saborsky, having changed seats during the fruit-basket-upset of the intermission. Miss Peavey leaned over to congratulate Mr. Saborsky on his wife's mastery of the monologue form, which made him duck his head; Miss Frye then leaned forward to confide. 'What *I* want to know,' she whispered, 'is about your experience of the hospitals—Miss Peavey is our district nurse, and she will certainly be enthralled.'

Victor could not answer. He shook his head stiffly. The air seemed to be full of eyes. He got up and limped along the row, and went back-stage instead, where he belonged, to find his wife.

Miss Frye was not much taken aback by Mr. Saborsky's behaviour; everyone knew him to be suffering from shell shock. But Miss Peavey whispered that they ought not to have presumed to speak to him about his war experiences. Chastened, Miss Frye sat back to watch as the curtains unfurled—and there was lovely Mrs. Mayhew and such a very handsome gent with shiny shoes. The music for the *Castle Walk* number was enchanting.

Lewis Ridgeway sat beside Dr. Graham, watching Aurora dance with that negligible jackanapes. She had thrown off her disguise tonight, and he saw her more clearly now, in company with her sisters. Not in any sense the wife of a superintendent of schools. All evening he had hovered on the verge of saying to himself irrevocable words. He had been puzzling over what an honourable person ought to do, but there was only one answer. The men he most admired, Chum and Dean Barr-Smith, had seen active service. Victor Saborsky was entirely admirable too—even the comical Mr. Verrall was going to sign up. It seemed they had all beaten him to the punch. Miss Frye would make an adequate principal while he was away. He could discover for himself what Aleck Graham knew, and all those other men. If he came back, perhaps things would look different all around.

The frail, exquisite grace of the dancing made ripples of breath go through the audience over and over. Bella whispered to Nando that Jimmy was better than he'd ever been before.

'But a bit of a flatfish, don't you think?' Nando said. He was happy now that the tilting of the wings had gone without a hitch, and his head was mostly full of ways to make the plane do more, when he had the chance of a really big theatre, like the Palace or Ziegfeld's or—or when he would be able to fly a real plane. His head went into cloud.

Bella ran down to change into her white dress for *They Didn't Believe Me*, leaving Nando to his dreaming. She had stripped to her corselette when the door handle turned. Hearing Jimmy's voice she ducked down behind the screen, onto the little cushioned stool for putting shoes on.

'Just a little—a very little something,' Jimmy was saying.

Aurora thanked him, paper tore, and she said, 'Oh, Jimmy, what a kind memento.'

Not the thing a lady says when she's over the moon, Bella thought. Through the hinge-crack in the screen, she saw Jimmy lean forward and kiss Aurora's cheek, and his arms go round her, but Aurora was out of that very quick. You could take lessons from her, Bella thought.

'I made the wrong choice,' Jimmy said, in a heartfelt, legitimate-theatre voice—the younger lover in that seabird melodrama! Bella almost laughed. 'I know that now,' he said.

'Yes, you did,' Aurora said, and she *was* laughing. 'But it was very nice to dance with you again.'

She's over it, Bella thought. That's for certain.

'Actually, I'm going up to Keith's in the fall, you know, in a play with Ethel Barrymore. But I'm thinking about the pictures, I've had a couple of offers.'

Bella found it hard to listen to his blather—East and Verrall were on, she wanted to see them.

'Anyhow, that bracelet's more worth keeping than the old one, and it comes straight from me to you with no hard feelings,' Jimmy said. 'Say a fond *adieu* to Bella for me . . . It's been a great gig.'

He took himself off as cleanly and neatly as he'd done everything else. It seemed he had erased himself, had become nothing but a handsome escort.

'Makes you a bit sad,' Aurora said through the screen to Bella. 'When you think how lovely he was when we first met him.'

'Let's go up and watch old East and Verrall,' Bella said, jumping up to pull on her frock. 'They only get better, you know.'

They crowded in backstage with all the others who wanted to see the number.

East had failed at his golf lessons many times, and Verrall, finally losing his temper completely, had whacked him over the head with a club that rebounded and hit his own head, bringing up a lump the size of a golf ball under his hat. In fact it *was* a golf ball. Verrall pocketed it thoughtfully.

East, glaring at him, said, 'There are times when I wonder if it wouldn't be better for us to part.'

'No, no,' said Verrall. 'I've got my temper back now. Let's turn to the book I brought for you, in my desperation: Launcelot Cressy Servos's *Practical Instruction in Golf.* Here, Verrall evinced a Moment of Discovery. 'Oh dear, I seem to have brought the wrong manual.'

'What have you brought?'

'*The Art of Flirtation. How to make a lady fall in love with you, for ten cents*,' Verrall said.

East hooted. 'A lady fell in love with *me* once and it cost me five-hundred dollars.'

'That's because you didn't have this book.'

Always in favour of saving money, East decided he did need flirtation lessons after all, and they settled down to work.

Mrs. Gower was laughing so hard already that Miss Peavey expressed a fear, to her other-side neighbour Miss North, that she might take an apoplexy.

But Verrall was giving a hands-on demonstration. 'Just to teach you how to flirt, I am going to take a walk through the park. I am a beautiful woman,' he said in a fluting voice.

East, puzzled, said, 'I thought you were a gentleman.'

Verrall was patient. 'No, no, just for an *example*, I am a lady. I will walk past in a reckless way, and make eyes at you.'

East would have none of that. 'If you do, I will smash up your face!'

'No, no, it's *pretend*. When I make eyes at you, you say something. What do you say?'

'Ten cents?'

Verrall moaned, but persevered: 'Now I'm the lady, I am coming. Get ready.' He did a glorious walk around the park, worthy of the sultriest of box-hall girls, melted along in front of East, dropped his handkerchief and swanned away.

East shouted after him, 'Hey! You dropped something.'

'I know, I know!' Verrall hissed back. 'I'm flirting! Pick up my handkerchief!'

But East was proud. 'I don't need any. I got one of my own.'

Mrs. Gower's mirth passed from merry to alarming at that point, and Dr. Graham leaned over to lay a cautious hand on her pulse.

In three, the little golden moon was being set up for Bella and Nando to sing in front of. 'I'm not a singer like that fellow's a dancer,' Nando said. 'It's not too late to bow out—you could do my verses.' Bella thumped his arm. Then, remembering the time she'd punched his eye, asked how long it had stayed black.

'Never went black at all,' he said stoutly. 'Or not for more than a month.'

'I hope it was embarrassing when you went to the sanatorium to get your dad, looking like another candidate.'

'Very funny,' he said, and the music was beginning, and they were on.

Now this was the sort of thing that she loved, thought Elsie, sitting comfortably in Chum's lee. '*How wonderful you are . . .*' That's the way she could imagine Chum talking to her, if they'd met when they were young. Not that it mattered, they didn't have to say things to know them. '*They'll never believe me, that from this great big world you've chosen me . . .*' It would make Chum laugh if she told him that, but the reason these nice songs worked was that they told the truth, a certain kind of truth. '*All I know is I said yes, hesitating more or less . . .*' But she had not needed to hesitate for an instant of course. Except for their dear baby's death, she was the happiest of women. And lucky, too, not to have had to worry about Chum while he was still in active service. Clover's face broke her heart, too often. This little Bella now, she was in the best of spirits. But she too looked as if she had been through the wars, overlaid now with the air of having been struck lucky that Elsie expected her own face showed. Faces gave out so much.

Chum's elbow squeezed her arm, and she gave a little pressure back.

At the last verse Nando Dent stood forward, and Bella turned her face away, suddenly grief-stricken. Was it acting? Elsie had heard that he was going to enlist.

'Now this is the verse they've been singing, over in France,' he said, and stood to a casual attention. 'A bit of a joke, of course, to keep the spirits up:

> '*And when they ask us, How dangerous it was,*
> *Oh! We'll never tell them—no, we'll never tell them,*
> *We spent our pay in some café,*
> *And fought wild women night and day,*
> *It was the cushiest job we ever had . . .*'

Chum bent his head down to hear his wife's whisper, as the curtains floated inward. 'Aurora tells me Clover's worried about poor Victor—she wants to leave tomorrow—and Aurora is going with her, to help with any—well, to see that they are all right.'

'She told me too,' Chum said. 'I said we'd be happy to keep Flora, if that's to your mind?'

'Well, of course,' Elsie said, a little doubt in her voice. The music was growing. 'Will she want to stay, though?' she said, close to his ear, but he was a little deaf.

The music blaring up had caught him—very martial, you could see the arousal in the faces around. His own heart strained upward to meet it. An American song, Clover had said. Be a useful recruitment tool. '*Tell your dad to be glad that he had such a lad . . .*'

That fellow East was good at his job, sawing along up there, with all Canadian girlhood getting in his way.

So were his nieces, good at their jobs. Watching this, knowing that they'd pulled it together from scratch, he saw they'd have to go. That Bella was a minx, sorry not to know her better. If he and Elsie kept Flora, the girls would have some reason to come back.

It would leave Mabel lonesome. Not everything could be fixed.

The audience was up and clapping, and the company assembled on the stage, a hullabaloo all round. It would be good to get home after all this. He reached for his hat but Elsie stopped him—oh, an encore. He sat back down, obedient to her hand.

He'd done very well for himself there. He'd advised Arthur not to marry, he recalled. If anyone had advised me like that, I'd have punched his lights out, Chum thought now. Advised him most strenuously not to marry Flora, of *all* people, no better than she should be, and very unlikely to be faithful to him. Temperamental to the point of throwing doubt upon her sanity. Had he said that to Arthur? He did remember offering him a thousand pounds in English money not to do it.

But she had raised these girls, and without much help from Arthur by the sounds of it. He'd be glad to give Flora a home. Elsie liked her very well, and Mabel did too.

Her pretty girls, singing together up there—some fluffery, but it had got to Elsie. Tears in her eyes. He was the luckiest man in the world: conscious that he was saying the same thing every moderately happy husband had said in the history of human interaction. Content to do so. *The rose that I keep in my heart . . .*

The crowd was applauding again, up on its feet in its animal way. Through the open windows of the hall some cool air blew.

Encore

JULY 2, 1917

Qu'Appelle, Saskatchewan

All acts should have an encore arranged that can be done in one, and acts that work in one are always in demand by managers.

FREDERICK LADELLE, *HOW TO ENTER VAUDEVILLE*

*J*he trunks went ahead to the station in the cart, Aurora's grey trunk among them. The girls petted and kissed Mama, still drowsing in bed after her exertions at the concert; they bid a fond goodbye to Chum and to Aunt Elsie, and gave Mabel all Bella's tour dates—which they were going to fill, now that Nando would be leaving, as some permutation of the Belle Auroras. It was a difficult parting for Aurora, but Avery was happy to travel on a train with his odd little cousin.

Chum piled them all into the Ford and blew a double honk to say goodbye to Elsie, as he always did.

In the bedroom upstairs, Flora sat up, a flood of understanding in her brain like a slung pail of water. Going, all going—*all* going.

Not without! Not without!

She threw nightgown, brush and her best dress into the carpet-bag Aurora had left unneeded by the bed. Into shoes. Her hands shook but she gripped the leather handles hard and the weight of it steadied her. Down the (forcing her dragging right foot to do its work on the stair-case), quiet mouse, cross hall—miss creaking board. The big door swung, she was out and down those steps, the car only just pulling out to the drive.

She ran, hobbling and wobbling, and she sang out as she ran, more to herself than to get their attention, '*Hope with a gentle persuasion, whispers her comforting word . . .*'

As the green car slowed to turn out onto the main road, she gathered her skirts together and pelted after them, and a shout gathered in her throat and leaped out.

'Wait!' she cried. 'Wait for me!'

Acknowledgements

This is a book of vaudeville. Everything in it is stolen, juggled, stitched together backwards and upside down, shined up and sent back out to see how it will play. I have been faithful to the vaudeville circuits in Alberta, Montana and Saskatchewan, although I invented an extra one, the Parthenon. In the shallows of the medium-time, very few big historical sharks swim into the Belle Auroras' ken; I regret any calumny done to Alexander Pantages' ghost, but he was, after all, convicted in 1929 of the rape of a 17-year-old vaudeville dancer. (His conviction was overturned when a second trial allowed the dancer to be portrayed as a woman of low morals.) The roof of a vaudeville theatre in Edmonton did cave in, as told in the wonderful book *Fallen Empires*, by Jon Orrell. Victor's elastic bouquet and sunburst bow is borrowed from Tomás Kubínek; the remarkable beauty of Kubínek's act was a prime instigator of this book. If you ever have a chance, see him! The Melodramas are All My Own Work. East & Verrall use period vaude routines, from Brett Page's *Writing for Vaudeville* (Mr. Page acknowledges their venerable age himself) and other classic comics; every joke is a genuine antique. The more absurd facts of Nando's life with the Knockabouts are true of Buster Keaton's life with his parents and their family act; as Avery is, Buster was born backstage. Gentry's scolding the girls on pushing is borrowed from Cicely Berry. His other voice lessons are amalgams of advice from Berry, Lili Lehmann and Peter Brook. When Mama and Victor disagree over art, their argument owes its vigour to Howard Barker; East & Verrall doff their hats to Beckett.

I thank the Canada Council for funding during the writing of this book, and the Augustana Faculty at the University of Alberta for research funds; thanks also to my research assistants, Sarah Haywood and Jordhana Rempel. Impossible to have written the book without Robert Earley's tour of the Bailey Theatre in Camrose (first known as the David), before their restoration project got underway; thanks also to Hugh Henry at the Swift Current Museum for his guided tour of the Lyric Theatre in Swift Current.

I'm indebted to my darling mother, Julianne Endicott, for an account of her experience of stroke and her memories of Qu'Appelle; and to my constant readers: Barbara Barnes, Thyra Endicott, Jeanne Harvie, Glenda MacFarlane, and Sara O'Leary. For the beautiful design of this book, a round of applause to Kelly Hill. For their skill, perspicacity and general loveliness, I thank Tracy Bohan, Kristin Cochrane, and my dear editor, Lynn Henry. Love as always to Rachel, Will and Peter Ormshaw for the continuous vaudeville of the everyday.

These girls and other artistes, these theatres and managers, are amalgams of hundreds of vaudeville performers known and forgotten. If you want to read more about vaudeville, and I certainly recommend it, start with Trav S.D.'s *No Applause, Just Throw Money*; if you're hooked, find Frank Cullen's massive encyclopedia, *Vaudeville Old & New*. For a full bibliography and list of sources and music, please visit www.marinaendicott.com

A NOTE ABOUT THE TYPE

Little Shadows has been set in Janson, a misnamed typeface designed in or about 1690 by Nicholas Kis, a Hungarian in Amsterdam. In 1919, the original matrices became the property of the Stempel Foundry in Frankfurt, Germany. Janson is an old-style book face of excellent clarity and sharpness, featuring concave and splayed serifs, and a marked contrast between thick and thin strokes.